What would you do if little men in purple uniforms filled your living room with impossible machinery?

A machine made it possible to bury your crimes in the future?

You were abandoned on an asteroid alone with a murderous living snake of metal?

Here are four collections of stories by the extraordinary Damon Knight, including the classic 'To Serve Man', made famous by its adaptation for *The Twilight Zone* and parodied in *The Simpsons*.

Far Out

In Deep

Off Centre

Turning On

Also by Damon Knight

Novels

Hell's Pavement (1955) (*aka* The Analogue Men)
A for Anything (1959) (*aka* The People Maker)
Natural State (1959) (*aka* Masters of Evolution)
Beyond the Barrier (1964)
Mind Switch (1965) (*aka* The Other Foot)
Double Meaning (1965) (*aka* The Rithian Terror)
World without Children and The Earth Quarter (1970)
(The Earth Quarter *aka* The Sun Saboteurs)
The World and Thorinn (1981)
The Man in the Tree (1984)
CV (1985)
The Observers (1987)
A Reasonable World (1991)
Why Do Birds (1992)
Humpty Dumpty: An Oval (1996)

Collections

Far Out (1961)
In Deep (1963)
Off Centre (1965)
Turning On (1966)
Rule Golden (1979)

Non-fiction

The Futurians (1977)
Turning Points: Essays on the Art of Science Fiction (1977)
In Search of Wonder: Essays on Modern Science Fiction (1996)

Damon Knight

SF GATEWAY OMNIBUS

FAR OUT
IN DEEP
OFF CENTRE
TURNING ON

GOLLANCZ
LONDON

First published in Great Britain in 2014 by
Gollancz
An imprint of the Orion Publishing Group
Orion House, 5 Upper St Martin's Lane,
London WC2H 9EA

An Hachette UK Company

A CIP catalogue record for this book
is available from the British Library

ISBN 978 0 575 11121 9

1 3 5 7 9 10 8 6 4 2

Typeset by Jouve (UK), Milton Keynes

Printed and bound by CPI Group (UK) Ltd, Croydon, CR0 4YY

The Orion Publishing Group's policy is to use papers
that are natural, renewable and recyclable products and
made from wood grown in sustainable forests. The logging
and manufacturing processes are expected to conform to
the environmental regulations of the country of origin.

www.orionbooks.co.uk
www.gollancz.co.uk

CONTENTS

ENTER THE SF GATEWAY . . .

Towards the end of 2011, in conjunction with the celebration of fifty years of coherent, continuous science fiction and fantasy publishing, Gollancz launched the SF Gateway.

Over a decade after launching the landmark SF Masterworks series, we realised that the realities of commercial publishing are such that even the Masterworks could only ever scratch the surface of an author's career. Vast troves of classic SF and fantasy were almost certainly destined never again to see print. Until very recently, this meant that anyone interested in reading any of those books would have been confined to scouring second-hand bookshops. The advent of digital publishing changed that paradigm for ever.

Embracing the future even as we honour the past, Gollancz launched the SF Gateway with a view to utilising the technology that now exists to make available, for the first time, the entire backlists of an incredibly wide range of classic and modern SF and fantasy authors. Our plan, at its simplest, was – and still is! – to use this technology to build on the success of the SF and Fantasy Masterworks series and to go even further.

The SF Gateway was designed to be the new home of classic science fiction and fantasy – the most comprehensive electronic library of classic SFF titles ever assembled. The programme has been extremely well received and we've been very happy with the results. So happy, in fact, that we've decided to complete the circle and return a selection of our titles to print, in these omnibus editions.

We hope you enjoy this selection. And we hope that you'll want to explore more of the classic SF and fantasy we have available. These are wonderful books you're holding in your hand, but you'll find much, much more ... through the SF Gateway.

www.sfgateway.com

INTRODUCTION

from The Encyclopedia of Science Fiction

Damon Knight (1922–2002) was a US editor, critic and author; his third marriage was to Kate Wilhelm. Like many SF writers, Knight became involved in SF Fandom at an early age, and by 1941 was a member of the Futurians in New York, where he shared an apartment with Robert A. W. Lowndes and met Isaac Asimov, James Blish, Judith Merril, C. M. Kornbluth, Frederik Pohl and others. In *The Futurians: The Story of the Science Fiction 'Family' of the 30's that Produced Today's Top SF Writers and Editors* (1977) he published a candid history of the group and its era, full of sometimes scathing portraits but also arguing with conviction that these young men and women, the first generation to have been brought up within the relatively new field, would shape SF for decades. Knight's first professional sale was a cartoon to *Amazing*. His first published story (for which he received no payment) was 'Resilience' for *Stirring Science Stories* in February 1941, a journal edited by another Futurian, Donald A. Wollheim; his career as a short-story writer then lay fallow for several years. In 1943 he became an assistant editor with Popular Publications, a Pulp-magazine chain. Later he worked for a literary agency, then returned to Popular Publications as assistant editor of *Super Science Stories*. In 1950–1951 he was editor of *Worlds Beyond*, but the magazine ran for only three issues; later he edited *If* for three issues 1958–1959.

Knight made his initial strong impact on the field as a book reviewer, and is generally acknowledged to have been the first outstanding Genre-SF critic. His first piece – a fanzine review of the 1945 *Astounding* serial version of A. E. Van Vogt's *The World of Ā* (1948) – remains perhaps his best known; it is in any case one of the most famous works of critical demolition ever published in the field, inspiring considerable revisions in the eventually published book, and being credited (perhaps a touch implausibly) for Van Vogt's eventual slide from pre-eminence. Knight later reviewed books for a number of amateur and professional magazines, notably *Infinity* and *The Magazine of Fantasy and Science Fiction*, expressing throughout a sane and consistent insistence on the relevance of literary standards to SF. His early reviews were collected in *In Search of Wonder: Essays on Modern Science Fiction* (1956)) and won him a Hugo in 1956; the second edition (1967) adds a considerable amount of material published up to 1960; the third edition (1996) adds six further pieces. He ceased his regular magazine reviewing when *The Magazine of Fantasy and*

Science Fiction declined to print a negative response to Judith Merril – this review, of *The Tomorrow People* (1960), appears in the revised edition of *In Search of Wonder*. In 1975, primarily for his criticism, he received a Pilgrim Award from the Science Fiction Research Association.

Knight's 1940s stories – including occasional collaborations with Blish – were of only mild interest until the release in 1949 of his ironic End of the World tale 'Not with a Bang' (1950), which appeared in one of the first issues of *The Magazine of Fantasy and Science Fiction*. This magazine, and *Galaxy* even more so, provided markets in which Knight could develop his urbane and darkly humorous short stories – including the famous 'To Serve Man' (1950), 'Four in One' (1953), 'Babel II' (1953), 'The Country of the Kind' (1956) and 'Stranger Station' (1956) – though as the decade advanced, and as his perspectives on the human enterprise darkened, even these markets proved too narrow, and he was forced to publish some of his finest work in lesser journals, where his scouring, revisionary, anatomical rewrites of the genre's already sclerotic conventions could appear in safe obscurity. Knight's reputation as a writer has primarily rested on the short stories published during the 1950s and, to a lesser extent, the 1960s; they are adult and sane and have not dated. His best work has been assembled in various collections, primarily *Far Out* (1961), *In Deep* (1963), *Off Centre* (1965) and *Turning On* (1966) (for all four collections see below). Later collections include *Rule Golden* (1979), *Late Knight Edition* (1985), *One Side Laughing: Stories Unlike Other Stories* (1991) and *God's Nose* (1991); they tend to mix early and late work.

From the first, the novel form presented something of a difficulty for Knight. Most of his efforts – like his first, *Hell's Pavement* (1955), a Dystopian story of a future society with humanity under psychological control, or *Masters of Evolution* (1959), or *The Sun Saboteurs* (1961) – were expanded from stories, and lose in the process the compressed drivenness of his short work. Some of them – like *The People Maker* (1959), which thoughtfully examines Matter Duplication, and the late *The World and Thorinn* (fixup 1981), a scintillating picaresque derived from some 1960s tales – do seem comfortably to fill the longer format; but by the mid-1960s he appeared to have turned his attention permanently elsewhere.

Like Frederik Pohl, Knight had soon become adept at many aspects of the writing business, having worked as magazine editor, short-story writer, novelist and critic. This mastery soon widened, and he began to work to formalize the professional collegiality so important to the SF field. He co-founded, with Blish and Merril, the Milford Science Fiction Writers' Conference in 1956, which he ran (soon with Wilhelm) for over 20 years; and later participated in its highly successful spiritual offspring, the Clarion Science Fiction Writers' Workshop writing seminar, for which he edited *The Clarion Writers' Handbook* (1978). He was responsible for arguing the need of, and for founding the

Science Fiction Writers of America serving as its first president 1965–1967. At the same time he began to issue well-conceived reprint Anthologies like *A Century of Science Fiction* (1962), *First Flight* (1963), *Tomorrow × 4* (1964), *A Century of Great Short Science Fiction Novels* (1964) and many others. But his greatest editorial achievement during these years was the Orbit series of Original Anthologies that he began in 1966 – beginning with *Orbit 1: A Science Fiction Anthology* (1966) and closing with *Orbit 21* (1980) – and which would become the longest-running and most influential series of that sort yet seen in the field; among writers strongly identified with Orbit were Gardner Dozois, R. A. Lafferty, Kate Wilhelm and Gene Wolfe, the latter publishing in the series eighteen of his most powerful early stories and novellas, one in almost every volume.

In the 1980s, after the end of Orbit, Knight became more active as a writer again, though without making a huge impression on a new generation of readers. But if *The Man in the Tree* (1984) may seem somewhat slack and irony-poor in its presentation of a contemporary Messiah figure, Knight returned to something like form, though without quite the energy of earlier efforts, in the wickedly Utopian sequence comprising *CV* (1985), *The Observers* (1988) and *A Reasonable World* (1991), about Alien parasites who turn out not to be the Paranoia-justifying Invasion of 1950s SF but moralistic symbionts who enforce something like rational behaviour upon humanity's leaders – echoing the central gimmick of Knight's much earlier story 'Rule Golden' (1954) – where artificially boosted empathy makes it impossible to be cruel without experiencing the victim's pain. In the third volume, a plethora of SF devices and appeals to reason somewhat weakens the pleasurable sting, but the series as a whole seems young at heart, and Knight's cognitive energy remains clearly evident. This is also demonstrated by the autumnal ironies of *Why Do Birds* (1992), in which the world is brought to an end and humanity's scant hope of salvation has the aura of a gigantic con-trick; and in *Humpty Dumpty: An Oval* (1996), a surreal tragi-farce which may be read as Posthumous Fantasy: the protagonist has been shot in the head, fractures and upheavals in Earth's crust may echo the state of his skull, bizarre conspiracy theories abound, and the lyric stillness of the final scene gently suggests the peace of death.

In 1995, he was granted the SFWA Grand Master Award – which from 2002 became formally known, in his honour, as the Damon Knight Grand Master Award. He was posthumously inducted into the Science Fiction Hall of Fame in 2003. He amply deserved these honours, but to the very end of his life there remained a sense that Knight had retained an impish tendency to shock the SF world, and perhaps to mock us all.

There is unmistakeably something impish, something mocking, in his best short stories, which were assembled as *Far Out* (1961), *In Deep* (1963), *Off*

Centre (1965) and *Turning On* (1966), and which are presented here in one volume. They give delight and they sting. They honour the rules of SF, but they use those rules to demonstrate to us that the world itself may not be amenable to those rules. Knight's Thought Experiments do not build a better world for technology; they are demolition derbies, where the costs (sometimes hilarious) of forging ahead can be anatomized. Written half a century ago, they tell us how it is today. They should be read for that. They should also be read because they are a joy to read.

For a more detailed version of the above, see Damon Knight's author entry in *The Encyclopedia of Science Fiction*: http://sf-encyclopedia.com/entry/knight_damon

Some terms above are capitalised when they would not normally be so rendered; this indicates that the terms represent discrete entries in *The Encyclopedia of Science Fiction*.

FAR OUT

CONTENTS

Acknowledgments

'To Serve Man' published in *Galaxy Science Fiction*
Copyright 1950 Galaxy Publishing Corp.

'Idiot Stick' published in *Star Science Fiction*
Copyright © 1958 by Ballantine Books, Inc.

'Thing of Beauty' published in *Galaxy Magazine*
Copyright © 1958 by Galaxy Publishing Corp.

'The Enemy' published in *Venture Science Fiction*
Copyright © 1957 by Mercury Press, Inc.

'Not with a Bang' published in *The Magazine of Fantasy & Science Fiction*
Copyright © 1949 by Mercury Press, Inc.

'Babel II' published in *Beyond Fantasy Fiction*
Copyright © 1953 by Galaxy Publishing Corp.

'Anachron' published in *If Science Fiction*
Copyright © 1953 by Quinn Publishing Co., Inc.

'Special Delivery' published in *Galaxy Science Fiction*
Copyright © 1953 by Galaxy Publishing Corp.

'You're Another' published in *The Magazine of Fantasy & Science Fiction*
Copyright © 1955 by Mercury Press, Inc.

'Time Enough' published in *Amazing Science Fiction Stories*
Copyright © 1960 by Ziff-Davis Publishing Co.

'Extempore' published in *Infinity Science Fiction*
Copyright © 1956 by Royal Publications, Inc.

'Cabin Boy' published in *Galaxy Science Fiction*
Copyright © 1951 by Galaxy Publishing Corp.

'The Last Word' published in *Satellite Science Fiction*
Copyright © 1956 by Renown Publications

TO SERVE MAN

The Kanamit were not very pretty, it's true. They looked something like pigs and something like people, and that is not an attractive combination. Seeing them for the first time shocked you; that was their handicap. When a thing with the countenance of a fiend comes from the stars and offers a gift, you are disinclined to accept.

I don't know what we expected interstellar visitors to look like – those who thought about it at all, that is. Angels, perhaps, or something too alien to be really awful. Maybe that's why we were all so horrified and repelled when they landed in their great ships and we saw what they really were like.

The Kanamit were short and very hairy – thick, bristly brown-grey hair all over their abominably plump bodies. Their noses were snout-like and their eyes small, and they had thick hands of three fingers each. They wore green leather harness and green shorts, but I think the shorts were a concession to our notions of public decency. The garments were quite modishly cut, with slash pockets and half-belts in the back. The Kanamit had a sense of humour, anyhow.

There were three of them at this session of the U.N., and, Lord, I can't tell you how queer it looked to see them there in the middle of a solemn plenary session – three fat pig-like creatures in green harness and shorts, sitting at the long table below the podium, surrounded by the packed arcs of delegates from every nation. They sat correctly upright, politely watching each speaker. Their flat ears drooped over the earphones. Later on, I believe, they learned every human language, but at this time they knew only French and English.

They seemed perfectly at ease – and that, along with their humour, was a thing that tended to make me like them. I was in the minority; I didn't think they were trying to put anything over.

The delegate from Argentina got up and said that his government was interested in the demonstration of a new cheap power source, which the Kanamit had made at the previous session, but that the Argentine government could not commit itself as to its future policy without a much more thorough examination.

It was what all the delegates were saying, but I had to pay particular attention to Señor Valdes, because he tended to sputter and his diction was bad. I got through the translation all right, with only one or two momentary hesitations, and then switched to the Polish-English line to hear how Gregori was doing with Janciewicz. Janciewicz was the cross Gregori had to bear, just as Valdes was mine.

Janciewicz repeated the previous remarks with a few ideological variations, and then the Secretary-General recognized the delegate from France, who introduced Dr Denis Lévèque, the criminologist, and a great deal of complicated equipment was wheeled in.

Dr Lévèque remarked that the question in many people's minds had been aptly expressed by the delegate from the U.S.S.R. at the preceding session, when he demanded, 'What is the motive of the Kanamit? What is their purpose in offering us these unprecedented gifts, while asking nothing in return?'

The doctor then said, 'At the request of several delegates and with the full consent of our guests, the Kanamit, my associates and I have made a series of tests upon the Kanamit with the equipment which you see before you. These tests will now be repeated.'

A murmur ran through the chamber. There was a fusillade of flashbulbs, and one of the TV cameras moved up to focus on the instrument board of the doctor's equipment. At the same time, the huge television screen behind the podium lighted up, and we saw the blank faces of two dials, each with its pointer resting at zero, and a strip of paper tape with a stylus point resting against it.

The doctor's assistants were fastening wires to the temples of one of the Kanamit, wrapping a canvas-covered rubber tube around his forearm, and taping something to the palm of his right hand.

In the screen, we saw the paper tape begin to move while the stylus traced a slow zigzag pattern along it. One of the needles began to jump rhythmically; the other flipped over and stayed there, wavering slightly.

'These are the standard instruments for testing the truth of a statement,' said Dr Lévèque. 'Our first object, since the physiology of the Kanamit is unknown to us, was to determine whether or not they react to these tests as human beings do. We will now repeat one of the many experiments which were made in the endeavour to discover this.'

He pointed to the first dial. 'This instrument registers the subject's heartbeat. This shows the electrical conductivity of the skin in the palm of his hand, a measure of perspiration, which increases under stress. And this –' pointing to the tape-and-stylus device – 'shows the pattern and intensity of the electrical waves emanating from his brain. It has been shown, with human subjects, that all these readings vary markedly depending upon whether the subject is speaking the truth.'

He picked up two large pieces of cardboard, one red and one black. The red one was a square about three feet on a side; the black was a rectangle three and a half feet long. He addressed himself to the Kanama.

'Which of these is longer than the other?'

'The red,' said the Kanama.

Both needles leaped wildly, and so did the line on the unrolling tape.

'I shall repeat the question,' said the doctor. 'Which of these is longer than the other?'

'The black,' said the creature.

This time the instruments continued in their normal rhythm.

'How did you come to this planet?' asked the doctor.

'Walked,' replied the Kanama.

Again the instruments responded, and there was a subdued ripple of laughter in the chamber.

'Once more,' said the doctor. 'How did you come to this planet?'

'In a spaceship,' said the Kanama, and the instruments did not jump.

The doctor again faced the delegates. 'Many such experiments were made,' he said, 'and my colleagues and myself are satisfied that the mechanisms are effective. Now –' he turned to the Kanama – 'I shall ask our distinguished guest to reply to the question put at the last session by the delegate of the U.S.S.R. – namely, what is the motive of the Kanamit people in offering these great gifts to the people of Earth?'

The Kanama rose. Speaking this time in English, he said, 'On my planet there is a saying, "There are more riddles in a stone than in a philosopher's head." The motives of intelligent beings, though they may at times appear obscure, are simple things compared to the complex workings of the natural universe. Therefore I hope that the people of Earth will understand, and believe, when I tell you that our mission upon your planet is simply this – to bring to you the peace and plenty which we ourselves enjoy, and which we have in the past brought to other races throughout the galaxy. When your world has no more hunger, no more war, no more needless suffering, that will be our reward.'

And the needles had not jumped once.

The delegate from the Ukraine jumped to his feet, asking to be recognized, but the time was up and the Secretary-General closed the session.

I met Gregori as we were leaving the chamber. His face was red with excitement. 'Who promoted that circus?' he demanded.

'The tests looked genuine to me,' I told him.

'A circus!' he said vehemently. 'A second-rate farce! If they were genuine, Peter, why was debate stifled?'

'There'll be time for debate tomorrow, surely.'

'Tomorrow the doctor and his instruments will be back in Paris. Plenty of things can happen before tomorrow. In the name of sanity, man, how can anybody trust a thing that looks as if it ate the baby?'

I was a little annoyed. I said, 'Are you sure you're not more worried about their politics than their appearance?'

He said, 'Bah,' and went away.

The next day reports began to come in from government laboratories all over the world where the Kanamit's power source was being tested. They were wildly enthusiastic. I don't understand such things myself, but it seemed that those little metal boxes would give more electrical power than an atomic pile, for next to nothing and nearly for ever. And it was said that they were so cheap to manufacture that everybody in the world could have one of his own. In the early afternoon there were reports that seventeen countries had already begun to set up factories to turn them out.

The next day the Kanamit turned up with plans and specimens of a gadget that would increase the fertility of any arable land by 60 to 100 per cent. It speeded the formation of nitrates in the soil, or something. There was nothing in the newscasts any more but stories about the Kanamit. The day after that, they dropped their bombshell.

'You now have potentially unlimited power and increased food supply,' said one of them. He pointed with his three-fingered hand to an instrument that stood on the table before him. It was a box on a tripod, with a parabolic reflector on the front of it. 'We offer you today a third gift which is at least as important as the first two.'

He beckoned to the TV men to roll their cameras into close-up position. Then he picked up a large sheet of cardboard covered with drawings and English lettering. We saw it on the large screen above the podium; it was all clearly legible.

'We are informed that this broadcast is being relayed throughout your world,' said the Kanama. 'I wish that everyone who has equipment for taking photographs from television screens would use it now.'

The Secretary-General leaned forward and asked a question sharply, but the Kanama ignored him.

'This device,' he said, 'generates a field in which no explosive, of whatever nature, can detonate.'

There was an uncomprehending silence.

The Kanama said, 'It cannot now be suppressed. If one nation has it, all must have it.' When nobody seemed to understand, he explained bluntly, 'There will be no more war.'

That was the biggest news of the millennium, and it was perfectly true. It turned out that the explosions the Kanama was talking about included gasoline and Diesel explosions. They had simply made it impossible for anybody to mount or equip a modern army.

We could have gone back to bows and arrows, of course, but that wouldn't have satisfied the military. Besides, there wouldn't be any reason to make war. Every nation would soon have everything.

Nobody ever gave another thought to those lie-detector experiments, or asked the Kanamit what their politics were. Gregori was put out; he had nothing to prove his suspicions.

I quit my job with the U.N. a few months later, because I foresaw that it was going to die under me anyhow. U.N. business was booming at the time, but after a year or so there was going to be nothing for it to do. Every nation on Earth was well on the way to being completely self-supporting; they weren't going to need much arbitration.

I accepted a position as translator with the Kanamit Embassy, and it was there that I ran into Gregori again. I was glad to see him, but I couldn't imagine what he was doing there.

'I thought you were on the opposition,' I said. 'Don't tell me you're convinced the Kanamit are all right.'

He looked rather shamefaced. 'They're not what they look, anyhow,' he said.

It was as much of a concession as he could decently make, and I invited him down to the embassy lounge for a drink. It was an intimate kind of place, and he grew confidential over the second daiquiri.

'They fascinate me,' he said. 'I hate them instinctively still – that hasn't changed – but I can evaluate it. You were right, obviously; they mean us nothing but good. But do you know –' he leaned across the table – 'the question of the Soviet delegate was never answered.'

I am afraid I snorted.

'No, really,' he said. 'They told us what they wanted to do – "to bring to you the peace and plenty which we ourselves enjoy". But they didn't say *why*.'

'Why do missionaries—'

'Missionaries be damned!' he said angrily. 'Missionaries have a religious motive. If these creatures have a religion, they haven't once mentioned it. What's more, they didn't send a missionary group; they send a diplomatic delegation – a group representing the will and policy of their whole people. Now just what have the Kanamit, as a people or a nation, got to gain from our welfare?'

I said, 'Cultural—'

'Cultural cabbage soup! No, it's something less obvious than that, something obscure that belongs to their psychology and not to ours. But trust me, Peter, there is no such thing as a completely disinterested altruism. In one way or another, they have something to gain.'

'And that's why you're here,' I said. 'To try to find out what it is.'

'Correct. I wanted to get on one of the ten-year exchange groups to their home planet, but I couldn't; the quota was filled a week after they made the announcement. This is the next best thing. I'm studying their language, and you know that language reflects the basic assumptions of the people who use it. I've got a fair command of the spoken lingo already. It's not hard, really, and there are hints in it. Some of the idioms are quite similar to English. I'm sure I'll get the answer eventually.'

'More power,' I said, and we went back to work.

I saw Gregori frequently from then on, and he kept me posted about his progress. He was highly excited about a month after that first meeting; said he'd got hold of a book of the Kanamit's and was trying to puzzle it out. They wrote in ideographs, worse than Chinese, but he was determined to fathom it if it took him years. He wanted my help.

Well, I was interested in spite of myself, for I knew it would be a long job. We spent some evenings together, working with material from Kanamit bulletin boards and so forth, and with the extremely limited English-Kanamit dictionary they issued to the staff. My conscience bothered me about the stolen book, but gradually I became absorbed by the problem. Languages are my field, after all. I couldn't help being fascinated.

We got the title worked out in a few weeks. It was *How to Serve Man*, evidently a handbook they were giving out to new Kanamit members of the embassy staff. They had new ones in, all the time now, a shipload about once a month; they were opening all kinds of research laboratories, clinics and so on. If there was anybody on Earth besides Gregori who still distrusted those people, he must have been somewhere in the middle of Tibet.

It was astonishing to see the changes that had been wrought in less than a year. There were no more standing armies, no more shortages, no unemployment. When you picked up a newspaper you didn't see H-BOMB or SATELLITE leaping out at you; the news was always good. It was a hard thing to get used to. The Kanamit were working on human biochemistry, and it was known around the embassy that they were nearly ready to announce methods of making our race taller and stronger and healthier – practically a race of supermen – and they had a potential cure for heart disease and cancer.

I didn't see Gregori for a fortnight after we finished working out the title of the book; I was on a long-overdue vacation in Canada. When I got back, I was shocked by the change in his appearance.

'What on earth is wrong, Gregori?' I asked. 'You look like the very devil.'

'Come down to the lounge.'

I went with him, and he gulped a stiff Scotch as if he needed it.

'Come on, man, what's the matter?' I urged.

'The Kanamit have put me on the passenger list for the next exchange ship,' he said. 'You too, otherwise I wouldn't be talking to you.'

'Well,' I said, 'but—'

'They're not altruists.'

I tried to reason with him. I pointed out they'd made Earth a paradise compared to what it was before. He only shook his head.

Then I said, 'Well, what about those lie-detector tests?'

'A farce,' he replied, without heat. 'I said so at the time, you fool. They told the truth, though, as far as it went.'

'And the book?' I demanded, annoyed. 'What about that – *How to Serve Man*? That wasn't put there for you to read. They *mean* it. How do you explain that?'

'I've read the first paragraph of that book,' he said. 'Why do you suppose I haven't slept for a week?'

I said, 'Well?' and he smiled a curious, twisted smile.

'It's a cookbook,' he said.

IDIOT STICK

The ship came down out of a blue sky to land in a New Jersey meadow. It sank squashily into the turf. It was about a mile long, colored an iridescent blue-green, like the shell of a beetle.

A door opened, and a thin, stick-bodied man came out to sniff the cool air. The sky overhead was full of fluffy cumulus clouds and crisscrossing contrails. Across the river, the tall buildings of Greater New York were picturesquely gilded by the early sun.

A dun-colored Army copter came into view, circling the ship at a cautious distance. The thin man saw it, blinked at it without interest, and looked away.

The river was smooth and silvery in the sunlight. After a long time, the sound of bullhorns came blaring distantly across the marshes. Then there was a clanking and a roaring, and two Army tanks pulled into sight, followed by two more. They deployed to either side, and slewed around with their 90-mm. guns pointing at the ship.

The alien watched them calmly. More helicopters appeared, circling and hovering. After a while a grey-painted destroyer steamed slowly into view up the river.

More tanks arrived. There was a ring of them around the spaceship, rumbling and smelling of Diesel oil. Finally a staff car pulled up, and three perspiring general officers got out of it.

From his low platform the alien looked down with a patient expression. His voice carried clearly. 'Good morning,' he said. 'This is a ship of the Galactic Federation. We come in peace. Your guns will not fire; please take them away. Now, then. I shall tell you what I am going to do. The Federation wishes to establish a cultural and educational organization upon your continent; and for your land and your co-operation, we will pay you generously. Here, catch these.' He raised his arm, and a cloud of glittery objects came toward them.

One of the officers, white-faced, tugged at the pistol in his belt holster; but the objects dropped harmlessly in and around the car. The senior officer picked one up. It was insubstantial to the touch, more like a soap bubble than anything else. Then it tingled suddenly in his palm. He sat down, glassy-eyed.

The other two shook him. 'Frank! Frank!'

His eyes slowly cleared; he looked from one to the other. 'Are you still here?' he said faintly, and then: 'My God!'

'Frank, what was it? Did it knock you out?'

The senior officer looked down at the glittery thing in his hand. It felt now like nothing in particular – just a piece of plastic, perhaps. There was no more tingle. The zip was gone out of it.

'It was … happiness,' he said.

The rest of the objects glittered and gleamed in the rank grass around the car. 'Go on,' called the alien encouragingly, 'take all you want. Tell your superiors, tell your friends. Come one, come all! We bring happiness!'

Within half a day, the word was out. Work stopped in New York offices; by ferry and tube, people poured across the river. The governor flew in from Trenton and was closeted with the aliens for half an hour, after which he emerged with a dazed and disbelieving look on his face, wearing a shoulder bag full of the glittering little capsules.

The crowd, muddy to the knees, milled around the ship. Every hour the thin alien appeared and tossed out another handful of capsules. There were shouts and screams; the crowd clotted briefly where the capsules fell, and spread apart again like filings released from a magnet.

Dull, used-up capsules littered the grass. Everywhere you saw the dazed expression, the transported look of a man who had had one.

Some few of the capsules got carried home to wives and children. The word continued to spread. No one could describe the effect of the capsules satisfactorily. It lasted only a few seconds, yet seemed to take a long time. It left them satiated and shaken. It was not pleasure of any specific kind, they said; it was happiness, and they wanted more.

Expropriation measures passed the state and national legislatures with blinding speed. There was furious debate elsewhere, but nobody who had had one of the capsules was in any doubt that he was getting a bargain. And the kicker was 'What else can we do?'

The aliens, it appeared, wanted five hundred acres of level ground to put up certain buildings and other structures. Their explanations to the press and public were infrequent and offhand in tone; some people found them unsatisfactory. When asked why the aliens had chosen a site so near heavily populated centres, rather than wasteland which would have been plentiful elsewhere, the spokesman replied (he was either the same stick-thin man who had appeared first, or one just like him), 'But then who would build us our buildings?'

New York, it seemed, represented a source of native labour to the aliens.

The pay would be generous: three capsules a day a man.

When the aliens announced they were hiring, half the population of Greater New York tried to get over onto the Jersey flats. Three-quarters of the population of Hoboken, Jersey City, Hackensack and Paterson was already there.

In the queues that eventually formed out of the confusion, the mayor of New York City was seen alongside an upstate senator and two visiting film stars.

Each person, as he reached the head of the line, was handed a light metal or plastic rod, five feet long, with a curved handle and a splayed tip. The lucky workers were then herded out onto the designated acreage. Some of it was marshland, some was a scraggly part of the New Jersey Parks System, some was improved land. The buildings on the site – a few homes, some factories and warehouses -had all been evacuated but not torn down. The workers with their rods were lined up at one edge of this territory, facing the opposite side.

'When the command "Go" is heard,' said the alien's voice clearly, 'you will all proceed directly forward at a slow walking pace, swinging your sticks from side to side.'

The voice stopped. Apparently that was going to be all.

In the middle of the line, young Ted Cooley looked at his neighbour, Eli Baker. They both worked in the same pharmaceuticals house and had come out together to try their luck. Cooley was twenty-five, blond and brawny; Baker, about the same age, was slight and dark. Their eyes met, and Baker shrugged, as if to say, Don't ask me.

It was a clear, cool day. The long line of men and women stood waiting in the sunlight.

'Go!' said the alien's voice.

The line began to move. Cooley stepped forward and waggled his stick hesitantly. There was no feeling of movement in the stick, but he saw a line of darkness spring out on the ground ahead of him. He paused instinctively, thinking that the stick must be squirting oil or some other liquid.

Up and down the line, other people were stopping, too. He looked more closely and saw that the ground was not wet at all. It was simply pressed down flat – dirt, stones, weeds, everything all at once – to form one hard, dark surface.

'Keep going,' said the alien's voice.

Several people threw down their sticks and walked away. Others moved forward cautiously. Seeing that nothing happened to them when they stepped on the dark strip, Cooley moved forward also. The dark ground was solid and firm underfoot. As he moved forward, swinging the stick, the dark area spread; and, looking closely now, he could see the uneven ground leap downward and darken as the stick swept over it.

'Get in rhythm,' called the voice. 'Leave no space between one man's work and the next.'

The line moved forward, a little raggedly at first, then faster as they got the hang of it. The dark, hard strip, running the whole length of the area, widened as they moved. It was as if everything under the business end of the stick were instantly compressed and smoothed down. Looking closely, you could see the traces of anything that had been there before, like the patterns in marbled linoleum: stones, sticks, grass and weeds.

'How the heck does it work?' said Baker, awed.

'Search me,' said Cooley. In his hands, the tube felt light and empty, like the aluminium shaft of a tank vacuum cleaner. He didn't see how it could possibly have any mechanism inside. There were no controls; he hadn't turned anything on to make it operate.

A few yards ahead, there was a stone wall, overgrown with weeds. 'What's going to happen when we come to that?' Baker asked, pointing.

'Search me.' Cooley felt bewildered; he walked mechanically forward, swinging the stick.

The wall grew nearer. When they were within a few paces of it, a rabbit burst suddenly out of cover. It darted one way, then the other, hind legs pumping hard. Confused by the advancing line, it leaped for the space between Baker and Cooley.

'Look out!' shouted Cooley instinctively. Baker's swinging stick went directly over the rabbit.

Nothing happened. The rabbit kept on going. Cooley and a few others turned to watch it: it bounded away across the level strip and disappeared into the tall grass on the other side.

Baker and Cooley looked at each other. 'Selective,' said Cooley through dry lips. 'Listen, if I—' He shortened his grip on the stick moving the splayed end toward himself.

'Better not,' said Baker nervously.

'Just to see—' Cooley slowly brought the stick nearer, slowly thrust the tip of one shoe under it.

Nothing happened. He moved the stick nearer. Bolder, he ran it over his leg, his other foot. Nothing. 'Selective!' he repeated. 'But how?'

The weeds were dried vegetable fibre. The stick compressed them without hesitation, stamped them down flat like everything else. His trousers were dried vegetable fibre, part of them, anyhow – cotton. His socks, his shoelaces – how did the stick know the difference?

They kept on going. When they came to the stone wall, Cooley waved his stick at it. A section of the wall slumped, as if a giant had taken a bite out of it. He waved it again. The rest of the wall fell.

Somebody laughed hysterically. The line was advancing. The wall was just a lighter stripe in the smooth floor over which they walked.

The sun crept higher. Behind the line of men and women stretched a level, gleaming floor. 'Listen,' said Cooley nervously to Baker, 'how bad do you want those happiness gadgets?'

Baker looked at him curiously. 'I don't know. What do you mean?'

Cooley moistened his lips. 'I'm thinking. We get the gadgets, we use them up—'

'Or sell them,' Baker interrupted.

'Or sell them, but then, either way, they're gone. Suppose we walked off with *these*.' He hefted his stick. 'If we could find out what makes it do what it does—'

'Are you kidding?' said Baker. His dark face was flushed; beads of sweat stood out on his forehead. He waved his stick. 'You know what this is? A shovel. An idiot stick.'

'How's that?' said Cooley.

'A shovel,' Baker told him patiently, 'is a stick with some dirt on one end and an idiot on the other. Old joke. Didn't you ever do any common labour?'

'No,' said Cooley.

'Well, you're doing some now. This thing that looks so wonderful to us – that's just a shovel, to them. An idiot stick. And we're the idiots.'

'I don't like that,' said Cooley.

'Who likes it?' Baker demanded. 'But there isn't a thing you can do about it. Do your work, take your pay, and that's all. Don't kid yourself we can ever get the bulge on them; we haven't got what it takes.'

Cooley thought hard about it, and he was one of the fifty-odd people who walked off the site with Galactic tools that day. The Galactics made no complaint. When daylight failed, they called in the first crew and sent another out under floating lights. The work went on, around the clock. The tools were stolen at a steady rate; the Galactics handed out more indifferently.

The site became level and smooth; the surface was glassy-hard, almost too slick to walk on. The next thing the aliens did was to set up a tall pole on a tripod in the middle of the site. Most of the floating lights went out and drifted away. In the dusk, a network of fluorescent lines appeared on the glassy surface. It looked like the ground plan for a huge building. Some of the pale lines went a little askew because of minor irregularities in the surface, but the Galactics did not seem to mind. They called in part of the crew and made some adjustment in each man's stick. A narrow tab, something like the clip in an automatic, came out of the butt; a different one went in.

So equipped, the reduced crew was sent back onto the site and scattered along the diagram, one man to every two hundred yards or so. They were instructed to walk backward along the lines, drawing their sticks after them.

There was some confusion. The tools now worked only on contact, and instead of flattening the surface down, they made it bulge up, like suddenly rising dough, to form a foot-high ridge. The ridge was pale in colour and felt porous and hard to the touch, like styrene foam.

A few men were called in and had still another set of control tabs put into their sticks. Wherever somebody had jumped, or twitched, and made a ridge where it didn't belong, these men wiped it out like wiping chalk with a wet sponge: the expanded material shrank again and became part of the dark surface.

Meanwhile, the rest of the crew, finishing the first set of lines, was walking along beside them, making the ridges twice as wide. They repeated this process until each ridge was nearly a yard across. Then they stepped up on top of the ridges and began again, making a second foot-high bulge on top of the first.

The building was going up. It was irregularly shaped, a little like an arrowhead, with an outer shell composed of many small compartments. The interior was left unpartitioned, a single area more than half a mile across.

When the shell was up ten feet, the aliens had connecting doorways cut between all the small chambers. A stick, looking no different from the others, was tossed into each chamber from the wall above. Where it landed, clear liquid immediately began to gush. The liquid rose, covered the stick, and kept on rising. It rose until it reached the level of the walls, and then stopped. A few minutes later, it was cold to the touch. In half an hour, it was frozen solid.

The control tabs were changed again, and a crew began walking across the frozen surface, forming another layer of the hard, dark, glassy substance. Afterward, more doorways were cut in the outer shell, and the liquid drained off toward the river. The sticks that had been dropped into the chambers were recovered. Each had left a slight irregularity in the floor, which was smoothed out.

The second storey went up in the same way. Walking backward along the high walls, a good many people fell off. Others quit. The aliens hired more, and the construction went on.

Hardly anybody except a few high government officials got to see the inside of the alien spaceship; but the Galactics themselves became familiar sights in the towns and cities of the eastern seaboard. They walked the streets in inquisitive, faintly supercilious pairs, looking at everything, occasionally stopping to aim little fist-size machines which might or might not have been cameras.

Some of them fraternized with the populace, asking many earnest questions about local laws and customs. Some bought vast quantities of potatoes, playing cards, Cadillacs, junk jewellery, carpets, confetti, nylons and other goods, paying, as usual, with the happiness capsules. They ate local foods with interest and drank heroically without getting drunk, or even tipsy. Skin-tight clothes cut in imitation of the Galactics' bottle-green uniform began to appear on the market. There were Galactic dolls and Galactic spaceship toys.

Legislatures everywhere were relaxed and amiable. Wherever the Galactics had trouble, or sensed it coming, they smoothed the way with more of the happiness capsules. Prices were beginning to be marked not only in '$' and 'c', but in 'Hc', for 'Hapcap'. Business was booming.

In the laboratories of the Bureau of Standards in Washington there was a concerted programme – one of many – to discover the secrets of the Galactic all-purpose tool. Specimens had been measured, X-rayed and cut apart. The material, whatever it was, seemed to have been formed in one piece. It was light, chemically inert and fairly strong. The hollow inside was irregularly curbed, according to no discernible principle.

There were only two parts – the tool proper and the control tab which fitted into a slot in the handle. With the tab in, the tool functioned. It did work, while the dials of every test instrument calmly reported that no energy was being released. With the tab out, nothing happened at all.

The tabs for various functions could be distinguished by colour; otherwise, in shape and dimensions, they seemed identical.

The first – and last – breakthrough came when the tabs were examined by X-ray microscopy. The substance, which had seemed amorphous, was found to have a crystalline structure, permanently stressed in patterns which differed consistently between tabs that produced different functions.

By an elaborate series of test heatings, compressions and deformations, Dr Crawford Reed succeeded in altering the stress pattern of a type 'A' tab to approximately that of a type 'C' tab.

When the tab was inserted in a tool, the laboratory went up in an explosion that demolished buildings within a radius of three city blocks.

The explosion was recorded by instruments in the giant spaceship. When he saw the record, the bored officer on duty smiled.

One of the aliens, who said his name was Pendrath go Pendrath, showed up frequently in the pleasant little town of Riverdale, New Jersey. He poked his nose into church bazaars, Little League baseball games, soda fountains, summer camps, chamber of commerce meetings. At first he gathered crowds wherever he went; then the natives, and even the tourists, got used to him.

Three nights after the rough shell of the building was finished, a young *Star-Ledger* reporter named Al Jenkins found him in the back of a bar, maudlin drunk.

Pendrath looked up as Jenkins slid into the booth next to him. 'Ah, my friend,' he said blurrily, 'how I regret your poor planet.'

'You don't like our planet?' said Jenkins.

'No, it is a nice little planet. Extremely picturesque. Pardon me.' Pendrath sipped from the glass he was holding. He blinked, and straightened up slightly.

'You must understand, that is Galactic progress,' he said. 'It cannot be helped. We all must go some day.'

Jenkins looked at him critically. 'You've been having quite a few of those, haven't you?' he said. 'I thought you people were immune to alcohol, or something.'

'No, it is the aps – as – aspirin,' said the alien. He produced a small bottle, and solemnly shook a tablet out into his palm. 'Your liquors gave me a headache, and so I took an apsirin – aspirin – and your aspirin is wonderful.' He looked lugubrious. 'To think, no more aspirin. No more church bazaar. No more baseball.'

'Why, what's going to happen to them?'

Pendrath spread his fingers and made an expressive fizzing noise with his mouth. 'Blooie,' he said.

Jenkins said incredulously, 'You're going to blow up the world?'

The alien nodded sadly. 'Soon our building will be finished. Then we will put in the big machines, and drill, drill.' He made twisting motions downward with one hand. 'We will drill to the core. Then we will drop the transformer and close up the shaft. Then we will go away. Then your poor little planet will go' – he made the fizzing noise again – 'Blooie.'

Jenkins' fists were clenched. 'But why? Why would you do a thing like that?'

'For dust,' Pendrath explained. 'Your little planet will all be dust. No big pieces left – nothing bigger than this.' He pinched his thumb and forefinger together, squinting, to show how tiny. 'We are making defences for the Galaxy. This sector is too open. We will make a little screen of dust here. If there is dust, a ship cannot go very fast. The dust slows it down. Some places, there is already dust. Other places, we will make it. It is the only way to protect ourselves from invasion.'

'Invasion by whom?'

Pendrath shrugged. 'Who can tell? We have to look ahead.'

Jenkins' hands began to shake. He took a dog-eared notebook out of his pocket, thumbing it open automatically; he looked at it and put it back. His hands didn't want to do anything but make fists. He said thickly, 'You lousy—' and swung a left to Pendrath's beaky face.

The blow never landed. His fist slowed down and stopped; strain as hard as he would, he couldn't push it any farther.

'No, no,' said Pendrath, smiling sadly. 'No use. I regret very much.'

Jenkins' heart was thumping. 'Why us?' he burst out angrily. 'If you had to have dust, why couldn't you take one of the other planets? Jupiter, Venus – any of them – why pick the one we live on?'

Pendrath blinked at him. 'But on your other planets no one lives,' he said. 'Who, then, would do the work for us?' He popped another tablet into his mouth. 'And besides,' he said 'remember that this dust will make a blanket around your sun. It will make the planets very cold. You see, I have thought of all these things. And then suppose we went to some other sun, and did not come here at all. It would be just the same. You would make big spaceships, and we would have to come and finish you anyway. This way, it will be very quick – you will not feel a thing.'

Jenkins had lost his hat. He fumbled on the floor for it. 'We'll stop you,' he said, red-faced over the table-top. 'You'll be sorry you ever opened your mouth to me, mister, I'll spread this from here to Belfast.'

'You are going to tell?' the alien asked, in dull surprise.

'You bet your sweet life I'm going to tell!'

Pendrath nodded owlishly. 'It does not matter now. The work is nearly done. You cannot stop us, my poor friend.'

The story broke the following day, when the installation of the complex system of girders and braces in the interior of the building had already been finished. A hatch in the side of the ship was open, and under the aliens' direction, crews were carrying out a steady stream of machine parts to be assembled inside the building.

There were a thousand and one pieces of different sizes and shapes: gigantic torus sections, tubes, cylinders, globes; twisted pipes, jigsaw-puzzle pieces. The material was not metal, but the same light substance the tools were made of.

Some of the tools were serving as grip-sticks: they clung like magnets to the machine parts, and to nothing else. Some, applied to massive pieces of equipment, made them extraordinarily slippery, so that it was easy to slide them across the site and into the building. Others were used in assembling: drawn along the join between two pieces, they made the two flow together into one.

The story did not reach the day shift at all. The second and third shifts turned up a little under strength; the aliens hired enough people from the crowd of curiosity-seekers to make up the difference.

At his regular press conference, the alien spokesman, Mr Revash go Ren, said, 'Mr Jenkins' story is a malicious fabrication. The machines you mention will provide pleasant heating, air conditioning, Galactic standard gravitation, and other necessary services for the clerical workers in our offices. We are accustomed to have many conveniences of this kind, and that is why we cannot live or work in buildings suitable for you.'

Hersch of the *Times* demanded, 'Why does that take a half-mile area, when your office space is only a thin ring around the outside of the building?'

Revash smiled. 'Why do you take a whole cellar to heat your buildings?' he asked. 'One of your savages would say that a fire of sticks and a hole in the ceiling are sufficient.'

Hersch had no answer to that; nevertheless, belief in the story spread. By the end of the week, half a dozen newspapers were thumping the drum for a crusade. A Congressional investigating committee was appointed. More workers quit. When the labour supply slackened, the aliens doubled the pay, and got more applicants than there were jobs. Riots broke out on the Jersey side of the tubes. There were picket lines, fulminations from the pulpit, attempts at sabotage. The work went on just the same.

'The whole problem is psychological,' said Baker. 'We know what kind of people they are – it sticks out all over them – they're decadent. That's their weak point; that's where we've got to hit them. They've got the perfect machines, but they don't know how to use them. Not only that, they don't want to; it would soil their lily-white hands. So they come here, and they get us to do their dirty work, even though it means an extra risk.'

'That doesn't sound so decadent to me,' said Cooley argumentatively. It was past midnight, and they were still sitting in Baker's living room over a case of beer, hashing it all out. Cooley's face was flushed, and his voice a little loud. 'Take an archaeological expedition, say – I don't know, maybe to Meso-potamia or somewhere. Do they drag along a lot of pick and shovel men? They do not; they take the shovels, maybe, but they hire native labour on the spot. That isn't decadence, that's efficiency.'

'All right, but if we had to, we could get out there and pick up a shovel. They can't. It just wouldn't occur to them. They're over-refined, Ted; they've got to the point where the machines *have* to be perfect, or they couldn't stay alive. That's dangerous; that's where we've got to hit them.'

'I don't see it. Wars are won with weapons.'

'So what are we supposed to do, hit them with atom bombs that don't go off, or guns that don't shoot?'

Cooley put down his stein and reached for the tool that lay on the floor. It had rolled the last time he put it down. He said, 'Damn,' and reached farther. He picked it up, the same 'idiot stick' he had stolen from the Galactic site the first day. 'I'm betting on this,' he said. 'You know and I know they're working on it, day and night, I'm betting they'll crack it. *This* is a weapon, boy – a Galactic weapon. If we just get that—'

'Go ahead, wish for the moon,' said Baker bitterly. 'What you're talking about happens to be impossible. We can change the stress patterns in the control tabs, yes. We can even duplicate the formative conditions, probably, and get as many tabs as you want with the same pattern. But it's empirical, Ted, just blind chance. We don't know *why* such and such a stress pattern makes the tool do a certain thing, and until we know that, all we can do is vary it at random.'

'So?'

'So there are millions of wrong patterns for every right one. There're the patterns that make things explode, like in Washington; there're the ones that boil the experimenter alive or freeze him solid, or bury him in a big lump of solid lead. There're the radioactive ones, the corrosive ones – and for every wrong guess, we lose at least one man.'

'Remote control?' said Cooley.

'First figure out what makes the tools operate when somebody's holding them, and stop when they let go.'

Cooley drank, frowning.

'And remember,' said Baker, 'there's just about one choice that would do us any good against the Galactics. One pattern, out of millions. No. It won't be technology that licks them; it'll be guts.'

He was right; but he was wrong.

Al Jenkins was in the *Star-Ledger* city room, gloomily reading a wire story about denunciations of the aliens issued by governors of eight states. 'What good is that?' he said, tossing it back onto the city editor's desk. 'Look at it.'

Through the window, they could see the top of the alien building shining in the distance. Tiny figures were crawling over the domed roof. The aliens had inflated a hemispherical membrane, and now the workers were going over it with the tools, forming a solid layer.

The dome was almost finished. Work on the interior of the building had stopped two days before.

'He knew what he was talking about,' said Jenkins. 'We couldn't stop them. We had three weeks to do it in, but we just couldn't get together that fast.'

Cigarette ash was spilling down the front of his shirt. He scrubbed at it absently, turned, and walked out of the office. The editor watched him go without saying anything.

One morning in July, two months after the aliens' landing, a ragged mob armed with Galactic tools appeared near the spaceship. Similar mobs had formed several times during the last few nights. When a native grew desperate, he lost what little intelligence he had.

The officer in charge, standing in the open doorway, looked them over disdainfully as they approached. There was no need for any defensive measures; they would try to club him with the tools, fail, and go away.

The native in the lead, a big, burly male, raised his tool like a pitchfork. The Galactic watched him with amusement. The next instant, he was dead, turned into bloody mush on the floor of the airlock.

The mob poured into the ship. Inside, the greenlit hallways were as dim and vast as a cathedral. Bored Galactics looked out of doorways. Their bland expressions changed to gapes of horror. Some ran; some hid. The tools cut them down.

The long corridors echoed to the rattle of running feet, to shouts of excitement and triumph, screams of dismay. The mob swept into every room; it was over in fifteen minutes.

The victors stopped, panting and sweaty, looking around them with the beginnings of wonder. The high-ceilinged rooms were hung with gleaming gold-and-green tapestries; the desks were carved crystal. Music breathed from somewhere, soothing and quiet.

A tray of food was steaming on a table. A transparent chart had been pulled out of a wall. Under each was a pulpy red smear, a puddle of disorganized tissue.

Baker and Cooley looked up and recognized each other. 'Guts,' said Baker wryly.

'Technology,' said Cooley. 'They underrated us; so did you.' He raised the tool he held, careful not to touch the butt. 'Ten thousand tries, I hear – and ten thousand dead men. All right, have it your way. I call that guts, too.' He lifted his head, staring off into the distance, trying to imagine the hundreds of research stations, hidden in remote areas, with their daily, ghastly toll of human life. 'Ten thousand' he said.

Baker was shaking with reaction. 'We were lucky; it might have been a million ...' He tried to laugh. 'Have to find a new name for this now – no more idiot stick.'

Cooley glanced at the floor. 'It depends,' he said grimly, 'which end of the stick the idiot's on.'

THING OF BEAUTY

There was a time slip in Southern California at about one in the afternoon. Mr Gordon Fish thought it was an earthquake. He woke up confused and sullen from his midday nap, blinking fiercely, as pink as a spanked baby's behind, with his sandy-yellow beard and eyebrows bristling. He got off the sofa and listened. No screams, no rumble of falling buildings, so probably it was all right.

He heard a knock.

Squinting uneasily, Fish went to the door. He had left his glasses on the table, but never mind; it might be a client, or even an investigator from the city. In which case ... He opened the door.

A slender man in purple was standing there. He was small, hardly an inch taller than Gordon Fish. He said, 'Three twenty-two and a half Platt Terrace?' His face was an oval blur; he seemed to be wearing some kind of tight uniform, like a bellboy's – but purple?

'That's right, three twenty-two and a half, this is it,' said Fish, straining to make out the fellow's salmon-coloured face. He caught sight of some other people standing behind him, and a shadowy bulk, like a big box of some kind. 'I don't know if you—'

'All right, fezh, bring it in,' said the man, turning to speak over his shoulder. 'Bung, did we have a time finding you,' he said to Fish, and pushed his way into the living room. Behind him, other men in tight purple clothing came staggering under the weight of boxes, first a big one, then two smaller ones, then a *really* big one, then a clutter of smaller boxes.

'Listen, wait, there must be some mistake,' said Fish, dancing out of the way. 'I didn't order—'

The first man in purple looked at some papers in his hand. 'Three twenty-two and a *half* Piatt *Terrace*?' he said. His voice sounded slurred and angry, as if he were half drunk or had just woken up, like Fish himself.

Fish was unreasonably irritated. 'I tell you I didn't order anything! I don't care if – You walk in here, into a man's home, just like – Listen! You get out of there!' Infuriated, he rushed at two of the men who were setting down one of the smaller boxes on the sofa.

'This is the address,' said the first man in a bored voice. He shoved some papers into Fish's hand. 'You don't want 'em, send 'em back. We just deliver 'em.' The purple men began to move toward the door.

The spokesman went out last. 'Bung, are *you* a dvich!' he said, and closed the door.

Raging, Fish fumbled for his glasses. They ought to be right *there*, but the movers had upset everything. He went to the door anyway, twitching with anger. Dammit, if he could just find his glasses he'd *report* them, but ... He opened the door. The purple-uniformed men, a little knot of them, were standing in the courtyard looking bewildered. One of them turned a salmon-coloured dot of a face. 'Hey, which way is ...' Something. It sounded like 'enchmire'.

There was a tremor, and Fish lurched against the door frame. It felt like an earth shock, a heavy one, but when he looked up the palm trees in the street were not swaying, and the buildings were solid and firm. But the purple men were gone.

Swearing frantically to himself, Fish went back into the living room and slammed the door behind him. The biggest box was in his way. He kicked it, and a slat fell out. He kicked it again, grunting with angry satisfaction. The whole side fell down with a clatter, revealing a black-enamelled panel. Fish kicked that, and bruised his toe.

'Hm,' said Fish, looking at the sleek black finish of whatever it was. 'Hah.' It looked like money. Peering, he ran his finger along the metal. Cool and smooth. Why, it might be almost anything. Industrial machinery, worth thousands of dollars to the right party. With rising excitement, Fish ran to the table, found his glasses pushed into some magazines, and ran back, fitting the glasses over his mean little eyes.

He pulled some more slats aside. The box fell away, disclosing an oddly shaped hunk of metal with knobs, dials and switches in the top. An engraved white plate read: 'TECKNING MASKIN', and then some numbers. It sounded ominous and important. Heart beating, Fish rubbed his fingers over the knurled knobs and the gleaming switch handles. There was a faint click. He had accidentally moved one switch, he saw, from 'Av' to 'På'. The dials were lighting up, and a set of long hooked arms, like claws, were slowly drifting out over the flat empty space in the middle.

Hastily, Fish turned the switch back to 'Av'. The lights went out; the arms, looking disappointed, he thought, drifted back into their enclosures.

Well, it *worked*, whatever it was, which was funny, because come to think of it he hadn't plugged it in anywhere. Fish stared at the machine uneasily, rubbing his podgy hands together. Batteries? In a machine that size? And those funny dials, the peculiar *expression* the whole thing had, and 'Teckning Maskin' – not even English. There it sat, all eight or nine pieces of it, filling up his living room – one crate, he saw with a pang, blocked off his view of the TV. Suppose it was all some kind *of joke?*

The instant he thought of it, he saw the whole thing in a flash. The crates sitting here, and then in a few days the bill would come in the mail – maybe they wouldn't even take the things away until he'd paid the shipping – and all the time, the joker would be laughing himself sick. Laughing, whoever it was that had ordered the machines in Fish's name – some old enemy, or it could even be someone he thought of as a *friend.*

With tears of rage in his eyes, he rushed to the door again, flung it open and stood panting, staring around the courtyard. But there was nobody there. He slammed the door and stood looking helplessly at the crates. If they would fight *fair!* How was he going to watch *Dragnet,* and, good heaven, where was he going to talk to clients – in the *kitchen?*

'Oh!' said Fish, and he kicked another crate hard. Slats gave, and something fell out, a little yellow booklet. Fish glimpsed more black-enamelled machinery inside. He bent wildly to pick up the booklet and tried to tear it across, but it hurt his hands. He threw it across the room, shouting, 'Well, then!' He danced from one crate to another, kicking. Slats littered the floor. Gleaming machines stood up from the mess, some with dials, some without. Fish stopped, out of breath, and stared at them with a new bewilderment.

A trick – no, it couldn't be. Big industrial machines like that – it wasn't like ordering something from a department store. But then what? A mistake. Fish sat down on the arm of a chair and frowned, scrubbing his beard with his fingers.

In the first place, now, he hadn't *signed* anything. Even if they came back tomorrow, if he could manage to get rid of say one piece, he could always claim there had been *eight* instead of *nine.* Or suppose he even got rid of all of it, discreetly of course, then when they came back he could simply deny the whole thing. Say he never heard of any machinery. Fish's nerves began to twitch. He jumped up, looked around, sat down again. Speed, speed, that was the thing. Get it over with. But what kind of machinery *was* it?

Fish frowned, squirmed, got up and sat down. Finally he went to the phone, looked up a number and dialled. He smoothed down his vest, cleared his throat musically. 'Ben? This is Gordon Fish, Ben … Just fine. Now, Ben –' his voice dropped confidentially– 'I happen to have a client who wants to dispose of a Teckning Maskin. Eight – What? Teckning Maskin. It's machinery, Ben. T-E-C-K-N-I-N-G -No? Well, that's the name they gave me. I have it written down right here. You never— Well, that's funny. Probably some mistake. I tell you, Ben, I'll check back and see. Yes, thanks a lot. Thanks, Ben, bye-bye.'

He hung up, chewing his whiskers in vexation. If Ben Abrams had never *heard* of it, then there couldn't be any market for it, not in *this* part of the country anyhow … Something funny. He was beginning to have a hunch about this thing now. Something … He prowled around the machines, looking at them this way and that. Here was another engraved white plate; it said 'TECKNING MASKIN', and Under that 'BANK 1', and then two columns of numbers and words: '3 Folk, 4 Djur, 5 Byggnader', and so on, a lot more. Crazy words; it didn't even look like any language he'd ever *heard* of. And then those maniacs in the purple uniforms … Wait a minute! Fish snapped his fingers, stopped, and stood in a pose of thought. Now what was it that fellow had said just as he was leaving? It had made him mad, Fish remembered – something like, 'Boy, are you a dvich.' Made him mad as a hornet; it *sounded* insulting, but what did it *mean?*

And then that kind of earthquake just before they got here – woke him up out of a sound sleep, left him feeling all funny. And then another one after they left – only *not* an earthquake, because he remembered distinctly that the palm trees didn't even tremble.

Fish ran his finger delicately over the shining curved edge of the nearest machine. His heart was thumping; his tongue came out to lick his lips. He had a feeling – no, he really *knew* – nobody would be coming back for the machines.

They were his. Yes, and there was money in them, somewhere; he could smell it. But how? What did they *do?*

He opened all the crates carefully. In one of them, instead of a machine, there was a metal box full of creamy-thick sheets of paper. They were big rectangular sheets, and they looked as if one would just about fit onto the flat centre space on the biggest machine. Fish tried one, and it did.

Well, what could go wrong? Fish rubbed his fingers nervously, then turned the switch on. The dials lighted and the hooked arms drifted out, as before, but nothing else happened. Fish leaned nearer again and looked at the other controls. There was a pointer and a series of marks labelled 'Av', 'Bank 1', 'Bank 2', and so on down to 'Bank 9'. He moved the pointer cautiously to 'Bank 1'. The arms moved a little, slowly, and stopped.

What else? Three red buttons marked 'Utplåna', 'Torka' and 'Avslå'. He pressed one down, but nothing happened. Then a series of white ones, like on an adding machine, all numbered. He pressed one down at random, then another, and was about to press a third when he leaped back in alarm. The hooked arms were moving, rapidly and purposefully. Where they passed over the paper, thin dark-grey lines were growing.

Fish leaned closer, his mouth open and his eyes bulging. The little points under the ends of the arms were riding smoothly over the paper, leaving graceful lines behind them. The arms moved, contracted on their little pivots and springs, swept this way and that, lifted slightly, dropped again and moved on. Why, the machine was drawing – drawing a picture while he watched!

27

There was a face forming under the arm over on the right, then a neck and shoulder – kind of a sappy-looking man, it was, like a Greek statue. Then over here on the left, at the same time, another arm was drawing a bull's head, with some kind of flowers between the horns. Now the man's body – he was wearing one of those Greek togas or whatever you call them – and the back of the bull curving around up on top. And now the man's arm, and the bull's tail, and now the other arm, and the bull's hind legs.

There it was. A picture of a man throwing flowers at this bull, who was kind of leaping and looking at the man over his shoulder. The arms of the machine stopped moving, and then pulled back out of sight. The lights went out, and the switch clicked by itself back to 'På'.

Fish took the paper and looked it over, excited but a little disappointed. He didn't know anything about *art*, of course, but he knew this was no good – all flat looking and kind of simple, like a kid would draw. And that bull – whoever saw a bull dancing like that? With flowers between its horns? Still, if the machine would draw this, maybe it would draw something better; he couldn't quite see the angle. Where would you sell drawings, even good ones? But it was there, somewhere. Exhibit the machine, like in a fair of science and industry? No, his mind hurriedly buried the thought – too exposed, too many questions. Heavens, if Vera found out he was still alive, or if the police in Scranton …

Drawings. A machine that made drawings. Fish looked at it, all eight lumpy black-enamelled massive pieces of it scattered around his living room. It seemed like a lot of machinery just to make *drawings*. He admitted it: he was disappointed. He had expected, well, metal stampings or something like that, something real. Crash, bang, the big metal jaw comes down, and tink, the bright shaped piece falls out into the basket. There was machinery for you; but this …

Fish sat back and pondered, twitching the paper disapprovingly between his fingers. Things were always letting him down like this. Really, his best line was marriage. He had been married five times, and always made a little profit out of it. He smoothed the vest down over his suety front. Between times, he turned to whatever was handy – marital counselling some years, or gave life readings if he could get enough clients, or naturopathy. It all depended. But somehow every time it looked as if he had a real gold mine, it slipped out from under his hand. He reddened with discomfort as he thought of the one winter he had been forced to go to work in a *shoe store* … Having this house had softened him up, too, he had been getting lazy – just a client or two a week for life readings. He ought to be getting busy, working up new contacts before his money ran out.

The thought of poverty made him ravenously hungry, as it always did. He kneaded his stomach. Time for lunch. He got his jacket hurriedly, and, as an afterthought, rolled up the drawing – it would not fold – and tucked it under his arm.

He drove to the barbecue place three blocks down the boulevard where he had been eating a lot of his meals lately, to save funds. The counterman was a young fellow named Dave, lean and pale, with a lock of straight dark hair falling over his forehead. Fish had got into friendly conversation with him and knew he was going to art school nights, over in Pasadena. Fish had tried to get him over for a life reading, but the youngster had said frankly that he 'didn't believe in it' in such an honest and friendly way that Fish bore him no ill-will.

'Bowl o' chile, Dave,' he said cheerfully, hoisting himself up on a stool with the rolled drawing precariously on his lap. His feet dangled; the paper was squeezed tight between his vest and the counter.

'Hello, Doc. Coming up.' Fish hunched forward over the bowl, loosening his collar. The one other customer paid and left.

'Say, Dave,' said Fish indistinctly, munching, 'like to get your opinion of something. Unh.' He managed to get the rolled paper free and opened it on the counter. 'What do you think – is it any good?'

'Say,' said Dave, coming nearer. 'Where'd you get *that*?'

'Mm. Nephew of mine,' Fish answered readily. 'He wants me to advise him, you know, if he should go on with it, because—'

'Go on with it! Well, say. Where's he been studying, anyhow?'

'Oh, just by himself, you know – back home.' Fish took another mouthful. 'Ver' bright boy, you understand, but—'

'Well, if he learned to draw like that all by himself, why he must be a world-beater.'

Fish forgot to chew. 'You really mean it?'

'Why, sure. Listen, are you sure he drew this himself, Doc?'

'Oh, certainly.' Fish waved the imputation of dishonesty away. 'Ver' honest boy, I know'm well. No, 'f he tells me he drew it, why' – he swallowed – 'he drew it. But now don't fool me, is it – do you really think it's as *good*—'

'Well, I tell you the truth, when I first saw it, *I* thought Picasso. You know, his classical period. Of course I see now it's different, but, my gosh, it's good. I mean, if you want *my* opinion, why—'

Fish was nodding to indicate that this only confirmed his own diagnosis. 'M-hm. M-hm. Well, I'm glad to hear you say it, son. You know, being a relative of the boy, I thought – Of course, I'm very impressed. Very impressed. I thought of Pricasso, too, same as you. Of course, now from the money end of it' – he wagged his head dolefully – 'you know and I know ...'

Dave scratched his head under the white cap. 'Oh, well, he ought to be able to get commissions, all right. I mean, if I had a line like that –' He traced in air the outline of the man's lifted arm.

29

'Now, when you say *commissions*,' Fish said, squirming with eagerness.

'Oh, well, you know, for portraits, or industrial designs or, you know, whatever he wants to go in for.' Dave shook his head in admiration, staring at the drawing. 'If this was only in colour.'

'How's that, Dave?'

'Why, I was just thinking – see, there's a competition up in San Gabriel for a civic centre mural. Ten-thousand-dollar prize. Now I don't know, it might not win, but why don't you have him render this in colour and send it in?'

'Colour,' said Fish blankly. The machine wouldn't colour anything, he was sure. He could get a box of water colour paints, but ... 'Well, now, the fact is,' he said, hastily revolving ideas, 'you know, the boy is laid up. Hurt his hand – oh, not serious,' he said reassuringly (Dave's mouth had fallen into an *O* of sympathy), 'but won't be able to draw any more pictures for a while. It's a shame, he could use the money, you know, for doctor bills.' He chewed and swallowed. 'Tell you, this is just a wild idea, now, but why couldn't you colour it up and send it in, Dave? 'Course if it doesn't win, I couldn't pay you, but—'

'Well, gee, I don't know how he'd like that, Doc. I mean suppose he'd have something else in mind, like some other colour scheme altogether. You know, I wouldn't like to—'

'I'll take full responsibility,' said Fish firmly. 'Don't you worry about that, and if we win, why I'll see that you're paid handsomely for your work, Dave. Now there, how's that?'

'Well, sure, then, Doc. I mean, sure,' said Dave, nodding and blushing. 'I'll do it tonight and tomorrow, and get it right off in the mail. Okay? Then – oh, uh, one thing, what's your nephew's name?'

'George Wilmington,' said Fish at random. He pushed the cleaned chile bowl away. 'And, uh, Dave, I believe I'll have an order of ribs, with French fries on the side.'

Fish went home with a vastly increased respect for the machine. The civic centre competition, he was positive, was in the bag. Ten thousand dollars! For one drawing! Why, there was millions in it! He closed and locked the front door carefully behind him, and pulled down the Venetian blinds to darken the gloomy little living room still further. He turned on the lights. There the machine still was, all eight gleaming pieces of it, scattered around on the floor, the furniture, everywhere. He moved excitedly from one piece to another, caressing the slick black surfaces with his palm. All that expensive machinery – all his!

Might as well put it through its paces again, just to see. Fish got another sheet of creamy paper from the stack, put it in position, and turned the switch to 'På'. He watched with pleasure as the dials lighted, the hooked arms drifted out and began to move. Lines grew on the paper: first some wavy ones at the top – could be anything. And farther down, a pair of long, up-curved lines, kind of like handlebars. It was like a puzzle, trying to figure out what it was going to be.

Under the wavy lines, which Fish now perceived to be hair, the pointer drew eyes and a nose. Meanwhile the other one was gliding around the outline of what, it became clear in a moment, was a bull's head. Now here came the rest of the girl's face, and her arm and one leg – not bad, but kind of beefy – and now the bull's legs, sticking out all different ways, and then, whoops, it wasn't a bull: there was the whatyoumaycallum with the teats swinging; it was a cow.

So, a girl riding on a cow, with flowers between its horns like before.

Fish looked at the drawing in disappointment. People and cows – was that all the thing could do?

He scrubbed his beard in vexation. Why, for heaven's sake, suppose somebody wanted a picture of something *besides* bulls and people? It was ridiculous – eight big pieces of machinery …

Wait a minute. 'Don't go off half cocked, Gordon,' he told himself aloud. That was what Florence, his second, always used to say, except she always called him 'Fishy'. He winced with discomfort at the memory. Well, anyway, he noticed now that the same buttons he had pressed down before were still down. That must have something to do with it. Struck by another thought, he trotted over and looked at the machine marked 'Bank 1'. Now this list here, number 3 was 'Folk', and number 4 was 'Djur'. Those were the numbers he had pressed on the big machine, so … maybe 'folk' meant *people*, and 'djur', why, that might be some crazy word for *bulls*. Then if he pressed a different set of buttons, why, the machine would have to draw something else.

In fifteen minutes he verified that this was the case. Pressing down the first two buttons, 'Land' and 'Planta', gave him drawings of outdoor scenes, just hills and trees. 'Folk' was people, and 'Djur' seemed to be animals; now he got goats or dogs instead of bulls. 'Byggnader' was buildings. Then it got more complicated.

A button marked 'Arbete' gave him pictures of people at work; one labelled 'Kärlek' produced scenes of couples kissing – all in the kind of Greek-looking clothes – and the landscapes and buildings were sort of vague and dreamy. Then there was a whole row of buttons under the heading 'Plats', and another headed 'Tid', that seemed to control the time and place of the pictures. For instance, when he pressed 'Egyptisk' and 'Gammal', along with 'Folk', 'Byggnader' and, on a hunch, the word he had decided meant *religion*, he got a picture of some priests in Egyptian headdresses bowing in front of a big statue of Horus. Now *there* was something!

The next day he nailed up the crates again, leaving the tops loose so that he could remove them whenever he wanted to use the machines. In the process, he came across the little yellow booklet he had thrown away. There were dia-grams in it, some of which made sense and some didn't, but the printing was all in the same unfamiliar language. Fish put the booklet away in a bureau drawer, under an untidy heap of clothes, and forgot about it. Grunting and sweating, he managed to push the smaller crates into corners and rearranged the furniture so there was room to put the big one against the wall. It still looked terrible, but at least he could get around, and have clients in, and he could see the TV again.

Every day he ate lunch at the barbecue place, or at least stopped in, and every day, when Dave saw him come in, he shook his head. Then all after-noon he would sit with a glass of beer, or maybe a plate of nuts or fudge, watching the machine draw. He used up all the paper in the stack and started turning them over to use the other sides.

But where was the money coming from? After some thought, Fish built a simple magic-writing box, and used it with his Egyptian drawings – he had a dozen, all of different gods, but after the first one the machine didn't draw any priests – to show clients what they had been up to in previous incarna-tions. He began to get a little more business, and once or twice his instinct told him he could raise the fee on account of the drawings, but that was only pocket money. He knew there was *millions* in it, he could almost taste it, but where?

Once it occurred to him that maybe he could take out a patent on the machine and sell it. Trouble with that was, he didn't have any idea how the thing worked. It seemed like the little machines must have pictures inside, or pieces of pictures, and the big machine put them together – how? Fuming with impatience, Fish took the big crate apart again, moved furniture out of the way, and fumbled at the smooth black side of the machine to see if there was any way of opening it up.

After a moment his fingers found two shallow depressions in the metal; he pushed experimentally, then pressed upward, and the side plate of the machine came off in his hands.

It weighed almost nothing. Fish put it aside, staring doubtfully into the interior of the machine. It was all dark in there, nothing but a few very tiny specks of light, like mica dust hanging motionless. No wires, no nothing. Fish got a sheet of paper and put it in position, and turned the machine on. Then he squatted down. The tiny specks of light seemed to be moving, circling slowly around one another in time to the motion of the drawing arms. It was darker in there, and looked farther away, somehow, than it had any right to.

Holding the front of the machine, Fish touched another shallow depres-sion and, without really meaning to, he pushed upward. The whole front of the machine fell off, and the other side with it.

He sprawled backward frantically to get out of the way, but the top of the machine didn't fall. It stayed there, rock-steady, although there was nothing holding it up but the back panel.

And underneath, nothing. No framework, just the thick darkness, with the little stars going slowly around as the machine drew.

Fish hastily picked up the front and side panels and put them back. They slid easily and perfectly into place, and fitted so closely that he couldn't see any line between them.

After that, he put the crate back together and never tried to look inside the machine again.

Dave hurried around the end of the counter to him. 'Doc! Where have you been?' He was drying his hands on his apron and grinning nervously, with a sort of poleaxed expression around his eyes. A customer around the other side of the counter looked up, then went on chewing with his mouth open.

'Well, I had quite a lot of things to do,' Fish began automatically. Then he began to feel excited. 'Say! You don't mean—'

Dave fished a long white envelope out of his back pocket. 'Came yesterday! Look here!' The envelope crackled in his nervous fingers. He pulled out a folded letter, and Fish seized it. Dave looked over his shoulder, breathing heavily, as he read.

DEAR MR WILMINGTON:

It is my very great pleasure to inform you that your design has been awarded the First Prize in the San Gabriel Civic Centre Mural Competition. In the opinion of the judges, the classic simplicity of your entry, together with its technical mastery, made it far superior to anything else submitted,

Enclosed please find our check for three thousand dollars ($3,000.00)...

'Where?' cried Fish, looking up.

'Right here,' said Dave, with a grin that looked painful. He held up a salmon-coloured strip of paper. The red-printed lettering read: 'EXACTLY 3,000.^{00} DOLLARS*****.'

Fish hugged Dave, who hugged him back, and then looked at the letter again.

... the remainder to be paid when the design is executed to the satis-faction of the Committee ...

'Executed?' said Fish, with a sinking feeling. 'What's that mean? Dave, what's he mean here, where he says—'

'When he paints the mural on the wall. Gee, Doc, I just can't tell you—'

'Who?'

'Your nephew. George Wilmington. See, when he paints the mural—'

'Oh,' said Fish. 'Oh. Well, you see, Dave, the fact *is*—'

Dave's long face grew solemn. 'Oh, gosh, I never thought. You mean he's not well enough to draw yet?'

Fish shook his head mournfully. 'No, sir. It's a terrible shame, Dave, but –' He folded the cheque absently and slipped it into his pocket.

'I thought you said, I mean, it wasn't serious or anything …'

Fish continued to shake his head. 'Turned out, there was more to it than they thought. It looks like now, they just don't know when he'll ever be able to draw again.'

'Oh, Doc,' said Dave, stricken.

'That's the way it is. These things – the doctors don't know as much about 'em as they'd like you to think, Dave.' Fish went on staring fiercely at the letter, barely listening to the sound of his own voice. *To be paid when the design is executed …*

'Look here,' he said, interrupting Dave's murmurs of commiseration. 'It don't say *who* has to execute it, now does it? Notice right there? Says "when the design is executed".'

'How about a glassa water over here?' called the customer.

'Coming right up, sir. Look, Doc, I think you got an idea.' He retired side-wise toward the counter, still talking. 'You know, anybody could scale that up and do the actual painting – any competent artist, I mean. Gee, I'd do it myself, I mean if George didn't care. And if it was all right with the commit-tee, why, you know, it would be an opportunity for me.' He gave the customer his water, mopped the counter blindly and came back.

Fish leaned over the counter, beard in hand, frowning. 'Wilmington' was just a name. Dave could take the part, just as well as not, and it would be a lot better in one way, because then Fish himself could stay out of sight. But, whoops, if they did that, then Dave would *be* Wilmington, and he might want to take off on his own …

'Well, Dave,' he said, 'are you a *good* artist?'

Dave looked embarrassed. 'Gee, Doc, you put me on the spot, but, well, anyway, they liked how I rendered the design, didn't they? See, I used a col-our scheme of deep aqua and a kind of buff, with accents of rose, you know, to make it cheerful? And, gee, if I did it on the paper, I could do it on a wall.'

'Sold!' said Fish heartily, and clapped Dave on the shoulder. 'George don't know it yet, but he just got himself an assistant!'

A slim female figure popped up at him suddenly from beside a potted palm. 'Mr Wilmington? If I could just have a moment …'

Fish paused, one hand going to his chin in the old gesture, although he had shaved off the beard over a year ago. He felt exposed without it, and his fea-tures tended to twitch when he was startled like this. 'Why, yes, uh, miss …'

'My name is Norma Johnson. You don't know me, but I have some draw-ings here …'

She was carrying a big black portfolio fastened with tapes. Fish sat down beside her and looked at the drawings. They looked all right to him, but skimpy, like the kind of thing he turned out mostly himself. What he *liked* was pictures with some meat to them, like Norman Rockwell, but the one time he had set the machine to draw something like that, his agent – the first one, Connolly, that crook! – had told him there was no market for 'genre stuff.

The girl's fingers were trembling. She was very neat and pale, with black hair and big expressive eyes. She turned over the last drawing. 'Are they any good?' she asked.

'Well, now, there's a good deal of spirit there,' said Fish comfortably. 'And a very fine sense of design.'

'Could I ever be successful at it?'

'Well …'

'See, the thing is,' she said rapidly, 'my Aunt Marie wants me to stay here in Santa Monica and come out next season. But I don't want to. So she agreed, if you said I had real talent, that she would send me abroad to study. But if you didn't, I'd give up.'

Fish looked at her intently. Her fingernails were short but looked cared for. She was wearing a simple white blouse and a little blue jacket and skirt; there was a whiff of woodsy perfume. Fish smelled money.

He said, 'Well, my dear, let me put it this way. Now you could go to Europe and spend a lot of money – ten thousand, twenty thousand dollars.' She watched him without blinking. 'Fifty thousand,' said Fish delicately. 'But what would be the point of it? Those fellows over there don't know as much as they'd like you to think.'

She fumbled blindly for her purse and gloves. 'I see.' She started to get up.

Fish put a pudgy hand on her arm. 'Now what *I* would suggest,' he said, 'why don't you come and study with me for a year instead?'

Her pale face lengthened. 'Oh, Mr Wilmington, *would* you?'

'Well, anybody with as much talent as these drawings' – Fish patted the portfolio on her knee – 'why, we have to do something, because—'

She stood up excitedly. 'Will you come tell that to Aunt Marie?'

Fish smoothed down the front of his pink shirt. 'Why, gladly, my dear, gladly.'

'She's right here in the lounge.'

Fish followed her and met Aunt Marie, who was a handsome woman of about fifty, plump but beautifully tailored in brown linen. They agreed that Norma would take a studio near Mr Wilmington's home in Santa Monica, and that Mr Wilmington would look in several times a week and give her the full benefit of his great experience, in return for ten thousand dollars per annum. It was, as Fish pointed out to them, less than half the amount he usually got now for major commissions; but, never mind, every little bit helped. Murals, institutional advertising, textile designs, private sales to collectors – my God, how it was rolling in!

The only thing that really worried him was the machine itself. He kept it now in a locked inner room of the house he was renting – twenty rooms, furnished, terrific view of the Pacific Ocean, lots of room for parties – and up to a point he could work it like a kiddy car. One time or another, he had figured out and memorized every one of the dozens of labelled buttons on the 'Bank' machines, and just by combining the right ones, he could get any kind of a drawing he wanted. For instance, that commission for stained glass for a church – 'Religion', 'People', 'Palestine', 'Ancient', and there you were.

The trouble was, the machine wouldn't draw the same thing twice in a row. On that church window job, he got one picture of Christ and then couldn't get another, no matter how long he tried, so he had to fill out with saints and martyrs. The church put up a beef, too. Then sometimes at night, for his own amusement, he used to put the machine through its paces – for instance, set it for 'Historical figures' and 'Romantisk', which seemed to be the machine's name for the present era, and then push the button marked 'Överdriva', and watch the famous faces come out with big cartoony noses, and teeth like picket fences.

Or he would set it for 'Love', and then various interesting times and places – ancient Rome gave him some spicy ones, and Samoa was even better.

But every time he did this, the machine turned out fewer drawings; and finally it wouldn't do any more like that at all.

Was there some kind of a censor built into the thing? Did it *disapprove* of him?

He kept thinking of the funny way those men in purple uniforms had delivered the thing. They had the right address, but the wrong … time? Whatever it was, he knew the machine wasn't intended for him. But who was it meant for? What was a 'dvich'?

There were eight pieces – six banks, the master machine, and one which he had discovered would enlarge any detail of a drawing to almost full size. He could handle all that. He could manage the controls that governed the complexity or simplicity of a drawing, gave it more or less depth, changed its style and mood. The only buttons he wasn't sure of were the three red ones marked 'Utplåna', 'Torka', and 'Avslå'. None of them seemed to *do* anything. He had tried all three both ways, and they didn't seem to make any difference. In the end he left them the way they had been: 'Torka' down, the other two up, for lack of any better idea. But big and red like that, they must be important.

He found them mentioned in the booklet, too: '*Utplåna en teckning, press knappen "Utplåna". Avtägsna ett mönster från en bank efter användning, press knappen "Torka". A vslå en teckning innan slutsatsen, press knappen "Avslå".*'

Press knappen, press knappen, that must be 'push button'. But *when?* And that business about 'monster', that made him a little nervous. He had been pretty lucky so far, figuring out how to work the whole machine without any accidents. Suppose there was still something that could go wrong – suppose the booklet was a *warning?*

He prowled restlessly around the empty house – empty, and untidy, because he wouldn't have any servants in the place. You never knew who was going to spy on you. A woman came in two days a week to clean the place up – all but the locked room – and once in a while he'd bring a couple of girls up for a party, but he always threw them out the next morning. He was busy, all right, seeing a lot of people, travelling around, but he'd had to drop all his old friends when he decided to become Wilmington, and he didn't dare make any new ones for fear of giving himself away. Besides, everybody was out for something. The fact was, dammit, he wasn't *happy*. What the hell good was all the money he was making, all the things he'd bought, if they didn't make him happy? Anyhow, pretty soon now that oil stock would start paying off – the salesman had assured him that the drillers were down within a few hundred feet of oil right now – and then he'd be a millionaire; he could retire – move to Florida or some place.

He paused in front of his desk in the library. The booklet was still there, lying open. The thing was, even suppose that was some language anybody had ever heard of, who would he dare show it to? Who could he trust?

An idea occurred to him, and he leaned over, staring at the yellow pages with their incomprehensible text. After all, he could already figure out some of the words; he didn't have to show anybody the whole book, or even a whole sentence … Then there was that information business that came with his de luxe set of the Encyclopaedia Britannica – he ought to have it right here somewhere. Fish hunted in the file drawers and finally came up with a folder and a sheet of gummed yellow stamps.

Grunting, he sat down at the desk, and after much cigar-chewing, scribbling and crossing out, he typed the following:

DEAR SIRS
Kindly inform me as to what language the enclosed words are, and also what they mean. Kindly give this matter your best attention, as I am in a hurry.

On a separate sheet he wrote all the doubtful words from the paragraph about the red buttons, cannily mixing them up so no one could guess what order they came in. Feeling a little foolish, he carefully drew in all the tiny circles and dots. Then he addressed an envelope, stuck one of the yellow stamps to his letter, and mailed the thing off before he could regret it.

'My rhetorical question is,' said Fish craftily to the young physicist, shouting over the hum of cocktail-party conversation, 'purely in interest of science, could you make a machine that would draw?' He beamed over his glasses at the horn-rimmed blur of the young man's face. He had had three martinis, and whew! he was floating. But fully in command of his senses, of course.

'Well, draw what? If you mean charts and graphs, sure, or something like a pantograph, to enlarge—'

'No, no. Draw *beau'fill* pictures.' The last word sprayed a little. Fish rocked forward and back again. 'Purely rhetorical question.' He put his glass down with precision on a passing tray and took another one, which spilled icy liquid down his wrist. He gulped to save it.

'Oh. Well, in that case, no. I would say not. I assume you mean it would originate the drawings, not just put out what was programmed into it. Well, that would mean, in the first place, you'd have to have an incredibly big memory bank. Say if you wanted the machine to draw a horse, it would have to know what a horse looks like from every angle and in every position. Then it would have to select the best one out of say ten or twenty billion – and then draw it in proportion with whatever else is in the drawing, and so on. Then, for God's sake, if you wanted *beauty*, too, I suppose it would have to consider the relation of every part to every other part, on some kind of aesthetic principle. *I* wouldn't know how to go about it.'

Fish, thick-fingered, probed for his olive. 'Say it's impossible, hey?' he asked.

'Well, with present techniques, anyhow. I guess we'll be staying out of the art business for another century or two.' The blur smiled and lifted its highball glass.

'Ah,' said Fish, putting a hand on the young man's lapel to support himself and keep the other from moving out of the corner. 'Now, suppose you had a machine like that. Now, suppose that machine kept forgetting things. What would be the reason for that?'

'Forgetting things?'

'What I said.' With a disastrous sense that he was talking too much. Fish was about to go on, but a sudden hand on his arm forestalled him. It was one of the bright young men – beautiful suit, beautiful teeth, beautiful handkerchief in pocket. 'Mr Wilmington, I just wanted to say, what an absolutely marvellous piece of work that new mural is. One enormous foot. I don't know what the significance is, but the draftsmanship is marvellous. We must get you on *Five Seven* some afternoon and have you explain it.'

'Never go on television,' said Fish, frowning. He had been fending off invitations like this one for almost a year.

'Oh, too bad. Nice to have met you. Oh, by the way, somebody asked me to tell you there's a phone call for you over there.' He waved his arm and drifted away.

Fish excused himself and set an adventurous course across the room. The phone was lying on one of the side tables giving him a black look. He picked it up jauntily. 'Helloo.'

'Dr Fish?'

Fish's heart began to knock. He put the martini glass down. 'Who's that?' he demanded blankly.

'This is Dave Kinney, Doc.'

Fish felt a wave of relief. 'Oh, Dave. I thought you were in Boston. Or, I suppose you *are*, but the connection—'

'I'm right here in Santa Monica. Look, Doc, something's come up that—'

'What? what're you doing here? Now I hope you haven't quit school, because—'

'This is summer vacation, Doc. Look, the fact is, I'm here in Norma Johnson's studio.'

Fish stood with the sweaty black phone in his hand and said nothing. Silence hummed in the wires.

'Doc? Mrs Prentice is here too. We've been kind of talking things over, and we think you ought to come over and explain a few things.'

Fish swallowed, with difficulty.

'Doc, you hear me? I think you ought to come over. *They're* talking about calling the police, but I wanted to give you a chance first, so—'

'I'll be right over,' said Fish hoarsely. He hung up the phone and stood bemused, with his hands to his flushed forehead. Oh, Lord, three – no, four – martinis and this had to happen! He felt dizzy. Everybody seemed to be standing at a slight angle on the Kellygreen carpet, all the bright young men in glossy summer jackets and the pastel women in cocktail dresses with bright, phony smiles on their faces. What did they care if all he could get out of the machine any more was parts of bodies? His last one a big clenched fist, and now a foot, and don't you think the committee didn't beef. They beefed plenty but they had to take it, because they had already announced the commission. Now this morning his agent had called up. Some church group in Indiana, they wanted sample sketches. So it was all going down the drain while he watched, and now this. Dave, good God, you'd think at least he would stay stuck off in Boston, and how the *hell* did he ever run into Norma?

One of the newspaper reporters turned away from the free lunch and planted himself in Fish's path as he lurched toward the door. 'Oh, Mr Wilmington, what would you say was the real significance of that foot?'

'Gow my way,' said Fish, staggering around him.

He took a cab home, told the driver to wait, ducked in for a quick shower and a cup of black coffee, and came out again, shaky but not as drunk as before. Those Goddamn cocktails … He never used to get like this when he just drank beer. Things were better back on Platt Terrace; how did he ever get mixed up in this crazy art game anyway?

His stomach felt hollow. He hadn't eaten any lunch, he remembered. Well, too late now. He braced himself and rang the bell.

Dave opened the door. Fish greeted him with cries of pleasure, shaking his limp hand. 'Dave, boy! Good to see you! How long has it been, anyway?' Without waiting for a reply, he bustled on into the room. It was a grey, windowless place that always made him nervous; instead of a roof there was one big slanting skylight, high overhead; the light filtered down cool and colourless through the translucent panes. There was an easel in one corner and some drawings pinned up on the otherwise bare walls. Down at the far end, Norma and her aunt were sitting on the redpadded bench. 'Norma, how are you, honey? And Mrs Prentice – now this is a real pleasure!'

That wasn't hard to say – she really did look good in that new dark-blue suit. He could tell he was projecting the old charm, and he thought he saw her eyes glint with pleasure. But it was only for an instant, and then her expression hardened. 'What's this I hear about your not even coming to see Norma?' she demanded.

Fish registered deep surprise. 'Why … why, Norma, didn't you explain to your aunt? Excuse me a minute.' He darted over to the drawings on the wall. 'Well. Now these are really excellent, Norma; there's a good deal of improvement here. The symmetry, you see, and the dynamic *flow—*'

Norma said, 'Those are three months old.' She was wearing a man's shirt and dungarees, and looked as if she might have been crying recently, but her face was carefully made up.

'Well, honey, I wanted to come back, even after what you said. I did come around, twice, you know, but you didn't answer your bell.'

'That's not so.'

'Well, I suppose you might have been out,' said Fish cheerfully. He turned to Mrs Prentice. 'Norma was upset, you know.' His voice dropped. 'About a month after we started, she told me to get out and not come back.'

Dave had drifted back across the room. He sat down beside Norma without comment.

'The idea of taking the poor child's money for *nothing*,' said Mrs Prentice vehemently. 'Why didn't you give it back?'

Fish pulled up a folding chair and sat down close to her. 'Mrs Prentice,' he said quietly, 'I didn't want Norma to make a mistake. I told her, now, if you'll live up to your agreement and study with me for a year, I said, and then if you're not satisfied, why, I'll gladly refund every cent.'

'You weren't doing me any good,' said Norma, with a hysterical note in her voice.

Fish gave her a look of sorrowful patience.

'He'd just come in, and look at my work, and say something like, "This has a good feeling," or "The symmetry is good," or some *meaningless* thing like that. I was getting so nervous I couldn't even *draw*. That's when I wrote you, Aunt Marie, but you were in Europe. My golly, I had to do something didn't I?' Her hands were clenched white in her lap.

'There, dear,' Mrs Prentice murmured, and gave her arm a little squeeze.

'I've been going to day classes at the Art Centre,' Norma said between her teeth. 'It was all I could *afford*.'

Mrs Prentice's eyes sparkled with indignation. 'Mr Wilmington, I don't think we have to discuss this much longer. I want you to return the money I paid you. I think it's disgraceful, a well-known artist like you, *stooping*—'

'Mrs Prentice,' said Fish, pitching his voice lower again, 'if it wasn't for my faith in Norma's great future as an artist, why I would hand you over every cent. But as it is she would be making a great mistake, so I suggest again—'

'Doc,' said Dave rudely, 'you give her back that money pretty damn quick.' He leaned forward to speak to the older woman. 'You want to know what his real name is, it's Fish. Anyhow, it was when I met him. This whole thing is just a joke. Why, he's no artist. The real George Wilmington is his nephew; he's an invalid out in Wisconsin. Doc here has just been fronting for him, because he's too sick to stand the publicity and all. Now, that's the truth. Or as much of it as I know.'

Fish said sorrowfully, 'Dave, is this the thanks I get for putting you through art school?'

'You got me the scholarship, but it didn't cost you anything. I found that out from the director. I guess you just wanted to put me out of the way so I wouldn't talk too much. Hell, Doc, that was all right. But when I met Norma here, over at your place yesterday—'

'What? When was that?'

'About ten o'clock.' Fish winced; he had been in bed with a bad head and hadn't answered the bell; if he'd only known! 'You weren't home, so we got to talking, and – well, pretending to be your nephew, that's one thing, but when you promise to teach somebody when you can't even draw a line yourself!'

Fish raised a hand. 'Now, Dave, there's a thing or two you don't know. You say my real name is Fish. Now did you ever see my birth certificate, or did you know anybody that knew me as a child? How do you know my name is Fish?'

'Well, you *told* me.'

'That's right, Dave, I did. And you say the real George Wilmington is an

41

invalid out in Wisconsin. You ever see him, Dave? You ever been in Wisconsin?'

'Well, no but—'

'Neither have I. No, Dave' – he lowered his voice solemnly – 'every single thing I told you about that was just a lie. And I admit it.' Now here was the place for a tear. Fish turned his mind to the creditors, the trouble with the machine, the oil stock salesman who had gone south with his money, the lawyers who were robbing him blind trying to get it back, the ungratefulness of everybody. A warm trickle crept out onto his cheek and, lowering his head, he knuckled it away.

'Well, what?' said Dave, bewildered.

Fish said with an effort. 'I had reasons. Certain reasons. You know, it's … it's hard for me to talk about 'em. Mrs Prentice, I wonder if I could just see you alone for a minute.'

She was leaning forward a little, looking at him with concern. It never failed – a woman like that couldn't stand to see a man cry.

'Well, it's certainly all right with me,' said Norma, getting up. She walked away, and Dave followed her. After a moment the door closed behind them.

Fish blew his nose, dabbed unobtrusively at his eyes, straightened up bravely and put his handkerchief away. 'Mrs Prentice, I don't s'pose you know that I'm a widower.' Her eyes widened a little. 'It's true, I lost my dear wife. I don't usually talk about it, as a matter of fact, but somehow – I don't know if you've been bereaved yourself, Mrs Prentice.'

She said nervously, 'Didn't Norma tell you? I'm a widow, Mr Wilmington.'

'No!' said Fish. 'Isn't that strange? I felt something – you know, a *vibration*. Well, Mrs Prentice – can I call you Marie? – yoü know, after my loss –' time for another tear now; once started, they came easily – 'I just went to pieces. I don't excuse myself, I didn't want to live. I couldn't touch a pencil for a year. And even to this day I can't draw a line if there's anybody watching me. Now – there's the reason for the whole mixup. That business about my nephew and all, that was just a story I made up to make things a little easier. That's what *I thought*. I don't know, I'm so clumsy where it takes a little tact. I'm just like a bull in a china closet, Marie. And that's the whole story.' He sat back, blew his nose vigorously again.

Mrs Prentice's eyes were moist, but her handsome face had a wary expression. 'I honestly don't know what to think, Mr Wilmington. You say you can't draw in public—'

'Call me George. You see, it's what the psychologists call a trauma.'

'Well, how would this be? I'll step outside for a few minutes, and you draw a picture. Now, I think that would be—'

Fish was shaking his head sadly. 'It's worse than I told you. I can't draw *anywhere* except in one room in my house – I've got it fixed up with her picture, and some mementoes.' He gulped hard, but decided against a third tear. 'I'm sorry, I'd do it for you if I could, but ...'

She sat quietly in thought for a moment. 'Then let's say this. You go home, Mr Wilmington, and draw something – a sketch of me, my face, from memory. I believe any competent artist could do that?'

Fish hesitated, not liking to say no.

'Now, you see, that will settle it. You couldn't get a snap-shot of me and send it off to Wisconsin – there wouldn't be time. I'll give you, oh, half an hour.'

'Half an—'

'That should be enough, shouldn't it? So that when I come to call on you, in half an hour from now, if you have a sketch of me – a likeness – why then I'll know that you're telling the truth. If not ...'

Boxed in, Fish made the best of it. He got to his feet with a confident smile. 'Well, now, that's fair enough. One thing, I know I could never forget *your* face. And I want to tell you how relieved I am that we had this little talk, incidentally, and – well, I better go and get that drawing started. I'll expect you in half an hour, Marie!' He paused at the door.

'I'll be there ... George,' she said.

Grunting and twitching, Fish stormed into the house banging doors behind him. Place was a mess – sofa cushions and newspapers all over the living room – but, never mind, she might marry him to clean up his house. Thing was – he unlocked the private room, feverishly swept the cover off the big machine, and began pushing buttons on one of the banks – thing was, get that sketch made. One chance in a hundred. But better than no chance at all. He switched on the machine, watched in helpless impatience while the arms drifted out and hung motionless.

A face – and a likeness! Only hope he had was to put it together from bits and pieces. Nothing left now that would work in the whole machine but some useless items, mechanical drawings and architecture, and a few scraps of anatomy. Let there be enough for one more face! And let it be something like Marie's face!

The machine clicked suddenly and began to trace a line. Fish stood over it in hand-wringing anxiety, watching how the combined motion of the two revolving pivots translated the straight push of the arm into a subtle line. Pretty thing to watch, even if he never could like what it made. Now here it came curving around; now the arm was lifting, going back. A nose! It was drawing a nose!

It was a kind of Greek nose, shapely but thick, not much like Marie's fine curved nose, but, never mind, he could talk her into it – give him the raw material, he could always sell. Let there be *any* kind of a female face, so long as it wasn't ugly. Come on, now, an eye!

But the arms stopped and hung motionless again. The machine hummed quietly, the dials were lighted; nothing happened.

Eaten by impatience, Fish looked at his watch, clapped his palm over it, peeked, swore, and wandered rapidly out of the room. Sometimes lately the machine would just sit like that for minutes at a time, as if it were trying and trying to work, but somehow not succeeding, and then, *click*, off it would go again. He hurried back, looked – still nothing – and went back, pacing the empty rooms, looking for something to do.

For the first time he noticed there was some mail in the basket under the letter drop. Mostly bills. He threw them behind the living-room sofa, but one was a long, bulky brown envelope with 'Encyclopaedia Britannica Library Research Service' in the corner.

It had been so long ago, it took him a moment to remember. A couple of weeks after he sent in his letter, there had been a polite printed postcard acknowledging it, then nothing for months. Somewhere along the line he had decided he wasn't going to get an answer. There wasn't any such language … Well, let's see. He picked the end of the envelope open.

His restless eye was caught by the dining-room clock. Look at the time! Clutching the envelope forgetfully, he rushed into the private room again. The machine was still sitting motionless, humming, lighted. There was nothing on the paper but a noble nose.

Fish pounded on the side of the big machine, with no result except to his fist, and then on the bank that was in use. Nothing. He turned away, noticed he was still holding the envelope, and irritably plucked out the papers inside.

There was a stiff orange folder, stapled at the top. When he lifted the cover, there was a single sheet of paper inside. At the top, the Britannica letterhead, and 'V. A. Sternback, Director'. Then, in the middle, 'SWEDISH WORDS'.

His eyes ran down the list, startled. There were all the words he had copied off, and opposite each one a word in English. *Teckning* … drawing. *Mönster* … pattern. *Utplåna* … to erase. *Användning* … application, use.

Fish looked up. Then that was why nothing had happened when he pressed the *Utplåna* button – he'd always tried it before the machine made a drawing, never while there was a finished one on the board. Now why hadn't he thought of that? Yes, and here was *Avslä* … to reject. And *slutsatsen* … completion. 'To reject a drawing before completion, press …' He'd never done that, either.

What about the middle button? *Torka* … to wipe. To wipe? Let's see, there was another word – *Avlägsna*, that was it. Sometimes the phrase '*Avlägsna ett monster*' would be running through his head when he was half awake, like a whispered warning … Here it was. *Avlägsna* … to remove.

His hands were shaking. 'To remove a pattern from bank after use, press button "Wipe". He let the folder fall. All this time, not knowing, he'd been systematically using up the precious patterns in the machine, throwing them away one by one, until now there was nothing left – just eight big hunks of useless machinery, made for somebody somewhere who spoke Swedish ...

The machine clicked softly and the other arm began to move. It traced a graceful upright line, some distance in front of the nose. It looped over and came back down again, then up ...

Somewhere distant, the doorbell rang imperiously.

Fish stared, mesmerized, at the paper. The moving point traced another graceful open loop, then another, like a squeezed-together roller coaster. Then another one, moving inexorably and without hurry: now there were four. Without pausing, it extended the last line downward and then brought it across. The line met the tip of the nose and curved back.

The four open loops were fingers. The fifth one was a thumb.

The machine, humming quietly, withdrew its arms into their recesses. After a moment the lights went dark and the hum stopped. Outside, the doorbell rang again, and went on ringing.

THE ENEMY

The spaceship lay on a rockball in the middle of the sky. There was a brilliance in Draco; it was the sun, four billion miles away. In the silence, the stars did not blink or waver: they burned, cold and afar. Polaris blazed overhead. The Milky Way hung like a frozen rainbow above the horizon.

In the yellow circle of the airlock, two figures appeared, both women, with pale, harsh faces behind the visors of their helmets. They carried a folding metal disk a hundred yards away and set it up on three tall insulators. They went back to the ship, moving lightly on tiptoe, like dancers, and came out again with a bulky collection of objects wrapped in a transparent membrane.

They sealed the membrane to the disk and inflated it by means of a hose from the ship. The objects inside were household articles: a hammock on a metal frame, a lamp, a radio transceiver. They entered the membrane through its flexible valve and set the furniture in order. Then, carefully, they brought in three last items – three tanks of growing green things, each in its protective bubble.

They unloaded a spidery vehicle with six enormous puffed wheels and left it standing on three insulators of its own.

The work was done. The two women stood facing each other beside the bubble house. The elder said, 'If your finds are good, stay here till I return in ten months. If not, leave the equipment and return in the escape shell.'

They both glanced upward, where a faint spark was moving against the field of stars. The parent ship had left it in orbit before landing. If needed, it could be called down to land automatically by radio; otherwise, there was no need to waste fuel.

'Understood,' said the younger one. Her name was Zael; she was fifteen, and this was her first time away from the space city alone. Isar, her mother, went to the ship and entered it without another glance. The lock door closed; the spark overhead was drifting down toward the horizon. A short burst of flame raised the parent ship; it drifted, rising and turning as it went. Then the torch blazed out again, and in a few moments the ship was only a brighter star.

Zael turned off her suit light and stood in the darkness under the enormous half-globe of the sky. It was the only sky she knew; like her mother's mother before her, she was space-born. Centuries ago, driven out of the fat green worlds, her people had grown austere, like the fields of stars they roamed among. In the five great space cities, and on Pluto, Titan, Mimas, Eros and a thousand lesser worlds, they struggled for existence. They were few; life was hard and short; it was no novelty for a fifteen-year-old child to be left alone to mine a planetoid.

The ship was a dim spark, climbing up the long slant toward the ecliptic. Up there, Isar and her daughters had deliveries to make and cargoes to take on at Pluto. Gron, their city, had sent them down this long detour to make a survey. The planetoid was now approaching the sun, on its eccentric cometary orbit, for the first time in twenty thousand years. Once here, it would be folly not to surface-mine the planetoid for whatever it might be worth. One child could do that, and survey the planetoid as well.

Alone, Zael turned impassively to the six-wheeled crawler. She might have rested awhile in the bubble house, but she had some hours of suit time left, and there was no need to waste it. She lifted herself easily against the slight gravity into the cab; turned on the lights and started the motor.

The spidery vehicle crawled ahead on its six individually sprung wheels. The terrain was astonishingly broken; giant spires and craters alternated with ravines and with fissures, some of them forty feet wide and thousands of feet deep. The planetoid's orbit passed near the sun, according to the astronomers, perhaps nearer than the orbit of Venus. Even now, the temperature of the rocks was a few degrees above absolute zero. This was a cold beyond anything Zael had ever experienced. She could feel it drawing at her feet through the long insulator spikes of her boot soles. The molecules of every stone were slowed to stillness; the whole world was one frozen yawn of hunger.

But once it had been a hot world. The record was here. At every perihelion passage, the rocks must have split, again and again, to make this nightmare of tumbled stone.

The surface gravitation was only one tenth G, almost like free-fall; the light, puffywheeled vehicle crawled easily up slopes within a few degrees of the vertical. Where it could not climb, it went around. Narrow fissures were bridged by the crawler's extensible legs; when she came to larger ones, Zael fired a harpoon which soared across the gap and embedded itself on the other side. The crawler edged forward, toppled and swung at the end of its cable; but while the slight gravity drew it toward the far side of the fissure, the crawler's winch motor was reeling in the cable. It arrived with a faint jar at the opposite side and, without pausing, inched up and over.

Sitting erect behind her instruments, Zael was charting the mineral deposits she passed over. It was a satisfaction to her to find they were rich enough to repay surface mining. The cities could make almost anything out of anything, but they needed a primary source: they had to have metals.

Methodically, she spiralled outward from the bubble house, charting a region no more than thirty miles in diameter. In the unpressurized crawler, it was not feasible to take in a larger area.

Labouring alone, hour after hour under the unchanging sky, she identified the richest lodes, marked them and established routes. Between times, she ate and slept in the bubble house, tended her necessary plants, serviced her equipment. Out of her armour, she was slender and spare, quick in her movements, with the harsh, thin-lipped comeliness of her people.

When her chart was made, she rode out again. At each marked spot, she dropped two widely separated poles. Self-embedding, each pair generated a current which ionized the metals or metallic salts and would slowly deposit pure metal around the cathode. Eventually the concentration would be such that the metal could be sawed out in blocks for convenient loading.

Only then did she turn her attention to the traces of shaped metal that clung here and there to the rocks. They were fragments, for the most part, such as were commonly found on cold satellites like Mimas and Titan, and occasionally on stony asteroids. It was not a matter of any importance; it simply meant that the planetoid had been inhabited or colonized at one time by the same pre-human civilization that had left its traces throughout the solar system.

But she had been sent to see whatever was to be seen. Her real work was almost done; she conscientiously examined the traces, photographed some, took others for specimens. She beamed regular radio reports to Gron; sometimes, five days later, there would be a curt acknowledgment waiting for her in the printer; sometimes not. Regularly she made the rounds of the poles, testing the concentration of metal. She was ready to replace any faulty poles she might find, but the occasion did not arise; Gron equipment seldom failed.

The planetoid hung in its millennial arc. The sky imperceptibly turned around it. The moving spark that was the escape shell traced its path, again and again. Zael grew restless and took the crawler on wider explorations. Deep in the cold crannies of the mountains, she found some metal constructions that were not mere fragments but complete works – dwellings or machines. The dwellings, if they were that, were made for some creature smaller than man; the doorways were ovals not more than a foot across. She dutifully radioed this information back to Gron and received the usual acknowledgment.

Then, one day the printer came to life out of season. The message read: I AM COMING, ISAR.

The ship would be three months slower than the message. Zael kept her calendar, rode her rounds, her starlit face impassive. Above her the escape shell, unneeded now, made its monotonous passage over and over. Zael was tracing the remnants of a complex of surface structures that had

48

miraculously survived, some half buried, others naked to the stars. She found where they led, in a crater only forty miles from her base, a week before the ship was due.

In the crater was a heavily reinforced globe of metal, dented and scarred, but not smashed. As Zael's light shone steadily on it, a sudden puff of vapour went out; the globe seemed to haze over briefly. Zael peered, interested: the minute warmth of the light beam must have thawed some film of frozen gas.

Then it happened again, and this time she could see distinctly: the jet escaped from a thin, dark seam that had not been there before.

The seam widened as she watched. The globe was splitting. In the narrow gap between the two halves, something moved. Startled, Zael threw the crawler into reverse. The cab lights dipped as the crawler retreated up-slope. In the dimness outside the light beams, she saw the globe expanding still more. There was an ambiguous motion between the barely visible halves of the globe, and she wished she had not taken the light away.

The crawler was tilting sidewise up a steep, broken slab of rock. Zael turned downward, still backing at a sharp angle. The light swung away from the globe altogether, then came back to it as she levelled out.

The two halves of the globe had separated completely. In the middle, something jerked as the light struck it. She could see nothing but a thick, gleaming coil of metal. While she hesitated, there was new motion between the halves of the globe. Something gleamed briefly; there was a short ground shock, and then something struck the cab a hard, resonant blow. The lights whirled bewilderingly and went out.

In the darkness, the cab was tipping. Zael clutched at the controls, but she was too slow. The crawler went over on its back.

Zael felt herself being flung out of the cab. As she rolled over, ears ringing, her first and sharpest impression was of the cold that struck through her armour at gauntlet and knee. She scrambled up quickly to a kneeling position, supporting herself on the brush-like spiked soles of her boots.

Even the brief contact had made her fingers smart with cold. She searched automatically for the crawler, which meant safety and warmth. She saw it smashed on the mountainside. Even so, her instinct drew her toward it, but she had hardly taken a first step before the wrecked machine leaped again and rolled another dozen yards down the slope.

She turned now, for the first time fully realizing that something down there was shooting at the crawler. Then she saw a glimmering shape that writhed up toward the wrecked machine. Her helmet light was not turned on; she crouched still and felt two grinding, metallic shocks transmitted through the rock.

The moving thing appeared again on the other side of the crawler, vanished inside, and after a long time came out again. Zael caught a glimpse of a narrow head upraised, and two red eyes gleaming. The head dropped; the sinuous form glided down into a ravine, coming toward her. Her only thought was to get away. She scrambled up in the dark, circled a spire. She saw the gleaming head upraised farther down, among a tangle of boulders, and went at a head-long, dangerous run across the slope to the wrecked crawler.

The control board was ruined, levers bent off or flattened down, dials smashed. She straightened to look at the engine and transmission, but saw at once that it was no use; the heavy drive shaft was bent out of true. The crawler would never run again without shop repairs.

Down in the bowl, she caught sight of the silvery shape casting along the edge of a fissure. Keeping it in view, she examined her suit and instruments all over. As far as she could tell, the suit was tight, her oxygen tanks and recirculation system undamaged.

She was thinking coldly and clearly as she looked at the split globe, gaping empty under the stars. The thing must have been coiled in there, inert, for thousands of years. Perhaps there had been a light-sensitive device in the globe, designed to open it when the planetoid approached the sun again. But her light had broken the globe prematurely; the thing inside was awake before its time. What was it, and what would it do, now that it was alive again?

Whatever happened, her first duty was to warn the ship. She turned on the broadcast transmitter in her suit; its range was small, but now that the ship was so near, there was a chance.

She waited long minutes, but no answer came. From where she stood, the sun was not visible; one of the high crags must be blocking her transmission.

The loss of the crawler had been a disaster. She was alone and afoot, forty miles across an impassable terrain from the bubble house. Her chances of survival now, she knew, were very small.

Still, to save herself now, without finding out more about the thing, would be less than her duty. Zael looked doubtfully down at the empty globe in the starlight. The way between was broken and dangerous; she would have to go slowly, for fear of attracting the thing if she used a light.

She started down nevertheless, picking her way carefully among the tumbled stones. Several times she leaped fissures too long to by-pass. When she was halfway down the slope, she saw movement, and froze. The thing writhed into view over a broken ridge – she saw the triangular head again, and a waving ruff of tentacles – and then disappeared inside the open globe.

Zael moved cautiously nearer, circling to get a view directly into the gap. After a few moments the thing emerged again, curiously stiff and thick-looking. On a level place outside the globe, it separated into two parts, and she saw now that one was the thing itself, the other a rigid metal framework, narrow and perhaps ten feet long. The thing retreated inside the globe again.

When it came out, it was burdened with a bulbous mechanism which it fitted on somehow to one end of the framework. It continued working for some time, using the tentacle-like jointed members that sprouted from just behind its head. Then it returned to the globe, and this time came out with two large cubical objects. These it began to attach to the opposite end of the framework, connecting them by a series of tubes to the bulbous mechanism.

For the first time, the suspicion entered her mind that the thing was building a spacecraft. Nothing could look less like a conventional ship, to be sure: there was no hull, nothing but a narrow shaft on which the thing could lie, the bulbous object which might be an engine, and the two big containers for reaction mass. Abruptly, she was certain. She had no Geiger with her – it was back in the crawler – but she felt sure there must be radioactives in the bulbous mechanism – a micropile, unshielded, for a spaceship without a hull! It would kill any living creature that rode on it – but what creature of flesh and blood could survive for twenty thousand years on this airless planetoid, at close to absolute zero?

She stood gravely still. Like all her people, she had seen the evidences of an eons-old war among the cold planetoids. Some thought the war had ended with the deliberate destruction of the fourth planet, the one which had formerly occupied the place of the asteroids. A bitter war, that one must have been; and now Zael thought she could understand why. If one side had been human-like, and the other like this thing, then neither could rest until it had wiped out the other. And if this thing were now to escape, and perhaps breed more of its kind …

Zael inched forward, making her way from stone to stone, moving only when the thing was out of sight. The alien had finished attaching several small ambiguous objects to the front of the frame. It went back inside the globe. To Zael, the structure looked almost complete. It did not seem possible to encumber it any more and still leave space for the rider.

Her heart was thudding. She left her concealment and went forward in a clumsy tiptoe pace that was faster than leaping. When she was almost in reach of the framework, the thing came out of the open globe. It glided toward her, enormous in the starlight, with its metal head rearing high.

Out of pure instinct she hit the light switch. The helmet beams flared: she had an instant's glimpse of skeletal metal ribs and gleaming jaws. Then the thing was thrashing away from her into the darkness. For a moment more she was stunned. She thought, it can't stand light! And she scrambled forward desperately into the globe.

The thing was coiled there, hiding. When the light struck it, it hurled itself out the other side. Zael pursued again, and caught it once more on the far side of the low ridge. It dived into a ravine and was gone.

She turned back. The framework lay on the rock where it had been left.

Zael picked it up tentatively. It had more mass than she had expected, but she was able to swing it at arm's length until it gained a respectable speed. She dashed it against the nearest stone; the impact numbed her fingers. The framework leaped free, slid to rest on the stone. The two containers were detached: the bulbous mechanism was bent away from the frame. She picked it up again, and again swung it hard against the rock. The frame bent and buckled; small pieces came loose. She swung it again, and again, until the frame broke and the bulbous part came free.

The alien thing was not in sight. Zael carried the pieces of the framework to the nearest fissure and dropped them in. In her helmet beams, they drifted silently down and were gone.

She returned to the globe. The creature was still nowhere to be seen. She examined the interior: it was full of oddly shaped partitions and of machines, most too large to be moved, some that were detached and portable. She could not with certainty identify any of them as weapons. To be safe, she took all the movable objects and dropped them after the framework.

She had done all she could, and perhaps more than was prudent. Her task now was to survive – to get back to the bubble house, call the escape shell down, and get away.

She turned back up the slope, past the wrecked crawler, retracing her route until she came to the crater wall.

The crags loomed over her, hundreds of feet above her head, and so sheer that when she tried to climb them, even her momentum would not keep her upright; she began to topple back and had to dance her way slowly down again to firmer footing.

She made the full circuit of the crater before she was convinced; there was no way out.

She was sweating under the armour: a bad beginning. The ragged tops of the mountains seemed to bend forward, peering down at her mockingly. She stood still to calm herself, took a salt pill and a sip of water from the dispenser in her helmet. The indicators showed that she had less than five hours of air left. It was little enough. She had to get out.

She chose what seemed to be the easiest slope within reach. She went up with a rush. When her momentum began to fall, she used her hands. The cold bit through her gauntlets like needles of fire. The slightest contact was painful; to grasp firmly became an agony. She was within yards of the top when her fingers began to grow numb. She clawed upward furiously, but her fingers refused to grip; her hands slid uselessly away from the rock.

She was falling. She toppled slowly down the slope she had climbed with so much pain; caught herself with an effort and came to rest, shaken and trembling, at the bottom.

Cold despair settled at her heart. She was young; she had no taste for death, even for a quick and clean one. To die slowly, gasping for air in a foul suit, or bleeding out her warmth against the stone, would be horrible.

Out across the crater floor, she saw a dim movement in the starlight. It was the alien thing; what could it be doing, now that she had destroyed its means of escape? The thought came to her slowly that perhaps it could not get out of the crater, either. After a moment, hesitantly, she went down the slope toward it.

Halfway down, she remembered to turn off her suit lights so as not to drive it away. The crater floor was criss-crossed with innumerable fissures. As she came nearer, she saw that the split sphere was surrounded by them on all sides. Down at one end of this long, irregular island of rock, the alien was throwing itself back and forth.

It turned to face her as she leaped the last gap. She could see its red eyes gleaming in the darkness, and the circle of thin, jointed arms that formed a collar behind its head. As she approached, the head reared higher, and the jaws gaped.

The sight of the thing, so near, filled her with a cold loathing she had never experienced before. It was not only that the creature was metal, and alive; it was some radiance of evil that seemed to reach her directly from the thing, as if to say, I am the death of all you love.

The blind, red eyes stared with implacable hatred. How could she make it understand?

The body of the thing was sinuous and strong; its jointed arms could grasp and hold. It was made for climbing, but not for jumping.

Abruptly, her loathing for the alien was more than she could master. She turned and jumped the chasm again. On the far side, she looked back. The alien was swaying high, with more than half its length raised from the rock. She saw now that there was another cluster of gripping members at its tail. The thing glided forward to the very edge of the fissure and swayed upright again, jaws agape, eyes glaring.

They had nothing in common but hatred – and fear. Staring across at the alien, Zael realized that it must be as afraid as she. Metal though it was, it could not live for ever without warmth. She had broken its machines, and now, like her, it was trapped. But how could she make it understand?

She moved a few yards away along the edge of the fissure, and then jumped again, back to the alien's side. It watched her alertly. The thing was intelligent; it must be. It must know that she was not native to the planetoid, and therefore that she must have a ship, or some means of escape.

She spread her arms. The alien's circle of limbs widened in response; but was that a gesture of invitation or of menace? Suppressing her fear and repugnance, she walked nearer. The tall shape swayed above her in the starlight. She saw now that the segments of the alien's body were metal rings that slid smoothly upon one another. Each ring was slightly open at the bottom, and inside she could glimpse some mechanism.

Such a thing could never have evolved on any world; it must have been made, for some unguessable purpose. The long, supple body was built for pursuit and capture; the jaws were for killing. Only a depth of hatred beyond her comprehension could have conceived this horror and let it loose in the world of the living.

She forced herself to move a step nearer. She pointed to herself, then back to the crater wall. She turned and leaped across the fissure, recovered herself and leaped back.

It seemed to her that the alien's attitude, as it stared at her, was an almost human parody of wariness and doubt. She pointed to herself, and to the alien; again, she turned and leaped across the chasm, then leaped back. She pointed to herself and to the alien, and then gestured across the fissure, a wide, slow motion of one arm. She waited.

After a long time the alien moved slowly forward. She retreated, as slowly, until she was at the edge of the fissure. Trembling, she held out her arm. Slowly the great head dipped; the circle of grasping members waved forward to wrap themselves around her sleeve. The red eyes stared blindly into hers from a few inches away.

She turned and kicked off strongly. She tried to allow for the alien's mass, but the unaccustomed drag on her arm tipped her backward in mid-air. They landed together with a grating jar. Awkwardly, Zael scrambled up, away from the cold that searched through her armour. The alien was swaying erect, near – too near.

By instinct again, she hit the light switch. The thing writhed away in silvery coils.

Zael was trembling with reaction. Her heart pounded at her throat. With an effort, she turned off the light again. The thing rose into view, waiting for her, a dozen yards away.

When she moved, it moved, keeping its distance. When they reached the next fissure, she stood still until it again approached and laid its grasping members on her arm.

On the far side, they separated once more. In this way, they traversed four of the islands of rock before they came to the crater wall.

The alien thrust its body slowly up along the steep incline. At full stretch, the gripping arms found a hold; the tail swung free. The long body looped gracefully up; the tail members found another hold above the alien's head.

It paused there, looking down at her. Zael spread her arms; she pantomimed climbing, then stepped back, shaking her head. She held out her arms again.

The alien hesitated. After a long moment, the head members gripped again; the tail swung down. Zael braced herself as the alien slid nearer. The smooth, shining head loomed over her. In that frozen moment, Zael found herself thinking that to the alien, the universe might be like a photographic negative: all the evil things good, the good things evil. It gave her a queer sense of exhilaration to realize when they met, the alien too might be embracing darkness.

Then the head glided past her shoulder; the heavy coils looped around her body with a faint scraping sound. The thing was cold, but not with the numbing supercold of the rocks. As the coils tightened, she felt the chill, constrictive strength of the great body. Then she was being lifted off her feet. The steep wall tilted and swung at a crazy angle.

A faintness sapped her strength as she lay in the metal coils. The stars swung around her head; they steadied and burned still. The alien had set her down at the top of the crater wall.

The cold coils slowly slipped away. Shaken and stunned, Zael followed the alien down the broken, tilted land. The touch still burned in her flesh. It was like a meaning that lay so heavily and coldly inside her that she had to puzzle to make it out. It was like a ring that, having been worn so long, still seems to be there after it has been removed.

Down in the tumbled vastness of the valley, the alien's head was upraised, waiting for her. Humbly she went down to it, where it lay at the edge of a fissure. This time, instead of clutching her arm, the heavy mass coiled itself around her.

She leaped. At the other side, slowly, almost reluctantly, the supple body slid down and away from her. When they came to a high place, again the alien took her in its cold embrace and swung her up, weightlessly, like a woman in a dream.

The sun was in the sky, low over the horizon. Zael put her hand to the radio switch, hesitated, and let her hand fall away. What could she tell them? How could she make them understand?

Time slipped away. When they passed one of her mining areas, where the cold purple light flickered from the rocks, she knew they were on the right path. She steered by that, and by the sun. At each fissure, the alien coiled itself around her shoulders; at each steep ascent, it cradled her about the waist and lifted her in long, free arcs to the top.

When, standing on a height, she saw the bubble house, she realized with a shock that she had lost account of time. She looked at the indicators. There was half an hour of air left.

The knowledge brought to wakefulness some part of her mind which had been submerged and asleep. She knew that the other had seen the bubble house too; there was a new tension in its manner, a new fixity in the way it stared ahead. She tried to recall the topography that lay between this spot and the house. She had been over it dozens of times, but always in the crawler. It was very different now. The high ridges that had been only momentary obstacles before were now impassable. The whole aspect of the country was changed; she could not be certain even of her landmarks any longer.

They were passing the last of the mining areas. The cold purple light rolled across the rocks. Just beyond this point, Zael recalled, there should be a wide fissure; the alien, a few yards distant, was not looking her way. Bending forward, she broke into a stiff-toed run. The fissure was there; she reached the edge, and jumped.

On the far side, she turned to look. The alien was writhing back and forth at the edge of the fissure, its collar of limbs extended in fury, its red eyes blazing. After a moment, its motion slowed and stopped. They stared at each other across the gap of silence; then Zael turned away.

The indicators gave her fifteen minutes more. She set off at a brisk pace and soon found herself descending into a deep ravine she recognized. All around her were the landmarks of the route she was accustomed to take in the crawler. Ahead and to the right, where stars gleamed in a gap, must be the place where a broken fall of rock formed a natural stairway to the top of the ravine. But as she neared the place, something made her uneasy. The far wall of the ravine was too sheer and too tall.

She stood beneath the gap at last, and there was no stairway.

She must have mistaken the spot. There was nothing for it but to cast along the ravine until she came to the right place. After a moment's indecision, she set off hurriedly to the left.

At every step, the ravine promised to become familiar. Surely, she could not have gone so far wrong in so short a time! The dots of light from her helmet beams danced ahead of her, mockingly elusive. Abruptly, she realized that she was lost.

There were seven minutes of air left.

The thought came to her that the alien must still be where she had left it, trapped on one of the islands of rock. If she went straight back to it, now, without hesitating a second, there might still be time.

With an involuntary groan of protest, she turned back. Her movements were hurried and unsure; once she stumbled and caught herself barely in time to prevent a bad fall. Yet she dared not slow down or stop for a moment. Inside the helmet, her breath was laboured; the familiar reek of the recirculated air seemed to have grown stuffier and more foul.

She looked at the indicators: five minutes.

Topping a rise, she saw a liquid glint of metal moving down among the purple fires. She leaped the last fissure and came to a wary halt. The alien was approaching her slowly. The great metal head was expressionless, the jaws closed; the ruff of grasping members was almost still; only now and then, one of the jointed limbs twitched abruptly. There was a grim, waiting stillness about it that she found disquieting, but she had no time for caution.

Hurriedly, with abrupt gestures, she tried to pantomime her need. She held out her arms. The alien glided forward slowly, and slowly wrapped its coils around her.

She scarcely felt the leap, or the landing. The alien glided beside her: close, this time, near enough to touch. Down into the starlit half-darkness of the ravine they went, Zael treading uncertainly because she could not use her helmet lights. They paused at the foot of the precipice. The alien turned to look at her for a moment.

Zael's ears were ringing. The great head swayed toward her and passed by. The metal arms gripped the rock; the great body swung up, over her head. She looked up to see it looping diagonally across the face of the rock; it glimmered briefly against the stars and then was gone.

Zael stared after it in incredulous horror. It had happened too quickly; she did not understand how she could have been so stupid. She had not even tried to grasp the coils as they passed!

The indicators were blurred; the needles hung near the zero mark. Staggering a little, she set off down the ravine to the right. She had perhaps a minute or two of air left, and then five or six minutes of slow asphyxiation. She might still find the stair; she was not dead yet.

The ravine wall, instead of sinking to an easier level, rose in spires and pinnacles. Zael stopped, cold and sodden with weariness. The silent peaks rose high against the stars. There was no help there, nor in all the dead, vampirish world around her.

Something leaped out of the stone at her feet. Startled, she drew back. The thing was spinning away under the stars. As she watched, another fragment of rock burst into view, and then another. This time she saw it fall, strike the stone and rebound.

She jerked her head back. Halfway down the rock face, swinging easily from hold to hold, came the alien. A cloud of rock fragments, dislodged by its passage, floated slowly down and rebounded about her head. The alien slid the last few yards and came to rest beside her.

Her head was swimming. She felt the heavy coils wind themselves around her; felt herself lifted and carried. The coils were too tight; she could not get her breath. When she was released, the pressure did not relax.

Reeling, she went forward toward the bubble house, where it winked and beckoned from the low horizon. Her throat was afire. Beside her, the alien went like quicksilver among the rocks.

Once she fell – an appalling, slow, helpless fall into the bruising cold – and the alien's heavy coils helped her up.

They came to a fissure. Zael stood tottering on the lip of it, dimly understanding now why the alien had come back for her. It was tit for tat; and now she was too bemused to play that game again. The alien's grasping members were on her sleeve.

Up there, somewhere in Draco, Isar's ship was on the way. Zael fumbled for the radio switch. Her voice came hoarse and strange: 'Mother …'

The heavy body was winding itself around her shoulders. Breathing hurt her chest, and her vision was dim. Gathering her strength, she jumped.

On the far side, she moved with a blurred slowness. She could see the bubble-house light winking prismatically at the end of an avenue of mist, and she knew that she had to get to it. She was not sure why; perhaps it had something to do with the silvery being that glided beside her.

The hum of a carrier wave suddenly filled her earphones. 'Zael, is that you?'

She heard the words, but their meaning slipped away. The bubble house was near now; she could see the flexible valve of its doorway. She had the idea that the silver thing must not be allowed to go inside, or it might breed there, and then there would be a plague of metal creatures running everywhere.

She turned clumsily to prevent it but lost her balance and fell against the side of the bubble. The great, silvery head was looming over her. She saw the jaws open and a pair of gleaming fangs slide into view. The head dipped delicately, the jaws seized her thigh, and the fangs went in, once. Without haste, the thing coiled itself way, out of her range of vision.

A coldness was spreading outward from her thigh. She saw two thin jets of vapour escaping from the armour where it was pierced. She turned her head; the alien creature was just disappearing through the flexible valve into the bubble. Inside, she could see it coursing back and forth, avoiding the one tiny light. It nosed at the hammock, the lamp, then the radio transceiver. Remembering, Zael said plaintively, 'Mother?'

As if in answer, the carrier hum came again, and the voice said, 'Zael, what is it?'

She tried to respond, but her thick tongue could not find the words. She felt weak and cold, but not at all afraid. Fumbling in her kit, she found the adhesive paste and smeared it over the punctures. The paste bubbled for a moment, then hardened. Something slow and languorous was spreading from the icy hurt in her thigh. As she turned again, she saw that the alien was still curved over the radio transceiver. Even from here, she could see the bright red knob of the escape shell signaller. As she watched, one of the alien's limbs grasped it and pushed it down.

She glanced up. After a moment the crawling orange spark in the sky seemed to pause and then grow slowly larger. The light burned to a bright star, then to a golden flare.

The escape shell came down on the rocky plain a hundred yards away. The torch winked out. Dazzled, she saw the dark shape of the alien come gliding down out of the bubble house.

It stopped, and for a moment the cruel head was poised, looking down at her. Then it flowed on.

The airlock door was a circle of yellow light. The alien seemed to hesitate before it; then it moved on and disappeared inside. The door closed. After a few moments the torch blazed again, and the shell rose on a pillar of fire.

Zael lay cradled against the bubble's resilient curve. Dimly the thought was in her mind that inside the bubble, a few feet away, were air and warmth. Whatever venom the alien had deposited in her flesh, perhaps it would not kill her for a long time. Her mother's ship was coming. She had a chance to live.

But the escape shell was still rising on its long golden plume; and she had eyes for nothing but that terrible beauty ascending into the night.

NOT WITH A BANG

Ten months after the last plane passed over, Rolf Smith knew beyond doubt that only one other human being had survived. Her name was Louise Oliver, and he was sitting opposite her in a department-store café in Salt Lake City. They were eating canned Vienna sausages and drinking coffee.

Sunlight struck through a broken pane like a judgment. Inside and outside, there was no sound; only a stifling rumour of absence. The clatter of dishware in the kitchen, the heavy rumble of streetcars: never again. There was sunlight; and silence; and the watery, astonished eyes of Louise Oliver.

He leaned forward, trying to capture the attention of those fish-like eyes for a second. 'Darling,' he said, 'I respect your views, naturally. But I've got to make you see that they're impractical.'

She looked at him with faint surprise, then away again. Her head shook slightly. *No, No, Rolf, I will not live with you in sin.*

Smith thought of the women of France, of Russia, of Mexico, of the South Seas. He had spent three months in the ruined studios of a radio station in Rochester, listening to the voices until they stopped. There had been a large colony in Sweden, including an English cabinet minister. They reported that Europe was gone. Simply gone; there was not an acre that had not been swept clean by radioactive dust. They had two planes and enough fuel to take them anywhere on the Continent; but there was nowhere to go. Three of them had the plague; then eleven; then all.

There was a bomber pilot who had fallen near a government radio station in Palestine. He did not last long, because he had broken some bones in the crash; but he had seen the vacant waters where the Pacific Islands should have been. It was his guess that the Arctic ice fields had been bombed.

There were no reports from Washington, from New York, from London, Paris, Moscow, Chungking, Sydney. You could not tell who had been destroyed by disease, who by the dust, who by bombs.

Smith himself had been a laboratory assistant in a team that was trying to find an antibiotic for the plague. His superiors had found one that worked sometimes, but it was a little too late. When he left, Smith took along with him all there was of it – forty ampoules, enough to last him for years.

Louise had been a nurse in a genteel hospital near Denver. According to her, something rather odd had happened to the hospital as she was approaching it the morning of the attack. She was quite calm when she said this, but a vague look came into her eyes and her shattered expression seemed to slip a little more. Smith did not press her for an explanation.

Like himself, she had found a radio station which still functioned, and when Smith discovered that she had not contracted the plague, he agreed to meet her. She was, apparently, naturally immune. There must have been others, a few at least; but the bombs and the dust had not spared them.

It seemed very awkward to Louise that not one Protestant minister was left alive.

The trouble was, she really meant it. It had taken Smith a long time to believe it, but it was true. She would not sleep in the same hotel with him, either; she expected, and received, the utmost courtesy and decorum. Smith had learned his lesson. He walked on the outside of the rubble-heaped sidewalks; he opened doors for her, when there were still doors; he held her chair; he refrained from swearing. He courted her.

Louise was forty or thereabouts, at least five years older than Smith. He often wondered how old she thought she was. The shock of seeing whatever it was that had happened to the hospital, the patients she had cared for, had sent her mind scuttling back to her childhood. She tacitly admitted that everyone else in the world was dead, but she seemed to regard it as something one did not mention.

A hundred times in the last three weeks, Smith had felt an almost irresistible impulse to break her thin neck and go his own way. But there was no help for it; she was the only woman in the world, and he needed her. If she died, or left him, he died. Old bitch! he thought to himself furiously, and carefully kept the thought from showing on his face.

'Louise, honey,' he told her gently, 'I want to spare your feelings as much as I can. You know that.'

'Yes, Rolf,' she said, staring at him with the face of a hypnotized chicken.

Smith forced himself to go on. 'We've got to face the facts, unpleasant as they may be. Honey, we're the only man and the only woman there are. We're like Adam and Eve in the Garden of Eden.'

Louise's face took on a slightly disgusted expression. She was obviously thinking of fig leaves.

'Think of the generations unborn,' Smith told her, with a tremor in his voice. Think about me for once. Maybe you're good for another ten years, maybe not. Shuddering, he thought of the second stage of the disease – the helpless rigidity, striking without warning. He'd had one such attack already, and Louise had helped him out of it. Without her, he would have stayed like that till he died, the hypodermic that would save him within inches of his rigid hand. He thought desperately, If I'm lucky, I'll get at least two kids out of you before you croak. Then I'll be safe.

He went on, 'God didn't mean for the human race to end like this. He spared us, you and me, to –' he paused; how could he say it without offending her? 'parents' wouldn't do – too suggestive '– to carry on the torch of life,' he ended. There. That was sticky enough.

Louise was staring vaguely over his shoulder. Her eyelids blinked regularly, and her mouth made little rabbit-like motions in the same rhythm.

Smith looked down at his wasted thighs under the table-top. I'm not strong enough to force her, he thought. Christ, if I were strong enough!

He felt the futile rage again, and stifled it. He had to keep his head, because this might be his last chance. Louise had been talking lately, in the cloudy language she used about everything, of going up in the mountains to pray for guidance. She had not said 'alone', but it was easy enough to see that she pictured it that way. He had to argue her around before her resolve stiffened. He concentrated furiously and tried once more.

The pattern of words went by like a distant rumbling. Louise heard a phrase here and there; each of them fathered chains of thought, binding her reverie tighter. 'Our duty to humanity ...' Mama had often said – that was in the old house on Waterbury Street, of course, before Mama had taken sick – she had said, 'Child, your duty is to be clean, polite, and God-fearing. Pretty doesn't matter. There's plenty of plain women that have got themselves good, Christian husbands.'

Husbands ... To have and to hold ... Orange blossoms, and the bridesmaids; the organ music. Through the haze, she saw Rolf's lean, wolfish face. Of course, he was the only one she'd ever get; *she* knew that well enough. Gracious, when a girl was past twenty-five, she had to take what she could get.

But I sometimes wonder if he's really a nice man, she thought.

'... in the eyes of God ...' She remembered the stained-glass windows in the old First Episcopalian Church, and how she always thought God was looking down at her through that brilliant transparency. Perhaps He was still looking at her, though it seemed sometimes that He had forgotten. Well, of course she realized that marriage customs changed, and if you couldn't have a regular minister ... But it was really a shame, an outrage almost, that if she were actually going to marry this man, she couldn't have all those nice things ... There wouldn't even be any wedding presents. Not even that. But of course Rolf would give her anything she wanted. She saw his face again, noticed the narrow black eyes staring at her with ferocious purpose, the thin mouth that jerked in a slow, regular tic, the hairy lobes of the ears below the tangle of black hair.

He oughtn't to let his hair grow so long, she thought. It isn't quite decent. Well, she could change all that. If she did marry him, she'd certainly make him change his ways. It was no more than her duty.

He was talking now about a farm he'd seen outside town – a good big house and a barn. There was no stock, he said, but they could get some later. And they'd plant things, and have their own food to eat, not go to restaurants all the time.

She felt a touch on her hand, lying pale before her on the table. Rolf's brown, stubby fingers, black-haired above and below the knuckles, were touching hers. He had stopped talking for a moment, but now he was speaking again, still more urgently. She drew her hand away.

He was saying, '… and you'll have the finest wedding dress you ever saw, with a bouquet. Everything you want, Louise, everything …'

A wedding dress! And flowers, even if there couldn't be any minister! Well, why hadn't the fool said so before?

Rolf stopped halfway through a sentence, aware that Louise had said quite clearly, 'Yes, Rolf, I will marry you if you wish.'

Stunned, he wanted her to repeat it but dared not ask, 'What did you say?' for fear of getting some fantastic answer, or none at all. He breathed deeply. He said, 'Today, Louise?'

She said, 'Well, *today* … I don't know quite … Of course, if you think you can make all the arrangements in time, but it does seem …'

Triumph surged through Smith's body. He had the advantage now, and he'd ride it. 'Say you will, dear,' he urged her. 'Say yes, and make me the happiest man …'

Even then, his tongue balked at the rest of it; but it didn't matter. She nodded submissively. 'Whatever you think best, Rolf.'

He rose, and she allowed him to kiss her pale, sapless cheek. 'We'll leave right away,' he said. 'If you'll excuse me for just a minute, dear?'

He waited for her 'Of course' and then left, making footprints in the furred carpet of dust down toward the end of the room. Just a few more hours he'd have to speak to her like that, and then, in her eyes, she'd be committed to him for ever. Afterward, he could do with her as he liked – beat her when he pleased, submit her to any proof of his scorn and revulsion, use her. Then it would not be too bad, being the last man on earth – not bad at all. She might even have a daughter …

He found the washroom door and entered. He took a step inside, and froze, balanced by a trick of motion, upright but helpless. Panic struck at his throat as he tried to turn his head and failed; tried to scream, and failed. Behind him, he was aware of a tiny click as the door, cushioned by the hydraulic check, shut for ever. It was not locked; but its other side bore the warning MEN.

BABEL II

I

From the front he looked a little like Happy Hooligan, if you remember that far back. From the side, where you got a better view of that silver-white crest, he looked more like a cross between George Arliss and a cockatoo.

He stood just under four feet tall, big head, crest and all. He had a wrinkled violet-grey skin, curious S-whorled ears, and a Tweedledum tummy; he was dressed in an electric-blue jacket and small-clothes of some crinkly material that glittered when he moved, with jackboots on his stubby legs and a white-metal disk, a quarter as big as he was, slung by a baldric from one narrow shoulder.

Lloyd Cavanaugh saw the apparition first, at eleven o'clock on a Wednesday morning in May, in the living room of his studio apartment on East 50th Street in Manhattan. It stepped into view, seemingly, from behind the drawing table at the far end of the room.

Which was nonsense. The drawing table, with its top horizontal and the breakfast dishes still on it, was shoved back against the closed drapes of the window. On the right, between the table and the record cabinet, there was about six inches clearance; on the left, between the table and the keg he kept his ink and brushes on, even less.

Cavanaugh, a bad-tempered young man with a long morose face casually connected to a knobbly, loose-jointed body, scowled across the pool of brilliance on the model table and said, 'What the hell?' He switched off the floods and turned on the room lights.

Suddenly illuminated, the Hooligan-thing blazed at him like a Christmas tree ornament. Its eyes blinked rapidly; then the long upper lip curled up in an astonishing crescent-shaped bucktoothed smile. It made a sound like '*Khakhptui!*' and nodded its head several times.

Cavanaugh's first thought was for the Hasselblad. He picked it up, tripod and all, carried it crabwise backward to safety behind the armchair, then crossed the room and took a poker out of the fireplace rack. Gripping this weapon, he advanced on the Hooligan.

The thing came to meet him, grinning and nodding. When they were two strides apart it stopped, bowed jerkily, and lifted the white disk at the end of the baldric, holding it at the top, with one of the flat sides toward Cavanaugh.

A picture formed in the disk.

In stereo and full colour, it showed a ten-inch Cavanaugh bending over something on a tripod. The hands moved swiftly, fitting pieces together; then the figure stepped back and stared with evident approval at an oblong box shape at the top of the tripod, with a chromed cylinder projecting from the front of it. The Hasselblad.

Cavanaugh lowered the poker. Jaw unhinged, he stared at the disk, which was now blank, then at the Hooligan's violet face and the silvery growth above it, which was neither hair nor feathers, but something in between ... 'How did you do that?' he demanded.

'Szu szat,' said the Hooligan alertly. He jiggled the disk at Cavanaugh, pointed to his head, then to the disk, then to Cavanaugh's head, then to the disk again. Then he held the thing out at arm's length, cocking his head to one side.

Cavanaugh took the disk gingerly. Gooseflesh was prickling along his arms. 'You want to know if I made the camera?' he said tentatively. 'Is that it?'

'Szat it,' said the Hooligan. He bowed again, nodded twice, and opened his eyes very wide.

Cavanaugh reflected. Staring at the disk, he imagined an enormous machine with a great many drive belts and moving parts, all whirling furiously. There it was, a little blurred, but not bad. He put a hopper on one side of it, made a man walk up and pour in a bucketful of scrap metal, and then showed a stream of cameras coming out the other side.

The Hooligan, who had been peering intently at the other side of the disk, straightened up and took the disk back with another bow. Then he whirled around rapidly three times, holding his nose with one hand and making violent gestures with the other.

Cavanaugh fell back a step, gripping his poker more firmly.

The Hooligan darted past him, moving so fast his legs twinkled, and fetched up with his chin on the edge of the model table, staring up at the setup in the middle of the tabletop.

'Hey!' said Cavanaugh angrily, and followed him. The Hooligan turned and held out the disk again. Another picture formed: Cavanaugh bending over the table, this time, putting tiny figures together and arranging them in front of a painted backdrop.

... Which was substantially what had happened. Cavanaugh was, by profession, a comic-book artist. He was indifferent to the work itself; it was automatic; it paid him well; but it had ruined him as a draftsman. He couldn't draw, paint or etch for fun any more. So he had taken up photography – specifically, tabletop photography.

He built his models out of clay and papier-mâché and wire and beads and bits of wood and a thousand other things; he painted or dyed them, composed them, lighted them – and then, with the Hasselblad and a special, very expensive shallow-focus lens, he photographed them. The results, after the first year, had begun to be surprising.

The setup on the table now was a deceptively simple one. Background and middle distance were a tangle of fir and mountain laurel, scaled half an inch to a foot. In the foreground were three figures grouped around the remains of a campfire. They were not human; they were attenuated, grey, hairless creatures with big mild eyes, dressed in oddly cut hiking clothes.

Two, with their backs to a block of crumbling masonry half sunken in the ground, were leaning together over a sheet of paper unrolled from a metal cylinder. The third was seated on a stone, nearer the camera, with a shank of meat in its hand. The shape of the half-gnawed bones was disturbingly familiar; and when you looked more closely you would begin to wonder if those projections at the end could be fingers, all but concealed by the eater's hand. As a matter of fact, they were; but no matter how long you looked at the photograph you would never be quite sure.

The Hooligan was thrusting the disk at him again, grinning and winking and teetering on his heels. Cavanaugh, suppressing annoyance in favour of curiosity, accepted it and ran through the same sequence the Hooligan had shown him.

'That's right,' he said. 'I made it. So what?'

'Szo khvat!' The Hooligan's hand made a gesture, too swift to follow, and suddenly contained what looked like a large fruit, like a purple pear with warts. Seeing Cavanaugh's uncomprehending expression, he put it back wherever it had come from and produced a wadded mass of translucent pink threads. Cavanaugh scowled irritably. 'Look—' he began.

The Hooligan tried again. This time he came up with a brilliant, faceted white stone about the size of a cherry.

Cavanaugh felt his eyes bulging. If that was a diamond …

'Khoiptoo!' said the Hooligan emphatically. He pointed to the stone and to Cavanaugh, then to himself and the model setup. His meaning was clear; he wanted to trade.

It was a diamond, all right; at least, it scribed a neat line in the glass of an empty beer bottle. It was also brilliant, pure white and, so far as Cavanaugh could tell, flawless. He put it on his postage scale; it weighed a little less than an ounce. Say twenty grams, and a carat was two hundred milligrams … It worked out to a preposterous one hundred carats, a little less than the Hope diamond in its prime.

He stared at the thing suspiciously. There *had* to be a catch in it, but with the best will in the world he couldn't see any. The models were a means to an end; once he was finished with them, they simply took up room. So what could he lose?

The Hooligan was gazing at him, owl-eyed. Cavanaugh picked up the disk and gave him his answer: a series of pictures that showed Cavanaugh photographing the models, processing the film, and then ceremoniously accepting the diamond and handing the models over.

The Hooligan bowed repeatedly, capered, stood briefly on his hands, and patted Cavanaugh's sleeve, grinning. Taking this for consent, Cavanaugh put the Hasselblad back in place, turned on the floods, and began where he had left off. He took half a dozen colour shots, then reloaded with black-and-white film and took half a dozen more.

The Hooligan watched everything with quivering attention. He followed Cavanaugh into the darkroom and goggled over the edge of the workbench while Cavanaugh developed the black-and-white film, fixed it, washed and dried it, cut it apart and printed it.

And as soon as the first print came out of the frame, the Hooligan made urgent gestures and held out another diamond, about half the size of the first. He wanted the prints, too!

Sweating, Cavanaugh dug into his files and brought up colour prints and transparencies of his other work: the Hansel and Gretel series, Cavor and the Grand Lunar, *Walpurgisnacht*, Gulliver extinguishing the palace fire in Lilliput, the Head of the N.I.C.E. The Hooligan bought them all. As each bargain was struck, he picked up his purchase and put it away wherever it was that he got the diamonds. Cavanaugh watched him closely, but couldn't figure out where they went.

For that matter, where had the Hooligan come from?

Assured that Cavanaugh had no more pictures, the Hooligan was darting around the room, peering into corners, bending to look into bookshelves, standing on tiptoe to see what was on the mantelpiece. He pointed at a five-inch wooden figurine, a squatting, hatchet-faced man-shape with its arms crossed, elbows on knees – an Ifugao carving that Cavanaugh had brought home from the Philippines. In the disk, a copy of the Goldberg machine Cavanaugh had used, to explain cameras, appeared for an instant. The Hooligan cocked his head at him.

'No,' said Cavanaugh. 'Handmade.' He took the disk and gave the Hooligan a view of a brown-skinned man gouging splinters out of a block of mahogany. Then, for kicks, he made the man shrink to a dot on an island on a globe that slowly turned, with Asia and Australia vanishing around one limb while the Americas rolled into sight from the other. He made a red dot for New York, and pointed at himself.

'Khrrrzt,' said the Hooligan thoughtfully. He turned away from the Ifuago and pointed to a bright diamond-patterned rug on the wall over the couch. 'Khandmate?'

Cavanaugh, who had just made up his mind to give up the Ifugao for another diamond, was nonplussed. 'Wait a minute,' he said, and made another moving picture in the disk: himself handing over the Ifugao for the standard emolument.

The Hooligan leaped back, ears flapping, crest aquiver. Recovering somewhat, he advanced again and showed Cavanaugh a revised version: the Hooligan receiving a wood carving from, and handing a diamond to the brown-skinned man Cavanaugh had pictured as its creator.

'Khandmate?' he said again, pointing to the rug.

Somewhat sourly, Cavanaugh showed him the rug being woven by a straw-hatted Mexican. Still more sourly, he answered the Hooligan's pictographed 'Where?' with a map of Mexico; and more sourly still, he identified and located the artists responsible for a Swedish silver pitcher, a Malay kris, an Indian brass hubble-bubble, and a pair of loafers hand-cobbled in Greenwich Village.

The Hooligan, it appeared, bought only at the source.

At any rate, if he wasn't going to get any more diamonds, he could get some information. Cavanaugh took the disk and projected a view of the Hooligan popping into sight and moving forward across the room. Then he ran it backward and looked inquiringly at the Hooligan.

For answer, he got a picture of a twilit depthless space where crested little creatures like the Hooligan walked among tall fungoid growths that looked like tiers of doughnuts on a stick. Another planet? Cavanaugh touched the disk and made the viewpoint tilt upward; the Hooligan obligingly filled in more of the featureless violet haze. No sun, no moon, no stars.

Cavanaugh tried again: a picture of himself, standing on the globe of the earth and peering at the night sky. Suddenly a tiny Hooligan-figure appeared, uncomfortably perched on a star.

The Hooligan countered with a picture that left Cavanaugh more confused than before. There were two globes, swinging in emptiness. One was solid-looking, and standing on it was a tiny man-shape; the other was violet mist, with the tubby, crested figure of a Hooligan inside it. The two spheres revolved very slowly around each other, coming a little nearer with each circuit, while the solid globe flickered light-dark, light-dark. Eventually they touched, clung, and the Hooligan-figure darted across. The solid globe flickered once more, the Hooligan shot back to the misty one, and the spheres separated, moving very gradually apart as they circled.

Cavanaugh gave up.

The Hooligan, after waiting a moment to be sure that Cavanaugh had no more questions, made his deepest bow to date and conjured up a final diamond: a beauty, larger than all but one or two that Cavanaugh already had.

Picture of Cavanaugh accepting the diamond and handing over something blurred: *What for?*

Picture of the Hooligan rejecting the blur: *For nothing.* Picture of the Hooligan patting Cavanaugh's sleeve: *For friendship.*

Feeling ashamed of himself, Cavanaugh got a bottle of May wine and two glasses out of the bookshelf. He explained to the Hooligan, via the disk, what the stuff was and – sketchily – what it was supposed to do to you.

This was a mistake.

The Hooligan, beaming enormously between sips, drank the wine with every sign of enjoyment. Then, with an impressive flourish, he put a smallish green and white doodad on the table. It had a green crystalline base with a slender knob-tipped metal shaft sprouting upright from the centre of it. That was all.

Feeling abnormally open-minded and expectant, Cavanaugh studied the Hooligan's pictograph explanation. The gadget, apparently, was the Hooligan equivalent of alcoholic beverages. (Picture of Cavanaugh and the Hooligan, with enormous smiles on their faces, while coloured lights flashed on and off inside their transparent skulls.) He nodded when the little man glanced at him for permission. With one thick finger, the Hooligan carefully tapped the doodad's projecting knob. Knob and shaft vibrated rapidly.

Cavanaugh had the odd sensation that someone was stirring his brains with a swizzle stick. It tickled. It was invigorating. It was delightful. 'Ha!' he said.

'Kho!' said the Hooligan, grinning happily. He picked up the doodad, put it away – Cavanaugh *almost* saw where it went – and stood up. Cavanaugh accompanied him to the door. He patted Cavanaugh's sleeve; Cavanaugh pumped his hand. Then, cheerfully bouncing three steps at a time, he disappeared down the stairwell.

From the window, a few minutes later, Cavanaugh saw him riding by – atop a Second Avenue bus.

II

The euphoric feeling diminished after a few minutes, leaving Cavanaugh in a relaxed but bewildered state of mind. To reassure himself, he emptied his bulging trouser pockets onto the table. Diamonds – solid, cool, sharp-edged, glowingly beautiful. He counted them; there were twenty-seven, ranging from over a hundred carats to about thirty; worth, altogether – how much?

Steady, he warned himself. There may be a catch in it yet. The thing to do was to get downtown to an appraiser's and find out. Conveniently, he knew where there was one – in the French Building, across the hall from Patriotic Comics. He picked out two of the stones, a big one and a little one, and zipped them into the inner compartment of his wallet. Jittering a little with excitement, he dumped the rest into a paper bag and hid them under the kitchen sink.

A yellow cab was cruising down the avenue. Cavanaugh hailed it and got in. 'Forty-fifth and Fifth,' he said.

'Boo?' said the driver, twisting to look at him.

Cavanaugh glowered. 'Forty-fifth Street,' he said distinctly, 'and Fifth Avenue. Let's go.'

'Zawss,' said the driver, pushing his cap up, 'owuh kelg trace wooj'l, fook. Bnog nood ig ye nolik?'

Cavanaugh got out of the cab. 'Pokuth*chowig'w!*' said the driver, and zoomed away, grinding his gears.

Jaw unhinged, Cavanaugh stared after him. He felt his ears getting hot. 'Why didn't I get his licence number?' he said aloud. 'Why didn't I stay upstairs where it was safe? Why do I live in this idiotic goddamn city?'

He stepped back onto the sidewalk. 'Lowly, badny?' said a voice in his ear.

Cavanaugh whirled. It was an urchin with a newspaper in his hand, a stack of them under his arm. 'Will you kindly mind your own business?' Cavanaugh said. He turned, took two steps toward the corner, then froze, faced around again, and marched back.

It was as he had thought: the headline of the paper in the boy's hand read, MOTN LNIUL IMAP QYFRAT.

The name of the paper, which otherwise looked like the *News*, was *Pionu Vajl*.

The newsboy was backing away from him, with a wary look in his eyes.

'Wait,' said Cavanaugh hastily. He clutched in his pocket for change, found none, and got a bill out of his wallet with trembling fingers. He thrust it at the child. 'I'll take a paper.'

The boy took the bill, glanced at it, threw it on the pavement at Cavanaugh's feet, and ran like sixty.

Cavanaugh picked up the bill. In each corner of it was a large figure 4. Over the familiar engraving of G. Washington were the words FRA EVOFAP LFIFAL YK IQATOZI. Under it, the legend read, YVA PYNNIT.

He clutched his collar, which was throttling him. That vibrating gadget – But that couldn't be it; it was the world that was scrambled, not Cavanaugh. And *that* was impossible, because …

A dirty little man in a derby rushed at him, grabbing for his lapels 'Poz'k,' he gabbled, 'fend gihekn, fend gihekn? Fwuz eeb l' mwukd sahtz' kn?'

Cavanaugh pushed him away and retreated.

The little man burst into tears, 'FWUH!' he wailed. 'Fwuh vekn r' NAHP shaoo?'

Cavanaugh stopped thinking. Out of the corner of his eye, he saw that a crosstown bus had just pulled up down at the end of the block. He ran for it.

The red-faced driver was half out of his seat, bellowing gibberish at a fat woman who was shrieking back at him, brandishing a dangerous parasol. Beyond them the narrow aisle was packed full of bewildered faces, annoyed faces, shouting faces. The air bristled with dislocated consonants.

Farther down, somebody shrieked and hammered on the rear door. Cursing, the driver turned around to open it. The fat woman seized this opportunity to clout him on the head, and when the resulting melee was over, Cavanaugh found himself halfway down the bus, well wedged in, without having paid his fare.

The bus moved. Hysterical passengers got off at every stop, but the ones that crowded on were in no better shape. Nobody, Cavanaugh realized numbly, could understand anybody; nobody could read anything written.

The din was increasing; Cavanaugh could hear the driver's bellowing voice getting steadily hoarser and weaker. Up ahead, horns were blowing furiously. Concentrating with the greatest difficulty, he managed: *How far?* That was the crucial point – had whatever it was happened simultaneously all over New York ... or all over the world? Or, horrid thought, was it a sort of infection that he was carrying with him?

He had to find out.

The traffic got thicker. At Sixth Avenue the bus, which had been moving by inches, stopped altogether and the doors slammed open. Peering forward, Cavanaugh saw the driver climb down, hurl his uniform cap to the street and disappear, shoulders hunched, into the crowd.

Cavanaugh got out and walked west into bedlam. Auto horns were howling, sirens shrieking; there was a fight every fifteen yards and a cop for every tenth fight. After a while it became obvious that he would never get to Broadway; he battled his way back to Sixth and turned south.

The loudspeaker over a record store was blaring a song Cavanaugh knew and detested; but instead of the all-too-familiar words, the raucous female voice was chanting:

'Kee-*ee* tho-*iv i-if* zeg*mlit Podn mawgeth oo-oou-gaatch* ...'

It sounded just as good.

The street sign directly ahead of him read, 13FR, LF. Even the *numbers* were cockeyed.

Cavanaugh's head hurt. He went into a bar.

It was well patronized. Nobody in a white coat was in evidence, but about a third of the customers were behind the bar, serving the rest – a bottle at a time.

Cavanaugh elbowed his way into the first tier and hesitated between two bottles labelled respectively CIF 05 and ZITLFIOTL. Neither sounded particularly appetizing, but the amber liquid in each looked to be what he needed. He settled for the Zitlfiotl. After his second swallow, feeling more alert, he scanned the backbar and located the radio.

It was, he found when he reached it, already turned on, but nothing was coming out but a power hum. He twiddled with the knobs. At the right of the dial – which was eccentrically numbered from 77 to 408 – he picked up an orchestra playing *Pictures at an Exhibition*; otherwise, nothing.

That, he decided, settled it. WQXR, with an all-music programme, was on the air; the others were off. That meant that speech was coming out double-talk, not only New York and New Jersey broadcasts, but in network programmes from the West Coast. Or – wait a minute – even if a radio performer in Hollywood were able to speak straight English, wouldn't it be nonsense to an engineer in Manhattan?

This led him by easy stages to the next problem. Selecting an unfrequented table in the rear, and carrying his Zitlfiotl with him, he seated himself with circumspection and carefully laid out on the table the following important articles:

A partially used envelope.

A fountain pen.

A one-dollar bill.

His social-security card.

A salvaged newspaper.

Now, the question was, did any order remain in the patterns of human speech, or was all reduced to utter chaos? Scientific method, encouraged by Zitlfiotl, would discover the answer.

As a preliminary gambit, he wrote the letters of the alphabet, in a severely vertical line, on the unused surface of the envelope.

Next, after reflection, he copied down the text of the one-dollar bill. Thusly:

FRA EVOFAP LFIFAL YK IQATOZI YVA PYNNIT

Under each line, letter by letter, he added what *ought* to be the text of the one-dollar bill.

This gave him fifteen letters, which he wrote down in their proper places opposite the already established letters of the alphabet. Following the identical procedure with the *Pionu Vajl*, or *Daily News*, and, with his own signature, which appeared on the card as *Nnyup Ziciviemr*, gave him four letters more, with the result:

A	E	H		O	I	V	N
B		I	A	P	D	W	
C	V	J	W	Q	M	X	
D		K	F	R	H	Y	O
E	U	L	S	S		Z	C
F	T	M	G	T	R		
G		N	L	U	Y		

Now came the supreme test. He copied down the *Vajl*'s puzzling headline and transliterated it according to his findings:

MOTN LNIUL
GIRL SLAYS
IMAP QYFRAT
AGED MOTHER

A triumphant success. He could now communicate.

The point is, he told himself lucidly, when I think I am saying 'Listen to me,' in actuality I am saying 'Nolfav fy qa,' and this is why nobody understands anyone else. And therefore, if I were to think I am saying 'Nolfav fy qa,' I would actually be saying 'Listen to me.' And in this way will we build the Revolution.

But it didn't work.

Some time later he found himself in a disused classroom with an unruly student body consisting of three men with spectacles and beards and a woman with hair in her eyes; he was attempting to teach them by means of blackboard exercises a new alphabet which began, E, blank, V, blank, U, T, blank. The blanks, he explained, were most important.

At a later period he was standing on the first landing of the left-hand staircase in the lobby of the Forty-second Street Branch of the New York Public Library shouting to an assembled crowd, over and over, 'Myppiqvap opoyfl! Myppiqvap opoyfl!'

And at a still later time he woke up, cold sober, leaning on an imitation-marble-topped table in a partially wrecked cafeteria. Sunlight was slanting through the plate glass onto the wall to his left; it must be either late afternoon or early morning.

Cavanaugh groaned. He had gone into that bar, he remembered, because his head hurt: about like taking a mickey finn for nausea.

And as for the rest of it – before *and* after … how much of that had he imagined?

He raised his head and stared hopefully at the lettering on the windows. Even back-to-front he could tell that it wasn't in English. The first letter was a Z.

He groaned again and propped his chin up with his hands, carefully, so as not to slosh. He tried to stay that way, not moving, not looking, not noticing, but eventually an insistent thought brought him upright again.

How long?

How long was this going to last? How long could it last before the whole world went to hell in a hand basket? Not very long.

Without language, how could you buy anything, sell anything, order anything? And if you could, what would you use for money – four-dollar bills marked YVA PYNNIT?

… Or, he amended bitterly, something equally outlandish. Because that was the point he had overlooked a few drunken hours ago – everybody's alphabet was different. To Cavanaugh, YVA PYNNIT. To somebody else, AGU MATTEK, or ENY ZEBBAL, or …

Twenty-six letters in the alphabet. Possible combinations, $26 \times 25 \times 24 \times 23 \times 22$ and so on down to $\times 1$ … figure roughly one decimal place for each operation …

Something in the *septillions*.

Not as many if vowels were traded for vowels, consonants for consonants, as seemed to have happened in his case, but still plenty. More than the number of people alive in the world.

That was for the written word. For speech, he realized suddenly, it would be just about twenty-five decimal places worse. Not letters, phonemes – forty of them in ordinary spoken English.

A swizzle stick that stirred up your brains – that switched the reflex arcs around at random, connecting the receptor pattern for *K* with the response pattern for *H*, or *D* or anything …

Cavanaugh traced a letter with his forefinger on the table-top, frowning at it. Hadn't he always made an A like that – a vertical stroke with three horizontal ones?

But, damn it, that was the fiendish thing about it – memory didn't mean a thing, because all the memories were still there but they were scrambled. As if you had ripped out all the connections in a telephone switchboard and put them back differently.

Of course: it *had* to be that way – nobody had gone around repainting all the signs or reprinting all the newspapers or forging a phoney signature on Cavanaugh's social-security card. That half-circle first letter of his name, even though it looked like a Z to him, was still a C.

Or was it? If a tree falls with nobody to hear it, is there a sound? And if beauty is in the eye of the beholder, then which way is up? Or, rather, thought Cavanaugh, repressing a tendency toward hysteria, *which way is out?*

First things first.

The Hooligan.

He came from some place that wasn't exactly a place, across a distance that wasn't exactly a distance. But it must be a difficult journey, because there was no record of any previous appearances of little cockatoo-crested art collectors …

He bought the local handicrafts with stones that were priceless on this planet, and very likely dirt-common where he came from. Pretty beads for the natives. In politeness, you offered him a drink. And being polite right back at you, he gave you a shot of swizzle-sticks-in-the-head.

Firewater. A mild stimulant to the Hooligan, hell on wheels to the aborigines. Instead of getting two people mildly confused, it turned a whole planet pole over equator … and, communicating by pictures as he did, it was probable that the Hooligan *still* didn't know what damage he had done. He would finish his tour and go happily back home with his prizes, and then a few thousand years from now, maybe, when the human race had put itself together again into half-acre nations and two-for-a-nickel empires, another Hooligan would come along …

Cavanaugh upset his chair.

Icicles were forming along his spine.

This wasn't the first time. It had happened at least once before, a few thousand years ago, in the valley of the Euphrates.

Not Bedlam – Babel.

III

The sun was quartering down toward the west, gilding a deserted Forty-second Street with the heartbreaking false promise of spring in New York. Leaning dizzily against the door frame, Cavanaugh saw broken display windows and dark interiors. He heard a confused roaring from somewhere uptown, but the few people who passed him were silent, bewildered.

There was a nasty wreck at the corner of Seventh Avenue, and another at Eighth; that accounted, he saw with relief, for the lack of traffic in this block. Holding the top of his head down with one hand, he scuttled across the street and dived into the black maw of the IRT subway.

The arcade and the station itself were empty, echoing. Nobody behind the news-stands, nobody playing the pinball machines, nobody in the change booth. Swallowing hard, Cavanaugh went through the open gate and clattered down the stairs to the downtown platform.

A train was standing in the express lane, doors open, lights burning, motor chuffing quietly. Cavanaugh ran down to the first car and went across the vestibule to the motorman's cubicle.

The control lever was missing.

Cursing, Cavanaugh climbed back to the street. He had to find the Hooligan; he had one chance in a million of doing it, and one wasted minute now might be the one minute that mattered.

The little man could be anywhere on the planet by now. But he'd expressed interest in objects in Cavanaugh's apartment that came variously from the Philippines, Mexico, Malaya, Sweden, India – and Greenwich Village. If, improbably, he hadn't got around to the Village yet, then Cavanaugh might be able to catch him there; it was the only hope he had.

On Eighth Avenue south of Forty-first, he came upon a yellow cab parked at the kerb. The driver was leaning against the wall under a Zyzi-Zyni sign, talking to himself, with gestures.

Cavanaugh clutched him by the sleeve and made urgent motions southward. The driver looked at him vaguely, cleared his throat, moved two feet farther down the wall and resumed his interrupted discourse.

Fuming, Cavanaugh hesitated for a moment, then fumbled in his pockets for pen and paper. He found the envelope with his world-saving alphabet on it, tore it open to get a blank space, and sketched rapidly:

The driver looked at it boredly, then with a faint gleam of intelligence. Cavanaugh pointed to the first picture and looked at him interrogatively.

'Oweh?' said the driver.

'That's right,' said Cavanaugh, nodding violently. 'Now the next—'

The driver hesitated. 'Mtshell?'

That couldn't be right, with a consonant at the end of it. Cavanaugh shook his head and pointed to the blacked-in circle.

'Vcode,' said the driver.

Cavanaugh moved his finger to the white circle.

'Mah.'

'Right!' said Cavanaugh. 'Oweh mah—' He pointed to the third picture.

That was the tough one; the driver couldn't get it. 'Vnakjaw?' he hazarded.

Not enough syllables. Cavanaugh shook his head and passed on to the fourth picture.

'Vbzyetch.'

Cavanaugh nodded, and they started through the sequence again.

'Oweh – mah – vbzyetch.' A look of enlightenment spread over the driver's face. '*Jickagl! Jickagl!* Vbzyetch!'

'You've got it,' Cavanaugh told him: 'Sheridan Square. *Jickagl* Vbzyetch.'

Halfway to the cab, the driver stopped short, with a remembering look on his face, and held out his hand insinuatingly.

Cavanaugh took the bills out of his wallet and fanned them at him. The driver shook his head. 'Ngupjoke,' he said sadly, and turned back toward his wall.

Twenty minutes later Cavanaugh was poorer by one thirty-carat diamond, and the cab-driver, with a smile on his honest face, was opening the door for him at the western corner of Sheridan Square (which is triangular), a few yards from the bullet-coloured statue of the General.

Cavanaugh made signs to him to wait, and got a happy grin and a nod in reply, and ran down the block.

He passed Janigian's shop once without recognizing it, and for an excellent reason: there was not a shoe or a slipper visible anywhere in the big, bare work-and sales-room.

The door was ajar. Cavanaugh went in, stared suspiciously at the empty shelves and then at the door to the back room, which was closed by a hasp and the largest, heaviest padlock he had ever seen in his life. This was odd (a) because Janigian did not believe in locking his doors, and this one, in fact, had never even had a latch, and (b) because Janigian never went anywhere – having been permanently startled, some years ago, by E. B. White's commentary on the way the pavement comes up to meet your foot when you lift it.

Cavanaugh stepped forward, got his fingernails into the crack between the door and the jamb, and pulled.

The hasp, being attached to the jamb only by the sawed-off heads of two screws, came free; the door swung open.

Inside was Janigian.

He was sitting cross-legged on a small wooden chest, looking moderately wild-eyed. He had a rusty shotgun across his thighs, and two ten-inch butcher knives were stuck into the floor in front of him.

When he saw Cavanaugh he raised the gun, then lowered it a trifle. 'Odeh!' he said. Cavanaugh translated this as 'Aha!' which was Janigian's standard greeting.

'Odeh yourself,' he said. He took out his wallet, removed his other diamond – the big one – and held it up.

Janigian nodded solemnly. He stood up, holding the shotgun carefully under one arm, and with the other, without looking down, opened the lid of the chest. He pulled aside a half-dozen dirty shirts, probed deeper, and scrabbled up a handful of something.

He showed it to Cavanaugh.

Diamonds.

He let them pour back into the chest, dropped the shirts back on top, closed the lid and sat down again. 'Odeh!' he said.

This time it meant 'Good-bye.' Cavanaugh went away.

His headache, which had left him imperceptibly somewhere on Forty-second Street, was making itself felt again. Cursing without inspiration, Cavanaugh walked back up to the corner.

Now what? Was he supposed to pursue the Hooligan to the Philippines, or Sweden, or Mexico?

Well, why not?

If I don't get him, Cavanaugh told himself, I'll be living in a cave a year from now. I'll make a lousy caveman. Grubs for dinner *again* …

The cabman was still waiting on the corner. Cavanaugh snarled at him and went into the cigar store across the street. From an ankle-deep layer of neckties, pocketbooks and mashed candy bars he picked out a five-borough map. He trudged back across the street and got into the cab.

The driver looked at him expectantly. 'Your mother has hairy ears,' Cavanaugh told him.

'Zee kwa?' said the driver.

'Three of them,' Cavanaugh said. He opened the map to the Queens-Long Island section, managed to locate Flushing Bay, and drew an X – which, on second thought, he scribbled into a dot – where La Guardia Field ought to be.

The driver looked at it, nodded – and held out his meaty hand.

Cavanaugh controlled an impulse to spit. Indignantly, he drew a picture of the diamond he had already given the man, pointed to it, then to the cabman, then to the map.

The driver shrugged and gestured outside with his thumb.

Cavanagh gritted his teeth, shut his eyes tight, and counted to twenty. Eventually, when he thought he could trust himself to hold anything with a sharp point, he picked up the pen, found the Manhattan section of the map, and made a dot at Fiftieth and Second Avenue. He drew another picture of a diamond, with an arrow pointing to the dot.

The driver studied it. He leaned farther over the seat and put a stubby finger on the dot. 'Fa mack alaha gur'l hih?' he demanded suspiciously.

'Your father comes from a long line of orangutans with loathsome diseases,' said Cavanaugh, crossing his heart.

Reassured by the polysyllables, the driver put his machine into motion.

At the apartment, while the driver lurked heavily in the living room, Cavanaugh picked out the very smallest diamond to pay his fare, and twelve others, from middling to big, for further emergencies. He also took two cans of hash, a can of tamales, an opener, a spoon, and a bottle of tomato juice in a paper bag; the thought of food revolted him at the moment, but he would have to eat some time. Better than grubs, anyway …

All the main arteries out of New York, Cavanaugh discovered, were choked – everybody who was on the island was apparently trying to get off, and vice versa. Nobody was paying much attention to traffic signals, and the battered results were visible at nearly every intersection.

It took them two hours to get to La Guardia.

Some sort of a struggle was going on around a car parked in front of the terminal building. As Cavanaugh's cab pulled up, the crowd broke and surged toward them; Cavanaugh had barely time to open the door and leap out. When he had bounced off the hood, tripped over somebody's feet, butted someone else in the stomach, and finally regained his balance a few seconds later, he saw the cab turning on two wheels, with one rear door hanging open, and a packed mass of passengers bulging out like a bee swarm. The cab's tail-lights wavered off down the road, a few stragglers running frantically after it.

Cavanaugh walked carefully around the diminished mob, still focused on the remaining car, and went into the building. He fought his way through the waiting room, losing his paper bag, several buttons from his shirt and nine-tenths of his temper, and found an open gate onto the field.

The huge, floodlighted area was one inextricable confusion of people, dogs and airplanes – more planes than Cavanaugh had ever seen in one place before; forests of them – liners, transports, private planes of every size and shape.

The dogs were harder to account for. There seemed to be several dozen of them in his immediate vicinity, all large and vociferous. One especially active Dalmatian, about the size of a cougar, circled Cavanaugh twice and then reared up to put two tremendous forepaws on his chest. Cavanaugh fell like a tree. Man and dog stared at each other, eye to eye, for one poignant moment; then the beast whirled, thumping Cavanaugh soundly in the ribs, and was gone.

Raging, Cavanaugh arose and stalked forth onto the field.

Somebody grabbed his sleeve and shouted in his ear; Cavanaugh swung at him, whirled completely around, and cannoned into somebody else, who hit him with a valise. Some time later, confused in mind and bruised of body, he found himself approaching a small, fragile-looking monoplane on whose wing sat an expressionless man in a leather jacket.

Cavanaugh climbed up beside him, panting. The other looked at him thoughtfully and raised his left hand, previously concealed by his body. There was a spanner in it.

Cavanaugh sighed. Raising one hand for attention, he opened his wallet and took out one of the larger gems.

The other man lowered the spanner a trifle.

Cavanaugh felt for his fountain pen; it was gone. Dipping one finger in the blood that was trickling from his nose, he drew a wobbly outline map of North America on the surface of the wing.

The other winced slightly, but watched with interest.

Cavanaugh drew the United States-Mexico border, and put a large dot, or blob, south of it. He pointed to the plane, to the dot, and held up the diamond.

The man shook his head.

Cavanaugh added a second.

The man shook his head again. He pointed to the plane, made motions as if putting earphones on his head, cocked his head in a listening attitude, and shook his head once more. *No radio.*

With one flattened hand, he made a zooming motion upward; with the other, he drew a swift line across his throat. *Suicide.*

Then he sketched an unmilitary salute. *Thanks just the same.*

Cavanaugh climbed down from the wing. The next pilot he found gave him the same answer; and the next; and the next. There wasn't any fifth, because, in taking a shortcut under a low wing, he tripped over two silently struggling gentlemen who promptly transferred their quarrel to him. When he recovered from a momentary inattention, they were gone, and so was the wallet with the diamonds.

Cavanaugh walked back to Manhattan.

Counting the time he spent asleep under a trestle somewhere in Queens, it took him twelve hours. Even an Oregonian can find his way around in Manhattan, but a Manhattanite gets lost anywhere away from his island. Cavanaugh missed the Queensborough Bridge somehow, wandered south into Brooklyn without realizing it (he would rather have died), and wound up some sixty blocks off his course at the Williamsburg Bridge; this led him via Delancey Street into the Lower East Side, which was not much improvement.

Following the line of least resistance, and yearning for civilization (i.e., midtown New York), Cavanaugh moved northwestward along that erstwhile cowpath variously named the Bowery, Fourth Avenue and Broadway. Pausing only to rummage in a Union Square fruit-drink stand for cold frankfurters, he reached Forty-second Street at half-past ten, twenty-three and one half hours after his introduction to the Hooligan.

Times Square, never a very inspiring sight in the morning, was very sad and strange. Traffic, a thin trickle, was moving spasmodically. Every car had its windows closed tight, and Cavanaugh saw more than one passenger holding a rifle. The crowds on the littered sidewalks did not seem to be going anywhere, or even thinking about going anywhere. They were huddling.

Bookstores were empty and their contents, scattered over the pavement; novelty shops, cafeterias, drug-stores … the astonishing thing was that, here and there, trade was still going on. Money would still buy you a bottle of liquor, or a pack of cigarettes, or a can of food – the necessities. Pricing was a problem, but it was being solved in a forthright manner: above each counter, the main items of the store's stock-in-trade were displayed, each with one or two bills pasted to it. Cigarettes – George Washington. A fifth of whisky – Alexander Hamilton and Abraham Lincoln. A can of ersatzized meat – Andrew Jackson.

There was even one movie house open for business. It was showing a Charlie Chaplin Festival.

Cavanaugh was feeling extremely light-headed and unsubstantial. Babylon, that great city! he thought; and somewhere, patently, in the ginnandgo gap between antediluvious and annadominant the copyist must have fled with his scroll …

The human race had now, in effect, Had It. New York was no longer a city; it was simply the raw material for an archaeologist's puzzle – a midden heap. And thinking of *Finnegan* again, he remembered, What a mnice old mness it all mnakes!

He looked at the faces around him, blank with a new misery, the misery of silence. That's what hits them the hardest, he thought. The speechlessness. They don't care about not being able to read – it's a minor annoyance. But they like to talk.

And yet, the human race could have survived if only the spoken word had been bollixed up, not the written word. It would have been easy enough to work out universal sound symbols for the few situations where speech was really vital. Nothing could replace the textbooks, the records, the libraries, the business letters.

By now, Cavanaugh thought bitterly, the Hooligan was trading shiny beads for grass skirts in Honolulu, or carved walrus tusks in Alaska, or …

Or was he? Cavanaugh stopped short. He had, he realized, been thinking of the Hooligan popping into view all over the globe the way he had appeared in his apartment – and, when he was through, popping back to where he belonged from wherever he happened to be.

But, if he could travel that way, *why had he left Cavanaugh's place on a Second Avenue bus?*

Cavanaugh scrabbled frantically through his memory. His knees sagged.

The Hooligan had showed him, in the disk, that the two – universes, call them – came together rarely, and when they did, touched at one point only. Last time, the plain of Shinar. This time, Cavanagh's living room.

And that one flicker, light-dark-light, before the pictured Hooligan moved back to its own sphere …

Twenty-four hours.

Cavanaugh looked at his watch. It was 10:37.

He ran.

Lead-footed, three quarters dead, and cursing himself, the Hooligan, the human race, God the Creator and the entire imaginable cosmos with the last breath in his body, Cavanaugh reached the corner of Forty-ninth and Second just in time to see the Hooligan pedalling briskly up the avenue on a bicycle.

He shouted, or tried to; nothing but a wheeze came out.

Whistling with agony, he lurched around the corner and ran to keep from falling on his face. He almost caught up with the Hooligan at the entrance to the building, but he couldn't stop to get the breath to make a noise. The Hooligan darted inside and up the stairs; Cavanaugh followed.

He can't open the door, he thought, halfway up. But when he reached the third-floor landing, the door was open.

Cavanaugh made one last effort, leaped like a salmon, tripped over the doorsill, and spreadeagled himself on the floor in the middle of the room.

The Hooligan, one step away from the drawing table, turned with a startled 'Chayadnih?'

Seeing Cavanaugh, he came forward with an expression of pop-eyed concern. Cavanaugh couldn't move.

Muttering excitedly to himself, the Hooligan produced the green-and-white doodad from somewhere – much, presumably, as a human being might have gone for the medicinal brandy – and set it on the floor near Cavanaugh's head.

'*Urgh!*' said Cavanaugh. With one hand, he clutched the Hooligan's disk.

The pictures formed without any conscious planning: the doodad, the lights flashing off and on in a skull – dozens, hundreds of skulls – then buildings falling, trains crashing, volcanoes erupting …

The Hooligan's eyes bulged half out of their sockets. 'Hakdaz!' he said, clapping his hands to his ears. He seized the disk and made conciliatory pictures – the doodad and a glass of wine melting into each other.

'I know that,' said Cavanaugh hoarsely, struggling up to one elbow. 'But *can you fix it?*' He made a picture of the Hooligan gesturing at the flashing lights, which promptly vanished.

'Deech, deech,' said the Hooligan, nodding violently. He picked up the doodad and somehow broke the green base of it into dozens of tiny cubes, which he began to reassemble, apparently in a different order, with great care.

Cavanaugh hauled himself up into an armchair and let himself go limp as a glove. He watched the Hooligan, telling himself drowsily that if he wasn't careful, he'd be asleep in another minute. There was something odd about the room, something extraordinarily soothing … After a moment he realized what it was.

The silence.

The two fishwives who infested the floor below were not screaming pleasantries across the courtyard at each other. Nobody was playing moron music on a radio tuned six times too loud for normal hearing.

The landlady was not shouting instructions from the top floor to the janitor in the basement.

Silence. Peace.

For some reason, Cavanaugh's mind turned to the subject of silent films: Chaplin, the Keystone Cops, Douglas Fairbanks, Garbo … they would have to bring them out of the cans again, he thought, for everybody, not just the patrons of the Museum of Modern Art Film Library …

Congress would have to rig up some sort of Telautograph system, with a screen above the Speaker's desk, perhaps.

Television. Television, thought Cavanaugh dreamily, would have to shut up and put up.

No more campaign oratory.

No more banquet speeches.

No more singing commercials.

Cavanaugh sat up. 'Listen,' he said tensely. 'Could you fix just the writing – not the speech?'

The Hooligan goggled at him and held out the disk

Cavanaugh took it and slowly began putting the idea into careful pictures …

The Hooligan was gone – vanished like a burst soap bubble at the end of a head-first dive across Cavanaugh's drawing table.

Cavanaugh sat where he was, listening. From outside, after a moment, came a confused, distance-muted roar. All over the city – all over the world, Cavanaugh supposed – people were discovering that they could read again; that the signs meant what they said; that each man's sudden island had been rejoined to the main.

It lasted twenty minutes and then faded slowly. In his mind's eye, Cavanaugh saw the orgy of scribbling that must be beginning now. He sat, and listened to the blessed silence.

In a little while a growing twinge forced itself upon his attention, like a forgotten toothache. After a moment, Cavanaugh identified it as his conscience. Just who are you, conscience was saying, to take away the gift of speech – the thing that once was all that distinguished man from the apes?

Cavanaugh dutifully tried to feel repentant, but it didn't work. Who said it was a gift? he asked his conscience. What did we use it for?

I'll tell you, he said. In the cigar store: Hey, waddya think of them Yankees? Yeah, that was som'n, wasn't it? Sure was! I tell you …

At home: So, how was the office t'day? Aa. Same goddamn madhouse. How'd it go with you? Awright. I can't complain. Kids okay? Yaa. Uh-huh. What's f-dinner?

At a party: Hello, Harry! Whattaya say, boy! How are ya? That's good. How's the … so I said to him, you can't tell me what I'm gonna … like to, but it don't agree with me. It's my stummick; th' doctor says … organdy, with little gold buttons … Oh, yeah? Well, how would you like a poke in the snoot?

On the street corners: Lebensraum … Nordische Blut …

I, said Cavanaugh, rest my case.

Conscience did not reply.

In the silence, Cavanaugh walked across the room to the record cabinet and pulled out an album. He could read the lettering on its spine: MAHLER, *The Song of the Earth*.

He picked out one of the disks and put it on the machine – the 'Drunkard's Song' in the fifth movement.

Cavanaugh smiled beatifically, listening. It was an artificial remedy, he was thinking; from the Hooligan's point of view the human race was now permanently a little tipsy. And so what?

The words the tenor was singing were gibberish to Cavanaugh – but then they always had been; Cavanaugh spoke no German. He knew what the words meant.

Was geht mich denn der Frühling an!?

Lasst mich betrunken sein?

'What then is the spring to me?

… Let me be drunk!'

ANACHRON

The body was never found. And for that reason alone, there was no body to find.

It sounds like inverted logic – which, in a sense, it is – but there's no paradox involved. It was a perfectly orderly and explicable event, even though it could only have happened to a Castellare.

Odd fish, the Castellare brothers. Sons of a Scots-Englishwoman and an expatriate Italian, born in England, educated on the Continent, they were at ease anywhere in the world and at home nowhere.

Nevertheless, in their middle years, they had become settled men. Expatriates like their father, they lived on the island of Ischia, off the Neapolitan coast, in a palace – *quattrocento*, very fine, with peeling cupids on the walls, a multitude of rats, no central heating and no neighbours.

They went nowhere; no one except their agents and their lawyers came to them. Neither had ever married. Each, at about the age of thirty, had given up the world of people for an inner world of more precise and more enduring pleasures. Each was an amateur – a fanatical, compulsive amateur.

They had been born out of their time.

Peter's passion was virtu. He collected relentlessly, it would not be too much to say savagely; he collected as some men hunt big game. His taste was catholic, and his acquisitions filled the huge rooms of the palace and half the vaults under them – paintings, statuary, enamels, porcelain, glass, crystal, metalwork. At fifty, he was a round little man with small, sardonic eyes and a careless patch of pinkish goatee.

Harold Castellare, Peter's talented brother, was a scientist. An amateur scientist. He belonged in the nineteenth century, as Peter was a throwback to a still earlier epoch. Modern science is largely a matter of teamwork and drudgery, both impossible concepts to a Castellare. But Harold's intelligence was in its own way as penetrating and original as a Newton's or a Franklin's. He had done respectable work in physics and electronics, and had even, at his lawyer's instance, taken out a few patents. The income from these, when his own purchases of instruments and equipment did not consume it, he gave to his brother, who accepted it without gratitude or rancour.

Harold, at fifty-three, was spare and shrunken, sallow and spotted, with a bloodless, melancholy countenance; on his upper lip grew a neat hedge of pink-and-salt moustache, the companion piece and antithesis of his brother's goatee.

On a certain May morning, Harold had an accident.

Goodyear dropped rubber on a hot stove; Archimedes took a bath; Curie left a piece of uranium ore in a drawer with a photographic plate. Harold Castellare, working patiently with an apparatus which had so far consumed a great deal of current without producing anything more spectacular than some rather unusual corona effects, sneezed convulsively and dropped an ordinary bar magnet across two charged terminals.

Above the apparatus a huge, cloudy bubble sprang into being.

Harold, getting up from his instinctive crouch, blinked at it in profound astonishment. As he watched, the cloudiness abruptly disappeared and he was looking *through* the bubble at a section of tesselated flooring that seemed to be about three feet above the real floor. He could also see the corner of a carved wooden bench, and on the bench a small, oddly shaped stringed instrument.

Harold swore fervently to himself, made agitated notes, and then began to experiment. He tested the sphere cautiously with an electroscope, with a magnet, with a Geiger counter. Negative. He tore a tiny bit of paper from his notepad and dropped it toward the sphere. The paper disappeared; he couldn't see where it went.

Speechless, Harold picked up a metre stick and thrust it delicately forward. There was no feeling of contact; the rule went into and through the bubble as if the latter did not exist. Then it touched the stringed instrument, with a solid click. Harold pushed. The instrument slid over the edge of the bench and struck the floor with a hollow thump and jangle.

Staring at it, Harold suddenly recognized its tantalizingly familiar shape.

Recklessly he let go the metre stick, reached in and picked the fragile thing out of the bubble. It was solid and cool in his fingers. The varnish was clear, the colour of the wood glowing through it. It looked as if it might have been made yesterday.

Peter owned one almost exactly like it, except for preservation – a viola d'amore of the seventeenth century.

Harold stooped to look through the bubble horizontally. Gold and rust tapestries hid the wall, fifty feet away, except for an ornate door in the centre. The door began to open; Harold saw a flicker of umber.

Then the sphere went cloudy again. His hands were empty; the viola d'amore was gone. And the metre stick, which he had dropped inside the sphere, lay on the floor at his feet.

'Look at that,' said Harold simply.

Peter's eyebrows went up slightly. 'What is it, a new kind of television?'

'No, no. Look here.' The viola d'amore lay on the bench, precisely where it had been before. Harold reached into the sphere and drew it out.

Peter started. 'Give me that.' He took it in his hands, rubbed the smoothly finished wood. He stared at his brother. 'By God and all the saints,' he said. 'Time travel.'

Harold snorted impatiently. 'My dear Peter, "time" is a meaningless word taken by itself, just as "space" is.'

'But, barring that, time travel.'

'If you like, yes.'

'You'll be quite famous.'

'I expect so.'

Peter looked down at the instrument in his hands. 'I'd like to keep this, if I may.'

'I'd be very happy to let you, but you can't.'

As he spoke, the bubble went cloudy; the viola d'amore was gone like smoke.

'There, you see?'

'What sort of devil's trick is that?'

'It goes back ... Later you'll see. I had that thing out once before, and this happened. When the sphere became transparent again, the viol was where I had found it.'

'And your explanation for this?'

Harold hesitated. 'None. Until I can work out the appropriate mathematics—'

'Which may take you some time. Meanwhile, in layman's language—'

Harold's face creased with the effort and interest of translation. 'Very roughly, then – I should say it means that events are conserved. Two or three centuries ago—'

'Three. Notice the sound holes.'

'Three centuries ago, then, at this particular time of day, someone was in that room. If the viola were gone, he or she would have noticed the fact. That would constitute an alteration of events already fixed; therefore it doesn't happen. For the same reason, I conjecture, we can't see into the sphere, or' – he probed at it with a fountain pen – 'I thought not – or reach into it to touch anything; that would also constitute an alteration. And anything we put into the sphere while it is transparent comes out again when it becomes opaque. To put it very crudely, we cannot alter the past.'

'But it seems to me that we did alter it. Just now, when you took the viol out, even if no one of that time saw it happen.'

'This,' said Harold, 'is the difficulty of using language as a means of exact communication. If you had not forgotten all your calculus ... However. It may be postulated (remembering of course that everything I say is a lie, because I say it in English) that an event which doesn't influence other events is not an event. In other words—'

'That, since no one saw you take it, it doesn't matter whether you took it or not. A rather dangerous precept, Harold; you would have been burned at the stake for that at one time.'

'Very likely. But it can be stated in another way or, indeed, in an infinity of ways which only seem to be different. If someone, let us say God, were to remove the moon as I am talking to you, using zero duration, and substitute an exact replica made of concrete and plaster of Paris, with the same mass, albedo and so on as the genuine moon, it would make no measurable difference in the universe as we perceive it – and therefore we cannot certainly say that it hasn't happened. Nor, I may add, does it make any difference whether it has or not.'

' "When there's no one about on the quad," ' said Peter.

'Yes. A basic and, as a natural consequence, a meaningless problem of philosophy. Except,' he added, 'in this one particular manifestation.'

He stared at the cloudy sphere. 'You'll excuse me, won't you, Peter? I've got to work on this.'

'When will you publish, do you suppose?'

'Immediately. That's to say, in a week or two.'

'Don't do it till you've talked it over with me, will you? I have a notion about it.'

Harold looked at him sharply. 'Commercial?'

'In a way.'

'No,' said Harold. 'This is not the sort of thing one patents or keeps secret, Peter.'

'Of course. I'll see you at dinner, I hope?'

'I think so. If I forget, knock on the door, will you?'

'Yes. Until then.'

'Until then.'

At dinner, Peter asked only two questions.

'Have you found any possibility of changing the time your thing reaches – from the seventeenth century to the eighteenth, for example, or from Monday to Tuesday?'

'Yes, as a matter of fact. Amazing. It's lucky that I had a rheostat already in the circuit; I wouldn't dare turn the current off. Varying the amperage varies the time set. I've had it up to what I think was Wednesday of last week – at any rate, my smock was lying over the workbench where I left it, I remember, Wednesday afternoon. I pulled it out. A curious sensation, Peter – I was wearing the same smock at the time. And then the sphere went opaque and of course the smock vanished. That must have been myself, coming into the room.'

'And the future?'

'Yes. Another funny thing, I've had it forward to various times in the near future, and the machine itself is still there, but nothing's been done to it – none of the things I'm thinking I might do. That might be because of the conservation of events, again, but I rather think not. Still farther forward there are cloudy areas, blanks; I can't see anything that isn't in existence now, apparently, but here, in the next few days, there's nothing of that.

'It's as if I were going away. Where do you suppose I'm going?'

Harold's abrupt departure took place between midnight and morning. He packed his own grip, it would seem, left unattended, and was seen no more. It was extraordinary, of course, that he should have left at all, but the details were in no way odd. Harold had always detested what he called 'the tyranny of the valet'. He was, as everyone knew, a most independent man.

On the following day Peter made some trifling experiments with the time-sphere. From the sixteenth century he picked up a scent bottle of Venetian glass; from the eighteenth, a crucifix of carved rosewood; from the nine-teenth, when the palace had been the residence of an Austrian count and his Italian mistress, a hand-illuminated copy of De Sade's *La Nouvelle Justine*, very curiously bound in human skin.

They all vanished, naturally, within minutes or hours – all but the scent bottle. This gave Peter matter for reflection. There had been half a dozen flickers of cloudiness in the sphere just futureward of the bottle; it ought to have vanished, but it hadn't. But then, he had found it on the floor near a wall with quite a large rat hole in it.

When objects disappeared unaccountably, he asked himself, was it because they had rolled into rat holes, or because some time fisher had picked them up when they were in a position to do so?

He did not make any attempt to explore the future. That afternoon he telephoned his lawyers in Naples and gave them instructions for a new will. His estate, including his half of the jointly owned Ischia property, was to go to the Italian government on two conditions: (1) that Harold Castellare should make a similar bequest of the remaining half of the property and (2) that the Italian government should turn the palace into a national museum to house Peter's collection, using the income from his estate for its administration and for further acquisitions. His surviving relatives – two cousins in Scotland – he cut off with a shilling each.

He did nothing more until after the document had been brought out to him, signed and witnessed. Only then did he venture to look into his own future.

Events were conserved, Harold had said – meaning, Peter very well understood, events of the present and future as well as of the past. But was there only one pattern in which the future could be fixed? Could a result exist before its cause had occurred?

The Castellare motto was *Audentes fortuna juvat* – into which Peter, at the age of fourteen, had interpolated the word *'prudentesque'*: 'Fortune favours the bold – and the prudent.'

Tomorrow: no change; the room he was looking at was so exactly like this one that the time sphere seemed to vanish. The next day: a cloudy blur. And the next, and the next …

Opacity, straight through to what Peter judged, by the distance he had moved the rheostat handle, to be ten years ahead. Then, suddenly, the room was a long marble hall filled with display cases.

Peter smiled wryly. If you were Harold, obviously you could not look ahead and see Peter working in your laboratory. And if you were Peter, equally obviously, you could not look ahead and know whether the room you saw was an improvement you yourself were going to make, or part of a museum established after your death, eight or nine years from now, or …

No. Eight years was little enough, but he could not even be sure of that. It would, after all, be seven years before Harold could be declared legally dead …

Peter turned the vernier knob slowly forward. A flicker, another, a long series. Forward faster. Now the flickering melted into a greyness; objects winked out of existence and were replaced by others in the showcases; the marble darkened and lightened again, darkened and lightened, darkened and remained dark. He was, Peter judged, looking at the hall as it would be some five hundred years in the future. There was a thick film of dust on every exposed surface; rubbish and the carcass of some small animal had been swept carelessly into a corner.

The sphere clouded.

When it cleared, there was an intricate trail of footprints in the dust, and two of the showcases were empty.

The footprints were splayed, trifurcate, and thirty inches long.

After a moment's deliberation Peter walked around the workbench and leaned down to look through the sphere from the opposite direction. Framed in the nearest of the four tall windows was a scene of picture-postcard banality: the sun-silvered bay and the foreshortened arc of the city, with Vesuvio faintly fuming in the background. But there was something wrong about the colours, even greyed as they were by distance.

Peter went and got his binoculars.

The trouble was, of course, that Naples was green. Where the city ought to have been, a rankness had sprouted. Between the clumps of foliage he could catch occasional glimpses of grey-white that might equally well have been boulders or the wreckage of buildings. There was no movement. There was no shipping in the harbour.

But something rather odd was crawling up the side of the volcano. A rust-orange pipe, it appeared to be, supported on hairline struts like the legs of a centipede, and ending without rhyme or reason just short of the top.

While Peter watched, it turned slowly blue.

One day further forward: now all the display cases had been looted; the museum, it would seem, was empty.

Given, that in five centuries the world, or at any rate the department of Campania, had been overrun by a race of Somethings, the human population being killed or driven out in the process; and that the conquerors take an interest in the museum's contents, which they have accordingly removed.

Removed where, and why?

This question, Peter conceded, might have a thousand answers, nine hundred and ninety-nine of which would mean that he had lost his gamble. The remaining answer was: to the vaults, for safety.

With his own hands Peter built a hood to cover the apparatus on the workbench and the sphere above it. It was unaccustomed labour; it took him the better part of two days. Then he called in workmen to break a hole in the stone flooring next to the interior wall, rig a hoist, and cut the power cable that supplied the time-sphere loose from its supports all the way back to the fuse box, leaving him a single flexible length of cable more than a hundred feet long. They unbolted the workbench from the floor, attached casters to its legs, lowered it into the empty vault below, and went away.

Peter unfastened and removed the hood. He looked into the sphere.

Treasure.

Crates, large and small, racked in rows into dimness.

With pudgy fingers that did not tremble, he advanced the rheostat. A cloudy flicker, another, a leaping blur of them as he moved the vernier faster – and then there were no more, to the limit of the time-sphere's range.

Two hundred years, Peter guessed – AD 2700 to 2900 or thereabout – in which no one would enter the vault. Two hundred years of 'unliquidated time'.

He put the rheostat back to the beginning of that uninterrupted period. He drew out a small crate and prised it open.

Chessmen, ivory with gold inlay, Florentine, fourteenth century. Superb.

Another, from the opposite rack.

Tang figurines, horses and men, ten to fourteen inches high. Priceless.

The crates would not burn, Tomaso told him. He went down to the kitchen to see, and it was true. The pieces lay in the roaring stove untouched. He fished one out with a poker; even the feathery splinters of the unplaned wood had not ignited.

It made a certain extraordinary kind of sense. When the moment came for the crates to go back, any physical scrambling that had occurred in the meantime would have no effect; they would simply put themselves together as they had been before, like Thor's goats. But burning was another matter; burning would have released energy which could not be replaced.

That settled one paradox, at any rate. There was another that nagged at Peter's orderly mind. If the things he took out of that vault, seven hundred-odd years in the future, were to become part of the collection bequeathed by him to the museum, preserved by it, and eventually stored in the vault for him to find – then precisely where had they come from in the first place?

It worried him. Peter had learned in life, as his brother had in physics, that one never gets anything for nothing.

Moreover, this riddle was only one of his perplexities, and that not among the greatest. For another example, there was the obstinate opacity of the time-sphere whenever he attempted to examine the immediate future. How-ever often he tried it, the result was always the same: a cloudy blank, all the way forward to the sudden unveiling of the marble gallery.

It was reasonable to expect the sphere to show nothing at times when he himself was going to be in the vault, but this accounted for only five or six hours out of every twenty-four. Again, presumably, it would show him no changes to be made by himself, since foreknowledge would make it possible for him to alter his actions. But he laboriously cleared one end of the vault, put up a screen to hide the rest and made a vow – which he kept – not to alter the clear space or move the screen for a week. Then he tried again – with the same result.

The only remaining explanation was that some time during the next ten years something was going to happen which he would prevent if he could; and the clue to it was there, buried in that frustrating, unbroken blankness.

As a corollary, it was going to be something which he *could* prevent if only he knew what it was … or even when it was supposed to happen.

The event in question, in all probability, was his own death. Peter therefore hired nine men to guard him, three to a shift – because one man alone could not be trusted, two might conspire against him, whereas three, with the very minimum effort, could be kept in a state of mutual suspicion. He also under-went a thorough medical examination, had new locks installed on every door and window, and took every other precaution ingenuity could suggest. When he had done all these things, the next ten years were as blank as before.

Peter had more than half expected it. He checked through his list of safe-guards once more, found it good, and thereafter let the matter rest. He had done all he could; either he would survive the crisis or he would not. In either case, events were conserved; the time-sphere could give him no forewarning.

Another man might have found his pleasure blunted by guilt and fear; Peter's was whetted to a keener edge. If he had been a recluse before, now he was an eremite; he grudged every hour that was not given to his work.

Mornings he spent in the vault, unpacking his acquisitions; afternoons and evenings, sorting, cataloguing, examining and – the word is not too strong – gloating. When three weeks had passed in this way, the shelves were bare as far as the power cable would allow him to reach in every direction, except for crates whose contents were undoubtedly too large to pass through the sphere. These, with heroic self-control, Peter had left untouched.

And still he had looted only a hundredth part of that incredible treasure house. With grappling hooks he could have extended his reach by perhaps three or four yards, but at the risk of damaging his prizes; and in any case this would have been no solution but only a postponement of the problem. There was nothing for it but to go through the sphere himself and unpack the crates while on the other 'side' of it.

Peter thought about it in a fury of concentration for the rest of the day. So far as he was concerned, there was no question that the gain would be worth any calculated risk; the problem was how to measure the risk and if possible reduce it.

Item: He felt a definite uneasiness at the thought of venturing through that insubstantial bubble. Intuition was supported, if not by logic, at least by a sense of the dramatically appropriate. Now, if ever, would be the time for his crisis.

Item: Common sense did not concur. The uneasiness had two symbols. One was the white face of his brother Harold just before the water closed over it; the other was a phantasm born of those gigantic, splayed footprints in the dust of the gallery. In spite of himself, Peter had often found himself trying to imagine what the creatures that made them must look like, until his visualization was so clear that he could almost swear he had seen them.

Towering monsters they were, with crested ophidian heads and great unwinking eyes; and they moved in a strutting glide, nodding their heads, like fantastic barnyard fowl.

But, taking these premonitory images in turn: first, it was impossible that he should ever be seriously inconvenienced by Harold's death. There were no witnesses, he was sure; he had struck the blow with a stone; stones also were the weights that had dragged the body down, and the rope was an odd length Peter had picked up on the shore. Second, the three-toed Somethings might be as fearful as all the world's bogies put together; it made no difference, he could never meet them.

Nevertheless, the uneasiness persisted. Peter was not satisfied; he wanted a lifeline. When he found it, he wondered that he had not thought: of it before.

He would set the time-sphere for a period just before one of the intervals of blankness. That would take care of accidents, sudden illnesses, and other unforeseeable contingencies. It would also insure him against one very real and not at all irrational dread: the fear that the mechanism which generated the time-sphere might fail while he was on the other side. For the conservation of events was not a condition created by the sphere but one which limited its operation. No matter what happened, it was impossible for him to occupy the same place-time as any future or past observer; therefore, when the monster entered that vault, Peter would not be there any more.

There was, of course, the scent bottle to remember. Every rule has its exception; but in this case, Peter thought, the example did not apply. A scent bottle could roll into a rat hole; a man could not.

He turned the rheostat carefully back to the last flicker of greyness; past that to the next, still more carefully. The interval between the two, he judged, was something under an hour: excellent.

His pulse seemed a trifle rapid, but his brain was clear and cool. He thrust his head into the sphere and sniffed cautiously. The air was stale and had a faint, unpleasant odour, but it was breathable.

Using a crate as a stepping stool, he climbed to the top of the workbench. He arranged another crate close to the sphere to make a platform level with its equator. And seven and a half centuries in the future, a third crate stood on the floor directly under the sphere.

Peter stepped into the sphere, dropped, and landed easily, legs bending to take the shock. When he straightened, he was standing in what to all appearances was a large circular hole in the workbench; his chin was just above the top of the sphere.

He lowered himself, half squatting, until he had drawn his head through and stepped down from the crate.

He was in the future vault. The sphere was a brightly luminous thing that hung unsupported in the air behind him, its midpoint just higher than his head. The shadows it cast spread black and wedge-shaped in every direction, melting into obscurity.

Peter's heart was pounding miserably. He had an illusory stifling sensation, coupled with the idiotic notion that he ought to be wearing a diver's helmet. The silence was like the pause before a shout.

But down the aisles marched the crated treasures in their hundreds.

Peter set to work. It was difficult, exacting labour, opening the crates where they lay, removing the contents and nailing the crates up again, all without disturbing the positions of the crates themselves, but it was the price he had to pay for his lifeline. Each crate was in a sense a microcosm, like the vault itself – a capsule of unliquidated time. But the vault's term would end some fifty minutes from now, when crested heads nodded down these aisles; those of the crates' interiors, for all that Peter knew to the contrary, went on for ever.

The first crate contained lacework porcelain; the second, shakudô sword hilts; the third, an exquisite fourth-century Greek ornament in *repoussé* bronze, the equal in every way of the Siris bronzes.

Peter found it almost physically difficult to set the thing down, but he did so; standing on his platform crate in the future with his head projecting above the sphere in the present – like (again the absurd thought!) a diver rising from the ocean – he laid it carefully beside the others on the workbench.

Then down again, into the fragile silence and the gloom. The next crates were too large, and those just beyond were doubtful. Peter followed his shadow down the aisle. He had almost twenty minutes left: enough for one more crate, chosen with care, and an ample margin.

Glancing to his right at the end of the row, he saw a door.

It was a heavy door, rivet-studded, with a single iron step below it. There had been no door there in Peter's time; the whole plan of the building must have been altered. *Of course!* he realized suddenly. If it had not, if so much as a single tile or lintel had remained of the palace as he knew it, then the sphere could never have let him see or enter this particular here-and-now, this – what would Harold have called it – this nexus in spacetime.

For if you saw any now-existing thing as it was going to appear in the future, you could alter it in the present – carve your initials in it, break it apart, chop it down – which was manifestly impossible, and therefore …

And therefore the first ten years were necessarily blank when he looked into the sphere, not because anything unpleasant was going to happen to him, but because in that time the last traces of the old palace had not yet been eradicated.

There was no crisis.

Wait a moment, though! Harold had been able to look into the near future … But – of course – Harold had been about to die.

In the dimness between himself and the door he saw a rack of crates that looked promising. The way was uneven; one of the untidy accumulations of refuse that seemed to be characteristic of the Somethings lay in windrows across the floor. Peter stepped forward carefully – but not carefully enough.

Harold Castellare had had another accident – and again, if you choose to look at it in that way, a lucky one. The blow stunned him; the old rope slipped from the stones; flaccid, he floated where a struggling man might have drowned. A fishing boat nearly ran him down, and picked him up instead. He was suffering from a concussion, shock, exposure, asphyxiation and was more than three-quarters dead. But he was still alive when he was delivered, an hour later, to a hospital in Naples.

There were, of course, no identifying papers, labels or monograms in his clothing – Peter had seen to that – and for the first week after his rescue

Harold was quite genuinely unable to give any account of himself. During the second week he was mending but uncommunicative, and at the end of the third, finding that there was some difficulty about gaining his release in spite of his physical recovery, he affected to regain his memory, gave a circumstantial but entirely fictitious identification and was discharged.

To understand this as well as all his subsequent actions, it is only necessary to remember that Harold was a Castellare. In Naples, not wishing to give Peter any unnecessary anxiety, he did not approach his bank for funds but cashed a cheque with an incurious acquaintance, and predated it by four weeks. With part of the money so acquired he paid his hospital bill and rewarded his rescuers. Another part went for new clothing and for four day's residence in an inconspicuous hotel, while he grew used to walking and dressing himself again. The rest, on his last day, he spent in the purchase of a discreetly small revolver and a box of cartridges.

He took the last boat to Ischia and arrived at his own front door a few minutes before eleven. It was a cool evening, and a most cheerful fire was burning in the central hall.

'Signor Peter is well, I suppose,' said Harold, removing his coat.

'Yes, Signor Harold. He is very well, very busy with his collection.'

'Where is he? I should like to speak to him.'

'He is in the vaults, Signor Harold. But ...'

'Yes?'

'Signor Peter sees no one when he is in the vaults. He has given strict orders that no one is to bother him, Signor Harold, when he is in the vaults.'

'Oh, well,' said Harold. 'I daresay he'll see me.'

It was a thing something like a bear trap, apparently, except that instead of two semi-circular jaws it had four segments that snapped together in the middle, each with a shallow, sharp tooth. The pain was quite unendurable.

Each segment moved at the end of a thin arm, cunningly hinged so that the ghastly thing would close over whichever of the four triggers you stepped on. Each arm had a spring too powerful for Peter's muscles. The whole affair was connected by a chain to a staple solidly embedded in the concrete floor; it left Peter free to move some ten inches in any direction. Short of gnawing off his own leg, he thought sickly, there was very little he could do about it.

The riddle was, what could the thing possibly be doing here? There were rats in the vaults, no doubt, now as in his own time, but surely nothing larger. Was it conceivable that even the three-toed Somethings would set an engine like this to catch a rat?

Lost inventions, Peter thought irrelevantly, had a way of being rediscovered. Even if he suppressed the time-sphere during his lifetime and it did not happen to survive him, still there might be other time-fishers in the remote future – not here, perhaps, but in other treasure houses of the world. And that might account for the existence of this metal-jawed horror. Indeed, it might account for the vault itself – a better man-trap – except that it was all nonsense; the trap could only be full until the trapper came to look at it. Events, and the lives of prudent time-travellers, were conserved.

And he had been in the vault for almost forty minutes. Twenty minutes to go, twenty-five, thirty at the most, then the Somethings would enter and their entrance would free him. He had his lifeline; the knowledge was the only thing that made it possible to live with the pain that was the centre of his universe just now. It was like going to the dentist, in the bad old days before procaine; it was very bad, sometimes, but you knew that it would end.

He cocked his head toward the door, holding his breath. A distant thud, another, then a curiously unpleasant squeaking, then silence.

But he had heard them. He knew they were there. It couldn't be much longer now.

Three men, two stocky, one lean, were playing cards in the passageway in front of the closed door that led to the vault staircase. They got up slowly.

'Who is he?' demanded the shortest one.

Tomaso clattered at him in furious Sicilian; the man's face darkened, but he looked at Harold with respect.

'I am now,' stated Harold, 'going down to see my brother.'

'No, Signor,' said the shortest one positively.

'You are impertinent,' Harold told him.

'Yes, Signor.'

Harold frowned. 'You will not let me pass?'

'No, Signor.'

'Then go and tell my brother I am here.'

The shortest one said apologetically but firmly that there were strict orders against this also; it would have astonished Harold very much if he had said anything else.

'Well, at least I suppose you can tell me how long it will be before he comes out?'

'Not long, Signor. One hour, no more.'

'Oh, very well, then,' said Harold pettishly, turning half away. He paused. 'One thing more,' he said, taking the gun out of his pocket as he turned, 'put your hands up and stand against the wall there, will you?'

The first two complied slowly. The third, the lean one, fired through his coat pocket, just like the gangsters in the American movies.

It was not a sharp sensation at all, Harold was surprised to find; it was more as if someone had hit him in the side with a cricket bat. The racket seemed to bounce interminably from the walls. He felt the gun jolt in his hand as he fired back, but couldn't tell if he had hit anybody. Everything seemed to be happening very slowly, and yet it was astonishingly hard to keep his balance. As he swung around he saw the two stocky ones with their hands half inside their jackets, and the lean one with his mouth open, and Tomaso with bulging eyes. Then the wall came at him and he began to swim along it, paying particular attention to the problem of not dropping one's gun.

As he weathered the first turn in the passageway the roar broke out afresh. A fountain of plaster stung his eyes; then he was running clumsily, and there was a bedlam of shouting behind him.

Without thinking about it he seemed to have selected the laboratory as his destination; it was an instinctive choice, without much to recommend it logically. In any case, he realized halfway across the central hall, he was not going to get there.

He turned and squinted at the passageway entrance; saw a blur move and fired at it. It disappeared. He turned again awkwardly, and had taken two steps nearer an armchair which offered the nearest shelter, when something clubbed him between the shoulder-blades. One step more, knees buckling, and the wall struck him a second, softer blow. He toppled, clutching at the tapestry that hung near the fireplace.

When the three guards, whose names were Enrico, Alberto and Luca, emerged cautiously from the passage and approached Harold's body, it was already flaming like a Viking's in its impromptu shroud; the dim horses and men and falcons of the tapestry were writhing and crisping into brilliance. A moment later an uncertain ring of fire wavered toward them across the carpet.

Although the servants came with fire extinguishers and with buckets of water from the kitchen, and although the fire department was called, it was all quite useless. In five minutes the whole room was ablaze; in ten, as windows burst and walls buckled, the fire engulfed the second storey. In twenty a mass of flaming timbers dropped into the vault through the hole Peter had made in the floor of the laboratory, utterly destroying the time-sphere apparatus and reaching shortly thereafter, as the authorities concerned were later to agree, an intensity of heat entirely sufficient to consume a human body without leaving any identifiable trace. For that reason alone, there was no trace of Peter's body to be found.

The sounds had just begun again when Peter saw the light from the time-sphere turn ruddy and then wink out like a snuffed candle.

In the darkness, he heard the door open.

SPECIAL DELIVERY

Len and Moira Connington lived in a rented cottage with a small yard, a smaller garden and too many fir trees. The lawn, which Len seldom had time to mow, was full of weeds, and the garden was overgrown with blackberry brambles. The house itself was clean and smelled better than most city apartments, and Moira kept geraniums in the windows; however, it was dark on account of the firs and on the wrong side of town. Approaching the door one late spring afternoon, Len tripped on a flagstone and scattered examination papers all the way to the porch.

When he picked himself up, Moira was giggling in the doorway. 'That was funny.'

'The hell it was,' said Len. 'I banged my nose.' He picked up his Chemistry B papers in a stiff silence; a red drop fell on the last one. 'God *damn* it!'

Moira held the screen door for him, looking contrite and faintly surprised. She followed him into the bathroom. 'Len, I didn't mean to laugh. Does it hurt much?'

'No,' said Len, staring fiercely at his scraped nose in the mirror, although in point of fact it was throbbing like a gong.

'That's good. It was the funniest thing – I mean, funny-peculiar,' she said hastily.

Len stared at her; the whites of her eyes were showing. 'Is there anything the matter with you?' he demanded.

'I don't know,' she said on a rising note. 'Nothing like that ever happened to me before. I didn't think it was funny at all, I was worried about you, and I didn't know I was going to laugh—' She laughed again, a trifle nervously. 'Maybe I'm cracking up?'

Moira was a dark-haired young woman with a placid, friendly disposition; Len had met her in his senior year at Columbia, with – looking at it impartially, which Len seldom did – regrettable results. At present, in her seventh month, she was shaped like a rather bosomy kewpie doll.

Emotional upsets, he remembered, may occur frequently during this period. He leaned to get past her belly and kissed her forgivingly. 'You're probably tired. Go sit down and I'll get you some coffee.'

... Except that Moira had never had any hysterics till now, or morning sickness, either – she burped instead – and anyhow, was there anything in the literature about fits of giggling?

After supper he marked seventeen sets of papers desultorily in red pencil, then got up to look for the baby book. There were four dog-eared paper-bound volumes with smiling infants' faces on the covers, but the one he wanted wasn't there. He looked behind the bookcase and on the wicker table beside it. 'Moira!'

'Hm?'

'Where the bloody hell is the other baby book?'

'I've got it.'

Len went and looked over her shoulder. She was staring at a mildly obscene drawing of a fetus lying in a sort of upside-down Yoga position inside a cut-away woman's body.

'That's what he looks like,' she said. 'Mama.'

The diagram was of a fetus at term. 'What was that about your mother?' Len asked, puzzled.

'Don't be silly,' she said abstractedly.

He waited, but she didn't look up or turn the page. After a while he went back to his work.

He watched her. Eventually she leafed through to the back of the book, read a few pages, and put it down. She lighted a cigarette and immediately put it out again. She fetched up a resounding belch.

'That was a good one,' said Len admiringly. Moira's belches surpassed any-thing ever heard in the men's locker rooms at Columbia; they shook doors and rattled windows.

Moira sighed.

Feeling tense, Len picked up his coffee cup and started toward the kitchen. He halted beside Moira's chair. On the side table was her after-dinner cup, still full of coffee: black, scummed with oil droplets, stone cold.

'Didn't you want your coffee?'

She looked at the cup. 'I did, but ...' She paused and shook her head, look-ing perplexed. 'I don't know.'

'Well, do you want another cup now?'

'Yes, please. No.'

Len, who had begun a step, rocked back on his heels. 'Which, damn it?'

Her face got all swollen. 'Oh, Len, I'm so mixed up,' she said, and began to tremble.

Len felt part of his irritation spilling over into protectiveness. 'What you need,' he said firmly, 'is a drink.'

He climbed a stepladder to get at the top cabinet shelf which housed their liquor when they had any; small upstate towns and their school boards being what they were, this was one of many necessary precautions.

Inspecting the doleful three fingers of whisky in the bottle, Len swore under his breath. They couldn't afford a decent supply of booze, or new clothes for Moira, or— The original idea had been for Len to teach for a year while they saved enough money so that he could go back for his master's; more lately, this proving unlikely, they had merely been trying to put aside enough for summer school, and even that was beginning to look like the wildest optimism.

High-school teachers without seniority weren't supposed to be married. Or graduate physics students, for that matter.

He mixed two stiff highballs and carried them back into the living room. 'Here you are. Skoal.'

'Ah,' she said appreciatively. 'That tastes— Ugh.' She set the glass down and stared at it with her mouth half open.

'What's the matter now?'

She turned her head carefully, as if she were afraid it would come off. 'Len, I don't know. Mama.'

'That's the second time you've said that. What is this all—'

'Said what?'

'Mama. Look kid, if you're—'

'I didn't.' She looked a little feverish.

'Sure you did,' said Len reasonably. 'Once when you were looking at the baby book, and then again just now, after you said ugh to the highball. Speaking of which—'

'Mama drink milk,' said Moira, speaking with exaggerated clarity.

Moira hated milk. Len swallowed half his highball, turned and went silently into the kitchen.

When he came back with the milk, Moira looked at it as if it contained a snake. 'Len, I didn't say that.'

'Okay.'

'I didn't. I didn't say mama and I didn't say that about the milk.' Her voice quavered. 'And I didn't laugh at you when you fell down.'

'It was somebody else.'

'It *was*.' She looked down at her gingham-covered bulge. 'You won't believe me. Put your hand there. A little lower.'

Under the cloth her flesh was warm and solid against his palm. 'Kicks?' he inquired.

'Not yet. Now,' she said in a strained voice. 'You in there. If you want your milk, kick three times.'

Len opened his mouth and shut it again. Under his hand there were three squirming thrusts, one after the other.

Moira closed her eyes, held her breath and drank the milk down in one long horrid gulp.

*

'Once in a great while,' Moira read, 'cell cleavage will not have followed the orderly pattern that produces a normal baby. In these rare cases some parts of the body will develop excessively, while others do not develop at all. This disorderly cell growth, which is strikingly similar to the wild cell growth that we know as cancer—' Her shoulders moved convulsively. 'Bluh.'

'Why do you keep reading that stuff if it makes you feel that way?'

'I have to,' she said absently. She picked up another book from the stack. 'There's a page missing.'

Len attacked the last of his egg in a noncommittal manner. 'Wonder it's held together this long,' he said. This was perfectly just; the book had had something spilled on it, partially dissolving the glue, and was in an advanced state of anarchy; however the fact was that Len had torn out the page in question four nights ago, after reading it carefully: the topic was 'Psychoses in Pregnancy'.

Moira had now decided that the baby was male, that his name was Leonardo (not referring to Len but to da Vinci), that he had informed her of these things along with a good many others, that he was keeping her from her favourite foods and making her eat things she detested, like liver and tripe, and that she had to read books of his choice all day long in order to keep him from kicking her in the bladder.

It was miserably hot; Commencement was only two weeks away, Len's students were fish-eyed and galvanic by turns.

Then there was the matter of his contract for next year, and the possible opening at Oster High, which would mean more money, and the Parent-Teacher's thing tonight at which Superintendent Greer and his wife would be regally present …

Moira was knee-deep in Volume I of *Der Untergang des Abendlandes*, moving her lips; an occasional guttural escaped her.

Len cleared his throat. 'Moy?'

'… *und also des tragichen* – what in God's name he means by that – What, Len?'

He made an irritated noise. 'Why not try the English edition?'

'Leo wants to learn German. What were you going to say?'

Len closed his eyes for a moment. 'About this PTA business – you sure you want to go?'

'Well, of *course*. It's pretty important, isn't it? Unless you think I look too sloppy—'

'No. No, damn it. But are you feeling up to it?'

There were faint violet crescents under Moira's eyes; she had been sleeping badly. 'Sure,' she said.

'All right. And you'll go see the sawbones tomorrow.'

'I said I would.'

'And you won't say anything about Leo to Mrs Greer or anybody—'

She looked slightly embarrassed. 'No. Not till he's born, I think, don't you? It would be an awful hard thing to prove – you wouldn't even have believed me if you hadn't felt him kick.'

This experiment had not been repeated, though Len had asked often enough; all little Leo had wanted, Moira said, was to establish communication with his mother – he didn't seem to be really interested in Len at all. 'Too young,' she explained.

And still ... Len recalled the frogs his biology class had dissected last semester. One of them had had two hearts. This disorderly cell growth ... like a cancer. Unpredictable: extra fingers or toes – or a double helping of cortex?

'And I'll burp like a lady, if at all,' Moira said cheerfully.

When the Conningtons arrived, the room was empty except for the ladies of the committee, two nervously smiling male teachers and the impressive bulk of Superintendent Greer. Card-table legs *skreeked* on the bare floor; the air was heavy with wood polish and musk.

Greer advanced, beaming fixedly. 'Well, isn't this nice. How are you young folks this warm evening?'

'Oh, we thought we'd be *earlier*, Mr Greer,' said Moira with pretty vexation. She looked surprisingly schoolgirlish and chic; the lump that was Leo was hardly noticeable unless you caught her in profile. 'I'll go right now and help the ladies. There must be *something* I can still do.'

'No, now, we won't hear of it. But I'll tell you what you can do – you can go right over there and say hello to Mrs Greer. I know she's dying to sit down and have a good chat with you. Go ahead now – don't worry about this husband of yours; I'll take care of him.'

Moira receded into a scattering of small shrieks of pleasure, at least half of them arching across a gap of mutual dislike.

Greer, exhibiting perfect dentures, exhaled Listerine. His pink skin looked not only scrubbed but disinfected; his gold-rimmed glasses belonged in an optometrist's window, and his tropical suit had obviously come straight from the cleaner's. It was impossible to think of Greer unshaven, Greer smoking a cigar, Greer with a smudge of axle grease on his forehead, or Greer making love to his wife.

'Well, sir, this weather ...'

'When I think of what this valley was like twenty years ago ...'

'At today's prices ...'

Len listened with growing admiration, putting in comments where required; he had never realized before that there were so many absolutely neutral topics of conversation.

A few more people straggled in, raising the room temperature about half a degree per capita. Greer did not perspire, he merely glowed.

Across the room Moira was now seated chummily with Mrs Greer, a large-bosomed woman in an outrageously unfashionable hat. Moira appeared to be telling a joke; Len knew perfectly well that it was a clean one, but he listened tensely, all the same, until he heard Mrs Greer yelp with laughter. Her voice carried well. 'Oh, that's *priceless*! Oh, dear, I *only* hope I can remember it!'

Len, who had resolutely not been thinking of ways to turn the conversation toward the Oster vacancy, stiffened again when he realized that Greer had abruptly begun to talk shop. His heart began pounding absurdly; Greer was asking highly pertinent questions in a good-humoured but business-like way – drawing Len out, and not even bothering to be Machiavellian about it.

Len answered candidly, except when he was certain he knew what the superintendent wanted to hear; then he lied like a Trojan.

Mrs Greer had conjured up a premature pot of tea; and oblivious to the stares of the thirstier teachers present, she and Moira were hogging it, heads together, as if they were plotting the overthrow of the Republic or exchanging recipes.

Greer listened attentively to Len's final reply, which was delivered with as pious an air as if Len had been a Boy Scout swearing on the *Manual*; but since the question had been 'Do you plan to make teaching your career?' there was not a word of truth in it.

He then inspected his paunch and assumed a mild theatrical frown. Len, with that social sixth sense which is unmistakable when it operates, knew that his next words were going to be: 'You may have heard that Oster High will be needing a new science teacher next fall ...'

At this point Moira barked like a seal.

The ensuing silence was broken a moment later by a hearty scream, followed instantly by a clatter and a boneshaking thud.

Mrs Greer was sitting on the floor; legs sprawled, hat over her eye, she appeared to be attempting to perform some sort of orgiastic dance.

'It was Leo,' Moira said incoherently. 'You know she's English – she said of course a cup of tea wouldn't hurt me, and she kept telling me to go ahead and drink it while it was hot, and I couldn't—'

'No. No. Wait,' said Len in a controlled fury. 'What—'

'So I *drank* some. And Leo kicked up and made me burp the burp I was saving. And—'

'Oh, Christ.'

'Then he kicked the teacup out of my hand into her lap, and I wish I was *dead*.'

On the following day, Len took Moira to the doctor's office, where they read dog-eared copies of *The Rotarian* and *Field and Stream* for an hour.

Dr Berry was a round little man with soulful eyes and a twenty-four hour bedside manner. On the walls of his office, where it is customary for doctors to hang at least seventeen diplomas and certificates of membership, Berry had three; the rest of the space was filled with enlarged, coloured photographs of beautiful, beautiful children.

When Len followed Moira determinedly into the consulting room. Berry looked mildly shocked for a moment, then apparently decided to carry on as if nothing *outré* had happened. You could not say that he spoke, or even whispered; he rustled.

'Now, Mrs Connington, we're looking just fine today. How have we been feeling?'

'Just fine. My husband thinks I'm insane.'

'That's g— Well, that's a funny thing for him to think, isn't it?' Berry glanced at the wall midway between himself and Len, then shuffled some file cards rather nervously. 'Now. Have we had any burning sensations in our urine?'

'No. Not as far as I'm— No.'

'Any soreness in our stomach?'

'Yes. He's been kicking me black and blue.'

Berry misinterpreted Moira's brooding glance at Len, and his eyebrows twitched involuntarily.

'The baby,' said Len. 'The baby kicks her.'

Berry coughed. 'Any headaches? Dizziness? Vomiting? Swelling in our legs or ankles?'

'No.'

'All rightie. Now let's just find out how much we've gained, and then we'll get up on the examining table.'

Berry drew the sheet down over Moira's abdomen as if it were an exceptionally fragile egg. He probed delicately with his fat fingertips, then used the stethoscope.

'Those X-rays,' said Len. 'Have they come back yet?'

'Mm-hm,' said Berry. 'Yes, they have.' He moved the stethoscope and listened again.

'Did they show anything unusual?'

Berry's eyebrows twitched a polite question.

'We've been having a little argument,' Moira said in a strained voice, 'about whether this is an ordinary baby or not.'

Berry took the stethoscope tubes out of his ears. He gazed at Moira like an anxious spaniel. 'Now let's not worry about *that*. We're going to have a perfectly healthy, wonderful baby, and if anybody tells us differently, why, we'll just tell them to go jump in the lake, won't we?'

'The baby is absolutely normal?' Len said in a marked manner.

'Absolutely.' Berry applied the stethoscope again. His face blanched.

'What's the matter?' Len asked after a moment. The doctor's gaze was fixed and glassy.

'*Vagitus uterinus*,' Berry muttered. He pulled the stethoscope off abruptly and stared at it. 'No, of course it couldn't be. Now isn't that a nuisance: we seem to be picking up a radio broadcast with our little stethoscope here. I'll just go and get another instrument.'

Moira and Len exchanged glances. Moira's was almost excessively bland.

Berry came confidently in with a new stethoscope, put the diaphragm against Moira's belly, listened for an instant and twitched once all over, as if his mainspring had broken. Visibly jangling, he stepped away from the table. His jaw worked several times before any sound came out.

'Excuse me,' he said, and walked out in an uneven line.

Len snatched up the instrument he had dropped.

Like a bell ringing under water, muffled but clear, a tiny voice was shouting: '*You bladder-headed pill-pusher! You bedside vacuum! You fifth-rate tree surgeon! You inflated enema bag!*' A pause. '*Is that you, Connington? Get off the line; I haven't finished with Dr Bedpan yet.*'

Moira smiled, like a Buddha-shaped bomb. 'Well?' she said.

'We've got to think,' Len kept saying over and over.

'*You've* got to think.' Moira was combing her hair, snapping the comb smartly at the end of each stroke. 'I've had plenty of time to think, ever since it happened. When you catch up—'

Len flung his tie at the carved wooden pineapple on the corner of the footboard. 'Moy, be *reasonable*. The chances against the kid kicking three times in any one-minute period are only about one in a hundred. The chances against anything like—'

Moira grunted and stiffened for a moment. Then she cocked her head to one side with a listening expression, a new mannerism of hers that was beginning to send intangible snakes crawling up Len's spine.

'What?' he asked sharply.

'He says to keep our voices down, he's thinking.'

Len's fingers clenched convulsively, and a button flew off his shirt. Shaking, he pulled his arms out of the sleeves and dropped the shirt on the floor. 'Look. I just want to get this straight. When he talks to you, you don't hear him shouting all the way up past your liver and lights. What—'

'You know perfectly well. He reads my mind.'

'That isn't the same as—' Len took a deep breath. 'Let's not get off on that. What I want to know is what is it like, do you seem to hear a real voice, or do you just know what he's telling you, without knowing how you know, or—'

Moira put the comb down in order to think better. 'It isn't like hearing a voice. You'd never confuse one with the other. It's more – The nearest I can come to it, it's like remembering a voice. Except that you don't know what's coming.'

'My God.' Len picked his tie off the floor and abstractedly began knotting it on his bare chest. 'And he sees what you see, he knows what you're think-ing, he can hear when people talk to you?'

'Of course.'

'But damn it, this is tremendous!' Len began to blunder around the bed-room, not looking where he was going. 'They thought Macaulay was a genius. This kid isn't even *born*. Quints, schmints. I *heard* him. He was cussing Berry out like Monty Woolley.'

'He had me reading *The Man Who Came to Dinner* two days ago.'

Len made his way around a small bedside table by trial and error. 'That's another thing. How much could you say about his ... his personality? I mean, does he seem to know what he's doing, or is he just striking out wildly in all directions?' He paused. 'Are you sure he's really conscious at all?'

Moira began, 'That's a silly—' and stopped. 'Define consciousness,' she said doubtfully.

'All right, what I really mean is— Why am I wearing this necktie?' He ripped it off and threw it over a lampshade. 'What I mean—'

'Are you sure you're really conscious?'

'Okay. You make joke, I laugh, ha. What I'm trying to ask you is, have you seen any evidence of creative thought, organized thought, or is he just ... integrating, along the lines of, of instinctive responses. Do you—'

'I know what you mean. Shut up a minute ... I don't know.'

'I mean, is he awake, or asleep and dreaming about us, like the Red King?'

'I don't *know*.'

'And if that's it, what'll happen when he wakes up?'

Moira took off her robe, folded it neatly, and manoeuvred herself between the sheets. 'Come to bed.'

Len got one sock off before another thought struck him. 'He reads your mind. Can he read other people's?' He looked appalled. 'Can he read mine?'

'He doesn't. Whether it's because he can't, I don't know. I think he just doesn't care.'

Len pulled the other sock halfway down and left it there. In another tone he said, 'One of the things he doesn't care about is whether I have a job.'

'No ... He thought it was funny. I wanted to sink through the floor, but I had all I could do to keep from laughing when she fell down ... Len, what are we going to do?'

He swivelled around and looked at her. 'Look,' he said, 'I didn't mean to sound that gloomy. We'll do something. We'll fix it. Really.'

'All right.'

Careful of his elbows and knees, Len climbed into the bed beside her. 'Okay now?'

'Mm … Ugh.' Moira tried to sit up suddenly and almost made it. She wound up propped on one elbow and said indignantly, 'Oh, no.'

Len stared at her in the dimness. 'What?'

She grunted again. 'Len, get up. All *right*. Len, *hurry!*'

Len fought his way convulsively past a treacherous sheet and staggered up, goose-pimpled and tense. 'Now what?'

'You'll have to sleep on the couch. The sheets are in the bottom—'

'On that couch? Are you crazy?'

'I can't help it,' she said in a thin voice. 'Please don't let's argue, you'll just have to—'

'*Why?*'

'We can't sleep in the same bed,' she wailed. 'He says it's – oh! – unhygienic!'

Len's contract was not renewed. He got a job waiting on tables in a resort hotel, an occupation which pays more money than teaching future citizens the rudiments of three basic sciences, but for which Len had no aptitude. He lasted three days at it; he was then idle for a week and a half, until his four years of college physics earned him employment as a clerk in an electrical shop. His employer was a cheerfully aggressive man who assured Len that there were great opportunities in radio-TV, and firmly believed that atom-bomb tests were causing all the bad weather.

Moira, in her eighth month, walked to the county library every day and trundled a load of books home in the perambulator. Little Leo, it appeared, was working his way simultaneously through biology, astrophysics, phrenology, chemical engineering, architecture, Christian Science, psychosomatic medicine, marine law, business management, Yoga, crystallography, metaphysics and modern literature.

His domination of Moira's life remained absolute, and his experiments with her regimen continued. One week, she ate nothing but nuts and fruit washed down with distilled water; the next, she was on a diet of porterhouse steak, dandelion greens and Hadacol.

With the coming of full summer, fortunately, few of the high-school staff were in evidence. Len met Dr Berry once on the street. Berry started, twitched, and walked off rapidly in an entirely new direction.

The diabolical event was due on or about July 29. Len crossed off each day on their wall calendar with an emphatic black grease pencil. It: would, he supposed, be an uncomfortable thing at best to be the parent of a superprodigy – Leo would no doubt be dictator of the world by the time he was fifteen, unless he was assassinated first – but almost anything would be a fair price for getting Leo out of his maternal fortress.

Then there was the day when Len came home to find Moira weeping over the typewriter, with a half-inch stack of manuscript beside her.

'It isn't anything, I'm just tired. He started this after lunch. Look.'

Len turned the face-down sheaf the right way up.

> Droning. Abrasing
> the demiurge.
> Hier begrimms the tale:
> Eyes undotted, grewling
> and looking, turns off
> a larm, seizes cloes.
> Stewed! Bierly a wretch!
> Pence, therefore jews we. Pons!
> Let the pants take air of themsulves.
> Searches in the bottom of a hole
> for soap; hawks up a good job.
> Flayed on fable, a
> round cut of cat's meat ...

The first three sheets were all like that. The fourth was a perfectly good Petrarchan sonnet reviling the current administration and the party of which Len was an assenting member.

The fifth was hand-lettered in the Cyrillic alphabet and illustrated with geometric diagrams. Len put it down and stared shakily at Moira.

'No, go on,' she said. 'Read the rest.'

The sixth and seventh were dirty limericks, and the eighth, ninth and so on to the end of the stack were what looked like the first chapters of a rattling good historical adventure novel.

Its chief characters were Cyrus the Great, his gallon-bosomed daughter Lygea, of whom Len had never previously heard, and a one-armed Graeco-Mede adventurer named Xanthes; there were also courtesans, spies, apparitions, scullery slaves, oracles, cut-throats, lepers, priests, whoremasters and men-at-arms, in magnificent profusion.

'He's decided,' said Moira, 'what he wants to be when he's born.'

Leo refused to be bothered with mundane details. When there were eighty pages of the manuscript, Moira invented a title and byline for it – *The Virgin of Persepolis*, by Leon Lenn – and mailed it off to a literary agent in New York. His response, a week later, was cautiously enthusiastic and a trifle plaintive. He asked for an outline of the remainder of the novel.

Moira replied that this was impossible, trying to sound as unworldy and impenetrably artistic as she could. She enclosed the thirty-odd pages Leo had turned out in the meantime.

Nothing was heard from the agent for two weeks. At the end of this time Moira received an astonishing document, exquisitely printed and bound in imitation leather, thirty-two pages including the index, containing three times as many clauses as a lease.

This turned out to be a book contract. With it came the agent's cheque for nine hundred dollars.

Len tilted his mop handle against the wall and straightened carefully, conscious of every individual gritty muscle in his back. How did women do housework every day, seven days a week, fifty-two bloody weeks a year? It was a little cooler now that the sun was down, and he was working stripped to shorts and bath slippers, but he might as well have been wearing an overcoat in a Turkish bath.

The clatter of Moira's monstrous new typewriter stopped, leaving a faint hum. Len went into the living room and sagged on the arm of a chair. Moira, gleaming sweatily in a flowered housecoat, was lighting a cigarette.

'How's it going?'

She switched off the machine wearily. 'Page two-eighty-nine. Xanthes killed Anaxander.'

'Thought he would. How about Ganesh and Zeuxias?'

'I don't know.' She frowned. 'I can't figure it out. You know who it was that raped Miriam in the garden?'

'No, who?'

'*Ganesh.*'

'You're kidding.'

'Nope.' She pointed to the stack of typescript. 'See for yourself.'

Len didn't move. 'But Ganesh was in Lydia, buying back the sapphire. He didn't get back till—'

'I know, I know. But he *wasn't*. That was Zeuxias in a putty nose and his beard dyed. It's all perfectly logical, the way he explains it. Zeuxias overheard Ganesh talking to the three Mongols – you remember, Ganesh thought there was somebody behind the curtain, only that was when they heard Lygea scream, and while their backs were turned—'

'All right, but for God's sake this fouls everything up. If Ganesh never went to Lydia, then he *couldn't* have had anything to do with distempering Cyrus's armour. And Zeuxias couldn't, either, because—'

'*I know*. It's exasperating. I know he's going to pull another rabbit out of the hat and clear everything up, but I don't see how.'

Len brooded. 'It beats me. It had to be either Ganesh or Zeuxias. Or Philomenes. But look, damn it, if Zeuxias knew about the sapphire all the time, that rules out Philomenes once and for all. Unless … No. I forgot about that business in the temple. Whuff. Do you think he really knows what he's doing?'

'I'm certain. Lately I've been able to tell what he's thinking even when he isn't talking to me – I mean just generally, like when he's puzzling over something, or when he's feeling mean. It's going to be something brilliant, and he knows what it is, but he won't tell me. We'll just have to wait.'

'I guess.' Len stood up, grunting. 'You want me to see if there's anything in the pot?'

'Please.'

Len wandered into the kitchen, turned the flame on under the Silex, stared briefly at the dishes waiting in the sink, and wandered out again. Since the onslaught of The Novel, Leo had relinquished his interest in Moira's diet, and she had been living on coffee. Small blessings …

Moira was leaning back with her eyes closed, looking very tired. 'How's the money?' she asked without moving.

'Lousy. We're down to twenty-one bucks.'

She raised her head and opened her eyes wide. 'We couldn't be. Len, how could anybody go through nine hundred dollars that fast?'

'Typewriter. And the dictaphone that Leo thought he wanted, till about half an hour after it was paid for. We spent about fifty on ourselves, I guess. Rent. Groceries. It goes, when there isn't any coming in.'

She sighed. 'I thought it would last longer.'

'So did I … If he doesn't finish this thing in a few days, I'll have to go look for work again.'

'Oh. That isn't so good.'

'I know it, but—'

'All right, if it works out, fine, if it doesn't … He must be near the end by now.' She stubbed out her cigarette abruptly and sat up, hands poised over the keyboard. 'He's getting ready again. See about that coffee, will you?'

Len poured two cups and carried them in. Moira was still sitting in front of the typewriter, with a curious half-formed expression on her face.

Abruptly the carriage whipped over, muttered to itself briefly and thumped the paper up twice. Then it stopped. Moira's eyes got bigger and rounder.

'What's the matter?' said Len. He went and looked over her shoulder.

The last line on the page read:

(TO BE CONTINUED IN OUR NEXT)

Moira's hands curled into small, helpless fists. After a moment she turned off the machine.

'What?' said Len incredulously. 'To be continued— What kind of talk is that?'

'He says he's bored with the novel,' Moira replied dully. 'He says he knows the ending, so it's artistically complete; it doesn't matter whether anybody else thinks so or not.' She paused. 'But he says that isn't the real reason.'

'Well?'

'He's got two. One is that he doesn't want to finish the book till he's certain he'll have complete control of the money it earns.'

'Well,' said Len, swallowing a lump of anger, 'that makes a certain amount of sense. It's his book. If he wants guarantees ...'

'You haven't heard the other one.'

'All right, let's have it.'

'He wants to teach us, so we'll never forget, who the boss is in this family.'

'Len, I'm awfully tired.'

'Let's go over it once more; there has to be some way— He still isn't talking to you?'

'I haven't felt anything from him for the last twenty minutes. I think he's asleep.'

'All right, let's suppose he *isn't* going to listen to reason—'

'We might as well.'

Len made an incoherent noise. 'Okay. I still don't see why we can't write the last chapter ourselves – a few pages—'

'*Who* can?'

'Well, not me, but you've done a little writing – damned good, too. And if you're so sure all the clues are there— Look, if you say you can't do it, okay, we'll hire somebody. A professional writer. It happens all the time. Thorne Smith's last novel—'

'Ugh.'

'Well, it *sold*. What one writer starts, another can finish.'

'Nobody ever finished *The Mystery of Edwin Drood*.'

'Oh, hell.'

'Len, it's impossible. It *is*. Let me finish. If you're thinking we could have somebody rewrite the last part Leo did—'

'Yeah, I just thought of that.'

'Even that wouldn't do any good, you'd have to go all the way back, almost to page one, it would be another story when you got through. Let's go to bed.'

'Moy, do you remember when we used to worry about the law of opposites?'

'Mm?'

'The law of *opposites*. When we used to be afraid the kid would turn out to be a pick-and-shovel man with a pointy head.'

'Uh. Mm.'

He turned. Moira was standing with one hand on her belly and the other behind her back. She looked as if she were about to start practising a low bow but doubted she could make it.

'What's the matter now?' he asked.

'Pain in the small of my back.'

'Bad one?'

'No ...'

'Belly hurt, too?'

She frowned. 'Don't be foolish. I'm feeling for the contraction. There it comes.'

'The ... but you just said the small of your back.'

'Where do you think labour pains usually start?'

The pains were coming at twenty-minute intervals, and the taxi had not arrived. Moira was packed and ready. Len was trying to set her a good example by remaining calm. He strolled over to the wall calendar, gazed at it in an offhand manner, and turned away.

'Len, I know it's only the fifteenth of July.'

'Huh? I didn't say that aloud.'

'You said it seven times. Sit down; you're making me nervous.'

Len perched on the corner of the table, folded his arms, and immediately got up to look out the window. On the way back he circled the table in an aimless way, picked up a bottle of ink and shook it to see if the cap was on tight, stumbled over a wastebasket, carefully upended it and sat down with an air of *J'y suis, j'y reste*. 'Nothing to worry about,' he said firmly. 'Women do this all the time.'

'True.'

'What for?' he demanded violently.

Moira grinned at him, then winced slightly and looked at the clock. 'Eighteen minutes. This is a good one.'

When she relaxed, Len put a cigarette in his mouth and lighted it in only two tries. 'How's Leo taking it?'

'Isn't saying. He feels—' She concentrated. 'Apprehensive. He's feeling strange and he doesn't like it ... I don't think he's entirely awake. Funny.'

'I'm glad this is happening now,' Len announced.

'So am I, but ...'

'Look,' said Len, moving energetically to the arm of her chair, 'we've always had it pretty good, haven't we? Not that it hasn't been tough at times, but – you know.'

'I know.'

'Well, that's the way it'll be again, once this is over. I don't care how much of a superbrain he is, once he's born – you know what I mean? The only reason he's had the bulge on us all this time is he could get at us and we couldn't get at him. He's got the mind of an adult, he can learn to act like one. It's that simple.'

Moira hesitated. 'You can't take him out to the woodshed. He's going to be a helpless baby, physically, like anybody else's. He has to be taken care of. You can't—'

'No, all right, but there are plenty of other ways. If he behaves, he gets read to. Like that.'

'That's right, but – there's one other thing I thought of. You remember when you said suppose he's asleep and dreaming … and what happens if he wakes up?'

'Yeah.'

'Well, that reminded me of something else, or maybe it's the same thing. Did you know that a fetus in the womb gets only about half the amount of oxygen in his blood that he'll have when he starts to breathe?'

Len looked thoughtful. 'Forgot. Well, that's just one more thing Leo does that babies aren't supposed to do.'

'Use as much energy as he does, you mean. All right, but what I'm getting at is, it can't be because he's getting more than the normal amount of oxygen, can it? I mean, he's the prodigy, not me. He must be using it more efficiently … And if that's it, what happens when he's getting twice as much?'

They had soaped and shaved and disinfected her, along with other indignities, and now she could see herself in the reflector of the big delivery-table light – the image clear and bright, like everything else, but very haloed and swimmy, and looking like a statue of Sita. She had no idea how long she had been here – that was the scopolamine, probably – but she was getting pretty tired.

'Bear down,' said the staff doctor kindly, and before she could answer, the pain came up like violins and she had to gulp at the tingly coldness of laughing gas. When the mask lifted she said, 'I *am* bearing down,' but the doctor had gone back to the other end of her and wasn't listening.

Anyhow, she had Leo. *How are you feeling?*

His answer was muddled – because of the anaesthetic? – but she didn't really need it; her perception of him was clear: darkness and pressure, impatience, a slow Satanic anger … and something else. Uncertainty? Apprehension?

'Two or three more ought to do it. Bear down.'

Fear. Unmistakable now. And a desperate determination.

'Doctor, he doesn't want to be born!'

'Seems that way sometimes, doesn't it? Now bear down good and hard.'

Tell him stop blurrrrrr too dangerrrrrrr stop I feel wowrrrr stop I tellrrrr stop.

'What, Leo, what?'

'Bear down.'

Faintly, like a voice far under water: *Hurry I hate you tell him … sealed incubator … tenth oxygen, nine tenths inert gases … Hurry.*

The pressure abruptly relaxed.

Leo was born.

The doctor was holding him up by the heels, red, bloody, wrinkled, trailing a lumpy soft snake. The voice was still there, very small, very far away: *Too late. The same as death.* Then a hint of the old cold arrogance: *Now you'll never know ... who killed Cyrus.*

The doctor slapped him smartly on the minuscule buttocks. The wizened, malevolent face writhed open; but it was only the angry squall of an ordinary infant that came out. Leo was gone, like a light turned off under the measureless ocean.

Moira raised her head weakly. 'Give him one for me,' she said.

YOU'RE ANOTHER

I

It was a warm spring Saturday, and Johnny Bornish spent the morning in Central Park. He drew sailors lying on the grass with their girls; he drew old men in straw hats, and Good Humour men pushing their carts. He got two quick studies of children at the toy-boat pond, and would have had another, a beauty, except that somebody's damned big Dalmatian, romping, blundered into him and made him sit down hard in the water.

A bright-eyed old gentleman solemnly helped him arise. Johnny thought it over, then wrung out his wet pants in the man's rest room, put them back on and spread himself like a starfish in the sun. He dried before his sketchbook did, so he took the bus back downtown, got off at Fourteenth Street and went into Mayer's.

The only clerk in sight was showing an intricate folding easel to a tweedy woman who didn't seem to know which end was which. Johnny picked up the sketchbook he wanted from a pile on the table and pottered around looking at lay figures, paper palettes and other traps for the amateur. He glimpsed some interesting textured papers displayed in the other aisle and tried to cross over to them, but misjudged his knobby-kneed turning circle, as usual, and brought down a cascade of little paint cans. Dancing for balance, somehow he managed to put one heel down at an unheard-of angle, buckle the lid of one of the cans and splash red enamel all over hell.

He paid for the paint, speechless, and got out. He had dropped the sketchbook somewhere, he discovered. Evidently God did not care for him to do any sketching today.

Also, he was leaving little red heel prints across the pavement. He wiped off his shoe as well as he could with some newspaper from the trash basket at the corner, and walked down to the Automat for coffee.

The cashier scooped in his dollar and spread two rows of magical dimes on the marble counter, all rattling at once like angry metal insects. They were alive in Johnny's palm; one of them got away, but he lunged for it and caught it before it hit the floor.

Flushed with victory, he worked his way through the crowd to the coffee dispenser, put a china cup under the spigot and dropped his dime in the slot. Coffee streamed out, filled his cup and went on flowing.

Johnny watched it for a minute. Coffee went on pouring over the lip and handle of the cup, too hot to touch, splashing through the grilled metal and gurgling away somewhere below.

A white-haired man shouldered him aside, took a cup from the rack and calmly filled it at the spigot. Somebody else followed his example, and in a moment there was a crowd.

After all, it was his dime. Johnny got another cup and waited his turn. An angry man in a white jacket disappeared violently into the crowd, and Johnny heard him shouting something. A moment later the crowd began to disperse.

The jet had stopped. The man in the white jacket picked up Johnny's original cup, emptied it, set it down on a bus-boy's cart, and went away.

Evidently God did not care for him to drink any coffee, either. Johnny whistled a few reflective bars of 'Dixie' and left, keeping a wary eye out for trouble.

At the kerb a big pushcart was standing in the sunshine, flaming with banana yellows, apple reds. Johnny stopped himself. 'Oh, no,' he said, and turned himself sternly around, and started carefully down the avenue, hands in pockets, elbows at his sides. On a day like what this one was shaping up to be, he shuddered to think what he could do with a pushcart full of fruit.

How about a painting of that? Semi-abstract – 'Still Life in Motion'. Flying tangerines, green bananas, dusty Concord grapes, stopped by the fast shutter of the artist's eye. By Cézanne, out of Stuart Davis. By heaven, it wasn't bad.

He could see it, big and vulgar, about a 36 by 30 (stretchers: he'd have to stop at Mayer's again, or on second thoughts somewhere else, for stretchers), the colours greyed on a violet ground, but screaming at each other all the same like a gaggle of parakeets. Black outlines here and there, weaving a kind of cock-eyed carpet pattern through it. No depth, no light-and-dark – flat Easter-egg colours, glowing as enigmatically as a Parrish cut up into jigsaw pieces. Frame it in oyster-white moulding – wham! The Museum of Modern Art!

The bananas, he thought, would have to go around this way, distorted, curved like boomerangs up in the foreground. Make the old ladies from Oshkosh duck. That saturated buttery yellow, transmuted to a poisonous green … He put out a forefinger absently to stroke one of the nearest, feeling how the chalky smoothness curved up and around into the dry hard stem.

'How many, Mac?'

For an instant Johnny thought he had circled the block, back to the same pushcart; then he saw that this one had only bananas on it. He was at the corner of Eleventh Street; he had walked three blocks, blind and deaf.

'No bananas,' he said hurriedly, backing away. There was a shriek in his ear. He turned; it was a glitter-eyed tweedy woman, brandishing an enormous handbag.

'Can't you watch where you're—'

'Sorry, ma'am,' he said, desperately trying to keep his balance. He toppled off the kerb, grabbing at the pushcart. Something slithery went out from under his foot. He was falling, sliding like a bowling ball, feet first toward the one upright shaft that supported the end of the pushcart …

The first thing that he noticed, as he sat there up to his chest in bananas, with the swearing huckster holding the cart by main force, was that an alert, white-haired old gentleman was in the front rank of the crowd, looking at him.

The same one who—?

And come to think of it, that tweedy woman—

Ridiculous.

All the same, something began to twitch in his memory. Ten confused minutes later he was kneeling asthmatically on the floor in front of his closet, hauling out stacks of unframed paintings, shoeboxes full of letters and squeezed paint tubes, a Scout axe (for kindling), old sweaters and mildewed magazines, until he found a battered suitcase.

In the suitcase, under untidy piles of sketches and water colours, was a small cardboard portfolio. In the portfolio were two newspaper clippings.

One was from the *Post*, dated three years back: it showed Johnny, poised on one heel in a violent adagio pose, being whirled around by the stream of water from a hydrant some Third Avenue urchins had just opened. The other was two years older, from *the Journal*: in this one Johnny seemed to be walking dreamily up a wall – actually, he had just slipped on an icy street in the upper Forties.

He blinked incredulously. In the background of the first picture there were half a dozen figures, mostly kids.

Among them was the tweedy woman.

In the background of the second, there was only one. It was the white-haired old man.

Thinking it over, Johnny discovered that he was scared. He had never actually enjoyed being the kind of buffoon who gets his shirttail caught in zippers, is trapped by elevators and revolving doors, and trips on pebbles; he had accepted it humbly as his portion, and in between catastrophes he'd had a lot of fun.

But suppose somebody was *doing* it to him?

A lot of it was not funny, look at it any way you like. There was the time the bus driver had closed the door on Johnny's foot and dragged him for three yards, bouncing on the pavement. He had got up with nothing worse than bruises – but what if that passenger hadn't seen him in time?

He looked at the clippings again. There they were, the same faces – the same clothing, even, except that the old man was wearing an overcoat. Even in the faded half-tones, there was a predatory sparkle from his rimless eye-glasses; and the tweedy woman's sharp beak was as threatening as a hawk's.

Johnny felt a stifling sense of panic. He felt like a man waiting helplessly for the punchline of a long bad joke; or like a mouse being played with by a cat.

Something bad was going to happen next.

The door opened; somebody walked in. Johnny stared, but it was only the Duke, brawny in a paint-smeared undershirt, with a limp cigarette in the corner of his mouth. The Duke had a rakish Errol Flynn moustache, blending furrily now into his day-old beard, and a pair of black, who-are-you-varlet brows. He was treacherous, clever, plausible, quarrelsome, ingenious, a great brawler and seducer of women – in short, exactly like Cellini, except he had no talent.

'*Hiding*?' said Duke, showing his big teeth.

Johnny became aware that, crouched in front of the closet that way, he looked a little as if he were about to dive into it and pull overcoats over his head. He got up stiffly, tried to put his hands in his pockets, and discovered he still had the clippings. Then it was too late. Duke took them gently, inspected them with a judicial eye, and stared gravely at Johnny. 'Not flattering,' he said. 'Is that blood on your forehead?'

Johnny investigated; his fingers came away a little red, not much. 'I fell down,' he said uncomfortably.

'My boy,' Duke told him, 'you are troubled. Confide in your old uncle.'

'I'm just – Look, Duke, I'm busy. Did you want something?'

'Only to be your faithful counsellor and guide,' said Duke, pressing Johnny firmly into a chair. 'Just lean back, loosen the sphincters and say the first thing that comes into your mind.' He looked expectant.

'Ugh,' said Johnny.

Duke nodded sagely. 'A visceral reaction. Existentialist. You wish to rid yourself of yourself – get away from it all. Tell me, when you walk down the street, do you feel the buildings are about to close in on you? Are you being persecuted by little green men who come out of the woodwork? Do you feel an overpowering urge to leave town?'

'Yes,' said Johnny truthfully.

Duke looked mildly surprised. 'Well?' he asked, spreading his hands.

'Where would I go?'

'I recommend sunny New Jersey. All the towns have different names – fascinating. Millions of them. Pick one at random. Hackensack, Perth Amboy, Passaic, Teaneck, Newark? No? You're quite right – too suggestive. Let me see. Something farther north? Provincetown. Martha's Vineyard – lovely this time of the year. Or Florida – yes, I can really see you, Johnny, sitting on a rotten wharf in the sunshine, fishing with a bent pin for pompano. Peaceful, relaxed, carefree ...'

Johnny's fingers stirred the change in his pocket. He didn't know what was in his wallet – he never did – but he was sure it wasn't enough. 'Duke, have you seen Ted Edwards this week?' he asked hopefully.

'No. Why?'

'Oh. He owes me a little money, is all. He said he'd pay me today or tomorrow.'

'If it's a question of money …' said the Duke after a moment.

Johnny looked at him incredulously.

Duke was pulling a greasy wallet out of his hip pocket. He paused with his thumb in it. 'Do you really want to get out of town, Johnny?'

'Well, sure, but …'

'Johnny, what are friends *for*? Really, I'm wounded. Will fifty help?'

He counted out the money and stuffed it into Johnny's paralysed palm. 'Don't say a word. Let me remember you just as you are.' He made a frame of his hands and squinted through it. He sighed, then picked up the battered suitcase and went to work with great energy throwing things out of the dresser into it. 'Shirts, socks, underwear. Necktie. Clean handkerchief. There you are.' He closed the lid. He pumped Johnny's hand, pulling him toward the door. 'Don't think it hasn't been great, because it hasn't. So on the ocean of life we pass and speak to each other. Only a look and a voice; then darkness and silence.'

Johnny dug in his heels and stopped. 'What's the matter?' Duke inquired.

'I just realized – I can't go now. I'll go tonight. I'll take the late train.'

Duke arched an eyebrow. 'But why wait, Johnny? When the sunne shineth, make hay. When the iron is hot, strike. The tide tarrieth for no man.'

'They'll see me leave,' said Johnny, embarrassed.

Duke frowned. 'You mean the little green men actually are after you?' His features worked; he composed them with difficulty. 'Well, this is – Pardon me. A momentary aberration. But now don't you see, Johnny, you haven't got any time to lose. If they're following you, they must know where you live. How do you know they won't come here?'

Johnny, flushing, could think of no adequate reply. He had wanted to get away under cover of darkness, but that would mean another five hours at least …

'Look here,' said Duke suddenly, 'I know the very thing. Biff Feldstein – works at the Cherry Lane. Your own mother won't admit she knows you. Wait here.'

He was back in fifteen minutes, with a bundle of old clothes and an object which turned out, on closer examination, to be a small brown beard.

Johnny put it on unwillingly, using gunk from a tube Duke had brought along. Duke helped him into a cast-off jacket, colour indistinguishable, shiny with grease, and clapped a beret on his head. The result, to Johnny's horrified gaze, looked like an old-time Village phoney or a peddlar of French post-cards. Duke inspected him judicially. 'It's magnificent, but it isn't war,' he said. 'However, we can always plant vines. *Allons!* I am the grass; I cover all!'

*

Walking toward Sixth at a brisk pace, hand firmly on Johnny's elbow, Duke suddenly paused. 'Ho!' he said. He sprang forward, bent, and picked something up.

Johnny stared at it glassily. It was a five-dollar bill.

Duke was calmly putting it away. 'Does that happen to you often?' Johnny asked.

'Now and again,' said Duke. 'Merely a matter of keeping the eyes in focus.'

'Luck,' said Johnny faintly.

'Never think of it,' Duke told him. 'Take the word of an older and wiser man. You make your own luck in this world. Think of Newton. Think of O'Dwyer. Hand stuck in the jam jar? You asked for it. Now the trouble with you—'

Johnny, who had heard this theory before, was no longer listening. Look, he thought, at all the different things that had had to happen so that Duke could pick up that fiver. Somebody had to lose it, to begin with – say because he met a friend just as he was about to put the bill away, and stuffed it in his pocket instead so he could shake hands, and then forgot it, reached for his handkerchief – All right. Then it just had to happen that everybody who passed this spot between then and now was looking the other way, or thinking about something else. And Duke, finally, had to glance down at just the right moment. It was all extremely improbable, but it happened, somewhere, every day.

And also every day, somewhere, people were being hit by flowerpots knocked off tenth-storey window ledges, and falling down manholes, and walking into stray bullets fired by law enforcement officers in pursuit of malefactors. Johnny shuddered.

'Oh-oh,' said Duke suddenly. 'Where's a cab? Ah – Cabby!' He sprang forward to the kerb, whistling and waving.

Looking around curiously, Johnny saw a clumsy figure hurrying toward them down the street. 'There's Mary Finigan,' he said, pointing her out.

'I know,' said Duke irascibly. The cab was just pulling in toward them, the driver reaching back to open the door. 'Now here we go, Johnny—'

'But I think she wants to talk to you,' said Johnny. 'Hadn't we—'

'No time now,' said Duke, helping him in with a shove. 'She's taken to running off at the mouth – that's why I had to give her up. Get moving!' he said to the driver, and added to Johnny, 'Among other things, that is ... Here will be an old abusing of God's patience, and the King's English.'

As they pulled away into traffic, Johnny had a last glimpse of the girl standing on the kerb watching them. Her dark hair was straggling down off her forehead; she looked as if she had been crying.

Duke said comfortably, 'Every man, as the saying is, can tame a shrew but he that hath her. Now there, John boy, you have just had an instructive object lesson. Was it luck that we got away from that draggletailed earbender? It was not ...'

But, thought Johnny, it was. What if the cab hadn't come along at just the right time?

'... in a nutshell, boy. Only reason you have bad luck, you go hunting for it.'

'That isn't the reason,' said Johnny.

He let Duke's hearty voice fade once more into a kind of primitive background music, like the muttering of the extras in a Tarzan picture when the Kalawumbas are about to feed the pretty girl to the lions. It had just dawned on him, with the dazzling glow of revelation, that the whole course of anybody's life was determined by improbable accidents. Here he stood, all five feet ten and a hundred and thirty pounds of him – a billion-to-one shot from the word go. (What were the chances against any given sperm's uniting with any given ovum? *More* than a billion to one – unimaginable.) What if the apple hadn't fallen on Newton's head?

What if O'Dwyer had never left Ireland? And what did free will have to do with the decision not to become, say, a Kurdish herdsman, if you happened to be born in Ohio?

... It meant, Johnny thought, that if you could control the random factors – the way the dice fall in a bar in Sacramento, the temper of a rich uncle in Keokuk, the moisture content of the clouds over Sioux Falls at 3:03 CST, the shape of a pebble in a Wall Street newsboy's sock – you could do anything. You could make an obscure painter named Johnny Bornish fall into the toyboat pond in Central Park and get red paint all over his shoe and knock down a pushcart ...

But why would you want to?

The airport waiting room was a little like a scene out of *Things to Come*, except that the people were neither white-robed, leisurely nor cool.

Every place on every bench was taken. Duke found a couple of square feet of floor space behind a pillar and settled Johnny there, seated on his upended suitcase.

'Now you're all set. Got your ticket. Got your magazine. Okay.' Duke made an abrupt menacing gesture in order to look at his wristwatch.

'Got to run. Now, remember, boy, send me your address as soon as you get one, so I can forward your mail and so on. Oh, almost forgot.' He scribbled on a piece of paper, handed it over. 'Mere formality. Payable at any time. Sign here.'

He had written, 'IOU $50.' Johnny signed, feeling a little more at home with Duke.

'Right. Oll korrect.'

'Duke,' said Johnny suddenly. 'Mary's pregnant, isn't she?' His expression was thoughtful.

'It has been known to happen,' said Duke good-humouredly.

'Why don't you give her a break?' Johnny asked with difficulty.

Duke was not offended. 'How? Speak the truth to me, Johnny – do you see me as a happy bridegroom? Well …' He pumped Johnny's hand. 'The word must be spoken that bids you depart – though the effort to speak it should shatter my heart – though in silence, with something I pine – yet the lips that touch liquor much never touch mine!' With a grin that seemed to linger, like the Cheshire cat's, he disappeared into the crowd.

II

Uncomfortably astride his suitcase, solitary among multitudes, Johnny found himself thinking in words harder and longer at a time than he was used to. *The* kind of thinking he did when he was painting, or had painted, or was about to paint was another process altogether, and there were days on end when he did nothing else. He had a talent, Johnny Bornish. A talent is sometimes defined as a gift of the gods, a thing that most people, who have not had one, confuse with a present under a Christmas tree.

It was not like that at all. It tortured and delighted him, and took up so much room in his skull that a lot of practical details couldn't get in. Without exaggeration, it obsessed him, and when occasionally, as now, its grip relaxed, Johnny had the comical expression of a man who has just waked up to find his pocket picked and a row of hotfoot scars around his shoes.

He was thinking about luck. It was all right to talk about everybody making his own, and to a certain extent he supposed it was true, but Duke *was* the kind of guy who found money on the street. Such a thing had happened to Johnny only once in his life, and then it wasn't legal tender, but a Japanese coin – brass, heavy, about the size of a half dollar, with a chrysanthemum symbol on one side and a character on the other. He thought of it as his lucky piece; he had found it on the street, his last year in high school, and here – he took it out of his pocket – it still was.

… Which, when you came to think of it, was odd. He was not superstitious about the coin, or especially fond of it. He called it a lucky piece for want of a better name, because the word *keepsake* had gone out of fashion; and in fact he believed that his luck in the last ten years had been lousy. The coin was the only thing he owned that was anywhere near that old. He had lost three wristwatches, numberless fountain pens, two hats, three or four cigarette lighters and genuine U.S. nickels and dimes by the handful. But here was the Japanese coin.

Now, how could you figure a thing like that, unless it was luck … or *interference?*

Johnny sat up straighter. It was a foolish notion probably born of the fact that he hadn't had any lunch; but he was in a mood to read sinister significance into almost anything.

He already knew that the old man and the tweedy woman had been interfering in his life for at least five years, probably longer. Somehow, they were responsible for the 'accidents' that kept happening to him – and *there* was a foolish and sinister notion for you, if you liked. Believing that, how could he help wondering about other odd things that had happened to him, no matter how small – like finding and keeping the Japanese coin?

With that kind of logic, you could prove anything. And yet, he couldn't rid himself of the idea.

Idly, he got up holding the coin and dropped it into a nearby waste can. He sat down on his suitcase again with a feeling of neurosis well quelled. If the coin somehow found its way back to him, he'd have evidence for thinking the worst of it; if it didn't, as of course it wouldn't, small loss.

'Excuse me,' said a thinnish prim-faced little man in almost clerical clothes. 'I believe you dropped this. A Japanese coin. Quite nice.'

Johnny found his tongue. 'Uh, thank you. But I don't want it; you keep it.'

'Oh, *no*,' said the little man, and walked stiffly away.

Johnny stared after him, then at the coin. It was lumpishly solid, a dirty-looking brown, nicked and rounded at the edges. Ridiculous!

His mistake, no doubt, had been in being too obvious. He palmed the coin, trying to look nonchalant. After a while he lighted a cigarette, dropped it, and as he fumbled for it, managed to shove the coin under the leg of the adjoining bench.

He had taken one puff on the retrieved cigarette when a large hulk in a grey suit, all muscles and narrowed eyes, knelt beside him and extracted the coin. The hulk looked at it carefully, front and back; weighed it in his palm, rang it on the floor, and finally handed it over to Johnny. 'This yours?' he asked in a gravelly voice.

Johnny nodded. The hulk said nothing more but watched grimly until Johnny put the coin away in his pocket. Then he got up, dusted off his knees, and went away into the crowd.

Johnny felt a cold lump gather at the pit of his stomach. The fact that he had seen this same routine in at least half a dozen bad movies gave him no comfort; he did not believe in the series of natural coincidences that made it impossible to get rid of the neatly wrapped garbage, or the incriminating nylon stocking, or whatever.

He stood up. It was already twenty minutes after his plane's scheduled departure time. He *had* to get rid of the thing. It was intolerable to suppose that he couldn't get rid of it. Of course he could get rid of it.

The low false roof of the baggage counter looked promising. He picked up his suitcase and worked his way toward it, and got there just as the p. a. system burst forth with '*Flight number mnglang for Buzzclickville, now loading at Gate Lumber Lide.*' Under cover of this clamour, Johnny swiftly took the coin out of his pocket and tossed it out of sight on the roof.

Now what? Was somebody going to fetch a ladder and climb up there after the coin, and come down and hand it to him?

Nothing at all happened, except that the voice on the p. a. emitted its thunderous mutter again, and this time Johnny caught the name of his destination, Jacksonville.

Feeling better, he stopped at the news-stand for cigarettes. He paid for them with a half dollar, which was promptly slapped back into his palm.

'*Flight mumble sixteen for Jagznbull, now loading at Gate Number Nine,*' said the p. a.

After a moment Johnny handed back the cigarettes, still staring at the Japanese coin that lay, infuriatingly solid, on his palm. He had had a fifty-cent piece in his pocket; it didn't seem to be there now; ergo, he had thrown it up on top of the baggage counter. A natural mistake. Only, in ten years of carrying the coin around with him, he had never once mistaken it for a half-buck, or vice versa, until now.

'*Flight number sixteen ...*'

The tweedy woman, Johnny realized with a slow chill crawling down his back, had been ahead of him in the art store, talking to a clerk. She couldn't have been following him – on the bus, in a cab, or any other way; there wouldn't have been time. She had known where he was going, and when he was going to get there.

It was as if, he thought, while the coin seemed to turn fishily cold and smooth in his fingers, it was just as if the two of them, the tweedy woman and the old man, had planted a sort of beacon on him ten years ago, so that wherever and whenever he went, he was a belled cat. It was as if they might be looking in a kind of radarscope, when it pleased them, and seeing the track of his life like a twisted strand of copper wire coiling and turning ...

But of course there was no escape, if that was true. His track went winding through the waiting room and onto a particular aircraft and down again, where that plane landed, and into a particular room and then a particular restaurant, so that a day from now, a month, a year, ten years from now, they could reach out and touch him wherever he might be.

There was no escape, because there was a peculiarity built into this brown Japanese coin, a combination of random events that added up to the mirth-provoking result that he simply couldn't lose it.

He looked around wildly, thinking, Blowtorch. Monkey wrench. Sledge hammer. But there wasn't anything. It was a great big phoney *Things-to-Come*ish wildcat-airline waiting room, without a tool in it anywhere.

A pretty girl came out from behind the counter to his right, swinging up the hinged section of counter and letting it down again behind her. Johnny stared after her stupidly, then at the way she had come out. His scalp twitched. He stepped to the counter, raised the hinged section.

A bald man a few feet away stopped talking to wave a telephone handset at Johnny. 'No admittance here, sir! No admittance!'

Johnny put the Japanese coin down at an angle on the place that supported the end of the hinged section. He made sure it was the Japanese coin. He wedged it firmly.

The bald man dropped his telephone and came toward him, hand outstretched.

Johnny slammed the hinged section down as hard as he could. There was a dull *bonk*, and an odd feeling of tension; the lights seemed to blur. He turned and ran. Nobody followed him.

The plane was a two-engined relic that looked faintly Victorian from the outside; inside, it was a slanting dark cavern with an astonishing number of seats crammed into it. It smelled like a locker room. Johnny stumbled down the narrow aisle to what seemed to be the only remaining place, next to a large dark gentleman in an awning-striped tie.

He sat down, a little awkwardly. He had had a peculiar feeling ever since he had bashed the coin with the counter section, and the worst of it was that he couldn't pin it down. It was a physical something-wrong feeling, like an upset stomach or too little sleep or a fever coming on, but it wasn't exactly any of those things. He was hungry, but not that hungry. He thought the trouble might be with his eyes, but whenever he picked out anything as a test, it looked perfectly normal and he could see it fine. It was in his skin, perhaps? A kind of not-quite-prickling that … No, it wasn't his skin.

It was a little like being drunk, at the fraction of an instant when you realize how drunk you are and regret it – it was like that, but not very much. And it was partly like the foreboding, stronger and more oppressive than before – *Something bad was going to happen.*

The pilot and co-pilot walked up the aisle and disappeared into the forward compartment. The door was shut; the stewardess, back in the tail, was poring over the papers on her clipboard. After a while the starters whined and the engines came to life; Johnny, who had flown only once before, and on a scheduled airline at that, was startled to find what a devil of a racket they made. There was another interminable wait, and then the plane was crawling forward, swinging its nose around, crawling a little faster, while an endless blank expanse of concrete slipped by – lumbering along, then, like some huge, preposterous and, above all, flightless bird – and lifting incredibly, a few inches up, airborne, the runway falling back, tilted, dwindling until they were up, high above the mist on the water, steady as a hammock in the rasping monotone drone of the engines.

Something went *flip* at the corner of Johnny's vision. He turned his head. *Flop*.

It was a little metallic disk that went *flip* up the carpet like a tiddly-wink or a Mexican jumping bean, and paused for an instant while his jaw began to come loose at the hinge, and went *flop*. It lay on the carpet next to his seat, and went *hop*.

It landed on his knee, a little brown metallic disk with a chrysanthemum design, bent across the middle. He brushed at it. It hopped, and clung to his hand like a magnet to steel.

'Good heavens!' said an explosive voice in his ear.

Johnny had no attention to spare. He had taken hold of the coin with his other hand – a horrid feeling; it clung clammily to his fingers, and pulled away from his palm with reluctance – and now he was trying to scrape it off against the fabric of the seat. It was like trying to scrape off his own skin. He gave up and furiously began shaking his hand.

'Here, friend, don't do that!' The dark man in the next seat half rose, and there was a moment of confusion; Johnny heard a sharp click and thought he saw something leap from the dark man's vest pocket. Then, for an instant, he had clinging to his fingers a brown Japanese coin *and* a pair of glittering pince-nez. And then the two had somehow twisted together in a nasty, writhing way that hurt his eyes to watch, and uncurled again – no coin, no pince-nez, but an impossible little leather change purse.

Had the coin ever been a coin at all? Was the change purse a change purse?

'Now look what you've done! *Ugh!*' The dark man, his face contorted with passion, reached gingerly fingers toward the purse. 'Don't move, friend. Let me—'

Johnny pulled away a trifle. 'Who are you?'

'F.B.I.,' said the dark man impatiently. He flapped a billfold at Johnny; there was some kind of official-looking shield inside. 'Now you have torn it, my God! Hold that still – just like that. Don't move.' He pulled back his sleeves like a conjurer, and began to reach very cautiously for the little brown bit of leather that clung to Johnny's hand.

The thing twitched slightly in his fingers. The next moment, people all around them began getting up and crowding into the aisle, heading for the single washroom back in the tail of the plane.

Palpably, the plane tilted. Johnny heard the stewardess shrieking, 'One at a time! One at a time! Take your seats, everyone – you're making the airplane tail-heavy!'

'Steady, steady,' moaned the dark man. 'Hold it absolutely still!'

Johnny couldn't. His fingers twitched again, and abruptly all the passengers in the aisle were tumbling the other way, fighting to get away from the dangerous tail. The stewardess came helplessly after them, squalling futile orders.

'Am I doing that?' Johnny gasped, staring in horror at the thing in his palm.

'The gadget is. Hold it steady, friend—'

But his hand twitched again, and abruptly all the passengers were back in their seats, quietly sitting as if nothing had happened. Then a chorus of shrieks arose. Looking out the window, Johnny saw a terrifying sea of tree-tops just below, where nothing but empty air had been the moment before. As the plane nosed up sharply, his hand moved again—

And the shrieks grew louder. Up ahead loomed a blue-violet wall of mountain, topless, gigantic.

His fingers twitched still again: and once more the plane was droning peaceably along between earth and heaven. The passengers were bored or sleeping. There was no mountain, and no trees.

Sweat was beaded on the dark man's forehead. 'Now ...' he said, gritting his teeth and reaching again.

'Wait a minute,' said Johnny, pulling away again. 'Wait – This is some kind of top secret thing, is it, that I'm not supposed to have?'

'Yes,' said the dark man, agonized. 'I tell you, friend, don't move it!'

The purse was slowly changing colour, turning a watery violet around the edges.

'And you're from the F.B.I.?' Johnny asked, staring hard at the dark man.

'Yes. Hold it steady—'

'No,' said Johnny. His voice had a disposition to tremble, but Johnny held it firmly in check. 'You forgot about your ears,' he said. 'Or are they too hard to change?'

The dark man showed his teeth. 'What are you talking about?'

'The *ears*,' Johnny said, 'and the jawbone. No two people have ears alike. And before, when you were the old man, your neck was too thick. It bothered me, only I was too busy to think about it.' He swallowed hard. 'I'm thinking about it now. You don't want me to move this thing?'

'Right, friend, right.'

'*Then tell me what this is all about.*'

The dark man made placating gestures. 'I can't do that, friend. I really can't. Look –' the tiny weight shifted in Johnny's hand – 'out!' shouted the dark man.

Tiny flickerings gathered in the air about them. In the plane window, the clear blue of the sky abruptly vanished. Instead, Johnny saw a tumbling waste of grey cloud. Rain drummed against the window, and the plane heeled suddenly as if a gust had caught it.

Scattered shrieks arose from up forward. Johnny swallowed a large lump, and his fingers twitched. The flickering came again.

The cloud and rain were gone; the sky was an innocent blue again. '*Don't do that,*' said the dark man. 'Listen, look. You want to know something? Watch me try to tell you.' He moistened his lips and began, 'When you have trouble ...' But on the fourth word his throat seemed to tighten and lock. His lips went on moving, his eyes bulged with effort, but nothing came out.

After a moment he relaxed, breathing heavily. 'You see?' he said.

'You can't talk,' said Johnny. 'About that. Literally.'

'Right! Now, friend, if you'll just allow me—'

'Easy. Tell me the truth: is there any way you can get around this, whatever it is, this block or whatever?' He let his fingers twitch, deliberately, as he spoke. 'Any gadget, or anything you can take?'

The dark man glanced nervously out the window, where blue sky had given way to purple twilight and a large sickle moon. 'Yes, but—'

'There is? What?'

The man's throat tightened again as he tried to speak.

'Well, whatever it is, you'd better use it,' said Johnny. He saw the dark man's face burden with resolution, and jerked his hand away just in time as the dark man grabbed—

III

There was a whirling moment, then the universe steadied. Johnny clutched at the seat with his free hand. The plane and all the passengers were gone. He and the dark man were sitting on a park bench in the sunshine. Two pigeons took alarm and flapped heavily away.

The dark man's face was twisted unhappily. 'Now you have done it! Oh, what time is it, anyway?' He plucked two watches out of his vest and consulted them in turn. 'Wednesday, friend, at the latest! Oh, oh, they'll ...' His mouth worked soundlessly.

'Wednesday?' Johnny managed. He looked around. They were sitting in Union Square Park, the only ones there. There were plenty of people on the streets, all hurrying, most of them women. It looked like a Wednesday, all right.

He opened his mouth and shut it again carefully. He looked down at the limp bit of leather and metal in his hand. Start from the beginning. What did he know?

The coin, which had evidently been some kind of telltale or beacon, had in some way joined itself, after Johnny had damaged it, to some other instrument of the dark man's – apparently the gadget that enabled him to control probability, and move from one time to another, and small chores like that.

In their present fused state, the two gadgets were ungovernable – dangerous, the dark man seemed to think – and no good to anybody.

And that was absolutely all he knew.

He didn't know where the dark man and his companion had come from, what they were up to, anything that would be useful to know, and he wasn't getting any nearer finding out. Except that there was some way of loosening the dark man's tongue. Drugs, which were out of the question … liquor …

Well, he thought, sitting up a trifle straighter, there was no harm in trying, anyhow. It might not work, but it was the pleasantest thought he had had all afternoon.

He said, 'Come on,' and stood up carefully; but his motion must have been too abrupt, because the scene around them melted and ran down into the pavement, and they were standing, not in the park, but on the traffic island at Sheridan Square.

It looked to be a little after noon, and the papers on the stand at Johnny's elbow bore today's date.

He felt a little dizzy. Say it was about one o'clock: then he hadn't got out to the airport yet; he was on his way there now, with Duke, and if he could hop a fast cab, he might catch himself and tell himself not to go …

Johnny steadied his mind by a strenuous effort. He had, he told himself, one single, simple problem now in hand, and that was how to get to a bar. He took a careful step toward the edge of the island. The thing in his hand bobbled; the world reeled and steadied.

With the dark man beside him, Johnny was standing on the gallery of the Reptile Room of the Museum of Natural History. Down below, the poised shapes of various giant lizards looked extremely extinct and very dry.

Johnny felt the rising rudiments of a vast impatience. At this rate, it was clear enough, he would never get anywhere he wanted to go, because every step changed the rules. All right, then; if Mohammed couldn't go to the mountain …

The dark man, who had been watching him, made a strangled sound of protest.

Johnny ignored him. He swung his hand sharply down. And up. And down.

The world swung around them like a pendulum, twisting and turning. Too far! They were on a street corner in Paris. They were in a dark place listening to the sound of machinery. They were in the middle of a sandstorm, choking, blinding …

They were sitting in a rowboat on a quiet river. The dark man was wearing flannels and a straw hat.

Johnny tried to move the thing in his hand more gently: it was as if it had a life of its own; he had to hold it back.

Zip!

They were seated on stools at a marble-topped counter. Johnny saw a banana split with a fly on it.

Zip!

A library, a huge low-ceilinged place that Johnny had never seen before.

Zip!

The lobby of the Art Theatre; a patron bumped into Johnny, slopping his demitasse.

Zip!

They were sitting opposite each other, the dark man and he, at a table in the rear of Dorrie's Bar. Dust motes sparkled in the late-afternoon sun. There was a highball in front of each of them.

Gritting his teeth, Johnny held his hand perfectly upright while he lowered it, so slowly that it hardly seemed to move, until it touched the worn surface of the table. He sighed. 'Drink up,' he said.

With a wary eye on the thing in Johnny's hand, the dark man drank. Johnny signalled the bartender, who came over with a faintly puzzled expression. 'How long you guys been here?'

'I was just going to ask you,' said Johnny at random. 'Two more.'

The bartender retired and came back, looking hostile, with the drinks, after which he went down to the farthermost end of the bar, turned his back on them and polished glasses.

Johnny sipped his highball. 'Drink up,' he told the dark man. The dark man drank.

After the third swift highball, the dark man looked slightly wall-eyed. 'How you feeling?' Johnny asked.

'Fine,' said the dark man carefully. 'Jus' fine.' He dipped two fingers into his vest pocket, drew out a tiny flat pillbox and extracted from it an even tinier pill, which he popped into his mouth and swallowed.

'What was that?' said Johnny suspiciously.

'Just a little pill.'

Johnny looked closely at him. His eyes were clear and steady; he looked exactly as if he had not drunk any highballs at all. 'Let me hear you say "The Leith police dismisseth us,"' said Johnny.

The dark man said it.

'Can you say that when you're drunk?' Johnny demanded.

'Don't know, friend. I never tried.'

Johnny sighed. Look at it any way you like, the man had been high, at least, before he swallowed that one tiny pill. And now he was cold sober. After a moment, glowering, he pounded on his glass with a swizzle stick until the bartender came and took his order for two more drinks. 'Doubles,' said Johnny as an afterthought. When they arrived, the dark man drank one down and began to look faintly glassy-eyed. He took out his pillbox.

Johnny leaned forward. 'Who's that standing outside?' he whispered hoarsely.

The dark man swivelled around. 'Where?'

'They ducked back,' said Johnny. 'Keep watching.' He brought his free hand out of his trousers pocket, where it had been busy extracting the contents of a little bottle of anti-histamine tablets he had been carrying around since February. They were six times the size of the dark man's pills, but they were the best he could do. He slid the pillbox out from under the dark man's fingers, swiftly emptied it onto his own lap, dumped the cold tablets into it and put it back.

'I don't see anybody, friend,' said the dark man anxiously. 'Was it a man or—' He picked out one of the bogus tablets, swallowed it, and looked surprised.

'Have another drink,' said Johnny hopefully. The dark man, still looking surprised, swilled it down. His eyes closed slowly and opened again. They were definitely glassy.

'How do you feel now?' Johnny asked.

'Dandy, thanks. *Vad heter denna ort?*' The dark man's face spread and collapsed astonishingly into a large, loose, foolish smile.

It occurred to Johnny that he might have overdone it. 'How was that again?' Swedish, it had sounded like, or some other Scandinavian language ...

'*Voss hot ir gezugt?*' asked the dark man wonderingly. He batted his head with the heel of his hand several times. '*Favour de desconectar la radio.*'

'The radio isn't—' began Johnny, but the dark man interrupted him. Springing up suddenly, he climbed onto the bench, spread his arms and began singing in a loud operatic baritone. The melody was that of the 'Toreador Song' from *Carmen*, but the dark man was singing his own words to it, over and over: '*Dove è il gabinetto?*'

The bartender was coming over with an unpleasant expression. 'Cut that out!' Johnny whispered urgently. 'You hear? Sit down, or I'll move this thing again!'

The dark man glanced at the object in Johnny's hand. 'You don't scare me, bud. Go ahead and move it. *Me cago en su* highball.' He began singing again.

Johnny fumbled three five-dollar bills out of his wallet – all he had – and shoved them at the bartender as he came up. The bartender went away.

'Well, why were you scared before, then?' Johnny asked, furiously.

'Simple,' said the dark man. '*Vänta ett ögenblick*, it'll come back to me. Sure.' He clapped a hand to his brow. '*Herr Gott im Himmel!*' he said, and sat down abruptly. 'Don't move it,' he said. He was pale and sweat-beaded.

'*Why not?*'

'No control,' whispered the dark man. 'The instrument is tuned to you – sooner or later you're going to meet yourself. Two bodies can't occupy the same space-time, friend.' He shuddered. '*Boom!*'

Johnny's hand and wrist, already overtired, were showing a disposition to tremble. He had the hand propped against a bowl of pretzels, and that helped some, but not enough. Johnny was close to despair. The chief effect of the drinks seemed to have been to make the dark man babble in six or seven foreign tongues. The anti-drink pills were safely in his pocket; there was a fortune in those, no doubt, just as a byproduct of this thing if he ever got out of it alive – but that seemed doubtful.

All the same, he checked with a glare the dark man's tentative move toward the object in his hand. His voice shook. 'Tell me now, or I'll wave this thing until something happens. I haven't got any more patience! What are you after? What's it all about?'

'*Un autre plat des pets de nonne, s'il vous plaît, garçon*,' murmured the dark man.

'And cut that out,' said Johnny. 'I mean it!' Intentionally or not, his hand slipped, and he felt the table shudder under them.

Zip!

They were sitting at a narrow table in a Sixth Avenue cafeteria, full of the echoing clatter of inch-thick crockery.

'Well?' said Johnny, close to hysteria. The glasses on the table between them were full of milk, not whisky. Now he was in for it. Unless he could break the dark man's nerve before he sobered up – or unless, which was unlikely in the extreme, they happened to hit another bar …

'It's like this, friend,' said the dark man. 'I'm the last surviving remnant of a race of Lemurians, see, and I like to persecute people. I'm bitter, because you upstarts have taken over the world. You can't—'

'Who's the lady I saw you with?' Johnny asked sourly.

'Her? She's the last surviving remnant of the Atlanteans. We have a working agreement, but we hate each other even more than—'

Johnny's fingers were clammy with sweat around the limp leather that clung to them. He let his hand twitch, not too much.

Zip!

They were sitting facing each other on the hard cane seats of an almost empty subway train, rackety-clacking headlong down its dark tunnel like a consignment to hell. 'Try again,' said Johnny through his teeth.

'It's like this,' said the dark man. 'I'll tell you the truth. This whole universe isn't real, get me? It's just a figment of your imagination, but you got powers you don't know how to control, and we been trying to keep you confused, see, because otherwise—'

'Then you don't care if I do this!' said Johnny, and he made a fist around the leather purse and slammed it on his knee.

Zip!

A wind thundered in his ears, snatched the breath from his mouth. He could barely see the dark man, through a cloud of flying sleet, hunkered like himself on a ledge next to nowhere. 'We're observers from the Galactic Union,' the dark man shouted. 'We're stationed here to keep an eye on you people on account of all them A-bomb explosions, because—'

'Or this!' Johnny howled, and jerked his fist again.

Zip!

They were sprawled on a freezing plain, staring at each other in the icy glitter of starlight. 'I'll tell you!' said the dark man. 'We're time travellers, and we got to make sure you never marry Piper Laurie, because—'

Gently, Johnny told himself.

Zip!

They were sliding side by side down the giant chute in the fun house at Jantzen's Beach in Portland, Oregon. 'Listen!' said the dark man. 'You're a mutant superman, see? Don't get sore – we had to test you before we could lead you into your glorious heritage of—'

As Johnny started to get to his feet, the movement jarred the thing in his hand, and …

Zip!

They were standing on the observation platform on top of the Empire State. It was a cold, raw day. The dark man was shivering – cold, or frightened enough to talk, or too frightened to stay drunk? His voice trembled. 'Okay, this is it, friend. You aren't human; you're an android, but such a good imitation, you don't even know it. But we're your inventors, see—'

Gently: it was the little jumps that were dangerous, Johnny reminded himself.

Zip! They were in a revolving door, and *zip!* Johnny was on the staircase of his own rooming house, looking down at the dark man who was goggling up at him, trying to say something, and *zip!* they were standing beside a disordered banana cart while a cold chill ran up Johnny's spine, and …

'All right!' the dark man shouted. There was raw sincerity in his voice. 'I'll tell you the truth, but *please—*'

Johnny's hand tilted in spite of himself.

Zip!

They were on the top deck of a Fifth Avenue bus parked at the kerb, waiting for a load. Johnny lowered his hand with infinite care to the shiny rail top of the seat ahead. 'Tell,' he said.

The dark man swallowed. 'Give me a chance,' he said in an undertone. 'I can't tell you. If I do, they'll break me, I'll never get a post again—'

'Last chance,' said Johnny, looking straight ahead. '*One … Two …*'

'It's a livie,' the dark man said, pronouncing the first *i* long. His voice was resigned and dull.

'A what?'

'Livie. Like movies. You know. You're an actor.'

'What is this now?' said Johnny uneasily. 'I'm a painter. What do you mean, I'm an ac—'

'You're an *actor, playing* a painter!' said the dark man. 'You actors! Dumb cows! You're an actor! Understand? It's *a livie.*'

'What is the livie about?' Johnny asked carefully.

'It's a musical tragedy. All about poor people in the slums.'

'I don't live in the slums,' said Johnny indignantly.

'*In* the *slums.* You want to tell me, or should I tell you? It's a big dramatic show. You're the comic *relief.* Later on you *die.*' The dark man stopped short, and looked as if he wished he had stopped shorter. 'A detail,' he said. 'Not important. We'll fix it up, next script conference.' He put his hands to his temples suddenly. 'Oh, why was I decanted?' he muttered. 'Glorm will split me up the middle. He'll pulverize me. He'll shove me back into the—'

'You're serious?' said Johnny. His voice cracked. 'What is this, I die? I die how?' He twitched uncontrollably.

Zip!

The Fifth Avenue bus was gone. They were sitting in the second row of a movie theatre. The house lights had just gone up; the audience was shuffling out. Johnny seized the dark man by the shirt front.

'I forget,' said the dark man sullenly. 'You fall off something, I think. Right before the end of the livie, when the hero gets to bed with the girl. You want to know who's the hero? Somebody you know. Duke—'

'Fall off what?' said Johnny, tightening his grip.

'Off a building. Into a trash can. Half.'

'Comic relief?' said Johnny with an effort.

'Sure. Pratfalls! You'll steal the livie! The lookers'll have heart attacks laughing!'

The sounds of the departing audience abruptly stopped. The walls and ceiling flickered alarmingly; when they steadied, Johnny saw with total bewilderment that they were in a different room altogether. It was nowhere he had ever been before – nowhere, he realized abruptly, with his heart racing, that he ever *could* have been before.

Out across the great silvery bowl, under a cloud-high ceiling, men were floating in the air like gnats, some drifting, some moving quickly around a bulbous metal shape that hung over the centre of the huge room. Down below, twenty feet lower than the balcony on which they sat, there was a little puff of light and exploding shape – a brilliant unfolding that lasted only an instant, leaving a crazy memory of moving trees and buildings. After a moment, it happened again.

Johnny was aware that the dark man beside him had stiffened and some-how shrunk into himself.

He turned. Behind them, in the eerie stillness, a silvery man came striding through a doorway.

'Glorm,' said the dark man, gasping, 'ne estis mia kulpo. Li—'

Glorm said, 'Fermu vian truon.' He was slender and sinewy, dressed in something that looked like tinfoil. He had bulging eyes under a broad shelf of brow. He turned them on Johnny. 'Now you vill give me d'instrument,' he said.

Johnny found his breath. The bit of leather in his hand, he discovered, was now as rigid as if it were part of an invisible pillar in the air; but he tightened his grip on it, anyhow. 'Why should I give it to you?' he demanded.

Glorm gestured impatiently. 'Vait.' He turned to look out over the enor-mous sunken bowl, and his voice suddenly echoed everywhere, somehow a hundred times magnified: 'Giŝpinu!'

Again came that flowering of colour and movement under the hanging bulge of metal, but this time it sprang into full life and didn't collapse again.

Fascinated, Johnny stared down over the balcony rim. The floor of the bowl was gone now, buried by a glittering marble street. On either side were white buildings, all porticoes and pillars, and down at the end loomed some-thing that looked like the Parthenon, only as big as the main U.N. building in New York.

The street was aboil with people, dwarfed by distance. They scattered as a four-horse chariot came hurtling past, then flowed together again. Johnny could hear them muttering angrily, like so many bees. There was a curious acrid scent in the air.

Puzzled, he glanced at Glorm and the dark man. 'What's that?' he asked, pointing.

Glorm made a gesture. 'Rome,' said the dark man, shaking as if with a chill. 'They're making a spectacle, back in 44 BC. This here's the scene where Julius Caesar burns the place down because they won't make him emperor.'

Sure enough, the acrid scent was stronger; down below, a thin veil of grey-black smoke was beginning to rise …

'But he didn't,' Johnny protested, stung. 'That isn't even Rome – the Par-thenon's in Athens.'

'It used to be,' said the dark man. His teeth were chattering. 'We changed it. The last outfit that made livies there, they were okay on the little scenes, but they didn't understand spectacle. Glorm –' he cast a furtive glance at the silver man and raised his voice slightly – 'he understands spectacle.'

'Let me get this straight now,' said Johnny with a thick tongue. 'You went to all the trouble of building that phoney set, with that crazy Parthenon and all, when you could just go back in time and shoot the real thing?'

'*Bona!*' shouted Glorm's amplified voice. '*Gi estu presata!*' The scene down below whirled in upon itself and winked out.

Glorm turned impatiently to Johnny. 'Now,' he said. 'You do not understand. Dat vich you see dere *is* vat you call d'real ding. Ve not built set – built riot set – not set – *Kiel oni ĝi dims?*'

' "We din't build no set," ' said the dark man.

'*Putra lingvo!* Ve din build no set. Ve made dat Romans build it. Dey din build no set – dey build Rome, di*ff*erent. Un*d*erstand? No*body* din build no set! Real Rome! Real fire! Real dead! Real his*t*ory!'

Johnny gaped at him. 'You mean you're changing history, just to make movies?'

'Livies,' the dark man muttered.

'Livies, then. You must all be loopies. Where does that leave the people up in the future? Look – where are we now? What time?'

'Your calendar, uh, 4400-something. About twenty-five hundred years from your time.'

'Twenty-five hundred – Well, what does it do to you, when you change the Romans all around?'

'Noddin',' said Glorm emphatically.

'Noddin'?' said Johnny obtusely.

'Noddin' at all. Vat happens to dog ven you cut off his modder's tail?'

Johnny thought about it. 'Noddin'.'

'*Korekti.* You dink it is big job?'

Johnny nodded.

'It *is* big job. But ve do it tventy, forty times *every* year. You know how many people live on d' planet now?' Without pausing, he answered himself. 'Tirty billion. You know how many go to livies? Half. Fifteen billion. Seven times more people dan live on d'planet in your time. Old, young. Stupid, smart. Livies got to en*t*ertain dem all. Not like your Hol*l*yvood. Dat vas not art, not spec*t*acle. Ven d'people tink, deep down –' he tapped his head – 'someting is true, den I make it true, and it *is* true! Dat is art! Dat is spec*t*acle!'

'You haven't changed New York much, anyway,' said Johnny in self-defence.

Glorm's bulging eyes grew bulgier. 'Not change!' He snorted, turned. His amplified voice rang out again: '*Donu al mi flugantan kvieton de Nov-Jorko natura!*'

There was a stirring of floating figures out around the hanging bulge of metal. Glorm cracked his knuckles impatiently. After a long moment the floor of the bowl blossomed again.

Johnny caught his breath.

The illusion was so perfect that the floor seemed to have dropped away: a thousand feet down, Manhattan Island lay spread in the morning sunlight; he could see ships at anchor in the harbour, and the clear glints of the Hudson and the East River running up northward into the mists over the Bronx.

The first thing he noticed was that the chaotic chequer-board of low buildings spread over the whole island: the cluster of skyscrapers at the southern tip, and the scattering at midtown, were missing.

'Guess vat year,' said Glorm's voice.

He frowned. 'About 1900?' But that couldn't be right, he thought uneasily – there were too many bridges: more, even, than in his own time.

Glorm laughed heartily. 'Dat vich you see is Nov-York, 1956 – before ve change it. You dink you invent skyscrapers? Oh, no. Me *invent* it.'

'For *Wage Slaves of Broadway*,' said the dark man reverently. 'That was his first livie. What a spectacle!'

'Now you un*der*stand?' Glorm asked patronizingly. 'Long time I vanted to tell dis to actor, see his face. Good – you understand now.' His lean face was shining. 'You are actor; I am producer, director. Producer, director is everything. Actor is dirt! So you vill give me d'ins*tru*ment.'

'Won't,' said Johnny weakly.

'You vill,' Glorm said. 'In a minute you have to let go.'

Johnny discovered with a shock that his hand was growing numb. So this was what they had all been stalling for, all this time. And now they'd got it. He *was* about to let go; he could feel it. So ...

'Listen!' he said desperately. 'What about the people in the future – I mean your future? Do they make livies, too? If they do, are you an actor to them?'

Glorm's face tautened with fury. '*Kraċajo!*' he said. 'Vait *until* –' He stared at the thing in Johnny's hand, and his fingers clenched.

Johnny's grip loosened. He was going to let go, and then what? Back to his own time, and more pratfalls, leading inexorably to ...

His whole arm was tired. He was going to have to let go.

... And there was nothing he could do about it. That endless chain of tinkerers, Glorms standing on each others' shoulders, all the way up into the unguessable future – that was too big to change. It was, he supposed, no more frightening or terrible than other kinds of macrocosmic tyranny the human mind had imagined; it would be possible to live with it, if only his part weren't so unpleasant ...

His hand dropped.

Smiling, Glorm reached out to the suspended bit of leather. His fingers did something to it that Johnny couldn't follow, and abruptly it sagged into his palm.

It shuddered and flickered there for a moment like a top running down. All at once it split into a brown coin and a pair of pince-nez. The flickering came again, a blur of bright shapes: fountain pen, notebook, watch, cigarette lighter. Then both objects came to rest, tiny and metallic and dead.

Glorm put them into a fold of his clothing.

'Bona,' he said indifferently over his shoulder. '*Resendu tion al Nov-Jorkon.*'

Desperation limbered Johnny's tongue. He started talking before he even knew what he was going to say. 'What if I don't stay in New York?'

Glorm paused, looking annoyed. '*Kio?*'

'You've got your gadget back,' said Johnny, as the idea took shape in his head. 'All right, but what are you going to do if I decide to move to Chicago, or some place? Or get myself arrested and sent to jail? I mean, you can shuffle the probabilities around, but if I try hard enough, I can put myself where it's *impossible* to have what you want to have happen, happen.' He took a deep breath. 'See what I mean?'

'*Plejmalpuro,*' said Glorm. From his expression, he saw.

'Listen,' Johnny said. 'Let me get the picture. This Duke you say is the hero – that's the Duke I know?' He got a nod from Glorm. 'And that was part of the script, when he helped me get out of town?'

'Dress rehearsal,' said the dark man. 'You fall in a swamp in Florida – come up all over mud and leeches. A real boff.'

Johnny shuddered and turned his mind resolutely away from leeches and falls from high buildings … 'What I want to know is, what was Duke's angle? Why did he think he wanted to get me out of town?'

They told him. The answer was brutally simple, and Johnny had been half afraid that he knew it already.

He waited until his nails unclenched from his palms, and he felt able to talk sensibly again. And even then, he found he had nothing to say. How could you talk to people who would do a thing like that and call it art, or entertainment? It was logical, he supposed, that a culture whose taste demanded Glorm's ruthless spec*tac*les should have such a concept of a 'hero'. It was also terrifying.

His time was running out again. But the answer to that one occurred to him too.

If Duke were here, what would he say?

'Okay, look,' Johnny said rapidly, 'I'm just spitballing, you understand, talking off the top of my head—'

Glorm and the dark man leaned forward with interested, wary expressions.

'– but here's how I see it. Instead of this clown type for your comedy relief, we have this suave man-of-the-world type. It's a switch. A really great, uh, producer-director could put it over. I can really see it. Take for instance – here, show me where it says in the script …'

*

Johnny materialized on the quiet side street a few steps from his door. He felt heavy and tired. The sun was still high over the tops of the old buildings; it was about 2:30 – an hour and a half after Duke had left him at the airport.

He leaned against a railing and waited. Sure enough, here came Mary Finigan across the street, her hair uncombed, dark circles under her eyes.

'Go home, Mary,' he said.

She was startled. 'What's the matter, isn't he there? I mean, Duke called me – he said he was at your place.'

'He's got an axe,' said Johnny. 'I'm telling you the truth. He was going to kill you in my apartment, with my Scout axe that I use for kindling, with my fingerprints on it.'

When she was gone, Johnny went on around the corner and into the foyer. Duke was there with his hand in Johnny's mailbox. He turned around and swore, and his hand twitched a long fat envelope out of the box. 'What the devil are you doing here, Johnny?'

'I decided not to go.'

Duke leaned against the wall, grinning. 'Well, every coming together again gives a foretaste of the resurrection. Whew!' He glanced at the envelope he was holding as if he had just noticed it. 'Now I wonder what this might be.'

'You know what it is,' said Johnny without rancour. 'Ted Edwards' fifty bucks that he owed me. That was what gave you the idea, when he told you he'd put it in the mail. Then this Mary business came up, and I suppose it just seemed to you like a God-given opportunity.'

Duke's eyes were narrow and hard. 'You know about that, too, do you? What were you planning to do about it, would you tell an old friend that?'

'Nothing,' said Johnny. 'Just give me my IOU, and we'll call it square.'

Duke fished in his pocket for the folded scrap of paper and handed it over. He peered into Johnny's eyes, looking baffled. 'Well, well. You're sure, are you?'

Johnny nodded and turned to go up the stairs.

'I believe you are,' said Duke. He was shaking his head, arms akimbo. 'Johnny, my boy, you're a character.'

Johnny looked down at him for a moment. 'You're another,' he said.

TIME ENOUGH

The walls and the control panel were grey, but in the viewscreen it was green summer noon.

'That's the place,' said the boy's voice in Vogel's ear.

The old man gently touched the controls, and the viewpoint steadied, twenty feet or so above the ground. In the screen, maple leaves swayed in a light breeze. There was just a glimpse of the path below, deep in shadow.

The display, on the tiny screen, was as real as if one could somehow squeeze through the frame and drop into those sunlit trees. A warm breath of air came into the room.

'Guess I could go there blindfold, I remember it so well,' he heard Jimmy say. The boy seemed unable to stop talking; his hands tightened and relaxed on his knees. 'I remember, we were all standing around in front of the drugstore in the village, and one of the kids said let's go swimming. So we all started off across town, and first thing I knew, we weren't going down to the beach; we were going out to the old quarry.'

The leaves danced suddenly in a stronger breeze. 'Guess we'll see them in about a minute,' Jimmy said. 'If you got the right time, that is.' His weight shifted, and Vogel knew he was staring up at the dials on the control board, even before his high voice read aloud: 'May twenty-eight, nineteen sixty. Eleven-nine-thirty-two A.M.'

His voice grew higher. 'Here they come.'

In the screen, a flicker of running bodies passed under the trees. Vogel saw bare brown backs, sports shirts, tee shirts, dark heads and blond. There were eight or nine boys in the pack, all aged about twelve; the last, lagging behind, was a slender brown-haired boy who seemed a little younger. He paused, clearly visible for a moment through the leaves, and looked up with a white face. Then he turned and was gone into the dark flickering green.

'There I go,' said Jimmy's raw voice. 'Now we're climbing up the slope to the quarry. Dark and kind of clammy up there, so many old spruces you can't even see the sky. That moss was just like cold mud when you stepped on it barefoot.'

'Try to relax,' said Vogel carefully. 'Would you like to do it later?'

'No, now,' said Jimmy convulsively. His voice steadied. 'I'm a little tensed up, I guess, but I can do it. I wasn't really *scared*; it was the way it happened, so sudden. They never gave me time to get ready.'

'Well, that's what the machine is for,' said Vogel soothingly. 'More time – time enough for everything.'

'I know it,' said Jimmy in an inattentive voice.

Vogel sighed. These afternoons tired him; he was not a young man any more and he no longer believed in his work. Things did not turn out as you expected. The work had to be done, of course; there was always the chance of helping someone, but it was not the easy, automatic thing that youth in its terrible confidence believed.

There was a rustle in the screen, and Vogel saw Jimmy's hands clench into desperate fists on his knees.

A boy flashed into view, the same boy, running clumsily with one hand over his face. His head rocked back and forth. He blundered past, whipped by undergrowth, and the swaying branches closed behind him.

Jimmy's hands relaxed slowly. 'There I go,' his voice said, low and bitter. 'Running away. Crying like a baby.'

After a moment Vogel's spidery fingers reached out to the controls. The viewpoint drifted slowly closer to the ground. Galaxies of green leaves passed through it like bright smoke, and then the viewpoint stopped and tilted, and they were looking up the leaf-shadowed path, as if from a point five feet or so above the ground.

Vogel asked carefully, 'Ready now?'

'Sure,' said Jimmy, his voice thin again.

The shock of the passage left him stumbling for balance, and he fetched up against a small tree. The reeling world steadied around him; he laughed. The tree trunk was cool and papery under his hand; the leaves were a dancing green glory all around. He was back in Kellogg's Woods again, on that May day when everything had gone wrong, and here it was, just the same as before. The same leaves were on the trees; the air he breathed was the same air.

He started walking up the trail. After a few moments he discovered that his heart was thumping in his chest. He *hated* them, all the big kids with their superior, grinning faces. They were up there right now, waiting for him. But this time he would show them, and then afterward, slowly, it would be possible to stop hating. He knew that. But oh, Christ, how he hated them now!

It was dark under the spruces as he climbed, and the moss was squashy underfoot. For a passing moment he was sorry he had come. But it was costing his family over a thousand dollars to have him sent back. They were giving him this golden chance, and he wouldn't waste it.

Now he could hear the boys' voices, calling hollow, and the cold splash as one of them dived.

Hating and bitter, he climbed to where he could look down across the deep shadowed chasm of the old quarry. The kids were all tiny figures on the other side, where the rock slide was, the only place where you could climb out of the black water. Some of them were sitting on the rocks, wet and shivering. Their voices came up to him small with distance.

Nearer, he saw the dead spruce that lay slanting downward across the edge of the quarry, with its tangled roots in the air. The trunk was silvery grey, perhaps a foot thick at the base. It had fallen straight down along the quarry wall, an old tree with all the stubs of limbs broken off short, and its tip was jammed into a crevice. Below that, there was a series of ledges you could follow all the way down.

But first you had to walk the dead tree.

He climbed up on the thick, twisting roots, trying not to be aware just yet how they overhung the emptiness below. Down across the shadowed quarry, he could see pale blurs of faces turning up one by one to look at him.

Now he vividly remembered the way it had been before, the line of boys tightrope-walking down the tree, arms waving for balance, bare or tennis-shoed feet treading carefully. If only they hadn't left him till last!

He took one step out onto the trunk. Without intending to, he glanced down and saw the yawning space under him – the black water, and the rocks.

The tree swayed under him. He tried to take the next step and found he couldn't. It was just the same as before, and he realized now that it was *impossible* to walk the tree – you would slip and fall, down, down that cliff to the rocks and the cold water. Standing there fixed between the sky and the quarry, he could tell himself that the others had done it, but it didn't help. What good was that, when he could see, when anybody could see, it was impossible?

Down there, the boys were waiting, in their cold and silent comradeship.

Jimmy stepped slowly back. Tears of self-hatred burned his lids, but he climbed over the arching roots and left the quarry edge behind him, hearing the clear, distant shouts begin again as he stumbled down the path.

'Don't blame yourself too much,' said Vogel in his grey voice. 'Maybe you just weren't ready, this time.'

Jimmy wiped his eyes angrily with the heel of his hand. 'I wasn't ready,' he muttered. 'I thought I was, but ... Must have been too nervous, that's all.'

'Or, maybe ...' Vogel hesitated. 'Some people think it's better to forget the past and solve our problems in the present.'

Jimmy's eyes widened with shock. 'I couldn't give up *now!*' he said. He stood up, agitated. 'Why, my whole life would be ruined – I mean, I never thought I'd hear a thing like that from you, Mr Vogel. I mean, the whole *point* of this machine, and everything ...'

'I know,' said Vogel. 'The past can be altered. The scholar can take his exam over again, the lover can propose once more, the words that were thought of too late can be spoken. So I always believed.' He forced a smile. 'It's like a game of cards. If you don't like the hand that is dealt to you, you can take another, and after that, another ...'

'That's right,' said Jimmy, sounding appeased. 'So if you look at it that way, how can I lose?'

Vogel did not reply but stood up courteously to see him to the door.

'So, then, I'll see you tomorrow, Mr Vogel,' Jimmy said.

Vogel glanced at the wall calendar; it read, *21 April 1978*. 'Yes, all right,' he answered.

In the doorway, Jimmy looked back at him with pathetic hopefulness – a pale, slender thirty-year-old man, from whose weak eyes a lost boy seemed to be staring, pleading ... 'There's always tomorrow, isn't there, Mr Vogel?' he asked.

'Yes,' said Vogel wearily. 'There's always tomorrow.'

EXTEMPORE

Everybody knew; everybody wanted to help Rossi the time-traveller. They came running up the scarlet beach, naked and golden as children, laughing happily.

'Legend is true,' they shouted. 'He is here, just like greatgrandfathers say!'

'What year is this?' Rossi asked, standing incongruously shirtsleeved and alone in the sunlight – no great machines bulking around him, no devices, nothing but his own spindling body.

'Thairty-five twainty-seex, Mista Rossi!' they chorused.

'Thank you. Goodbye.'

'Goodbyee!'

Flick. Flick. Flick. Those were days. *Flicketaflicketaflick* – weeks, months, years, WHIRRR ... Centuries, millennia streaming past like sleet in a gale!

Now the beach was cold, and the people were buttoned up to their throats in stiff black cloth. Moving stiffly, like jointed stick people, they unfurled a huge banner: 'SORI WI DO NOT SPIC YOUR SPICH. THIS IS YIR 5199 OF YOUR CALINDAR. HELO MR ROSI.'

They all bowed, like marionettes, and Mr Rossi bowed back. *Flick. Flick. Flicketaflicketa* WHIRRR ...

The beach was gone. He was inside an enormous building, a sky-high vault, like the Empire State turned into one room. Two floating eggs swooped at him and hovered alertly, staring with poached eyes. Behind them reared a tilted neon slab blazing with diagrams and symbols, none of which he could recognize before *flicketa* WHIRRRR ...

This time it was a wet stony plain, with salt marshes beyond it. Rossi was not interested and spent the time looking at the figures he had scrawled in his notebook. 1956, 1958, 1965 and so on, the intervals getting longer and longer, the curve rising until it was going almost straight up. If only he'd paid more attention to mathematics in school ... *flickRRR* ...

Now a white desert at night, bitter cold, where the towers of Manhattan should have been. Something mournfully thin flapped by over *flkRRRR* ...

Blackness and fog was all he could *fkRRRR* ...

Now the light and dark blinks in the greyness melted and ran together, flickering faster and faster until Rossi was looking at a bare leaping landscape as if through soap-smeared glasses – continents expanding and contracting, icecaps slithering down and back again, the planet charging towards its cold death while only Rossi stood there to watch, gaunt and stiff, with a disapproving, wistful glint in his eye.

His name was Albert Eustace Rossi. He was from Seattle, a wild bony young man with a poetic forelock and the stare-you-down eyes of an animal. He had learned nothing in twelve years of school except how to get passing marks, and he had a large wistfulness but no talents at all.

He had come to New York because he thought something wonderful might happen.

He averaged two months on a job. He worked as a short-order cook (his eggs were greasy and his hamburgers burned), a platemaker's helper in an offset shop, a shill in an auction gallery. He spent three weeks as a literary agent's critic, writing letters over his employer's signature to tell hapless reading-fee clients that their stories stank. He wrote bad verse for a while and sent it hopefully to all the best magazines, but concluded he was being held down by a clique.

He made no friends. The people he met seemed to be interested in nothing but baseball, or their incredibly boring jobs, or in making money. He tried hanging around the Village, wearing dungarees and a flowered shirt, but discovered that nobody noticed him.

It was the wrong century. What he wanted was a villa in Athens; or an island where the natives were childlike and friendly, and no masts ever lifted above the blue horizon; or a vast hygienic apartment in some future underground Utopia.

He bought certain science-fiction magazines and read them defiantly with the covers showing in cafeterias. Afterward, he took them home and marked them up with large exclamatory blue and red and green pencil and filed them away under his bed.

The idea of building a time machine had been growing a long while in his mind. Sometimes in the morning on his way to work, looking up at the blue cloud-dotted endlessness of the sky, or staring at the tracery of lines and whorls on his unique fingertips, or trying to see into the cavernous unexplored depths of a brick in a wall, or lying on his narrow bed at night, conscious of all the bewildering sights and sounds and odours that had swirled past him in twenty-odd years, he would say to himself, Why not?

Why not? He found a second-hand copy of J. W. Dunne's *An Experiment with Time* and lost sleep for a week. He copied off the charts from it, Scotch-taped them to his wall; he wrote down his startling dreams every morning as soon as he awoke. There was a time outside time, Dunne said, in which to measure time; and a time outside that, in which to measure the time that measured time, and a time outside that ... Why not?

An article in a barbershop about Einstein excited him, and he went to the library and read the encyclopedia articles on relativity and space-time, frowning fiercely, going back again and again over the paragraphs he never did understand, but filling up all the same with a threshold feeling, an expectancy.

What looked like time to him might look like space to somebody else, said Einstein. A CLOCK ran slower the faster it went. Good, fine. Why not? But it wasn't Einstein, or Minkowski or Wehl who gave him the clue; it was an astronomer named Milne.

There were two ways of looking at time, Milne said. If you measured it by things that moved, like clock hands and the earth turning and going around the sun, that was one kind; Milne called it dynamical time and his symbol for it was T. But if you measured it by things happening in the atom, like radioactivity and light being emitted, that was another kind; Milne called it kinematic time, or t. And the formula that connected the two showed that it depended on which you used whether the universe had ever had a beginning or would ever have an end – yes in T time, no in t.

Then it all added together: Dunne saying you didn't really have to travel along the timetrack like a train, you just thought you did, but when you were asleep you forgot, and that was why you could have prophetic dreams. And Eddington: that all the great laws of physics we had been able to discover were just a sort of spidery framework, and that there was room between the strands for an unimaginable complexity of things.

He believed it instantly; he had known it all his life and had never had any words to think it in – that this reality wasn't all there was. Pay cheques, grimy window sills, rancid grease, nails in the shoes – how could it be?

It was all in the way you looked at it. That was what the *scientists* were saying – Einstein, Eddington, Milne, Dunne, all in a chorus. So it was a thing anybody could do, if he wanted it badly enough and was lucky. Rossi had always felt obscurely resentful that the day was past when you could discover something by looking at a teakettle or dropping gunk on a hot stove; but here, incredibly, was one more easy road to fame that everybody had missed.

Between the tip of his finger and the edge of the soiled plastic cover that hideously draped the hideous table, the shortest distance was a straight line containing an infinite number of points. His own body, he knew, was mostly empty space. Down there in the shadowy regions of the atom, in t time, you could describe how fast an electron was moving or where it was, but never both; you could never decide whether it was a wave or a particle; you couldn't even prove it existed at all, except as the ghost of its reflection appeared to you.

Why not?

It was summer, and the whole city was gasping for breath. Rossi had two weeks off and nowhere to go; the streets were empty of the Colorado vacationers; the renters of cabins in the mountains, the tailored flyers to Ireland, the Canadian Rockies, Denmark, Nova Scotia. All day long the sweaty subways had inched their loads of suffering out to Coney Island and Far Rockaway and back again, well salted, flayed with heat, shocked into a fishy torpor.

Now the island was still; flat and steaming, like a flounder on a griddle; every window open for an unimagined breath of air; silent as if the city were under glass. In dark rooms the bodies lay sprawled like a cannibal feast, all wakeful, all moveless, waiting for Time's tick.

Rossi had fasted all day, having in mind the impressive results claimed by Yogis, early Christian saints and Americans; he had drunk nothing but a glass of water in the morning and another at blazing noon. Standing now in the close darkness of his room, he felt that ocean of Time, heavy and stagnant, stretching away for ever. The galaxies hung in it like seaweed, and down at the bottom it was silted unfathomably deep with dead men. (Seashell murmur: I am.)

There it all was, temporal and eternal, *t* and tau, everything that was and would be. The electron dancing in its imaginary orbit, the May fly's moment, the long drowse of the sequoias, the stretching of continents, the lonely drifting of stars; it cancelled them all against each other, and the result was stillness.

The sequoia's truth did not make the May fly false. If a man could only see some other aspect of that totality, feel it, believe it – another relation of tau time to *t* ...

He had chalked a diagram on the floor – not a pentacle but the nearest thing he could find, the quadrisected circle of the Michelson apparatus. Around it he had scrawled, 'e = mc^2', 'Z^2/n^2', 'M = M$_0$+3K+2V'. Pinned up shielding the single bulb was a scrap of paper with some doggerel on it:

$$\frac{t, \tau, t, \tau, t\,\tau\,t}{c}$$

R $\sqrt{3}$

Cartesian co-ordinates x, y, z

$-c^2t^2 = me$

It was in his head, hypnotically repeating: *t tau, t, tau, t taut* ...

As he stood there, the outlines of the paper swelled and blurred, rhythmically. He felt as if the whole universe were breathing, slowly and gigantically, all one, the smallest atom and the farthest star.

c over R times the square root of three ...

He had a curious drunken sense that he was standing *outside*, that he could reach in and give himself a push, or a twist – no, that wasn't the word, either ... But something was happening; he felt it, half in terror and half in delight.

less c squared, t squared, equals ...

An intolerable tension squeezed Rossi tight. Across the room the paper, too, near the bulb, crisped and burned.

And (as the tension twisted him somehow, finding a new direction for release) that was the last thing Rossi saw before *flick*, it was daylight, and the room was clotted with moist char, *flick*, someone was moving across it, too swift to *flick. Flick. Flick. Flick, flick, flicketa-flicketa ...*

And here he was. Most incredibly, what had seemed so true *was* true: by that effort of tranced will, he had transferred himself to another time rate, another relationship of t to τ – a variable relationship, like a huge merry-go-round that whirled, and paused, and whirled again.

He had got on; how was he going to get off?

And – most terrifying question – where was the merry-go-round going? Whirling headlong to extinction and cold death, where the universe ended – or around the wheel again, to give him a second chance?

The blur exploded into white light. Stunned but safe inside his portable anomaly, Rossi watched the flaming earth cool, saw the emerging continents furred over with green, saw a kaleidoscope whirl of rainstorm and volcanic fury, pelting ice, earthquake, tsunami, fire!

Then he was in a forest, watching the branches sway as some great shape passed.

He was in a clearing, watching as a man in leather breeches killed a copper-skinned man with an axe.

He was in a log-walled room, watching a man in a wide collar stand up, toppling table and crockery, his eyes like onions.

He was in a church, and an old man behind the pulpit flung a book at him.

The church again, at evening, and two lonely women saw him and screamed.

He was in a bare, narrow room reeking of pitch. Somewhere outside, a dog set up a frenzied barking. A door opened and a wild, whiskery face popped in; a hand flung a blazing stick and flame leaped up ...

He was on a broad green lawn, alone with a small boy and a frantic white duck. 'Good morrow, sir. Will you help me catch this pesky ...'

He was in a little pavilion. A grey-bearded man at a desk turned, snatching up a silver cross, whispering fiercely to the young man at his side, '*Didn't I tell you!*' He pointed the cross, quivering. 'Quick, then! Will New York continue to grow?'

Rossi was off guard. 'Sure. This is going to be the biggest city ...'

*

The pavilion was gone; he was in a little perfumed nook, facing a long room across a railing. A red-haired youth, dozing in front of the fire, sat up with a guilty start. He gulped. 'Who ... who's going to win the election?'

'What election?' said Rossi. 'I don't—'

'Who's going to win?' The youth came forward, pale-faced. 'Hoover or Roosevelt? Who?'

'Oh, that election. Roosevelt.'

'Uh, will the country ...'

The same room. A bell was ringing; white lights dazzled his eyes. The bell stopped. An amplified voice said, 'When will Germany surrender?'

'Uh, 1945,' said Rossi, squinting. 'May, 1945. Look, whoever you are—'

'When will Japan surrender?'

'Same year. September. Look, whoever you are ...'

A tousle-headed man emerged from the glare, blinking, wrapping a robe around his bulging middle. He stared at Rossi while the mechanical voice spoke behind him.

'Please name the largest new industry in the next ten years.'

'Uh, television, I guess. Listen, you right there, can't you ...'

The same room, the same bell ringing. This was all wrong, Rossi realized irritably. Nineteen thirty-two, 1944 (?) – the next ought to be at least close to where he had started. There was supposed to be a row of cheap rooming houses – his room, *here* ...

'... election, Stevenson or Eisenhower?'

'Stevenson. I mean, Eisenhower. Now look, *doesn't anybody*—'

'When will there be an armistice in Korea?'

'Last year. *Next year*. You're mixing me up. Will you turn off that—'

'When and where will atomic bombs next be used in—'

'Listen!' Rossi shouted. 'I'm getting mad! If you want me to answer questions, let me ask some! Get me some help! Get me—'

'What place in the United States will be safest when—'

'*Einstein!*' shouted Rossi.

But the little grey man with the bloodhound eyes couldn't help him, nor the bald moustachioed one who was there the next time. The walls were inlaid now with intricate tracings of white metal. The voice began asking him questions he couldn't answer.

The second time it happened, there was a *puff* and a massive rotten stench rolled into his nostrils. Rossi choked. 'Stop that!'

'Answer!' blared the voice. 'What's the meaning of those signals from space?'

'I don't know!' *Puff.* Furiously: 'But there isn't any New York past here! It's all gone – nothing left but ...' *Puff!*

Then he was standing on the lake of glassy obsidian, just like the first time.

And then the jungle, and he said automatically, 'My name is Rossi. What year ...' But it wasn't the jungle, really. It had been cleared back, and there were neat rows of concrete houses, like an enormous tank trap, instead of grasstopped verandas showing through the trees.

Then came the savanna, and that was all different, too – there was a looming piled ugliness of a city rising half a mile away. Where were the nomads, the horsemen? And next ...

The beach: but it was dirty grey, not scarlet. One lone dark figure was hunched against the glare, staring out to sea; the golden people were gone.

Rossi felt lost. Whatever had happened to New York, back there – to the whole world, probably – something he had said or done had made it come out differently. Somehow they had saved out some of the old grimy, rushing civilization, and it had lasted just long enough to blight all the fresh new things that ought to have come after it. The stick men were not waiting on their cold beach.

He caught his breath. He was in the enormous building again, the same tilted slab blazing with light, the same floating eggs bulging their eyes at him. That hadn't changed, and perhaps nothing he could do would ever change it; for he knew well enough that that wasn't a human building.

But then came the white desert, and after it the fog, and his glimpses of the night began to blur together, faster and faster ...

That was all. There was nothing left now but the swift vertiginous spin to the end-and-beginning, and then the wheel slowing as he came around again.

Rossi began to seethe. This was worse than dishwashing – his nightmare, the worst job he knew. Standing here, like a second hand ticking around the face of Time, while men who flickered and vanished threaded him with questions: a thing, a tool, a gyrating information booth!

Stop, he thought, and pushed – a costive pressure inside his brain – but nothing happened. He was a small boy forgotten on a carousel, a bug trapped between window and screen, a moth circling a lamp ...

It came to him what the trouble was. There had to be the yearning, that single candle-cone focus of the spirit: that was the moving force, and all the rest – the fasting, the quiet, the rhymes – was only to channel and guide.

He would have to get off at the one place in the whole endless sweep of time where he wanted to be. And that place, he knew now without surprise, was the scarlet beach.

Which no longer existed, anywhere in the universe.

While he hung suspended on that thought, the flickering stopped at the prehistoric jungle; and the clearing with its copper dead man; and the log room, empty; the church, empty, too.

And the fiery room, now so fiercely ablaze that the hair of his forearms puffed and curled.

And the cool lawn, where the small boy stood agape.

And the pavilion: the greybeard and the young man leaning together like blasted trees, livid-lipped.

There was the trouble: they had believed him, the first time around, and acting on what he told them, they had changed the world.

Only one thing to be done – destroy that belief, fuddle them, talk nonsense, like a ghost called up at a séance!

'Then you tell me to put all I have in land,' says grey-beard, clutching the crucifix, 'and wait for the increase!'

'Of course!' replied Rossi with instant cunning. 'New York's to be the biggest city – in the whole state of Maine!'

The pavilion vanished. Rossi saw with pleasure that the room that took its place was high-ceilinged and shabby, the obvious forerunner of his own roach-haunted cubbyhole in 1955. The long panelled room with its fireplace and the youth dozing before it: were gone, snuffed out, a mighthave-been.

When a motherly looking woman lurched up out of a rocker, staring, he knew what to do.

He put his finger to his lips. 'The lost candlestick is under the cellar stairs!' he hissed, and vanished.

The room was a little older, a little shabbier. A new partition had been added, bringing its dimensions down to those of the room Rossi knew, and there was a bed, and an old tin washbasin in the corner. A young woman was sprawled open-mouthed, fleshy and snoring, in the bed; Rossi looked away with faint prim disgust and waited.

The same room: *his* room, almost: a beefy stubbled man smoking in the armchair with his feet in a pan of water. The pipe dropped from his sprung jaw.

'I'm the family banshee,' Rossi remarked. 'Beware, for a short man with a long knife is dogging your footsteps.' He squinted and bared his fangs; the man, standing up hurriedly, tipped the basin and stumbled half across the room before he recovered and whirled to the door, bellowing, leaving fat wet tracks and silence.

Now; *now* … It was night, and the sweaty unstirred heat of the city poured in around him. He was standing in the midst of the chalk marks he had scrawled a hundred billion years ago. The bare bulb was still lighted; around it flames were licking tentatively at the edges of the table, cooking the plastic cover up into lumpy hissing puffs.

Rossi the shipping clerk; Rossi the elevator man; Rossi the *dishwasher!*

He let it pass. The room kaleidoscope-flicked from brown to green; a young man at the washbasin was pouring something amber into a glass, gurgling and clinking.

'Boo!' said Rossi, flapping his arms.

The young man whirled in a spasm of limbs, a long arc of brown droplets hanging. The door banged him out, and Rossi was alone, watching the drinking glass roll, counting the seconds until …

The walls were brown again; a calendar across the room said 1965 MAY 1965. An old man, spidery on the edge of the bed, was fumbling spectacles over the rank crests of his ears. 'You're real,' he said.

'I'm not,' said Rossi indignantly. He added, 'Radishes. Lemons. Grapes. Blahhh!'

'Don't put me off,' said the old man. He was ragged and hollow-templed, like a bird skull, coloured like earth and milkweed floss, and his mouth was a drum over porcelain, but his oystery eyes were burning bright. 'I knew the minute I saw you – you're Rossi, the one that disappeared. If you can do that –' his teeth clacked – 'you must know, you've got to tell me. Those ships that have landed on the moon – what are they building there? What do they want?'

'I don't know. Nothing.'

'Please,' said the old man humbly. 'You can't be so cruel. I tried to warn people, but they've forgotten who I am. If you know: if you could just tell me …'

Rossi had a qualm, thinking of heat flashing down in that one intolerable blow that would leave the city squashed, glistening, as flat as the thin film of a bug. But remembering that, after all, the old man was not real, he said, 'There isn't anything. You made it up. You're dreaming.'

And then, while the pure tension gathered and strained inside him, came the lake of obsidian.

And the jungle, just as it ought to be – the brown people carolling, 'Hello, Mister Rossi, hello again, hello!'

And the savanna, the tall black-haired people reining in, breeze-blown, flash of teeth: 'Hillo, Misser Rossi!'

And the *beach*.

The scarlet beach with its golden, laughing people: 'Mista Rossi, Mista Rossi!' Heraldic glory under the clear sky, and out past the breakers the clear heart-stirring glint of sun on the sea: and the tension of the longing breaking free (stop), no need for symbols now (stop), a lifetime's distillation of *I wish* … spurting, channeled, done.

There he stands where he longed to be, wearing the same pleased expression, for ever caught at the beginning of a hello – Rossi, the first man to travel in Time, and Rossi, the first man to Stop.

He's not to be mocked or mourned. Rossi was born a stranger; there are thousands of him, unconsidered gritty particles in the gears of history: the ne'er-do-wells, the superfluous people, shaped for some world that has never yet been invented. The air-conditioned Utopias have no place for them; they would have been bad slaves and worse masters in Athens. As for the tropic isles – the Marquesas of 1800, or the Manhattan of 3256 – could Rossi swim a mile, dive six fathoms, climb a fifty-foot palm? If he had stepped alive onto that scarlet shore, would the young men have had him in their canoes, or the maidens in their bowers? But see him now, stonily immortal, the symbol of a wonderful thing that happened. The child-like golden people visit him every day, except when they forget. They drape his rock-hard flesh with garlands and lay little offerings at his feet; and when he lets it rain, they thump him.

CABIN BOY

I

The cabin boy's name was unspeakable, and even its meaning would be diffi-cult to convey in any human tongue. For convenience, we may as well call him Tommy Loy.

Please bear in mind that all these terms are approximations. Tommy was not exactly a cabin boy, and even the spaceship he served was not exactly a spaceship, nor was the Captain exactly a captain. But if you think of Tommy as a freckled, scowling, red-haired, wilful, prank-playing, thoroughly abhor-rent brat, and of the Captain as a crusty, ponderous old man, you may be able to understand their relationship.

A word about Tommy will serve to explain why these approximations have to be made, and just how much they mean. Tommy, to a human being, would have looked like a six-foot egg made of greenish gelatin. Suspended in this were cer-tain dark or radiant shapes which were Tommy's nerve centres and digestive organs, and scattered about its surface were star-shaped and oval markings which were his sensory organs and gripping mechanisms – his 'hands'. At the lesser end was an orifice which expelled a stream of glowing vapour – Tommy's means of propulsion. It should be clear that if instead of saying, 'Tommy ate his lunch', or, 'Tommy said to the Captain …' we reported what really happened, some pretty complicated explanations would have to be made.

Similarly, the term 'cabin boy' is used because it is the closest in human meaning. Some vocations, like seafaring, are so demanding and so complex that they simply cannot be taught in classrooms; they have to be lived. A cabin boy is one who is learning such a vocation and paying for his instruc-tion by performing certain menial, degrading, and unimportant tasks.

That describes Tommy, with one more similarity – the cabin boy of the sailing vessel was traditionally occupied after each whipping with preparing the mischief, or the stupidity, that earned him the next one.

Tommy, at the moment, had a whipping coming to him and was fighting a delaying action. He knew he couldn't escape eventual punishment, but he planned to hold it off as long as he could.

Floating alertly in one of the innumerable corridors of the ship, he watched as a dark wave sprang into being upon the glowing corridor wall and sped

155

toward him. Instantly, Tommy was moving away from it, and at the same rate of speed.

The wave rumbled: 'Tommy! Tommy Loy! Where *is* that obscenity boy?'

The wave moved on, rumbling wordlessly, and Tommy moved with it. Ahead of him was another wave, and another beyond that, and it was the same throughout all the corridors of the ship. Abruptly the waves reversed their direction. So did Tommy, barely in time. The waves not only carried the Captain's orders but scanned every corridor and compartment of the ten-mile ship. But as long as Tommy kept between the waves, the Captain could not see him.

The trouble was that Tommy could not keep this up for ever, and he was being searched for by other lowly members of the crew. It took a long time to traverse all of those winding, interlaced passages, but it was a mathematical certainty that he would be caught eventually.

Tommy shuddered, and at the same time he squirmed with delight. He had interrupted the Old Man's sleep by a stench of a particularly noisome variety, one of which he had only lately found himself capable. The effect had been beautiful. In human terms, since Tommy's race communicated by odours, it was equivalent to setting off a firecracker beside a sleeper's ear.

Judging by the jerkiness of the scanning waves' motion, the Old Man was still unnerved.

'Tommy!' the wave rumbled. 'Come out, you little piece of filth, or I'll smash you into a thousand separate stinks! By Spore, when I get hold of you—'

The corridor intersected another at this point, and Tommy seized his chance to duck into the new one. He had been working his way outward ever since his crime, knowing that the search parties would do the same. When he reached the outermost level of the ship, there would be a slight possibility of slipping back past the hunters – not much of a chance, but better than none.

He kept close to the wall. He was the smallest member of the crew – smaller than any of the other cabin boys, and less than half the size of an Ordinary; it was always possible that when he sighted one of the search party, he could get away before the crewman saw him. He was in a short connecting corridor now, but the scanning waves cycled endlessly, always turning back before he could escape into the next corridor. Tommy followed their movement patiently, while he listened to the torrent of abuse that poured from them. He snickered to himself. When the Old Man was angry, everybody suffered. The ship would be stinking from stem to stern by now.

Eventually the Captain forgot himself and the waves flowed on around the next intersection. Tommy moved on. He was getting close to his goal by now; he could see a faint gleam of starshine up at the end of the corridor.

The next turn took him into it – and what Tommy saw through the semi-transparent skin of the ship nearly made him falter and be caught. Not merely the fiery pinpoints of stars shone there, but a great, furious glow which could only mean that they were passing through a star system. It was the first time this had happened in Tommy's life, but of course it was nothing to the Captain, or even to most of the Ordinaries. Trust them, Tommy thought resentfully, to say nothing to him about it!

Now he knew he was glad he'd tossed that surprise at the Captain. If he hadn't, he wouldn't be here, and if he weren't here …

A waste capsule was bumping automatically along the corridor, heading for one of the exit pores in the hull. Tommy let it catch up to him, then englobed it, but it stretched him so tight that he could barely hold it. That was all to the good; the Captain wouldn't be likely to notice that anything had happened.

The hull was sealed, not to keep atmosphere inside, for there was none except by accident, but to prevent loss of liquid by evaporation. Metals and other mineral elements were replaceable; liquids and their constituents, in ordinary circumstances, were not.

Tommy rode the capsule to the exit sphincter, squeezed through, and instantly released it. Being polarized away from the ship's core, it shot into space and was lost. Tommy hugged the outer surface of the hull and gazed at the astonishing panorama that surrounded him.

There was the enormous black half-globe of space – Tommy's sky, the only one he had ever known. It was sprinkled with the familiar yet always changing patterns of the stars. By themselves, these were marvels enough for a child whose normal universe was one of ninety-foot corridors and chambers measuring, at most, three times as much. But Tommy hardly noticed them. Down to his right, reflecting brilliantly from the long, gentle curve of the greenish hull, was a blazing yellow-white glory that he could hardly look at. A star, the first one he had ever seen close at hand. Off to the left was a tiny, milky-blue disk that could only be a planet.

Tommy let go a shout, for the sheer pleasure of its thin, hollow smell. He watched the thin mist of particles spread lazily away from his body, faintly luminous against the jet blackness. He shivered a little, thickening his skin as much as he could. He could not stay long, he knew; he was radiating heat faster than he could absorb it from the sun or the ship's hull.

But he didn't want to go back inside, and not only because it meant being caught and punished. He didn't want to leave that great, dazzling jewel in the sky. For an instant he thought vaguely of the future time when he would be grown, the master of his own vessel, and could see the stars whenever he chose; but the picture was too far away to have any reality. Great Spore, that wouldn't happen for twenty thousand years!

Fifty yards away, an enormous dark spot on the hull, one of the ship's vision devices, swelled and darkened. Tommy looked up with interest. He could see nothing in that direction, but evidently the Captain had spotted something. Tommy watched and waited, growing colder every second, and after a long time he saw a new pinpoint of light spring into being. It grew steadily larger, turned fuzzy at one side, then became two linked dots, one hard and bright, the other misty.

Tommy looked down with sudden understanding, and saw that another wide area of the ship's hull was swollen and protruding. This one showed a pale colour under the green and had a dark ring around it: it was a polarizer. The object he had seen must contain metal, and the Captain was bringing it in for fuel. Tommy hoped it was a big one; they had been short of metal every since he could remember.

When he glanced up again, the object was much larger. He could see now that the bright part was hard and smooth, reflecting the light of the nearby sun. The misty part was a puzzler. It looked like a crewman's voice, seen against space – or the ion trail of ship in motion. But was it possible for metal to be alive?

II

Leo Roget stared into the rearview scanner and wiped beads of sweat from his brown, half-bald scalp. Flaming gas from the jets washed up toward him along the hull; he couldn't see much. But the huge dark ovoid they were headed for was still there, and it was getting bigger. He glanced futilely at the control board. The throttle was on full. They were going to crash in a little more than two minutes, and there didn't seem to be a single thing he could do about it.

He looked at Frances McMenamin, strapped into the acceleration harness beside his own. She said, 'Try cutting off the jets, why don't you?'

Roget was a short, muscular man with thinning straight black hair and sharp brown eyes. McMenamin was slender and ash-blonde, half an inch taller than he was, with one of those pale, exquisitely shaped faces that seem to be distributed equally among the very stupid and the very bright. Roget had never been perfectly sure which she was, although they had been companions for more than three years. That, in a way, was part of the reason they had taken this wild trip: she had made Roget uneasy, and he wanted to break away, and at the same time he didn't. So he had fallen in with her idea of a trip to Mars – 'to get off by ourselves and think' – and here, Roget thought, they were, not thinking particularly.

He said, 'You want us to crash quicker?'

'How do you know we will?' she countered. 'It's the only thing we haven't tried. Anyhow, we'd be able to see where we're going, and that's more than we can do now.'

'All right,' said Roget, 'all *right*.' She was perfectly capable of giving him six more reasons, each screwier than the last, and then turning out to be right.

He pulled the throttle back to zero, and the half-heard, half-felt roar of the jets died.

The ship jerked backward suddenly, yanking them against the couch straps, and then slowed.

Roget looked into the scanner again. They were approaching the huge object, whatever it was, at about the same rate as before. Maybe, he admitted unwillingly, a little slower. Damn the woman! How could she possibly have figured that one out in advance?

'And,' McMenamin added reasonably, 'we'll save fuel for the takeoff.'

Roget scowled at her. 'If there is a takeoff,' he said. 'Whatever is pulling us down there isn't doing it to show off. What do we do – tell them that was a very impressive trick and we enjoyed it, but we've got to be leaving now?'

'We'll find out what's doing it,' said McMenamin, 'and stop it if we can. If we can't, the fuel won't do us any good anyway.'

That was, if not Frances' most exasperating trick, at least high on the list. She had a habit of introducing your own argument as if it were not only a telling point on her side, but something you had been too dense to see. Arguing with her was like swinging at someone who abruptly disappeared and then sandbagged you from behind.

Roget was fuming, but he said nothing. The greenish surface below was approaching more and more slowly, and now he felt a slight but definite tightening of the couch straps that could only mean deceleration. They were being manoeuvred in for a landing as carefully and efficiently as if they were doing it themselves.

A few seconds later, a green horizon line appeared in the direct-view ports, and they touched. Roget's and McMenamin's couches swung on their gimbals as the ship tilted slowly, bounced and came to rest.

Frances reached inside the wide collar of her pressure suit to smooth a ruffle that had got crumpled between the volcanic swell of her bosom and the front of the transparent suit. Watching her, Roget felt a sudden irrational flow of affection and – as usually happened – a simultaneous notification that his body disagreed with his mind's opinion of her. This trip, it had been tacitly agreed, was to be a kind of final trial period. At the end of it, either they would split up or decide to make it permanent, and up to now, Roget had been silently determined that it was going to be a split. Now he was just as sure that, providing they ever got to Mars or back to Earth, he was going to nail her for good.

He glanced at her face. She knew, all right, just as she'd known when he'd felt the other way. It should have irritated him, but he felt oddly pleased and comforted. He unstrapped himself, fastened down his helmet and moved toward the airlock.

He stood on a pale-green, almost featureless surface that curved gently away in every direction. Where he stood, it was brilliantly lighted by the sun, and his shadow was sharp and as black as space. About two-thirds of the way to the horizon, looking across the short axis of the ship, the sunlight stopped with knife-edge sharpness, and he could make out the rest only as a ghostly reflection of starlight.

Their ship was lying on its side, with the pointed stern apparently sunk a few inches into the green surface of the alien ship. He took a cautious step in that direction, and nearly floated past it before he could catch himself. His boot magnets had failed to grip. The metal of this hull – if it *was* metal – must be something that contained no iron.

The green hull was shot through with other colours here, and it rose in a curious, almost rectangular mound. At the centre, just at the tip of the earth vessel's jets, there was a pale area; around that was a dark ring which lapped up over the side of the ship. He bent to examine it. It was in shadow, and he used his helmet light.

The light shone through the mottled green substance; he could see the skin of his own ship. It was pitted, corroding. As he watched, another pin-point of corruption appeared on the shiny surface, and slowly grew.

Roget straightened up with an exclamation. His helmet phones asked, 'What is it, Leo?'

He said, 'Acid or something eating the hull. Wait a minute.' He looked again at the pale and dark mottlings under the green surface. The centre area was not attacking the ship's metal; that might be the muzzle of whatever instrument had been used to pull them down out of their orbit and hold them there. But if it was turned off now … He had to get the ship away from the dark ring that was destroying it.

He couldn't fire the jets otherwise, because they were half buried; he'd blow the tubes if he tried.

He said, 'You still strapped in?'

'Yes.'

'All right, hold on.' He stepped back to the centre of the little ship, braced his corrugated boot soles against the hard green surface, and shoved.

The ship rolled. But it rolled like a top, around the axis of its pointed end. The dark area gave way before it, as if it were jelly-soft. The jets still pointed to the middle of the pale area, and the dark ring still lapped over them. Roget moved farther down and tried again, with the same result. The ship would move freely in every direction but the right one. The attracting power, clearly enough, was still on.

He straightened dejectedly and looked around. A few hundred yards away, he saw something he had noticed before, without attaching any significance to it; a six-foot egg, of some lighter, more translucent substance than the one on which it lay. He leaped toward it. It moved sluggishly away, trailing a cloud of luminous gas. A few seconds later he had it between his gloved hands. It squirmed, then ejected a thin spurt of vapour from its forward end. It was alive.

McMenamin's head was silhouetted in one of the forward ports. He said, 'See this?'

'Yes! What is it?'

'One of the crew, I think. I'm going to bring it in. You work the airlock – it won't hold both of us at once.'

'... All right.'

The huge egg crowded the cabin uncomfortably. It was pressed up against the rear wall, where it had rolled as soon as Frances had pulled it into the ship. The two human beings stood at the other side of the room, against the control panel, and watched it.

'No features,' said Roget, 'unless you count those markings on the surface. This thing isn't from anywhere in the solar system, Frances – it isn't even any order of evolution we ever heard of.'

'I know,' she said abstractedly. 'Leo, is he wearing any protection against space that you can see?'

'No,' said Roget. 'That's *him*, not a spacesuit. Look, you can see halfway into him. But—'

Frances turned to look at him. 'That's it,' she said. 'It means this is his natural element – space!'

Roget looked thoughtfully at the egg. 'It makes sense,' he said. 'He's adapted for it, anyhow – ovoid, for a high volume-to-surface ratio. Tough outer shell. Moves by jet propulsion. It's hard to believe, because we've never run into a creature like him before, but I don't see why not. On earth there are organisms, plants, that can live and reproduce in boiling water, and others that can stand near-zero temperatures.'

'He's a plant, too, you know,' Frances put in.

Roget stared at her, then back at the egg. 'That colour, you mean? Chlorophyll. It could be.'

'Must be,' she corrected firmly. 'How else would he live in a vacuum?' And then, distressedly, 'Oh, what a smell!'

They looked at each other. It *had* been something monumental in the way of smells, though it had only lasted a fraction of a second. There had been a series of separate odours, all unfamiliar and all overpoweringly strong. At least a dozen of them, Roget thought; they had gone past too quickly to count.

'He did it before, outside, and I saw the vapour.' He closed his helmet abruptly and motioned McMenamin to do the same. She frowned and shook her head. He opened his helmet again. 'It might be poisonous!'

'I don't think so,' said McMenamin. 'Anyway, we've got to try something.'

She walked toward the green egg. It rolled away from her, and she went past it into the bedroom.

In a minute she reappeared, carrying an armload of plastic boxes and bottles. She came back to Roget and knelt on the floor, lining up the containers with their nipples toward the egg.

'What's this for?' Roget demanded. 'Listen, we've got to figure some way of getting out of here. The ship's being eaten up—'

'Wait,' said McMenamin. She reached down and squeezed three of the nipples quickly, one after the other. There was a tiny spray of face powder, then one of cologne (*Nuit Jupitérienne*), followed by a jet of good Scotch.

Then she waited. Roget was about to open his mouth when another blast of unfamiliar odours came from the egg. This time there were only three: two sweet ones and one sharp.

McMenamin smiled. 'I'm going to name him Stinky,' she said. She pressed the nipples again, in a different order. Scotch, face powder, *Nuit Jupitérienne*. The egg replied: sharp, sweet, sweet.

She gave him the remaining combination, and he echoed it; then she put a record cylinder on the floor and squirted the face powder. She added another cylinder and squeezed the cologne. She went along the line that way, releasing a smell for each cylinder until there were ten. The egg had responded, recognizably in some cases, to each one. Then she took away seven of the cylinders and looked expectantly at the egg.

The egg released a sharp odour.

'If ever we tell anybody,' said Roget in an awed tone, 'that you taught a six-foot Easter egg to count to ten by selective flatulence—'

'Hush, fool,' she said. 'This is a tough one.'

She lined up three cylinders, waited for the sharp odour, then added six more to make three rows of three. The egg obliged with a penetrating smell which was a good imitation of citron extract, Frances' number nine. He followed it immediately with another of his own rapid, complicated series of smells.

'He gets it,' said McMenamin. 'I think he just told us that three times three are nine.' She stood up. 'You go out first, Leo. I'll put him out after you and then follow. There's something more we've got to show him before we let him go.'

Roget followed orders. When the egg came out and kept on going, he stepped in its path and held it back. Then he moved away, hoping the thing would get the idea that they weren't trying to force it but wanted it to stay. The egg wobbled indecisively for a moment and then stayed where it was. Frances came out the next minute, carrying one of the plastic boxes and a flashlight.

'My nicest powder,' she said regretfully, 'but it was the only thing I could find enough of.' She clapped her gloved hands together sharply, with the box between them. It burst, and a haze of particles spread around them, glowing faintly in the sunlight.

The egg was still waiting, somehow giving the impression that it was watching them alertly. McMenamin flicked on the flashlight and pointed it at Roget. It made a clear, narrow path in the haze of dispersed particles. Then she turned it on herself, on the ship, and finally upward, toward the tiny blue disk that was Earth. She did it twice more, then stepped back toward the airlock, and Roget followed her.

They stood watching as Tommy scurried off across the hull, squeezed himself into it and disappeared.

'That was impressive,' Roget said. 'But I wonder just how much good it's going to do us.'

'He knows we're alive, intelligent, friendly, and that we come from Earth,' said McMenamin thoughtfully. 'Or, anyhow, we did our best to tell him. That's all we can do. Maybe he won't want to help us; maybe he can't. But it's up to him now.'

III

The mental state of Tommy, as he dived through the hull of the ship and into the nearest radial corridor, would be difficult to describe fully to any human being. He was the equivalent of a very small boy – that approximation still holds good – and he had the obvious reactions to novelty and adventure. But there was a good deal more. He had seen living, intelligent beings of an unfamiliar shape and substance, who lived in metal and had some connection with one of those enormous, enigmatic ships called planets, which no captain of his own race dared approach.

And yet Tommy *knew*, with all the weight of knowledge accumulated, conified and transmitted over a span measured in billions of years, that there was no other intelligent race than his own in the entire universe, that metal, though life-giving, could not itself be alive, and that no living creature, having the ill luck to be spawned aboard a planet, could ever hope to escape so tremendous a gravitational field.

The final result of all this was that Tommy desperately wanted to go somewhere by himself and think. But he couldn't; he had to keep moving, in time with the scanning waves along the corridor, and he had to give all his mental energy to the problem of slipping past the search party.

The question was – how long had he been gone? If they had reached the hull while he was inside the metal thing, they might have looked for him outside and concluded that he had somehow slipped past them, back to the centre of the ship. In that case, they would probably be working their way back, and he had only to follow them to the axis and hide in a chamber as soon as they left it. But if they were still working outward, his chances of escape were almost nil. And now it seemed more important to escape than it had before.

There was one possibility which Tommy, who, in most circumstances, would try anything, hated to think about. Fuel lines – tubes carrying the rushing, radiant ion vapour that powered the ship – adjoined many of these corridors, and it was certain that if he dared to enter one, he would be perfectly safe from detection as long as he remained in it. But, for one thing, these lines radiated from the ship's axis and none of them would take him where he wanted to go. For another, they were the most dangerous places aboard ship. Older crew members sometimes entered them to make emergency repairs, but they got out as quickly as they could. Tommy did not know how long he could survive there; he had an unpleasant conviction that it would not be long.

Only a few yards up the corridor was the sealed sphincter which gave entrance to such a tube. Tommy looked at it indecisively as the motion of the scanning waves brought him nearer. He had still not made up his mind when he caught a flicker reflected around the curve of the corridor behind him.

Tommy squeezed himself closer to the wall and watched the other end of the corridor approach with agonizing slowness. If he could only get around that corner …

The flicker of motion was repeated, and then he saw a thin rind of green poke into view. There was no more time to consider entering the fuel line, no time to let the scanning waves' movement carry him around the corner. Tommy put on full speed, cutting across the next wave and down the cross-corridor ahead.

Instantly the Captain's voice shouted from the wall, 'Ah! Was that him, the dirty scut? After him, lads!'

Tommy glanced behind as he turned another corner, and his heart sank. It was no cabin boy who was behind him, or even an Ordinary, but a Third Mate – so huge that he filled nearly half the width of the corridor, and so powerful that Tommy, in comparison, was like a boy on a bicycle racing an express train.

He turned another corner, realizing in that instant that he was as good as caught: the new corridor ahead of him stretched straight and without a break for three hundred yards. As he flashed down it, the hulk of the Mate appeared around the bend behind.

The Mate was coming up with terrifying speed, and Tommy had time for only one last desperate burst. Then the other body slammed with stunning force against his, and he was held fast.

As they coasted to a halt, the Captain's voice rumbled from the wall. '*That's it, Mister. Hold him where I can see him!*'

The scanning areas were stationary now. The Mate moved Tommy forward until he was squarely in range of the nearest.

Tommy squirmed futilely. The Captain said, '*There's* our little jokester. It's a pure pleasure to see you again, Tommy. What – no witty remarks? Your humour all dried up?'

Tommy gasped, 'Hope you enjoyed your nap, Captain.'

'Very good,' said the Captain with heavy sarcasm. 'Oh *very* entertaining, Tommy. Now would you have anything more to say, before I put the whips to you?'

Tommy was silent.

The Captain said to the Mate, 'Nice work, Mister. You'll get extra rations for this.'

The Mate spoke for the first time, and Tommy recognized his high, affected voice. It was George Adkins, who had recently spored and was so proud of the new life inside his body that there was no living with him. George said prissily, 'Thank you, sir, I'm sure. Of course, I really shouldn't have exerted myself the way I just did, in my state.'

'Well, you'll be compensated for it,' the Captain said testily. 'Now take the humorist down to Assembly Five. We'll have a little ceremony there.'

'Yes, sir,' said the Mate distantly. He moved off, shoving Tommy ahead of him, and dived into the first turning that led downward.

They moved along in silence for the better part of a mile, crossing from one lesser passage to another until they reached a main artery that led directly to the centre of the ship. The scanning waves were still stationary, and they were moving so swiftly that there was no danger of being overheard.

Tommy said politely, 'You won't let them be too hard on me, will you, sir?'

The Mate did not reply for a moment. He had been baited by Tommy's mock courtesy before, and he was as wary as his limited intelligence allowed. Finally he said, 'You'll get no more than what's coming to you, young Tom.'

'Yes, sir. I know that, sir. I'm sorry I made you exert yourself, sir, in your condition and all.'

'You should be,' said the Mate stiffly, but his voice betrayed his pleasure. It was seldom enough that even a cabin boy showed a decent interest in the Mate's prospective parenthood. 'They're moving about, you know,' he added, unbending a little.

'Are they, sir? Oh, you must be careful of yourself, sir. How many are there, please, sir?'

'Twenty-eight,' said the Mate, as he had on every possible occasion for the past two weeks. 'Strong and healthy – so far.'

'That's remarkable, sir!' cried Tommy. 'Twenty-eight! If I might be so bold, sir, you ought to be careful of what you eat. Is the Captain going to give you your extra rations out of that mass he just brought in topside, sir?'

'I'm sure *I* don't know.'

'Gosh!' exclaimed Tommy. 'I wish I could be sure ...'

He let the pause grow. Finally the Mate said querulously, 'What do you mean? Is there anything wrong with the metal?'

'I don't really know, sir, but it isn't like any we ever had before. That is,' Tommy added, 'since I was spored, sir.'

'Naturally,' said the Mate. '*I*'ve eaten all kinds myself, you know.'

'Yes, sir. But doesn't it usually come in ragged shapes, sir, and darkish?'

'Of course it does. Everybody knows that. Metal is non-living, and only living things have regular shapes.'

'Yes, sir. But I was topside, sir, while I was trying to get away, and I saw this metal. It's quite regular, except for some knobs at one end, sir, and it's as smooth as you are, sir, and shiny. If you'll forgive me, sir, it didn't look at all appetizing to me.'

'Nonsense,' said the Mate uncertainly. 'Nonsense,' he repeated, in a stronger tone. 'You must have been mistaken. Metal can't be alive.'

'That's just what I thought, sir,' said Tommy excitedly. 'But there are live things in this metal, sir. I saw them. And metal wasn't just floating along the way it's supposed to, sir. I saw it when the Captain brought it down, and ... But I'm afraid you'll think I'm lying, sir, if I tell you what it was doing.'

'Well, what was it doing?'

'I swear I saw it, sir,' Tommy went on. 'The Captain will tell you the same thing, sir, if you ask him – he must have noticed.'

'Sterilize it all, what *was* it doing?'

Tommy lowered his voice. 'There was an ion trail shooting from it, sir. It was trying to get away!'

While the Mate was trying to absorb that, they reached the bottom of the corridor and entered the vast globular space of Assembly Five, lined with crewmen waiting to witness the punishment of Tommy Loy.

This was not going to be any fun at all, thought Tommy, but at least he had paid back the Third Mate in full measure. The Mate, for the moment, at any rate, was not taking any joy in his promised extra rations.

When it was over, Tommy huddled in a corner of the crew compartment where they had tossed him, bruised and smarting in every nerve, shaken by the beating he had undergone. The pain was still rolling through him in faint, uncontrollable waves, and he winced at each one, in spite of himself, as though it were the original blow.

In the back of his mind, the puzzle of the metal ship was still calling, but the other experience was too fresh, the remembered images too vivid.

The Captain had begun, as always, by reciting the Creed.

In the beginning was the Spore, and the Spore was alone. (And the crew: *Praised be the Spore!*)

Next there was light, and the light was good. Yea, good for the Spore and the Spore's First Children.

(*Praised be they!*)

But the light grew evil in the days of the Spore's Second Children.

(*Woe unto them!*)

And the light cast them out. Yea, exiled were they, into the darkness and the Great Deep.

(*Pity for the outcasts in the Great Deep!*)

Tommy had mumbled his responses with the rest of them, thinking rebellious thoughts. There was nothing evil about light; they lived by it still. What must have happened – the Captain himself admitted as much when he taught history and natural science classes – was that the earliest ancestors of the race, spawned in the flaming heart of the Galaxy, had grown too efficient for their own good.

They had specialized, more and more, in extracting energy from starlight and the random metal and other elements they encountered in space; and at last they absorbed, willy-nilly, more than they could use. So they had moved, gradually and naturally, over many generations, out from that intensely radiating region into the 'Great Deep' – the universe of thinly scattered stars. And the process had continued, inevitably; as the level of available energy fell, their absorption of it grew more and more efficient.

Now, not only could they never return to their birthplace, but they could not even approach a single sun as closely as some planets did. Therefore the planets, and the stars themselves, were objects of fear. That was natural and sensible. But why did they have to continue this silly ritual, invented by some half-evolved, superstitious ancestor, of 'outcasts' and 'evil'?

The Captain finished:

Save us from the Death that lies in the Great Deep …

(*The creeping Death that lies in the Great Deep!*)

And keep our minds pure …

(*As pure as the light in the days of the Spore, blessed be He!*)

And our course straight …

(*As straight as the light, brothers!*)

That we may meet our lost brothers again in the Day of Reuniting.

(*Speed that day!*)

Then the pause, the silence that grew until it was like the silence of space. At last the Captain spoke again, pronouncing judgment against Tommy, ending, 'Let him be whipped!'

Tommy tensed himself, thickening his skin, drawing his body into the smallest possible compass. Two husky Ordinaries seized him and tossed him at a third. As Tommy floated across the room, the crewman pressed himself tightly against the wall, drawing power from it until he could contain no more. And as Tommy neared him, he discharged it in a crackling arc that filled Tommy's body with the pure essense of pain, and sent him hurtling across the chamber to the next shock, and the next, and the next.

Until the Captain had boomed, 'Enough!' and they had carried him out and left him here alone.

He heard the voices of crewmen as they drew their rations. One of them was grumbling about the taste, and another, sounding happily bloated, was telling him to shut up and eat, that metal was metal.

That would be the new metal, however much of it had been absorbed by now, mingled with the old in the reservoir. Tommy wondered briefly how much of it there was, and whether the alien ship – if it *was* a ship – could repair even a little damage to itself. But that assumed life in the metal, and in spite of what he had seen, Tommy couldn't believe in it. It seemed beyond question, though, that there were living things inside the metal; and when the metal was gone, how would they live?

Tommy imagined himself set adrift from the ship, alone in space, radiating more heat than his tiny volume could absorb. He shuddered.

He thought again of the problem that had obsessed him ever since he had seen the alien, five-pointed creatures in the metal ship. Intelligent life was supposed to be sacred. That was part of the Creed, and it was stated in a sloppy, poetic way like the rest of it, but it made a certain kind of sense. No crewman or captain had the right to destroy another for his benefit, because the same heredity was in them all. They were all potentially the same, none better than another.

And you ate metal, because metal was nonliving and certainly not intelligent. But if that stopped being true …

Tommy felt he was missing something. Then he had it: In the alien ship, trying to talk to the creatures that lived in metal, he had been scared almost scentless – but underneath the fright and the excitement, he had felt wonderful. It had been, he realized suddenly, like the mystic completion that was supposed to come when all the straight lines met, in the 'Day of Reuniting' – when all the far-flung ships, parted for all the billions of years of their flight, came together at last. It was talking to someone different from yourself.

He wanted to talk again to the aliens, teach them to form their uncouth sounds into words, learn from them … Vague images swirled in his mind. They were products of an utterly different line of evolution. Who knew what they might be able to teach him?

And now the dilemma took shape. If his own ship absorbed the metal of theirs, they would die; therefore he would have to make the Captain let them go. But if he somehow managed to set them free, they would leave and he would never see them again.

A petty officer looked into the cubicle and said, 'All right, Loy, out of it. You're on garbage detail. You eat after you work, if there's anything left. Lively, now!'

Tommy moved thoughtfully out into the corridor, his pain almost forgotten. The philosophical problems presented by the alien ship, too, having no apparent solution, were receding from his mind. A new thought was taking their place, one that made him glow inside with the pure rapture of the devoted practical jokester.

The whipping he was certainly going to get – and, so soon after the last offence, it would be a beauty – scarcely entered his mind.

IV

Roget climbed in, opening his helmet, and sat down warily in the acceleration couch. He didn't look at the woman.

McMenamin said quietly, 'Bad?'

'Not good. The outer skin's gone all across that area, and it's eating into the lead sheathing. The tubes are holding up pretty well, but they'll be next.'

'We've done as much as we can, by rolling the ship around?'

'Just about. I'll keep at it, but I don't see how it can be more than a few hours before the tubes go. Then we're cooked, whatever your fragrant little friend does.'

He stood up abruptly and climbed over the slanting wall which was now their floor, to peer out the direct view port. He swore, slowly and bitterly. 'You try the radio again while I was out?' he asked.

'Yes.' She did not bother to add that there had been no response. Here, almost halfway between the orbits of earth and Mars, they were hopelessly out of touch. A ship as small as their couldn't carry equipment enough to bridge the distance.

Roget turned around, said, 'By God—' and then clenched his jaw and strode out of the room. McMenamin heard him walk through the bedroom and clatter around in the storage compartment behind.

In a few moments he was back with a welding torch in his hand. 'Should have thought of this before,' he said. 'I don't know what'll happen if I cut into that hull – damn thing may explode, for all I know – but it's better than sitting doing nothing.' He put his helmet down with a bang and his voice came tinnily in her helmet receiver. 'Be back in a minute.'

'Be careful,' McMenamin said again.

Roget closed the outer lock door behind him and looked at the ravished hull of the ship. The metal had been eaten away in a broad band all around the ship, just above the tail, as if a child had bitten around the small end of a pear. In places the clustered rocket tubes showed through. He felt a renewed surge of anger, with fear deep under it.

A hundred years ago, he reminded himself, the earliest space voyagers had encountered situations as bad as this one, maybe worse. But Roget was a city man, bred for city virtues. He didn't, he decided, know quite how to feel or act. What were you supposed to do when you were about to die, fifteen million miles from home? Try to calm McMenamin – who was dangerously calm already – or show your true nobility by making one of those deathbed speeches you read in the popular histories? What about suggesting a little suicide pact? There was nothing in the ship that would give them a cleaner death than the one ahead of them. About all he could do would be to stab Frances, then himself, with a screwdriver.

Her voice said in the earphones, 'You all right?'

He said, 'Sure. Just going to try it.' He lowered himself to the green surface, careful not to let his knees touch the dark, corrosive area. The torch was a small, easily manageable tool. He pointed the snout at the dark area where it lapped up over the hull, turned the switch on and pressed the button. Flame leaped out, washing over the dark surface. Roget felt the heat through his suit. He turned off the torch to see what effect it had had.

There was a deep, charred pit in the dark stuff, and it seemed to him that it had pulled back a little from the area it was attacking. It was more than he had expected. Encouraged, he tried again.

There was a sudden tremor under him and he leaped nervously to his feet, just in time to avoid the corrosive wave as it rolled under him. For a moment he was only conscious of the thick metal of his boot soles and the thinness of the fabric that covered his knees; then, as he was about to step back out of the way, he realized that it was not only the dark ring that had expanded, that was still expanding.

He moved jerkily – too late – as the pale centre area swept toward and under him. Then he felt as if he had been struck by a mighty hammer.

His ears rang, and there was a mist in front of his eyes. He blinked, tried to raise an arm. It seemed to be stuck fast at the wrist and elbow. Panicked, he tried to push himself away and couldn't. As his vision cleared, he saw that he was spreadeagled on the pale disk that had spread out under him. The metal collars of his wrist and elbow joints, all the metal parts of his suit, were held immovably. The torch lay a few inches away from his right hand.

For a few moments, incredulously, Roget still tried to move. Then he stopped and lay in the prison of his suit, looking at the greenish-cream surface under his helmet.

Frances' voice said abruptly, 'Leo, is anything wrong?'

Roget felt an instant relief that left him shaken and weak. His forehead was cold. He said after a moment, 'Pulled a damn fool trick, Frances. Come out and help me if you can.'

He heard a click as her helmet went down. He added anxiously, 'But don't come near the pale part, or you'll get caught too.'

After a while she said, 'Darling, I can't think of anything to do.'

Roget was feeling calmer, somehow not much afraid any more. He wondered how much oxygen was left in his suit, not more than an hour, he thought. He said, 'I know. I can't, either.'

Later he called, 'Frances?'

'Yes?'

'Roll the ship once in a while, will you? Might get through to the wiring or something, otherwise.'

'... All right.'

After that, they didn't talk. There was a great deal to be said, but it was too late to say it.

V

Tommy was on garbage detail with nine other unfortunates. It was a messy, hard, unpleasant business, fit only for a cabin boy – collecting waste from the compartment and corridor receptacles and pressing it into standard capsule shapes, then hauling it to the nearest polarizer. But Tommy, under the suspicious eye of the petty officer in charge, worked with an apparent total absorption until they had cleaned out their section of the six inmost levels and were well into the seventh.

This was the best strategic place for Tommy's departure, since it was about midway from axis to hull, and the field of operations of any pursuit was correspondingly broadened. Also, the volume in which they laboured had expanded wedgewise as they climbed, and the petty officer, though still determined to watch Tommy, could no longer keep him constantly in view.

Tommy saw the officer disappear around the curve of the corridor, and kept on working busily. He was still at it, with every appearance of innocence and industry, when the officer abruptly popped into sight again about three seconds later.

The officer stared at him with baffled disapproval and said unreasonably, 'Come on, come on, Loy. Don't slack.'

'Right,' said Tommy, and scurried faster.

A moment later Third Mate Adkinshove majestically into view. The petty officer turned respectfully to face him.

'Keeping young Tom well occupied, I see,' said the Mate.

'Yes, sir,' said the officer. 'Appears to be a reformed character, now, sir. Must have learned a lesson, one way or another.'

'Ha!' said the Mate. 'Very good. Oh, Loy, you might be interested in this – the Captain himself has told me that the new metal is perfectly all right. Unusually rich, in fact. I've had my first ration already – very good it was, too – and I'm going to get my extras in half an hour or so. Well, good appetite, all.' And, while the lesser crewmen clustered against the walls to give him room, he moved haughtily off down the corridor.

Tommy kept on working as fast as he could. He was draining energy he might need later, but it was necessary to quiet the petty officer's suspicions entirely, in order to give himself a decent start. In addition, his artist's soul demanded it. Tommy, in his own way, was a perfectionist.

Third Mate Adkins was due to get his extras in about half an hour, and if Tommy knew the Captain's habits, the Captain would be taking his first meal from the newly replenished reservoir at about the same time. That set the deadline. Before the half hour was up, Tommy would have to cut off the flow of the new metal, so that stomachs which had been gurgling in anticipation would remain desolately void until the next windfall.

The Mate, in spite of his hypochondria, was a glutton. With any luck, this would make him bitter for a month. And the Old Man – but it was better not to dwell on that.

The petty officer hung around irresolutely for another ten minutes, then dashed off down the corridor to attend to the rest of his detail. Without wasting a moment, Tommy dropped the capsule he had just collected and shot away in the other direction.

The rest of the cabin boys, as fearful of Tommy as they were of constituted authority, would not dare to raise an outcry until they spotted the officer coming back. The officer, because of the time he had wasted in watching Tommy, would have to administer a thorough lecture on slackness to the rest of the detail before he returned.

Tommy had calculated his probable margin to a nicety, and it was enough, barring accidents, to get him safely away. Nevertheless, he turned and twisted from one system of corridors to another, carefully confusing his trail, before he set himself to put as much vertical distance behind him as he could.

This part of the game had to be accomplished in a fury of action, for he was free to move in the corridors only until the Captain was informed that he was loose again. After that, he had to play hounds and hares with the moving strips through which the Captain could see him.

When the time he had estimated was three-quarters gone, Tommy slowed and came to a halt. He inspected the corridor wall minutely, and found the almost imperceptible trace that showed where the scanning wave nearest him had stopped. He jockeyed his body clear of it, and then waited. He still had a good distance to cover before he dared play his trump, but it was not safe to move now; he had to wait for the Captain's move.

It came soon enough: the scanning waves erupted into simultaneous motion and anger. 'Tommy!' they bellowed. 'Tommy Loy! Come back, you unmentionable excrescence, or by Spore you'll regret it! Tommy!'

Moving between waves, Tommy waited patiently until their motion carried him from one corridor to another. The Captain's control over the waves was not complete: in some corridors they moved two steps upward for one down, in others the reverse. When he got into a downward corridor, Tommy scrambled out of it again as soon as he could and started over.

Gradually, with many false starts, he worked his way up to the thirteenth level, one level short of the hull.

Now came the hard part. This time he had to enter the fuel lines, not only for sure escape, but to gather the force he needed. And for the first time in his life, Tommy hesitated before something that he had set himself to do.

Death was a phenomenon that normally touched each member of Tommy's race only once – only captains died, and they died alone. For lesser members of the crew, there was almost no mortal danger; the ship protected them. But Tommy knew what death was, and as the sealed entrance to the fuel line swung into view, he knew that he faced it.

He made himself small, as he had under the lash. He broke the seal. Quickly, before the following wave could catch him, he thrust himself through the sphincter.

The blast of ions gripped him, flung him forward, hurting him like a hundred whips. Desperately he held himself together, thickening his insulating shell against that deadly flux of energy; but still his body absorbed it, till he felt a horrid fullness.

The walls of the tube fled past him, barely perceptible in the rush of glowing haze. Tommy held in that growing tautness with his last strength, meanwhile looking for an exit. He neither knew nor cared whether he had reached his goal; he had to get out or die.

He saw a dim oval on the wall ahead, hurled himself at it, clung, and forced his body through.

He was in a horizontal corridor, just under the hull. He drank the blessed coolness of it for an instant, before moving to the nearest sphincter. Then he was out, under the velvet-black sky and the diamond blaze of stars.

He looked around. The pain was fading now; he felt only an atrocious bloatedness that tightened his skin and made all his movements halting. Forward of him, up the long shallow curve of the hull, he could see the alien ship, and the two five-pointed creatures beside it. Carefully, keeping a few feet between himself and the hull, he headed toward it.

One of the creatures was sprawled flat on the polarizer that had brought its ship down. The other, standing beside it, turned as Tommy came near, and two of its upper three points moved in an insane fashion that made Tommy feel ill. He looked away quickly and moved past them, till he was directly over the centre of the polarizer and only a few inches away.

Then, with a sob of relief, he released the energy his body had stored. In one thick, white bolt, it sparked to the polarizer's centre.

Shaken and spent, Tommy floated upward and surveyed what he had done. The muzzle of the polarizer was contracting, puckering at the centre, the dark corrosive ring following it in. So much energy, applied in one jolt, must have shorted and paralysed it all the way back to the ship's nerve centre. The Captain, Tommy thought wryly, would be jumping now!

And he wasn't done yet. Tommy took one last look at the aliens and their ship. The sprawled one was up, and the two of them had their upper points twined around each other in a nauseating fashion. Then they parted suddenly, and, facing Tommy, wiggled their free points. Tommy moved purposefully off across the width of the ship, heading for the three heavy-duty polarizers.

He had to go in again through that hell not once more, but twice. Though his nerves shrank from the necessity, there was no way of avoiding it. For the ship could not alter its course, except by allowing itself to be attracted by a sun or other large body – which was unthinkable – but it could rotate at the Captain's will. The aliens were free now, but the Captain had only to spin ship in order to snare them again.

Four miles away, Tommy found the second polarizer. He backed away a carefully calculated distance before he re-entered the hull. At least he could know in advance how far he had to go – and he knew now, too, that the energy he had stored the first time had been adequate twice over. He rested a few moments; then, like a diver plunging into a torrent, he thrust himself into the fuel line.

He came out again, shuddering with pain, and pushed himself through the exit. He felt as bloated as he had before. The charge of energy was not as great, but Tommy knew that he was weakening. This time, when he discharged over the polarizer and watched it contract into a tiny, puckered mass, he felt as if he could never move again, let alone expose himself once more to that tunnel of flame.

The stars, he realized dully, were moving in slow, ponderous arcs over his head. The Captain was spinning ship. Tommy sank to the hull and lay motionless, watching half attentively for a sight of the alien ship.

There it was, a bright dot haloed by the flame of its exhaust. It swung around slowly, gradually, with the rest of the firmament, growing smaller slowly.

'He'll get them before they're out of range,' Tommy thought. He watched as the bright dot climbed overhead, began to fall on the other side.

The Captain had one polarizer left. It would be enough.

Wearily Tommy rose and followed the bright star. It was not a joke any longer. He would willingly have gone inside to the bright, warm, familiar corridors that led downward to safety and deserved punishment. But somehow he could not bear to think of those fascinating creatures – those wonderful playthings – going to fill the Captain's fat belly.

Tommy followed the ship until he could see the pale gleam of the functioning polarizer. Then he crawled through the hull once more, and again he found a sealed entrance to the fuel tube. He did not let himself think about it. His mind was numb already, and he pushed himself through uncaring.

This time it was worse than ever before; he had not dreamed that it could be so bad. His vision dimmed and he could barely see the exit, or feel its pressure when he dragged himself out. Lurching drunkenly, he passed a scanning wave on his way to the hull sphincter, and heard the Captain's voice explode.

Outside, ragged black patches obscured his vision of the stars. The pressure inside him pressed painfully outward, again and again, and each time he held it back. Then he felt rather than saw that he was over the pale disk, and, as he let go the bolt, he lost consciousness.

When his vision cleared, the alien ship was still above him, alarmingly close. The Captain must have had it almost reeled in again, he thought, when he had let go that last charge.

Flaming, it receded into the Great Deep, and he watched it go until it disappeared.

He felt a great peace and a great weariness. The tiny blue disk that was a planet had moved its apparent position a little nearer its star. The aliens were going back there, to their unimaginable home, and Tommy's ship was forging onward into new depths of darkness – toward the edge of the Galaxy and the greatest Deep.

He moved to the nearest sphincter as the cold bit at him. His spirits lifted suddenly as he thought of those three stabs of energy, equally spaced around the twelve-mile perimeter of the ship. The Captain would be utterly speechless with rage, he thought, like an aged martinet who had had his hands painfully slapped by a small boy.

For, as we warned you, the Captain was not precisely a captain, nor the ship precisely a ship. Ship and captain were one and the same, hive and queen bee, castle and lord.

In effect, Tommy had circumnavigated the skipper.

THE LAST WORD

The first word, I like to think, was 'Ouch.' Some cave man, trying to knock a stone into better shape with another stone, slipped, hit his thumb – and there you are. Language.

I have an affection for these useless and unverifiable facts. Take the first dog. He, I feel sure, was an unusually clever but cowardly wolf, who managed to terrorize early man into throwing him a scrap. Early man himself was a terrible coward. Man and wolf discovered that they could hunt together, in their cowardly fashion, and there you are again. 'Domesticated animals'.

I admit that I was lax during the first few thousand years. By the time I realized that Man needed closer supervision, many of the crucial events had already taken place. I was then a young – well, let us say a young fallen angel. Had I been older and more experienced, history would have turned out very differently.

There was that time when I happened across a young Egyptian and his wife sitting on a stone near the bank of the Nile. They looked glum; the water was rising. A hungry jackal was not far away, and it crossed my mind that if I distracted the young people's attention for a few minutes, the jackal might surprise them.

'High enough for you?' I asked agreeably, pointing to the water.

They looked at me rather sharply. I had put on the appearance of a human being, as nearly as possible, but the illusion was no good without a large cloak, which was odd for the time of year.

The man said, 'If it never got any higher, it would suit me.'

'Why, I'm surprised to hear you say that,' I replied. 'If the river didn't rise, your fields wouldn't be so fertile – isn't that right?'

'True,' said the man, 'but also if it didn't rise, my fields would still be my fields.' He showed me where the water was carrying away his fences. 'Every year we argue over the boundaries, after the flood, and this year my neighbour has a cousin living with him. The cousin is a big, unnecessarily muscular man.' Broodingly, he began to draw lines in the dirt with a long stick.

These lines made me a little nervous. The Sumerians, up north, had recently discovered the art of writing, and I was still suffering from the shock.

'Well, life is a struggle,' I told the man soothingly. 'Eat or be eaten. Let the strong win, and the weak go to the wall.'

The man did not seem to be listening. 'If there was some way,' he said, staring at his marks, 'that we could keep tally of the fences, and put them back exactly the way they were before—'

'Nonsense,' I interrupted. 'You're a wicked boy to suggest such a thing. What would your old dad say? Whatever was good enough for him ...'

All this time, the woman had not spoken. Now she took the long stick out of the man's hand and examined it curiously. 'But why not?' she said, pointing to the lines in the dirt. The man had drawn an outline roughly like that of his fields, with the stone marking one corner.

It was at that moment that the jackal charged. He was gaunt and desperate, and his jaws were full of sharp yellow teeth.

With the stick she was holding, the woman hit him over the snout. The jackal ran away, howling piteously.

'Tut,' I said, taken aback. 'Life is struggle ...'

The woman said a rude word, and the man came at me with a certain light in his eye, so I went away. And do you know, when I came back after the next flood, they were measuring off the field with ropes and poles?

Cowardice again – that man did not want to argue about the boundaries with his neighbour's muscular cousin. Another lucky accident, and there you are. Geometry.

If only I had had the foresight to send a cave bear after the first man who showed that original, lamentable spark of curiosity ... Well, it was no use wishing. Not even I could turn the clock back.

Oh, I gained a few points as time went on. Instead of trying to suppress the inventive habit, I learned to direct it along useful lines. I was instrumental in teaching the Chinese how to make gunpowder. (Seventy-five parts saltpetre, thirteen parts brimstone, twelve parts charcoal, if you're interested. But the grinding and mixing are terribly difficult; they never would have worked it out by themselves.) When they used it only for fireworks, I didn't give up; I introduced it again in Europe. Patience was my long suit. I never took offence. When Luther threw an inkwell at me, I was not discouraged. I persevered.

I did not worry about my occasional setbacks; it was my successes that threatened to overthrow me. After each of my wars, there was an impulse that drew men closer together. Little groups fought each other until they formed bigger groups; then the big groups fought each other until there was only one left.

I had played this game out over and over, with the Egyptians, the Persians, the Greeks, and, in the end, I had destroyed every one. But I knew the danger. When the last two groups spanned the world between them, the last war might end in universal peace, because there would be no one left to fight.

My final war would have to be fought with weapons so devastating, so unprecedently awful, that man would never recover from it.

It was.

On the fifth day, riding the gale, I could look down on a planet stripped of its forests, its fields, even its topsoil: there was nothing left but the bare rock, cratered like the moon. The sky shed a sickly purple light, full of lightnings that flickered like serpents' tongues. Well, I had paid a heavy price, but Man was gone.

Not quite. There were two left, a man and a woman. I found them alive and healthy, for the time being, on a crag that overhung the radioactive ocean. They were inside a transparent dome, or field of force, that kept out the contaminated air.

You see how near I had come to final defeat? If they had managed to distribute that machine widely before my war started … But this was the only one they had made. And there they were inside it, like two white mice in a cage.

They recognized me immediately. The woman was young and comely, as they go.

'This is quite an ingenious device,' I told them courteously.

In actuality, it was an ugly thing, all wires and tubes and so on, packed layers deep under the floor, with a big semi-circular control board and a lot of flashing lights. 'It's a pity I didn't know about it earlier; we might have put it to some use.'

'Not this one,' said the man grimly. 'This is a machine for peace. Just incidentally, it generates a field that will keep out an atomic explosion.'

'Why do you say, "just incidentally"?' I asked him.

'It's only the way he talks,' the woman said. 'If you had held off another six months, we might have beaten you. But now I suppose you think you've won.'

'Oh, indeed,' I said. 'That is, I will have, before long. Meanwhile, we might as well make ourselves comfortable.'

They were standing in tense, aggressive attitudes in front of the control board, and took no notice of my suggestion. 'Why do you say I "think" I've won?' I asked.

'It's just the way I talk. Well, at least we gave you a long fight of it.'

The man put in, 'And now you're brave enough to show yourself.' He had a truculent jaw. There had been a good many like him in the assault planes, on the first day of the war.

'Oh,' I said, 'I've been here all the time.'

'From the very beginning?' the woman asked.

I bowed to her. 'Almost,' I said, to be strictly fair.

There was a little silence, one of those uncomfortable pauses that interrupt the best of talks. A tendril of glowing spray sprang up just outside. After a moment, the floor settled slightly.

The man and woman looked anxiously at their control board. The coloured lights were flashing. 'Is that the accumulators?' I heard the woman ask in a strained, low voice.

'No,' the man answered. 'They're all right – still charging. Give them another minute.'

The woman turned to me. I was glad of it, because there was something about their talk together that disturbed me. She said, 'Why couldn't you let things alone? Heaven knows we weren't perfect, but we weren't that bad. You didn't have to make us do that to each other.'

I smiled. The man said slowly, 'Peace would have poisoned him. He would have shrivelled up like a dried apple.' It was the truth, or near enough, and I did not contradict him. The floor lurched again.

'You're waiting to watch us suffer,' the woman said. 'Aren't you?'

I smiled.

'But that may take a long time. Even if we fall into the ocean, this globe will keep us alive. We might be in here for months before our food gives out.'

'I can wait,' I said pleasantly.

She turned to her husband. 'Then we *must* be the last,' she said. 'Don't you see? If we weren't, would he be here?'

'That's right,' said the man, with a note in his voice that I did not like. He bent over the control board. 'There's nothing more to keep us here. Ava, will you ...' He stepped back, indicating a large red-handled switch.

The woman stepped over and put her hand on it. 'One moment,' I said uneasily. 'What are you doing? What is that thing?'

She smiled at me. 'This isn't just a machine to generate a force field,' she said.

'No?' I asked. 'What else?'

'It's a time machine,' the man said.

'We're going back,' the woman whispered, 'to the beginning.'

Back, to the beginning, to start all over.

Without me.

The woman said, 'You've won Armageddon, but you've lost Earth.'

I knew the answer to that, of course, but she was a woman and had the last word.

I gestured toward the purple darkness outside. 'Lost Earth? What do you call this?'

She poised her hand on the switch.

'Hell,' she said.

And I have remembered her voice, through ten thousand lonely years.

IN DEEP

CONTENTS

Acknowledgments

'Four in One' published in *Galaxy Science Fiction*
Copyright © 1953, by Galaxy Publishing Corp.

'An Eye for a What?' published in *Galaxy Science Fiction*
Copyright © 1957, by Galaxy Publishing Corp.

'Stranger Station' published in *The Magazine of Fantasy and Science Fiction*
Copyright © 1956, by Fantasy House, Inc.

'Ask Me Anything' published in *Galaxy Science Fiction*
Copyright © 1951, by World Editions Inc.

'The Country of the Kind' published in *The Magazine of Fantasy and Science Fiction*
Copyright © 1955, by Fantasy House, Inc.

'Ticket to Anywhere' published in *Galaxy Science Fiction*
Copyright © 1952, by Galaxy Publishing Corp.

'Beachcomber' published in *Imagination*
Copyright © 1952, by Greenleaf Publishing Company

FOUR IN ONE

I

George Meister had once seen the nervous system of a man – a display specimen, achieved by coating the smallest of the fibers until they were coarse enough to be seen, then dissolving all the unwanted tissue and replacing it with clear plastic. A marvellous job; that fellow on Torkas III had done it – what was his name? At any rate: having seen the specimen, Meister knew approximately what he himself must look like at the present moment.

Of course, there were distortions: for example, he was almost certain that the neurons between his visual center and his eyes had produced themselves by at least thirty centimeters. Also, no doubt, the system as a whole was curled up and spread out rather oddly, since the musculature it had originally controlled was gone; and he had noticed certain other changes which might or might not be reflected by gross structural differences. The fact remained that he – all that he could still call *himself* – was nothing more than a brain, a pair of eyes, a spinal cord and a spray of neurons.

George closed his eyes for a second. It was a thing he had learned to do only recently, and he was proud of it. That first long period, when he had had no control whatever, had been very bad. He had decided later that the paralysis had been due to the lingering effects of some anaesthetic – the agent, whatever it was, that had kept him unconscious while his body was being— Well.

Either that, or the neuron branches had simply not yet knitted firmly in their new positions. Perhaps he could verify one or the other suppositions some future time. But at first, when he had only been able to see and not to move, knowing nothing beyond the moment when he had fallen face first into that mottled green and brown puddle of gelatin ... that had been upsetting.

He wondered how the others were taking it. There were others, he knew, because occasionally he would feel a sudden acute pain down where his legs belonged, and at the same instant the motion of the landscape would stop with a jerk. That could only be some other brain, trapped like his, trying to move their common body in another direction.

Usually the pain stopped immediately, and George could go on sending messages down to the nerve endings which had formerly belonged to his fingers and toes, and the gelatinous body would keep on creeping slowly forward. When the pains continued, there was nothing to do but to stop moving until the other brain quit – in which case George would feel like an unwilling passenger in a very slow vehicle – or try to alter his own movements to coincide, or at least produce a vector with the other brain's.

He wondered who else had fallen in – Vivian Bellis? Major Gumbs? Miss McCarty? Or all three of them? There ought to be some way of finding out.

He tried looking down once more, and was rewarded with a blurry view of a long, narrow strip of mottled green and brown, moving very slowly forward along the dry stream bed they had been crossing for the last hour or more. Twigs and shreds of dry vegetable matter were stuck to the dusty, translucent surface.

He was improving; the last time, he had only been able to see the thinnest possible edge of his new body.

When he looked up again, the far edge of the stream bed was perceptibly closer. There was a cluster of stiff-looking, dark-brown vegetable shoots just beyond, on the rocky shoulder; George was aiming slightly to the left of it. It had been a plant very much like the one that he'd been reaching for when he lost his balance and got himself into this condition. He might as well have a good look at it, anyhow.

The plant would probably turn out to be of little interest. It would be out of all reason to expect every new life form to be a startling novelty; and George was convinced that he had already stumbled into the most interesting organism on this planet.

Something *meisterii*, he thought. He had not settled on a species name – he would have to learn more about it before he decided – but *meisterii* certainly. It was his discovery, and nobody could take it away from him. Or – unhappily – him away from it.

It was a really lovely organism, though. Primitive – less structure of its own than a jellyfish, and only on a planet with light surface gravity, like this one, could it ever have hauled itself up out of the sea. No brain, no nervous system at all, apparently. But it had the perfect survival mechanism. It simply let its rivals develop highly organised nervous tissue, sat in one place (looking exactly like a deposit of leaves and other clutter) until one of them fell into it, and then took all the benefit.

It wasn't parasitism, either; it was a true symbiosis, on a higher level than any other planet, so far as George knew, had ever developed. The captive brain was nourished by the captor; wherefore it served the captive's interest to move the captor toward food and away from danger. *You steer me, I feed you*. It was fair.

They were close to the plant now, almost touching it. George inspected it; as he had thought, it was a common grass type, of no particular interest.

Now his body was tilting itself up a ridge he knew to be low, although from his eye level it looked tremendous. He climbed it laboriously and found himself looking down into still another gully. This could go on, no doubt, indefinitely. The question was, did he have any choice?

He looked at the shadows cast by the low-hanging sun. He was heading approximately northwest, or directly away from the encampment. He was only a few hundred meters away; even at a crawl, he could make the distance easily enough … if he turned back.

He felt uneasy at the thought, and didn't know why. Then it struck him that his appearance was not obviously that of a human being in distress; the chances were that he looked rather more like the monster which had eaten and partially digested one or more people.

If he crawled into camp in his present condition, it was a certainty that he would be shot at before any questions were asked, and only a minor possibility that narcotic gas would be used instead of a machine rifle.

No, he decided, he was on the right course. The idea was to get away from camp so that he wouldn't be found by the relief party which was probably searching for him now. Get away, bury himself in the forest and study his new body: find out how it worked and what he could do with it, whether there actually were others in it with him, and if so, if there was any way of opening communications with them.

It would take a long time, he thought, but he could do it.

Limply, like a puddle of mush oozing over the edge of a tablecloth, George started down into the gully.

The circumstances leading up to George's fall into the something *meisterii* were, briefly as follows:

Until as late as the mid-twenty-first century, a game invented by the ancient Japanese was still played by millions in the eastern hemisphere of Terra. The game was called *go*. Although its rules were almost childishly simple, its strategy included more permutations and was more difficult to master than that of chess.

Go was played, at the height of its development – just before the geological catastrophe that wiped out most of its devotees – on a board with nine hundred shallow holes, using small pill-shaped counters. At each turn, one of the two players placed a counter on the board, wherever he chose, the object being to capture as much territory as possible by surrounding it completely.

There were no other rules; and yet it had taken the Japanese almost a thousand years to work up to that thirty-by-thirty board, adding perhaps one rank and file per century. A hundred years was not too long to explore all the possibilities of that additional rank and file.

At the time George Meister fell in to the gelatinous green-and-brown monster, toward the end of the twenty-third century AD, a kind of *go* was being played in a three-dimensional field which contained more than ten billion positions. The galaxy was the board, the positions were star systems, men were the counters. The loser's penalty was annihilation.

The galaxy was in the process of being colonised by two opposing federations. In the early stages of this conflict, planets had been raided, bombs dropped, and a few battles had even been fought by fleets of spaceships. Later that haphazard sort of warfare became impossible. Robot fighters, carrying enough armament to blow each other into dust, were produced in trillions. In the space around the outer stars of a cluster belonging to one side or the other, they swarmed like minnows.

Within such a screen, planets were utterly safe from attack and from any interference with their commerce … unless the enemy succeeded in colonising enough of the circumambient star systems to set up and maintain a second screen outside the first. It was *go*, played for desperate stakes and under impossible conditions.

Everyone was in a hurry; everyone's ancestors for seven generations had been in a hurry. You got your education in a speeded-up, capsulised form. You mated early and bred frantically. And if you were assigned to an advance ecological team, as George was, you had to work without any decent preparation.

The sensible, the obvious thing to do in opening up a new planet with unknown life forms would have been to begin with at least ten years of immunological study conducted from the inside of a sealed station. After the worst bacteria and viruses had been licked, you might proceed to a little cautious field work and exploration. Finally – total elapsed time fifty years, say – the colonists would be shipped in.

There simply wasn't that much time.

Five hours after the landing, Meister's team had unloaded fabricators and set up barracks enough to house its two thousand, six hundred and twenty-eight members. An hour after that, Meister, Gumbs, Bellis and McCarty started out across the level cinder and ash left by the transport's tail jets to the nearest living vegetation, six hundred meters away. They were to trace a spiral path outward from the camp site to a distance of a thousand meters, and then return with their specimens – providing nothing too large and hungry to be stopped by a machine rifle had previously eaten them.

Meister, the biologist, was hung with collecting boxes to the point that his slender torso was totally invisible. Major Gumbs had a survival kit, binoculars and a machine rifle. Vivian Bellis, who knew exactly as much mineralogy as had been contained in the three-month course prescribed for her rating, and no more, carried a light rifle, a hammer and a specimen sack. Miss McCarty – no one knew her first name – had no scientific function. She was the group's Loyalty Monitor. She wore two squat pistols and a bandolier bristling with cartridges. Her only job was to blow the cranium off any team member caught using an unauthorised communicator, or in any other way behaving oddly.

All of them were heavily gloved and booted, and their heads were covered by globular helmets, sealed to their tunic collars. They breathed through filtered respirators, so finely meshed that – in theory – nothing larger than an oxygen molecule could get through.

On their second circuit of the camp, they had struck a low ridge and a series of short, steep gullies, most of them choked with the dusty-brown stalks of dead vegetation. As they started down into one of these, George, who was third in line – Gumbs leading, then Bellis, and McCarty behind George – stepped out onto a protruding slab of stone to examine a cluster of plant stalks rooted on its far side.

His weight was only a little more than twenty kilograms on this planet, and the slab looked as if it were firmly cemented into the wall of the gully. Just the same, he felt it shift under him as soon as his weight was fully on it. He felt himself falling, shouted, and caught a flashing glimpse of Gumbs and Bellis, standing as if caught by a high-speed camera. He heard a rattling of stones as he went by. Then he saw what looked like a shabby blanket of leaves and dirt floating toward him, and he remembered thinking, *It looks like a soft landing, anyhow* ... That was all, until he woke up feeling as if he had been prematurely buried, with no part of him alive but his eyes.

Much later, his frantic efforts to move had resulted in the first fractional success. From then on, his field of vision had moved fairly steadily forward, perhaps a meter in every fifty minutes, not counting the times when someone else's efforts had interfered with his own.

His conviction that nothing remained of the old George Meister except a nervous system was not supported by observation, but the evidence was regrettably strong. To begin with, the anaesthesia of the first hours had worn off, but his body was not reporting the position of the torso, head and four limbs he had formerly owned. He had, instead, a vague impression of being flattened and spread out over an enormous area. When he tried to move his fingers and toes, the response he got was so multiplied that he felt like a centipede. He had no sense of cramped muscles, such as would normally be expected after a long period of paralysis: and he was not breathing. Yet his brain was evidently being well supplied with food and oxygen; he felt clear-headed, at ease and healthy.

He wasn't hungry, either, although he had been using energy steadily for a long time. There were, he thought, two possible reasons for that, depending on how you looked at it ... one, that he wasn't hungry because he no longer had any stomach lining to contract; two, that he wasn't hungry because the organism he was riding in had been well nourished by the superfluous tissues George had contributed ...

Two hours later, when the sun was setting, it began to rain. George saw the big, slow-falling drops and felt their dull impacts on his 'skin.' He did not know whether rain would do him any damage or not, rather thought not, but crawled under a bush with large, fringed leaves just to be on the safe side. When the rain stopped it was dark, and he decided he might as well stay where he was until morning. He did not feel tired, and it occurred to him to wonder whether he still needed to sleep. He composed himself as well as he could to wait for the answer.

He was still wakeful after a long time had passed, but had made no progress toward deciding whether this answered the question or prevented it from being answered, when he saw a pair of dim lights coming slowly and erratically toward him.

George watched them with an attentiveness compounded of professional interest and apprehension. Gradually, as they came closer, he made out that the lights were attached to long, thin stalks which grew from an ambiguous shape below – either light organs, like those of some deep-sea fish, or simply luminescent eyes.

George noted a feeling of tension in himself which seemed to suggest that adrenalin or an equivalent was being released somewhere in his system. He promised himself to follow this lead at the first possible moment; meanwhile he had a more urgent problem to consider. Was this approaching organism the kind which the something *meisterii* ate, or the kind which devoured the something *meisterii*? If the latter, what would he do about it?

For the present, at any rate, sitting where he was seemed to be indicated. The body he inhabited made use of camouflage in its normal, and untenanted state, and was not equipped for speed. So George held still and watched, keeping his eyes half closed, while he considered the possible nature of the approaching animal.

The fact that it was nocturnal, he told himself, meant nothing. Moths were nocturnal; so were bats – no, the devil with bats, they were carnivores The light-bearing creature came nearer, and George saw the faint gleam of a pair of long, narrow eyes below the two stalks.

Then the creature opened its mouth.

It had a great many teeth.

George found himself crammed into some kind of crevice in a wall of rock, without any clear recollection of how he had got there. He remembered a flurry of branches as the creature sprang at him, and a moment's furious pain, and then nothing but vague, starlit glimpses of leaves and earth.

The thing was impossible. How had he got away?

He puzzled over it until dawn came, and then, looking down at himself, he saw something that had not been there before. Under the smooth edge of gelatinous flesh three or four projections of some kind were visible. It struck George that his sensation of contact with the stone underneath him had changed, too: he seemed to be standing on a number of tiny points instead of lying flat.

He flexed one of the projections experimentally, then thrust it out straight ahead of him. It was a lumpy, single-jointed caricature of a finger – or a leg.

George lay still for a long time and thought about it with as much coherence as he could muster. Then he waggled the thing again. It was there, and so were all the others, as solid and real as the rest of him.

He moved forward experimentally, sending the same messages down to his finger-and-toe nerve ends as before. His body lurched out of the cranny with a swiftness that very nearly tumbled him down over the edge of a minor precipice.

Where he had crawled like a snail before, he now scuttled like an insect.

But how … No doubt, in his terror when the thing with the teeth attacked, he had unconsciously tried to run as if he still had legs. Was that all there was to it?

George thought of the carnivore again, and of the stalks supporting the organs which he had thought might be eyes. That would do as an experiment. He closed his own eyes and imagined them rising outward, imagined the mobile stalks growing, growing … He tried to convince himself that he had eyes like that, had always had them – that everyone who was anyone had eyes on stalks.

Surely, something was happening?

George opened his eyes again, and found himself looking straight down at the ground, getting a view so close up that it was blurred, out of focus. Impatiently he tried to look up. All that happened was that his field of vision moved forward a matter of ten or twelve centimeters.

It was at this point that a voice shattered the stillness. It sounded like someone trying to shout through half a meter of lard. 'Urghh! Lluhh! *Eeraghh!*'

George leaped convulsively, executed a neat turn and swept his eyes around a good two hundred and forty degrees of arc. He saw nothing but rocks and lichens. On a closer inspection, it appeared that a small green-and-orange larva or grub of some kind was moving past him. George regarded it with suspicion for a long moment, until the voice broke out again:

'Ellfff! Ellfffneee!'

The voice, somewhat higher this time, came from behind.

George whirled again, swept his mobile eyes around

Around an impossible wide circuit. His eyes *were* on stalks, and they were mobile – whereas a moment ago he had been staring at the ground, unable to look up. George's brain clattered into high gear. He had grown stalks for his eyes, all right, but they'd been limp – just extensions of the jelly-like mass of his body, without a stiffening cell structure of muscular tissue to move them. Then, when the voice had startled him, he'd got the stiffening and the muscles in a hurry.

That must have been what had happened the previous night. Probably the process would have been completed, but much more slowly, if he hadn't been frightened. A protective mechanism, obviously. As for the voice—

George rotated once more, slowly, looking all around him. There was no question about it: he was alone. The voice, which had seemed to come from someone or something standing just behind him, must in fact have issued from his own body.

The voice started again, at a less frantic volume. It burbled a few times, then said quite clearly in a high tenor, 'Whass happen'? Wheh am I?'

George was floundering in a sea of bewilderment. He was in no condition to adapt quickly to more new circumstances, and when a large, desiccated lump fell from a nearby bush and bounced soundlessly to within a meter of him, he simply stared at it.

He looked at the hard-shelled object, and then at the laden bush from which it had dropped. Slowly, painfully, he worked his way through to a logical conclusion. The dried fruit had fallen without a sound. That was natural, because he had been totally deaf ever since his metamorphosis. But – he had heard a voice!

Ergo, hallucination, or telepathy.

The voice began again. 'Heelp. Oh, dear, I wish someone would answer!'

Vivian Bellis. Gumbs, even if he affected that tenor voice, wouldn't say, 'Oh, dear.' Neither would McCarty.

George's shaken nerves were returning to normal. He thought intently, *I get scared, grow legs. Bellis gets scared, grows a telepathic voice. That's reasonable, I guess – her first and only instinct would be to yell.*

George tried to put himself into a yelling mood. He shut his eyes and imagined himself cooped up in a terrifyingly alien medium, without any control or knowledge of his predicament. He tried to shout: 'Vivian!'

He kept on trying, while the girl's voice continued at intervals. Finally she stopped abruptly in the middle of a sentence. George said, 'Can you hear me?'

'Who's that – what do you want?'

'This is George Meister, Vivian. Can you understand what I'm saying?'

'What'

George kept at it. His pseudo-voice, he judged, was a little garbled, just as Bellis's had been at first. At least the girl said, 'Oh, George – I mean Mr Meister! Oh, I've been so frightened. Where are you?'

George explained, apparently not very tactfully, because Bellis shrieked when he was through and then went back to burbling. George sighed, and said, 'Is there anyone else on the premises? Major Gumbs? Miss McCarty?'

A few minutes later two sets of weird sounds began almost simultaneously. When they became coherent, it was no trouble to identify the voices. Gumbs, the big, red-faced professional soldier, shouted, 'Why the hell don't you watch where you're going, Meister? If you hadn't started that rock slide we wouldn't be in this mess!'

Miss McCarty, who had had a seamed white face, a jutting jaw, and eyes the color of mud, said coldly, 'Meister, all of this will be reported. *All* of it.'

It appeared that only Meister and Gumbs had kept the use of their eyes. All four of them had some muscular control, though Gumbs was the only one who had made any serious attempt to interfere with George's locomotion. Miss McCarty, not to George's surprise, had managed to retain a pair of functioning ears.

But Bellis had been blind, deaf and dumb all through the afternoon and night. The only terminal sense organs she had been able to use had been those of the skin – the perceptors of touch, heat and cold, and pain. She had heard nothing, seen nothing, but she had felt every leaf and stalk they had brushed against, the cold impact of every raindrop, and the pain of the toothy monster's bite. George's opinion of her went up several notches when he learned this. She had been terrified, but she hadn't been driven into hysteria or insanity.

It further appeared that nobody was doing any breathing, and nobody was aware of a heartbeat.

George would have liked nothing better than to continue this discussion, but the other three were united in believing that what had happened to them after they got in was of less importance than how they were going to get out.

'We can't get *out*,' said George. 'At least, I don't see any possibility of it in the present state of our knowledge. If we—'

'But we've got to get out!' said Vivian.

'We'll go back to camp,' said McCarty coldly. 'Immediately. And you'll explain to the Loyalty Committee why you didn't turn back as soon as you regained consciousness.'

'That's right,' Gumbs put in self-consciously. 'If you can't do anything, Meister, maybe the other technical fellows can.'

George patiently explained his theory of their probable reception by the guards at the camp. McCarty's keen mind detected a flaw. 'You grew legs, and stalks for your eyes, according to your own testimony. If you weren't lying, you can also grow a mouth. We'll announce ourselves as we approach.'

'That may not be easy,' George told her. 'We couldn't get along with just a mouth, we'd need teeth, tongue, hard and soft palates, lungs or the equivalent, vocal cords, and some kind of substitute for a diaphragm to power the whole business. I'm wondering if it's possible at all, because when Miss Bellis finally succeeded in making herself heard, it was by the method we're using now. She didn't—'

'You talk too much,' said McCarty. 'Major Gumbs, Miss Bellis, you and I will try to form a speaking apparatus. The first to succeed will receive a credit mark on his record. Commence.'

George, being left out of the contest by implication, used his time in trying to restore his hearing. It seemed to him likely that the whatever-it-was *meisterii* had some sort of division-of-labor principle built into it, since Gumbs and he – the first two to fall in – had kept their sight without making any special effort in that direction, while matters like hearing and touch had been left for the latecomers. This was fine in principle, and George approved of it, but he didn't like the idea of Miss McCarty's being the sole custodian of any part of the apparatus.

Even if he were able to persuade the other two to follow his lead – and at the moment this prospect seemed dim – McCarty was certain to be a holdout. And it might easily be vital to all of them, at some time in the near future, to have their hearing hooked into the circuit.

He was distracted at first by muttered comments between Gumbs and Vivian – 'Getting anywhere?' 'I don't think so. Are you?' – interspersed between yawps, humming sounds and other irritating noises as they tried unsuccessfully to switch over from mental to vocal communication. Finally McCarty snapped, 'Be quiet. Concentrate on forming the necessary organs – don't bray like jackasses.'

George settled down to his work, using the same technique he had found effective before. With his eyes shut, he imagined that the thing with all the teeth was approaching in darkness – tap, slither; tap; click. He wished valiantly for ears to catch the faint approaching sounds. After a long time he thought he was beginning to succeed – or were those mental sounds, unconsciously emitted by one of the other three? *Click. Slither. Swish. Scrape.*

George opened his eyes, genuinely alarmed. A hundred meters away, facing him across the shallow slope of rocky ground, was a uniformed man just emerging from a stand of black, bamboo like spears. As George raised his eye stalks, the man paused, stared back at him, then shouted and raised his rifle.

George ran. Instantly there was a babble of voices inside him, and the muscles of his 'legs' went into wild spasms. 'Run, dammit!' he said frantically. 'There's a trooper with—'

The rifle went off with a deafening roar, and George felt a sudden hideous pain aft of his spine. Vivian Bellis screamed.

The struggle for possession of their common legs stopped, and they scut-tled full speed ahead for the cover of a nearby boulder. The rifle roared again, and George heard rock splinters screeching through the foliage overhead. Then they were plunging down the side of a gully, up the other slope, over a low hummock and into a forest of tall, bare-limbed trees.

George spotted a leaf-filled hollow and headed for it, fighting somebody else's desire to keep on running in a straight line. They plopped into the hollow and stayed there while three running men went past them, and for an hour afterward.

Vivian was moaning steadily. Raising his eye stalks cautiously, George was able to see that several jagged splinters of stone had penetrated the monster's gelatinous flesh near the far rim … They had been very lucky. The shot had apparently been a near miss – accountable only on the grounds that the trooper had been shooting downhill at a moving target – and had shattered the boulder behind them.

Looking more closely, George observed something which excited his professional interest. The whole surface of the monster appeared to be in constant slow ferment: tiny pits opening and closing as if the flesh were boiling … except that here the bubbles of air were not forcing their way outward, but were being engulfed at the surface and pressed down into the interior.

He could also see, deep under the mottled surface of the huge lens-shaped body, four vague clots of darkness which must be the living brains of Gumbs, Bellis, McCarty – and Meister.

Yes, there was one which was radially opposite his own eye stalks. It was an odd thing, George reflected, to be looking at your own brain. No doubt you could get used to it in time.

The four dark spots were arranged close together in an almost perfect square at the center of the lens. The spinal cords, barely visible, crossed between them and rayed outward from the center.

Pattern, George thought. The thing was designed to make use of more than one nervous system. It arranged them in an orderly fashion, with the brains inward for greater protection – and perhaps for another reason. Perhaps there was even a provision for conscious cooperation among the passengers: a matrix that somehow promoted the growth of communication cells between separate brains … If that were so, it would account for their ready success with telepathy. George wished most acutely that he could get inside and find out.

Vivian's pain was diminishing. Hers was the brain opposite George's, and she had taken most of the effect of the rock splinters. But the fragments were sinking now, slowly, through the gelid substance of the monster's tissues. Watching carefully, George could see them move. When they got to the bottom, they would be excreted, no doubt – just as the indigestible parts of their clothing and equipment had been.

George wondered idly which of the remaining two brains was McCarty's and which Gumbs's. The answer was easy to find. To George's left, as he looked back toward the center of the mound, was a pair of blue eyes set flush with the surface. They had lids apparently grown from the monster's substance, but thickened and opaque.

To his right, George could make out two tiny openings, extending a few centimeters into the body, which could only be Miss McCarty's ears. George had an impulse to see if he could devise a method of dropping dirt into them.

Anyhow, the question of returning to camp had been settled, at least for the moment. McCarty said nothing more about growing a set of speech organs, although George was sure she herself was determined to keep on trying.

He didn't think she would succeed. Whatever the mechanism was by which these changes in bodily structure were accomplished, it seemed probable that amateurs like themselves could succeed only under the pressure of considerable emotional strain, and then only with comparatively simple tasks which involved one new structure at a time. And as he had already told McCarty, the speech organs in man were extraordinarily diverse and complicated.

It occurred to George that the thing just might be done by creating a thin membrane to serve as a diaphragm, and an air chamber behind it, with a set of muscles to produce the necessary vibrations and modulate them. He kept the notion to himself. He didn't want to go back. George was a rare bird: a scientist who was actually fitted for his work and loved it for its own sake. And at the moment he was sitting squarely in the middle of the most powerful research tool that had ever existed in his field: a protean organism, with the observer inside it, able to order its structure and watch the results; able to devise theories of function and test them on the tissues of what was effectively his own body – able to construct new organs, new adaptations to environment!

George saw himself at the point of an enormous cone of new knowledge; and some of the possibilities he glimpsed humbled and awed him.

He *couldn't* go back, even if it were possible to do it without getting killed. If only he had fallen into the damned thing alone No, then the others would have pulled him out and killed the monster.

There were, he felt, too many problems demanding solutions all at once. It was hard to concentrate; his mind kept slipping maddeningly out of focus.

Vivian, whose pain had stopped some time ago, began to wail again. Gumbs snapped at her. McCarty cursed both of them. George himself felt that he had had very nearly all he could take – cooped up with three idiots who had no more sense than to—

Wait a minute,' he said. 'Do you all feel the same way? Irritable? Jumpy? As if you'd been working for sixty hours straight and were too tired to sleep?'

'Stop talking like a video ad,' Vivian said angrily. 'Haven't we got enough trouble without—'

'We're hungry,' George interrupted. 'We didn't realise it, because we haven't got the organs that usually signal hunger. But the last thing this body ate was us, and that was at least twenty hours ago. We've got to find something to ingest.'

'Good Lord, you're right,' said Gumbs. 'But if this thing only eats people – I mean to say—'

'It never met any people until we landed,' George said curtly. 'Any protein should do, but the only way we can find out is to try. The sooner we start, the better.'

He started off in what he hoped was the direction they had been following all along – directly away from camp. At least, he thought, if they put enough distance behind them, they might get thoroughly lost.

II

They moved out of the trees and down the long slope of a valley, over a wiry carpet of dead grasses, until they reached a watercourse in which a thin trickle was still flowing. Far down the bank, partly screened by clumps of skeletal shrubbery, George saw a group of animals that looked vaguely like miniature pigs. He told the others about it, and started cautiously in that direction.

'Which way is the wind blowing, Vivian?' he asked. 'Can you feel it?'

She said, 'No. I could before, when we were going downhill, but now I think we're facing into it.'

'Good,' said George. 'We may be able to sneak up on them.'

'But – we're not going to eat *animals*, are we?'

'Yes, how about it, Meister?' Gumbs put in. 'I don't say I'm a squeamish fellow, but after all—'

George, who felt a little squeamish himself – like all the others, he had been brought up on a diet of yeasts and synthetic protein – said testily, 'What else can we do? You've got eyes – you can see it's autumn here. Autumn after a hot summer, at that. Trees bare, streams dried up. We eat meat, or go without – unless you'd rather hunt for insects?'

Gumbs, shocked to the core, muttered for a while and then gave up.

Seen at closer range, the animals looked less porcine and even less appetising than before. They had lean, segmented, pinkish-gray bodies, four short legs, flaring ears and blunt scimitar-like snouts with which they were rooting in the ground, occasionally turning up something which they gulped, ears flapping.

George counted thirty of them, grouped fairly closely in a little space of clear ground between the bushes and the river. They moved slowly, but their short legs looked powerful; he guessed that they could run when they had to.

He inched forward, keeping his eye stalks low, stopping instantly whenever one of the beasts looked up. Moving with increasing caution, he had got to within ten meters of the nearest when McCarty said abruptly:

'Meister, has it occurred to you to wonder just *how* we are going to eat these animals?'

'Don't be foolish,' he said irritably. 'We'll—' He stopped.

Wait a minute – did the thing's normal method of assimilation stop as soon as it got a tenant? Were they supposed to grow fangs and a gullet and all the rest of the apparatus? Impossible; they'd starve to death first. But on the other hand – *damn* this fuzzy-headed feeling – wouldn't it have to stop, to prevent the tenant from being digested with the first meal?

'Well?' McCarty demanded.

That was wrong, George knew, but he couldn't say why; and it was a distinctly unpleasant thought. Or – even worse – suppose the meal became the tenant, and the tenant the meal?

The nearest animal's head went up, and four tiny red eyes stared at George. The floppy ears snapped to attention.

It was no time for speculation. 'He's seen us!' George shouted mentally. '*Run!*'

The scene exploded into motion. One instant they were lying still in the prickly dry grass; the next they were skimming at express-train speed across the ground, with the herd galloping away straight ahead of them. The hams of the nearest beast loomed up closer and closer, bounding furiously; then they had run it down and vaulted over it.

Casting an eye backward, George saw that it was lying motionless in the grass – unconscious or dead.

They ran down another one. *The anaesthetic*, George thought lucidly. *One touch does it* And another, and another. *Of course we can digest them*, he thought with relief. *It has to be selective to begin with, or it couldn't have separated out our nervous tissue.*

Four down. Six down. Three more together as the herd bunched between the last arm of the thicket and the steep river bank; then two that tried to double back; then four stragglers, one after the other.

The rest of the herd disappeared into the tall grass up the slope; but fifteen bodies were strewn behind them.

Taking no chances, George went back to the beginning of the line and edged the monster's body under the first carcass.

'Crouch down, Gumbs,' he said. 'We have to slide under it ... that's far enough. Leave the head hanging over.'

'What for?' said the soldier.

'You don't want his brain in here with us, do you? We don't know how many this thing is equipped to take. It might even like this one better than one of ours. But I can't see it bothering to keep the rest of the nervous system, if we make sure not to eat the head—'

'Oh!' said Vivian faintly.

'I beg your pardon, Miss Bellis,' George said contritely. 'It shouldn't be too unpleasant, though, if we don't let it bother us. It isn't as if we had taste buds, or—'

'It's all right,' she said. 'Just please let's not talk about it.'

'I should think not,' Gumbs put in. 'A little more tact, don't you think, Meister?'

Accepting this reproof, George turned his attention to the corpse that lay on the monster's glabrous surface, between his section and Gumbs's. It was sinking, just visibly, into the flesh. A cloud of opacity was spreading around it.

When it was almost gone, and the neck had been severed they moved on to the next. This time, at George's suggestion, they took aboard two at once. Gradually their irritable mood faded; they began to feel at ease and cheerful, and George found it possible to think consecutively without having vital points slip out of his reach.

They were in their eighth and ninth courses, and George was happily engaged in an intricate chain of speculation as to the monster's circulatory system, when Miss McCarty broke a long silence to announce:

'I have now perfected a method by which we can return to camp safely. We will begin at once.'

Startled and dismayed, George turned his eyes toward McCarty's quadrant of the monster. Protruding from the rim was a stringy, jointed something that looked like – yes, it was! – a grotesque but recognisable arm and hand. As he watched, the lumpy fingers fumbled with a blade of grass, tugged, uprooted it.

'Major Gumbs!' said McCarty. 'It will be your task to locate the following articles, as quickly as possible. One. A surface suitable for writing. I suggest a large leaf, light in color, dry but not brittle. Or a tree from which a large section of bark can be easily peeled. Two. A pigment. No doubt you will be able to discover berries yielding suitable juice. If not, mud will do. Three. A twig or reed for use as a pen. When you have directed me to all these essential items, I will employ them to write a message outlining our predicament. You will read the result and point out any errors, which I will then correct. When the message is completed, we will return with it to the camp, approaching at night, and deposit it in a conspicuous place. We will retire until daybreak, and when the message has been read we will approach again. Begin, Major.'

'Well, yes,' said Gumbs, 'that ought to work, except – I suppose you've worked out some system for holding the pen, Miss McCarty?'

'Fool,' she replied, 'I have made a hand, of course.'

'Well, in that case, by all means. Let's see, I believe we might try this thicket first—' Their common body gave a lurch in that direction.

George held back. 'Wait a minute,' he said desperately. 'Let's at least have the common sense to finish this meal before we go. There's no telling when we'll get another.'

McCarty demanded, 'How large are these creatures, Major?'

'Oh – about sixty centimeters long, I should say.'

'And we have consumed nine of them, is that correct?'

'Nearer eight,' George said. 'These two are only half gone.'

'In other words,' McCarty said, 'we have had two apiece. That should be ample. Don't you agree, Major?'

George said earnestly, 'You're wrong, Miss McCarty. You're thinking in terms of human food requirements, whereas this organism has a different metabolic rate and at least three times the mass of four human beings. Look at it this way – the four of us together had a mass of about three hundred kilos, and yet twenty hours after this thing absorbed us, it was hungry again. Well, these animals wouldn't weigh much more than twenty kilos apiece at one G – and according to your scheme we've got to hold out until sometime after daybreak tomorrow.'

'Something in that,' Gumbs said. 'Yes, on the whole, Miss McCarty, I think we had better forage while we can. It won't take us more than half an hour longer, at this rate.'

'Very well. Be as quick as you can.'

They moved on to the next pair of victims. George's brain was working furiously. It was no good arguing with McCarty, and Gumbs was not much better, but he had to try. If he could only convince Gumbs, then Bellis would fall in with the majority – maybe. It was the only hope he had.

'Gumbs,' he said, 'have you given any thought to what's going to happen to us when we get back?'

'Not quite my line, you know. Leave that to the technical fellows like yourself.'

'No, that isn't what I mean. Suppose you were the C.O. of this team, and four people had fallen into this organism instead of us—'

'What, what? I don't follow.'

George patiently repeated it.

'Yes, I see what you mean. And so—'

'What orders would you give?'

Gumbs thought a moment. 'Turn the thing over to the bio section, I suppose. What else?'

'You don't think you might order it destroyed as a possible menace?'

'Good Lord, I suppose I might. No, but you see, we'll be careful what we say in the note. We'll point out that we're a valuable specimen, and so on. Handle with care.'

'All right,' George said, 'but suppose that works, then what? Since it's out of your line, I'll tell you. Nine chances out of ten, bio section will classify us as a possible enemy weapon. That means, first of all, that we'll go through a full-dress interrogation – and I don't have to tell you what that can be like.'

'Major Gumbs,' said McCarty stridently, 'Meister will be executed for disloyalty at the first opportunity. You are forbidden to talk to him, under the same penalty.'

'But she can't stop you from listening to me,' George said tensely. 'In the second place, Gumbs, they'll take samples. Without anaesthesia. And finally, they'll either destroy us just the same, or they'll send us back to the nearest strong point for more study. We will then be Federation property, Gumbs, in a top-secret category, and since nobody in Intelligence will ever dare to take the responsibility of clearing us, we'll *stay* there.

'Gumbs, this *is* a valuable specimen, but it will never do anybody any good if we go back to camp. Whatever we discover about it, even if it's knowledge that could save billions of lives, that will be top-secret too, and it'll never get past the walls of Intelligence … If you're still hoping that they can get you out of this, you're wrong. This isn't like limb grafts, *your whole body* has been destroyed, Gumbs, everything but your nervous system and your eyes. The only new body we'll get is the one we make ourselves. We've got to stay here and – and work this out ourselves.'

'Major Gumbs,' said McCarty, 'I think we have wasted quite enough time. Begin your search for the materials I need.'

For a moment Gumbs was silent, and their collective body did not move.

Then he said: 'Yes, that was a leaf, a twig and a bunch of berries, wasn't it? Or mud. Miss McCarty, unofficially of course, there's one point I'd like your opinion on. Before we begin. That is to say, I daresay they'll be able to patch together some sort of bodies for us, don't you think? I mean, one technical fellow says one thing, another says the opposite. Do you see what I'm driving at?'

George had been watching McCarty's new limb uneasily. It was flexing rhythmically and, he was almost certain, growing minutely larger. The fingers groped occasionally in the dry grass, plucking first a single blade, then two together, finally a whole tuft. Now she said: 'I have no opinion, Major. The question is irrelevant. Our duty is to return to camp. That is all we need to know.'

'Oh, I quite agree with you there,' said Gumbs. 'And besides, there really isn't any alternative, is there?'

George, staring down at one of the fingerlike projections visible below the rim of the monster, was passionately willing it to turn into an arm. He had, he suspected, started much too late.

'The alternative,' he said, 'is simply to keep on going as we are. Even if the Federation holds this planet for a century, there'll be places on it that will never be explored. We'll be safe.'

'I mean to say,' added Gumbs as if he had only paused for thought, 'a fellow can't very well cut himself off from civilisation, can he?'

Again George felt a movement toward the thicket; again he resisted it. Then he found himself overpowered, as another set of muscles joined themselves to Gumbs's. Quivering, crabwise, the something *meisterii* moved half a meter. Then it stopped, straining.

And for the second time that day, George was forced to revise his opinion of Vivian Bellis.

'I believe you, Mr Meister – George,' she said. 'I don't want to go back. Tell me what you want me to do.'

'You're doing beautifully now,' George said after a speechless instant. 'Except if you can grow an arm, I imagine that will be useful.'

The struggle went on.

'Now we know where we are,' said McCarty to Gumbs.

'Yes. Quite right.'

'Major Gumbs,' she said crisply, 'you are opposite me, I believe?'

'Am I?' said Gumbs doubtfully.

'Never mind. I believe you are. Now: is Meister to your right or left?'

'Left. I know that, anyhow. Can see his eye stalks out of the corner of my eye.'

'Very well.' McCarty's arm rose, with a sharp-pointed fragment of rock clutched in the blobby fingers.

Horrified, George watched it bend backward across the curve of the monster's body. The long, knife-sharp point probed tentatively at the surface three centimeters short of the area over his brain. Then the fist made an abrupt up-and-down movement, and a fierce stab of pain shot through him.

'Not quite long enough, I think,' McCarty said. She flexed the arm, then brought it back to almost the same spot and stabbed again.

'No,' she said thoughtfully. 'It will take a little longer,' then, 'Major Gumbs, after my next attempt you will tell me if you notice any reaction in Meister's eye stalks.'

The pain was still throbbing along George's nerves. With one half-blinded eye he watched the embryonic arm that was growing, too slowly, under the rim; with the other, fascinated, he watched McCarty's arm lengthen slowly toward him.

It was growing visibly, he suddenly realised – but it wasn't getting any nearer. In fact, incredibly enough, it seemed to be losing ground.

The monster's flesh was flowing away under it, expanding in both directions.

McCarty stabbed again, with vicious strength. This time the pain was less acute.

'Major?' she said. 'Any result?'

'No,' said Gumbs, 'no, I think not. We seem to be moving forward a bit, though, Miss McCarty.'

'A ridiculous error,' she replied. 'We are being forced *back*. Pay attention, Major.'

'No, really,' he protested. 'That is to say, we're moving toward the thicket. Forward to me, backward to you.'

'Major Gumbs, *I* am moving forward, *you* are moving back.'

They were both right, George discovered: the monster's body was no longer circular, it was extending itself along the Gumbs-McCarty axis. A suggestion of concavity was becoming visible in the center. Below the surface, too, there was motion.

The four brains now formed an oblong, not a square.

The positions of the spinal cords had shifted. His own and Vivian's seemed to be about where they were, but Gumbs's now passed under McCarty's brain, and vice versa.

Having increased its mass by some two hundred kilos, the something *meisterii* was fissioning into two individuals – and tidily separating its tenants, two to each. Gumbs and Meister in one, McCarty and Bellis in the other.

The next time it happened, he realised, each product of the fission would be reduced to one brain – and the time after that, one of the new individuals out of each pair would be a monster in the primary or untenanted state, quiescent, camouflaged, waiting to be stumbled over.

But that meant that, like the common amoeba, this fascinating organism was immortal. It never died, barring accidents; it simply grew and divided.

Not the tenants, though, unfortunately – their tissues would wear out and die.

Or would they? Human nervous tissue didn't proliferate as George's and Miss McCarty's had done; neither did *any* human tissue build new cells fast enough to account for George's eye stalks or Miss McCarty's arm.

There was no question about it: none of that new tissue could possibly be human; it was all counterfeit, produced by the monster from its own substance according to the structural blueprints in the nearest genuine cells. And it was a perfect counterfeit: the new tissues knit with the old, axones coupled with dendrites, muscles contracted or expanded on command. The imitation *worked*.

And therefore, when nerve cells wore out, they could be replaced. Eventually the last human cell would go, the human tenant would have become totally monster – but 'a difference that makes no difference is no difference.' Effectively, the tenant would still be human – and he would be immortal.

Barring accidents.

Or murder.

Miss McCarty was saying, 'Major Gumbs, you are being ridiculous. The explanation is quite obvious. Unless you are deliberately deceiving me, for what reason I cannot imagine, then our efforts to move in opposing directions must be pulling this creature apart.'

McCarty was evidently confused by her geometry. Let her stay that way – it would keep her off balance until the fission was complete. No, that was no good. George himself was out of her reach already, and getting farther away – but how about Bellis? Her brain and McCarty's were, if anything, closer together

What to do? If he warned the girl, that would only draw McCarty's attention to her sooner. Unless he could misdirect her at the same time

There wasn't much time left, he realised abruptly. If he was right in thinking that some physical linkage between the brains had occurred to make communication possible, those cells couldn't hold out much longer; the gap between the two pairs of brains was widening steadily.

'Vivian!' he said.

'Yes, George?'

Relieved, he said rapidly, 'Listen, we're not pulling this body apart, it's splitting. That's the way it reproduces. You and I will be in one half, Gumbs and McCarty in the other. If they don't give us any trouble, we can all go where we please—'

'Oh, I'm so glad!'

What a warm voice she had ... 'Yes,' said George nervously, 'but we may have to fight them; it's up to them. So *grow an arm*, Vivian.'

'I'll try,' she said doubtfully. 'I don't know—'

McCarty's voice cut across hers. 'Ah. Major Gumbs, since you have eyes, it will be your task to see to it that those two do not escape. Meanwhile, I suggest that you, also, grow an arm.'

'Doing my best,' said Gumbs.

Puzzled, George glanced downward, past his own half-formed arm: there, almost out of sight, was a fleshy bulge under Gumbs's section of the rim! The major had been working on it in secret, keeping it hidden ... and it was already better developed than George's.

'Oh-oh,' said Gumbs abruptly. 'Look here, Miss McCarty, Meister's been leading you up the garden path. Look here, I mean, you and I aren't going to be in the same half. How could we be? We're on *opposite sides* of the blasted thing. It's going to be you and Miss Bellis, me and Meister.'

The monster was developing a definite waistline. The spinal cords had rotated, now, so that there was clear space between them in the center.

'Yes,' said McCarty faintly. '*Thank* you, Major Gumbs.'

'George!' came Vivian's frightened voice, distant and weak. 'What shall I do?'

'Grow an arm!' he shouted.

There was no reply.

III

Frozen, George watched McCarty's arm, the rock-fragment still clutched at the end of it, rise into view and swing leftward at full stretch over the bubbling surface of the monster. He had time to see it bob up and viciously down again; time to think, *Still short, thank God – that's McCarty's right arm, it's farther from Vivian's brain than it was from mine;* time, finally, to realise that he could not possibly help her before McCarty lengthened the arm a few centimeters more than were necessary. The fission was not more than half complete; and he could no more move to where he wanted to be than a Siamese twin could walk around his brother.

Then his time was up. A flicker of motion warned him, and he looked back to see a lumpy, distorted pseudo-hand clutching for his eye stalks.

Instinctively he brought his own hand up, grasped the other's wrist and hung on desperately. It was half again the size of his, and so strongly muscled that although his leverage was better, he couldn't force it back or hold it away; he could only keep the system oscillating up and down, adding his strength to Gumbs's so that the mark was overshot.

Gumbs began to vary the force and rhythm of his movements, trying to catch him off guard. A thick finger brushed the base of one eye stalk.

'Sorry about this, Meister,' said Gumbs's voice. 'No hard feelings in it, oh my side. Between us (oof) I don't fancy that McCarty woman much – but (ugh! almost had you that time) beggars can't be choosers. Ah. Way I see it, I've got to look after myself; mean to say (ugh) if I don't, who will? See what I mean?'

George did not reply. Astonishingly enough, he was no longer afraid, either for himself or for Vivian; he was simply overpoweringly, ecstatically, monomaniacally angry. Power from somewhere was surging into his arm; fiercely concentrating, he thought *Bigger! Stronger! Longer! More arm!*

The arm grew. Visibly it added substance to itself, it lengthened, thickened, bulged with muscle. So did Gumbs's.

He began another arm. So did Gumbs.

All around him the surface of the monster was bubbling violently. And, George realised finally, the lenticular bulk of it was perceptibly shrinking. Its curious breathing system was inadequate; the thing was cannibalising itself, destroying its own tissues to make up the difference.

How small could it get and still support two human tenants?

And which brain would it dispense with first?

He had no leisure to think about it. Scrabbling in the grass with his second hand, Gumbs had failed to find anything that would serve as a weapon; now, with a sudden lurch, he swung their entire body around.

The fission was complete.

That thought reminded George of Vivian and McCarty. He risked a split second's glance behind him, saw nothing but a featureless ovoid mound, and looked back in time to see Gumbs's half-grown right fist pluck a long, sharp-pointed dead branch out of the grass. In the next instant the thing came whipping at his eyes.

The lip of the river bank was a meter away to the left. George made it in one abrupt surge. They slipped, tottered, hesitated, hands clutching wildly- and toppled, end over end, hurtling in a cloud of dust and pebbles down the breakneck slope to a meaty smash at the bottom.

The universe made one more giant turn around them and came to rest. Half blinded, George groped for the hold he had lost, found the wrist and seized it.

'Oh, Lord,' said Gumbs's voice, 'that's done me. I'm hurt, Meister. Go on, man, finish it, will you? Don't waste time.'

George stared at him suspiciously, without relaxing his grip. 'What's the matter with you?'

'I tell you I'm done,' said Gumbs pettishly. 'Paralysed. I can't move.'

They had fallen, George saw, onto a small boulder, one of many with which the river bed was strewn. This one was roughly conical; they were draped over it, and the blunt point was directly under Gumbs's spinal cord, a few centimeters from the brain.

'Gumbs,' he said, 'that may not be as bad as you think. If I can show you it isn't, will you give up and put yourself under my orders?'

'How do you mean? My spine's crushed.'

'Never mind that now. Will you or won't you?'

'Why, yes,' said Gumbs. 'That's very decent of you, Meister, matter of fact. You have my word, for what it's worth.'

'All right,' said George. Straining hard, he managed to get their body down off the boulder. Then he stared up at the slope down which they had tumbled. Too steep; he'd have to find an easier way back. He turned and started off to eastward, paralleling the thin stream that still flowed in the center of the watercourse.

'What's up now?' Gumbs asked after a moment.

'We've got to find a way up to the top,' George said impatiently. 'I may still be able to help Vivian.'

'Ah, yes. Afraid I was thinking about myself, Meister. If you don't mind telling me—'

She couldn't still be alive, George was thinking despondently, but if there were any small chance 'You'll be all right,' he said. 'If you were still in your old body that would be a fatal injury, or permanently disabling, anyhow, but not in this thing. You can repair yourself as easily as you can grow a new limb.'

'Good Lord,' said Gumbs. 'Stupid of me not to think of that. But look here, Meister, does that mean we were simply wasting our time trying to kill one another? I mean to say—'

'No. If you'd crushed my brain, I think the organism would have digested it, and that would be the end of me. But short of anything that drastic, I believe we're immortal.'

'Immortal,' said Gumbs. 'Good Lord ... That does rather put another face on it, doesn't it?'

The bank was becoming a little lower, and at one point, where the raw earth was thickly seeded with boulders, there was a talus slope that looked as if it could be climbed. George started up it.

'Meister,' said Gumbs after a moment.

'What do you want?'

'You're right, you know – I'm getting some feeling back already ... Look here, Meister, is there anything this beast *can't* do? I mean, for instance, do you suppose we could put ourselves back together the way we were, with all the – appendages, and so on?'

'It's possible,' George said curtly. It was a thought that had been in the back of his mind, but he didn't feel like discussing it with Gumbs just now.

They were halfway up the slope.

'Well, in that case—' said Gumbs meditatively. 'The thing has *military* possibilities, you know. Man who brought a thing like that direct to the War Department could write his own ticket, more or less.'

'After we split up,' George said, 'you can do whatever you please.'

'But, dammit,' said Gumbs in an irritated tone, 'that won't do.'

'Why not?'

'Because,' said Gumbs, 'they might find you.' His hands reached up abruptly, grasped a small boulder, and before George could stop him, pried it sidewise out of its socket in the earth.

The larger boulder above it trembled, dipped and leaned ponderously outward. George, directly underneath, found that he could move neither forward nor back.

'Sorry again,' he heard Gumbs saying, with what sounded like genuine regret. 'But you know the Loyalty Committee. I simply can't take the chance.'

The boulder seemed to take forever to fall. George tried twice more, with all his strength, to move out of its path. Then, instinctively, he put his arms straight under it.

At the last possible instant he moved them to the left, away from the center of the toppling gray mass.

It struck.

George felt his arms breaking like twigs, and saw a looming grayness that blotted out the sky; he felt a sledge-hammer impact that made the earth shudder beneath him.

He heard a splattering sound.

And he was still alive. That astonishing fact kept him fully occupied for a long time after the boulder had clattered its way down the slope into silence. Then, finally, he looked down to his right.

The resistance of his stiffened arms, even while they broke, had been barely enough to lever the falling body over, a distance of some thirty centimeters … The right half of the monster was a flattened shattered ruin. He could see a few flecks of pasty gray matter, melting now into green-brown translucence as the mass flowed slowly together again.

In twenty minutes the last remains of a superfluous spinal cord had been reabsorbed, the monster had collected itself back into its normal lens shape, and George's pain was diminishing. In five minutes more his mended arms were strong enough to use. They were also more convincingly shaped and colored than before – the tendons, the fingernails, even the wrinkles of the skin were in good order. In ordinary circumstances this discovery would have left George happily bemused for hours; now, in his impatience, he barely noticed it. He climbed to the top of the bank.

Thirty meters away a humped green-brown body like his own lay motionless in the dry grass.

It contained, of course, only one brain. Whose?

McCarty's, almost certainly; Vivian hadn't had a chance. But then how did it happen that there was no visible trace of McCarty's arm?

Unnerved, George walked around the creature for a closer inspection.

On the far side he encountered two dark-brown eyes, with an oddly unfinished appearance. They focused on him after an instant, and the whole body quivered slightly, moving toward him.

Vivian's eyes had been brown; George remembered them distinctly. Brown eyes with heavy dark lashes in a tapering slender face … But did that prove anything? What color had McCarty's eyes been? He couldn't remember for certain.

There was only one way to find out. George moved closer, hoping fervently that the something *meisterii* was at least advanced enough to conjugate, instead of trying to devour members of its own species …

The two bodies touched, clung and began to flow together. Watching, George saw the fissioning process reverse itself: from paired lenses the alien flesh melted into a slipper shape, to an ovoid, to lens shape again. His brain and the other drifted closer together, the spinal cords crossing at right angles.

And it was only then that he noticed an oddity about the other brain: it seemed to be lighter and larger than his, the outline a trifle sharper.

'Vivian?' he said doubtfully. 'Is that you?'

No answer. He tried again; and again.

Finally:

'George! Oh dear – I want to cry, but I can't seem to do it.'

'No lachrymal glands,' George said automatically. 'Uh, Vivian?'

'Yes, George.' That warm voice again …

'What happened to Miss McCarty? How did you – I mean, what happened?'

'I don't know. She's gone, isn't she? I haven't heard her for a long time.'

'Yes,' said George, 'she's gone. You mean you don't *know?* Tell me what you did.'

'Well, I wanted to make an arm, because you told me to, but I didn't think I had time enough. So I made a skull instead. And those things to cover my spine—'

'Vertebrae.' *Now why*, he thought dazedly, *didn't I think of that?* 'And then?' he said.

'I think I'm crying now,' she said. 'Yes, I am. It's such a relief. And then, after that, nothing. She was still hurting me, and I just lay here and thought how wonderful it would be if she weren't in here with me. And then, after a while, she wasn't. Then I grew eyes to look for you.'

The explanation, it seemed to George, was more perplexing than the enigma. Staring around in a vague search for enlightenment, he caught sight of something that had escaped his notice before. Two meters to his left, just visible in the grass, was a damp-looking grayish lump, with a suggestion of a stringy extension trailing off from it …

There must, he decided suddenly, be some mechanism in the something *meisterii* for disposing of tenants who failed to adapt themselves – brains that went into catatonia, or hysteria, or suicidal frenzy. An eviction clause.

Somehow, Vivian had managed to stimulate that mechanism – to convince the organism that McCarty's brain was not only superfluous but dangerous – 'poisonous' was the word.

Miss McCarty – it was the final ignominy – had not been digested, but excreted.

*

By sunset, twelve hours later, they had made a good deal of progress. They had reached an understanding very agreeable to them, both; they had hunted down another herd of the pseudo-pigs for their noon meal; and, for divergent reasons – on George's side because the monster's normal metabolism was grossly inefficient when it had to move quickly, and on Vivian's because she refused to believe that any man could be attracted to her in her present condition – they had begun a serious attempt to reshape themselves.

The first trials were extraordinarily difficult, the rest surprisingly easy. Again and again they had to let themselves collapse back into amoeboid masses, victims of some omitted or malfunctioning organ; but each failure smoothed the road; eventually they were able to stand breathless but breathing, swaying but erect, face to face – two protean giants in the fortunate dimness, two sketches of self-created Man.

They had also put thirty kilometers between themselves and the Federation camp. Standing on the crest of a rise and looking southward across the shallow valley, George could see a faint funereal glow: the mining machines, chewing out metals to feed the fabricators that would spawn a billion ships.

'We'll never go back, will we?' said Vivian.

'No,' said George soberly. 'They'll come to us, in time. We have lots of time. We're the future.'

And one thing more, a small thing, but important to George; it marked his sense of accomplishment, of one phase ended and a new one begun. He had finally completed the name of his discovery – not, as it turned out, anything *meisterii* at all. *Spes hominis:* Man's hope.

AN EYE FOR A WHAT?

I

On his way across the wheel one morning, Dr Walter Alvarez detoured down to C level promenade. A few men were standing, as usual, at the window looking out at the enormous blue-green planet below. They were dressed alike in sheen-gray coveralls, a garment with detachable gauntlets and hood designed to make inconvertible into a spacesuit. It was uncomfortable, but regulation: according to the books, a Survey and Propaganda Satellite might find itself under attack at any moment.

Nothing so interesting had happened to SAPS 3107A, orbiting the seventh planet of a G-type star in Ophiuchus. They had been here for two years and a half, and most of them had not even touched ground yet.

There it was, drifting by out there, blue-green, fat and juicy – an oxygen planet, two-thirds land, mild climate, soil fairly bursting with minerals and organics.

Alvarez felt his mouth watering when he looked at it. He had 'wheel fever'; they all did. He wanted to get *down* there, to natural gravity and natural ailments.

The last month or so, there had been a feeling in the satellite that a break-through was coming. Always coming: it never arrived.

A plump orthotypist named Lola went by, and a couple of the men turned with automatic whistles. 'Listen,' said Olaf Marx conspiratorially, with a hand on Alvarez's arm, 'that reminds me, did you hear what happened at the big banquet yesterday?'

'No,' said Alvarez, irritably withdrawing his arm. 'I didn't go. Can't stand banquets. Why?'

'Well, the way I got it, the Commandant's wife was sitting right across from George—'

Alvarez's interest sharpened. 'You mean the gorgon? What did he do?'

'I'm *telling* you. See, it looked like he was watching her all through dinner. Then up comes the dessert – lemon meringue. So old George—'

The shift bell rang. Alvarez started nervously and looked at his thumb-watch. The other men were drifting away. So was Olaf, laughing like a fool. 'You'll die when you hear,' he called back. 'Boy, do I wish I'd been there myself! So long, Walt.'

Alvarez reluctantly went the other way. In B corridor, somebody called after him, 'Hey, Walt? Hear about the banquet?'

He shook his head. The other man, a baker named Pedro, grinned and waved, disappearing up the curve of the corridor. Alvarez opened the door of Xenology Section and went in.

During his absence, somebody had put a new chart on the wall. It was ten feet high and there were little rectangles all over it, each connected by lines to other rectangles. When he first saw it, Alvarez thought it was a new table of organisation for the Satellite Service, and he winced: but on closer inspection, the chart was *too* complex, and besides, it had a peculiar disorganised appearance. Boxes had been white-rubbed out and other boxes drawn on top of them. Some parts were crowded illegibly together and others were spacious. The whole thing looked desperately confused; and so did Elvis Womrath, who was on a wheeled ladder erasing the entire top right-hand corner. '*N* panga,' he said irritably. 'That right?'

'Yes,' a voice piped unexpectedly. Alvarez looked around, saw nobody. The voice went on, 'but he is *R* panga to his cousins and all their *N* pangas or bigger, except when—'

Alvarez leaned over and peered around the desk. There on the carpet was the owner of the voice, a pinkish-white spheroid with various appendages sprouting in all directions, like a floating mine: 'George' the gorgon. 'Oh, it's you,' said Alvarez, producing his echo sounder and humidometer.

'What's all this nonsense I hear—' He began to prod the gorgon with the test equipment, making his regular morning examination. It was the only bright moment of his day; the infirmary could wait.

'All right,' Womrath interrupted, scrubbing furiously. '*R* panga to cousins – wait a minute, now.' He turned with a scowl. 'Alvarez, I'll be through in a minute. *N* panga or bigger, except when ...' He sketched in half a dozen boxes, labeled them and began to draw connecting lines. 'Now is *that* right?' he asked George.

'Yes, only now it is wrong panga to *mother's* cousins. Draw again, from father's cousins' *N* pangas, to mother's cousins' *O* pangas or bigger ... Yes, and now from father's uncles' *R* pangas, to mother's uncles' pangas *cousins*—'

Womrath's hand faltered. He stared at the chart; he had drawn such a tangle of lines, he couldn't tell what box connected with which. 'Oh, God,' he said hopelessly. He climbed down off the ladder and slapped the stylus into Alvarez's palm. '*You* go nuts.' He thumbed the intercom on the desk and said, 'Chief, I'm going off now. *Way* off.'

'*Did you get that chart straightened out?*' the intercom demanded.

'No, but—'

'*You're on extra duty as of now. Take a pill. Is Alvarez here?*'

'Yes,' said Womrath resignedly.

'*Both of you come in, then. Leave George outside.*'

'Hello, Doctor,' the spheroid piped. 'Are you panga to me?'

'Don't let's go into *that*,' said Womrath, twitching, and took Alvarez by the sleeve. They found the chief of the Xenology Section, Edward H. Dominick, huddled bald and bearlike behind his desk. The cigar in his hand looked chewed. 'Womrath,' he said, 'when can you give me that chart?'

'I don't know. Never, maybe.' When Dominick scowled at him irritably, he shrugged and lit a sullen cigarette.

Dominick swiveled his gaze to Alvarez. 'Have you,' he asked, 'heard about what happened at the banquet in George's honor yesterday?'

'No, I have not,' said Alvarez. 'Will you be so kind to tell me, or else shut up about it?'

Dominick rubbed his shaven skull, absorbing the insult. 'It was during the dessert,' he said. 'George was sitting opposite Mrs Carver, in that little jump seat. Just as she got her fork into the pie – it was lemon meringue – George rolled up over the table and grabbed the plate away. Mrs Carver screamed, pulled back – thought she was being attacked, I suppose – and the chair went out from under her. It-was-a-mess.'

Alvarez ended the awed silence. 'What did he do with the pie?'

'Ate it,' said Dominick glumly. 'Had a perfectly good piece of his own, that he didn't touch.' He popped a lozenge into his mouth.

Alvarez shook his head. 'Not typical. His pattern is strictly submissive. I don't like it.'

'That's what I told Carver. But he was livid. Shaking. We all sat there until he escorted his wife to her room and came back. Then we had an interrogation. All we could get out of George was, "I thought I was panga to her."'

Alvarez shifted impatiently in his chair, reaching automatically for a bunch of grapes from the bowl on the desk. He was a small, spare man, and he felt defensive about it. 'Now what is all this panga business?' he demanded.

Womrath snorted, and began to peel a banana.

'Panga,' said Dominick, 'would appear to be some kind of complicated authority-submission relationship that exists among the gorgons.' Alvarez sat up straighter. 'They never mentioned it to us, because we never asked. Now it turns out to be crucial.' Dominick sighed. 'Fourteen months, just getting a three-man base down on the planet. Seven more to get the elders' permission to bring a gorgon here experimentally. All according to the book. We picked the biggest and brightest-looking one we could find: that was George. He seemed to be coming along great. And now this.'

'Well, chief,' said Womrath carefully, 'nobody has any more admiration than I have for Mrs Carver as a consumer – she really puts it away, but it seems to me the question is, is *George* damaged—'

Dominick was shaking his head. 'I haven't told you the rest of it. This panga thing stopped Carver cold, but not for long. He beamed down to the planethead and had Rubinson ask the elders. "Is George panga to the Commandant's wife?"'

Alvarez grinned mirthlessly and clicked his tongue.

'Sure,' Dominick nodded. 'Who knows what a question like that may have meant to them? They answered back, in effect, "Certainly not," and wanted to know the details. Carver *told* them.'

'And?' said Alvarez.

'They said George was a shocking criminal who should be appropriately punished. Not by them, you understand – by us, because we're the offended parties. Moreover – now this must make sense to their peculiar way of looking at things – if *we* don't punish George to their satisfaction, *they'll* punish Rubinson and his whole crew.'

'How?' Alvarez demanded.

'By doing,' Dominick said, 'whatever it is we should have done to George – and that could be anything.'

Womrath pursed his lips to whistle, but no sound came out. He swallowed a mouthful of banana and tried again. Still nothing.

'You get it?' said Dominick with suppressed emotion. They all looked through the open doorway at George, squatting patiently in the other room. 'There's no trouble about "punishment" – we all know what it means, we've read the books. But how do you punish an alien like that? *An eye for a what?*'

'Now let's see if we have this straight,' said Dominick, sorting through the papers in his hand. Womrath and Alvarez looked on from either side. George tried to peek, too, but his photoceptors were too short. They were all standing in the outer office, which had been stripped to the bare walls and floor. 'One. We know a gorgon changes color according to his emotional state. When they're contented, they're a kind of rose pink. When they're unhappy, they turn blue.'

'He's been pink ever since we've had him on the Satellite,' said Womrath, glancing down at the gorgon.

'Except at the banquet,' Dominick answered thoughtfully. 'I remember he turned bluish just before ... If we could find out what it was that set him off— Well, first things first.' He held down another finger. 'Two, we don't have any information at all about local systems of reward and punishment. They may cut each other into bits for spitting on the sidewalk, or they may just slap each other's – um, wrists—' He looked unhappily down at George, all his auricles and photoceptors out on stalks.

'– for arson, rape and mopery,' Dominick finished. 'We don't know; we'll have to play it by ear.'

'What does George say about it?' Alvarez asked. 'Why don't you ask him?'

'We thought of that,' Womrath said glumly. 'Asked him what the elders would do to him in a case like this, and he said they'd quabble his infarcts, or something.'

'A dead end,' Dominick added. 'It would take us years ...' He scrubbed his naked scalp with a palm. 'Well, number three, we've got all the furniture out of here – it's going to be damned crowded, with the whole staff working in my office, but never mind ... Number four, there's his plate with the bread and water. And number five, that door has been fixed so it latches on the out-side. Let's give it a dry run.' He led the way to the door; the others followed, including George. 'No, you stay in here,' Womrath told him. George stopped, blushing an agreeable pink.

Dominick solemnly closed the door and dropped the improvised latch into its socket. He punched the door button, found it satisfactorily closed. Through the transparent upper pane, they could see George inquisitively watching.

Dominick opened the door again. 'Now, George,' he said, 'pay attention. This is a *prison*. You're being *punished*. We're going to keep you in here, with nothing to eat but what's there, until we think you're punished enough. Understand?'

'Yes,' said George doubtfully.

'All right,' said Dominick, and closed the door. They all stood watching for a while, and George stood watching them back, but nothing else happened. 'Let's go into my office and wait,' said Dominick with a sigh. 'Can't expect miracles, all at once.'

They trooped down the corridor to the adjoining room and ate peanuts for a while. 'He's a sociable creature,' Womrath said hopefully. 'He'll get lone-some after a while.'

'And hungry,' Alvarez said. 'He never turns down a meal.'

Half an hour later, when they looked in, George was thoughtfully chewing up the carpet. 'No, no, no, no, George,' said Dominick, bursting in on him; 'You're not supposed to eat anything except what we give you. This is a *prison*.'

'Good carpet,' said George, hurt.

'I don't care if it is. You don't eat it, understand?'

'Okay,' said George cheerfully. His color was an honest rose pink.

Four hours later, when Alvarez went off shift, George had settled down in a corner and pulled in all his appendages. He was asleep. If anything, he looked pinker that ever.

When Alvarez came on shift again, there was no doubt about it. George was sitting in the middle of the room, photoceptors out and waving rhythmi-cally; his color was a glowing pink, the pink of a rose pearl. Dominick kept him in there for another day, just to make sure; George seemed to lose a little weight on the austere diet, but glowed a steady pink. He liked it.

II

Goose Kelly, the games instructor, tried to keep up a good front, but he had the worst case of wheel fever on SAPS 3107A. It had got so that looking out of that fat, blue-green planet, swimming there so close, was more than he could bear. Kelly was a big man, an outdoorman by instinct; he longed for natural air in his lungs, and turf under his feet. To compensate, he strode faster, shouted louder, got redder of face and bulgier of eye, bristled more fiercely. To quiet an occasional trembling of his hands, he munched sedative pills. He had dreams of falling, with which he bored the ship's Mother Hubbard and the Church of Marx padre by turns.

'Is that it?' he asked now, disapprovingly. He had never seen the gorgon before; Semantics, Medical and Xenology Sections had been keeping him pretty much to themselves.

Dominick prodded the pinkish sphere with his toe. 'Wake up, George.'

After a moment, the gorgon's skin became lumpy at half a dozen points. The lumps grew slowly into long, segmented stems. Some of these expanded at the tips into 'feet' and 'hands'; others flowered into the intricate patterns of auricles and photoceptors – and one speech organ, which looked like a small trumpet. 'Hello,' said George cheerfully. 'He can pull them back in any time?' Kelly asked, rubbing his chin.

'Yes. Show him, George.'

'All right.' The feather stalks became blank-tipped, then rapidly shrank, segment by segment. In less than two seconds, George was a smooth sphere again.

'Well, that makes for a little problem here,' said Kelly. 'You see what I mean? If you can't get a grip on him, how are you going to *punish* him like you say?'

'We've tried everything we could think of,' said Dominick. 'We locked him up, kept him on short rations, didn't talk to him … He doesn't draw any pay, you know, so you can't fine him.'

'Or downgrade him on the promotion lists, either,' said Womrath gloomily.

'No. And it's a little late to use the Pavlov-Morganstern treatments we all had when we were children. We can't prevent a crime he's already committed. So our thought was, since you're the games instructor—'

'We thought,' Womrath said diplomatically, 'you might have noticed something that might be useful. You know, rough-housing and so on.'

Kelly thought this over. 'Well, there's low blows,' he said, 'but I mean, hell—' He gestured futilely at George, who had just decided to put his auricles out again. 'What would you—'

'No, that's out of the question,' Dominick said heavily. 'Well, I'm sorry, Kelly. It was nice of you to help out.'

'No, now, wait a minute,' said Kelly. 'I got something coming to me, maybe.' He nibbled a thumbnail, staring down at the gorgon. 'How would this be? I was thinking – sometimes the boys in the pool, they get kind of frisky, they take to ducking each other. Under the water. Now what I was thinking, he breathes air, doesn't he? You know what I mean?'

Dominick and Womrath looked at each other. 'It sounds possible,' said Dominick.

'Out of the question. We don't know what his tolerance is. Suppose Kelly should damage him severely, or even—'

'Oh,' said Dominick. 'No, you're right, we couldn't take a chance.'

'I've been a games instructor for seventy-three years – two rejuvenations—' Kelly began, bristling.

'No, it isn't that, Kelly,' said Womrath hastily. 'We're just thinking, George isn't human. So how do we know how he'd react to a ducking?'

'On the other hand,' Dominick said, 'gorgons *do* turn blue when they're not happy – we have Rubinson's assurance for that. It seems to me George wouldn't be happy when smothering; that would be the whole point, wouldn't it? Dr Alvarez would supervise closely, of course. Really, Alvarez, I don't see why not. Kelly, if you'll tell what time would be most convenient for you—'

'Well,' said Kelly, looking at his thumbwatch, 'hell, the pool is empty now – it's ladies' day, but all the girls are down in Section Seven, hanging around Mrs Carver. I hear she's still hysterical.'

Struck by a thought, Alvarez was bending over to speak to the gorgon. 'George, you breathe by spiracles, is that correct? Those little tubes all over your skin?'

'Yes,' said George.

'Well, do they work under water?'

'No.'

Dominick and Kelly were listening with interest.

If we held you under water, would it hurt you?'

George flickered uncertainly, from rose to pale magenta. 'Don't know. Little bit.'

The three men leaned closer. 'Well, George,' said Dominick tensely, 'would that be a *punishment?*'

George flickered again, violently. 'Yes. No. Maybe. Don't know.'

They straightened again, disappointed; Dominick sighed gustily. 'He always gives us those mixed-up answers. I don't know. Let's try it – what else can we do?'

Kelly found himself paired off with George, following Dominick and Dr Alvarez, and preceding Womrath and an orderly named Josling who was wheeling one of the dispensary pul-motors. The up-curving corridors were deserted. Kelly lagged a little, adjusting his pace to George's waddling steps. After a moment, he was surprised to feel something small and soft grip his fingers. He looked down; George the gorgon had put one seven-fingered 'hand' into his. The gorgon's flower-like photoceptors were turned trustfully upward.

Kelly was taken by surprise. No children were allowed on the Satellite, but Kelly had been the father of eight in a previous rejuvenation. The confiding touch stirred old memories. 'That'll be all right,' said Kelly gruffly. 'You just come along with me.'

The pool, as he had predicted, was empty. Ripples reflected faint threads of light up the walls. 'The shallow end would be better,' said Kelly. His voice was hollow, and echoed back flatly. Pausing to peel off his coverall, he led George carefully down the steps into the pool. Half submerged, George floated. Kelly drew him gently out into deeper water.

Dominick and the others arranged themselves along the brink in interested attitudes. Kelly cleared his throat. 'Well,' he said, 'the way it generally happens, one of the boys will grab ahold of another one, like this—' He put his hands on the smooth floating globe, and hesitated.

'Go ahead now, Kelly,' called Dominick. 'Remember, you have a direct order to do this.'

'Sure,' said Kelly. 'Well—' he turned to the gorgon.

'Hold your breath now!' He pressed downward. The gorgon seemed lighter than he had expected, like an inflated ball; it was hard to force it under.

Kelly pushed harder. George went under briefly and slipped out of Kelly's hands, bobbing to the surface. The gorgon's speaking trumpet cleared itself of water with a *phonk* and said, 'Nice. Do again, Kelly.'

Kelly glanced over at Dominick, who said, 'Yes. Again.' Dr Alvarez stroked his thin beard and said nothing.

Kelly took a deep sympathetic breath, and shoved the gorgon under. A few bubbles came to the surface; George's speaking trumpet broke water, but made no sound. Down below, Kelly could see his own pale hands gripping the gorgon's body; the water made them look bloodless; but not George; he was a clear, unblemished pink.

There was a discouraged silence when Kelly brought him back up.

'Listen,' said Dominick, 'I've got another idea. George, can you breathe through that speaking trumpet, too?'

'Yes,' said George cheerfully.

There was a chorus of disgusted 'Oh, wells.' Everybody brightened perceptibly. Josling polished his pul-motor with a rag. 'Go ahead, Kelly,' said Dominick. 'And this time, you hold him under.'

George went down for the third time. The bubbles swirled upward. The gorgon's speaking trumpet swayed toward the surface, but Kelly leaned farther over, blocking it with his forearm. After a moment, all of George's appendages began to contract. Kelly craned his neck downward anxiously. Was a hint of blue beginning to show?

'Keep him down,' said Alvarez sharply.

George was a blank sphere again. Then one or two of the limbs began to reappear; but they looked different somehow.

'Now?' said Kelly.

'Give him a second more,' said Dominick, leaning over precariously. 'It seems to me—'

Kelly's back muscles were knotted with tension. He did not like the way George's new limbs seemed to be flattening out, trailing limply – it was as if something had gone wrong in the works.

'I'm bringing him up,' he said hoarsely.

To Kelly's horror, when he lifted his hands. George stayed where he was. Kelly made a grab for him, but the gorgon slipped out from under his fingers. The new limbs stiffened and sculled vigorously; George darted away, deep under the water.

Leaning, open-mouthed, Dominick slipped and went into the pool with a majestic splash. He floundered and rose up, a moment later, streaming with water like a sea lion. Kelly, wading anxiously toward him, stopped when he saw that Dominick was safe. Both men looked down. Between them and around them swam George, darting and drifting by turns, as much at home in the pool as a speckled trout.

'Fins!' said Dominick, stack-jawed. 'And *gills!*'

It may as well be said that Dr Walter Alvarez was a misanthrope. He did not like people; he liked diseases. Down there on Planet Seven, once the trade mission was established, he could confidently expect enough new and startling ailments to keep him happy as a lark for years. Up here, all he got was sprained ankles, psychosomatic colds, hives and indigestion. There was one cook's helper named Samuels who kept coming back every Wednesday with the same boil on the back of his neck. It got so that in spite of himself, Alvarez spent the whole week dreading Wednesday. When he saw Samuels's earnest face coming through the door, something seemed to wind itself a little tighter inside him.

Some day, when Samuels opened his mouth to say, 'Hey, Doc' – Samuels always called him 'Doc' – the something inside him was going to break with a sound like a banjo string. What would happen then, Dr Alvarez was unable to imagine.

When the gorgon had first been brought up to the Satellite, there had been two or three delightful little fungus infections, then nothing. A great disappointment. Alvarez had isolated and cultured almost a hundred microorganisms found in smears he had taken from George, but they were all non-viable in human tissue. The viable bacteria, viruses, parasites that always turned up on a life-infested planet, were evidently lurking in some organism other than the gorgons. They swam, at night, across the optical field of Dr Alvarez's dreaming mind – rod-shaped ones, lens-shaped ones, wriggly ones, leggy ones and ones with teeth.

One morning Dr Alvarez awoke with a desperate resolve. It was a Tuesday. Alvarez went directly to the infirmary, relieved Nurse Trumble, who was on duty, and, opening a locked cabinet, filled a hypodermic from an ampule of clear straw-colored fluid. The trade name of this substance was Bets-off; it was a counter-inhibitant which stunned the censor areas of the forebrain chiefly affected by the Pavlov-Morganstern treatments. (By an odd coincidence, the patentee was a Dr Jekyll.) Alvarez injected two c.c.'s of it directly into the median basilic vein and sat down to wait.

After a few minutes his perpetual bad humor began to lift. He felt a pleasant ebullience; the colors of things around him seemed brighter and clearer. 'Ha!' said Alvarez. He got up and went to his little refrigerator, where, after some search, he found half a dozen of the cultures he had made of microorganisms taken from gorgon smears. They were quiescent, of course – deep-frozen. Alvarez warmed them cautiously and added nutrients. All morning, while the usual succession of minor complaints paraded through the infirmary, the cultures grew and multiplied. Alvarez was jovial with his patients; he cracked a joke or two, and handed out harmless pills all around.

By noon, four of the cultures were flourishing. Alvarez carefully concentrated them into one, and loaded another hypodermic with the resulting brew. To his liberated intelligence, the matter was clear: No organism, man or pig or gorgon, was altogether immune to the microbes it normally carried in its body. Upset the balance by injecting massive colonies of any one of them, and you were going to have a sick gorgon – i.e. Alvarez thought, a punished gorgon.

The treatment might also kill the patient, but Alvarez light-heartedly dismissed this argument as a quibble. (Or quabble?) Armed with his hypo, he went forth looking for George.

He found him in the small assembly room, together with Dominick, Womrath, and a mechanic named Bob Ritner. They were all standing around a curious instrument, or object of art, built out of bar aluminum. 'It's a rack,' Ritner explained proudly. 'I saw a picture of it once in a kid's book.'

The chief feature of the 'rack' was a long, narrow table, with a windlass at one end. It looked like a crude device for stretching something.

'We thought the time had come for stern measures,' Dominick said, mopping his head.

'In the olden days,' Ritner put in, 'they used these on the prisoners when they wouldn't talk.'

'I talk,' said George unexpectedly.

'It's another punishment, George,' Dominick explained kindly. 'Well, Alvarez, before we go ahead, I suppose you want to examine your patient.'

'Yes, just so, ha ha!' said Alvarez. He knelt down and peered keenly at George, who swiveled his photoceptors interestedly around to stare back. The doctor prodded George's hide; it was firm and resilient. The gorgon's color was a clear pink; the intricate folds of his auricles seemed crisp and alert.

Alvarez took a hand scale from his kit; it was preset for A-level gravity. 'Climb up here, George.' Obediently, the gorgon settled himself on the pan of the scale while Alvarez held it up. 'Hm,' said Alvarez. 'He's lost a good deal of weight.'

'He has?' asked Dominick hopefully.

'But he seems to be in unusually good condition – better than a week ago, I would say. Perhaps just a little sugar solution to pep him up—' Alvarez withdrew the hypo from his kit, aimed it at George's smooth skin and pressed the trigger. Dominick sighed. 'Well, I suppose we might as well go ahead. George, just hop up there and let Ritner tie those straps onto you.'

George obediently climbed onto the table. Ritner buckled straps around four of his limbs and then began to tighten the cylinder. 'Not too much,' said George anxiously.

'I'll be careful,' Ritner assured him. He kept on winding the cylinder up. 'How does that feel?' George's 'arms' and 'legs' were half again their usual length, and still stretching.

'Tickles,' said George.

Ritner went on turning the handle. Womrath coughed nervously and was shushed. George's limbs kept on getting longer; then his body started to lengthen visibly.

'Are you all right, George?' Dominick asked.

'All right.'

Ritner gave the handle a last despairing twist. George's elongated body stretched all the way in comfort from one end of the rack to the other: there was no place else for him to go. 'Nice,' said George. 'Do again.' He was glowing a happy pink.

Ritner, who seemed about to cry, petulantly kicked his machine. Alvarez snorted and went away. In the corridor, unseen, he jumped up and clicked his heels together. He was having a wonderful time; his only regret was that it was not tomorrow. Come to think of it, why wait till Wednesday?

Commandant Charles Watson Carver, S.S., had been trained to make quick and courageous decisions. Once you began to entertain a doubt of your own rightness, you would hesitate too much, begin to second-guess yourself, fall prey to superstition and anxiety, and end up without any power of decision at all.

The trouble was, you could never be right all the time. Following the book to the letter, or improvising brilliantly, either way, you were bound to make mistakes. The thing was, to cross them off and go ahead just the same.

Carver firmed his chin and straightened his back, looking down at the sick gorgon. It was sick, all right, there was no question about that: the thing's limbs drooped and weaved slightly, dizzily. Its hide was dry and hot to the touch. 'How long has he been like this?' Carver demanded, hesitating only slightly over the 'he': aliens were 'it' to him and always had been, but it didn't do to let anybody know it.

'Twenty minutes, more or less,' said Dr Nasalroad. 'I just got here myself' – he stifled a yawn – 'about ten minutes ago.'

'What are you doing here, anyway?' Carver asked him. 'It's Alvarez's shift.'

Nasalroad looked embarrassed. 'I know. Alvarez is in the hospital, as a patient. I think he assaulted a cook's helper named Samuels – poured soup over his head. He was shouting something about boiling the boil on Samuel's neck. We had to put him under sedation; it took three of us.'

Carver set his jaw hard. 'Nasalroad, what in thunder is happening on this wheel, anyhow? First this thing attacks my wife – then Alvarez—' He glared down at George. 'Can you pull him out of this, whatever it is?'

Nasalroad looked surprised. 'That would be a large order. We don't know any gorgon medicine – I was assuming you'd want to beam down and ask *them*.'

That was reasonable, of course: the only hitch was, as usual, a matter of interpretation. Was this something they had negligently allowed to happen to an important alien representative, or was it the necessary and proper punishment they had all been looking for? Carver glanced at his thumbwatch: it was just about three hours before the elders' deadline.

He asked Nasalroad, 'What color would you say he is now? Not pink, certainly.'

'No-o. But not blue, either. I'd call it a kind of violet.'

'Hm. Well, anyhow, he's got smaller than he was, isn't that right? *Conspicuously* smaller.'

Nasalroad admitted it.

Carver made his decision. 'Do the best you can,' he said to Nasalroad. He lifted his wristcom, said briskly, 'Have you got a line-of-sight to the planethead?'

'Yes, sir,' the operator answered.

'All right, get me Rubinson.'

A few seconds passed. *'Planethead.'*

'Rubinson, this is Carver. Tell the elders we've got a pretty unhappy gorgon here. We're not sure just what did it – might have been any one of a lot of things – but he's lost a good deal of weight, and his color' – Carver hesitated – 'it's bluish. Definitely *bluish*. Got that?'

'*Yes, chief. Thank goodness! I'll pass the message along right away, and call you back.*'

'Right.' Carver closed the wristcom with an assertive snap. The gorgon, when he glanced down at it, looked sicker than ever, but never mind. What happened to the gorgon was its lookout; Carver was doing his duty.

III

Alvarez awoke with a horrible headache and a sense of guilt. He was not in his own cubicle, but in one of the hospital bunks, dressed in a regulation set of hospital pajamas (with removable hood and gloves, capable of being converted into a spacesuit). He could just see the wall clock at the far end of the room. It was twenty-three hours – well into his shift. Alvarez scuttled out of bed, groaning, and looked at the chart beside it. *Mania, delusions. Sedation. Signed Nasalroad.*

Delusions: yes, he was having one now. He imagined he could remember heaving up a big tureen of mock-turtle soup over Samuels's startled face – splash, a smoking green torrent. Good heavens! If that was *real* – Samuels! And the gorgon!

Groaning and lurching, Alvarez darted out of the room, past the orderly, Munch, who was sitting with a story viewer on his lap and couldn't get up fast enough. 'Dr Alvarez! Dr Nasalroad said—'

'Never mind Nasalroad,' he snapped, pawing in the refrigerator. He remembered those cultures being right back *there:* but now they were gone.

'– not to let you up until you acted normal again. Uh, how do you feel, Doctor?'

'I feel fine! What difference does that make? How is *he*?'

Munch looked puzzled and apprehensive. 'Samuels? Just superficial burns. We put him to bed in his own cubby, because—'

'Not Samuels!' Alvarez hissed, grabbing Munch by the front of his suit. 'The gorgon!'

'Oh, well, he's been sick, too. How did you know, though, Doctor? You were snoring when it happened. Listen, let go my suit, you're making me nervous.'

'Where?' Alvarez demanded, thrusting his scrawny face close to the other's.

'Where what? Oh, you mean the *gorgon*? Up in the little assembly room, the last I—'

Alvarez was gone, out the door and down the corridor like a small, bearded fireball. He found an anxious crowd assembled – Commandant and Mrs Carver, Dominick and his staff, Urban and two assistants from Semantics, orderlies, porters, and Dr Nasalroad. Nasalroad had the gaunt and bright-eyed appearance of a man who has been on wake-up pills too long. He started when he saw Alvarez.

'What's up?' Alvarez demanded, grabbing his sleeve. 'Where's the gorgon? What—'

'Be quiet,' said Nasalroad. 'George is over in that corner behind Carver. We're waiting for the delegation from planet-side. Rubinson said they were coming up, three of them with some kind of a box …'

A loudspeaker said suddenly, 'I have the tender locked on. Contact. Contact is made. The lock is opening; get ready, here they come.'

Alvarez couldn't see past Carver's bulk; he tried to get away, but Nasalroad stopped him. 'I want to *see*,' he said irritably.

'Listen,' Nasalroad said. 'I know what you did. I checked the Bets-off and those cultures against inventory. The gorgon seems to be recovering nicely, no thanks to you. Now has the stuff worn off you, or not? Because if not—'

A rustle went over the group. Alvarez and Nasalroad turned in time to see the door opening. Two large, vigorous-looking gorgons waddled through; they were carrying an enameled metal box between them. *'Foop!'* said the first one, experimentally. 'Where is gorgon George?'

'I'm all right,' Alvarez muttered. 'If I wasn't, I'd have done something uncivilised to you by now, wouldn't I?'

'I guess so,' said Nasalroad. They elbowed closer as the group shifted, making a space around the three gorgons. Peering, on tiptoe, Alvarez could see George standing shakily beside the other two. 'He looks terrible. Those are big ones, those other two, aren't they?'

'Not as big as George was when we got him,' Nasalroad muttered. 'Listen, Walt, if it turns out you've ruined the whole thing, I'll take a dose of Bets-off myself, and—'

'Listen!' snarled Alvarez. One of the gorgons was explaining. 'This is panga box. What you call? You know panga?'

'Well, uh, yes and no,' said Dominick uncomfortably. 'But what about the punishment? We understood—'

'Punishment later. You George, go in box.' Obediently, George waddled over and squatted beside the mouth of the box. He bobbed uncertainly; he looked for all the world like a large woman trying to get into a small sports copter. There was a minor outbreak of nervous laughter, quickly suppressed.

George leaned, retracting most of his upper appendages. His round body began to be composed into a squarish shape, wedging itself into the box.

The other gorgons watched with an air of tension, photoceptors rigidly extended. A hush fell. Among the humans present there was a general air of Why-are-we-all-whispering?

George wriggled and oozed farther into the box. Momentarily he stuck. He flicked blue, then pink. His 'feet,' almost retracted, scrabbled feebly at the bottom of the box. Then he was in.

One of the other gorgons solemnly closed the lid on him and fastened it to make sure, then opened it again and helped him out. All three gorgons began to make rhythmic swaying motions with their 'arms' and other appendages. George, Alvarez thought, looked smug. He felt a sudden premonitory pang. What had he done? 'What's it all about?' Nasalroad demanded. 'Are they measuring him for a coffin, or—'

Dominick, overhearing, turned and said, 'I don't think so. Now this is interesting. You remember they said a panga box. What I'm afraid of is, they may have a standard of size. You see what I mean, they're measuring George to see if he falls below the minimum standard of, uh, panga relations.'

'Oh, heavens,' said another voice. It was Urban of Semantics, who had been neglected of late; they hadn't needed him since George learned English. He was peering over Dominick's shoulder, looking dumbfounded. He said, 'But don't you know the word we've been translating as "elders" really means "smallest ones"? Good heavens—'

'I don't see—' Dominick began, but the Commandant's voice drowned him out. 'Quiet! Quiet please!' Carver was trumpeting. He went on, 'Our friends from Seven have an announcement to make. Now, then.'

To everyone's surprise, it was George who spoke, in the lisping accents of the gorgon language. No human present understood a word of it except Urban, who turned pale under his tan and began stammering inaudibly to himself.

One of the larger gorgons began to speak when George stopped. 'Most elder person, known to you by name George, wishes me to thank you all for kindness done him when he was humble youth.'

('Youth,' muttered Urban. 'But it really means "ungainly one" – or "fat boy"! Oh, my *heavens*!') 'Now that he has become an elder, it will be his most pleasure to repay all kindness in agreeable legislative manner.'

('What does that mean?' Alvarez said aggrievedly. 'Why can't he talk for himself, anyway?'

'It would be beneath *his* dignity now,' said Nasalroad. 'Hush!')

'– If,' said the gorgon, 'you will succeed in giving elder person, known by name George, proper punishment as aforesaid.'

While the others stared with dumb dismay, Carver briskly snapped open his wristcom. 'Exactly how long have we got till that gorgon deadline is up?' he demanded.

There was a pause, while ears strained to catch the tiny voice.
'Just under half an hour.'

'This meeting will come to order!' said Carver, banging on the table. George and the other two gorgons were sitting opposite him, with the centerpiece of nasturtiums and ferns between them. Grouped around Carver were Dominick, Urban, Womrath, Alvarez, Nasalroad, Kelly and Ritner.

'Now this is the situation,' Carver said aggressively. 'This gorgon turns out to be a member of their ruling council, I don't understand why, but never mind that now – the point is, he's friendly disposed towards us, so we've succeeded in this mission *if* we can find that proper punishment – otherwise we're in the soup. Suggestions.'

(Dominick craned his bald head toward Alvarez across the table. 'Doctor, I had a thought,' he murmured. 'Would you say – is there anything peculiar about the gorgon's body constitution, as compared say to ours?'

'Certainly,' said Alvarez, dourly. 'Any number of things. You name it, they—')

Giving them a dirty look, Carver nodded to Ritner. 'Yes?'

'Well, I was thinking. I know the rack was a washout, but there was another thing they used to use, called the Iron Virgin. It had a door, like, with spikes on it—'

('What I had in mind,' Dominick said, 'is there anything that would tend to limit their body size – any danger or disadvantage in growing large?'

Alvarez frowned and looked at Nasalroad, who hitched his chair closer. 'The pressure?' said Nasalroad tentatively. They rubbed their chins and looked at each other with professional glints in their eyes.

'What *about* the pressure?' Dominick prompted eagerly.)

'How long would it take you to build a thing like that?' Carver was asking Ritner.

'Well – ten, eleven hours.'

'Too long. That's out. Next!'

('They're actually a single cell – all colloidal fluid, at a considerable osmotic pressure. The bigger they get, the more pressure it takes to keep that shape. If they got too big, I rather imagine—' Alvarez snapped his fingers, awed. 'They'd burst!')

Carver turned with an indignant glare. 'Gentlemen, if I could get a little cooperation out of you, instead of this continual distraction— All right, Womrath?'

'Sir, I was just wondering, suppose if we let him turn into a fish, the way he did before in the pool – but then we'd net him and take him out of the water fast. That way, maybe—'

'It wouldn't work,' said Kelly. 'He changed back in about a second, the other time.'

Nobody was paying any attention to him. One of the big gorgons, who had been staring fixedly at the flowers in the middle of the table, had suddenly grabbed a handful and was stuffing them into his mouth. George said something shrill in gorgon talk, and snatched the flowers away again. The other gorgon looked abashed, but flushed pink.

George, on the other hand, was distinctly blue.

His 'hand,' clutching the mangled flowers, hesitated. Slowly, as if with an effort, he put them back in the bowl.

The other two gorgons twined their 'arms' around him. After a moment George looked more like his old self, but a hint of blue remained.

'What is it?' said Carver alertly. 'Did we do something, finally?' He snapped open his wristcom. 'There's still ten minutes before the deadline, so—'

'Did you turn blue because we punished you, George?' Womrath asked.

'No,' said George unexpectedly. 'Hard for me to be elder.' He added a few words in his own language to the other gorgons, and their 'arms' twined around him again. 'Before, they panga to *me*,' added George.

('Then that's why he took the pie away from the Commandant's wife!' said Dominick, smiting himself on the forehead.

'Of course. They—')

'What's that? What's that?' Carver turned, bristling.

'Why, this explains that pie business,' said Dominick. 'He felt protective towards your wife, you see – that's what "panga" means. They none of them have much control over their own appetites, so they guard each other. As they grow older, and get more self-control, they're expected to get smaller, not bigger. George felt confused about his panga relationships to us, but in your wife's case, he was positive one more mouthful would make her explode—'

Carver was red to the ears. 'Nonsense!' he shouted, 'Dominick, you're being insulting, insubordinate and unpatriotic!'

George, looking on interestedly, piped a few words in the gorgon language. One of the other gorgons immediately spoke up: 'Elder person says, you with smooth head are a smart man. He says, the other big one who talks too much is wrong.'

Carver's jaws worked. He looked at the gorgons, then around the table. No one said anything.

Carver set his jaw heroically. 'Well, gentlemen,' he began, 'we certainly tried, but—'

'Wait a minute!' said Alvarez. Somewhere in his narrow skull a great light had dawned. 'George, am I panga to you?'

George's auricles weaved tensely. 'Yes,' he said. 'You very small man.'

'Good,' said Alvarez, dry-washing his bony hands. 'And you still have to be punished, for that mistake you made at the banquet?'

George's speaking tube buzzed unhappily. 'Yes,' he said.

'All right,' said Alvarez. Everybody was looking at him, with expressions varying from puzzlement to alarm. Alvarez took a deep breath. 'Then here are my orders to you,' he said. *Do as you please!*'

There was a hiss of indrawn breath from Urban. Most of the others looked at Alvarez as if he had grown snakes for hair.

'Doctor,' said Carver, 'have you gone off your—'

The chorus of gasps stopped him. Up on the table, flushing blue and bright pink by turns like a sky sign, George was gobbling up the flowers in the centerpiece. Next he ate the bowl. One of his flailing limbs raked in the scratch pad Urban had been doodling on. He ate that.

Next moment he was leaping to the floor, making Ritner duck wildly as he passed. Part of Dominick's detachable hood went with him, disappearing with hoarse munching sounds. With a gulp, George swallowed it and began on the carpet. He was eating greedily, frantically. The other two gorgons hovered around him with shrill gorgon cries, but he ate on, oblivious. Now he was bright blue and bulging, but still he ate.

'Stop it!' shouted Alvarez. 'George, *stop* that!' George rocked to a halt. Gradually his blueness faded. The other gorgons were prodding and patting him anxiously. George looked all right, but it was obvious as he stood there that he would never fit into the panga box again. He was as big as the other two; maybe a little bigger.

'Alvarez,' said Carver, wildly, 'why did you—'

'He was going to burst,' said Alvarez, twitching with excitement. 'Couldn't you tell? Another mouthful or two—'

Carver recovered himself. He straightened his coverall and thrust out his chin. 'At any rate,' he said, 'he was certainly blue that time. You all saw it – isn't that right?' He looked around triumphantly. 'And by heaven, it happened inside the time limit. So, unless I'm very much mistaken—'

One of the two attendant gorgons raised his photoceptors. It was hard to tell which was George, now, except that his color was still a little lavender. The other gorgon spoke two brief sentences in his own language, and then all three of them waddled off together toward the exit. 'What was that? What did he say?' demanded Carver. Urban cleared his throat; he had turned pale again. 'He said you should get the tender ready to take them back home.'

'The tender is there,' said Carver indignantly, 'they can go back any time they want. But what did he say about the punishment?'

Urban cleared his throat again, looking bemused. 'They say the punishment is good. More severe than any they ever thought of, in twenty thousand years. They say they won't have to punish Rubinson and the others, now, because you have done all the punishment necessary.'

'Well?' said Carver. 'Why are you looking that way? What's the hitch? Are they going to refuse to enter the Union, after all this?'

'No,' said Urban. 'They say we are all panga to them now. They'll do as we say – let us land and build the distribution centers, start them consuming in massive quantity …'

'But that'll destroy them!' someone interjected in a horrified tone.

'Oh, yes,' said Urban.

Carver sighed. He had been in the SAPS service most of his life and was proud of his record. He played it as a game; the new, virgin planets were the prizes, and he kept score with the row of tiny iridium buttons on his breast pocket. He said into his wristcom, 'Let me know when Rubinson and his crew are on the way up.'

There was a long wait. The silence grew oppressive. At length the wall screen lighted up with a view of Planet Seven, gilded along one cusp, blue-green and mysterious in the shadow. A silver spark was floating up out of the night side. 'Here they come now,' said the voice.

Carver sighed again. 'When they make contact,' he said, 'secure the tender and then signal for acceleration stations. We're leaving Seven – tell Mr Fruman to set a first approximation for our next star of call.'

Alvarez, twitching and frowning, clutched at the front of his coverall. 'You're letting them go?' he demanded. 'Not landing on Seven – after all this work?'

Carver was staring into the view plate. 'Some things,' he said slowly and unwillingly, 'are not meant to be consumed.'

STRANGER STATION

The clang of metal echoed hollowly down through the Station's many vaulted corridors and rooms. Paul Wesson stood listening for a moment as the rolling echoes died away. The maintenance rocket was gone, heading back to Home; they had left him alone in Stranger Station.

Stranger Station! The name itself quickened his imagination. Wesson knew that both orbital stations had been named a century ago by the then British administration of the satellite service; 'Home' because the larger, inner station handled the traffic of Earth, and its colonies; 'Stranger' because the outer station was designed specifically for dealings with foreigners … beings from outside the solar system. But even that could not diminish the wonder of Stranger Station, whirling out here alone in the dark – waiting for its once-in-two-decades visitor …

One man, out of all Sol's billions, had the task and privilege of enduring the alien's presence when it came. The two races, according to Wesson's understanding of the subject, were so fundamentally different that it was painful for them to meet. Well, he had volunteered for the job, and he thought he could handle it – the rewards were big enough.

He had gone through all the tests, and against his own expectations he had been chosen. The maintenance crew had brought him up as dead weight, drugged in a survival hamper; they had kept him the same way while they did their work, and then had brought him back to consciousness. Now they were gone. He was alone.

… But not quite.

'Welcome to Stranger Station, Sergeant Wesson,' said a pleasant voice. 'This is your alpha network speaking. I'm here to protect and serve you in every way. If there's anything you want, just ask me.' It was a neutral voice, with a kind of professional friendliness in it, like that of a good schoolteacher or rec supervisor.

Wesson had been warned, but he was still shocked at the human quality of it. The alpha networks were the last word in robot brains-computers, safety devices, personal servants, libraries, all wrapped up in one, with something so close to 'personality' and 'free will' that experts were still arguing the question. They were rare and fantastically expensive; Wesson had never met one before.

'Thanks,' he said now, to the empty air. 'Uh – what do I call you, by the way? I can't keep saying, "Hey, alpha network."'

'One of your recent predecessors called me Aunt Nettie,' was the response.

Wesson grimaced. Alpha network – Aunt Nettie. He hated puns; that wouldn't do. 'The aunt part is all right,' he said. 'Suppose I call you Aunt Jane. That was my mother's sister; you sound like her, a little bit.'

'I am honored,' said the invisible mechanism politely. 'Can I serve you any refreshments now? Sandwiches? A drink?'

'Not just yet,' said Wesson. 'I think I'll look the place over first.'

He turned away. That seemed to end the conversation as far as the network was concerned. A good thing; it was all right to have it for company, speaking when spoken to, but if it got talkative …

The human part of the Station was in four segments: bedroom, living room, dining room, bath. The living room was comfortably large and pleasantly furnished in greens and tans: the only mechanical note in it was the big instrument console in one corner. The other rooms, arranged in a ring around the living room, were tiny; just enough space for Wesson, a narrow encircling corridor, and the mechanisms that would serve him. The whole place was spotlessly clean, gleaming and efficient in spite of its twenty-year layoff.

This is the gravy part of the run, Wesson told himself. The month before the alien came – good food, no work, and an alpha network for conversation. 'Aunt Jane, I'll have a small steak now,' he said to the network. 'Medium rare, with hashed brown potatoes, onions and mushrooms, and a glass of lager. Call me when it's ready.'

'Right,' said the voice pleasantly. Out in the dining room, the autochef began to hum and cluck self-importantly. Wesson wandered over and inspected the instrument console. Airlocks were sealed and tight, said the dials; the air was cycling. The Station was in orbit, and rotating on its axis with a force at the perimeter, where Wesson was, of one g. The internal temperature of this part of the Station was an even 73.

The other side of the board told a different story; all the dials were dark and dead. Sector Two, occupying a volume some eighty-eight thousand times as great as this one, was not yet functioning.

Wesson had a vivid mental image of the Station, from photographs and diagrams – a five-hundred-foot duralumin sphere, onto which the shallow thirty-foot disk of the human section had been stuck apparently as an afterthought. The whole cavity of the sphere, very nearly – except for a honeycomb of supply and maintenance rooms, and the all-important, recently enlarged vats – was one cramped chamber for the alien …

'Steak's ready!' said Aunt Jane.

The steak was good, bubbling crisp outside the way he liked it, tender and pink inside. 'Aunt Jane,' he said with his mouth full, 'this is pretty soft, isn't it?'

'The steak?' asked the voice, with a faintly anxious note.

Wesson grinned. 'Never mind,' he said. 'Listen, Aunt Jane, you've been through this routine – how many times? Were you installed with the Station, or what?'

'I was not installed with the Station,' said Aunt Jane primly. 'I have assisted at three contacts.'

'Um. Cigarette,' said Wesson, slapping his pockets. The autochef hummed for a moment, and popped a pack of G.I.'s out of a vent. Wesson lit up. 'All right,' he said, 'you've been through this three times. There are a lot of things you can tell me, right?'

'Oh, yes, certainly. What would you like to know?'

Wesson smoked, leaning back reflectively, green eyes narrowed. 'First,' he said, 'read me the Pigeon report – you know, from the *Brief History*. I want to see if I remember it right.'

'Chapter Two,' said the voice promptly. 'First contact with a non-Solar intelligence was made by Commander Ralph C. Pigeon on 1 July, 1987, during an emergency landing on Titan. The following is an excerpt from his official report:

'"While searching for a possible cause for our mental disturbance, we discovered what appeared to be a gigantic construction of metal on the far side of the ridge. Our distress grew stronger with the approach to this construction, which was polyhedral and approximately five times the length of the *Cologne*.

'"Some of those present expressed a wish to retire, but Lt. Acuff and myself had a strong sense of being called or summoned in some indefinable way. Although our uneasiness was not lessened, we therefore agreed to go forward and keep radio contact with the rest of the party while they returned to the ship.

'"We gained access to the alien construction by way of a large, irregular opening ... The internal temperature was minus seventy-five degrees Fahrenheit; the atmosphere. appeared to consist of methane and ammonia ... Inside the second chamber, an alien creature was waiting for us. We felt the distress which I have tried to describe, to a much greater degree than before, and also the sense of summoning or pleading ... We observed that the creature was exuding a thick yellowish fluid from certain joints or pores in its surface. Though disgusted, I managed to collect a sample of this exudate, and it was later forwarded for analysis ..."

'The second contact was made ten years later by Commodore Crawford's famous Titan Expedition—'

'No, that's enough,' said Wesson. 'I just wanted the Pigeon quote.' He smoked, brooding. 'It seems kind of chopped off, doesn't it. Have you got a longer version in your memory banks anywhere?'

There was a pause. 'No,' said Aunt Jane.

'There was more to it when I was a kid,' Wesson complained nervously. 'I read that book when I was twelve, and I remember a long description of the alien … that is, I remember its being there.' He swung around. 'Listen, Aunt Jane – you're a sort of universal watchdog, that right? You've got cameras and mikes all over the Station?'

'Yes,' said the network, sounding – was it Wesson's imagination? – faintly injured.

'Well, what about Sector Two – you must have cameras up there, too, isn't that so?'

'Yes.'

'All right, then you can tell me. What do the aliens look like?'

There was a definite pause. 'I'm sorry, I can't tell you that,' said Aunt Jane.

'No,' said Wesson, 'I didn't think you could. You've got orders not to, I guess, for the same reason those history books have been cut since I was a kid. Now, what would the reason be? Have you got any idea, Aunt Jane?'

There was another pause. 'Yes,' the voice admitted.

'Well?'

'I'm sorry, I can't—'

'– tell you that,' Wesson repeated along with it. 'All right. At least we know where we stand.'

'Yes, Sergeant. Would you like some dessert?'

'No dessert. One other thing. *What happens to Station watchmen, like me, after their tour of duty?*'

'They are upgraded to Class Seven, students with unlimited leisure, and receive outright gifts of seven thousand stellors, plus free Class One housing …'

'Yeah, I know all that,' said Wesson, licking his dry lips. 'But here's what I'm asking you. The ones you know – what kind of shape were they in when they left here?'

'The usual human shape,' said the voice brightly. 'Why do you ask, Sergeant?'

Wesson made a discontented gesture. 'Something I remember from a bull session at the Academy. I can't get it out of my head; I know it had something to do with the Station. Just part of a sentence – "blind as a bat, and white bristles all over." Now, would that be a description of the alien … or the watchman when they came to take him away?'

Aunt Jane went into one of her heavy pauses. 'All right, I'll save you the trouble,' said Wesson. 'You're sorry, you can't tell me that.'

'I *am* sorry,' said the robot, sincerely.

As the slow days passed into weeks, Wesson grew aware of the Station almost as a living thing. He could feel its resilient metal ribs enclosing him, lightly bearing his weight with its own as it swung. He could feel the waiting emptiness 'up there' and he sensed the alert electronic network that spread around him everywhere, watching and probing, trying to anticipate his needs.

Aunt Jane was a model companion. She had a record library of thousands of hours of music; she had films to show him, and micro-printed books that he could read on the scanner in the living room; or if he preferred, she would read to him. She controlled the Station's three telescopes, and on request would give him a view of Earth, or the Moon, or Home …

But there was no news. Aunt Jane would obligingly turn on the radio receiver if he asked her, but nothing except static came out. That was the thing that weighed most heavily on Wesson, as time passed: the knowledge that radio silence was being imposed on all ships in transit, on the orbital stations, and on the planet-to-space transmitters. It was an enormous, almost a crippling handicap. Some information could be transmitted over relatively short distances by photophone, but ordinarily the whole complex traffic of the spacelanes depended on radio.

But this coming alien contact was so delicate a thing that even a radio voice, out here where the Earth was only a tiny disk twice the size of the Moon, might upset it. It was so precarious a thing, Wesson thought, than only one man could be allowed in the Station while the alien was there, and to give that man the company that would keep him sane, they had to install an alpha network …

'Aunt Jane?'

The voice answered promptly, 'Yes, Paul?'

'This distress that the books talk about – you wouldn't know what it is, would you?'

'No, Paul.'

'Because robot brains don't feel it, right?'

'Right, Paul.'

'So tell me this – why do they need a man here at all? Why can't they get along with just you?'

A pause. 'I don't know, Paul.' The voice sounded faintly wistful. Were those gradations of tone really in it, Wesson wondered, or was his imagination supplying them?

He got up from the living room couch and paced restlessly back and forth. 'Let's have a look at Earth,' he said. Obediently, the viewing screen on the console glowed into life: there was the blue Earth, swimming deep below him, in its first quarter, jewel bright. 'Switch it off,' Wesson said.

'A little music?' suggested the voice, and immediately began to play something soothing, full of woodwinds.

'No,' said Wesson. The music stopped.

Wesson's hands were trembling; he had a caged and frustrated feeling.

234

The fitted suit was in its locker beside the air lock. Wesson had been top-side in it once or twice; there was nothing to see up there, just darkness and cold. But he had to get out of this squirrel cage. He took the suit down and began to get into it.

'Paul,' said Aunt Jane anxiously, 'are you feeling nervous?'

'Yes,' he snarled.

'Then don't go into Sector Two,' said Aunt Jane.

'Don't tell me what to do, you hunk of tin!' said Wesson with sudden anger. He zipped up the front of his suit with a vicious motion.

Aunt Jane was silent.

Seething, Wesson finished his check-off and opened the lock door.

The air lock, an upright tube barely large enough for one man, was the only passage between Sector One and Sector Two. It was also the only exit from Sector One; to get here in the first place, Wesson had had to enter the big lock at the 'south' pole of the sphere, and travel all the way down inside, by drop hole and catwalk. He had been drugged unconscious at the time, of course. When the time came, he would go out the same way; neither the maintenance rocket nor the tanker had any space, or time, to spare.

At the 'north' pole, opposite, there was a third air lock, this one so huge it could easily have held an interplanet freighter. But that was nobody's business – no human being's.

In the beam of Wesson's helmet lamp, the enormous central cavity of the Station was an inky gulf that sent back only remote, mocking glimmers of light. The near walls sparkled with hoarfrost. Sector Two was not yet pres-surised; there was only a diffuse vapor that had leaked through the airseal and had long since frozen into the powdery deposit that lined the walls. The metal rang cold under his shod feet; the vast emptiness of the chamber was the more depressing because it was airless, unwarmed and unlit. *Alone*, said his footsteps; *alone* …

He was thirty yards up the catwalk when his anxiety suddenly grew stronger. Wesson stopped in spite of himself, and turned clumsily, putting his back to the wall. The support of the solid wall was not enough. The catwalk seemed threatening to tilt underfoot, dropping him into the lightless gulf.

Wesson recognized this drained feeling, this metallic taste at the back of his tongue. It was fear.

The thought ticked through his head, *They want me to be afraid.* But why? Why now? Of what?

Equally suddenly, he knew. The nameless pressure tightened like a great fist closing, and Wesson had the appalling sense of something so huge that it had no limits at all, descending, with a terrible endless swift slowness …

It was time.

His first month was up.

The alien was coming.

As Wesson turned, gasping, the whole huge structure of the Station around him seemed to dwindle to the size of an ordinary room … and Wesson with it, so that he seemed to himself like a tiny insect, frantically scuttling down the walls toward safety.

Behind him as he ran, the Station *boomed*.

In the silent rooms, all the lights were burning dimly. Wesson lay still, looking at the ceiling. Up there his imagination formed a shifting, changing image of the alien – huge, size, that kept on hideously falling toward his face … It was the dead puppy he had pulled out of the creek, that summer in Dakota … wet fur, limp head; cold, cold, *cold* …

With an effort, Wesson rolled over on the couch and lifted himself to one elbow. The pressure was an insistent chill weight on his skull; the room seemed to dip and swing around him in slow, dizzy circles.

Wesson felt his jaw muscles contorting with the strain as he knelt, then stood erect. His back and legs tightened; his mouth hung painfully open. He took one step, then another, timing them to hit the floor as it came upright.

The right side of the console, the one that had been dark, was lighted. Pressure in Sector Two, according to the indicator was about one and a third atmospheres. The airlock indicator showed a slightly higher pressure of oxygen and argon; that was to keep any of the alien atmosphere from contaminating Sector One, but it also meant that the lock would no longer open from either side. Wesson found that irrationally comforting.

'Lemme see Earth,' he gasped.

The screen lighted up as he stared into it. 'It's a long way down,' he said. A long, long way down to the bottom of that well … He had spent ten featureless years as a servo tech in Home Station. Before that, he'd wanted to be a pilot, but had washed out the first year – couldn't take the math. But he had never once thought of going back to Earth.

Now, suddenly, after all these years, that tiny blue disk seemed infinitely desirable.

'Aunt Jane, Aunt Jane, it's beautiful,' he mumbled.

Down there, he knew, it was spring; and in certain places, where the edge of darkness retreated, it was morning: a watery blue morning like the sea light caught in an agate, a morning with smoke and mist in it; a morning of stillness and promise. Down there, lost years and miles away, some tiny dot of a woman was opening her microscopic door to listen to an atom's song. Lost, lost, and packed away in cotton wool, like a specimen slide: one spring morning on Earth.

Black miles above, so fair that sixty Earths could have been piled one on another to make a pole for his perch, Wesson swung in his endless circle within a circle. Yet, vast as the gulf beneath him was, all this – Earth, Moon, orbital stations, ships; yes, the Sun and all the rest of his planets, too – was the merest sniff of space, to be pinched up between thumb and finger.

Beyond – there was the true gulf. In that deep night, galaxies lay sprawled aglitter, piercing a distance that could only be named in a meaningless number, a cry of dismay: O, O, O …

Crawling and fighting, blasting with energies too big for them, men had come as far as Jupiter. But if a man had been tall enough to lie with his boots toasting in the Sun and his head freezing at Pluto, still he would have been too small for that overwhelming emptiness. Here, not at Pluto, was the outermost limit of man's empire: here the Outside funneled down to meet it, like the pinched waist of an hour-glass: here, and only here, the two worlds came near enough to touch. Ours – and Theirs.

Down at the bottom of the board, now, the golden dials were faintly alight, the needles trembling ever so little on their pins.

Deep in the vats, the vats, the golden liquid was trickling down: '*Though disgusted, I took a sample of the exudate and it was forwarded for analysis …*'

Space-cold fluid, trickling down the bitter walls of the tubes, forming little pools in the cups of darkness; goldenly agleam there, half alive. The golden elixir. One drop of the concentrate would arrest aging for twenty years – keep your arteries soft, tonus good, eyes clear, hair pigmented, brain alert.

That was what the tests of Pigeon's sample had showed. That was the reason for the whole crazy history of the 'alien trading post' – first a hut on Titan, then later, when people understood more about the problem, Stranger Station.

Once every twenty years, an alien would come down out of Somewhere, and sit in the tiny cage we had made for him, and make us rich beyond our dreams – rich with life – and still we did not know why.

Above him, Wesson imagined he could see that sensed body a-wallow in the glacial blackness, its bulk passively turning with the station's spin, bleeding a chill gold into the lips of the tubes; drip, drop.

Wesson held his head. The pressure inside made it hard to think; it felt as if his skull were about to fly apart. 'Aunt Jane,' he said.

'Yes, Paul.' The kindly, comforting voice: like a nurse. The nurse who stands beside your cot while you have painful, necessary things done to you. Efficient, trained friendliness.

'Aunt Jane,' said Wesson, 'do you know why they keep coming back?'

'No,' said the voice precisely. 'It is a mystery.'

Wesson nodded. 'I had,' he said, 'an interview with Gower before I left Home. You know Gower? Chief of the Outerworld Bureau. Came up especially to see me.'

'Yes?' said Aunt Jane encouragingly.

'Said to me, "Wesson, you got to find out. Find out if we can count on them to keep up the supply. You know? There's fifty million more of us," he says, "than when you were born. We need more of the stuff, and we got to know if we can count on it. Because," he says, "you know what would happen if it stopped?" Do you know, Aunt Jane?'

'It would be,' said the voice, 'a catastrophe.'

'That's right,' Wesson said respectfully. 'It would. Like, he says to me, "What if the people in the Nefud area were cut off from the Jordan Valley Authority? Why, there'd be millions dying of thirst in a week.

' "Or what if the freighters stopped coming to Moon Base. Why," he says, "there'd be thousands starving and smothering to death."

'He says, "Where the water is, where you can get food and air, people are going to settle, and get married, you know? and have kids."

'He says, "If the so-called longevity serum stopped coming ..." Says, "Every twentieth adult of the Sol family is due for his shot this year." Says, "Of those, almost twenty per cent are one hundred fifteen or older." Says, "The deaths in that group in the first year would be at least three times what the actuarial tables call for." ' Wesson raised a strained face. 'I'm thirty-four, you know?' he said. 'That Gower, he made me feel like a baby.'

Aunt Jane made a sympathetic noise.

'Drip, drip,' said Wesson hysterically. The needles of the tall golden indicators were infinitesimally higher. 'Every twenty years we need more of the stuff, so somebody like me has to come out and take it for five lousy months. And one of *them* has to come out and sit there, and *drip. Why,* Aunt Jane? What for? Why should it matter to them whether we live a long time or not? Why do they keep on coming back? What do they take *away* from here?'

But to these questions, Aunt Jane had no reply.

All day and every day, the lights burned cold and steady in the circular gray corridor around the rim of Sector One. The hard gray flooring had been deeply scuffed in that circular path before Wesson ever walked there: the corridor existed for that only, like a treadmill in a squirrel cage; it said 'Walk,' and Wesson walked. A man would go crazy if he sat still, with that squirming, indescribable pressure on his head; and so Wesson paced off the miles, all day and every day, until he dropped like a dead man in the bed at night.

He talked, too, sometimes to himself, sometimes to the listening alpha network; sometimes it was difficult to tell which. 'Moss on a rock,' he muttered, pacing. 'Told him, wouldn't give twenty mills for any damn shell ... Little pebbles down there, all colors.' He shuffled on in silence for a while. Abruptly: 'I don't see *why* they couldn't have given me a cat.'

Aunt Jane said nothing. After a moment Wesson went on, 'Nearly everybody at Home has a cat, for God's sake, or a goldfish or something. You're all right, Aunt Jane, but I can't *see* you. My God, I mean if they couldn't send a man a woman for company, what I mean, my God, I never liked *cats*.' He swung around the doorway into the bedroom, and absent-mindedly slammed his fist into the bloody place on the wall.

'But a cat would have been *something*,' he said.

Aunt Jane was still silent.

'Don't pretend your damn feelings are hurt, I know you, you're only a damn machine,' said Wesson. 'Listen, Aunt Jane, I remember a cereal package one time that had a horse and a cowboy on the side. There wasn't much room, so about all you saw was their faces. It used to strike me funny how much they looked alike. Two ears on the top with hair in the middle. Two eyes. Nose. Mouth with teeth in it. I was thinking, we're kind of distant cousins, aren't we, us and the horses. But compared to that thing up there-we're *brothers*. You know?'

'Yes,' said Aunt Jane, quietly.

'So I keep asking myself, why couldn't they have sent a horse, or a cat, *instead* of a man? But I guess the answer is because only a man could take what I'm taking. God, only a man. Right?'

'Right,' said Aunt Jane with deep sorrow.

Wesson stopped at the bedroom doorway again and shuddered, holding onto the frame. 'Aunt Jane,' he said in a low, clear voice, 'you take pictures of *him* up there, don't you?'

'Yes, Paul.'

'And you take pictures of me. And then what happens? After it's all over, who looks at the pictures?'

'I don't know,' said Aunt Jane humbly.

'You don't know. But whoever looks at 'em, it doesn't do any good. Right? We got to find out why, why, why ... And we never do find out, do we?'

'No,' said Aunt Jane.

'But don't they figure that if the man who's going through it could see him, he might be able to tell something? That other people couldn't? Doesn't that make sense?'

'That's out of my hands, Paul.'

He sniggered. 'That's funny. Oh, that's funny.' He chortled in his throat, reeling around the circuit.

'Yes, that's funny,' said Aunt Jane.

'Aunt Jane, tell me what happens to the watchmen.'

'... I can't tell you that, Paul.'

He lurched into the living room, sat down before the console, beat on its smooth, cold metal with his fists. 'What are you, some kind of monster? Isn't there any blood in your veins, damn it, or oil or *anything?*'

'Please, Paul—'

'Don't you see, all I want to know, can they talk? Can they tell anything after their tour is over?'

'… No, Paul.'

He stood upright, clutching the console for balance. 'They can't? No, I figured. And you know why?'

'No.'

'Up there,' said Wesson obscurely. 'Moss on the rock.'

'Paul, what?'

'We get changed,' said Wesson, stumbling out of the room again. 'We get changed. Like a piece of iron next to a magnet. Can't help it. You – non-magnetic, I guess. Goes right through you, huh, Aunt Jane? You don't get changed. You stay here, wait for the next one.'

'… Yes,' said Aunt Jane.

'You know,' said Wesson, pacing, 'I can tell how he's lying up there. Head *that* way, tail the other. Am I right?'

'… Yes,' said Aunt Jane.

Wesson stopped, 'Yes,' he said intently. 'So you *can* tell me what you see up there, can't you, Aunt Jane?'

'No. Yes. It isn't allowed.'

'Listen, Aunt Jane, *we'll die* unless we can find out what makes those aliens tick! Remember that.' Wesson leaned against the corridor wall, gazing up. 'He's turning now – around this way. Right?'

'Well, what else is he doing? Come on, Aunt Jane, tell me!'

A pause. 'He is twitching his—'

'What?'

'I don't know the words.'

'My God, my God,' said Wesson, clutching his head, 'of course there aren't any words.' He ran into the living room, clutched the console and stared at the blank screen. He pounded the metal with his fist. 'You've got to show me, Aunt Jane, come on and show me, show me!'

'It isn't allowed,' Aunt Jane protested.

'You've got to do it just the same, or we'll *die,* Aunt Jane – millions of us, billions, and it'll be your fault, get it, *your fault,* Aunt Jane!'

'*Please,*' said the voice. There was a pause. The screen flickered to life, for an instant only. Wesson had a glimpse of something massive and dark, but half transparent, like a magnified insect – a tangle of nameless limbs, whip-like filaments, claws, wings …

He clutched at the edge of the console.

'Was that all right?' Aunt Jane asked.

'Of course! What do you think, it'll kill me to look at it? Put it back, Aunt Jane, put it back!'

Reluctantly, the screen lighted again. Wesson stared, and went on staring. He mumbled something.

'What?' said Aunt Jane.

'*Life of my love, I loathe thee,*' said Wesson, staring. He roused himself after a moment and turned away. The image of the alien stayed with him as he went reeling into the corridor again; he was not surprised to find that it reminded him of all the loathsome, crawling, creeping things the Earth was full of. That explained why he was not supposed to see the alien, or even know what it looked like – because that fed his hate. And it was all right for him to be afraid of the alien, but he was not supposed to hate it ... Why not? Why not?

His fingers were shaking. He felt drained, steamed, dried up and withered. The one daily shower Aunt Jane allowed him was no longer enough. Twenty minutes after bathing the acid sweat dripped again from his armpits, the cold sweat was beaded on his forehead, the hot sweat was in his palms. Wesson felt as if there were a furnace inside him, out of control, all the dampers drawn. He knew that under stress, something of the kind did happen to man: the body's chemistry was altered – more adrenalin, more glycogen in the muscles; eyes brighter, digestion retarded. That was the trouble – he was burning himself up, unable to fight the thing that tormented him, nor run from it.

After another circuit, Wesson's steps faltered. He hesitated, and went into the living room. He leaned over the console, staring. From the screen, the alien stared blindly up into space. Down in the dark side, the golden indicators had climbed: the vats were more than two-thirds filled.

... To *fight*, or *run* ...

Slowly Wesson sank down in front of the console. He sat hunched, head bent, hands squeezed tight between his knees, trying to hold onto the thought that had come to him.

If the alien felt a pain as great as Wesson's – or greater—

Stress might alter the alien's body chemistry, too.

Life of my love, I loathe thee.

Wesson pushed the irrelevant thought aside. He stared at the screen, trying to envisage the alien, up there, wincing in pain and distress – sweating a golden sweat of horror ...

After a long time, he stood up and walked into the kitchen. He caught the table edge to keep his legs from carrying him on around the circuit. He sat down.

Humming fondly, the autochef slid out a tray of small glasses – water, orange juice, milk. Wesson put the water glass to his stiff lips; the water was cool and hurt his throat. Then the juice, but he could only drink a little of it; then he sipped the milk. Aunt Jane hummed approvingly.

Dehydrated – how long had it been since he had eaten, or drunk? He looked at his hands. They were thin bundles of sticks, ropy-veined, with hard yellow claws. He could see the bones of his forearms under the skin, and his heart's beating stirred the cloth at his chest. The pale hairs on his arms and thighs – were they blond or white?

The blurred reflections in the metal trim of the dining room gave him no answers – only pale faceless smears of gray. Wesson felt light-headed and very weak, as if he had just ended a bout of fever. He fumbled over his ribs and shoulder-bones. He was thin.

He sat in front of the autochef for a few minutes more, but no food came out. Evidently Aunt Jane did not think he was ready for it, and perhaps she was right. *Worse for them than for us,* he thought dizzily. *That's why the Station's so far out; why radio silence, and only one man aboard. They couldn't stand it all, otherwise* ... Suddenly he could think of nothing but sleep – the bottomless pit, layer after layer of smothering velvet, numbing and soft ... His leg muscles quivered and twitched when he tried to walk, but he managed to get to the bedroom and fall on the mattress. The resilient block seemed to dissolve under him. His bones were melting.

He woke with a clear head, very weak, thinking cold and clear: *When two alien cultures meet, the stronger must transform the weaker with love or hate.* 'Wesson's Law,' he said aloud. He looked automatically for pencil and paper, but there was none, and he realised he would have to tell Aunt Jane, and let her remember it.

'I don't understand,' she said.

'Never mind, remember it anyway. You're good at that, aren't you?'

'Yes, Paul.'

'All right ... I want some breakfast.'

He thought about Aunt Jane, so nearly human, sitting up here in her metal prison, leading one man after another through the torment of hell ... nurse-maid, protector, torturer. They must have known that something would have to give ... But the alphas were comparatively new; nobody understood them very well. Perhaps they really thought that an absolute prohibition could never be broken.

... the stronger must transform the weaker ...

I'm *the stronger,* he thought. *And that's the way it's going to be.* He stopped at the console, and the screen was blank. He said angrily, 'Aunt Jane!' And with a guilty start, the screen flickered into life.

Up there, the alien had rolled again in his pain. Now the great clustered eyes were staring directly into the camera; the coiled limbs threshed in pain: the eyes were staring, asking, pleading ...

'*No,*' said Wesson, feeling his own pain like an iron cap, and he slammed his hand down on the manual control. The screen went dark. He looked up, sweating, and saw the floral picture over the console.

The thick stems were like antennae, the leaves thoraxes, the buds like blind insect eyes. The whole picture moved slightly, endlessly, in a slow waiting rhythm.

Wesson clutched the hard metal of the console, and stared at the picture, with sweat cold on his brow, until it turned into a calm, meaningless arrangement of lines again. Then he went into the dining room, shaking, and sat down.

After a moment he said, 'Aunt Jane, does it get worse?'

'No. From now on, it gets better.'

'How long?' he asked vaguely.

'One month.'

A month, getting better ... that was the way it had always been, with the watchman swamped and drowned, his personality submerged. Wesson thought about the men who had gone before him – Class Seven citizenship, with unlimited leisure, and Class One housing, yes, sure – in a sanatorium.

His lips peeled back from his teeth, and his fists clenched hard. *Not me!* he thought.

He spread his hands on the cool metal to steady them. He said, 'How much longer do they usually stay able to talk?'

'You are already talking longer than any of them ...'

Then there was a blank. Wesson was vaguely aware, in snatches, of the corridor walls moving past, and the console glimpsed, and of a thunderous cloud of ideas that swirled around his head in a beating of wings. The aliens: what did they want? And what happened to the watchmen in Stranger Station?

The haze receded a little and he was in the dining room again, staring vacantly at the table. Something was wrong.

He ate a few spoonsful of the gruel the autochef served him, then pushed it away; the stuff tasted faintly unpleasant. The machine hummed anxiously and thrust a poached egg at him, but Wesson got up from the table.

The Station was all but silent. The resting rhythm of the household machines throbbed in the walls, unheard. The blue-lit living room was spread out before him like an empty stage setting, and Wesson stared as if he had never seen it before.

He lurched to the console and stared down at the pictured alien on the screen: heavy, heavy, a-sprawl with pain in the darkness. The needles of the golden indicators were high, the enlarged vats almost full. *It's too much for him,* Wesson thought with grim satisfaction. The peace that followed the pain had not descended as it was supposed to; no, not this time!

He glanced up at the painting over the console: heavy crustacean limbs that swayed gracefully in the sea ...

He shook his head violently. *I won't let it; I won't give in!*

He held the back of one hand close to his eyes. He saw the dozens of tiny cuneiform wrinkles stamped into the skin over the knuckles, the pale hairs sprouting, the pink shiny flesh of recent scars. I'm *human*, he thought. But when he let his hand fall onto the console, the bony fingers seemed to crouch like crustaceans' legs, ready to scuttle.

Sweating, Wesson stared into the screen. Pictured there, the alien met his eyes, and it was as if they spoke to each other, mind to mind, an instantaneous communication that needed no words. There was a piercing sweetness to it, a melting, dissolving luxury of change into something that would no longer have any pain … A pull, a calling.

Wesson straightened up slowly, carefully, as if he held some fragile thing in his mind that must not be handled roughly, or it would disintegrate. He said hoarsely, 'Aunt Jane!'

She made some responsive noise.

He said, 'Aunt Jane, I've got the answer! The whole thing! Listen, now wait – listen!' He paused a moment to collect his thoughts. *'When two alien cultures meet, the stronger must transform the weaker with love or hate.* Remember? You said you didn't understand what that meant. I'll *tell* you what it means. When these – monsters – met Pigeon a hundred years ago on Titan, *they knew* we'd have to meet again. They're spreading out, colonising, and so are we. We haven't got interstellar flight yet, but give us another hundred years, we'll *get* it. *We'll wind up out there, where they are.* And they can't stop us. Because they're not killers, Aunt Jane, it isn't in them. They're *nicer* than us. See, they're like the missionaries, and we're the South Sea Islanders. *They* don't kill their enemies, oh no – perish the thought!'

She was trying to say something, to interrupt him, but he rushed on. 'Listen! The longevity serum – that was a lucky accident. But they played it for all it's worth. Slick and smooth – they come and give us the stuff free – they don't ask for a thing in return. Why not? Listen.

'They come here, and the shock of that first contact makes them sweat out that golden gook we need. Then, the last month or so, the pain always eases off. Why? Because the two minds, the human and alien, they stop fighting each other. Something gives way, it goes soft, and there's a mixing together. And that's where you get the human casualties of this operation – the bleary men that come out of here not even able to talk human language any more. Oh, I suppose they're happy – happier than I am! – because they've got something big and wonderful inside 'em. Something that you and I can't even understand. But if you took them and put them together again with the aliens who spent time here, *they could all live together – they're adapted.*

'That's what they're aiming for!' He struck the console with his fist. 'Not now – but a hundred, two hundred years from now! When we start expanding out to the stars – when we go a-conquering – we'll have already been conquered! Not by weapons, Aunt Jane, not by hate – by love! Yes, love! *Dirty, stinking, low-down, sneaking love!'*

Aunt Jane said something, a long sentence, in a high, anxious voice.

'What?' said Wesson irritably. He couldn't understand a word.

Aunt Jane was silent. 'What, what?' Wesson demanded, pounding the console. 'Have you got it through your tin head or not? *What?'*

Aunt Jane said something else, tonelessly. Once more, Wesson could not make out a single word.

He stood frozen. Warm tears started suddenly out of his eyes. 'Aunt Jane—' he said. He remembered, *You are already talking longer than any of them.* Too late? Too late? He tensed, then whirled and sprang to the closet where the paper books were kept. He opened the first one his hand struck.

The black letters were alien squiggles on the page, little humped shapes, without meaning.

The tears were coming faster, he couldn't stop them: tears of weariness, tears of frustration, tears of hate. *'Aunt Jane!'* he roared.

But it was no good. The curtain of silence had come down over his head. He was one of the vanguard – the conquered men, the ones who would get along with their strange brothers, out among the alien stars.

The console was not working any more; nothing worked when he wanted it. Wesson squatted in the shower stall, naked, with a soup bowl in his hands. Water droplets glistened on his hands and forearms; the pale short hairs were just springing up, drying.

The silvery skin of reflection in the bowl gave him back nothing but a silhouette, a shadow man's outline. He could not see his face.

He dropped the bowl and went across the living room, shuffling the pale drifts of paper underfoot. The black lines on the paper, when his eye happened to light on them, were worm shapes, crawling things, conveying nothing. He rolled slightly in his walk; his eyes were glazed. His head twitched, every now and then, sketching a useless motion to avoid pain.

Once the bureau chief, Gower, came to stand in his way. 'You fool,' he said, his face contorted in anger, 'you were supposed to go on to the end, like the rest. Now look what you've done!'

'I found out, didn't I?' Wesson mumbled, and as he brushed the man aside like a cobweb, the pain suddenly grew more intense. Wesson clasped his head in his hands with a grunt, and rocked to and fro a moment, uselessly, before he straightened and went on. The pain was coming in waves now, so tall that at their peak his vision dimmed out, violet, then gray.

It couldn't go on much longer. Something had to burst.

He paused at the bloody place and slapped the metal with his palm, making the sound ring dully up into the frame of the Station: *rroom, rroom.*

Faintly an echo came back: boo-oom.

Wesson kept going, smiling a faint and meaningless smile. He was only marking time now, waiting. Something was about to happen.

The kitchen doorway sprouted a sudden sill and tripped him. He fell heavily, sliding on the floor, and lay without moving beneath the slick gleam of the autochef.

The pressure was too great: the autochef's clucking was swallowed up in the ringing pressure, and the tall gray walls buckled slowly in …

The Station lurched.

Wesson felt it through his chest, palms, knees and elbows: the floor was plucked away for an instant and then swung back.

The pain in his skull relaxed its grip a little. Wesson tried to get to his feet.

There was an electric silence in the Station. On the second try, he got up and leaned his back against a wall. *Cluck*, said the autochef suddenly, hysterically, and the vent popped open, but nothing came out.

He listened, straining to hear. What?

The Station bounced beneath him, making his feet jump like a puppet's; the wall slapped his back hard, shuddered and was still; but far off through the metal cage came a long angry groan of metal, echoing, diminishing, dying. Then silence again.

The Station held its breath. All the myriad clickings and pulses in the walls were suspended; in the empty rooms the lights burned with a yellow glare, and the air hung stagnant and still. The console lights in the living room glowed like witchfires. Water on the dropped bowl, at the bottom of the shower stall, shone like quicksilver, waiting.

The third shock came. Wesson found himself on his hands and knees, the jolt still tingling in the bones of his body, staring at the floor. The sound that filled the room ebbed away slowly and ran down into the silences: a resonant metallic sound, shuddering away now along the girders and hull plates, rattling tinnily into bolts and fittings, diminishing, noiseless, gone. The silence pressed down again.

The floor leaped painfully under his body: one great resonant blow that shook him from head to foot.

A muted echo of that blow came a few seconds later, as if the shock had traveled across the Station and back.

The bed, Wesson thought, and scrambled on hands and knees through the doorway, along a floor curiously tilted, until he reached the rubbery block.

The room burst visibly upward around him, squeezing the block flat. It dropped back as violently, leaving Wesson bouncing helplessly on the mattress, his limbs flying. It came to rest, in a long reluctant groan of metal.

Wesson rolled up on one elbow, thinking incoherently, *Air, the air lock.* Another blow slammed him down into the mattress, pinched his lungs shut, while the room danced grotesquely over his head. Gasping for breath in the ringing silence, Wesson felt a slow icy chill rolling toward him across the room … and there was a pungent smell in the air. *Ammonia!* he thought; and the odorless, smothering methane with it.

His cell was breached. The burst membrane was fatal: the alien's atmosphere would kill him.

Wesson surged to his feet. The next shock caught him off balance, dashed him to the floor. He arose again, dazed and limping; he was still thinking confusedly, *The air lock, get out.*

When he was halfway to the door, all the ceiling lights went out at once. The darkness was like a blanket around his head. It was bitter cold now in the room and the pungent smell was sharper. Coughing, Wesson hurried forward. The floor lurched under his feet.

Only the golden indicators burned now: full to the top, the deep vats brimming, golden-lipped, gravid, a month before the time. Wesson shuddered.

Water spurted in the bathroom, hissing steadily on the tiles, rattling in the plastic bowl at the bottom of the shower stall. The lights winked on and off again. In the dining room, he heard the autochef clucking and sighing. The freezing wind blew harder: he was numb with cold to the hips. It seemed to Wesson abruptly that he was not at the top of the sky at all, but down, *down* at the bottom of the sea … trapped in this steel bubble, while the dark poured in.

The pain in his head was gone, as if it had never been there, and he understood what that meant: Up there, the great body was hanging like a butcher's carrion in the darkness. Its death struggles were over, the damage done.

Wesson gathered a desperate breath, shouted, 'Help me! The alien's dead! He kicked the Station apart – the methane's coming in! Get help, do you hear me? *Do you hear me?*'

Silence. In the smothering blackness, he remembered: *She can't understand me any more. Even if she's alive.*

He turned, making an animal noise in his throat. He groped his way on around the room, past the second doorway. Behind the walls, something was dripping with a slow cold tinkle and splash, a forlorn night sound. Small, hard, floating things rapped against his legs. Then he touched a smooth curve of metal: the airlock.

Eagerly he pushed his feeble weight against the door. It didn't move. Cold air was rushing out around the door frame, a thin knife-cold stream, but the door itself was jammed tight.

The suit! He should have thought of that before. If he just had some pure air to breathe, and a little warmth in his fingers … But the door of the suit locker would not move, either. The ceiling must have buckled.

And that was the end, he thought, bewildered. There were no more ways out. But there *had* to be— He pounded on the door until his arms would not lift any more; it did not move. Leaning against the chill metal, he saw a single light blink on overhead.

The room was a wild place of black shadows and swimming shapes – the book leaves, fluttering and darting in the air stream. Schools of them beat wildly at the walls, curling over, baffled, trying again; others were swooping around the outer corridor, around and around: he could see them whirling past the doorways, dreamlike, a white drift of silent paper in the darkness.

The acrid smell was harsher to his nostrils. Wesson choked, groping his way to the console again. He pounded it with his open hand, crying weakly: he wanted to see Earth.

But when the little square of brightness leaped up, it was the dead body of the alien that Wesson saw.

It hung motionless in the cavity of the Station, limbs dangling stiff and still, eyes dull. The last turn of the screw had been too much for it: but Wesson had survived ...

For a few minutes.

The dead alien face mocked him; a whisper of memory floated into his mind: *We might have been brothers* ... All at once Wesson passionately wanted to believe it – wanted to give in, turn back. That passed. Wearily he let himself sag into the bitter *now*, thinking with thin defiance, *It's done – hate wins. You'll have to stop this big giveaway – can't risk this happening again. And we'll hate you for that – and when we get out to the stars—*

The world was swimming numbly away out of reach. He felt the last fit of coughing take his body, as if it were happening to someone else besides him.

The last fluttering leaves of paper came to rest. There was a long silence in the drowned room.

Then:

'Paul,' said the voice of the mechanical woman brokenly; 'Paul,' it said again, with the hopelessness of lost, unknown, impossible love.

ASK ME ANYTHING

It began with the crutch. Then came the iron hook, then the first mechanical limbs. And finally—

Bedlam. Thin metal legs switching by, a moving forest of scissors. Metal arms flashing in balance; torsos of metal, like bright dented beetles. Round metal skulls – that cupped the swift wink and stare of human eyes.

Krisch, watching them in his desk scanner, kept the volume turned down. The unit walls were deliberately made sound-reflecting; the children grew up in the atmosphere of their own clattering noise, and they learned to shout against it. To soldiers so reared, there would be no terror in the roar of battle. But Krisch, who was only human, wore earplugs when he walked among them.

The river of metal funneled into classrooms, stopped. Lights flashed on over the scanners, on the board that covered the twenty-foot wall facing Krisch's desk. Instruction had begun.

Krisch watched the board for a while, then switched on the illuminated panel that carried his notes and began to dictate his weekly report. He was a small, spare man, with thinning strands of iron-gray hair roached stiffly back over his freckled brown scalp. His mouth was straight, and the lines around it showed that he never smiled; but there was a glint of controlled, ironic humor in his watchful eyes.

A bell spoke and a red light gleamed. Krisch looked up sharply, identified the scanner under the warning light, and transferred its image to his own desk screen. Half a thousand pairs of eyes stared back at him from the massed metal forms in the amphitheater.

Krisch set the playback cube for one minute preceding. The robot instructors were equipped to answer all permissible questions; therefore a nonpermissible question had just been asked.

The harsh voice of the robot said, '– along the inguinal canal and enters the abdomen through the internal abdominal ring. Yes? What is your question?'

There was a pause. Krisch scanned the rows of gleaming heads, could not tell which one had signaled 'Question.' Then the abnormally loud but still childish voice spoke, and simultaneously the student's number appeared in the recording circle at the lower left corner of the screen. Krisch statted it automatically. The ten-year-old voice bellowed:

'What is a kiss?'

There was a five-second pause. The robot answered, 'Your question is meaningless. It has been reported to the Director and you will hold yourself in readiness for his orders.' Then it resumed its lecture.

Krisch switched the scanner back to normal operation. The robot was now discussing the prostate gland. Krisch waited until it had reached the end of a sentence and then pressed the 'Attention' button on his console. He said, 'Cadet ER17235 will report to the Director's office immediately.' He cleared the board and sank into his cushioned chair, frowning.

A non-permissible question was bad enough in itself; there had not been one in the oldest class in the last six years of the Project's existence. It was not only bad; it was indefensible. Logically, it should not have happened – the entire student body of the unit, according to a check made not a week ago, was correctly conditioned.

But that was not all. The robot instructor had been perfectly truthful, to the extent of its own knowledge, when it had said the cadet's question was meaningless. The subject of normal human love relationships was not on the curriculum for two more years. To introduce it earlier, with the desired effect of repugnance, would seriously damage discipline.

Krisch turned his selector to the appropriate list, but he knew the answer already. The word 'kiss' was not in the student's vocabulary. And there was no one in the Unit, besides himself, from whom the cadet could have learned it.

Krisch stood up and went to the transparent wall behind his desk – one huge window that looked out on the parade ground and beyond it to the chill, airless surface of the planet. Only starlight gleamed from the jagged points of that landscape which faced eternally away from the sun; the force screen that maintained the Unit's atmosphere also acted as a light trap. Krisch could look up and see, one thousand light years away, the cold dim glow that was the cluster of which Cynara was a part, and the whole frightening majesty of space in between. But a hypothetical enemy scout, pausing in space to scan this waste planet, would see nothing but a tiny disk of blackness that might be a vitreous plain, or the crater of a long-dead volcano.

Krisch had been here a little more than ten years, moving along from one installation to the next with his class, turning over the vacated office and its duties to the next lowest man in the hierarchy. Each year a new Director was shipped out with a new load of embryos and equipment, and at the end of ten more years Krisch would be permanently installed as Director of the final Unit, and as senior officer of the entire Project. That was all he had to look forward to, for the rest of his life. Many ships arrived here, but none left, or would ever leave, except those that carried the troops themselves when they were needed. Krisch's rewards were solitude, achievement, power, and the partial satisfaction of boundless curiosity.

His penalty, if the Project were to fail or even be seriously delayed while it was under his command, would be painful in the extreme.

The door speaker said, 'Cadet ER17235 reporting as ordered, sir.'

Krisch returned to his desk. He said, 'Enter.'

The metal thing stalked into the room and stood at attention in front of the Director's desk. Only the irreducible minimum of it was organic: the boy's head, pared to a functional ball, the blue eyes staring through the metal skull piece, a surgically simplified torso, the limb stumps. By itself it would be no more than a disgusting, useless lump of meat; but, housed in the metal body, it was a sketch of the perfect fighting man.

The cadet, like the rest of his class, was only ten years old; the living part of him had been transferred many times from one articulated metal shell to another. For that reason his present body was comparatively crude. When he had reached his full growth he would be given his final body – so fantastically armored as to be almost indestructible, so powerful that it could outrun any land vehicle over broken terrain. The weapons built into his arms, controlled directly by his nerves, would be sufficient to destroy a city. And he would be completely without fear.

Krisch let the silence frown between them while the boy stood at attention. Just now the boy knew fear. It was necessary for discipline, and the repressed hostility toward Krisch would later be translated into a useful hatred for all non-mechanical human beings. To use physical pain as a means of punishment was out of the question. That, in fact, was the root idea of the entire Project.

The crutch went back to prehistoric times. The metal hook, to replace a lost hand, was born early in the Iron Age. The Twentieth Century knew prosthetic devices which looked almost like flesh, and adequately performed all mechanical functions of natural limbs. But it remained for the galactic culture and the warlike nation which Krisch was a part of to discover that artificial limbs could be more than a lesser evil; that the metal arm, the metal finger, was better than flesh. Better. Its cleverly articulated segments reported pressure, temperature and position as well as flesh. Its strength was incomparably greater. And it felt no pain.

Man is so soft, thought Krisch, in comparison with the metal he uses; so soft, and so easily hurt. Every cubic inch of flesh, excepting only the brain itself, contains its minuscule fuse of agony. But metal feels no pain. Those boys will conquer the galaxy; no human troops can stand against them.

He amended the thought. Five minutes ago that had been almost a certainty. Now, it was only possible.

He said, 'Where did you learn the word "kiss"?'

The boy's eyelids fluttered behind the steel mask. 'From a—' He hesitated. 'A training device, sir,' he finished uncertainly.

Krisch said sharply, 'Are you sure?'

A long pause. 'I – I think it was, sir.'

'You *think* it was,' said Krisch. 'Describe this "training device."'

'It's – like a human being, sir.'

'Mechanised, or all flesh?'

Silence. The boy's eyelids blinked, and Krisch could imagine the rest of the face, screwed up in an agony of uncertainty. 'Answer the question,' he said.

'Neither one, sir,' said the boy painfully. 'It was—'

'Well? What was it made of?'

'Of—'

'Well?'

'Of – just lines, sir.'

Krisch sat back a moment, looking at the cadet in frowning silence. The boy's hesitant answers showed either that he was lying – which was inconceivable – or that he was conscious of guilt.

'Of just lines,' he repeated. He put a skeptical note into his voice. 'Explain.'

'That's all, sir,' the boy said eagerly. 'It was made of lines, and it looked like a human being, and it talked to me.' His voice stopped abruptly.

Krisch pounced on that. 'What did it talk about?'

'About – about love, sir.'

Another word the cadets had not been taught. 'Go on,' said Krisch. 'What did it say about love?'

'About human beings meeting, flesh to flesh, and – how good it was. About one human being loving another one – it said that means when you know the other human being is lonely and afraid like you, and you give the other one part of the way you feel about yourself, instead of keeping it all. And you show how you feel by meeting flesh to flesh, and it makes you feel wonderful, like killing something, but much better.' The cadet paused. 'But I didn't understand about kisses. It seemed to be very complicated.'

Krisch felt a ball of coldness settle in his chest. This boy was ruined; he would have to be scrapped. And how many others?

Where did all this take place?' he demanded.

'During airless maneuvers yesterday, sir.'

Krisch tried to visualise it: the cadets scattered out there in the cold blackness, carrying out one of the prescribed war games under the direction of student squad leaders. One of them isolated from the rest, waiting for a signal. And while he waited – something – had approached him, and spoken to him of love …

'No one else saw or heard?'

'No, sir.'

'Why did you fail to report it?'

A pause. 'I – I thought it was part of the training.'

'Tell the truth!' Krisch snapped.

The cadet's eyes blinked. As Krisch watched, horrified, they grew unmistakably moist. 'I – don't know, sir! I don't know!'

The moisture brimmed over: two tears ran down the shining mask that was the boy's face.

Another signal light blinked red on the master board. Then another. Krisch knew, finally, that the test had come ten years ahead of time: the Project was at war.

Krisch strapped himself into the speedster and eased it out through the exit tunnel. He had put the entire student body through interrogation and a psych check, and had turned up fifty-three more cases of induced aberration. For the time being he had left them all at liberty but carefully monitored; he hoped that one of them might be approached again by the saboteur, whoever or whatever it was.

Something flashed dully in the starlight outside the transparent nose of the speedster. Krisch stared at it, then inched the speedster over until the object lay almost directly under him.

It was a cadet, without the space gear that should have closed the openings in his faceplate and made his body airtight. The body was sprawled lifelessly. The staring eyes were blood red with burst capillaries.

Krisch peered through the transparent metal and read the serial number etched into the cadet's foreskull. It was the boy he had interviewed an hour ago.

He contacted his desk relays and gave orders for the disposal of the body and the detention of the other fifty-three. For the moment, it was all he could do.

He took the speedster up and set its course toward Unit 1, three hundred miles away. After his interview with Cadet ER17235, he had called the Directors of the other nine installations and ordered immediate psych checks. The results, gathered two hours later, showed that every unit had been affected. Viar, Director of Unit 1 and the newest member of the Project's staff, had had an additional and equally disturbing report to make.

Krisch watched the backdrop of white fire and black velvet move ponderously past. Even if he were able to remove the disturbing factor before it had done further harm, it might prove impossible to knit the structure together again. The oldest of the cadets had not yet reached the stage in which the circle of their conditioning would be unbreakable. Normal emotions and a normal biological life had no place in that circle; but it was still possible to introduce them. The result was – insanity. A flood of emotion for which no outlet had been or could be provided; impossible desires: the classic insoluble dilemma.

He remembered the blood-red, staring eyes of the dead boy. The symbolism was appropriate. His eyes were the only organs of expression left to him; and he had certainly used them effectively enough.

For the first time in many years, the Director wished he had not been born into a nation with a history of thwarted development and a psychology of resentment. He wished that he were an underpaid pedagogue on a world at peace. He wished that he had not been forced by circumstances to put that boy in a metal cage.

Viar met him, by request, at the bottom level of Unit 1 – the level that housed the huge atomic converter which powered the unit. Viar was a young-ish man with a large, white, perspiring face that expressed conscientiousness and insecurity. His eyes were milk-blue, surrounded by white lashes. Krisch disliked him thoroughly.

They stood by the shaft that the converter had dug in the stone of the planet. Viar said nervously, 'I first noticed that we had stumbled on some-thing when I checked the meter readings. They showed mostly granite, but there were occasional fluctuations that indicated refined metal. I was curi-ous, so I set the converter to extract only the stone. Yesterday I shut off the converter briefly, and sent a cadet down to see what was left.'

Krisch looked at the curious array of objects spread out on the plastic floor. There were three metal tablets incised with neat rows of dots, ovals, squares, and crosses. There was a long curved trough, with an attachment at one end that suggested it might have been designed to fit a wrist – or a tentacle. There was a set of concentric ellipses, with little balls that seemed designed to run along them; clearly an orrery of this solar system. There was a six-foot metal box, curiously fashioned in a complexity of intersecting planes.

Krisch knew that this world could not have supported indigenous life more recently than ten million years ago; but there was not a trace of corro-sion in any of the artifacts.

He said, 'Why did you fail to report this until I called you?'

Viar said apologetically, 'I thought it could wait for my weekly report. It didn't seem to have any importance, until today. Then I noticed that this box was open.'

Krisch looked at it. The seam gaped very slightly around three sides. He tested it, and found that the enclosed face would not move in either direc-tion. It seemed unlikely that anything but a gas could have escaped.

He remembered the dead cadet's description of the strange thing that had spoken to him on the training ground. 'It was made of lines …' None of the others had duplicated this phrase: they had simply said that it was like a man, but different. The fanciful thought occurred to him that if the first descrip-tion was correct, and the word 'lines' had been used mathematically, even this millimeter gap would not have been necessary.

'Is it possible that one of the cadets could have opened it?' he demanded.

'Perhaps,' Viar granted, willing to consider every possibility, 'but it does not seem probable.' He gestured toward the box. 'I made several attempts to open it when I first got it out,' he said. 'Perhaps something I did had a delayed action. At any rate, I would swear that not only was it heavier then than it is now, but there was a force lock of some nature holding it shut. I've looked in with a microprobe, and there is a small mechanism of some kind attached to one corner. I believe the box can be opened fully now, but I thought I had better wait until you could inspect it.'

'You believe, then,' said Krisch, 'that there was a device in this thing which was still in operation until yesterday?'

Viar looked at him with a trace of hangdog defiance. 'I believe that there was something in that box which is still operating, *now.*'

Krisch controlled his irritation and said nothing. Viar escorted him back to the exit tube. Krisch told him, 'Proceed with normal activities, but monitor every cadet. And open that box, but not inside the Unit. And report to me hourly.' He strapped himself into the speedster again and turned its nose back to Unit Ten.

Three more cases of aberrant conduct were waiting for him, and the reports from the other units were similar and equally alarming. Krisch interviewed a few more, then cubed a standard interview form and turned the process over to robot mechanisms. Viar called him later in the day, to report that he had succeeded in opening the box but could make nothing of its contents.

Krisch got the collated reports from the robot interviewers and ran up a tentative prediction. In twenty-six hours the unknown agent – which might or might not have escaped from the box unearthed by Viar – had corrupted one hundred and fifty-three cadets, or approximately one every ten minutes. If it continued at the same rate, which of course could not be assumed with so little data, ten per cent of the total student body would have been aberrated at the end of three hundred hours. Twelve and a half Galactic Standard days-and at the end of that time, Krisch reckoned grimly, the Project would be hopelessly crippled.

Monitoring the cadets had been totally ineffective; Krisch ordered it discontinued. His only other defensive move would have been to suspend normal activities altogether and keep the cadets in monitored groups, but that would have had a psychological effect nearly as bad as the one he was trying to avert. He ordered the aberrees to be confined and then destroyed personally by the Director of each Unit, without the knowledge of the student leaders.

He carried out this duty himself in Unit Ten, and then went to bed.

He awoke from a nightmare in which he had been surrounded by silent metal bodies – the bodies of ten-year-old cadets; but instead of the egg-shaped headpieces, they had worn open helmets; and where their faces should have been were raw, bleeding disks of flesh.

Deliberately he relaxed his body and sank back onto the sweat-drenched cushion. Then he sat up again with a start, realising that what had waked him had been someone's entrance into the room.

And that was simply, starkly impossible. His apartment was guarded while he slept by armored walls and a massive door which would have held back a regiment. Moreover, there were alarm devices which would signal any attempt to enter. Still further, no one in this Unit or any other had the slightest sane motive for trying to enter without permission.

That realisation exploded in his mind, and faded against the fact registered by the outmost corner of his vision: there was someone in the room.

He raised his head, looking full at the archway that separated his sleeping room from his office. There was a dim glow from the instrument panels.

A strange man stood there.

That was his first dominant impression; and it was so strong that for a long minute, even while he saw that he was mistaken, he could not rid himself of it.

The eye does not see a man; it sees a grouping of lines which are capable of almost infinite variation. The visual center interprets those lines, compares them with a *gestalt*, a perception-of-form, and the mind says, 'Man.'

With an effort, Krisch put aside his preconceptions and accepted what he saw.

He saw a collection of lines that enclosed no form. The glow from his office shone between them. There was a series of curlicues that might have suggested hair; then a gap; then two incomplete spirals that vaguely suggested eyes; another gap; and a straight line for a nose; farther down, a line for the mouth, curved into an idiotic smile. On either side was a handle-shaped line for the ear.

The body was like that of a stick man drawn by a child; one line for the torso, two for the arms, two for the legs, and three stiffly curling lines for each hand.

The figure said, 'Ask me anything.'

The voice spoke without sound, the words coming spontaneously into Krisch's mind as if written with a phosphorescent crayon on a sheet of black glass. Krisch realised this without surprise, and briefly wondered why: then he recalled the interview with the first cadet. The boy had said he had spoken with the 'training device' outside the Unit area, during airless maneuvers.

Krisch thought, 'Who are you?'

The answer was immediate. 'I am a device to entertain and instruct you. Ask me anything.'

Krisch's hand rested on the button that controlled a battery of force pencils focused on the area in front of his couch, but he had no intention of using it. There was every reason to suspect that such methods would fail; and if they did he would have surrendered his only chance.

He decided to take the thing at its word. 'How can you be destroyed?'

'I cannot be destroyed.'

'How can you be immobilised, then?'

'By—' The figure went without a pause, but the visual images replaced the words. There were, Krisch realised, no words in his language for those images. They flashed briefly before him, each one trailing glimpses of the process that produced it. Krisch could not even retain the sequence, much less interpret it. 'Repeat,' he thought.

The same images came and went; and at the end of it, Krisch knew that he would never learn anything useful from them. What he was seeing was the terminal end of a thousand-year chain of technology. He could not expect to grasp it from one simple explanation, any more than a savage could be taught metallurgy in a sentence.

Krisch remembered, with panic, that the thing's average indoctrination period was ten minutes. He said, 'What governs the length of time you stay with one person?'

'If he asks me to stay, I stay.'

Krisch relaxed for the first time since he had seen the figure standing there in the doorway. If that were true then his battle was won. 'There are a great many questions I want to ask you,' he thought. 'Stay with me until I ask you to go.'

There was no reply. He demanded, 'Will you do as I ask?'

'Yes.'

Fully awake now, Krisch raised the backrest of the cushion and pressed the buttons for nourishment. His mind was racing. A thought was half born in his mind that made him tremble. He asked, 'Of what substance are you composed?'

The figure said, 'Of no substance. I am the Pattern.'

Krisch leaned forward. 'Do you mean that you are not material?' he demanded.

'I am not material. I am a pattern of forces which adapts itself to each individual I serve. You see the sketch of a man; my makers would see something quite different.'

'Are you intelligent?'

'I am not intelligent. I have no will or independent existence. I am merely a device for answering questions.'

Krisch thought for a moment. He said, 'A minute ago you described yourself as *the* Pattern. Does that mean you are the only one of your kind ever created?'

'No. There were many others, but those who came after my makers did not like us. We disturbed them. Therefore they imprisoned us, like the jinn in your legend, since they could not destroy us.'

Krisch asked, 'Are you capable of lying?'

'No.'

That was the central question, and unfortunately the answer meant nothing. But Krisch was beginning to see a strong possibility that his first estimate of the thing as a saboteur was mistaken. The other explanation fitted the facts more readily and completely. The Pattern was what it called itself, 'a device to entertain and instruct you.' It presented itself to a cadet who was alone and idle – probably it had been designed never to interfere with anyone who had something better to do. The cadet asked questions; the Pattern answered them. At the end of ten minutes or so – a cadet was rarely unoccupied for longer – the cadet released it and it looked for another client.

And because the fields about which the cadets were most curious were precisely those whose knowledge would destroy them – they went insane.

The Pattern had said that 'those who came after my makers did not like us.' It was understandable. Every culture had its areas of forbidden knowledge and politely ignored facts. The Pattern would be inhibited in those areas-where its own makers were concerned. But in an alien society, its truthful answers could be explosive.

He asked, 'Were you intended for the use of children, or of adults?'

'For the use of both.'

The knowledge he wanted was there, then, and by asking enough questions, he could get it. You could not teach metallurgy to a savage in one sentence, or even in one day – but you could teach him.

Assuming that the pattern was truthful, there was still one open question that gave Krisch reason to hesitate. An absolutely truthful oracle could be a dangerous thing: witness the insanity of the cadets, and the 'disturbance' of 'those who came after our makers.' Krisch's mind was not the artificial, delicately balanced creation that the cadets' were, but he knew very well that he had areas of instability; he could even concede that there might be such areas of which he was not aware. Could he ask the right questions – the ones which would not evoke dangerous answers?

He thought so. What he wanted from the pattern was nothing that could be intimately bound up with his emotional drives or the structure of his ego; he wanted technical information.

Prove to a religious fanatic that there is no God, and you destroy him. But give him a flame thrower, and he will destroy the ungodly.

Finally, there was the question that capped all others: just how had the Pattern kept up an average rate of one cadet every ten minutes – counting the time spent in traveling from one Unit to the next, and in finding an available subject?

The answer was the one he had suspected and hoped for: the Pattern moved by instantaneous transport, out of the normal fabric of space-time.

'How?' asked Krisch. Again he got a series of incomprehensible images. 'Explain that first picture,' said Krisch, and, 'Break that down further,' and 'What is that component?' And, very slowly, the Pattern began to teach him.

The problem of limiting the Pattern's activities while Krisch slept bothered him. He solved it, finally, by setting up a pool of cadets to be admitted by a robot monitor, one at a time, into a room where the Pattern could talk to them without interruption. As soon as one cadet stopped asking questions, he was removed and another was admitted. Krisch found that although the Pattern could plant the seeds of insanity in a cadet in less than ten minutes, it took an average of nearly two hours to reduce the same cadet to such a mindless state that he was no longer useful as a questioner. Thus, during each of Krisch's six-hour sleep periods, the Pattern disposed of only three cadets. During the remaining eighteen hours of each day, Krisch kept it fully occupied.

All knowledge is power, rightfully applied. But Krisch needed a particular kind of lever and a special place to stand. Slowly and painfully he was getting it.

The balance of forces which had made the cadets possible and necessary included, as one of its basic assumptions, transport at finite speeds. Under this limiting condition, attack from space on a fortified planet was enormously costly and by itself could not succeed. It was necessary for the attacker to expend twenty ships in order to land one: thereafter the war proceeded on the ground, under the enemy's own defensive umbrella, as wars had always been fought-in hand-to-hand, street-to-street combat. Superiority in ground troops, therefore, could be the decisive factor.

But an object moving instantaneously could not, by definition, be interrupted or affected in any way while in transit. And therefore: the man who brought the secret of such transport to Cynara or any other great power could ask his own price. Since the power which brought the secret would shortly rule the galaxy, the price would be high.

If Krisch had been required to understand everything he was taught, the project would have been nearly hopeless. As it was, his task was difficult enough. The Pattern's knowledge included minutely detailed plans for every stage of the operation that were required, and for all the subsidiary operations that produced the components, and the still more subsidiary operations that produced *them*. Krisch had to follow these step by painful step, like a savage smelting ore to build a smeltery to smelt the ore better, to build a foundry to cast the metal to make tools that made other tools that built a machine that built another machine to draw wire, that another machine shaped and threaded: result, a bolt.

He stopped sending his weekly reports. The next ship to Cynara was not due for six months, and it would take more than two years for a ship to reach him after his message carriers stopped arriving. He glanced at the master board in his office only twice a day, when he awoke and before he went to bed; the rest of the time he spent with the Pattern in the Unit's machine shops and laboratories. Minor breakdowns occurred, but he grudged the time to attend to them. Repair machines broke down and were not replaced from stock: thereafter, when anything went wrong with a robot instructor or monitor, it remained out of action. Cadets went to their assigned classrooms but heard no lectures. Krisch saw a few of these, with more initiative than the rest, wandering around the corridors. He ignored them. The Project simply did not matter any longer, by comparison with the weapon he was forging under the Pattern's direction.

He allowed the weekly cubes from the other nine Directors to pile up unread on his desk. On the fifteenth morning the green light of the inter-unit communicator was blinking as he entered his office. He clicked over the switch and saw Viar's round, perspiring face on the screen. Viar said: 'Director Krisch! I've been trying to get you since eighteen hours yesterday. Is anything wrong at your Unit?'

'Nothing's wrong,' said Krisch curtly. 'I've been very busy. What is it you want?'

'Why, I was only wondering if you'd decided what action to take on the special report I sent you last week. I don't want to press you, but—'

'I'm considering it,' Krisch said. 'I'll let you know as soon as I reach a decision. Is there anything else?'

'Just one other thing – I was wondering if there had been any more trouble with the saboteur in your Unit. I haven't had any for two weeks, now, and—'

'Nor I,' said Krisch. 'There's nothing we can do on that score until it appears again, if it does.'

He broke the contact and sorted the message cubes on his desk until he found the one labeled 'Unit 1-1/17/09-Special.' He dropped it into the viewer and scanned it quickly. It appeared that Viar had been doing more archeological research on his own initiative. Krisch repressed a stab of irritation and read on. Viar had widened the converter's field and increased its output, using the surplus to turn out ingots for small converter units, in order to excavate a pit two hundred feet square by one hundred feet deep. The objects he had so far extracted showed clearly, he said, that two entirely distinct cultures were represented. Those that Krisch had already seen, including the enigmatic box, belonged to the later culture, and these included several artifacts which Viar considered to be weapons. Krisch frowned over this section; it was not elaborated.

Viar's main point was that, judging, by pictograms and items shaped to the wearers' use, the first culture had been so alien biologically and sociologically as to be almost incomprehensible – but the latecomers had been men. Viar suggested, with a breathless tone showing through his careful phrases, that this was a discovery of enormous importance to galactic archeology and anthropology. Radioactive tests confirmed their previous estimate that the planet had been dead for more than ten million years. Therefore the conclusion was inescapable that mankind had not originated on Earth or Sol – that there had been a previous wave of colonisation, so ancient that no trace of it had ever been found before.

Viar, Krisch thought contemptuously, envisioned a future of academic glory. He wanted Krisch to authorise him to dispatch his finds immediately to Cynara, with the recommendation that a research group be set up on the Project planet – to be headed, no doubt, by Viar himself.

The notion of independent evolution did not even seem to have occurred to him.

The obvious thing to do was to keep him contented, and Krisch was inclined to doubt that Viar's discoveries had any importance compared with his own. However, the thought of Viar's cryptic reference to weapons returned to him. There were two remote but unpleasant possibilities there: one, that Viar might be hinting that if Krisch opposed him, he had force to back up his requests; the other, that among those weapons, just possibly, might be one whose strategic importance to Cynara would overshadow Krisch's.

It would be just as well to take care of both, and satisfy Viar at the same time, if it could be done. Krisch thought for a moment, then dictated a memo: 'Your suggestion is accepted. Send all artifacts and relevant data to this office for shipment. I will endorse your request for the establishment of a research group and will recommend your appointment as its head. In the meantime, however, I cannot authorise any further use of the Unit 1 converter for excavation purposes. Discontinue such activity, and use converter ingots pending a reply from Cynara.'

That tied it up. It was not only reasonable but accommodating; Viar could not disobey instructions without open hostility. If he did disobey, he could be dealt with; if he didn't, Krisch could end any possibility of future trouble by removing all weapons from the shipment.

There was, however, a third alternative which Krisch had not taken into account, as he discovered when he examined the crates Viar sent. They contained a considerable number and variety of artifacts, but not one of them, as far as Krisch could tell, could possibly be classed as a weapon.

It did not ring true, somehow: Viar was simply not the type to make even so definite a stand as this against a person in authority over him. He would intrigue, and he would undermine, but he would never risk his neck in open conflict. A new weapon would give him some false courage, but not, Krisch thought, that much.

A thought struck him. He said to the Pattern: 'Did you show yourself to Viar before you came to me?'

'Yes.'

Why didn't you tell me?' Krisch gestured impatiently. 'Never mind; I know. I didn't ask you. How long did you spend and what did you discuss with him?'

'An hour and twenty minutes. I answered his questions about myself, about himself, about those who came after my makers, and about their weapons. I told him where to look for three that were in the area he was excavating.'

That was like Viar, at least, Krisch thought wryly: to get his hands on a fountainhead of power and then let go.

And Viar's sudden aggressiveness was explained. He had been shown a path to power, and the Pattern had no doubt told him a few truths about his timidity and lack of drive. Viar was, for the time being, a reformed character – and an unstable one.

The crisis was unwelcome, since it came at a time when Krisch was almost at the end of his strenuous labors; but he was realist enough to see that it had to be dealt with immediately. He considered his problem, made his preparations – which took some time, since they included transferring all big shop and laboratory equipment to the end of a half-mile tunnel dug outward from the Unit's perimeter – and then called Viar.

Viar's face was arranged in an expression of careful deference, though which cunning and self-complacency were almost obscenely visible.

Krisch cut through his greeting with, 'Viar, your instructions were to send all the artifacts to me. Where are the weapons you mentioned in your report?'

Viar's features realigned themselves to produce an effect of utter surprise. 'Why, everything's there,' he said. 'I sent it all over, just as you stipulated.'

'Viar,' said Krisch coldly, 'you unspeakable worm, guilt is written all over your face. What do you hope to gain by lying?'

Viar's white eyelashes blinked, and his weak mouth hardened slightly; but he replied in the same careful, polite tone. 'Perhaps something was left out by error, Director Krisch. Let me suggest this – send me back the items I gave you, and I'll make a careful search before I dispatch the shipment to Cynara.'

'You mean,' Krisch said, 'that I had better do as you say, or I'll get the weapons – but not in the way I expect.'

Viar's eyes gleamed. 'If you care to put it that way, Director.'

Instantly, Krisch launched himself into a torrent of abuse. He had had nine years' more experience at this form of psychological punishment than Viar, and he was a past master of the art. He called Viar a majority of filthy names in his vocabulary, with special emphasis on Viar's putative masculinity, and he delivered the whole tirade in a tone of scathing, furious contempt. He continued without slackening his pace or lowering his voice until he saw Viar redden, then turn pale; then still without a pause, he accused Viar of sabotage and treason.

Viar exploded. 'You talk about treason!' he shrieked. 'I know what you've been up to over there – I know what's been keeping you so busy! You've got that thing that escaped from my box, and you're pumping secrets out of it, to sell to the highest bidder!'

'Suppose I am?' Krisch demanded swiftly. 'What can *you* do about it?'

Viar told him. He had warned the other eight Directors that Krisch was plotting against the Project. Krisch was one against nine – he'd never get away with it – and Viar himself had a beam projector that would cut through Krisch's force screen like paper.

Krisch had all the information he needed. Now he wanted just one thing more – to get Viar out from behind the protection of his own screen. He told Viar, in extremely vulgar terms, to come and try it, and added an epithet he had been holding in reserve.

Viar's moon face went whiter than before. His eyes bulged. He opened his mouth to speak, and Krisch, grinning with triumph, cut him off.

He had been about ten minutes. He checked carefully to make sure that the Pattern was being kept occupied in the interrogation room; then he got into his battle harness and strode down the corridor toward the lift.

Halfway along the corridor was a group of cadets. One of them was on the floor, his metal body contorted and writhing. As Krisch approached, the boy began to scream at the top of his lungs. Krisch winced. He glanced at the other cadets, one of whom wore a squad leader's insignia. 'Why isn't he in surgery?' he snapped.

The squad leader said in a bewildered tone of voice, 'Surgery doesn't work, sir. The control robot there is out of commission. What shall we do, sir?'

More of the unit's services must be out than Krisch had realised; the boy evidently had some acute malfunctioning of his internal organs which should have been detected in the incipient stage by robot examiners.

'Kill him,' said Krisch, and walked on.

The voice of the squad leader followed him. 'Sir, I don't understand. Are we all going to have pain, like the lower animals?'

Krisch did not answer. He stepped into the lift at the end of the corridor and dropped swiftly to the ground level. His speedster was waiting opposite the mouth of the exit tunnel. He climbed in, worked it through the tunnel, then pointed the speedster's nose at the sky and fed it power.

Five thousand feet above the Unit's force screen and some distance away from its perimeter, he leveled off and hovered, scanning the surface below at high magnification. He waited.

There it came now: a tiny, slim, metal shape darting straight toward the Unit from the direction of Unit 1. Viar must be furious, Krisch thought. He caught the shape on the screen of his computer and snapped the controls over to 'intercept.' Instantly his craft nosed over and shot downward. He counted seconds automatically. At 'three' the other speedster was nearly in the center of his forward screen. At 'four' it entered the field of the force cannon Krisch had installed in the nose of his ship. He pressed the trigger and flung the ship into a steep ascent.

When he came out of the blackout, he saw the fragments of Viar's ship still spreading, whirling crazily under the stars. Below, an amorphous column of dust and debris was rising from the site of Unit 10. The force screen was down, and every structure above ground level had been destroyed.

Krisch leveled off and turned on the scanner that was tuned to his cavern at the end of the tunnel. It responded immediately showing him a view of the machine shop, with his nearly complete assembly standing in the middle of the room. Beyond were the transparent chambers in which the Pattern worked. Krisch saw that there were still three cadets waiting in the outer of these. It was enough. After an hour there would be no more extraneous minds to ask the Pattern questions.

Satisfied, he turned his ship toward Unit 2. It was just as well that Viar had managed to destroy Krisch's own Unit; it saved him the inconvenience of doing it himself. Neglected, the cadets had become not only distasteful but a potential danger.

He descended cautiously on Unit 2, jockeying the ship until its discharge valve was directly over the center of the force screen. Everywhere else the screen was proof against any attack likely to be mounted by a spaceship, including radio-active dust; but here, at the node, it was vulnerable to a man who knew exactly what to do. Krisch tripped the release and let the deadly stuff filter down.

He repeated the process at every remaining Unit, taking Viar's Unit 1 last. He was reasonably certain that Viar had not waited to persuade any other Director to cooperate in the attack; if he had, that Director would find nothing to attack when he got there – and no place to go when he got back.

He returned to the shambles of Unit 10, reconnoitered carefully to make sure that no other speedster was waiting within attacking range, then descended and tunneled through the debris until he struck the end of excavation. He left the speedster, opened the airtight door, one of a series that had closed when the tunnel lost air, and walked back to the cavern.

The incredibly complex structure which Krisch had built was not, the final stage; it was only the final fabricator. The final product would be Krisch himself.

He experimented first with a tiny cylinder into which he had built an affinity device tuned to a target plate at the opposite end of the chamber. He lined it up so that it would pass through the field of the Pattern's machine on its way to the target, and arranged a photoelectric cell to track it and register the exact moment when it disappeared.

He released the cylinder. It streaked across the room, into the middle of the ten-foot framework of the machine – and abruptly sprouted from the target, fifty feet away. Trembling, Krisch read the meters. There was not one microsecond's difference between the time the cylinder had passed through the field and the time it had appeared on the target plate. To the limit of his equipment's ability to record, the passage had been instantaneous.

He examined the cylinder with sensitive instruments that had previously measured its dimensions, its weight and structure. The cylinder was unchanged, undistorted.

Krisch grinned at the Pattern. There was danger in that enigmatic structure of forces, he knew; but he had escaped it by a strategy that was perfect because it was so simple. There were a million questions he had wanted to ask the Pattern; they tingled within him like an internal itch; but he had not asked one. He had asked only for the technical information he needed to build the transport device – he had not even followed up any of the curious mathematical and philosophical implications of some of the steps involved. And he knew that his certainty of safety was not self-delusion: he had checked himself daily with the hypnotically given psych tests. He was sane. His self-confidence was up a few points; that was natural. His empathy rating was down about the same amount; that had never been high – if it had, he would never have been assigned to head the Project. Those were the only changes. His orientation was perfect. There were no signs of any incipient neuroses or psychoses, including the one he had most feared: a guilt complex centered around his destruction of the cadets.

He was able to think about that without remorse, now as ever. They had only been half alive. They were better off in oblivion.

He looked at the finished device once more. It was a hollow framework of curious, out-of-plumb angles. Over it and around it crawled a metal vine bearing odd fruits: metal roses, each petal mathematically aligned; lozenges of transparent metal, each with a tiny, glowing heart. It looked like nothing so much as some alien being's notion of a work of art; but Krisch looked at it with awe and respect, remembering the labor each tiny part had cost him.

Inside, in the field created by those metal blossoms, matter gained a new dimension – permanently. It was not like the half-efficient overdrive used in spaceships – that was an artificial condition, that collapsed when the power was withdrawn. Krisch had made a visual analogy to help himself understand the difference. He imagined normal spacetime as a sphere of viscous fluid. A ship going into overdrive extended itself half out of that sphere, and tilted its molecules so that the rest offered less resistance to the liquid. But the Pattern's device extended the matter it affected like an accordion – open, half out of the stream; closed, all the way out. The matter so treated, was not an uneasy visitor on the threshold of that abnormal space; it was at home there. And, once treated, it could be made to move from one space to the other at will.

It was, Krisch thought, the difference between a flying fish and an amphibian.

The test cylinder, though it now partook of the properties of both spaces, was useless for transport because it lacked control. It was set to home on the target plate where it now was. If you tried to move it away, the instant you succeeded by so much as the width of a molecule, the cylinder would return through hyperspace to its former position. The result, in gross terms, was that you simply could not budge it. It was an amusing toy, Krisch thought, and some use might later be found for it.

Target plates planted in enemy cities, for example, and radiating missiles.

But the principal military use of the device was going to involve human control. The human passenger *was* the control. You snapped into hyperspace, you selected your target in normal space, snapped through again, and you were there. In hyperspace there was a perceptible interval, long enough to choose; in normal space there was none.

Krisch checked his equipment once more. He had a semi-portable field generator which projected a spherical force screen around him, and a reaction motor which could be used for short-range travel. The assembly was much too bulky and awkward to be of any use in military operations, but it was a necessary safeguard. If anything went wrong Krisch did not propose to die for want of air in interplanetary space. Also, he meant to appear somewhat dramatically in the all but impregnable fortress that housed GHQ on Cynara. A startled staff officer might conceivably turn a weapon on him before he had a chance to explain.

He considered setting a charge to destroy the Pattern's device after he had used it, and regretfully abandoned the idea. It would be good insurance against any reluctance to meet his terms, but the model itself was the only thing he had to sell. He had not drawn any plans as he worked; the plans were now in the Pattern's memory, and he had saved time by working directly from the vivid images the Pattern gave him.

Krisch turned off the power, stepped into the middle of the framework and stood with his hand on the control. There was nothing more to be done. He looked at the Pattern and thought, 'Will you be here when I return?'

'Yes.'

Good enough. The thing was not alive, not intelligent, and was therefore, obviously, incapable of boredom. Its drives took it restlessly from one questioning mind to another – when there were minds available. When there were none, it would wait. It had been built on this planet; evidently no provision had ever been made for it to leave.

It knew too much, and was intrinsically too dangerous, ever to be allowed to contact another mind. Krisch could not destroy it, but it would be here when he returned; and he could make sure that no one else would ever come to this world.

Krisch thought to himself, 'Cynara. The spaceport outside Fortress One.' He visualised it, held the thought firmly in his mind. He turned on the power.

Stunned, Krisch tried to orient himself, to figure out what was the matter. He lay weightless in a gray space, somehow above and somehow surrounded by a frightening, tangled infinity of gray spheres and white, criss-crossing lines. Everything he saw was at the same time immensely distant and so close that he could almost touch it. The array changed and shifted bewilderingly, and he tried helplessly to follow it, read some sense into its morion, until he remembered: 'Cynara. The spaceport outside Fortress One.'

There it was, below him, like some incredible four-dimensioned map, at his fingertips. He saw it clearly. He willed himself toward it, into it. But nothing happened.

Time passed, without measure. The tiny gray figures of man and machine did not move; time was suspended, for them, at the instant Krisch had entered the field. Krisch realised suddenly that he was hungry. Terrified, he looked at the dial of the airmaker at his waist. It was hard to read; the new dimension made vision queer and uncertain; but he made out at last that he had used more than three hours' supply. Time had not stopped for him.

He thought desperately, 'The Project planet. The cavern.'

Instantly, there was the cavern; the framework standing in the middle of the shop floor, and, nearby, the Pattern. An instant later the Pattern vanished.

A voice said in his mind, 'Ask me anything.'

Krisch stared at it. Was there a mocking tone in that unaccented, polite, mental voice? He said hoarsely, aloud, 'What went wrong?'

'Nothing went wrong.'

Krisch mastered himself sufficiently to say evenly, 'I was not able to enter normal space at my destination. Why not?'

'You did not wait long enough. There is a great disparity between the time rates of this plenum and the normal one; that is why travel can be achieved at a rate which cannot be distinguished from simultaneity by your methods. In subjective terms, the trip to Cynara will take you a long time.'

'How long?' Krisch demanded. He felt helpless, fixed like a pinned specimen in the midst of this gray infinity.

'Approximately one thousand of your years.'

Krisch felt his face writhe and distort into the silent shape of a scream. Blood pounded at his temples; his eyes filmed. He said, 'How long – back to the cavern?'

'Only one year, if you were to start immediately to concentrate on the objective. If you allow yourself to drift, as you are doing now, the distance will widen rapidly.'

'But I've only got enough air for twenty hours!' Krisch shouted. 'I'll die!'

There was no response.

Krisch pulled himself back from the borderline of hysteria. He suppressed his rage and fear and uncertainty. At least – whatever the reason – the Pattern was here to answer questions. He said, 'What was your motive in lying to me?'

'I did not lie to you.'

'You told me,' Krisch said furiously, 'that there was a negligible time interval between departure and arrival. Why?'

'To me it is negligible.'

Krisch saw that it was true: it was his own fault for having phrased the question inadequately, for having refused to follow up all the implications of the science the Pattern had taught him. The Pattern, he remembered, was not alive, not intelligent – not capable of boredom.

He remembered another line of questioning that he had not followed up, and thought he saw the vague shape of a terrifying possibility.

He said, 'When you first came to me – you described yourself as a device to amuse and entertain. Was that the whole truth?'

'No.'

'What *is* the whole truth?'

The Pattern immediately began to recite the history of the race that had made it. Krisch realised petulantly that he had asked too sweeping a question, and was about to rephrase it; but the significance of what the Pattern was saying stopped him.

They had been entirely alien, those people; their psychology was incomprehensible to men. They did not fight; they did not explore; they did not rule or exploit; they had nothing that could be identified with human curiosity – that apelike trait that had made humanity what it was. Yet they had a great science. They had acquired it for some motive that Krisch could never grasp. They had, really, only two characteristics that would be recognisable to men: they loved each other, their homes, their world; and they had a deep, joyful, ironic sense of humor.

'Men came,' said the Pattern, 'eleven million of your years ago. They wanted my makers' world and therefore they killed my makers. My makers knew anguish of flesh and spirit, but they could not fight. Aggressiveness, conflict, were inconceivable to them. But remember that they understood irony. Before the last of them died they made us as a gift to their destroyers. We were a good gift. We contain all that they knew. We were truthful. We are immortal. We are made to serve.

'It is not our makers' fault,' said the Pattern, 'if men use the knowledge we give them to destroy themselves.'

There was only a thin shred left of Krisch's hold on his sanity. He said very carefully, 'Did your makers foresee this – the situation I am in?'

'Yes.'

'Is there any way for me to escape from it?'

The Pattern said, 'Yes. It is the final jest of my makers. To travel in hyperspace, you must become what I am – only a pattern of forces and memory, not alive, not intelligent, not capable of boredom. I can make this alteration, if you request it. It is simple: like the growth of one crystal from another, or like the transfer of pattern in living cells.'

Krisch choked. He said, 'Will I – remember?'

'Yes. You will have your own memories in addition to those I give you. But you will not retain your human character: you will not be aggressive, or cruel, or egotistic, or curious. You will be a device for answering questions.'

Krisch's mind revolted against the thought. But he looked at the dial of his airmaker and knew what his answer would be. And in a flash of prophetic insight, he knew what would happen thereafter. He would finish his journey to Cynara. He would tell the truth, and the truth would corrupt.

Wherever there were men, throughout the universe and to the end of time, his influence would follow them. In time there would be other unwary seekers of knowledge who would take the path he had taken. By choosing this way out he would become mankind's executioner.

But when had men hesitated to risk the survival of the race for their own advantage?

The pattern, Krisch thought, was clear.

THE COUNTRY OF THE KIND

The attendant at the car lot was daydreaming when I pulled up – a big, lazy-looking man in black satin chequered down the front. I was wearing scarlet, myself; it suited my mood. I got out, almost on his toes.

'Park or storage?' he asked automatically, turning around. Then he realised who I was, and ducked his head away.

'Neither,' I told him.

There was a hand torch on a shelf in the repair shed right behind him. I got it and came back. I knelt down to where I could reach behind the front wheel, and ignited the torch. I turned it on the axle and suspension. They glowed cherry red, then white, and fused together. Then I got up and turned the flame on both tires until the rubberoid stank and sizzled and melted down to the pavement. The attendant didn't say anything.

I left him there, looking at the mess on his nice clean concrete.

It had been a nice car, too; but I could get another any time. And I felt like walking. I went down the winding road, sleepy in the afternoon sunlight, dappled with shade and smelling of cool leaves. You couldn't see the houses; they were all sunken or hidden by shrubbery, or a little of both. That was the fad I'd heard about; it was what I'd come here to see. Not that anything the dulls did would be worth looking at.

I turned off at random and crossed a rolling lawn, went through a second hedge of hawthorn in blossom, and came out next to a big sunken games court.

The tennis net was up, and two couples were going at it, just working up a little sweat – young, about half my age, all four of them. Three dark-haired, one blonde. They were evenly matched, and both couples played well together; they were enjoying themselves.

I watched for a minute. But by then the nearest two were beginning to sense I was there, anyhow. I walked down onto the court, just as the blonde was about to serve. She looked at me frozen across the net, poised on tiptoe. The others stood.

'Off,' I told them. 'Game's over.'

I watched the blonde. She was not especially pretty, as they go, but compactly and gracefully put together. She came down slowly, flat-footed without awkwardness, and tucked the racket under her arm; then the surprise was over and she was trotting off the court after the other three.

I followed their voices around the curve of the path, between towering masses of lilacs, inhaling the sweetness, until I came to what looked like a little sunning spot. There was a sundial, and a birdbath, and towels lying around on the grass. One couple, the dark-haired pair, was still in sight farther down the path, heads bobbing along. The other couple had disappeared.

I found the handle in the grass without any trouble. The mechanism responded, and an oblong section of turf rose up. It was the stair I had, not the elevator, but that was all right. I ran down the steps and into the first door I saw, and was in the top-floor lounge, an oval room lit with diffused simulated sun-light from above. The furniture was all comfortably bloated, sprawling and ugly; the carpet was deep, and there was a fresh flower scent in the air.

The blonde was over at the near end with her back to me, studying the autochef keyboard. She was half out of her play-suit. She pushed it the rest of the way down and stepped out of it, then turned and saw me.

She was surprised again; she hadn't thought I might follow her down.

I got up close before it occurred to her to move; then it was too late: She knew she couldn't get away from me; she closed her eyes and leaned back against the paneling, turning a little pale. Her lips and her golden brows went up in the middle.

I looked her over and told her a few uncomplimentary things about herself. She trembled, but didn't answer. On an impulse, I leaned over and dialed the autochef to hot cheese sauce. I cut the safety out of the circuit and put the quantity dial all the way up. I dialed *soup tureen* and then *punch bowl.*

The stuff began to come out in about a minute, steaming hot. I took the tureens and splashed them up and down the wall on either side of her. Then when the first punch bowl came out I used the empty bowls as scoops. I clotted the carpet with the stuff; I made streamers of it all along the walls, and dumped puddles into what furniture I could reach. Where it cooled it would harden, and where it hardened it would cling.

I wanted to splash it across her body, but it would've hurt, and we couldn't have that. The punch bowls of hot sauce were still coming out of the autochef, crowding each other around the vent. I punched *cancel,* and then *sauterne (swt., Calif.).*

It came out well chilled in open bottles. I took the first one and had my arm back just about to throw a nice line of the stuff right across her midriff, when a voice said behind me:

'Watch out for cold wine.'

My arm twitched and a little stream of the wine splashed across her thighs. She was ready for it; her eyes had opened at the voice, and she barely jumped.

I whirled around, fighting mad. The man was standing there where he had come out of the stair well. He was thinner in the face than most, bronzed, wide-chested, with alert blue eyes. If it hadn't been for him, I knew it would have worked – the blonde would have mistaken the chill splash for a scalding one.

I could hear the scream in my mind, and I wanted it.

I took a step toward him, and my foot slipped. I went down clumsily, wrenching one knee. I got up shaking and tight all over. I wasn't in control of myself. I screamed, 'You – you—' I turned and got one of the punch bowls and lifted it in both hands, heedless of how the hot sauce was slopping over onto my wrists, and I had it almost in the air toward him when the sickness took me – that damned buzzing in my head, louder, louder, drowning everything out.

When I came to, they were both gone. I got up off the floor, weak as death, and staggered over to the nearest chair. My clothes were slimed and sticky. I wanted to die. I wanted to drop into that dark furry hole that was yawning for me and never come up; but I made myself stay awake and get out of the chair.

Going down in the elevator, I almost blacked out again. The blonde and the thin man weren't in any of the second-floor bedrooms. I made sure of that, and then I emptied the closets and bureau drawers onto the floor, dragged the whole mess into one of the bathrooms and stuffed the tub with it, then turned on the water.

I tried the third floor: maintenance and storage. It was empty. I turned the furnace on and set the thermostat up as high as it would go. I disconnected all the safety circuits and alarms. I opened the freezer doors and dialed them to defrost. I popped the stair well door open and went back up in the elevator.

On the second floor I stopped long enough to open the stairway door there – the water was halfway toward it, creeping across the floor – and then searched the top floor. No one was there. I opened book reels and threw them unwinding across the room; I would have done more, but I could hardly stand. I got up to the surface and collapsed on the lawn: that furry pit swallowed me up, dead and drowned.

While I slept, water poured down the open stair well and filled the third level. Thawing food packages floated out into the rooms. Water seeped into wall panels and machine housings; circuits and fuses blew. The air conditioning stopped, but the pile kept heating. The water rose.

Spoiled food, floating supplies, grimy water surged up the stair well. The second and first levels were bigger and would take longer to fill, but they'd fill. Rugs, furnishings, clothing, all the things in the house would be waterlogged and ruined. Probably the weight of so much water would shift the house, rupture the water pipes and other fluid intakes. It would take a repair crew more than a day just to clean up the mess. The house itself was done for, not repairable. The blonde and the thin man would never live in it again.

Serve them right.

The dulls could build another house; they built like beavers. There was only one of me in the world.

The earliest memory I have is of some woman, probably the cresh-mother, staring at me with an expression of shock and horror. Just that. I've tried to remember what happened directly before or after, but I can't. Before, there's nothing but the dark formless shaft of no-memory that runs back to birth. Afterward, the big calm.

From my fifth year, it must have been, to my fifteenth, everything I can remember floats in a pleasant dim sea. Nothing was terribly important. I was languid and soft; I drifted. Waking merged into sleep.

In my fifteenth year it was the fashion in love-play for the young people to pair off for months or longer. 'Loving steady,' we called it. I remember how the older people protested that it was unhealthy; but we were all normal juniors, and nearly as free as adults under the law.

All but me.

The first steady girl I had was named Elen. She had blonde hair, almost white, worn long; her lashes were dark and her eyes pale green. Startling eyes: they didn't look as if they were looking at you. They looked blind.

Several times she gave me strange startled glances, something between fright and anger. Once it was because I held her too tightly, and hurt her; other times, it seemed to be for nothing at all.

In our group, a pairing that broke up sooner than four weeks was a little suspect – there must be something wrong with one partner or both, or the pairing would have lasted longer.

Four weeks and a day after Elen and I made our pairing, she told me she was breaking it.

I'd thought I was ready. But I felt the room spin half around me till the wall came against my palm and stopped.

The room had been in use as a hobby chamber; there was a rack of plasti-craft knives under my hand. I took one without thinking, and when I saw it I thought, *I'll frighten her.*

And I saw the startled, half-angry look in her pale eyes as I went toward her; but this was curious: she wasn't looking at the knife. She was looking at my face.

The elders found me later with the blood on me, and put me into a locked room. Then it was my turn to be frightened, because I realised for the first time that it was possible for a human being to do what I had done.

And if I could do it to Elen, I thought, surely they could do it to me.

But they couldn't. They set me free: they had to.

And it was then I understood that I was the king of the world ...

The sky was turning clear violet when I woke up, and shadow was spilling out from the hedges. I went down the hill until I saw the ghostly blue of photon tubes glowing in a big oblong, just outside the commerce area. I went that way, by habit.

Other people were lining up at the entrance to show their books and be admitted. I brushed by them, seeing the shocked faces and feeling their bodies flinch away, and went on into the robing chamber.

Straps, aqualungs, masks and flippers were all for the taking. I stripped, dropping the clothes where I stood, and put the underwater equipment on. I strode out to the poolside, monstrous, like a being from another world. I adjusted the lung and the flippers, and slipped into the water.

Underneath, it was all crystal blue, with the forms of swimmers sliding through it like pale angels. Schools of small fish scattered as I went down. My heart was beating with a painful joy.

Down, far down, I saw a girl slowly undulating through the motion of a sinuous underwater dance, writhing around and around a ribbed column of imitation coral. She had a suction-tipped fish lance in her hand, but she was not using it; she was only dancing, all by herself, down at the bottom of the water.

I swam after her. She was young and delicately made, and when she saw the deliberately clumsy motions I made in imitation of hers, her eyes glinted with amusement behind her mask. She bowed to me in mockery, and slowly glided off with simple, exaggerated movements, like a child's ballet.

I followed. Around her and around I swam, stiff-legged, first more child-like, and awkward than she, then subtly parodying her motions; then improving on them until I was dancing an intricate, mocking dance around her.

I saw her eyes widen. She matched her rhythm to mine, then, and together, apart, together again we coiled the wake of our dancing. At last, exhausted, we clung together where a bridge of plastic coral arched over us. Her cool body was in the bend of my arm; behind two thicknesses of vitrin – a world away! – her eyes were friendly and kind.

There was a moment when, two strangers yet one flesh, we felt our souls speak to one another across that abyss of matter. It was a truncated embrace – we could not kiss, we could not speak – but her hands lay confidingly on my shoulders, and her eyes looked into mine.

That moment had to end. She gestured toward the surface and left me. I followed her up. I was feeling drowsy and almost at peace, after my sickness. I thought ... I don't know what I thought.

We rose together at the side of the pool. She turned to me, removing her mask: and her smile stopped, and melted away. She stared at me with a horrified disgust, wrinkling her nose.

'*Pyah!*' she said, and turned, awkward in her flippers. Watching her, I saw her fall into the arms of a white-haired man, and heard her hysterical voice tumbling over itself.

'But don't you remember?' the man's voice rumbled. 'You should know it by heart.' He turned. 'Hal, is there a copy of it in the clubhouse?'

A murmur answered him, and in a few moments a young man came out holding a slender brown pamphlet.

I knew that pamphlet. I could even have told you what page the white-haired man opened it to; what sentences the girl was reading as I watched.

I waited. I don't know why.

I heard her voice rising: 'To think that I let him *touch* me!' And the white-haired man reassured her, the words rumbling, too low to hear. I saw her back straighten. She looked across at me ... only a few yards in the scented, blue-lit air; a world away ... and folded up the pamphlet into a hard wad, threw it, and turned on her heel.

The pamphlet landed almost at my feet. I touched it with my toe, and it opened to the page I had been thinking of:

> ... sedation until his 15th year, when for sexual reasons it became no longer practical. While the advisors and medical staff hesitated, he killed a girl of the group by violence.

And farther down:

> The solution finally adopted was three-fold.
> 1. *A sanction* – the only sanction possible to our humane, permissive society. Excommunication: not to speak to him, touch him willingly, or acknowledge his existence.
> 2. *A precaution.* Taking advantage of a mild predisposition to epilepsy, a variant of the so-called Kusko analog technique was employed, to prevent by an epileptic seizure any future act of violence.
> 3. *A warning.* A careful alteration of his body chemistry was effected to make his exhaled and exuded wastes emit a strongly pungent and offensive odor. In mercy, he himself was rendered unable to detect this smell.
> Fortunately, the genetic and environmental accidents which combined to produce this atavism have been fully explained and can never again ...

The words stopped meaning anything, as they always did at that point. I didn't want to read any farther; it was all nonsense, anyway. I was the king of the world.

I got up and went away, out into the night, blind to the dulls who thronged the rooms I passed.

Two squares away was the commerce area. I found a clothing outlet and went in. All the free clothes in the display cases were drab: those were for worthless floaters, not for me. I went past them to the specials, and found a combination I could stand – silver and blue, with a severe black piping down the tunic. A dull would have said it was 'nice.' I punched for it. The automatic looked me over with its dull glassy eye, and croaked, 'Your contribution book, please.'

I could have had a contribution book, for the trouble of stepping out into the street and taking it away from the first passer-by; but I didn't have the patience. I picked up the one-legged table from the refreshment nook, hefted it, and swung it at the cabinet door. The metal shrieked and dented, opposite the catch. I swung once more to the same place, and the door sprang open. I pulled out clothing in handfuls till I got a set that would fit me.

I bathed and changed, and then went prowling in the big multi-outlet down the avenue. All those places are arranged pretty much alike, no matter what the local managers do to them. I went straight to the knives, and picked out three in graduated sizes, down to the size of my fingernail. Then I had to take my chances. I tried the furniture department, where I had had good luck once in a while, but this year all they were using was metal. I had to have sea-soned wood.

I knew where there was a big cache of cherry wood, in good-sized blocks, in a forgotten warehouse up north at a place called Kootenay. I could have carried some around with me – enough for years – but what for, when the world belonged to me?

It didn't take me long. Down in the workshop section, of all places, I found some antiques – tables and benches, all with wooden tops. While the dulls collected down at the other end of the room, pretending not to notice, I sawed off a good oblong chunk of the smallest bench, and made a base for it out of another.

As long as I was there, it was a good place to work, and I could eat and sleep upstairs, so I stayed.

I knew what I wanted to do. It was going to be a man, sitting, with his legs crossed and his forearms resting down along his calves. His head was going to be tilted back, and his eyes closed, as if he were turning his face up to the sun.

In three days it was finished. The trunk and limbs had a shape that was not man and not wood, but something in between: something that hadn't existed before I made it.

Beauty. That was the old word.

I had carved one of the figure's hands hanging loosely, and the other one curled shut. There had to be time to stop and say it was finished. I took the smallest knife, the one I had been using to scrape the wood smooth, and cut away the handle and ground down what was left of the shaft to a thin spike. Then I drilled a hole into the wood of the figurine's hand, in the hollow between thumb and curled finger. I fitted the knife blade in there; in the small hand it was the sword.

I cemented it in place. Then I took the sharp blade and stabbed my thumb, and smeared the blade.

I hunted most of that day, and finally found the right place – a niche in an outcropping of striated brown rock, in a little triangular half-wild patch that had been left where two roads forked. Nothing was permanent, of course, in a community like this one that might change its houses every five years or so, to follow the fashion; but this spot had been left to itself for a long time. It was the best I could do.

I had the paper ready: it was one of a batch I had printed up a year ago. The paper was treated, and I knew it would stay legible a long time. I hid a little photo capsule in the back of the niche, and ran the control wire to a staple in the base of the figurine. I put the figurine down on top of the paper, and anchored it lightly to the rock with two spots of all-cement. I had done it so often that it came naturally; I knew just how much cement would hold the figurine steady against a casual hand, but yield to one that really wanted to pull it down.

Then I stepped back to look: and the power and the pity of it made my breath come short, and tears start to my eyes.

Reflected light gleamed fitfully on the dark-stained blade that hung from his hand. He was sitting alone in that niche that closed him in like a coffin. His eyes were shut, and his head tilted back, as if he were turning his face up to the sun.

But only rock was over his head. There was no sun for him.

Hunched on the cool bare ground under a pepper tree, I was looking down across the road at the shadowed niche where my figurine sat.

I was all finished here. There was nothing more to keep me, and yet I couldn't leave.

People walked past now and then – not often. The community seemed half deserted, as if most of the people had flocked off to a surf party somewhere, or a contribution meeting, or to watch a new house being dug to replace the one I had wrecked ... There was a little wind blowing toward me, cool and lonesome in the leaves.

Up the other side of the hollow there was a terrace, and on that terrace, half an hour ago, I had seen a brief flash of color – a boy's head, with a red cap on it, moving past and out of sight.

That was why I had to stay. I was thinking how that boy might come down from his terrace and into my road, and passing the little wild triangle of land, see my figurine. I was thinking he might not pass by indifferently, but stop: and go closer to look: and pick up the wooden man: and read what was written on the paper underneath.

I believed that sometime it had to happen. I wanted it so hard that I ached.

My carvings were all over the world, wherever I had wandered. There was one in Congo City, carved of ebony, dusty-black; one on Cyprus, of bone; one in New Bombay, of shell; one in Chang-teh, of jade.

They were like signs printed in red and green, in a color-blind world. Only the one I was looking for would ever pick one of them up, and read the message I knew by heart.

TO YOU WHO CAN SEE, the first sentence said, I OFFER YOU A WORLD ...

There was a flash of color up on the terrace. I stiffened. A minute later, here it came again, from a different direction: it was the boy, clambering down the slope, brilliant against the green, with his red sharp-billed cap like a woodpecker's head.

I held my breath.

He came toward me through the fluttering leaves, ticked off by pencils of sunlight as he passed. He was a brown boy, I could see at this distance, with a serious thin face. His ears stuck out, flickering pink with the sun behind them, and his elbow and knee pads made him look knobby.

He reached the fork in the road, and chose the path on my side. I huddled into myself as he came nearer. *Let him see it, let him not see* me, I thought fiercely.

My fingers closed around a stone.

He was nearer, walking jerkily with his hand in his pockets, watching his feet mostly.

When he was almost opposite me, I threw the stone.

It rustled through the leaves below the niche in the rock. The boy's head turned. He stopped, staring. I think he saw the figurine then. I'm sure he saw it.

He took one step.

'Risha!' came floating down from the terrace.

And he looked up. 'Here,' he piped.

I saw the woman's head, tiny at the top of the terrace. She called something I didn't hear; I was standing up, tight with anger.

Then the wind shifted. It blew from me to the boy. He whirled around, his eyes big, and clapped a hand to his nose.

'Oh, what a stench!' he said.

He turned to shout, 'Coming!' and then he was gone, hurrying back up the road, into the unstable blur of green. My one chance ruined. He would have seen the image, I knew if it hadn't been for that damned woman and the wind shifting ... They were all against me, people, wind and all.

And the figurine still sat, blind eyes turned up to the rocky sky.

There was something inside me that told me to take my disappointment and go away from there, and not come back.

I knew I would be sorry. I did it anyway: took the image out of the niche, and the paper with it, and climbed the slope. At the top I heard his clear voice laughing.

There was a thing that might have been an ornamental mound, or the camouflaged top of a buried house. I went around it, tripping over my own feet, and came upon the boy kneeling on the turf. He was playing with a brown and white puppy.

He looked up with the laughter going out of his face. There was no wind, and he could smell me. I knew it was bad. No wind, and the puppy to distract him – everything about it was wrong. But I went to him blindly anyhow, and fell on one knee, and shoved the figurine at his face.

'Look' I said.

He went over backwards in his hurry: he couldn't even have seen the image, except as a brown blur coming at him. He scrambled up, with the puppy whining and yapping around his heels, and ran for the mound.

I was up after him, clawing up moist earth and grass as I rose. In the other hand I still had the image clutched, and the paper with it.

A door popped open and swallowed him and popped shut again in my face. With the flat of my hand I beat the vines around it until I hit the door-plate by accident and the door opened. I dived in, shouting, 'Wait,' and was in a spiral passage, lit pearl-gray, winding downward. Down I went head-long, and came out at the wrong door – an underground conservatory, humid and hot under the yellow lights, with dripping rank leaves in long rows. I went down the aisle raging, overturning the tanks, until I came to a vestibule and an elevator.

Down I went again to the third level and a labyrinth of guest rooms, all echoing, all empty. At last I found a ramp leading upward, past the conservatory, and at the end of it voices.

The door was clear vitrin, and I paused on the near side of it looking and listening. There was the boy, and a woman old enough to be his mother, just – sister or cousin, more likely – and an elderly woman in a hard chair holding the puppy. The room was comfortable and tasteless, like other rooms.

I saw the shock grow on their faces as I burst in: it was always the same, they knew I would like to kill them, but they never expected that I would come uninvited into a house. It was not done.

There was that boy, so close I could touch him, but the shock of all of them

DAMON KNIGHT

was quivering in the air, smothering, like a blanket that would deaden my voice. I felt I had to shout.

'Everything they tell you is lies!' I said. 'See here – here, this is the truth!' I had the figurine in front of his eyes, but he didn't see.

'Risha, go below,' said the young woman quietly. He turned to obey, quick as a ferret, I got in front of him again. 'Stay,' I said, breathing hard. 'Look—'

'Remember, Risha, don't speak,' said the woman.

I couldn't stand any more. Where the boy went I don't know; I ceased to see him. With the image in one hand and the paper with it, I leaped at the woman. I was almost quick enough; I almost reached her; but the buzzing took me in the middle of a step, louder, louder, like the end of the world.

It was the second time that week. When I came to, I was sick and too faint to move for a long time.

The house was silent. They had gone, of course ... the house had been defiled, having me in it. They wouldn't live here again, but would build elsewhere.

My eyes blurred. After a while I stood up and looked around the room. The walls were hung with a gray close-woven cloth that looked as if it would tear, and I thought of ripping it down in strips, breaking furniture, stuffing carpets and bedding into the oubliette ... But I didn't have the heart for it. I was too tired. Thirty years ... They had given me all the kingdoms of the world, and the glory thereof, thirty years ago. It was more than one man alone could bear, for thirty years.

At last I stooped and picked up the figurine, and the paper that was supposed to go under it – crumpled now, with the forlorn look of a message that someone has thrown away unread.

I sighed bitterly.

I smoothed it out and read the last part.

YOU CAN SHARE THE WORLD WITH ME. THEY CAN'T STOP YOU. STRIKE NOW – PICK UP A SHARP THING AND STAB, OR A HEAVY THING AND CRUSH. THAT'S ALL. THAT WILL MAKE YOU FREE. ANYONE CAN DO IT.

Anyone. Someone. Anyone.

TICKET TO ANYWHERE

I

Richard Falk was a sane man. Up until three months ago he had been, so far as he could discover, the only sane man left in a world of lunatics.

Now he was a dead man.

He lay in a metal coffin twenty yards long by three wide, airless, soundless. Behind the faceplate of his helmet, under the rime of frozen air, his lips were bright blue, his cheeks, nose, forehead a lighter color, almost violet. The flesh was stiff as frozen leather. He did not move, breathe, or think: he was dead.

Beside him, strapped to the bulging torso of his suit, was a metal box labeled: SCATO HEART PROBE. SEE INSTRUCTIONS INSIDE.

All around him, strapped tight to the walls by broad loops of webbing, were boxes, canisters, canvas bags, kegs. Cargo. His coffin was a freighter, going to Mars.

In his frozen brain the memories were neady stacked, just as he had left them. Not coupled now, each cell isolated, the entropy of his mind fallen to zero. But uppermost among them, waiting for the thaw that might never come, were the memories of his last few hours of life.

Once the ship was launched and free, he had had to wait until its dancing molecules had stilled, their heat all radiated away into space. Then to wait again, heater turned off, listening to the silence while his own life's heat drained away: fingers and toes numb first, ears and nose following, then lips, cheeks, and all his flesh; shivering in an agony of cold, watching his breath fill the helmet with cloud, the cold drops beading on the colder faceplate.

Tricky, that, and a thing that demanded courage. Act too soon, and the last drop into stillness would be too slow – the freezing liquids in his body would crystallize, gashing his cells with a million tiny stabs. Wait too long, and the cold would steal his ability to act at all.

He had waited until the false warmth of the dying had crept over him, the subtle destroyer, cumbering his limbs not with harshness but with too much peace. Twisting then in the dead center where he floated, he had drawn himself into the lane between two looped bundles of cargo, forcing them aside, until he reached the naked hull. There, spread-eagled against the chill metal, embracing it as one who crucifies himself gladly, he had died.

The ship, stillest of sepulchers, hung fixed in the center of the starry globe.

So it might have remained for time without end, changeless, knowing no time; for there was no time here, no 'events' – the ship and all its contents – except its robot control, inactive now but warmed by a minute trickle of electrons – now being very nearly at zero Absolute.

But a relay clicked, communicating its tremor through support frame and girder and hull. Time had begun again. The radar assembly in the prow began to emit timed clusters of radiation; presently other relays snapped over, and then the engine awoke, whispered to itself an instant, and was silent. For an instant the ship had become once more a thing in motion, a pebble flung between the stars. Another such instant came, then another; then, at long last, the hull shuddered to the whip and carom of atmospheric molecules. Lightly it dipped into Martian air, out again, in again, making a great circuit of the globe. A final relay clicked, and Falk's coffin hurled itself groundward, free of the skeletal ship whose rockets now flamed again, driving it back into the timeless deep.

A parachute opened as the cargo hull hurtled downward: a preposterous parasol that would not have held the weight a minute against Earth's gravity, in Earth's air; but here it slowed that plummeting fall until the box met Martian sand at not quite killing speed.

In the shell, Falk's corpse slowly thawed.

His heart was beating. That was Falk's first conscious realisation, and he listened to the tiny sound thankfully. His chest was rising and falling in a deep, slow rhythm; he heard the hiss and whisper of breath in his nostrils and felt the veins twitch at his temples.

Then came a prickling, half pain, in his arms and legs; then he saw a ruddy haze of light on his closed lids.

Falk opened his eyes.

He saw a pale glow that turned itself into a face. It went away briefly, and came back. Falk could see it a little better now. Young – about thirty – pale-skinned, with a blue beard shadow. Black straight hair, a little untidy. Black-rimmed spectacles. Ironic lines on either side of the thin mouth.

'All right now?' said the face.

Falk murmured, and the face bent closer. He tried again. Think so.

The young man nodded. He picked up something from the bed and began taking it apart, fitting the components into the cushioned troughs of a metal box. It was the heart probe, Falk saw: the bulky control box and the short, capillary-thin needle.

'Where did you get this?' the young man asked. 'And what the devil were you doing aboard that freighter?'

'Stole the probe,' said Falk. 'And the suit, and the rest of the stuff. Dumped enough cargo to match my weight. Wanted to get to Mars. Only way.'

The young man let his hands fall into his lap. 'You *stole* it,' he repeated incredulously. 'Then you never had the analogue treatment?'

Falk smiled. 'Had it, all right. Dozen times. Never took.' He felt very tired. 'Let me rest a minute, will you?'

'Of course. Sorry.'

The young man went away, and Falk closed his eyes, returning to the slow surge of memory that moved in his mind. He went through those last hours, painful as they were, and then again. There was trauma there; mustn't let it get buried to cause him trouble later. Accept it, know the fear, live with it.

After a while the young man came back, carrying broth that steamed in a cup, and Falk drank it gratefully. Then he fell unknowing into sleep.

When he awoke he was stronger. He tried to sit up, and found to his mild surprise that he could. The other, who had been sitting in an armchair across the room, put down his pipe and came over to thrust pillows behind Falk's back. Then he sat down again. The room was cluttered and had a stale odor. Floor, walls and ceiling were enameled metal. There were books and rolls of tape, records, in shelves; more piled on the floor. A dirty shirt was hanging from the doorknob.

'Want to talk now?' the young man asked. 'My name's Wolfert.'

'Glad to know you. Mine's Falk … You want to know about the analogue business first, I suppose.'

'And why you're here.'

'It's the same thing,' Falk told him. 'I'm immune to analogue treatment. I didn't know it for sure till I was ten, but I think I was born that way. From seven on, I remember the other kids talking about their Guardians, and me pretending I had one too. You know how kids are – anything to run with the mob.

'But for a long time, years, I wasn't certain whether everyone else was pretending like me, or whether I really was the only one without an invisible Guardian to talk to. I was pretty sure the kids were lying when they said they could see theirs, but whether they were there at all or not was another question. I didn't know; actually it didn't bother me much.

'When I was ten, I stole something. It was a book I wanted that my father wouldn't let me have. The clerk was looking the other way – I put it under my jacket. Funny, I was halfway through it before it struck me that I'd just proved I had no Guardian. By that time, you see, I'd decided that I'd just never seen mine because I'd never done anything bad. I was proud of that, a little prissy about it if you want the truth – only I wanted this book …

'I had sense enough, thank God, to burn that book after I'd finished it. If I hadn't, I don't suppose I would have lived to grow up.'

Wolfert grunted. 'Should think not,' he said. His eyes were fixed on Falk, interested, alert, wary. 'One man without any control could turn the whole applecart over. But I thought immunity was theoretically impossible?'

'I've thought about that a good deal. According to classic psychology, it is. I'm not unusually resistant to hypnotic drugs; I go under all right. But the censor mechanism just doesn't respond. I've had the fanciful notion that I may be a mutation, developed in response to the analogue treatment as an anti-survival factor. But I don't know. As far as I've ever been able to find out, there are no more like me.'

'Umm,' said Wolfert, puffing at his pipe. 'Should think your next move would be to get married, have children, see if they were immune too.'

Falk stared at him soberly. 'Wolfert – no offense, but can you imagine yourself settling down happily in a community of maniacs?'

The other's face flushed slowly. He took his pipe out of his mouth, looked down at it. Finally he said, 'All right, I know what you mean.'

'Maybe you don't,' said Falk, thinking, *I've offended him. Couldn't help it.* 'You've been out here ten years, haven't you?'

Wolfert nodded.

'Things are getting worse,' Falk told him. 'I've taken the trouble to look up some statistics. They weren't hard to find; the damned fools are proud of them. The number of persons in mental institutions has gone steadily down since 1980, when the world-wide analogue program got under way. Extension of analogue program, steadily up. The two curves cancel out perfectly.

'There are fewer and fewer people that have to be put away in madhouses – not because of any improvement in therapy, but because the analogue techniques are getting better and better. The guy who would have been hopelessly insane fifty years ago now has a little man inside his head, steering him around, making him act normal. On the outside he *is* normal; inside, he's a raving madman. Worse still, the guy who would have been just a little bit cracked fifty years ago – and gotten treatment for it – is now just as mad as the first guy. It doesn't matter any more. We could all be maniacs, and the world would go on just as before.'

Wolfert grimaced wryly. 'Well? It's a peaceful world, anyhow.'

'Sure,' said Falk. 'No war or possibility of war, no murders, no theft, no crime at all. That's because every one of them has a policeman inside his skull. But action begets reaction, Wolfert, in psychiatry as well as in physics. A prison is a place to get out of, if it takes you a lifetime. Push one plunger down, another will rise. Just a few years more, I think – ten or twenty, say – and you'll see that madhouse curve rise again. Because there's no escape from the repression of the Guardians except a further retreat into insanity. And eventually a point is reached where no amount of treatment can help. What are they going to do then?'

Wolfert tamped his pipe out slowly and stood up, sucking absently at the stem. 'You say *they*,' he said, 'meaning the psychiatrists who really govern Earth, I suppose. You've evidently figured out what you're going to do.'

Falk smiled. 'Yes. With your help – I'm going to the stars.'

The other stood frozen a moment. 'So you know about that,' he said. 'Well— Come into the next room. I'll show it to you.'

Falk had known about the Doorway, but not that it looked like this. It was a cubicle of something that looked like slick brown glass. Ten feet high, six wide and deep. Inside, at waist level on the far wall, a lever – curiously shaped, like the head of an old-fashioned walking stick, the slightly curved bar of the L parallel to the wall. Nothing more than that. The floor of Wolfert's hut had been assembled around it. It was the reason for the hut's existence, for Wolfert's dearly bought presence on Mars.

'So that's it,' said Falk. He took a step toward it.

'Stay where you are,' Wolfert said sharply. 'The area in front of the entrance is booby-trapped.'

Falk stopped and looked at Wolfert, then at the metal cabinets bolted to the floor on either side of the Doorway. Now that he looked at them closely, he could see the lenses of black-light beams and, above them, metal cones that he supposed were discharge points.

Wolfert confirmed it. 'If anything ever comes out, the current is supposed to get him. If it doesn't, I'm here.' He put his hand on the rapid-fire automatic at his belt.

Falk sat down slowly on a bench next to the wall. 'Why?' he asked. 'Why are they so afraid of whatever might come out of the Doorway?'

The other leaned awkwardly against the wall and began re-filling his pipe. 'You don't know the whole story, then,' he said. 'Tell me what you do know, and I'll fill in the gaps.'

Falk said slowly, 'I was able to find out that the Doorway existed – that the first Mars expedition, in '76 had found it here. Apparently it was known to be an interstellar transportation system, but as far as I could learn nobody had ever actually tried it out. I knew that a caretaker had been left here – your predecessor, I take it – after the idea of colonising Mars was abandoned. But I didn't know any of the reasons.'

Wolfert grinned briefly and straightened away from the wall. As he talked, he paced back and forth across the room, glancing at Falk only occasionally. 'It's a transportation system, all right. Put an object in that cubicle, press the lever down – the object vanishes. So does most of the crowbar or whatever you use to work the lever. *FffT* – gone.

'We don't know how old it is and have no way of telling. The material it's made of is harder than diamond. About half of it is underground. That was the way it was found – sitting perfectly level on the surface of the desert. I believe it must have some sort of self-leveling mechanism built into it so that it's always available no matter what happens to the surface.

'Other ruins have been found on Mars, but they're all stone and quite primitive; nothing like this. The first expedition tried to get into its innards and find out what made it go, of course, but they couldn't. You can *see* in, but there's nothing to see.' He gave his quick, bitter smile. 'It's frustrating. Makes a physicist feel like a backward student in a kindergarten.

'We know that it's part of an interstellar network. One man did try it out – a member of the first expedition, one of the group that found the Doorway in the first place. He saw the cubicle and the lever – stepped in and pressed it to find out what would happen. *He* found out, all right, but I don't suppose the rest of us will ever know. The second expedition brought along a batch of powerful all-wave senders and sent them through. They picked up the first signal five years later, from the general direction of Regulus. Two more after seven years, then four during the thirteenth year, all from different directions. The other eight have yet to be heard from.'

He stopped pacing and looked at Falk. 'Now do you understand? The thing has no selectivity – it's completely random. We could walk through here and step out onto the planet of another star, all right – but it would take us a million years to find the way back by trial and error.' He knocked his pipe out against the heel of his hand, letting the dottle fall on the floor. 'There it sits, the doorway to the stars. And we can't use it.'

Falk leaned back against the wall, trying to absorb the idea. 'Maybe there are only a dozen or so stars in the network,' he suggested.

Wolfert's thin mouth drew down at the corners. 'Don't be a fool,' he said. 'Would the race that could build *that*' – he gestured toward the cubicle – 'stop at a dozen stars, or a thousand? The devil! They owned the galaxy!' Nervously he began to fill his pipe again. 'Sixty billion stars,' he said. 'And according to current theory, all the mainliners have planets.'

He pointed to the cubicle again. 'Three hundred sixty cubic feet, about,' he said. 'Enough for one man and supplies for a month, or fifteen people and supplies for a week. That's the limit of the size of the colony we could send out. With no assurance,' he added bitterly, 'that they'd land anywhere they could live for a minute.'

'Frustrating,' Falk agreed. 'But I still don't see why you're here – with a gun. I can understand that if a member of the race that built that thing came through – and I must say it seems unlikely – that would be an important event. But why kill him when he steps out?'

'Dammit,' said Wolfert violently, 'it isn't my policy, Falk. I only work here.'

'I understand that,' Falk said. 'But do you have any idea what's behind the policy?'

'Fear,' said Wolfert promptly. 'They've got too much at stake.' He leaned against the wall again, gesturing with his pipestem. 'Do you realise,' he said, 'that we could have inter-stellar colonisation *without* this gadget, on our own? Certainly. Not now, but fifty, a hundred years from now – if we worked at it. Give us a fuel source efficient enough so that we can accelerate continuously for as long as eight months, and we could reach the stars well within a man's lifetime. But do you know why we won't?

'They're afraid. They're even afraid to plant colonies here on Mars, or on Jupiter's moons, simply because transportation takes too long. Imagine a colony cut off from Earth by a five-or ten-year trip. Say something goes wrong – a man like yourself, naturally immune to analogue treatment. Or a man who somehow evades the treatment, then manages to take it over, change it. Say he cuts out the one directive, "You must do nothing against the policy or interests of Earth." Then you've got two communities again, not one. And then?'

Falk nodded soberly. 'War. I see now. They don't dare take even the smallest chance of that.'

'It isn't a question of daring, they *can't*. That's one of the directives in their own conditioning, Falk.'

'So we'll never get to the stars.'

'Unless,' said Wolfert, 'somebody walks out of that Doorway who understands how it works. The voltage is high, but not high enough to kill – we hope. He's supposed to be stunned. If the current doesn't stop him, and he tries to get back into the Doorway, I'm supposed to shoot to cripple. But at all events, he's supposed to be stopped. He isn't to be allowed to go back and warn others to stay away from this station. Because if we had that knowledge – how to alter the system so that it would be selective—'

'Then we'd have colonies, all right,' finished Falk. 'Everyone just around the corner from Earth. All just alike. The loonies shall inherit the Universe ... I hope nobody ever comes through.'

'I don't think you're likely to be disappointed,' said Wolfert.

II

He prowled the rest of the cabin with Wolfert, resting at intervals until his strength returned. There wasn't much to see: the Doorway room, with a spyhole Falk had not noticed between it and the bedroom; the room that housed radio, radar, and the computer that controlled the grazing orbits of the supply rockets; the power plant, and the compressor that kept the cabin's air at breathable pressure; kitchen, bathroom, and two storage chambers.

The radio room had a window, and Falk stood there a long time, looking out over the alien desert, violet now as the sun dropped toward the horizon. Stars glittered with unfamiliar brilliance in the near-black sky, and Falk found his gaze drawn to them even against the tug of that unearthly landscape.

In his mind he sketched hairlines of fire across the sky – a cat's cradle of stars. The thought that tomorrow he would be standing on a planet of one of

those suns was like an icy douche; the mind recoiled from it as from the thought of personal death. But at the same time it lured him. He felt like a boy standing on the edge of an unsounded pool whose black water might hold treasure or death: he was afraid to dive, and yet he knew that he must.

How could a man feel otherwise, he wondered, knowing that the way was open, that he had only to step forward?

Wolfert said abruptly, 'You haven't asked me whether I reported to Earth when I found you in that freighter shell.'

Falk looked at him. 'You did, of course,' he said. 'It doesn't matter. I'll be gone long before they can do anything about me. You'll tell them that I overpowered you and escaped through the Doorway – they won't be able to prove otherwise – unless you're conditioned against lying?'

'No,' said Wolfert, 'I'm not. That part's all right, with one emendation: I'll say I revived you, then shot and buried you. But what made you so sure that I'd be – sympathetic?'

'You're here,' said Falk simply. 'You're a volunteer. They haven't got to the stage of conditioning people to do jobs they don't want to do, though I suppose they will eventually. And when I'd heard you speak, I knew you were intelligent. So – you're a hermit. You don't like the madhouse they're making out of Earth, any more than I do.'

'I don't know,' said Wolfert slowly. 'Perhaps you're assuming too much similarity.' He looked down at his ever-present pipe, tamping the tobacco with a horny thumb: 'I don't feel as you do about the analogue system, or the present government. I'm – adjusted, there. In my personal universe, it works. I can see that it will lead to disaster eventually, but that doesn't bother me much. I'll be dead.'

He looked at Falk earnestly. 'But I want the stars,' he said. 'That's an emotional thing with me ... There are no slugs in these cartridges.' He indicated the gun at his hip. 'Or in any of the ammunition I've got. They didn't condition me against that.'

Falk stared at him. 'Look,' he said abruptly, 'you've got a directive against stepping through that Doorway, is that right?'

The other nodded.

'Well, but is there any reason why I couldn't knock you over the head and drag you through?'

Wolfert smiled wryly, shaking his head slowly. 'No good,' he said. 'Somebody's got to stay, this end.'

'Why?'

'Because there's a chance that you'll find the secret out there, somewhere. That's what you're hoping, too, isn't it? You're not just looking for a place to hide – you could do that in a thousand places on Earth. You're after knowledge, and in spite of what I've told you, you're hoping you'll be able to bring it back and make the Earth over.'

'It sounds a little quixotic,' said Falk, 'but you're right.'

Wolfert shrugged, letting his gaze drift away again. 'Well, then ... there's got to be somebody here. Somebody with no slugs in his gun. If I went with you, they'd take good care to send a different sort of man next time.'

He met Falk's eyes briefly. 'Don't waste time feeling sorry for me,' he said. 'You may not believe it, but I'm quite happy here. When I'm ... alone, that is.'

Falk had been wondering why the government had not sent a married couple instead of a single man, who might go mad from sheer loneliness. Now it struck him that he had been stupid. Wolfert had a wife, undoubtedly; the best kind – one who suited him perfectly, who would never be fickle, or want to return to Earth; one who cost nothing to feed, consumed no air, and had not added an ounce of weight when Wolfert had been shipped out here. And on Mars it did not ordinarily matter that no one else could see her.

He felt an inward twinge of revulsion and instantly knew that Wolfert had seen and understood it. The man's cheeks flushed, and he turned away to stare through the window, his lips thin and hard.

After a moment Falk said, 'Wolfert, I like you better than any man I've ever met. I hope you'll believe that.'

Wolfert hauled out a pipe cleaner, a complicated thing of many hinged stems, the free ends stamped into shovel shapes, tamper, shapes, probes. He said, 'I'm afraid I dislike you, Falk, but it's nothing personal. I simply hate your guts a little, because you've got something I wasn't lucky enough to be born with. You're the master of your own mind.'

He turned and put out his hand, grinning. 'Aside from that trifling matter, I entirely approve of you. If that's good enough?'

Falk gripped his hand. 'I hope you're here when I get back,' he said.

'I'll be here,' said Wolfert, scraping his pipe, 'for another thirty-odd years, barring accidents. If you're not back by then, I don't suppose you'll be coming back at all.'

At Wolfert's suggestion, Falk put on one of the other's light Mars suits instead of the spacesuit he had worn in the freighter. The latter, designed for heavy-duty service in the orbital space station that circled Earth, was, as Wolfert pointed out, too clumsy for use on a planet's surface. The lighter suit furnished adequate protection in thin atmosphere and was equipped with gadgetry that the other lacked: a head lamp, climbing gear, built-in compasses, and traps for the occupant's ingestion and excretion. It carried air tanks, but also had a compression outfit – which, given an atmosphere at least as oxygen-rich as that of Mars, would keep the wearer alive for as long as the batteries held out.

'You'll have to find a place where you can live off the land, so to speak, any-how,' said Wolfert. 'If all the planets you hit should happen to be dead, so will you be, very shortly. But this suit will give you longer to look, at least, and the stuff in the knapsack will last you as long as you have air. I'd give you this gun, but it wouldn't do you any good – all the ammunition's dud, as I told you.'

He disconnected the booby trap and stood aside as Falk moved to the entrance. Falk took one last look around at the bare metal room and at Wolf-ert's spare figure and gloomy face. He stepped into the brown-glass cubicle and put his gloved hand on the lever.

'See you later,' he said.

Wolfert nodded soberly, almost indifferently. 'So long, Falk,' he said, and put his pipe back in his mouth.

Falk turned on his helmet lamp, put his free hand near the control box at his belt – and pressed the lever down.

Wolfert vanished. An instant later Falk was aware that the lever was no longer beneath his hand. He turned, dazedly, and saw that it was back in its original position, above his hand.

Then he remembered the curious blank that had taken Wolfert's place and he turned again to the entrance. He saw – nothing. A gray-white blankness, featureless, uncommunicative. Was this some kind of intermediary state – and if so, how long did it last? Falk felt a brief surge of panic as he realised they had only assumed the journey was instantaneous, and another as he recalled the eight transmitters that had never been heard from …

Then common sense took over, and he stepped forward to the entrance.

The gray-white shaded gradually, as his gaze traveled downward, into gray-blue and violet, and then a chaos of dim colors of which his eye made nothing. He gripped the edge of the Doorway and bent forward, looking downward and still downward. Then he saw the cliff, and all the rest of the scene fell into perspective.

He stood at the top of a sheer mountain – an impossible, ridiculous height. Down it went and again down, until whatever was at the bottom melted into a meaningless tapestry of grayed color. He looked to right and left and saw nothing else. No sound came through the diaphragm of his helmet. He had only the tactile and muscular responses of his own body, and the hard reality of the Doorway itself, to assure him that he was real and live.

The planet was dead; he felt irrationally sure of that. It *felt* dead; there was not even a whisper of wind: only the featureless blanket of gray cloud, the cliff, the meaningless colors below.

He looked at the kit slung to his belt: the pressure gauge, bottled litmus papers, matches. But there was no point in testing this atmosphere: even if it were breathable, there was clearly no way of getting out of the Doorway. The cliff began not more than an inch from the entrance.

Falk went back to the lever, pressed it down again.

This time he watched it as it reached the end of its stroke. There was no hint of a transition: the lever was there, under his hand, and then it was back in the starting position – as if it had passed unfelt through the flesh of his hand.

He turned.

Deep blue night, blazing with stars. Underneath, a flat blue-green waste that ran straight away into the far distance.

Falk stepped out onto the icy plain and looked around him, then upward. The sky was so like the one he had known as a boy in Michigan that it struck him almost as a conviction that this terminus was on Earth – in the Antarctic, perhaps, near the pole, where no explorer had ever happened across it. Then, as he looked automatically for the Dipper, Orion's Belt, he knew that he was wrong.

He saw none of the familiar patterns. These were alien stars, in an alien sky. He reviewed what he could remember of the configurations of Earth's southern hemisphere, but none of them fitted either.

Directly above him was a group of eight stars, two of them very brilliant- four arranged in a straight line, the rest spread out in an almost perfect semicircle. Falk knew that if he had ever seen that constellation before he would not have forgotten it.

Now he looked down toward the horizon, blacker than the sky. How could he know that light, warmth, safety, knowledge were not hiding just beyond the curve of the planet?

He turned back to the cubicle. He was here on sufferance, a man in a Mars suit, with weeks – or, with great luck, months or years – to live. He had to find what he sought within a pitifully small radius from the Doorway, or not at all.

Down went the lever again. Now it was still night – but when Falk went to the Doorway, he saw an avenue of great buildings under the stars.

Now the pressure gauge came out – low, but the compressor could handle it. The litmus papers – negative. The match burned – weakly, and only for an instant, but it burned.

Falk started the compressor and shut off the flow of air from the tanks slung at his back. Then he turned on his helmet light and marched off down the avenue.

The buildings were variations on a theme: pyramid, cone, and wedge shape, they sloped away as they rose, so that for all their enormous bulk they did not hide the sky. Falk looked up when he had taken a few steps, subconsciously expecting to see the half-circle constellation. But it was not there, and he realised with a shock that, for all he knew, he might be halfway across the galaxy from the spot where he had stood five minutes ago.

He drew a picture of the galaxy in his mind, an oval clot of mist against blackness. Near one focus of the ellipse he put a dot of brightness that stood for Sol. Then he made another dot and drew a shining line between them. Then another dot, and another line; then another. They made a sprawling letter N across the misty oval.

It was incomprehensible. A race that could span the galaxy, but could not choose one destination from another?

The only other alternative was: there was some function of the Doorways that men had failed to grasp, some method of selection had evaded them, as a savage might be bewildered in a modern tubeway system. But Falk's mind rejected that. The mechanism was simple and clear. A cubicle and a lever. Function is expressed by shape; and the shape of the Doorway said 'Go'; it did not say 'Where?'

He looked again at the buildings. The upper quarter of them, he saw now, was badly eroded: layers inches deep had been eaten away. He glanced at the fine orange sand that paved the avenue and saw that it filled doorways almost to the top. Evidently this city had lain all but buried for many years, and in some recent time the shifting sands had uncovered it again.

The space between the sand and the tops of the doorways was narrow, but he thought he could squeeze through. He picked out one, centering it in the brilliant disk of his head lamp – and stood there, in the middle of the avenue, reluctant to move.

He glanced back at the cubicle, as if for reassurance. It was still there, comfortably clear and sharp-lined, timeless. Now he realised what was troubling him. This city was dead – dead as the planet of the cliff or the planet of ice. The buildings were stone; they had crumbled under the weather. Their makers were dust.

He had agreed with Wolfert when the other had suggested that he was on a quest for knowledge; that he hoped the Doorway would eventually take him back to Sol, armed with knowledge, ready to remake the world. But it wasn't true. That had been his conscious idea, but it was a dream, a self-delusion – an excuse.

He had no love for Earth, or any conviction that humanity must be rescued from its own weakness. If that force had driven him, there would have been no logic in leaving Earth. He could have stayed, worked himself into the governing elite, organised a revolution from within. His chance of success would have been small, but there would have been some chance.

Yes, he might have done it – and for what? To remove the one control that kept humanity from destroying itself?

That coin had the same face on both sides. Uncontrolled, mankind was not fit to colonise. Controlled, it dared not take the risk. Human civilisation was not ready, was a dead end, an aborted experiment. Mankind was a dirty beast, ravaging its planet, befouling itself – capable of any imaginable perversion, degradation, horror.

But there had been another civilisation once – one that had been worthy of the stars. Falk did not believe it was dead. Stone crumbled; metal rusted; and the races that used them vanished and were not mourned. The Doorways still lived, still functioned, defying time.

That race was not here; it had left no trace of itself except the Doorway. Without another glance at the buildings around him, Falk turned and went back to the brown glass cubicle.

When he was three yards away from it, he saw the footprints.

There were five of them, lightly impressed into the sand near the Doorway's entrance. Search as he might, Falk could not find any more. Two, apparently, pointed away from the cubicle; the other three were the returning trail, for one overlapped one of the previous set.

They were smaller than Falk's booted prints, oval, slightly flattened along the sides. Falk stared at them as if the mere act of looking would make them give up more information; but they told him nothing.

They were not human; but what did that prove?

They had been made long since the time when the Doorways had been built; Falk did not know what winds swept this world, but it could only have been a few years, at most, since the sands had dropped to their present level. But even that train of logic led nowhere.

They could be the trace of a Doorway builder. Or they could have been made by a wanderer like himself, another barbarian venturing in the paths of his betters.

The bitterest thing of all was that, having found the trail, he could not follow it. For it led through the Doorway – to any one of sixty billion suns.

Falk stepped into the cubicle and pressed the lever down once more.

III

White light that sealed his eyes with pain, and a vicious torrent of heat. Gasping, Falk groped frantically for the lever.

The after-image faded slowly. He saw night again, and the stars. The last one, he thought, must have been the planet of a nova. How many of those was he likely to run into?

He stepped to the doorway. A wasteland: not a stick, not a stone.

He went back to the lever. Light again, of bearable intensity, and a riot of color outside.

Falk stepped cautiously to the entrance. Slowly his mind adapted to the unfamiliar shapes and colors. He saw a bright landscape under a tropic sun – gray-violet mountains in the distance, half veiled by mist; nearer, tall stalks that bore heavy leaves and fronds of startling blue-green; and directly ahead of him, a broad plaza that might have been cut from one monstrous boulder of jade. On either side were low, box-shaped structures of dark vitreous material: blue, brown, green and red. And in the middle of the plaza stood a group of slender shapes that were unquestionably alive, sentient.

Falk's heart was pounding. He stepped behind the shelter of the entrance hall and peered out. Curiously it was not the cluster of live things that drew him, but the buildings on either side.

They were made of the same enduring, clean-edged substance as the Doorway. He had come, by blind chance, at last to the right place.

Now he stared at the creatures grouped in the middle of the plaza. For some reason they were disappointing. They were slender S-shapes, graceful enough in repose: lizard shapes, upright on two legs; pink of belly and umber of back. But in spite of the bandoliers slung from their narrow shoulders, in spite of their quick patterned gestures as they spoke together, Falk could not convince himself that he had found the people he sought.

They were too manlike. One turned away while two others spoke; came back leaning at a passionate angle, thrust himself between the two, gesturing wildly. Shouted down, he again left and stalked a half circle around the group. He moved as a chicken moves, awkwardly, thrusting his long neck forward at each step.

Of the five others, two argued, two merely stood with drooping, attentive heads and watched; and the last stood a little apart, gazing around him disdainfully.

They were funny, as monkeys are funny – because they resemble men. We laughed at our mirrored selves. Even the races of man laugh at each other when they should weep.

They're tourists, Falk thought. *One wants to go to the Lido, another insists they see the Grand Canal first; the third is furious with both of them for wasting time, the next two are too timid to interfere, and the last one doesn't care.*

He couldn't imagine what their reaction to him would be. Nothing welcome, at any rate; they might want to take him home as a souvenir. He wanted to get into those buildings, but he'd have to wait until they were out of sight.

While he waited, he got out the atmosphere-testing kit. The pressure gauge showed the merest trifle less than Earth normal; the litmus papers did not react; the match burned cheerfully, just as it would have on Earth. Falk turned off the oxygen, cracked the helmet valve cautiously, and sniffed.

After the stale air of the suit, the breath he inhaled was so good that it brought tears to his eyes. It was fresh, faintly warm, and sweet with flower fragrance. Falk opened the helmet seam, tipped the helmet back, and let the breeze wash over his face and hair.

He peered out, and saw to his dismay that the party was trooping directly toward him. Falk ducked his head back inside, glanced instinctively at the lever, then looked out again.

They were running now; they had seen him. They ran very clumsily, heads darting strenuously forward and back. The one, in the lead was opening and shutting his triangular mouth, and Falk heard faint yawps. He leaped out of the cubicle, cut sharply to the right, and ran.

The nearest building with a visible opening, unfortunately, was some distance down the line, between Falk and the lizards. He glanced back when he was halfway there. The lizards were considerably strung out now, but the leader was only a few yards away.

They were faster than they looked. Falk put his head down and tried to make his heavy boots move to a quicker rhythm. Almost to the door, he looked back again. The lizard was one jump away, its grimy, ball-tipped fingers outspread.

Falk turned in desperation and, as the lizard came up, swung a knotted fist to the point of its snout. He heard its steam-whistle screech, saw it collapse, and then he was diving through the open door ahead.

The door closed gently behind him – a sheet of glassy substance, the same blue as the walls, gliding down to seal the opening.

Falk stared at it. Through its transparency he could see the dark shapes of the lizards crowding around, leaning to pry at the bottom of the door, gesticulating at each other. It was plain, at any rate, that the door was not going to open for them.

Whether it would open for him, when he wanted it to, was another matter.

He looked around him. The building was a single huge room, so long and deep that he could barely see the far walls. Scattered over the floor, patternless, were boxes, or chests, racks, shelves, little ambiguous mounds. Nearly all the objects Falk could see were fashioned of the same glass-like material.

There was no dust in the room; but now that Falk thought of it, he realised that there had been none in any of the Doorways, either. How that was done he could not conjecture. He moved to the nearest object, a file, or rack formed apparently to take many things of diverse shapes and sizes. It was a quarter empty now, and the remaining contents had a jumbled look.

He picked up an orange glass spindle, full of embedded threads, or flaws that looped in a curious pattern from one end to the other. He put it down, took a hollow sphere of opal. It was made in halves and seemed to be empty, but Falk could find no way to take it apart. He replaced it and took a brown object shaped like a double crescent, with a clear fracture plane running diagonally through it …

Half an hour later he realised that he was not going to find any picture books or engineering manuals or any one thing that would unlock the mystery of the Doorway people for him. If there were any knowledge to be gained here, it would have to come from the building as a whole.

The lizards distracted him. He could see them through the walls of the building, pressing their snouts against the glass, staring with little round eyes, gesturing at him. But he learned things from them.

The group broke up finally, leaving only one to guard the exit; the others dispersed. Falk saw one go into the building directly across the plaza. The door closed behind him. A little later another one approached and pounded on the door; but it did not open until the first lizard came close to it inside. Some automatic mechanism, beyond Falk's fathoming, evidently responded to the presence or absence of any living thing inside each building. When the last person left, the door stayed open; when another person entered, it shut and would not open for the next unless the first person allowed it.

That added one item to the description of the Doorway people that Falk was building in his mind. They were not property-conscious – not afraid that thieves would enter in their absence, for the doors stood open when they were gone-but they respected each other's love of privacy.

Falk had previously thought of this building as a vast factory or laboratory or dormitory – a place designed to serve a large number of people, anyhow. Now he revised his opinion. Each building, he thought, was the private domain of one person – or, if they had family groups, only two or three. But how could one person use all this space, all these possessions?

He made the comparison that by now was becoming automatic. He asked himself what a cliff dweller would make of a millionaire's triplex apartment in New York.

It helped, but not enough. The objects around him were all specialised tools; they would not function for him and so told him nothing about the Doorway builders. There was nothing that he could compare to a bed, to a table, to a shower bath. He could not see the people who had lived here.

With an effort, he forced himself to stop thinking in terms of men. The facts were important, not his prejudices. And then what had been a barrier became a road. There were no beds, tables, showers? Then the Doorway people did not sleep; they did not eat; they did not bathe.

Probably, thought Falk, they did not die.

They were fit to live among the stars …

The riddle of the deserted chamber mocked him. How, having built this city, would they leave it? How would they spread the network of the Doorways across the face of the galaxy, and then leave it unused?

The first question answered itself. Looking at the littered chamber, Falk thought of his comparison of the cliff dweller and the millionaire and humbly acknowledged his presumption. Not a millionaire's triplex, he told himself ... a tent.

Once there had been something of particular interest on this world. No telling what it had been, for that had been some millions of years ago when Mars was a living world. But the Doorway people, a few of them, had come here to observe it. When they were finished, they had gone away, leaving their tents behind, as a man might abandon a crude shelter of sticks and leaves.

And the other things they had left behind them? The cubes, cones, rods, odd shapes, each one beyond price to a man? *Empty cans*, thought Falk; *toothpaste tubes, wrapping paper.*

They had abandoned this city and the million things in it because they were of no value.

The sun was redder, nearer the horizon. Falk looked at the chronometer strapped to the wrist of his suit and found to his surprise that it was more than five hours since he had left Wolfert on Mars.

He had not eaten. He took food out of his pack and looked at the labels on the cans. But he was not hungry; he did not even feel tired.

He watched the lizards outside. They were scurrying around in the plaza now, bringing armloads of junk from the building, packing them into big red boxes. As Falk watched, a curious construction floated into view down at the end of the plaza. It was a kind of airboat, an open shell with two lizards riding it, supported by two wing-like extensions with streamlined, down-pointing shapes at their ends.

It drifted slowly until it hovered over the pile of boxes the lizards had gathered. Then a hatch opened in its belly, and a hook emerged at the end of three cords. The lizards on the plaza began slinging loops of cord from their boxes to the hook.

Falk watched them idly. The hook began to rise, dragging the boxes after it, and at the last moment one of the lizards tossed another loop over it.

The new box was heavy; the hook stopped when it took up the slack, and the airboat dipped slightly. Then it rose again, and the hook rose too, until the whole load was ten feet off the ground.

Abruptly one of the three cords snapped; Falk saw it whip through the air, saw the load lurch ponderously to one side, and the airboat dip. Simultaneously the pilot sent the boat down to take up the strain on the remaining cords.

The lizards were scattering. The load struck heavily; and a moment later so did the airboat. It bounced, skidded wildly, and came to rest as the pilot shut off the power.

The lizards crowded around again, and the two in the airboat climbed down for an interminable conference. Eventually they got aboard again, and the boat rose a few feet while the lizards beneath disengaged the hook. Then there was another conference. Falk could see that the doors of the boat's hatch were closed and had a crumpled look. Evidently they were jammed and could not be opened again.

Finally the boat came down once more, and with much argument and gesticulation the boxes were unpacked and some of their contents reloaded into two boxes, these being hoisted with much effort into the airboat's cockpit. The rest was left strewn around the plaza.

The airboat lifted and went away, and most of the lizards followed it. One straggler came over for a last look at Falk; he peered and gestured through the wall for a while, then gave it up and followed the rest. The plaza was deserted.

Some time passed, and then Falk saw a pillar of white flame that lifted, with a glint of silver at its tip, somewhere beyond the city, and grew until it arched upward to the zenith, dwindled, and vanished.

So they had spaceships, the lizards. They did not dare use the Doorways, either. Not fit, not fit … too much like men.

Falk went out into the plaza and stood, letting the freshening breeze ruffle his hair. The sun was dropping behind the mountains, and the whole sky had turned ruddy, like a great crimson cape streaming out of the west. Falk watched, reluctant to leave, until the colors faded through violet to gray, and the first stars came out.

It was a good world. A man could stay here, probably, and live his life out in comfort and ease. No doubt there were exotic fruits to be had from those trees; certainly there was water; the climate was good; and Falk thought sardonically that there could be no dangerous wild beasts, or those twittering tourists would never have come here.

If all a man wanted was a hiding place, there could be no better world than this. For a moment Falk was strongly tempted. He thought of the cold dead world he had seen and wondered if he would ever find a place as fair as this again. Also, he knew now that if the Doorway builders still lived, they must long ago have drawn in their outposts. Perhaps they lived now on only one planet, out of all the billions. Falk would die before he found it.

He looked at the rubble the lizards had left in the middle of the plaza. One box was still filled, but burst open; that was the one that had caused all the trouble. Around it was a child's litter of baubles – pretty glass toys, red, green, blue, yellow, white.

A lizard, abandoned here by his fellows, would no doubt be happy enough in the end.

With a sigh, Falk turned back to the building. The door opened before him, and he collected his belongings, fastened down his helmet, strapped on his knapsack again.

The sky was dark now, and Falk paused to look up at the familiar sweep of the Milky Way. Then he switched on his helmet light and turned toward the waiting Doorway.

The light fell across the burst box the lizards had left, and Falk saw a hard edge of something thrusting out. It was not the glassy adamant of the Doorway builders; it looked like stone.

Falk stooped and tore the box aside.

He saw a slab of rock, roughly smoothed to the shape of a wedge. On its upper face, characters were incised. They were in English.

With blood pounding in his ears, Falk knelt by the stone and read what was written there.

THE DOORWAYS STOP THE AGING PROCESS. I WAS 32 WHEN I LEFT MARS, AM HARDLY OLDER NOW THOUGH I HAVE BEEN TRAVELING FROM STAR TO STAR FOR A TIME I BELIEVE CANNOT BE LESS THAN 20 YEARS. BUT YOU MUST KEEP ON. I STOPPED HERE 2 YRS. FOUND MYSELF AGING – HAVE OBSERVED THAT MILKY WAY LOOKS NEARLY THE SAME FROM ALL PLANETS SO FAR VISITED. THIS CANNOT BE COINCIDENCE. BELIEVE THAT DOORWAY TRAVEL IS RANDOM ONLY WITHIN CONCENTRIC BELTS OF STARS & THAT SOONER OR LATER YOU HIT DOORWAY WHICH GIVES ENTRY TO NEXT INNERMOST BELT. IF I AM RIGHT, FINAL DESTINATION IS CENTER OF GALAXY. I HOPE TO SEE YOU THERE.

JAMES E. TANNER
NATIVE OF EARTH

Falk stood up, blinded by the glory of the vision that grew in his mind. He thought he understood now why the Doorways were not selective and why their makers no longer used them.

Once – a billion years ago, perhaps – they must have been uncontested owners of the galaxy. But many of their worlds were small planets like Mars – too small to keep their atmospheres and their water forever. Millions of years ago, they must have begun to fall back from these. And meanwhile, Falk thought, on the greater worlds just now cooling, the lesser breeds had arisen: the crawling, brawling things. The lizards. The men. Things not worthy of the stars.

But even a man could learn if he lived long enough, journeyed far enough. James Tanner had signed himself not 'TERRAN SPACE CORPS' or 'U.S.A.' but 'NATIVE OF EARTH.'

So the way was made long, and the way was made hard; and the lesser breeds stayed on their planets. But for a man, or a lizard, who would give up all that he called 'life' for knowledge, the way was open.

Falk turned off the beam of his lamp and looked up at the diamond mist of the galaxy. Where would he be a thousand years from today? Standing on that mote of light, or that, or that …?

Not dust, at any rate. Not dust, unmourned, unworthy. He would be a voyager with a destination, and perhaps half his journey would be done. Wolfert would wait in vain for his return, but it would not matter; Wolfert was happy – if you called that happiness. And on Earth, the mountains would rise and fall long after the question of human survival had been forgotten.

Falk, by that time, perhaps, would be home.

BEACHCOMBER

Maxwell and the girl with the astonishing bust had started their weekend on Thursday in Venice. Friday they went to Paris, Saturday to Nice, and on Sunday they were bored. The girl, whose name was Alice, pouted at him across the breakfast table. 'Vernon, let's go someplace else,' she said.

'Sure,' said Maxwell, not too graciously. 'Don't you want your bug eggs?'

'Urgh,' said Alice, pushing them away. 'If I ever did, I don't now. Why do you have to be so unpleasant in the morning?'

The eggs were insect eggs, all right, but they were on the menu as *oeufs Procyon Thibault*, and three of the half-inch brown spheres cost about one thousand times their value in calories. Maxwell was well paid as a script writer for the North American Unit Ministry of Information – he bossed a gang of six gagmen on the Cosmic Cocktail show – but he was beginning to hate to think about what these five days were costing him.

Maxwell was a small man, sturdily built and not bad-looking, except that he was a little pop-eyed. When he raised his eyebrows, which he did whenever he spoke, his brown forehead creased into accordion-like wrinkles. Some girls found this attractive; those who didn't were usually impressed by his hand-finished duroplast tunics and forty-credit cummerbunds. He had an unhappy suspicion that Alice, whose most prominent feature has already been mentioned, was one of the latter group.

'Where do you want to go?' asked Maxwell. Their coffee came out of the conveyor, steaming and fragrant, and he sipped his moodily. 'Want to run over to Algiers? Or up to Stockholm?'

'No,' said Alice. She leaned forward across the table and put up one long white hand to keep her honey-colored hair out of her eyes. 'You don't know what I mean. I mean, let's go to some other planet.'

Maxwell choked slightly and spilled coffee on the table top. 'Europe is all right,' Alice was saying with disdain, 'but it's all getting to be just like Chicago. Let's go some place different for once.'

'And be back by tomorrow noon?' Maxwell demanded. 'It's ten hours even to Proxima; we'd have just time to turn around and get back on the liner.'

Alice dropped her long lashes, contriving to look inviting and sullen at the same time. Not bad at that, Maxwell thought, for ten o'clock in the morning. 'You couldn't get Monday off, I suppose,' she said.

Maxwell's crew worked two weeks ahead, anyhow; it would only mean digging in harder when he got back. What the hell, why not play sick until Tuesday or Wednesday?

Alice's lashes rose again, slowly enough for one swift, sure look at Maxwell's face. Then her eye corners crinkled, and she gave him her A-Number-One smile. '*That's* why I love you so, Vernie,' she said with satisfaction.

They took the liner to Gamma Tauri IV, the clearing point for the system, then transferred to the interplanet shuttle for Three. Three was an almost undeveloped planet; there were perhaps a hundred cities near the equator, and some mines and plantations in the temperate zones – the rest was nothing but scenery. Maxwell had heard about it from people at the Ministry; he'd been warned to go within a year or so if he went at all – after that it would be as full of tourists as Proxima II.

The scenery was worth the trip. Sitting comfortably on their rented airscooters, stripped to shorts and shirts, with the polarised sunscreens moderating the blazing heat of Gamma Tauri, Maxwell and the girl could look in any horizontal direction and see a thousand square miles of exuberant blue-green foliage.

Two hundred feet below, the tops of gigantic tree ferns waved spasmodically in the breeze. They were following a chain of low mountains that bisected this continent; the treetops sloped away abruptly on either side, showing an occasional glimpse of reddish-brown undergrowth, and merged into a sea of blue-green that became bluer and mistier toward the horizon. A flying thing moved lazily across the clear, cumulus-dotted sky, perhaps half a mile away. Maxwell trained his binoculars on it: it was an absurd lozenge with six pairs of wings – an insect, perhaps; he couldn't tell. He heard a raucous cry down below, not far away, and glanced down hoping to see one of the carnivores; but the rippling sea of foliage was unbroken.

He watched Alice breathing deeply. Maxwell grinned. Her face was shiny with perspiration and pleasure. 'Where to now?' he asked.

The girl peered to the right, where a glint of silver shone at the horizon. 'Is that the sea over there?' she asked. 'If it is, let's go look for a nice beach and have our lunch.'

There were no nice beaches; they were all covered with inch-thick pebbles instead of sand; but Alice kept wanting to try the next place. After each abortive approach, they went up to two thousand feet to survey the shore line. Alice pointed and said, 'There's a nice-looking one. Oh! There's somebody on it.'

Maxwell looked, and saw a tiny figure moving along the shore. 'Might be somebody I know,' he said, and focused his binoculars. He saw a broad, naked back, dark against the silvery sea. The man was stooping, looking at something on the beach.

The figure straightened, and Maxwell saw a blazing crest of blond hair, then the strongly modeled nose and chin, as the man turned. 'Oh-oh,' he said, lowering the binoculars.

Alice was staring intently through her binoculars. 'Isn't he handsome,' she breathed. 'Do you know him?'

'Yes,' said Maxwell. 'That's the Beachcomber. I interviewed him a couple of times. We'd better leave him be.'

Alice kept staring. 'Honestly,' she said. 'I never saw such a— Look, Vernie, he's waving at us.'

Maxwell looked again. The Beachcomber's face was turned up directly toward them. As Maxwell watched, the man's lips moved unmistakably in the syllables of his name.

Maxwell shortened the range, and saw that the Beachcomber was indeed waving. He also saw something he had missed before: the man was stark naked.

'He's recognised me,' he said, with mingled emotions. 'Now we'll have to go down.'

Alice took her eyes away from the binoculars for the first time since they had sighted the man. 'That's silly,' she said.

'How could he— Vernon, you don't mean he can see us clearly from that far away?'

Maxwell waved back at the tiny figure and mouthed silently, 'Coming right down. Put some pants on, dammit.' He said to Alice, 'That's not all he can do. Weren't you listening when I said he's the Beachcomber?'

They started down on a long slant as the little figure below moved toward the jungle's edge. 'The who?' said Alice, looking through the binoculars again.

'Watch where you're going,' said Maxwell, more sharply than he had intended.

'I'm sorry. Who is he, dear?'

'The Beachcomber. The Man From the Future. Haven't you seen a newscast for the last five years?'

'I only tune in for the sports and fashions,' Alice said abstractedly. Then her mouth formed an O. 'My goodness! Is *he* the one who—'

'The same,' said Maxwell. 'The one who gave us the inertia-less drive, the anti-friction field, the math to solve the three-body problem, and about a thousand other things. The guy from three million years in the future. And the loneliest man in all creation, probably. This is the planet he showed up on, five years ago, now that I come to think of it. I guess he spends most of his time here.'

'But why?' asked Alice. She looked toward the tiny beach, which was now vacant. Her expression, Maxwell thought, said that there were better uses to which he could put himself.

Maxwell snorted. 'Did you ever read—' He corrected himself; Alice obviously never read. 'Did you ever see one of the old films about the South Seas? Ever hear of civilised men "going native" or becoming beachcombers?'

Alice said, 'Yes,' a trifle uncertainly.

'All right, imagine a man stranded in a universe full of savages – pleasant, harmless savages, maybe, but people who are three million years away from his culture. What's he going to do?'

'Go native,' said Alice, 'or comb beaches.'

'That's right,' Maxwell told her. 'His only two alternatives. And either one is about as bad as the other, from his point of view. Conform to native customs, settle down, marry, lose everything that makes him a civilised man – or just simply go to hell by himself.'

'That's what he's doing?'

'Right.'

'Well, but what is he combing those beaches *for?*'

Maxwell frowned. 'Don't be a cretin. These particular beaches have nothing to do with it; he just happens to be on one at the moment. He's a beachcomber because he lives like a bum – doesn't do any work, doesn't see people, just loafs and waits to be old enough to die.'

'That's awful,' said Alice. 'It's – such a waste.'

'In more ways than one,' Maxwell added drily. 'But what do you want? There's only one place he could be happy – three million years from now – and he can't go back. He says there isn't any place to go back to. I don't know what he means; he can't explain it any better than that, apparently.'

The Beachcomber was standing motionless by the edge of the forest as their scooters floated down to rest on the pebbly beach. He was wearing a pair of stained, weathered duroplast shorts, but nothing else; no hat to protect his great domed head, no sandals on his feet, no equipment, not even a knife at his belt. Yet Maxwell knew that there were flesh-eaters in the jungle that would gobble a man, outside the force field of his scooter, in about half a second. Knowing the Beachcomber, none of this surprised him. Whether it occurred to Alice to be surprised at any of it, he couldn't tell. She was eating the Beachcomber with her eyes as he walked toward them.

Maxwell, swearing silently to himself, turned off his scooter's field and stepped down. Alice did the same. *I only hope she can keep from trying to rape him,* Maxwell thought.

Aloud, he said, 'How's it, Dai?'

'All right,' said the Beachcomber. Up close, he ceased to be merely impressive and became a little frightening. He stood over seven feet tall, and there was an incredible strength in every line of him. His clear skin looked resilient but *hard*; Maxwell privately doubted that you could cut it with a knife. But it was the eyes that were really impressive: they had the same disquieting, alien quality as an eagle's. Dai never pulled his rank on anybody; he 'went native' perfectly when he had to, for social purposes; but he couldn't help making a normal human adult feel like a backward child.

'Dai, I'd like you to meet Alice Zwerling.' The Beachcomber acknowledged the introduction with effortless courtesy; Alice nearly beat herself to death with her eyelashes.

She managed to stumble very plausibly as they walked down to the water's edge, and put a hand on the giant's arm for support. He righted her casually with the flat of his hand on her back – at the same time giving a slight push that put her a step or two in advance – and went on talking to Maxwell.

They sat down by the water's edge, and Dai pumped Maxwell for the latest news on Earth. He seemed genuinely interested; Maxwell didn't know whether it was an act or not, but he talked willingly and well. The Beachcomber threw an occasional question Alice's way, just enough to keep her in the conversation. Maxwell saw her gathering her forces, and grinned to himself.

There was a pause in Maxwell's monologue, and Alice cleared her throat. Both men looked at her politely. Alice said, 'Dai, are there really man-eating animals in this jungle? Vernon says so, but we haven't seen one all the time we've been here. And—' Her gaze ran down the Beachcomber's smooth, naked torso, and she blushed very prettily. 'I mean—' she added, and stopped again.

The Beachcomber said, 'Sure, there are lots of them. They don't bother me, though.'

She said earnestly, 'You mean – you walk around, like that, *in* the jungle, and nothing can hurt you?'

'That's it.'

Alice drove the point home. 'Could you protect another person who was with you, too?'

'I guess I could.'

Alice smiled radiantly. 'Why, that's too good to be true! I was just telling Vernon, before we saw you down here, that I wished I could go into the jungle without the scooter, to see all the wild animals and things. Will you take me in for a little walk, Dai? Vernon can mind the scooters – you wouldn't mind, would you, Vernie?'

Maxwell started to reply, but the Beachcomber forestalled him. 'I assure you, Miss Zwerling,' he said slowly, 'that it would be a waste of your time and mine.'

Alice blushed again, this time not so prettily. 'Just what do you mean?' she demanded.

Dai looked at her gravely. 'I'm not quite such a wild man as I seem,' he said. 'I always wear trousers in mixed company.' He repeated, with emphasis, '*Always.*'

Alice's lips grew hard and thin, and the skin whitened around them. Her eyes glittered. She started to say something to the Beachcomber, but the words stuck in her throat. She turned to Maxwell. 'I think we'd better go.'

'We just got here,' Maxwell said mildly. 'Stick around.'

She stood up. 'Are you coming?'

'Nope,' said Maxwell.

Without another word she turned, walked stiffly to her scooter, got in and soared away. They watched the tiny shining speck dwindle and disappear over the horizon.

Maxwell grinned, a little sickly, and looked at the Beachcomber. 'She had that coming,' he said. 'Not that she's out anything – she's got her return ticket.' He put a hand behind him to hoist himself to his feet. 'I'll be going now, Dai. Nice to have—'

'No, stay a while, Vern,' said the giant. 'I don't often see people.' He looked moodily off across the water. 'I didn't spoil anything special for you, I hope?'

'Nothing special,' Maxwell said. 'Only my current light o' love.' The giant turned and stared at him, half frowning.

'What the hell!' said Maxwell disgustedly. 'There are plenty of other pebbles on the beach.'

'Don't say that!' The Beachcomber's face contorted in a blaze of fury. He made a chopping motion with his forearm. Violent as it was, the motion came nowhere near Maxwell. Something else, something that felt like the pure essence of wrath, struck him and bowled him over, knocking the breath from him.

He sat up, a yard away from the giant, eyes popping foolishly. 'Whuhh—' he said.

There was pain and contrition in the Beachcomber's eyes. 'I'm sorry,' he said. He helped Maxwell to sit up. 'I don't often forget myself that way. Will you forgive me?'

Maxwell's chest was still numb; it was hard to breathe. 'Don't know,' he said with difficulty. 'What did you do it for?'

Sunlight gleamed dazzlingly on the Beachcomber's bare head. His eyes were in deep shadow, and shadows sketched the bold outline of his nose, marked the firm, bitter lines of his mouth. He said, 'I've offended you.' He paused. 'I'll explain, Vernon, but there's one condition – don't tell anybody else, ever.'

He put his big hand on Maxwell's wrist and Maxwell felt the power that flowed from him. 'All right?'

'All right,' said Maxwell. A curious complex of emotions boiled inside him – anger and petulance, curiosity, and something else, deeper down: a vague, objectless fear. 'Go ahead.'

The Beachcomber talked. After a few minutes he seemed almost to forget

Maxwell; he stared out across the silver sea, and Maxwell, half hypnotised by the deep, resonant voice, watched his hawklike profile in silence.

Dimly, he saw the universe the Beachcomber spoke of: a universe of men set free. Over that inconceivable gap of time that stretched between Maxwell's time and theirs, they had purged themselves of all their frailties. Maxwell saw them striding among the stars, as much at home in the pitiless void as on the verdant planets they loved. He saw them tall and faultless and strong, handsome men and beautiful women, all with the power that glowed in the Beachcomber, but without a hint of his sadness. If they were angels, he was Lucifer.

He tried to imagine what the daily life of those people must be like, and couldn't; it was three million years beyond his comprehension. But when he looked at the Beachcomber's face, he knew that the last men were human beings like himself, capable of love, hate, joy and despair.

'We had mating customs that would seem peculiar to you,' said the Beachcomber after a while. 'Like elephants – because we were so long-lived, you know. We – married – late, and it was for life. My marriage was about to take place when we found the enemy.'

'The enemy?' said Maxwell. 'But – didn't you say you were the only dominant life form in the whole universe?'

'That's right.' The Beachcomber outlined an egg-shaped figure with a motion of his cupped hands, caressingly. 'The universe; all of it. Everything that existed in this space. It was all ours. But the enemy didn't come from this universe.'

'Another dimension?' Maxwell asked.

The Beachcomber looked puzzled. 'Another—' he said, and stopped. 'I thought I could say it better than that in English, but I can't. Dimension isn't right – call it another time-line; that's a little closer.'

'Another universe like ours, co-existent with this one, anyhow,' said Maxwell.

'No – not the same as ours, at all. Different laws, different—' He stopped again.

'Well, can you describe the enemy?'

'Ugly,' said the Beachcomber promptly. 'We'd been searching other – dimensions, if you want to use that word – for thousands of years, and this was the first intelligent race we found. We hated them on sight.' He paused. 'If I drew you a picture, it would look like a little spiny cylinder. But a picture wouldn't convey it. I can't explain.' His mouth contracted with distaste.

'Go on,' said Maxwell. 'What happened? They invaded you?'

'No. We tried to destroy them. We broke up the crystal spiderwebs they built between their worlds; we smashed their suns. But more than a quarter of them survived our first attack, and then we knew we were beaten. They were as powerful as we were, more so in some ways—'

307

'Wait, I don't get it,' said Maxwell unbelievingly. 'You – attacked them – without provocation? Wiped out three-quarters of them, simply because—'

'There was no possible peace between us and them,' said the Beachcomber. 'And it was only a matter of time before they discovered us; it was simply a chance that we made the contact first.'

What would an unspoiled South Sea Islander have made of the first atomic war? Maxwell wondered. Morals of one society didn't apply to another, he knew. Still – was it possible that the Beachcomber's people, Maxwell's own descendants, still had a taint of the old Adam? And was it accident that they were the only dominant life form in the entire universe, or had they eliminated all other contenders?

Not for him to judge, he decided; but he didn't like it. He said, 'Then what? They counterattacked?'

'Yes. We had time to prepare, and we knew what they were going to do. The trouble was, there simply was no defense against it.' He noticed Maxwell's wry smile. 'Not like the planet busters; there is a defense against those, you just haven't found it yet. But there actually was no defense whatever against their weapon. They were going to destroy our universe, down to the last quantum – wipe it right out of the series, make a blank where it had been.'

'And?' said Maxwell. He was beginning to understand why the Beachcomber had never told this story to anyone else; why the public at large must never know it. There was a feeling of doom in it that would color everything men did. It was possible, he supposed, to live with the knowledge that the end of it all was death, but fatalism was the mark of a dying culture.

'And there was just one thing we could do,' said the Beachcomber. 'Not a defense, but a trick. At the instant before their weapon was due to take effect, we planned to bring our universe back three million years along its own time-line. It would vanish, just as if it had been destroyed. Then, if it worked, we'd be able to return, but on a different time-line – because, obviously, on our own line nothing like this doubling back had already happened. Changing the past changes the future; you know the theory.'

'Yeah. So – you were too late, is that it? You got away, but all the rest were destroyed.'

'The timing was perfect,' said the Beachcomber. 'All the calculations were perfect. There's a natural limit to the distance in time any mass can travel, and we managed to meet it exactly. Three million years. I wish we hadn't. If we hadn't, I could go back again—' He stopped, and his jaw hardened.

'There isn't much more to tell,' he said. 'I happened to be chosen to execute the plan. It was a great honor, but not an easy one to accept. Remember, I was about to be married. If anything went wrong it meant that we'd be separated forever ... We couldn't even die together. But I accepted. I had one day with her – one day; and then I set up the fields and waited for the attack. Just one microsecond before it would have reached us, I released the energy that was channeled through me – and the next instant, I was falling into the ocean out there.'

He turned a tormented face to Maxwell. 'It was the worst possible luck!' he said. 'You can see for yourself, there was less chance of my landing anywhere near a planet than of – finding one given pebble on all the beaches of this planet.'

Maxwell felt as if he had missed the point of a joke. 'I still don't understand,' he said. 'You say *you* landed – but what about the universe? Where did it—'

The Beachcomber made an impatient gesture. 'You don't think we could bring it back into a space it already occupied, do you? It was in stasis, all but a fraction out of this time-line. Just a miniature left, so that it could be controlled. A model of the universe, so big.' He spread his thumb and forefinger an inch apart. 'Just a pebble.'

Maxwell's jaw dropped open. He stared at the giant. 'You don't mean – you—'

'Oh, yes,' said the Beachcomber. 'I landed about twenty miles out from shore – five years ago.' He stared out across the sea, while his fingers groped nervously among the pebbles at his feet.

'And when I hit the water,' he said, 'I dropped it.'

OFF CENTRE

CONTENTS

Acknowledgments

WHAT ROUGH BEAST

Mr Frank said to me, 'Hey, you. Get that corner cleaned up.' He was a big man with red face, mouth always open little bit, wet lips always pulling back suddenly over little yellow teeth. This I remember, late at night, just after rush from theaters and before bars close. Place was empty, all sick light on the tiles and brown tabletops. Outside, dark and wet. People going by with coat collars turned up and faces gray like rain.

On corner table was some dishes, some food spilled. I cleaned up, put dishes in kitchen sink on top of big stack, then came back to Mr Frank. He was cutting tomato for sandwiches, using his knife too quick and hard. Tip of his big pink thumb was white from holding knife.

I said to him, 'Mr Frank, I work here three weeks and you call me "Hey, you." My name is Kronski. If it is too hard to remember, say Mike. But not "Hey, you."'

He looked down on me, with lips twitching away from yellow teeth. Sides of his nose turned yellow-white, like I saw before when he was mad. And his knife went cut. He sucked air between teeth, and grabbed his hand. I saw the blood coming out dark as ink where he sliced the side of his thumb. Blood was dripping on board and pieces of tomato. It was deep cut, bleeding hard. He said through teeth, 'Now look what you made me do. Christ!'

From other end of counter, Mr Harry called out, 'What's the matter?' He started toward us – a thin man, bald, with big eyes blinking all time like afraid.

Was my fault. I went quickly to Mr Frank, but he pushed me away with his elbow. 'Get off of me, you creep!'

Now Mr Harry looked at Mr Frank's thumb and he whistled, then turned and went to the medicine box on wall Mr Frank was holding his wrist and cursing. From the cashier's desk at front of cafeteria, Mr Wilson the night manager was coming; I heard his footsteps click on the tiles.

Mr Harry was trying to put a bandage on, but it would not stick. Mr Frank pushed him out of the way, shouting, 'God damn it!' and pulled the medicine box off wall. Always bleeding.

I got quickly a fork and handkerchief, not clean, but best I could do. I tied a knot in the handkerchief, and tried to put it around Mr Frank's wrist, but he pushed me away again.

'Give me that,' says Mr Harry, and he took from me the fork and handkerchief. Now Mr Frank was leaning back against coffee machine looking white, and Mr Harry slipped the handkerchief over his wrist. In coffee machine I saw myself, like shadow standing – no face, just blackness – and I looked other way.

Always was blood, over counter, duckboards, steam tables, everything. Mr Harry tried to tighten the fork, but he dropped it and I picked up. He took it saying, 'Get out of the way, will you?' and started to turn the handkerchief.

'Better call a hospital,' says Mr Wilson's voice behind me. Then, 'Look out!'

Mr Frank had his eyes turned up and mouth open. His knees started to bend and then he was falling, and Mr Harry tried to catch, but too late, and he also went down.

Mr Wilson was going around end of counter, so I went the other way to telephone.

Was in my pocket, no dimes. I thought to go back and ask, but it would take minute. I thought maybe Mr Frank would the because I was not quick. So I put fingers in the metal hole where coin is supposed to come back, and was no coin there; but I felt deeper, down where turning place was, and I found it and I turned. Then, was a dime lying in coin hole. So I took it and put in top of telephone. I called ambulance for Mr Frank.

Then I went back to where he was lying, and they were by his side squatting, and Mr Wilson looked up and said, 'Did you call that hospital?' I say yes, but without stopping he said, 'Well, get out of my way then. Harry, you take the feet and we'll straighten him out a little.'

I could see Mr Frank's red shirt front, and hand wrapped now in gauze, also red, with tourniquet around his wrist He was lying without moving. To lose blood is for some not easy.

I went to stand at end of the counter, out of way. I was feeling very bad for Mr Frank. I saw he was mad, and I knew he was cutting with knife, as it was my fault.

After long while came a policeman, and he looked on Mr Frank, and I told how it happened. Mr Harry and Mr Wilson also told, but they did not see from beginning. Then came ambulance, and I ask Mr Wilson if I can go with Mr Frank to hospital. So he said, 'Go on, I don't care. We won't need you here after tonight anyhow, Kronski.' He looked on me from bright glasses. He was gray haired man, very neat, who always spoke cheerful but thought suspicious. I liked Mr Harry, and even Mr Frank, but him I could never like.

So I was fired. Not new feeling for me. But I thought how in a year, two years, or even sooner, those men would forget I was ever alive.

I was working in place three nights, night shift, cleaning up tables and stacking dishes in sink for dishwasher. It is not enough to make a place different because you are there. But if you make no difference, you are not living.

At the hospital, they wheeled Mr Frank up indoors and took him in elevator. Hospital woman asked me questions and wrote down on a big paper, then policeman came again, and was more questions.

'Your name is Michael Kronski, right? Been in this country long?'

'Since twenty years.' But I told a lie, was only one month. Policeman said, 'You didn't learn English very good, did you?'

'For some is not easy.'

'You a citizen?'

'Sure.'

'When naturalized?'

I said, 'Nineteen forty-five.' But was a lie.

He asked more questions, was I in army, how long belong to union, where I worked before, and always I would lie. Then he closed book.

'All right, you stick around till he comes to. Then if he says there was no assault you can go on home.'

In hospital was quiet like grave. I sat on hard bench. Sometimes doors opened, doctors shoes squeaked on floor. Then telephone went *brr* very quiet, hospital woman picked up and talked so I could not hear. She was blonde, I think from bottle, with hard lines in cheeks.

She put down telephone, talked to policeman for minute, then he came over to me. 'Okay, they fixed him up. He says he did it himself. You a friend of his?'

'We work together. *Did* work. Is something I can do?'

'They're going to let him go, they need the bed. But somebody ought to go home with him. I got to get back on patrol.'

'I will take him to his home, yes.'

'Okay.' He sat down on bench, looked on me. 'Say, what kind of an accent is that, anyhow? You chesky?'

'No.' I would say yes, but this man had the face of a Slav. I was afraid he should be Polish. Instead, I told different lie. 'Russian. From Omsk.'

'No,' he said slow, looking on me hard, and then spoke some words in Russian. I did not understand, it was too different from Russiche, so I said nothing.

'*Nyet?*' asked policeman, looking on me with clear gray eyes. He was young man, big bones in cheeks and jaw, and lines of smiling around mouth.

Just then came down the elevator with Mr Frank and nurse. He had a big white bandage on hand. He looked on me and turned away.

Policeman was writing in his book. He looked on me again. He said something more in Russian. I did not know the words, but one of them was like word for 'pig' in Russiche. But I said nothing, looked nothing.

Policeman scratched his head. 'You say you're from Russia, but you don't get the language. How come?'

I said, 'Please, when we leave Russia, I was young boy. In house was speaking only Yiddish.'

'Yeah? *It zent ah Yidishe' yingl?*'

'*Vi den?*'

Now was better, but still he did not look happy. 'And you only spoke Yiddish in the home?'

'Sometimes French. My mother spoke French, also my aunt.'

'Well – that might account for it, I guess.' He closed book and put away. 'Look, you got your naturalization papers on you?'

'No, is home in box.'

'Well, hell, you ought to carry them on you. Times like these. You remember what I said. All right, take it easy now.'

I looked up, and was no Mr Frank. I went quickly to desk. 'Where did he go?'

Woman said very cold, 'I don't know what you mean.' Each word separate, like to child.

'Mr Frank, was just here.'

She said, 'Down the hall, the payment office.' And pointed with yellow pencil over her shoulder.

I went, but in hall I stopped to look back. Policeman was leaning over desk to talk with woman, and I saw his book in pocket. I knew there would be more questions, maybe tomorrow, maybe next week. I took long breath, and closed eyes. I reached down where turning place of book was. I found it, and turned. I felt it happen.

Policeman never noticed; but next time he would look in book, would be no writing about me in it. Maybe would be empty pages, maybe something else written.

He would remember, but without writing is no good.

Mr Frank was by window in hall, pale in face, arguing with man in office. I came up, I heard him say, 'Twenty-three bucks, ridiculous.'

'It's all itemized, sir.' Man inside pointed to piece of paper in Mr Frank's hand.

'Anyway, I haven't got that much.'

I say quickly, 'I will pay.' I took out money, almost all I have in purse.

'I don't want your money,' said Mr Frank. 'Where would you get twenty-three bucks? Let the workmen's pay for it.'

'Please, for me is pleasure. Here, you take.' I pushed money at man behind window.

'Twenty-three seventeen.' I gave him the change.

'All right, give him the God damn money,' said Mr Frank, and turned away.

Man behind the window stamped bill and gave me. I quickly caught up Mr Frank and we went outdoors. Mr Frank could not walk straight. I took his elbow. First he pushed me away, but then he let me.

'That's it,' said Mr Frank. Was street of old thin houses with stone steps coming down like they stick out all their tongues. I paid the taxi driver, and helped Mr Frank up steps. 'What floor you live?'

'Fourth. I can make it.'

But I said, 'No, I help you,' and we went up stairs. Mr Frank was very weak, very tired, and now his lips did not pull back over teeth any more.

We went in kitchen and Mr Frank sat down by table under the sour yellow light. He leaned his head on hand. 'I'm all right. Just let me alone now, okay?'

'Mr Frank, you are tired. Eat something now, then sleep.'

He did not move. 'What sleep? In three hours I got to be on my day job.'

I looked on him. Now I understand why was cutting so hard with knife, why was so quick anger.

'How long you worked two jobs?' I say.

He leaned back in chair and put his hand with white bandage on the table. 'Year and a half.'

'Is no good. You should quit one job.'

'You don't know a thing about it.'

I wanted to ask something more, but then opened a door, and I saw someone in bathrobe standing. A voice said, 'Pop?' Was young girl's voice.

Mr Frank answered her, and I said quick, 'Well, I will go then. Goodbye.' And while the girl was coming into kitchen one way, I was going out other. I saw only face, pale, and brown hair, and I thought she was tall.

Downstairs I found mailbox with Mr Frank's name, and apartment number, and over door was number of house. I wrote on piece of paper, thinking when I go home I would make some money and send him by mail. From me he would not take, but if he finds in mailbox, is like from God, he must take it and give thanks.

On street, dawn was coming up, gray and cold. In gutter was papers blowing.

Since I was small boy in Novo Russie – what they call here Canada, but it is all different – always I could see where every thing in world, even every stone and stick, had shadow in past and in future. To me is hard thing to understand that other people only see what is *now*.

Sometimes I would say to my brother Misha when he would hurt himself, 'But didn't you *see* that it would happen?' And because I was stubborn, sometimes I would even say this when I saw that he would hit me because I said it.

But then I learned also to reach, not with hands but with mind. And in darkness where something could be or not be, I learned to turn it so that it is different. At first I did it without knowing, when I was very sick, and frightened that I would die. Without knowing it I reached, and turned, and suddenly I was not sick. Doctor was not believing, and my mother prayed a long time before icon, because she thought God had saved my life.

Then I learned I could do it. When I did badly in school, or if something else I did not like would happen, I could reach and turn, and change it. Little by little, I was changing pieces of world.

At first was not so bad, because I was young boy and I only did things for myself, my own pleasure.

But then I was growing up, and it was making me sad to see how other people were unhappy. So then I would begin to change more. My father had a bad knee, I made it well. Our cow broke her neck and died. And I made her alive again.

First I was careful, then not so careful. And at last they saw that I did it.

Then everyone said I was going to be a saint, they prayed over me, and big men talked to me so much that I believed it.

And I worked miracles.

Then one day I began to see that what I do is bad. I made so many patches in world that it was not world any more, but mistake. If you would try to make chair better by many patches, putting a piece oak wood here, and piece cherry wood there, until all was patches, you would make a worse chair than before.

So I saw every day that I was only making more patches, but I would not let myself know that it was bad. And at last I could not bear it, and I reached back far, I changed not little bit but whole country. I reached back before I was born, and I turned, and I changed it.

And when I looked up, all world around me was different houses, fields, people.

My father's house was not there. My mother, my brothers, my sisters, they were all gone; and I could not bring them back.

Then for first time, I knew what I was.

Next day after Mr Frank's accident, I found a new room. It was time for me to move anyway; in old room was becoming everything black so I could not see it. My new room was on second floor, not bad – maple furniture, oilcloth on table, washbowl, like usual. I moved in, and then I remembered about Mr Frank, and I took a dollar bill, my last one, and reached back and turned where man could have given me five dollar bill by mistake. Always it is possible this should happen, even if only once in hundred times. So I turned where it did happen, and in my hand was five dollar bill. Then I turned again where instead of five it is ten; and then instead of ten, ten one dollar bills.

And so I went on turning until I had three hundred dollars in ten dollar bills. And in drug store I bought envelope and stamps, and wrote Mr Frank's address on envelope, 'Mr Frank Verney, Apartment 4B.' When I put bills inside envelope, they are already becoming dark so I cannot read the numbers. This money is no good for me, I will always make mistakes if I try to spend it; but for Mr Frank it would be all right.

Next day I was angry with myself, and I lay on bed doing nothing. I told myself it would be no good to get different job, which I knew; but I did not tell myself without job I would be like dead man, which I also knew.

Next day, I went on Greenwich Avenue walking. Sky was deep blue over the building roofs. The sun was shining warm, and all buildings looked surprised and sad, as if they would say, 'I am dirty, but is best I can do.'

Here, in this same place, I have seen droshkies. Also steam cars, quiet, with white puffing like man smoking a pipe very quick I have seen people all dressed in black, and people in many colors like parrots. I know how wide is the world God made. Is so big, so deep, that heart turn small to feel it. But I would say to God, 'Why did you not make a world smaller? More like man?'

I went home, and in hall the door of Mr Brennan was standing open, the one they called landlord, but he was only janitor, and Mr Brennan was in doorway looking. He was a man with frozen face, mouth tight like he taste lemon, and eyes always big. I said, 'Hello, Mr Brennan,' but he said nothing, only looked while I went up the stairs. Behind him I saw his wife, small brown-haired woman with too much rouge.

I went in the room, and inside was policeman.

My heart was hurting chest, and I was so weak that I must lean against door. Policeman was same one that was at hospital before. He was sitting in my good chair, with hands on knees. The light was not good, but I saw his gray eyes burning.

'Shut that door.'

I did it.

'Come over here.'

I went.

'Okay, take everything out of your pockets and throw it on the bed.'

I took out wallet, money, handkerchief and so on. My hands were shaking.

'Sit down.'

I sat on wooden chair while he picked up the wallet and looked inside. Always was heart pounding, and hard to breathe.

Policeman said, 'I've been looking for you for three days. My wife thinks I'm nuts. I must have tried every rooming house in Chelsea before I hit this one.' He looked on me, with nostrils big.

'Nothing like this ever happened to me before,' he said. 'When I went to make my report out, it was all gone. Pretty soon I began to wonder if I dreamed the whole thing.'

He looked at cards from my wallet, then opened his book hard on knee, and wrote. Then he threw the wallet back on bed, and said, 'All right, now what's your real name?'

'I told you before, Michael Kronski.'

'You told me plenty. where are you from?'

'Odessa, Russia.'

'Didn't you tell me Omsk before?'

'No, Odessa.' He was right, I said Omsk, but I was too frightened to make up new lie.

'Who sent you here?'

'Nobody. Maybe God.'

He leaned and slapped me across mouth with his hand. 'Don't give me that sacrilegious crap.'

I jumped, and my chest got tight, harder to breathe. Inside was something like balloon wanting to burst.

I said, 'Please, you make mistake.'

'How did you do that trick to me?'

'If you would let me explain—'

'Well?' He waited, then slapped my face again. My body was trying to go through back of chair.

'Let's have it. By God, I'll get it out of you. Where are you from? What are you here for?' He slapped me again.

I said, 'Don't,' but already was inside me like a bursting, I felt big weight roll over inside, then nothing.

Yellow light was shining on empty chair.

Was no policeman. No one in room but me.

I was weak all over like a baby. With the hitting I could not think, could not stop it. Now I have reached back, maybe thirty years, I have made policeman not born.

Once more, I have killed a man.

I was crying. I thought, if only he would not have hit me in face. But it was me that made him so frightened that he must hit. It was me, my fault, always my fault.

To reach back again for same turning place is foolish, because I know I cannot do it, but I tried. Was like reaching where is nothing, like empty shelf in old dusty closet.

I sat in chair, looking at walls. Then I could not bear it. I went down stairs, past Mr Brennan and wife still in doorway watching. My knees were weak. I went like a drunk man.

I knew they would go up to my room and find no policeman, and would think I do not know what, but I had no time to worry. I went out in the street, looking for something.

My jaw was shaking, like cold, teeth going click. My hands, arms were shivering, and knees weak. But I must hurry. I crossed big avenue, running; then I was in quiet street with many old stone houses. In the street was playing two little girls with a ball.

While I stood looking, around corner came a car, too fast, tipping on wheels. I heard tires shout, and car was coming so quick that I could do nothing but stand and watch.

In street, little girls began to run. One had dark pigtails tied with pieces white ribbon, and her dress was blue and white. The other had blonde curly hair, and she was wearing pink dress. I saw their legs flashing, and I saw the ball rolling very slowly across street.

Then the car hit sideways into another car parked by side-walk, and it made a sound like hammer hitting tin cans. The car bounced away, still coming, and I saw driver, young man with blonde hair, bouncing in seat. Car was red, with no top. He was turning the wheel as hard as he could, but the car went by little girl with pigtails and just touched her going by, and she was down in street, not moving.

Then car hit fire plug on other side of street, and stopped. All up and down street was sound of hit metal. In the car, young man was leaning over wheel. Then I saw him straighten up, I look around. In doorways and windows now was people.

Now I was beginning to run. Now came a woman out of basement, and she was screaming, 'Jeannie!' But now the red car backed up away from fire plug, and the young man was twisting wheel quick, and now was grinding sound, and then red car jumped down street again, past me so close I felt the wind, and saw young man's red eyes. Then he was gone around the corner.

In middle of street was people gathering. Woman still screaming at top of voice, more people running from door-ways. I did not see the girl any more.

I could not run. I was sick inside. I bent over with hands on belly; inside my head was still shouting the tires, and red car still coming sidewise down street, to hit car, bang, hit girl, hit fire plug, bang.

Inside was reaching, turning. I felt the whole street, sky, turning all together. Then I was lying on cold pavement with ringing sound in my head.

When I looked up, I saw face hanging in the sky, men and women all looking down on me. Closer was two little girls. One blonde, pink dress, one dark pigtails, blue and white dress.

Woman's voice said, 'Jeannie, go on now. Get in the house.' Girl with dark pigtails turned slowly and went away, looking back over her shoulder to me. It was the same girl that I saw lying in street; but now she was not hurt, not dirty, not even frightened, only curious.

Then I began to understand. Without knowing it I had reached and turned where car would not hit girl, but would hit me instead. And now there was blood on pavement – but it was mine.

I closed my eyes, then opened them again. To lie on pavement was good, was like growing to earth. Overhead was sky very big, and here was peace. All day long would be people walking on this street, but how many would lie down?

If I was hurt, I did not feel it, only numb place on side of head. I pushed myself up on one elbow and with other hand tried to feel my head if it was broken. Then was hands helping me to sit up, even though I did not know I wanted to do it. I heard someone say 'hospital.'

I said, 'No. No hospital.' On side of head was only a cut, not big. To show them I was all right, I stood up. But could not stand straight, and with many hands they helped me.

'Where do you want to go? Where do you live?'

For minute, I could not remember. So often I move, I forget easily the old addresses and sometimes the new ones too. Always I tell myself to write down new address, and I never do it, but I felt in my pockets anyway. I found little piece of paper, squeezed together.

My fingers would not hold it, and so a man took it away from me, and opened it up, and read an address. It was man with new white cap on, like for golfing. He had face brown like coffee, and gold tooth. What he read did not sound right, but I saw paper, and it was my writing.

'Mister, don't you want to come inside and have a cup of coffee first?'

I said, 'No, please – just want to go home.'

Young man with many pimples said, 'It's just up the block.'

So they took me one on each side, with my arms around their necks, and we started. I thought we were going wrong way, but maybe it was short cut. Then we start to go up high stone stairway into building, and I stop and say, 'No. Wrong house.'

Man looked at paper again and said, 'Two twelve east? This is it. Apartment 4B. See, it says right here.' He showed me the paper, but I could not read what it said, only that the handwriting was mine.

Also we did not walk long enough to get back to my house; but I knew that I had seen this house before. And I could not understand it; except that I think in back of my mind, I did understand.

Man with white cap said, 'Well, it must be somebody that knows him, anyway. Let's take him up.' So we went up the stairs.

Then we knocked on a door, and I saw face of young woman, surprised, looking through crack. Then they were talking, and after minute door opened all the way, and they helped me in through kitchen, and narrow hall, then brown living room and they put me in a chair. Now my head was hurting. But I saw young woman, brown hair, tall, in blue dress. Then they were lifting me, putting me down on soft bed. Then I remember smell of perfume, and soft hands lifting head, giving me pills to take and glass of water. Then perhaps I sleep, because when I looked up, was no one in room.

Outside window by bed was iron fire escape, and then deep courtyard, gray stone, with clotheslines across and white clothes hanging. Clotheslines curved down, beautiful. Light came from somewhere, not bright, and clothes swung a little bit from wind. Was quiet, peaceful. Was best time of day in city, when people are working, not so crowded in buildings. Light was quiet and gray; bed where I was lying smelled good from laundry.

While I was looking, I heard small noise from next room, and turned my head. Young woman came in, tall, with hands together. She had brown hair soft and shiny, not curled straw like so many; face very clean and young, but also very big. She had a wide mouth, and I wanted to see her smile, because if teeth were good, she would be beautiful.

She said, 'Mr Kronski? Is that right?'

I nodded yes, still looking at her. Now I saw little bit in her past, not clear, but what I saw I did not like.

'I thought you must be.' She smiled a little, just enough to show teeth white. 'I wasn't sure, but you had our address in your pocket.'

'Yes.' Now I knew: she was Mr Frank's daughter.

Then I must have made a face, because she said, 'Are you all right? Does your head hurt?'

I said no, head was all right. With my fingers now I could feel where she had put a gauze bandage around my head, but even without feeling I could tell that underneath was nothing wrong: no cut, nothing. In sleep I had made myself well. Always, all my life it was so. On my whole body is no mark, no scar, not even pimple.

Now I was trying not to look on her, because I could see also a little bit the future, and I was afraid. But she sat down and said, 'Mr Kronski, if you're sure you're feeling all right—'

I said rough, 'You want to know if I sent money to your father.'

She said, 'Well – the writing on the envelope looked the same. Did you?'

'Yes. I will tell you. I sent it.'

'That was pretty nice of you. You know?'

'No, foolish. Now you are going to tell me you need more money, much more than I sent.'

Her eyes opened big. 'How did you know that?'

'Never mind, I know.'

She was pale, but now pink. She got up and said, 'You seem to think people are all alike.'

'No, every one different, but all foolish like me. I ran away from you so hard, I got myself knocked down on your street, with your address in pocket.'

She looked on me and said, 'I don't think I get that. What do you mean, about running away from me?'

I said, 'I did not want to help you. But now is no more use running.' Was hard to talk, because throat was swollen up. I held out my hand and said, 'Please. Let me see your shoulder.'

She went stiff all over, and one hand jumped to the shoulder of her blue dress. She looked on me with big eyes, bright and mad. 'Did my father—?'

'No,' I said, shaking my head hard, 'he didn't tell me nothing, but I know. Don't you see that I know? Now let me see it.'

She was again pink, and trying not to weep from shame. She sat down, still holding her shoulder, and did not look on me.

I said, 'If you want I will help you. Do you understand? Now let me see.'

She did not understand, but she looked on me. Eyes pink and wet, face swollen, not pretty. Was hard to look on her so, but I did it. After a minute she took a hard breath and turned away from me, and began to unbutton her dress in back.

I had my hands in fists, and I looked on them. After minute I heard her turn and say, 'All right.'

I looked, and she had pulled away the blue dress from one shoulder. By her neck, was skin smooth and like cream. But on the shoulder and across the chest was skin hard and white, standing up in strings and lumps, like something that had melted and boiled, and then hardened.

She had her head down, and eyes shut, crying. I was crying also, and inside was a big hurt trying to get out. I touched her with my hand, and said, 'My dear.'

She jumped when hand touched her, but then sat still. I felt under my fingertips cold skin, tough like lizard. Inside me was big hurt jumping, I could not hold in very long. I rubbed her very easy, very slow with my fingers, looking and feeling where was inside the wrong skin. Was not easy to do. But if I did not do it this way, then I knew I would do it without wanting, all at once, and it would be worse.

To make well all at once is no good. Each cell must fit with next cell. With my fingertips I felt where down inside the bottom part of bad skin was, and I made it turn, and change to good skin, one little bit at a time.

She held still and let me do it. After a while she said, 'It was a fire, two years ago. Dad left a blowtorch lit, and I moved it, and there was a can of plastic stuff with the top off. And it went up—'

I said, 'Not to talk. Not necessary. Wait. Wait.' And always I rubbed softly the bad skin.

But she could not bear to have me rub without talking, and she said, 'We couldn't collect anything. It said right on the can, keep away from flame. It was our fault. I was in the hospital twice. They healed it, but it just grew back the same way. It's what they call keloid tissue.'

I said, 'Yes, yes, dear one, I know.'

Now was one layer on the bottom, soft skin instead of hard; and she moved a little in the chair, and said in a small voice, 'It feels better.'

Under my fingertips the skin was still hard, but now more soft than before. When I pushed it, was not like lizard any more, but like glove.

I worked, and she forgot to be ashamed until it came a noise of door opening at front of apartment. She sat up straight, looking around and then on me. Her face got pink again, she grabbed my wrist. 'What are you doing?' Her voice was thin and not real.

In a minute I knew she would jump up and pull her dress together, and then she would run out of room, so whatever happened, it would not be her fault.

But I could not let her do it I was also ashamed, and my ears like on fire, but to stop now was impossible. I said loud, 'No, sit down.' I held her in the chair, and kept my fingers on her skin. I did not look up, but I heard a man's feet come into room.

I heard Mr Frank say, 'Hey, you. What do you think you're up to?'

And the girl was trying to get up again, but I held her still, and I said, 'Look. Look.' With tears running down my cheeks.

Under my fingers was a little piece of good, soft skin, smooth like cream. While I moved my fingers, slowly that place got bigger. She looked down, and she forgot to breathe.

Over her shoulder, I saw Mr Frank come nearer, with face mad and wondering. He said once more, 'Hey,' with lips pulling back hard over teeth, and then he looked on the shoulder of his daughter. He blinked his eyes like not believing, and then looked again. He put his hand on it, quick, hard, and then took away like burned.

Now was changing more fast the rest of skin. Was like rubbing from a window the frost. Still they were not moving, the daughter and Mr Frank, and then he went down on his knees beside the chair with arm around her and arm around me holding so hard that it hurt, and we were all three tight together, all three hot wet faces.

In living room was radio, so loud you could not think, and people laughing. I was sitting by table in kitchen when Mr Frank came out with glass in his hand, and fell against table, and sat down hard. His face was red like from steam bath. He looked on me and said, 'Well, there you are. I thought you got lost in the john or something. Well, why don't you join the party, for Christ sake? Get in there and have a little fun.'

I said, 'I'm feeling tired. Would like to just sit quietly for while.'

He blinked and said, 'Sure. You do whatever you want. You're the greatest, Mike, you know that? You just sit there and take it easy, old buddy.' He looked in his drink, and shook ice cubes, and then drank what was in bottom and put it down. 'You know,' he said, 'two years I had that hanging over me. Two years, would you believe it?' He shook his head. 'I use to belong to a bowling club. Had to give that up. Use to go out bowling every Tuesday night. Sold all my fishing stuff, too – never got much for it. Had to take the telephone out. You know we were living on franks and beans? Over two hundred bucks a week coming in, and living on franks and beans. Every cent went to the doctors. For two years. I don't take no credit, what the hell, I done the damage. And I paid for it too.' He reached for bottle on cabinet, and poured more whisky in glass. He drank some and put it down.

'You know she was engaged to a fellow. I never liked him. His name was Ernest. Ernest Nixon, he worked for a bank. But, she thought she loved him and all that. Then come her accident, and we never saw him again. I broke that up, all right. And don't you think she ever let me forget it.' He held up glass. 'You want some of this?'

I said, 'No, thank you. It makes me sick in stomach.'

'Too bad.' He drank again. 'Funny you can't fix a thing like that. I mean, after what you done for Anne.'

I said, 'I could fix it, but to me is not worth the trouble.'

'Oh, yeah?' He nodded without interest, and then looked up. 'Mean you can fix other stuff? Like if anybody got sick?'

'Some things I can fix. But not germ disease, because is too many little germs. But sometimes cancers I can fix, and things where body is not working right.'

He put down his glass. 'Cancer? You kidding? Yeah, you're kidding, you can't fix no cancer.' He drank again.

'No, not kidding.'

'Cut it out, will you? If you could do that, you'd be a millionaire, not a bus boy.'

Just then door from outside opened and two girls came in giggling, Anne and her girl friend Loraine. Anne said, 'Poppa, look?' They were both wearing pretty dresses, and Anne held open little jacket to show how low was neck of dress. Where bad skin was on her chest, was now only brown place you could hardly see – tanned from sun, because if not for her accident, she would have been at beach many times in bathing suit. And even this she had powdered now so it did not show. 'A strapless!' she said. 'Oh, you just don't know what it *means!*' In her eyes was tears. She kissed him, and then leaned over and kissed me also on forehead. Her lips were warm and greasy with lipstick, which I did not like. Then she and other one were rustling down hall toward where radio was going.

Mr Frank stood up, holding onto chair. He said, 'Excuse me a minute. Be right back.' He went down the hall.

I sat and listened to radio too loud with music I did not understand. After long time, Mr Frank came back, bumping into one side of hall and then other, with behind him Mr Pete, the round bald one who always smiled. Mr Frank sat down in chair so hard I thought he would break it, and Mr Pete tried to help him but he said, 'I'm all right.'

Mr Pete sat down on other side and put his hand on my shoulder. 'Well, how you doing, boy?'

'All right.'

'Frank here was just telling me, you have some kind of a secret where you cure cancer, is that right?' He smiled on me, with teeth gray and wet.

'I can cure it,' I said. I moved away little bit.

But he kept his hand on my shoulder. 'Well, like how do you do it? I mean, do you say some words, or what?'

'Is hard to explain.'

He nodded, smiling, and said to Mr Frank, 'See, Frank, a four-flusher. I seen them before. When he says it's hard to explain, that means he can't do it.'

He turned to me and said, 'Is that right?' On his breath was liquor. His head was bald and shiny brown under light.

I said, 'I can do it.'

'Well, you don't sound like you can do it. Look, can you do it or not?' He moved little closer to me. 'I mean, like if you can do it, do it, or if you can't do it, shut up.' Always smiling.

Mr Frank sat up straight and said, 'What have you, got a cancer? What's he going to cure, for Christ sake? Don't be such a jerk, will you, for Christ sake?'

Mr Pete said, 'Look. I got a wart, see?' He held up hand. There was a brown wrinkled wart on thumb. 'Now if he can cure a cancer, it stands to reason he can cure a wart, don't it?'

'Oh, don't be such a jerk, Pete.' Mr Frank was frowning and rolling himself from side to side in chair. 'Come on now, I don't like it.' He leaned forward suddenly and took hold of my arm. 'You and me are buddies, right, Mike?'

'Sure, Mr Frank.'

'You bet. So don't be such a jerk, Pete, I don't like it.' He sat back and closed his eyes.

Mr Pete was still holding up hand with wart. He was smiling, but not so wide. He said, 'Okay, how about it?'

I said, 'For wart is not worth it, and already I had a hard day, I am tired—'

'No, now,' said Mr Pete, holding wart in my face, 'you said you could do it, and I want to see you do it. Come on, boy, let's see you cure that wart. Go ahead, make her disappear. Go ahead.'

I looked on his face, and he was very hating man, very quiet and smiling, but always looking for reason to hurt someone. And I saw in his past a shadow that made me feel bad in stomach.

Now my heart was again jumping hard in chest, and I was afraid it would be again like with policeman. So I reached, and turned where there was no wart. And it was gone.

Mr Pete jumped like hit, and grabbed his hand. Mr Frank had eyes open and watching, and I saw him rub his own thumb, where was small bandage. But he was not thinking about it, he was looking on Mr Pete's hand. Then they both looked on me.

Mr Pete swallowed and said, 'He did it, by God.'

'Gone?'

'Look here. You can't even see where it was.'

Mr Pete looked on me again with small bright eyes, and smile almost gone. 'I don't know about this. I got to think.'

He rubbed his thumb, looked on it and then rubbed again. I smelled him sour and I knew he was afraid. He said, 'There's possibilities in it, Frank.'

'Aw, he's kidding you. Why ain't he a millionaire, then? He's nothing but a lousy bus boy. It's all a load of crap.'

I said, 'I could do it, but I would not. Sometimes I can help, like with Anne. But if I would cure everybody who is sick, first it would be like whirlpool, everyone coming, fighting. I could make well forty, fifty people a day, that is nothing. It is like throwing one piece bread to hundred people who are starving. Believe me, I have seen it and I know. You cannot imagine what ugliness, how terrible is a world where all life, all happiness depends on one man.'

But I stopped, because I saw they were looking on me but not listening. When I stopped, Mr Pete got up and went around table to Mr Frank. He bent down to whisper in his ear.

Then I thought it would be better if I should go, and I got up and went to the door. But with a crash of chair on floor they came after me, one on each side, both with red faces and liquor breath, and held my arms.

'Come on!' said Mr Pete, and they made me walk across kitchen, down hall, and they opened bedroom door and pushed me in.

They were both breathing hard. Mr Pete stood in doorway and took knife out of pocket, and showed me the blade. 'Listen,' he said, 'one peep out of you, and this. Understand?'

I said nothing. They backed out of door and closed it, and I heard a click.

In room it was dark then, but I found string hanging from ceiling and turned on light. It was one lightbulb, dim and sad. One wooden chair was in room, one bureau, and one little folding bed with thin mattress and Indian blanket on it. In air was smell of spray to kill insects.

I turned out light again and sat down on bed in the dark. Then I was very tired, and I lay down. After little while I heard voices and footsteps in hall, and then in kitchen, and door slammed. Then I heard only Anne's voice sounding mad asking some questions, and Mr Frank and Mr Pete answering, and then after while radio was turned off and it was quiet.

I lay still and closed eyes, but could not rest. First my leg would jump, then neck, then hand. And always I would think of Mr Pete and Mr Frank sitting in kitchen, under sick yellow light, with their wet eyes looking on me.

Then sometimes I would remember shiny black streets empty at night, and walls of brick and soot, and the faces of the people gray as they went down stairs into subway.

After long time, when house was quiet, I got up and went to door. Underneath in crack I could see light, very thin. I tried door and it would open little way, then click on something and stop. It was not a lock, but a bolt outside, the kind that slides across and then down into a slot.

I reached, and turned to make the bolt not be there. Then I opened door little by a little, and looked out. Hall was dark, only a little bit light coming from underneath kitchen door, which was now closed. Other way, all was black in living room, but I heard someone breathing slow.

Kitchen door also was closed by bolt, and this bolt also I removed. Carefully I opened door and looked in.

Mr Pete was asleep in chair, leaning back against wall in corner. He was partly against wall, partly against front door, so it could not open without hitting his chair. His head was hanging, and he was breathing loud. Every so often he would start to lean too far off the chair, and then he would pull himself back with a jerk, and his breathing would be quiet Then, noisy again, and he would lean, and so on. He was frowning, and looked worried.

I went quietly across floor. The front door was closed with a big spring lock, also a bolt, and a chain. To open them would be easy, but then if I would open door, it would knock down Mr Pete's chair and wake him up. So I reached, and turned to where whole door was not hung. And it flickered and disappeared. A cold air began to flow in through open doorway, and I stepped out into the hall.

When I was at the top of stairs, I heard a crash and a yell from inside apartment. I looked up as I started down stairs, and I saw Mr Pete in doorway, with eyes big. When he saw me he ducked back behind the doorway, and then I saw him coming out again, and suddenly was a flash of fire and a sound like house breaking apart. Then I was falling downstairs. In my shoulder, slowly, was a feeling like someone would have hit me with a stick.

I was lying with my head downstairs, feet up. The stairs were full of that noise that made in my ears a pain, and whole building was going slowly around. Then I saw over the railing Mr Pete's gray face looking down on me, and I saw his hand move, and inside me the fear came bursting up, and then suddenly was a black hole over my head. No Mr Pete, no hallway, all vanished.

I was feeling sick, and dizzy. Now when I moved I felt pain in my shoulder, and in my mind I said, 'He shot me. I am shot.' I put my hand on place, and there was blood.

For minutes I could not see, and I thought I would faint. Then upstairs I heard feet running, and dimly I saw Mr Frank standing on edge of hallway, where beginning of hole was, and trying not to fall over. He was in pajamas, top part open. When I saw him, the fear came up again, and then he was gone, like candle going out.

Downstairs I heard doors banging, voices. I was trying to feel inside shoulder and find bullet, but there was no bullet, only hole. Then I started to fix wound, but it was too hard, I could not think with all the voices calling, and feet running in hallways. Then I heard Anne: 'Pop! Pop!' And I saw her on edge of hallway upstairs, in blue bathrobe and pajamas. She was looking at hole in floor, holding on to railing with one hand, and with other brushing back her hair from face. I said, 'Go back,' and then she saw me but did not hear. She said, 'Mike!' and began to move sideways along railing, putting her feet in spaces between the bars.

She got safely to top of stairs and came down quickly. 'Mike, what *happened?* Gee, are you hurt? Let me—'

I said, 'Shot. Trying to fix it, but— Must get out.' I tried to get up, and she helped me.

'Mike, where's Pop? Oh, look out, you're bleeding!'

I got my feet down where should be, and stood up holding on to wall. Anne tried to help, but did not like to touch side where I was bleeding.

I said, 'Don't worry, doesn't matter,' and I started down stairs holding wall with one hand, and her arm with other. Still I was trying to fix bullet hole, little by little, but could not do much, only close up to make the blood stop.

Going down the next flight we met two men in bathrobes coming up. They began to ask questions, and one tried to help me and make Anne go back, but I pushed him away. Now my shoulder was hurting, but we went down, past more people in doorways, until finally we were in bottom hallway, and Anne helped me push open the big door to outside. And cool air was blowing in our faces.

I went down stone steps slow, holding on. I tried not to think, not feel, only lean against the cold stone and make well my hurt shoulder.

Behind me Anne's voice said, 'Mike, should I get a doctor?'

'No, wait, I can fix.' Looking up street to avenue I could see the red eyes of traffic lights, and it was so quiet that when the lights changed to green, I could hear the click all way from corner.

Still, inside me was the fear pushing to get out. I heard Anne coming down stairs behind me, and each footstep I heard like a touch on my skin. She came and looked on my face, and began to say something.

Then doors of houses opened bang, and again I was like shot: I saw a man standing in doorway with legs apart and mouth open – but only a flicker, and then doorway turned black and melted away. The man was gone. Inside house, was a rain of plaster falling into hallway like a cave: and a dirty cloud puffed out of hole where doors had been.

In my ears was pain, on my knees cold stone. Inside house, I heard a woman scream. Then the stairs shook like thunder with feet coming down; and I could not help it, the fear came up inside me again. And it was quiet inside house. Except for patter of dropping things.

Anne was calling in my ear, 'Mike, Mike, what is it?' Holding my arm till it hurt.

But I could not speak to her, because from few blocks away I heard a sound that made my skin cold. It was a siren of police car – coming nearer.

Then once more the bursting inside me, bigger than before; and the siren stopped like cut off with knife.

Then there was a rumble that shook street, and a cloud of dust crawled up over tops of buildings. Anne was shouting in my ear; I could not hear what she said.

I was seeing in my mind where buildings were cut in half, with people falling out.

I could not stop it. I put my hands over ears, but no good, I heard window opening, and my head jerked up; but all I saw was bricks flying from hole in building behind me. They winked out in middle of air, and never hit sidewalk. Then – one, two – the fear bulged again inside me, and there was nothing left of that building – not a brick, not a scream, only empty lot, color of ashes.

Anne said, in hoarse voice, 'Mike—'

But across the street was doors opening, and people standing … and then, nothing. Darkness. Empty lots, and dark backs of buildings on next street. The wind was blowing a piece white paper, like bird with broken wing. And we looked on it.

Then I heard in the air a sound like police car a million times bigger. It was air raid siren, howling, in pain, shaking the streets, up and down, up, down. I could not stand it, and there was inside me like explosion, and that sound also stopped.

Stillness came whispering down the street.

But it was no more a street, only flat gray land as far as I could look. Not a tree, not even weed, only rock. Where minute ago we were in bottom of the street, like bugs in a crack, now we could see to edge of the world, and over us was the whole sky.

Now, slowly, like one muscle unclenching after another, my fear went away.

I listened. Under stillness was no sound, not even cricket; only more stillness, deep and deep. Across the land came a cold strong wind, and it passed us and went on.

'What happened?' said Anne. Her voice was flat and dull.

I said, 'I killed them. Some I killed. Some cut in pieces. And the rest I made go away.'

She looked on me, and after minute whispered, long and slow, 'Why?'

'I was afraid.' I listened to that word, waiting for it to echo like hand slapped on a wall, but it only floated away into darkness.

She said, 'But what happened – to all the buildings? The—'

'I turned to where they were not built. Where was no city, and even no life. Now is a city on a world of gray rock, like this.'

'I don't understand.'

I said, 'The way I fix your shoulder. I turned each little bit to where your accident never happened. Many worlds, many Annes. It is to me like breathing. I could always do it, even when I did not want to do it.'

She did not seem to understand. She looked on me and said politely, 'How is your shoulder?'

I felt, and it was whole again. 'When I am asleep, or sometimes if I am very frightened, it is like inside me a small frightened child. Anything that is wrong with me, or anything it is afraid of, it will fix. To hurt other people – it does not know, it does not care.'

She shook her head, looking past me. 'It was all here, just a minute ago. Gee, I was sound asleep. Then I heard this big noise, and Pop got up and ran outside – and then I got up too, and went to see—' She laughed. 'I just can't believe it. I mean, it was all here.' She looked around, and said, 'Oh,' with her hand to mouth.

'What?'

'I just thought, Queens is gone too. That's where Phil lived.' I saw her eye shine. 'He's a boy where I work. He kept asking me for dates, and I liked him, but – Gee, I'll never know, will I? And Pop—'

She put face down into her hands and her body began to shake. Deep, hurting sounds came up from her belly. And it kept going on. I could not bear to listen, and I went close and said, 'Anne, don't cry. I will do anything, anything to help you.'

Still she wept, and between crying she said to me, 'Why couldn't you kill yourself instead!'

I said, 'Once I tried it. But inside would not let me. And I woke up, and I was alive.'

She was still weeping, and only to comfort her, I said, 'All must die sometime, Anne, but to be me is not easy.'

She raised her head and looked on me, blind with crying. I said, 'If I try to bring back a world where something has made me afraid, that frightened child will not let me. I tell you with shame, that it is stronger than me. And it never forgets. I could do for you only two things. Either I could take you over there' – I pointed – 'where is still other cities – Philadelphia, Boston—'

She said in thick voice, 'What's the other one?'

'I could turn where is another world, and another city – not New York, but it would be as much like New York as I could make.'

'Pop?' she asked.

'No. There will be no one that you knew, because I must turn before they were born. But you are young, pretty, you will make friends—'

She wiped her eyes with sleeve. 'Will they build New York up again?'

'In this world? They will build it, yes, but never in your life would it be the same. Also there will be hard times for a while, even if you would go to California. I tell you truth, so you will know. To lose such a city, is like to a man to lose his arm. There will be shock, and much unhappiness.'

'I lived here all my life,' she said. 'What would this other place be like?'

I said, 'I will reach back and turn where simple thing was different – maybe one man president of country instead of another man. From this will be all things a little bit different – there will be different people born, and even different buildings built. But it will look like New York to you, and you will soon feel at home in it That I promise.'

She found handkerchief in her pocket, and turned away. 'Don't look at me.'

Now I knew she would be better, so I went little bit away and sat looking across gray plain, where ash colored sky was turning slowly to a little bit green and pale gold.

'I'm sorry.'

I turned to her. She was sitting straight, with hands in lap. 'I'll take the other place you talked about. Can you do it right now?'

'Yes.' I reached back, feeling for place to turn. It was easy to find one, but not so easy to pick right one. After minute I said, 'Ready.'

I reached and turned. And like a light going on in dark room, so quick it hurts the eyes, around us was a street with high buildings of red brick: and down at corner, traffic lights were turning green, and a long car went by with swish of tires on pavement. Street lights were yellow and dusty, and sky was again black. Under the stillness was small sounds everywhere, and in air was smell of burned gasoline.

I heard Anne say, very small, 'Oh.'

It was almost like old street. Small different things wherever you look, but from corner of eye, almost the same.

I said, 'You will need some money,' and I stepped to curb. I reached, and turned one small part of gutter, like deck of cards, until I found place where money was dropped. I picked it up, it was a dollar bill, but in middle was a different face. Then I turned to where it was a five instead, and then a ten, and so on until there was five hundred dollars. And I gave it to her, but she was holding robe tight around her and looking if anyone should see her not *dressed*. 'Wait,' I said, 'I will fix it.'

Under stone stairway was cellar entrance with railing, and garbage cans. I climbed over railing, and turned until I found place where was a coat thrown away. It was lying beside garbage can, a fur coat, with fur rubbed off some places, but better than bathrobe. I climbed back, and gave it to her, and she put it on.

'Now what?' she said, trying to smile.

Up at corner, lights were red, and I saw a taxi, a yellow one with sign on top lit. I stood at curb and waved, and I saw driver's head turn, and then lights were yellow, then green, and the taxi came curving around. It rolled up to us and stopped. The driver looked at us out of his window without saying anything. He was young, with long, pale chin, and he was chewing gum. He saw me and he saw Anne in her bad fur coat, with bedroom slippers on her feet, but he did not look away with politeness, or stare with rudeness; he did not care.

I opened the door for her, and she got in. 'Take her to a good hotel,' I told driver, 'quiet, not too expensive.' I started to close door, but she held out her hand.

'Aren't you coming too?'

The driver was listening, but I said, 'Anne, this is not a world for me. If I would stay here, it would be same as last time. Better I should go now, and not take chances.'

She said, 'Go where?'

'Somewhere.'

'What's the use, if it always turns out the same?'

'It will not always be the same. Somewhere I know God has made a place, even for me.'

On her forehead was pain. She touched my hand and said, 'Mike, Mike—'

Then I closed door slowly. 'Goodbye. Please go on now, driver.'

She was rolling down her window as taxi made a metal sound, and gray smoke came out of tail pipe, and taxi began to roll away down empty street; and Anne's head came out of window looking back, getting smaller, and I saw her hand waving; then taxi turned corner and she was gone.

I did not think to lose her would be so hard.

But if I would have stayed with her now, first from loneliness and then from being grateful, she would have grown to need me. Other bad things there would be, but this worst of all.

At least I had not done that to her, to spoil her by making myself a little demon who would do miracles, whenever a pot would boil over or a finger-nail was broken.

Over roofs of buildings the sky was turning a bright, clear blue between streamers of purple-gray cloud. There was no use to wait any more. I was tired, but I could rest where I was going.

I took long breath, and reached back deep and far, farther than ever before – two thousand years or little bit less. I was thinking that maybe all my trouble was because I was trying to stay close to my own world, and always to be traveling around it even though I could never go back. If I must wander, why not go far?

I found place, where if one man was not born, all world would be different And I turned.

The buildings jumped like flames and disappeared. Then, under that same sky, there was another city.

Cold gray buildings climbing one behind another, all with peaked doors and windows, very big, and with domes of yellow stone or of powdery blue copper. Across the brightening sky was an airplane drifting – not cross-shaped, but round. The street was of cobblestones.

I was standing inside a little park with a railing of stone carved like loops of cloth. Behind me was a pedestal of stone, and two statues, one of hand-some young man in a hat with no brim, carrying a torch in his arms. And the other just the same, but with torch upside down. They looked down on me with blank stone eyes.

Is it you? They seemed to say.

And I, looking back, said, *Is it here?*

But we could not answer each other; and I left them standing there, and went into the city.

THE SECOND-CLASS CITIZEN

Though he was used to the tropical sun, a sliver of light reflected from one of the laboratory windows stabbed into Craven's head as he crossed the walkway, leading his little group of mainlanders. He felt uneasy and feverish, more than the previous night's drinking would account for. Perhaps he was coming down with something, God forbid – it would be a rotten time for it, with the rest of the staff over in Charlotte Amalie for the weekend.

'What time did you say that plane's coming from Miami?' asked the gray, paunchy man with the clipped mustache. Hurrying to catch up with Craven, and glancing at his wrist-watch, he stumbled and swore. 'I ought to be back in New York right now. I hate to be out of the country with the situation the way it is.'

'Two-fifteen,' said Craven shortly. 'You'll have plenty of time.'

'What do *you* think about the crisis, Dr Craven?' one of the women asked. She was plump and gray-haired. 'Aren't you worried to be out here all by yourself? My goodness, I would be.'

'Oh, I expect it'll blow over,' Craven said indifferently. 'They always do.'

'Well, that's right, they always *have*,' the paunchy man said, sounding relieved. He paused, squinting his eyes to peer out past the white concrete pens to the harbor. 'Saw something jump out there. There's another. Are those some of the animals?'

'Yes, those are the dolphins,' Craven said. Irritably he strode forward to open the laboratory door. 'This way, please.'

Inside, it was cooler than outdoors, but full of sunlight from the big windows overlooking the sea. On the wall was an alphabet chart, with brightly colored pictures of simple objects. The floor was a concrete slab, cut away across the far side of the room to form a channel open at both ends. The water in the channel rose and fell with a slow, vertiginous surge. Craven's head was beginning to ache.

'Here's where we do most of our work with the dolphins,' he said. 'Just a moment, I'll see if I can get one for you.' He stepped to a wall panel, pressed a switch, and spoke into the microphone. 'Pete, this is Charles. Come in, please.'

A quacking gobble of sound from the wall speaker answered him.

'Okay, come on in,' Craven said, and switched off the mike.

'What was that?' one of the matrons demanded. 'Was that one of the dolphins *talking?*'

Craven smiled. 'That's right – that was Pete, our star pupil. Look out the window. And stand back a little from the channel, please.'

There was a nervous shuffling of feet as some of the visitors moved away from the edge, others crowded closer to the windows. Down the concrete channel that led past the pens directly to the wall of the laboratory, something gray was moving with surprising speed. It was submerged, but kicked up an occasional burst of spray. The visitors began to murmur in alarm; some backed away from the window.

'Look out!' someone yelled. The gray shape burst into the room; the water in the channel lifted as if about to overflow, then fell back with a slapping sound. There was a shriek, then nervous laughter.

In the channel, balancing itself half out of the water, was a streamlined, water-bright shape. It spoke, in the same quacking gabble as before.

'Okay, Pete,' Craven said. 'Out you come.'

'Was it really *talking?*' someone asked behind him. 'Could you understand what it said?'

Craven, without bothering to reply, pressed a switch on the control panel. Out of a recess in the wall came an electric hoist supporting a curved, heavily braced metal platform. The platform lowered itself into the water; the dolphin swam into position over it. Craven pressed another switch; the platform rose, streaming water. The hoist moved forward again, then lowered its passenger onto a wheeled framework that stood beside the channel. There was a click. The supporting arms of the hoist, disengaged from the platform, rose out of the way.

On the platform, which now formed the bed of the wheeled cart, lay a bulky eight-foot mammal. One eye was cocked alertly at Craven. The mouth, open in what seemed a pleasant smile, was full of sharp conical teeth.

'Goodness!' said one of the women. 'I hope he doesn't bite!'

'Dolphins have never been known to attack a human being,' Craven said perfunctorily. He pressed a button on the control panel. 'Say hello to our visitors, Pete.'

The dolphin glanced alertly at the people standing behind Craven, then emitted one of its high-pitched bursts of sound. To Craven's accustomed ear the words were blurred but understandable. To the others, he knew, they were only noise.

He pressed another button on the panel. After a moment, the dolphin's recorded voice, slowed down and deeper in pitch, came out of the speaker.

'Hello, lat'ss and ge'men.'

There was a general murmur, some nervous laughter, one clear voice: 'What did he say?'

'His mouth didn't move when he talked,' someone commented suspiciously.

Craven grinned. 'He doesn't use it for talking – that's for fish. He talks through his blowhole – there, on the top of his head. Come on over, Pete, let's have a look at you.'

Obediently, the dolphin glided nearer on his cart, trailing a long plastic hose. Sprays of water had begun to spurt out of perforated tubes along either side of the cart, making the dolphin's skin gleam wetly. Out of this tiny personal rainstorm, the dolphin stared up at the visitors with friendly interest.

'He's shaped just like a jet plane!' one of the male visitors remarked. 'Look at the curve of his head and, uh, snout—'

Craven smiled at the man. 'Similar solutions for similar problems,' he said. 'Pete's streamlined, just like a jet. He's a bottle-nosed dolphin – *Tursiops truncatus* – the same specimens Lilly used in his original work. He weighs about four hundred pounds; his brain is a little bigger than a man's. Pete is more intelligent than a dog or a monkey. He can not only understand commands in English – he can talk back to us. That's why we feel this research is so important. What we're doing is teaching another species to enter the human community.'

There was a moment of impressed silence. *That will hold them.* Craven thought.

'What are all the gadgets for?' another man asked.

'He controls the cart motors with those bars under his flukes,' Craven said. 'The other levers on either side are for manipulation – he works those with his flippers. Pete's great lack is that he hasn't any hands or feet, you see – but we're trying to make up for that. Show them, Pete, okay?'

'Okay, Charless,' said the dolphin cheerfully. The cart wheeled, glided across the floor to the low bench on the far side, leaving a wet path behind it. Jointed arms extended from the front of the cart, groped for a pointer, picked it up in metal pincers.

'Show us the apple, Pete,' Craven said.

The pointer rose, wavered, came to rest with its tip on the bright picture of an apple on the wall chart.

'Now the boy,' Craven said. There were murmurs of admiration as the dolphin pointed to the boy, the dog, the boat 'Now spell cat, Pete,' said Craven. The pointer spelled out C-A-T.

'Good boy, Pete,' Craven said. 'Plenty of fish for you today.'

The dolphin opened his jaws wide, emitted a Bronx cheer, then a burst of crackling dolphin laughter. There was a nervous stir among the visitors.

'You said dolphins have never been known to attack a person,' said a gray-eyed girl. It was the first time she had spoken, but Craven had been aware of her; she was slender and pretty, held herself very erect.

'That's right,' he said, facing her. 'It isn't that they couldn't – you know they kill sharks – but they just never have.'

'Even when people have hurt them?' she asked. Her gray eyes were sober.

'That's correct,' Craven said.

'And it's true, isn't it, that many dolphins have been killed in the course of this research?'

Craven felt a little irritated. 'There were some fatalities, before we learned how to handle them,' he said shortly. He turned away. 'Now let's try something more difficult. Show them the chemistry experiment, Pete.'

As the dolphin turned toward the bench again, Craven commented, 'This is something Pete has just been learning. We're pretty proud of it.'

On the bench was a little stand with several stoppered bottles, a beaker and a row of test tubes. Controlling the jointed arms with his flippers, the dolphin reached out, picked up a bottle and pulled the stopper. One set of metal pincers held the bottle; the other picked up a test tube. Slowly Pete made the bottle pour into the test tube. It ran full and spilled over. The dolphin rocked back and forth nervously in his cart.

'Okay, Pete,' Craven said soothingly. 'Don't get nervous. It's all right – go ahead.'

The dolphin set the bottle down with a crash, poured the contents of the test tube into the beaker. The pincers reached for another bottle, slipped and tried again. They got the bottle on the second try, tilted it but missed the test tube. Over-correcting, the dolphin crashed bottle and test tube together, and the test tube broke. The bottle dropped, spilled.

The dolphin backed his cart away, swiveled toward Craven. 'Too hard, Charless,' he said plaintively. 'Too hard.'

Craven's fists clenched with disappointment. The creature had done it perfectly on the last three tries! 'Never mind, Pete,' he said. 'It's okay – you did fine. Go on out and play now.'

'All finiss?' Pete asked.

'Yes. So long.'

'So long.' The dolphin wheeled his cart around, glided over to the edge of the channel. The jointed arms retracted. The cart bed tilted slowly; the dolphin slid off it into the water, almost without a splash. There was a glimpse of his gray body darting underwater; then the channel was empty.

On the way down to the seaplane, Craven found himself walking beside the gray-eyed girl. 'Well, what did you make of it all?' he asked her.

'I thought it was *pathetic*,' she said. Her gray eyes were indignant. 'You talk about making them enter the human community. It's all wrong! He's a dolphin, not a man. He was trying so hard, but the best you could turn him into was something like a retarded, crippled child. I felt so *sorry*.'

Hours after the visitors were gone, Craven was still restless. He kept remembering what the girl had said; there was just enough truth in it to make it rankle. His headache had not improved; the sunlight was still oppressive. He prowled through his living quarters, glanced with distaste at the black headlines of the day-old Miami paper, finally turned on the television.

'... initials stand for "non-radioactive heat emitters,"' a chubby, gray-haired man was saying, enunciating each word clearly. 'Now the question is, what would be the consequence to *us* if these weapons—'

His voice cut off suddenly and a placard filled the screen: NEWS SPECIAL. Nothing more happened for a moment. Craven lit a cigarette and waited patiently: probably it was something more about the interminable peace talks in New Delhi.

A voice said abruptly, 'We interrupt this program to bring you—' Then it stopped, and the placard vanished. There was nothing on the screen but a raster, and nothing but a hiss coming out of the speaker.

After a moment Craven put his cigarette down and punched the channel selector. There was nothing on any of the channels except 13, where a faint gray picture came in for a moment, then vanished.

Craven stared at the machine, feeling abruptly frightened. If there was something wrong with the set, then why would channel 13—?

He discovered that he was shaking. Without trying to understand what he was doing, he began to rip off his shirt and trousers. Naked except for shoes, he ran to the locker, pulled out mask, flippers, air tanks and regulator.

The sky was bright and empty as he ran toward the dock – not even a plane in sight. Craven shrugged into his harness, buckled it hastily. He glanced toward the buoy that marked the underwater station, then dropped into the water.

Halfway out toward the station, swimming two fathoms deep, Craven knew he had been right. A sudden hissing patter came above him, and looking up, transfixed, he saw a shower of golden sparks descending, each in its furious cloud of bubbles. One came so near that he felt its heat on his skin. He writhed away from it, staring incredulously as it fell to the bottom ten fathoms below.

All around, the golden sparks were disappearing into the sand, each still marked by a boiling stream of bubbles. The water felt faintly warmer.

It came to Craven's stunned mind that the thing that must not happen had happened: someone had used the weapons that were too terrible for use.

The underwater station was in sixteen fathoms, as deep as it could have been built without pressuring the dome. It stood on a rocky shelf in deep water, and although several of the golden sparks had fallen around it, none seemed to have clung to the dome. Craven swam to the lock, let himself in, and sat hugging himself, shaken by chills, as air slowly filled the chamber.

Inside, he stared wildly around at the deserted dome – the two cots, recording instruments, shelves of supplies. The air seemed oppressively warm, and he bent to look at the thermometer, ready to cut off the surface air supply and turn on the tanks: but the temperature was normal.

He heard himself say aloud, 'My God, what am I going to do?' Scraps of information from other TV broadcasts came back to his mind. Those informal little pellets would go on emitting heat for months. And this must be only an accidental scattering: on the mainland, in populated centers, they would have fallen thick as hail. Anywhere they dropped, the land would shortly become too hot for life. Only the ocean could carry away so much heat …

There was a compressor here in the station, and a tide-driven standby generator; he could recharge his tanks indefinitely; but what about food, after the canned stuff on the shelves was gone?

Fish.

Craven felt weak with reaction, but could not be still. He adjusted his mask and mouthpiece again, went out through the lock.

There seemed to be no more of the pellets on the bottom than before, and none were falling. Craven plucked up his courage, swam to the surface. Treading water, he put his mask up and stared across at the island.

The laboratories were in flames. Behind them, the mountain was one mass of yellowish-white smoke: the whole island was on fire.

The sky seemed empty, but Graven could not endure its gigantic blue stare. He lowered his mask and dived again.

Down in the clear blue depths, Craven heard the high-pitched gabble of dolphin conversation, and once or twice saw their gray shapes flitting by. A school of plump blues swam into view. Craven started, then went after it.

There were spear-guns in the station, but he had not thought to bring one. He swam at the fish, grasping ineffectually with his hands, but they scattered easily around him.

I've got to learn, Craven's mind was telling him. *This is my element now, the sea – I've got to adapt …*

Something large and gray swam up toward him. Craven stiffened, but it was only Pete, gazing at him with friendly curiosity.

The school of blues had reformed not far away. Abruptly the dolphin wheeled, darted away with a lazy surge of his flukes. In a moment he was gliding back, with a fat blue-fish in his jaws.

'Look, Charless,' he said kindly, 'this is the way to catch a fiss …'

BE MY GUEST

I

The room was quiet; the man in front of the mirror was the only living thing there, and he was too horrified to utter a sound.

In the mirror, five faces stared back at him: one young and ruddy, which was his own, and four that did not belong in that place at all, for they were wrinkled, malevolent, small as crab-apples and as blue as smoke.

This is the way it happened:

After the funeral, the only thing that occurred to Kip Morgan was to go out and get boiled. It was one time when he didn't even want to see Angelica MacTavish, but she was there, looking open to suggestion, so he drove her down Sunset to a bar he knew that wasn't really a bar, but a chop house. It was quiet and dark; the wallpaper didn't yell at you because there wasn't any, there was old black paneling instead; there was a jukebox, but nobody ever played it; the waiters wore black jackets and gold-rimmed spectacles; and if a man wanted to get quietly, darkly drunk in there, the management would serve him and leave him alone.

'When I was a kid,' said Morgan to his scotch-and-water, 'nobody died. Except my Uncle Austin one time, and he fell off a ladder. Now all of a sudden they're dying like flies. I must be getting old.'

Angelica watched him and listened calmly. She was one of those slim, compact young women who wear collegiate sports clothes and next to no makeup, not because they want to particularly, but because they look like dressed-up little girls in anything else. They have structural-steel spines and muscles like a cat's, and when they are pretty, as they usually are, it would stop your heart to look at them. When they're intelligent as well, it's a great pity, for then they're too good for most men and they know it.

After a moment she said, 'You liked him a lot, didn't you.'

'Old George? Sure. He was—' Kip's square fingers tightened on his glass, trying to squeeze expression out of it. 'He was worth a million of me.' He frowned and tried again. 'He was the kind of a guy – it made you feel good, just to know that he was alive.'

'I never met him.'

'No. That's right.' Kip blinked at her. 'You were at the funeral, though.'

'Yes.'

'How come?'

'You asked me if I wanted to go. Last Wednesday.'

'*That's* right. Sure. He was only forty-six, the obituary said. Cerebral hemorrhage; that's a filthy thing. He should have lived to be a hundred and ninety.'

'What's going to happen to his work now?'

'His work?' said Kip.

'Didn't you tell me he'd discovered a new vitamin?'

'Oh, that. I dunno. Nothing, probably. It was his own private thing – he didn't have a grant. He had a couple of graduate students working with him, one time or another, but they weren't much good. Head of the department had all the hotshots tied up on a cancer project ... I washed bottles for him sometimes; so did his daughter, when she could get away from her mother. Except she broke more than she washed.'

'That would be the starry-eyed one, who didn't cry?'

'Uh, yeah. Nancy.'

'She was bearing down on you when we left. What's the matter with her, Kip?'

'Everything. All – bottled up inside. You ever see a spastic? Like that, only in her mind instead of her muscles. She can't *reach* people – keeps trying, all the time, it hurts you to watch her. She doesn't know how.'

He gulped the last of his drink and set the glass down carefully. 'I saw her coming at me, back there,' he said.

Angelica's eyebrows went up a trifle; otherwise her expression didn't change. 'Tell me some more about the vitamin,' she said. 'If it's as important as it sounds, why do you think nobody's going to pick it up?'

Kip shook his head. 'Not important. It was a bust. Contra-survival.'

She blinked slowly. 'A contra-survival *vitamin?*'

'Sure.'

'No,' she said positively. The waiter came and put down two fresh drinks and took the old glasses away, thinking about something else all the time.

'Kip, what's the source of this thing – where did Professor Liebert find it to begin with?'

'Pig liver.'

'Then it wasn't contra-survival for the pig.'

'No. Might have been, though, if it had turned out to be any good for people. See, the pig synthesizes this stuff. It isn't anything to him, one way or the other – just a by-product from something else he was doing at the time. Only way it could affect him is if it turned into another reason for slaughtering pigs.'

Angelica frowned slightly. 'Aren't you using "survival" in two different ways?'

'Well, yeah, but you have to. Like, take a Jersey heifer that breeds true – short horns and a big udder. Those are pro-survival factors, right?' He paused and added, 'As long as the farmer's around.'

She nodded.

'Or if you want vitamins, take C. It keeps us from getting skin hemorrhages and pulpy gums, and it gets the lemon cultivated – good for us, and good or bad for the lemon, we don't know yet. Or the L complex – good for you, if you ever have kids and want to nurse them, but lousy for me if it had the same effect on men, which God forbid.

'Another thing L does, we found out, is to break down George's vitamin in primates. He had to synthesize the stuff – took him six years. Got it pure, and the L let it alone – must have been a chain reaction with the natural vitamin and its impurities, and the L. So he tried it on rhesus monkeys.'

'And?'

'Well, it's a vitamin. Guinea pigs and rabbits got fatter and grew heavier fur than the control group, rats and mice were more active. The monkeys went into hysteria and convulsions. Last of them died two weeks ago Thursday … George put a poison label on twenty cc's of the stuff and stuck it in his lab for a keepsake; he poured the rest down the drain.'

Kip swallowed half his drink as if it were tincture of dubious vitamin, then put the glass into the patch of stained light from the tiny window overhead, and watched the ice cubes turn to amber, sapphire and ruby. Angelica, who never spoke merely to break a silence, sat as quietly as he.

The waiter came and went. The old pendulum clock over the archway paused to chime discreetly, and resumed its delicate funereal ticking, and after a long while chimed again. The patches of light moved imperceptibly across the table until the corner of it touched Angelica's folded hands.

The hands moved. Kip raised his head as Angelica drew back the forest-green sleeve and looked at her watch.

'Mm?' he said.

'It's two o'clock.'

'Oh. Uh – you got a date?'

'Yes.'

'Oh. Where? I'll drive you—' He started to get up.

'Here.'

He sat down again and looked at her dazedly. 'That's funny.'

'Kip.'

'Yeah?'

'It's *Monday*. Lunch. Remember?'

Kip looked startled, incredulous, then stricken. 'Monday,' he said. 'You've got the afternoon off.'

'Yes.'

'We were going to have lunch, and then go to the beach if it was nice, or dance if it wasn't.'

'*That* Monday,' she said, smiling.

Kip glanced at his watch, then craned his neck to look at the wall clock. 'It's two o'clock,' he said foolishly. He blundered up and looked for the waiter.

'Kip, we could just order here.'

'No. Not here – some place where there's a lot of plate glass, and parakeets in cages, and waitresses with Italian haircuts, and flowers all the hell over.' He looked at the bill the waiter was holding out, piled bills on top of it, and reached for Angelica's hand. 'Come on!'

So they had lunch, with exactly the right number of Martinis, and argued cheerfully about what kind of a day it was, because it was the late-fall kind that always turns out to be whatever you thought it wasn't; and finally Kip said: 'Look. If we go to the beach, either it'll rain or it'll be just one degree too cool, but we'll stick it out to show how tough we are. Right?'

'Right.'

'And if we go dancing, either it'll be a perfect day for the beach, or it'll rain and we'll wish we were someplace we could sit and listen to it.'

'Right.'

'And either way, we'll find ourselves eating burned lamb chops with a side of spaghetti and listening to Mario Lanza sing louder than human.'

'It figures.'

'All right. Let's go to my place and listen to Mahler, and I'll cook us an honest steak.'

Kip (for Kipling) Morgan lived in a cottage that went with his job and was more job than cottage – pro shop in the front, living room, kitchenette, bedroom and bath in the rear. There are a lot of golf pros in southern California, and hundreds of them were better than Kip, who had all the style in the world and no tournament spirit at all; but he was patient and friendly, he was ornamental, he didn't seduce the lady members, and by and large they couldn't seduce him; and everybody liked him, because Kip liked everybody.

The club was a wonderful place to meet people. He had met Angelica there; she played a strong, clean game of golf, because she couldn't help it, built the way she was, and because she took it seriously – which, Kip was guiltily aware, was the way you were supposed to take it.

Angelica worked as a research secretary for a city councilman who was going to be Mayor; she knew politics from the dirty end up and was intensely partisan about it; she spoke French and Spanish too fast for anybody but a native, had a Master's in sociology, and could sing harmony to anything without a score. Kip was a little frightened of her, because he wanted her more than he had wanted anything in the world since he was twelve.

The sky was a luminous water-agate color when they came up the walk; the air was cool and moist, and there was a little wind in the tops of the euca-lypti. It was going to rain.

Kip opened the door and ushered her in with one big hand warmly in the small of her back, where it seemed to belong. For a moment he thought she was leaning back against him; then he realized she had stopped, halfway through the door. Then he got a whiff from inside, and knew something was wrong.

He slid in behind her and closed the door. The Venetian blinds were closed, not the way he had left them, but he could see that the wall looked funny and there was something scattered whitely across the floor. He clicked the wall switch.

Light spilled out from the three lamps, yellow and strange against the watery gray light from outdoors. The multicolored mound on the long table was garbage: coffee grounds, wet newspaper, banana skins, lumps of pale grease, lettuce leaves, seaweed tendrils of spinach.

Eggshells crunched under his feet as he crossed the room. The green monk's-cloth drapes from one of the windows had been nailed to the wall over the couch to form a kind of garland. In the enclosed space something was written in red smeary letters:

$$LuO + Vi_2 + E \rightarrow i\ LOVE\ u_2$$

Angelica was at his elbow. She looked at him as he turned, her eyes wide and alert.

Kip walked over to the leather chair in the far corner. The thing propped up in it was a toilet seat, decorated with a red heart-shaped outline. It framed a piece of brown cardboard, apparently torn from a carton; the red lettering said:

WILL   U
BE   MY
VALENTINO?
???

He opened the bedroom door and glanced in, then went around the dog-leg past the tiny kitchenette and tried the door that led to the storeroom behind the shop. It opened. He stood in the doorway without moving for a moment, then closed the door and came back.

'Red lead all over hell,' he said. 'She must have opened a gallon.'

'She?' Angelica asked.

Kip bent and picked up a scrap of ruled paper; there were dozens of them on the floor, among the eggshells. This one was covered with lines of verse in a precise schoolgirl hand. Kip stared at it quietly, then dropped it and went over to the table. Angelica followed.

The garbage on the table was piled into three rough tiers. On the top one stood two little figures made of pipe cleaners and papier-mache, delicately tinted with water colors, a boy one and a girl one. The boy figure had bright yellow hair, and the girl figure was wearing a long white crepe-paper dress, with a veil.

'Who, Kip?'

He picked up the girl figure and tossed it gently in his hand. 'Nancy Liebert,' he said. 'She makes these things.'

Angelica looked at him curiously, then went to the couch and sat down, under the garland. 'George's daughter,' she said.

'George's daughter. She's – got a crush on me.'

'I can see that,' said Angelica. 'Has this been going on long?'

'No.' There was a small silence.

'I made a mistake,' said Kip, reddening slowly. 'It was last week, after her father died. She found him. She phoned me and I went over … she held up all right till the cops and the coroner were all through, and then she let go. She cried. You ever read about people crying buckets, and think it was funny? The front of my shirt was still wet the next morning … Warm tears down my chest – the damndest feeling. It was like she was bleeding all over me. And she kept saying that she was twenty-six years old and ugly, and the only one that had ever loved her was her father, and now he was dead.'

After a moment Angelica said unsteadily, 'What was your mistake?'

'I kissed her.'

'… Was that all?'

'No,' Kip said. 'I told her I loved her – and, God, I did – I do … But she took it – the other way.'

The rain began: first a tap, then a hammering at the windows, and then a steady scything sound, hollow from the roof, staccato on the flagstones, and the rushing gurgle in the downspouts.

Kip's head turned abruptly. 'What was that?'

'What?'

'Sounded like a door closing – in here.'

'I heard it. I thought it was a car door slamming, outside.'

'Maybe,' said Kip doubtfully. He glanced at her, then walked around the dogleg into the hall.

The bathroom door was ajar. It had been closed before. Kip pulled it open the rest of the way and stepped in. There was a steamy smell in the air, and a faint reek of after-shave lotion. The toilet-seat lid was propped against the wall under the medicine cabinet, in a litter of tubes and boxes. Kip's toothbrush lay in the middle of the floor, its bristles oozing a puddle of red.

He stepped over it, glanced at the moist gritty ring in the bathtub, and opened the door to the bedroom.

The bed was rumpled. There were two brown wads of nylon on the pillow, and a gray dress on the floor, draped over a lump that was probably a pair of shoes. Kip walked past them into the L-shaped room, around the corner that had been cut out to form the kitchenette on the other side.

The living-room door was open. Kip went through in time to hear Nancy Liebert say, 'Why don't you go home?'

She was standing by the table, barefoot, with a black cloth bag clenched in one red-knuckled hand. Her shoulder-blades were like plucked bony wings. Her slip was wrinkled and hung awry; one brassiere strap was fastened with a safety pin.

She turned to face him, hunched and awkward, with those big greenish eyes staring feverishly. 'Hello, Kip,' she said. 'Don't *you* think she ought to go home?'

Nancy's hair was red: not carrot-color, and not henna-color, but the real, dark, glossy red that you see once in a lifetime. She had the pale skin that goes with it, and that made it worse. Her thin face was scarred and blotched and lumped with acne. It looked like something that ought to have been covered up. Her eyes didn't belong in that face, or in any face; they were too large and too bright, and the whites had the yellowish tint of discolored teeth.

Kip said, 'Nancy, will you do me a favor?'

'She ought to go home. It isn't right for her to be here, Kip.'

'We'll talk about that afterward,' said Kip. His hands were curling involuntarily. 'First the favor, huh?'

'Well, what is it?'

'Go put your dress on. Please.'

She thought about it. 'Well,' she said confidentially, 'if she won't go, we'll just have to pretend she isn't here.' She marched past Kip into the bedroom. After a moment they heard the springs creak as she sat down.

'What are you going to do?' Angelica murmured.

He sat beside her, trying to unwind the tension. 'Take her home.'

'Kip, that girl ought to be in a psychiatric ward.'

'I know it. George wanted her to get help years ago, but her mother wouldn't hold still for it. Took it as a personal insult. I can't get her into a hospital; it needs a relative.'

'Call the police. Have her arrested for malicious mischief. I *know* how it sounds, but it's the best thing you can do for her.'

Nancy walked out of the kitchenette, wearing the gray dress, unbuttoned, and one stocking. She was still carrying the black bag in one hand; with the other, she held up a bottle of prune juice.

'Have some?' she said brightly.

'No, thanks,' said Kip. 'Nancy—'

She giggled and walked back out of sight. They heard bottles clinking in the refrigerator, then nothing but the rain.

When the silence alarmed them, a few minutes later, Kip first called to her and then went to look. A window in the bedroom was open, rain whipping in in gusts over the bed and half the floor. Nancy was gone.

The next morning was bad. The alarm rolled him out at 6:30 and Kip sang in the shower, out of habit, before he remembered. Then he wrapped himself in a towel and padded into the living room to make sure. It was true, all right: there were the nail holes in the wall over the couch, there were the faint stubborn smears of red paint that wouldn't come off, and there was the spot, by the door, where Angelica had said a word to him that would be hard to take back.

He brooded about it while his eggs turned leathery in the pan. After Nancy's disappearance, they had gone over the business about Kip's calling the police, with all the logic on Angelica's side, and nothing at all on Kip's except the knowledge that he'd feel like the executioner at Golgotha if he did it without trying all the other ways first.

From that, in some way that wasn't clear to Kip, they'd got onto the subject of his job. Kip didn't see anything wrong with it; he'd tried a lot of things since college, and had fun at all of them – lumberjack, boy's-camp counselor, zoo attendant, merchant seaman – but never a one had been as pleasant or congenial as this. He said so. He pointed out in passing that if he'd been doing any other work, he would very likely never have met Angelica. For no apparent reason, this seemed to infuriate her.

She was silent long enough to count ten; then her eyes narrowed. 'Kip, I just remembered something you said at lunch. Did you study bio-chemistry in college?'

'Sure. U.C.L.A. George was one of my profs – didn't I ever tell you?'

'Then am I wrong in thinking that you did a little more for Professor Liebert than just washing bottles? Were you one of his star pupils, by any chance?'

'Well, he gave me A's, but—'

'Well, then *why*—'

'Wait a minute. That was just a kind of a hobby – I wasn't majoring in it.'

That stopped her for a minute. 'What was your major – physical ed?'

'Physics. Nuclear.'

That stopped her again. Her eyes got big and round. 'I suppose you got As in that, too. Don't tell me, I know you did. Kip, I'm sorry, this isn't really my business – but how could you give that up, or even half of it, for this kind of a life?'

He groped for a way to tell her. 'It wasn't like that – not the way you mean it. See, when I was a kid I was a science nut. Skinny little guy with an armload of books. Well, all through high school and college I kept thinking that was what I wanted to do, but the work was getting tougher and tougher. All right, then I went back for p.g., figuring with the football and track out of the way, I'd really hit it. And I got sick. I didn't finish the first semester.

'When I got my strength back I tried it again – summer extension. And I got sick again. *Real* sick – anemia, hypertension, asthma, every damned thing, and a jolt of cerebrospinal meningitis on top of it. When I came out of that, I sat down and figured it out. All those things are psychomatic, except the meningitis, and by that time I was a sucker for any kind of bug. I was asking for it. I didn't *want* to spend the rest of my life getting hunchbacked and near-sighted over a lab bench, but I was kidding myself that I did. What for? To make bigger and better bombs?

'So I headed north and spent a season logging. I haven't been sorry once.'

Angelica's cheeks were pinker than usual. She said gravely, 'And you think that wasn't giving up anything? What are you going to do when you can't be a golf pro any more, Kip?'

'I may not wait that long. I've got my eye on a little place up in the sequoia country that I'd like to buy if I can raise the price. A tourist camp, on a lake.'

'A *tourist* camp!'

'Sure. I know there's more work in it than most people think – carpentry, plumbing, anything you want to name, but that's all right. I can do anything that—'

'You can do anything,' said Angelica hurriedly, getting up, 'but you *won't*.' She picked up her raincoat with one motion, got into it with two more. She had the door open before he could move. She turned.

'Why do they give talent to people like you?' she asked, looking at him as if he had a window in his forehead. And then she was gone …

The scrambled eggs were brown around the edges and a delicate greenish color in the middle. Kip nudged them off onto a plate, added underdone bacon, and carried the mess abstractedly into the living room. Rolls, butter, fruit juice, coffee. The coffee was cold.

He swore at it without enthusiasm and drank the prune juice, which bit him on the way down.

He choked, spraying brown droplets on the already colorful eggs, and stared at the empty glass. 'Brandy,' he said aloud, and then, 'Nancy.'

That was right: she'd come into the room with the bottle in her hand. She must have laced the stuff with cognac just before that, or else on the way back. Before, probably. Another little joke.

But it didn't fit. Everything else had followed one plain pattern: the toilet seat, the garbage wedding cake, even the eggshells: love and fear.

What was the symbolic significance of cognac? Of prune juice?

Kip stood up suddenly and walked into the kitchenette. He opened the refrigerator. There was the prune-juice bottle, and there, directly above it on the cabinet, was the cognac, but they didn't tell him anything.

He didn't understand it, and he didn't like it.

If it came to that, what about Nancy's exit through the window? That wasn't pattern, either; he had expected to spend the rest of the evening trying to get her home.

Could she have overheard what they were saying in the living room? Very likely; they'd been keeping their voices down, but there was no telling how long she'd been listening at the bedroom door or just around the corner in the hall.

That reminded him that nobody had answered the phone last night at the apartment Nancy shared with her mother. It was too early yet for anything but a fire or an earthquake; he'd give them till eight, anyhow, before he tried again.

He wandered back into the living room and looked moodily at the wall where Nancy's inscription was still faintly legible. '$LuO + Vi_2 + E \rightarrow i$ LOVE u_2.' That fitted, but not particularly well, unless you took chemistry to mean stinks.

Chemistry.

Question: Why would you put cognac in a bottle of prune juice?

Answer: To hide the taste of something else.

Kip felt a little odd. The room was blurry and there was a ringing in his head – no, not a ringing, a murmur.

Nancy could have got hold of all her father's keys. She might have found the lab safe combination among his papers.

And George had put a poison label on the …

Kip turned to the table, dipped his finger in the little puddle left in the prune-juice glass, and tasted it. Prime. Cognac. And something else, unmistakable now that he was looking for it: the dark oily taste of the vitamin solution.

He whirled and headed for the bathroom. The murmuring was getting louder: tinny little voices, as if a bunch of people were talking quietly at the bottom of a well. Sweating, Kip tried not to hear them, but he couldn't help it:

'… afraid of being poisoned.'

'Peculiar. Must be cracking up.'

They were talking about *him*. *Was* this what had happened to George's monkeys, to make them froth at the mouth, and bite themselves bloody, and die?

He skidded on the wet floor, grabbed the rim of the wash-bowl and found himself staring at his own flushed image in the cabinet mirror. For an instant he thought idiotically that someone had painted little malevolent faces on the wall behind him. Then they snapped into focus, and no matter how long he looked, he couldn't deny what he saw:

Four little men, smoke-blue and as insubstantial as soap bubbles, squatting on his shoulders.

II

Kip sat in the leather chair with his head in his hands, eyes shut, knuckles tight against his temples. There was one repeated thought in his mind: *A monkey isn't a man*. He had been thinking it so long and so hard that he wasn't quite sure what he meant by it any more, but it was a comforting thing: it was something to hold onto.

Keeping his eyes closed was an improvement, but he could still hear the voices; putting his fingers in his ears, he'd already discovered, didn't help. The sounds weren't ordinary physical vibrations, he was sure, although he was certainly hearing them with his ears; they were binaural and he could estimate their sources with exactness; for example, two of them were still on his left shoulder, but the other two were moving—

He sat bolt upright, with a thrill of pure horror.

One of the two abominable little voices was now coming from the general region of his lungs. The other was inside his skull.

There was a knocking on the storeroom door, and then a hoarse yell: 'Hey, Kip!' That was Lebeau, the caddy master.

He got up stiffly and went to the door without opening it. 'Yeah, Irving?'

'Mr Chase is out here – says you promised to work him out with his irons this morning.'

'*Vitamins?*' the voice in chest was saying. '*What the thunder and blazes are vitamins?*'

'*You know,*' said the voice in his head, '*those chemical things. Blast it, Alfie, try to be a little more help ...*'

'Tell him I'm sorry,' said Kip. 'I can't make it – feeling kind of rocky.'

'Okay. Hey, Kip.'

'Yeah.'

'You know who slopped all this paint around the storeroom?'

'Oh,' said Kip. The two voices inside him were still arguing about vitamins, and now the things on his shoulder had joined in; he could see them out of the corner of his eye. 'I did that myself, Irv – I'll straighten it out with the club.' He hesitated, then opened the door.

Lebeau looked at him, his sad face all lit up with concern and curiosity. 'Hey, you do look beat. You better go see a doctor.'

'Think I will. Look, Irv, will you square me with the paying customers, and so on? And about the paint – tell Olcutt I'll talk to him tonight or tomorrow. Okay?'

'Sure, Kip.'

… That settled one point, anyhow; not that he had been in much doubt about it: the little blue people were visible and audible only to him.

Next – Kip went grimly back into the bathroom, sponged the cold sweat off his forehead, and stared at the two little beings who were still visible on his shoulder. One had a long, hatchet-sharp face, the other was pudgy and shapeless. They stared back at him, and it was pretty hard to take.

'Who are you?' he said to the mirror in the empty room.

They blinked at each other. 'Think we ought to tell him?' asked the pudgy one. 'It seems only polite,' said Hatchet-face. 'But – of course – he is not real.'

Kip's jaw wouldn't close properly. While he was working on it a blue haze flowed out of him and solidified into the other two creatures, the lantern-jawed one with the bristly mustache and the squat sheep-faced one. 'What's this? What's this?' said Lantern-jaw.

'Talking to us,' explained the shapeless one. 'Wants to know who we are.'

Lantern-jaw looked affronted. 'Irregular,' he said.

'Still – why not?' asked Hatchet-face. 'I am Don Nobilio Hernandez San Juan Filippe Salvador Guevara de Cervera-Silva. These gentlemen are Captain Ephram Goodnews – Major Jocelyn Britt-Howard – and Dr Alfred R. O'Leary.'

'Doctor of dentistry,' piped up the sheep-faced one.

'How do you do,' said Kip insanely; and then, 'What's this all about? What are you doing here, what do you want? And what do you mean, *I'm* not real?'

Lantern-jaw snorted. 'My dear fellow,' he said, 'we're dreaming you.'

'You,' asked Kip carefully, 'are dreaming me?'

'Absolutely. Nothing odd in that, is there? I'll admit this is an uncommonly long dream, but that suits me. When I went to sleep, I don't mind telling you, I was a damn' sick man. *Damn'* sick.'

'I also,' sighed Hatchet-face. 'We are not as young as we used to be.'

'I can use the rest,' said the sheep-faced one. 'Have to be pretty careful – my heart, you know.'

'Spar knocked me into the scuppers,' the shapeless one said. 'Worst storm I ever saw. Don't know why we haven't foundered by now.'

Kip stared at them all in horror. The transparency of Major Britt-Howard's face was splotched and spotted. In Don Nobilio's right temple, just over the eye, there was a tiny, puckered hole. And Captain Goodnews, lumpy, swollen—

'What year is it?' he asked hoarsely. 'Not in your dream, but the real year?'

All four looked uneasy. 'Ought nine,' snapped the Major.

'It is the year of Our Lord eighteen sixty-seven,' said Don Nobilio.

'Nineteen twenty-one,' said Dr O'Leary.

'Eighty-nine,' said Captain Goodnews.

They glared at each other briefly. 'You're *dead*,' said Kip. He didn't want to, but he couldn't stop. He pointed to the Major. 'You and Dr O'Leary died of disease. You –' to Don Nobilio – 'were shot in your sleep. And you –' to Captain Goodnews – 'drowned.'

There was a babble of furious protest, dominated by Major Britt-Howard's 'Nonsense! Nonsense!' He added, 'Knew it was a mistake to talk to the beggar. Argue with a dream, deserve what you get. Come along, Alfie, Ephram, Billyoh.'

All four melted into a blue shimmer that sank into Kip's body and was gone. He heard their voices, down inside, muttering together angrily.

On the subject of survival after death, Kip's attitude had always been the cheerfully pragmatic one of a man who can count on its being a long way away – if it was true, he'd find out about it, and if it wasn't, it wouldn't matter.

Somewhat to his surprise, the notion was now violently repugnant to him. His mind kept shying away from it into sophistries: There was no reason to suppose that his senses were correctly interpreting the new information they were getting. Where Kip saw little blue ghosts, somebody else in his shoes might see purple beetles and hear them singing barbershop harmony; there was no way of telling.

But that was pure Berkeleian idealism, which could be used just as logically to explain away a ham sandwich. Worse yet, it violated the law of parsimony – it introduced one more assumption than you needed to explain the observed data. And finally, what was his objection to the idea of ghosts in the first place?

That there was no evidence for their existence? Well – hardly. Kip was uncomfortably aware that the case for disembodied spirits was as well documented as the case for meteorites; there was just no place to file it but under 'Superstition.'

That they were theoretically impossible? No, because you can't say that of anything until you know what the theory is.

True, ghosts were supposed to haunt places, not people; but— Wait a minute!

Kip got up from the couch and paced blindly across the room, avoiding the table by reflex and instinct.

Sure, there were recorded instances of spirits inhabiting people. There was a common word for it:

Possession.

Suppose the human body were the natural habitat of spectres, and that when they were seen floating around in ruined buildings, it wasn't from choice but because they had nowhere else to go? If, like the four he'd met, all earthbound spirits were those who couldn't bear to give up the pleasures of a bodily existence – or, indeed, even to admit to themselves that they were dead – what other explanation would do?

And that would account for the lugubrious aspect of house-haunting ghosts, compared to the complacency and general snottiness of Kip's tenants …

Tenants. Peaceful possession. *Possession,* said the disused dictionary in Kip's skull, dustily: *Condition of a person's having such control of property that he may legally enjoy it to the exclusion of all others having no better right than himself …*

'Hell in a bucket!' said Kip.

He wasn't a free agent, he was a piece of real estate – to be precise, a sort of private club for four elderly gentlemen. Hot running blood, dining hall, air conditioning, spectator sports; library in the top story, used for smoking in, probably; nobody ever read the books. Warranted of sound construction, desirable neighborhood, cooking on the premises. Plez cnoke if an rnsr is not reqid.

Did they have a lease? And if they did or if they didn't, how was he going to evict them?

Well, how did you evict anybody? By invoking a law. Exorcism …

But it depended on what kind of law you were talking about. In jurisprudence, a law was a rule of conduct or action *enforced by a sanction.* No policeman, no law.

Therefore, before invoking a law, consider the sanction. In the case of exorcism, what was it?

Very simple, he remembered. If the exorcism didn't work, the afflicted person was drowned or put to the stake. It was effective – if the tenants won't leave, burn down the house! – but extreme.

There was another kind of law that, in this universe at least, could never be revoked and needed no sanctions, and from which there was no appeal: physical law.

Kip was on friendly terms with at least a dozen doctors, none of whom had ever made a nickel off him. He phoned one at random, a bright young man named Latham who had offices in West L.A.

'You get beaned by a golf ball?' Latham asked in honest surprise.

'No, I'm okay; I just want a checkup. And, Al, I'm in kind of a hurry. Can I get the works this morning, basal, x-rays and everything?'

'When did you eat last?'

'About eleven last night.'

'All right, if you want the basal you'll have to wait till eleven today. Don't take any exercise, and don't eat or drink anything before you come over. Make it about ten-thirty; we'll get some of the other stuff done first. How about lunch afterward?'

Kip begged off and dialed another number.

Mike Vitale, a paunchy little man with nervous eyebrows and an inextinguishable grin, was devoted to golf, at which he was very bad, and to sonics, at which he was as good as they come. Kip spent most of the morning at his Westwood laboratory, looking at everything and asking questions, and contriving to get in the way of every non-lethal sub- and ultrasonic frequency known to man.

The subsconics made him feel depressed, happy, fighting mad, sleepy and as amorous as a mink – the latter when Vitale's good-naturedly plain lab assistant, who was used to the gag, happened to pass by. The ultrasonics, those that Vitale would let him try, didn't make him feel any particular way; and none of them, sub or ultra, made any apparent difference to the little blue people. *Buzz buzz buzz*, down there in his chest …

'That all there is?'

'That's all I can show you,' said Vitale, 'except a few frequencies that would set you afire or curdle your brains, little things like that. I tried 'em, and look at me.'

'Oh,' said Kip. 'Well – thanks, Mike.'

Vitale put a hand on his arm. 'Kip, what's it all about? You didn't come here because you're interested in the work.'

'Did it show?'

'Kip, you know what I said to you about five minutes ago? I said to you, "The resonator coils are built around a core of laminated cream cheese." And you said uh-huh.'

Kip grinned. 'You crumb.'

'Sure. And you know damn well I don't use cream cheese in there; it hasn't got the right squeak quotient. Pasteurized shoe polish, that's the stuff, right? Okay. Now how many hours did I put in showing you around the lab, because you're a friend of mine and you asked me? Two. What for, Kip?'

Kip hesitated. 'If I told you,' he said, 'you wouldn't even think I was crazy. You'd think I was kidding you, only it wouldn't be funny, Mike. I'm sorry.'

He went away from there, feeling about three feet high.

The basal metabolism test turned out normal; so did the knee-jerks and all the rest of it. Kip was depressed. He had had a lovely hunch that something would show up in the basal; if his visitors were parasitic, he ought to be burning more energy than he needed.

Latham fluoroscoped him and x-rayed him from every angle. It didn't bother the little blue men.

Latham, it presently appeared, believed that every M.D. ought to know a little about all the principal varieties of psychoquackery. 'Kip, what would you do if you found out you were seriously ill?'

'I dunno. Hey, Al, who do you know that has an encephalograph?'

'Why? What do you think it would show?'

Kip sighed. 'Nothing, probably.' He paid and got away with some difficulty from the lie-down-relax-and-tell-me-all-about-it gleam in Latham's eye. It was getting on toward noon, and he was so hungry he could hardly think straight any more, so he headed toward Olympic and stopped at the first restaurant he saw – which, unfortunately, was entirely paneled in peach-tinted mirrors, suitable for framing upside down in the canopy of a bed.

This meant Waldorf salad and chops with paper panties, followed by jello with carrot strips embalmed in it. It also meant that unless Kip took care not to look up, he couldn't help seeing the reflections of the four wraiths who were now once more squatting on his shoulders, clicking their lips and looking around for the waitress.

As soon as his order was brought, however, they all disappeared inside him again. Kip ate warily, listening to their very voices down below:

'Ghastly food.' (That was the Major.) 'These Americans simply don't know cooking; no offense, gentlemen, I'm still a bit nervy. The indecency of the fellow, saying a thing like that to our faces! Fellow that said a thing like that ought to be horsewhipped!'

'Then I take it,' said the calmer, wearier voice of Don Nobilio, 'that you are in favor of our looking for another host?'

Kip spilled his coffee.

'No,' said the Major reluctantly, but with conviction. 'If I had my choice, of course – but there, one seldom does.'

'I don't see why—' said Dr O'Leary.

'Well, we shouldn't expect you to, Alfie. You haven't seen what we've seen. Oh, I don't deny there are places that could be got tomorrow, if we decided to move. I've lived in some of 'em. I tell you, Alfie, we were *damn'* lucky to get this when the last one fell down. *Damn'* lucky, even with all the trouble we had. Perhaps you think that was extraordinary, but I can assure you it wasn't. No, you never get exactly what you want; you've got to tinker with it till you get something that suits you more or less. And then if you've made the wrong choice to begin with, the whole thing cracks up and you've got to start over. Isn't that right, Billyoh?'

'So I have always found it. But if we are all agreed that we wish to remain—'

Listening, Kip forgot to chew; and in a moment, when the implication of what the Major had just said sank home, he forgot to listen. '... got to tinker with it ...' Had they been tinkering with *him*?

He lost the thread altogether, then picked it up briefly: '... know you can't keep anything from the Committee, blasted nosy parkers, they've probably got wind of it already. And there's no telling what they'll decide to do, but what I say is, we've got to find out what's really at the bottom of this – even if it means going to that ghastly mobhouse, what's her name, Nancy Liebert—'

Nancy.

Kip started guiltily, looked at his watch, swore, and headed for the pay phone.

There was pure blind selfishness for you if you liked; he'd been thinking of nothing but his own trouble all day. The ringing signal pulsed in his ear, stopped with a click.

'Hello, who *is* this?' Mrs Liebert's voice, sounding more hysterical than usual.

'This is Kip Morgan, Mrs Liebert. I wanted to talk to you about—'

'Where is she? *What have you done with her?*'

'Who, Nancy? Didn't she come home—'

'You know very well what I mean. The idea, coming into my house without a word and taking her away – what's the *matter* with you? Why can't you leave Nancy alone?'

'Mrs Liebert—'

'She doesn't *want* you hanging around her. She's perfectly happy here with me, why can't you *realize* that?'

'Mrs Liebert, when did this happen? I haven't seen Nancy since last—'

'You know when it happened. Just *now!* A few *minutes* ago! I went into the kitchen for a *second*, and when I turned around she was gone: How can you stand there and pretend—'

'Mrs Liebert—'

'This excitement is very bad for me, but you don't care—'

'Mrs Liebert, please. Couldn't she just have stepped out for a minute?'

'*No*, because I looked in the hall, and then I looked out the window, it's right over the entrance, and I didn't see her come *out!*' Her voice sharpened. 'Nancy's told me about your disgusting behavior, Mr Morgan. She tells me everything, maybe you didn't realize that. Now you bring her right back, or I'm going to call for the *police!*'

She hung up.

Kip stared perplexedly at the phone. Angelica had been right, of course, and admitting that, Mrs Liebert's calling the police was probably the best thing that could happen – if she could be counted on to do it. This seemed a little doubtful; anyone who would accuse Kip of making off with Nancy, while in the same breath saying that she couldn't have left the building—

What *was* the answer to that, by the way?

The more he thought about it, the less he liked it. He didn't quite see Nancy jumping out a courtyard window, or going down to the cellar to cut her throat, but it was possible, he supposed. She might be hiding from some imaginary danger. She might have gone into fugue and be wandering around the building, or on the roof—

The waitress was nowhere in sight. The cashier was talking to a man in a seersucker jacket, and wouldn't turn to look at him. Exasperated, Kip dropped money on the counter and walked out, nearly running down a plump youth who seemed to have his mind on higher things.

The building was on 15th Street in Santa Monica. Kip had never been there and didn't know the neighborhood; the house numbers, as usual, were invisible, so he parked and got out to check.

In the third yard he came to, cross-legged under a lantern bush, sat Nancy Liebert.

She didn't move as he walked toward her. She looked at him or past him, he couldn't tell which. Remembering the cashier and the fat boy in the restaurant, Kip suddenly felt cold. What if those hadn't been coincidences? What would it be like if she couldn't see him – if *nobody* could see him?

'Nancy,' he said, tentatively.

Her head turned a little: toward him, or past him? She looked slowly surprised.

'Oh, of course,' she said. 'You're dead too, Kip.'

She got up. 'I'm glad I killed you, Kip,' she said confidingly. 'Now we can be together always, can't we?'

Kip's tenants were buzzing away inside him; he tried to ignore them. 'You didn't kill me. I'm alive,' he told her.

'Oh, no. If you were alive, you couldn't see me. Live people can't see dead people, Kip. Mother can't see me.'

Some high-school-aged kids were straggling down the pavement, all talking at once, clear treble and brand-new bass. Kip glanced at them, then back to Nancy.

'Look, your mother's worried about you – let's go tell her you're all right.' He put a hand persuasively on her arm.

She pivoted away from him and stepped back. 'Then you don't know yet. Do you want me to show you, Kip? Look.'

She backed down the lawn, keeping her eyes on him. She stepped onto the sidewalk squarely in front of the first group of kids.

A girl and two boys were walking abreast. The girl turned to speak to someone behind her, and at the same moment the middle boy jostled the other one; they staggered wrestling into the gutter. In the next breath a commotion broke out behind them: a tall boy dodged into the street with two girls after him, reaching for a handbag that he seemed to be trying to open as he ran. A whoop went up, and then the whole pack was pounding diagonally across the street. Nancy had not moved.

It was all perfectly reasonable – a pure coincidence – or was it?

'See?' said Nancy.

'You aren't invisible,' he told her. 'They didn't see you, but it was because they were all looking another way.'

Nancy nodded. 'That's how it was with Mother, too,' she said.

Chills paraded up his spine. It was, he realized, a question of definition. A thing that was completely transparent was invisible, like a non-reflecting window; and a thing that was perfectly camouflaged was invisible, too, like a stick-insect on a twig or a faun in dappled shade. And a thing that nobody ever happened to look at—

What about the feeling he had often had when he was a child, mostly in dark lonely places but sometimes in full daylight too – that he mustn't turn his head, that something horrible would happen if he did?

A man was coming toward them down the walk, striding rapidly, swinging a briefcase; moving a little awkwardly, because his head was turned away as if he were scanning the house-fronts opposite.

Kip moved into his path. 'Excuse me,' he said.

The man came on, humming under his breath. At the last moment his head jerked down, he darted to the right, stooping, reaching toward something that glittered dully on the pavement: a flattened wad of metal foil. His fingertips spurned it, he straightened, all in the same motion, and walked on. He hadn't touched Kip or looked at him: another coincidence.

Kip breathed heavily for a moment without speaking. Nancy was watching him with her fixed yellow stare and her fixed expectant smile. He took her arm. 'Come on,' he said.

The crowds on the avenue parted miraculously to let them through. They saw faces turned away, faces staring up, faces staring down. In the drugstore, the girls behind the fountain were in a whispering cluster; the customers were intent on the merchandise; the tobacco clerk was checking his stock.

A man at the directory rack turned away abruptly when Kip reached out to put his hand on the open book. Kip looked up two numbers and went into a booth. Nancy waited outside, with that same stare and that same frozen smile.

The police department did not answer.

Neither did the fire department.

The operator did not answer.

Kip hung up and sat looking at nothing much in the darkness of the narrow booth. He thought of the people who had disappeared, suddenly and completely and forever: Ambrose Bierce, Benjamin Bathurst, Judge Crater ... Had they spent the rest of their lives wandering among faces that were turned away, shouting across gulfs of silence, begging, weeping, praying, writing desperate letters that they knew would never be delivered?

There was one more number he was afraid to call. He dialed it, anyhow, with a steady hand.

Angelica's office did not answer.

… But that, it occurred to him after a long bitter moment, would be a switchboard operator like all the rest. He was trembling a little when he dialed Angelica's home number. There was no reason to suppose she'd be home at this hour, but—

'Hello? Hello?'

'Angelica!'

'Kip!' Her voice broke. 'Oh, *Kip*. I've been so— Where are you, are you home?'

'No, I'm in a phone booth. In Santa Monica. Look—'

A thin arm came sneaking past his face and tried to pull the receiver away. Nancy's ruined face was leaning into the booth. 'Don't talk to her!' she said urgently. 'She hasn't any *right*.'

He pried her loose and got the receiver back to his ear. '… or hear me, it's as if I wasn't there. I called you, but there wasn't any answer. Kip, try to believe me, this isn't a joke—'

'I know,' he said. 'It's the same with me. Look, my place is nearer. Can you meet me there in half an hour?'

'Yes, but— Yes.'

'I'm not kidding you,' said Kip tightly, 'and you're not going crazy, and it really is happening to both of us. And Nancy Liebert, too. I'll explain when I see you. Okay?'

'All right. See you … *Kip*.'

'Yeah.'

'Nothing – I'm all right, now. Goodbye.'

He discovered that he was still hanging onto Nancy's wrist, hard enough to hurt her. When he let go, her other hand came up to rub it, but otherwise she didn't move, and her too-bright, too-confident smile didn't change.

He hardly noticed. He was remembering something one of the blue men had said, not long ago. He hadn't been paying attention, and one word of it was all he could bring back now; but that was enough. One word:

Quarantine.

III

Nancy, who had not learned to like Angelica any better, was sitting on the edge of the leather chair by the bedroom door. Angelica was on the couch, feet together, hands in her lap, with an oddly watchful expression on her smooth face.

'Can you hear them now?' she asked. 'What are they saying?'

Kip listened. '... *three-goal man at Poona, tall fella, cast in one eye, couldn't stand the climate ... first shot, at over a hundred yards, you know; biggest buck I ever ...'*

'Nothing useful,' he said. 'The Major's talking about polo, and Dr O'Leary about hunting. That's all they've been talking about, the last half hour or so. I can't figure it; they sounded so worried before.'

'Kip, does it strike you that just maybe you're making all this up without realizing it – all these little blue men inside you?'

'And the quarantine, too?'

She frowned. 'No, of course not, but does that necessarily have anything to do—'

'No, look, it all fits together. When I drank the vitamin solution that Nancy put in the prune juice—'

Angelica stood up irritably and reached for an ashtray. 'If you had just called the police last night,' she said in an undertone, and sat down again.

'But that was after the damage was done,' Kip said reasonably. 'Anyhow—'

'All right, tell me this, then. This vitamin exists in natural form, doesn't it? Something else breaks it down in the body, you said, but there must have been times when a person had this vitamin in him and not the other thing, whatever it is—'

'L complex.'

'All right. Then why hasn't this ever happened to anyone before?'

Kip said, 'It *has*. That's what I was trying to tell you. Look, George's vitamin comes from pork liver; L_1 is found in beef liver and L_2 in yeast. There are other sources for all of them, probably, but those are the major ones. So you can figure that anybody who ate a lot of pork and little or no beef or yeast might have his system clear enough of L, every now and then, to catch just a glimpse or two of a ghost. Right? All right, whose diet does that describe – and where do all the traditional ghost stories come from? Goblins, kobolds, banshees; figure them in, too—'

Angelica's eyes widened slightly. 'The Irish?'

'The Irish, the Scots, middle Europeans – pastoral peoples, and not cattle herders, either: pig and goat farmers.' He ticked them off on his fingers: 'Pig. No beef. And unleavened bread – no yeast.

'Add the Chinese and other eastern peoples,' he said. 'Pig and rice, no bread at all – plenty of ghost stories *and ancestor worship*.'

Angelica was silent for a moment. 'And this is the first time the synthetic vitamin has been used,' she said. 'And that doesn't break down. I see. But surely it'll be used up, eliminated, sooner or later – then all we have to do is wait!'

'I don't think so,' said Kip. 'Theoretically it ought to, but if that were all there was to it, I can't figure why they'd be in such a sweat. I think they think it's going to last. And,' he added, 'if it was just waiting, I don't even know I could do that, for long. It's kind of rough.'

Nancy said unexpectedly, 'What does it feel like, Kip?'

He thought about it. 'Crawly,' he said. 'Dirty, inside.'

Angelica shuddered and looked away; Nancy merely nodded. 'That's what I thought.'

Kip looked at her intently; he started to speak, thought better of it, and turned to the paper parcel on the table.

'What's that?' asked Angelica.

Kip was taking bottles, vials, pasteboard boxes out of the parcel and arranging them neatly on the tabletop. 'I picked these up before I left the drugstore,' he said. 'Antispasmodics. Desiccants. Stimulants.' He showed her a vial and a hypodermic syringe. 'Adrenalin. Hope I won't need that, but you never know.'

Angelica's eyebrows went up and down in the are-you-kiddding gesture. 'And what's *that?*'

'Incense,' said Kip, spilling the little brown cones into an ashtray. 'I hate the stuff.'

Her lips tightened. 'Kip – if you don't mind—?'

'Just a minute.' He carried the hypodermic into the kitchenette, washed it, and put it into a saucepan to boil. He rummaged in the cabinet, found a bulb of garlic and a can of red pepper, and brought them back in with him.

'I wanted to get that started – it'll take a few minutes.' He grunted. 'They've shut up. I think they're beginning to catch on. Anyhow, it won't do any harm to tell you, I guess, because they'll know soon enough even if they haven't already read it in my mind. I'm going to exorcise them. E-x-o-r.'

Angelica said nothing. Nancy giggled suddenly.

'After I tried a couple of obvious things like radiation and vibration, and they didn't work, I got to thinking about the traditional approach. Incantation, prayer, fasting, flagellation and so on. I had the usual prejudice, I guess – I thought it was all a lot of nonsense, but it wasn't. Those are all perfectly good lease-breaking methods. When you want to get rid of a tenant who's wrecking the place, and he won't budge, what do you do? You annoy the bejesus out of him!

'The only trouble was, they didn't use the principle selectively enough. Suppose you happened to hit the ghost of a devout masochist with frugal tastes? The prayers wouldn't bother him, he wouldn't care about eating, and the whipping would make him feel right at home. But I *know* what my tenants don't like.'

Angelica was beginning to look interested. 'How can you be so sure?'

'Easy. I've got four tenants. One of 'em was a British army officer, one owned a hacienda, one was a sea captain, and the other was a dentist with a passion for hunting. All outdoor-men. Not one of them ever read a book for pleasure in his life. Okay. You remember that time I was telling you about yesterday – when I got sick? What did I do afterwards? I spent a season logging – and hunting when I had time. I shipped out, I worked on a ranch and in a boys' camp, and so on and so on … and here I am, in a job that keeps me outdoors and doesn't require me to read any books, and gives me plenty of free time to swim and play tennis and hike and hunt – and I don't mind telling you the thought's occurred to me more than once that if I ever got rich, I'd buy a string of polo ponies.'

Something kindled in Angelica's eyes that he'd been missing; something he thought he'd heard in her voice on the phone, only to be disappointed when she turned up half an hour later, cool and self-possessed and faintly watchful. 'Kip, that's— You've *got* to get rid of them!'

Sure.

'But what about the drugs? I don't see where they fit in.'

'If they can control other people, even at a distance, to make them forget to look where one of us happens to be – then I don't find it hard to believe they can play tunes on my nervous system if they feel like it. I think I'm going to get awful sick again.'

The hypodermic ought to be sterile by now; he fished it out, put it together, filled it from the ampule, and laid it ready on the table, with a clean dishtowel under it. 'You know how to use this, if you have to?' he asked Angelica. She nodded, her eyes big and intent.

He pulled down all the blinds and closed the curtains. In the dimness, the floor lamp made a sharp cone of yellow light. He moved it over near the table and put a straight chair under it; then he crossed to the bookcase and pulled out a thin volume in a red and yellowed-gray jacket. 'All my law books are in storage,' he said, 'but this ought to do. Wiener's *Cybernetics* – I bought it five years ago and never got past chapter one.'

He went back to the kitchenette and adjusted the faucet to a steady slow drip. He hesitated, looking over the collection of things on the table-but everything was ready; there was no reason to wait any longer.

He sat down under the light, touched a match to the incense cones and watched the gray smoke curl up. *Tonk*, said the faucet in the silence.

He opened the book and began to read aloud.

'If the original group is the translation group on the infinite line, so that the operator T changes x into $x+$T, (2.03) becomes: (*Tonk*)

$$\text{'(2.06) } f(x+T) = \propto(T)\, f(x),$$

'which is satisfied if $f(x) = e^{i\lambda x}$, $\propto(T) = e^{i\lambda T}$. The characters (*Tonk*) will be the functions $e^{i\lambda x}$, and the character group will be the group of translations changing λ into $\lambda+\pi$, thus having the same structure (*Tonk*) as the original group ...'

Kip's voice was hoarse. Beadlets of sweat were breaking in the furrow between his brows and trickling down; his eyes blurred and stung. He groped for the clove of garlic on the table, shaved off another bitter, oily bite of it between his front teeth, and kept on reading, concentrating, following the argument.

The incense was getting so thick that it was like trying to breathe cologne. His feet were asleep, and the hard chair was giving him a beautiful case of lecture-room cramp.

'In the case of the group of rotations on a circle, tills (*Tonk*) gives us directly that if

$$(2.10)\ f(x) = \Sigma\, a_n e^{inx},\ (Tonk)$$

His stomach lurched.

'then:

$$(2.11)\ a_n = \frac{1}{2\pi} \int^{2\pi} f(x)e^{inx}dx;'\ (Tonk)$$

It lurched again; Kip began to wonder if three antispasmodic pills were going to be enough. He took another, and washed it down with cola.

Time (*tonk*) passed.

He felt a growing reasonless panicky urge to turn his head aside, to get up from the chair, to close the book. It was a hard thing to fight, even though he knew what it was, but he found he could do it: it was knowing, and having a reason to fight, that made the difference.

He lit a cigarette from the butt of the old one, and kept on reading. When the equations blurred and jumped, or when he found himself reading without understanding, he grimly went back and started over.

His stomach squirmed. He took another pill.

His heartbeat speeded up. He took a sedative.

His nostrils began to itch. He sneezed convulsively, blew his nose, sneezed again. His eyes were watering, his nostrils filling with mucus, his lips and throat and the membranes of his eyelids were bloating. As the seizure mounted, he fumbled for the antispasmodics and desiccants and took a triple dose.

It got worse; his nose was so choked that he couldn't breathe through it; he couldn't see no matter how often he wiped his eyes. Then his throat began to constrict. Wheezing sounds came out of him. He couldn't take a full breath – he couldn't *breathe*.

It was worse than he had ever imagined it could be.

Somebody's fingers were prying at his wrist. He let go the book and felt small hard shapes being pressed into his palm – two of damned near everything, by the feel. He swallowed them, put out his hand again and found a glass. Water, thank God; he couldn't have stood any more of the cola.

'Kip, I'm *sorry*—' Angelica's voice said from a long way off.

Very slowly the worst of it went away. When he could speak he said, 'Thanks, Angel.' When he could see, and had enough breath left over, he raised the book again and began where he had left off, reading a phrase, stopping to breathe through his mouth, reading another.

(*Tonk*) 'Note that this expression (3.091) is positive, and that it is independent of *w*. It is one-half the logarithm of the ratio of the sum (*Tonk*) of the mean squares of *u* and *v*, to the mean square of *v*. If *v* has only a small range of variation, the amount of information concerning (*Tonk*) *u* which a knowledge of *u+v* gives is large ...'

The headache began. One massive dose of methadon – all he dared take, with half the pharmacopoeia in him already – sprung the jaws of the vise far enough apart to let him think again; and no farther.

He read on. The warmth of the light on the back of his neck spread around to his cheeks and forehead. It grew. Kip thought of fever, but the rest of his body was still cool, and he didn't have the light-headedness or the skin sensitivity that go with fever.

'Kip, your *face!*'

He touched his forehead, and felt squashy serum-filled blisters that broke under his fingers. There was nothing to do about blisters, and the pain wasn't intense; it was just bad enough to be a convenient distraction from his other troubles.

'That is, the transformation group (*Tonk*) consisting of the operators T which change *f(t)* into *f(t+λ)* leaves the probability of the ensemble Invariant. The group satisfies the prop- (*Tonk*) -erties that ...'

Little muscular tremors began to travel down his arms and legs and trunk. He was bouncing uncontrollably in the chair; the book joggled, his head nodded and his jaw shook. Stabs of pain tweaked him all over. Bursts of idiot emotion followed them: despair, hatred, fury, fear.

To Kip, it was as if his body had been taken away from him: he himself was somewhere inside, a tiny straphanger clinging desperately to one thread of purpose. As long as he hung on the letters would keep bouncing across the screen, and that giant voice that wasn't his any more would keep roaring and groaning and jerking out their meanings; but if he once let go—

The screen went dark.

The shock was enough to swell Kip out to man size again, and as he sat in the chair, in his own private darkness, feeling such a torrent of anguish and despair as he'd never known before.

Trumps. *If you can't see, you can't read.* He had no card to play against that. He was done.

The book twitched out of his hand.

A strained voice began reading: ' "For example, for quite a wide class of functions f of t where minus infinity is less than t which is less than infinity, we have fully determined f when we know the set of quantities: three seventeen – a sub n equals the integral between minus infinity and zero of e to the t, t to the n, f of t, d of t: n equals zero, one, two and so on. Now let A be some function of the values of t in the future: that is, for arguments greater than zero. Then we can determine the simultaneous distribution of a zero, a one and so on up to a sub n and A ..." '

He hung on gratefully in the roaring darkness. The tension in the room squeezed slowly tighter like a fist; everything grew more unbearable all at once, the pain, the nausea, the itch – and then, all at once, everything stopped.

The blindness lifted. He was free.

And he realized for the first time that the voice which was still reading was not Angelica's; it was Nancy's.

'Are they really gone?'

'I think so,' said Kip numbly. He felt peculiar inside; it was a thing he couldn't put a name to, a sensation he couldn't remember ever having felt before. He looked up. Angelica's eyes were shining; and he realized with a queer shock that he didn't feel any particular way about that. It was as if – there was nothing inside him telling him how he *ought* to feel. That was a funny thought, too. Had there ever been?

He was too busy exploring inside himself to wonder about it *Major?* he said silently. *Don Nobilio?* There was no answer, only a hollow feeling, a little like the echo in an empty apartment. It was peculiar. He wasn't even sure he liked it.

'Hm?'

'I said, sorry I couldn't help,' Angelica told him.

'Uh, but you did, didn't you? Those pills, before?'

She shook her head unhappily. 'I was over by the door. I'm sorry. Kip, I wanted to help, I thought I could. But that's something I can't stand – sickness, or any kind of—' She glanced at Nancy and looked away.

Deformity was the word, probably. Nancy was standing across the table, the book still in her hands, the same smile on her face. Kip was beginning to wish something would break that smile; it looked like a thing that had been fastened onto her, hurting her.

'... When the blisters started, I couldn't take it,' Angelica was saying. 'You look a lot better now; how do you feel?'

'All right,' said Kip abstractedly. 'Nancy, I owe you a lot. I mean – Thank you.'

'You're welcome,' said Nancy politely.

What was going on inside that head? She didn't do things at random; all her responses were ordered and purposeful, they just came out of the wrong

369

slots, kind of – like gum when you put a nickel in for candy. He knew what was wrong with her: at least he knew the name for it, but the name was only a label, useful for identification and for covering up ignorance. What's that?. Psychoneurosis. What's psychoneurosis? *That.*

But what was it really, that could get into your mind and change everything around so that everything that happened to you and everything you did was like an untranslatable passage in a foreign language?

'Kip, how do you feel about *things?*' said Angelica.

He looked at her blankly. 'Things?'

'Your work, and your job,' she said, her tone making it clear that she meant altogether different things.

'I don't know,' he said slowly. There was still that curious emptiness, and the more he tried to define it in some other way, the more forcibly it reminded him of an empty house: the vacancy where you expected to find a familiar table or chair or lamp. 'I can do whatever I want now, I suppose … Maybe I'll go back to school. At night.'

'Take you a long time to get your degree that way.'

He said, 'Huh?' and then, 'Oh. You mean the law. Funny, I hadn't even thought of it.'

'Well, what else—?'

'There were a lot of things I couldn't fit into my schedule before. Abnormal psych, sociology, comparative literature – and that course in the history of the movies … No more law, I don't think. I'd be picking it up a little late.'

'Well, but you can do it, Kip. My boss passed his bar exams when he was forty! If you want it badly enough—'

'That's just the thing,' Kip said. 'I don't.'

'You don't.'

'No. That must have been just a kid thing, after all. Hero worship, maybe – my Uncle Austin was a pretty well-known trial lawyer. You remember, the one I was telling you about—'

'The one who fell off the ladder,' said Angelica expressionlessly.

'Yeah, he— *Oh-oh.*'

'What's the matter?'

Kip blinked twice before his eyes focused again. 'Well, nothing, except – I just happened to remember. It was *after* Uncle Austin fell off the ladder that I got this big yen to be a lawyer. Right after; the same day. I remember, I felt all noble about it at the time – I was going to carry on where he left off, pick up the torch and so forth … Jesus.'

'I don't get it,' said Angelica.

He looked at her pretty, impatient face and at Nancy's frozen one. 'Suppose when Uncle Austin died, his gang of spooks moved into me? My God, is that what makes lawyers? I always kind of wondered about it, myself … I must have been about fourteen that year. And then along about eight years later – wait a minute, I've got to think.'

He knuckled his temples for a moment, then looked up.

'The only way it makes sense is if this happens to people a lot oftener than I thought. I get one gang at fourteen. For all I know there may have been others before that, but say there weren't. Maybe up till puberty a kid's no good for them – too sexless, too alien. But you'd think puberty itself'd scare them away; I was a mess—' His eyes widened. He glanced at Nancy involuntarily, then shook his head.

'No, it couldn't be. That would mean everybody's got them – it's bad enough this way. Anyway, eight years later – no, say six or seven – I remember the Major talking about how long it took them to whip me into line ...' He grimaced. 'Call it six – that would make me twenty, and that was the year I had my first serious love affair. You could argue that that marks another level of maturity, as important as adolescence. I know I felt that way about it, anyway. And wham, the first batch leaves or gets kicked out, and another one moves in. The question is—'

'Say what you were going to say before,' Nancy interrupted. 'Was it something about me?'

'No, not about you, Nancy. I was just thinking, what if I had it backwards – what if it was the first tenants moving in that caused all the – the skin disorders and the emotional upsets and so on? Instead of the other way around. But I hope to blazes that was just a wild thought, with nothing to back it up, because – Oh, *no!*'

Angelica stood up in one motion and took a step toward him. They were both staring at him, looking a question. After that first instant he didn't look at his shoulder, but he could hear the little voices mumbling and squeaking at him, like the sounds of mice inside a wall.

'Seven of them,' he said dully. 'Different ones.'

IV

'Have you found out anything?' Angelica asked.

Kip finished pouring the third cup of coffee and loaded it onto his tray. 'Some,' he said. 'Not enough.' He looked around for silverware, found it, and took three of everything. 'This stuff is going to get cold before we get it upstairs.'

'All right, but you don't want to eat it down here, do you?'

He looked at the backs of the two cooks, the salad-counter girl and the waitress, all clustered down at the other end of the kitchen. 'No, I guess not. Okay, eggs, toast, coffee, milk – what about that damned breakfast fodder for Nancy – oh, you got it? Let's go.'

They shouldered out through the swinging doors into the half-empty dining room. A hotel had seemed the obvious answer last night; the quarantine, they'd discovered, was still on, if it had ever been off at all, and there wasn't room for everybody at Kip's. They'd driven around downtown L.A. looking at room lists till they struck a place that had a vacant second-floor suite. Then all they had to do was take the key out of the box behind the room clerk's oblivious back, and move in.

One trouble was that there wasn't any room service.

They couldn't use the elevator, either, unless, they waited for somebody who was going to their floor. So far they hadn't even tried it. It was getting to be actively unpleasant to be near other people; for Kip and Angelica, at any rate – if Nancy found this state of affairs harder to take than her ordinary life, it didn't show.

Back in the suite, it was better. The sitting room was quiet and secure; the walls closed it in; there was an air of shipwreck about it, or of world's end, but at least all the corpses were outside.

The eggs were cold, all right, but the coffee was gratefully hot. 'Kip, *can* you tell us anything?' said Angelica.

Kip, who hadn't slept, rubbed his whiskery chin irritably. He had brought a razor along, but he didn't feel up to looking in any mirrors.

His population had increased to eight overnight.

'The two new ones are named Tom and Cliff,' he said. 'I don't know much about them, except they're brothers. The other ones – there's Pappacostas, he was a wine merchant. He sings hymns in Greek, but I don't think he sings them the way they were written; he laughs like hell when he gets through. Burke – had an auto agency, hated his wife. That's all he talks about. Schleiser – ran a pool room, likes the horses. Ottley – worked for the telephone company, talks about women. Freeman won't tell what he did for a living. Levinson was an offset stripper, whatever that is. Not burlesque, anyhow – something to do with commercial lithography. Leeuwerink – he was a jeweler, the kind that makes rings, not the kind that sells them. Used to raise pigeons.'

Angelica waited. 'Is that all?'

'Makes nine,' said Kip, and bit a piece of toast as if it were a throat.

'But is that all you know about them? I'm sorry – but it isn't enough, is it?'

'No.'

'You have to find out what they *don't* like.'

'Right.'

'How much longer do you think it'll take?'

Kip set his fork down. 'I don't know,' he said with great restraint. 'They don't like each other, most of them. That isn't much help. The other time, it was no problem, because they had me trained – what they didn't like, *I* didn't like. Maybe it'll take months or years for that to happen again. I dunno. I've been knocking myself out, trying to think of a way—'

'They don't sound like intellectuals. Why wouldn't the book work again?'

'Tried it last night. Nothing. Either it just didn't bother them, or one thing isn't enough – you have to hit them with half a dozen of the things they hate the most, all at once.'

Nancy patted her lips delicately with a paper napkin and said, 'Why don't you try doing a lot of different things?'

For a minute they had forgotten she was there. Kip blinked at her. 'It's an idea,' he said cautiously. 'Go to the zoo, drink beer, ride a bus, smell flowers, look at a policeman— Why not?'

'Ice cream and pickles,' said Kip gloomily, and crossed it off his list. 'Now what?'

They sat in a row on the curbstone and thought about it. The list was a long one: *beer, policeman, flowers, bus, concert, juke box, zoo, lecture, church, haute cuisine, chow mein, tamales* … Most of the items were crossed off; a few had question marks beside them.

They had one success, early in the day: half a glass of a popular alcoholic beverage, which tasted like sweetened grape juice only less so, had made Kip violently sick. He kept drinking the stuff between spasms, while Angelica chanted 'Kyrie Eleison,' and when the bottle was gone so was Pappacostas, the wine merchant.

But none of the others, apparently, was that simple.

'You've had enough to eat and drink for a while, I guess,' said Angelica. 'What about some more noises? Boiler factory?'

'Know where there is one?'

'No, but there are plenty of aircraft plants.'

So they tried an aircraft plant. They walked down a long aisle, under lights that turned all the pink in their skins to a hecotograph purple, and made Nancy's face into something you would only look at once; past an enclosure where a Negro girl was punching neat holes in an aluminum stamping; past a bigger place where two men and a girl in overalls were doing nothing at all to a partly assembled plane; past an office where a stout man was waddling rapidly on flat feet from a bench to a set of vertical files on the other side of the room, and back again; past the doorway of a beaverboard hut inside which, in front of a beaverboard barrier, sat a frog-faced plant policeman.

Angelica stopped and looked thoughtful. She said something Kip didn't catch, in the din.

'What?'

'Said that would be the experimental design section,' she shouted in his ear. 'Very hush-hush!'

'I guess so.' He started to move on, but she put a hand on his arm.

'Kip, we could just walk in there.'

'Well, sure. But why would you want to?'

She looked irritated. 'I *don't* want to. I was just thinking – I don't know why I never thought of this before—'

He waited, but she seemed to have forgotten about him. He touched her on the shoulder.

'Kip, you can spare me for a couple of hours, *can't* you?'

'Well – yeah but what's this about hush-hush—'

'Kip, listen, won't you? I know you're going to lick this thing soon, and then the quarantine will be over. I can't pass this up; I must have been blind – I could kick myself. Don't you see? If I can find out what Magnusson and Sweeney are going to do at the council meeting Thursday – it would mean so much! Is it all right? I'll meet you back at the hotel tonight sometime: okay?'

'Sure,' said Kip, trying not to notice how hollow he felt inside. 'Hey, wait – you want to take my car?'

She hesitated, then took the keys. 'All right, then – you can take the bus from here. See you!' She vanished down the aisle, running, people melting out of her path as she went.

It was a long ride back on the bus, and Nancy sat stiffly with her arm through his all the way.

He didn't want to be alone in any hotel room with Nancy, so he led her on a long tour up Broadway and down Spring, stopping every few yards to try something else, although he was sick of it and had no hope for it at all. They wandered through the five and dime handling the cutlery and tools, looking at goldfish, sniffing cosmetics; they tried oranges and gimcrack jewelry, stopped at a movie for twenty minutes of Betty Grable, looked at copies of the *Times*, the *Mirror* and the *Christian Science Monitor*, went into a garage for the smells and a ballroom for the noise, smoked rum-flavored cigarettes, watched Edward R. Murrow on television and petted a stray cat. It took them two hours; nothing did any good; and when they got back to the suite Angelica still was not there.

Kip got the Gideon Bible out of his room and read half the begats to Nancy because he was desperate, and some of the ordinances in Leviticus because they had once amused him, and David's lament for Jonathan because he liked it. And a little after midnight Angelica came in.

She was bright-eyed and rosy. She looked as if she had played three fast sets of tennis and swum a mile, and as if she were on her way now, not even breathing hard, to collect murderous looks from women at a cocktail party.

'How was it?' Kip asked.

She sat down beside him on the couch, not the way most women would have done it – in three stages, each preceded by a cautious peek at the area to be honored – but all at once, thump, as poised and sure as a flung javelin. 'It was wonderful. I couldn't locate Sweeney; he seems to be out of town. But I found Magnusson talking to Weiss, and I know they're going to meet Sweeney tomorrow morning, and I know where. How did you two make out?'

'Not so good.'

'I'm sorry. But you'll get it tomorrow, I know you will. As soon as I get back, we'll hit it together. It won't take long. You believe that, don't you, Kip?'

'Sure.'

'If we started now,' said Nancy to no one in particular, 'it would be quicker.'

Angelica glanced at her, frowned, and turned to Kip. 'I should have explained before, but there wasn't time – probably it sounds very silly, but this meeting Thursday isn't just an ordinary Council session; the whole election may turn on it ... and it is, or it could be, awfully important. How do you feel? Is it very bad, can you hold out till tomorrow afternoon?'

It was getting hard for Kip to listen to long sentences; he was like a man straining to hear the telephone at a Saturday night brawl. '... *comes up t' me with a mumble piecea pipe innis hand ... mumble pretty potted, so I grabbed her by the ... second time, you understand, twice in a row, mumble, and I don't take that kind of mumble ...*' 'It's okay,' he said fuzzily. 'Tomorrow's swell.'

'You're sure.'

'Sure.'

Angelica went off to bed, meaning to be up and stirring betimes, and after a while Kip went too, but not to sleep. He heard Nancy moving around in the bathroom, and then her door closed, and the silence settled down: the thick, muffled silence that belongs to hotels at night, and is deeper than most because its built of layer on layer of sounds just too faint to hear.

The voices inside him went on, loud against that background, and he lay blind in the darkness listening to them. How long could you go on like this? After a month or a year, if you lasted that long, could you get so used to that interior gabble that you wouldn't hear it at all?

It didn't seem to matter much. There was a slow shifting and settling in his mind, and it ended with the spark of his awareness on one side, and all the pain on the other: still there, close enough to touch, and just as bad as ever, but it was as if he were looking at it through a window ... or down into the darkening depths of ocean ...

The sedative he'd taken was beginning to work, he realized fuzzily. Then he was adrift, turning slowly in space, while his outlines melted and expanded, and the darkness flowed into him until they were one.

He came awake slowly with the fragment of a dream in his mind. For a moment he thought he was still dreaming, and that the voices were part of it, because they were talking about the blonde girl: but the bright, hot picture faded and the voices didn't.

'(chortle) boy, what a pair of ... how'd you like to (laughter) ...'

He was tangled in the bedclothes and clammy with sweat. The air was cool and fresh; the windows were visible as oblongs of gray on black. It must be near morning.

They were watching my dream, he thought, and was suddenly so sickened that he couldn't bear to hear the voices any longer. He set up a competing clamor in his own mind: songs, recorded memories of Sousa marches, football crowds, bowling alleys, anything. Gradually the voices quieted, but he clung to the memories, more coherent and more vivid now: Saturday afternoon, with the air crisp and cool and the bleachers a honeycomb of faces ... football tumbling slowly down the blue sky over the goalposts ... Evelyn Nesbitt, sitting across the table from him in the Grog Shop ... Mary Clyde, the little brunette he'd dated in Snoqualmie ... and Angelica. Angelica. Angelica ...

He was standing barefoot beside the bed with the switch of the bedside lamp in his fingers, blinking at the sudden warm light.

What *about* this?

He had found himself thinking about Angelica lying asleep in the next room: not Angelica the girl who meant 'No' when she said it and would never be coy about saying 'Yes' if she meant that; and not Angelica the eager politician, but just Angelica, softly and warmly asleep in the darkness.

It was wrong: not because it said so in any book but because it had never been like that between him and Angelica, and perhaps now it never would be.

And even now, he realized with shame and horror, he didn't care.

He didn't care if she fought him. He didn't care if she screamed.

There was a waiting silence inside him, and that somehow made it worse. It would have been easier if they had been talking to him, urging, insinuating; his anger would have helped.

He bent over numbly, found his clothes and began putting them on.

One lamp was glowing at the far end of the sitting room.

Someone was kneeling in front of it, a cusp of light along her red hair: Nancy. He tried to get past her quietly, but she turned before he reached the door.

'Kip?' She got up awkwardly and came toward him; her dress hung loosely on her, unbelted and unbuttoned. She saw his face, and stopped. 'What's the matter, Kip?'

'Nothing.' He got the door open. The voices were beginning again; it was intolerable – he hadn't even noticed that Nancy was wearing nothing under her dress, but *they* had ... He slammed the door on her 'Where you *going?*' and ran for the stairs.

A little rose-pearl light was beginning to filter up over the tops of the buildings to the east. Under it, the city was cold and gray. Kip paused for a moment to look at a ragged man asleep in a doorway. Was anybody inside him, watching his dreams?

Footsteps clattered after him down the pavement. He turned. It was Nancy. She had stopped to put on shoes and a coat, and she was carrying something under her arm.

She halted a few feet away, and held the things out – his raincoat, rolled up into a bundle. 'I thought you might need this,' she said doubtfully.

'Thanks.'

She stood waiting, and he realized that she wasn't going to make a stink, or follow him if he asked her not to. 'You really want to help, don't you?' he said.

She nodded soberly. 'I'm – trying.'

'All right. Come on.'

She trotted along beside him. 'Where are we going?'

'We're looking for a box,' he told her, and kept going, hands swinging clenched at his sides, while the blood beat at his temples *Angelica –'gelica –'gelica ...*

It took them a long time, wandering down back alleys, before Kip found what he wanted: a heavy crate, not quite five feet high and about twenty inches wide. He got into it to see if he could, and Nancy stared at him round-eyed but didn't ask any questions.

When he dropped the thing in the middle of the sitting-room carpet and straightened up, he noticed for the first time that his duffel bag was open and the things that ought to have been in it were scattered on the floor – all but one. The incense tray he'd bought yesterday at the drug store was on the end table under the lamp. It was a cheap piece of stamped, black-enameled tin, probably made in Brooklyn, and stuck onto the rim of it was a gold-enameled figurine of a cow.

A gilded cow.

Or a golden calf.

He turned and looked at Nancy. 'You weren't—'

'I've prayed,' she said, 'to everybody else.'

There was pain in those fixed eyes, so deep and so full that it hurt him to look, and he couldn't look away.

He put his hands on her shoulders. 'Nancy—'

'But nobody answers, ever – do they.'

After a moment he let go. 'No,' he said, 'I guess they don't.'

Angelica was coming into the room, fresh and rosy, knotting the belt of her robe. Her expression of faint surprise turned to something sharper when she saw the box. 'Kip, what's this for?'

'The usual thing,' he told her. 'I can't wait any more, Angel – I thought I could, last night, but it's a lot worse now. I can't even tell you how bad it is. It's got to be now. I'm sorry.'

'You—' she began, and sucked at her lower lip. 'All right, if that's how it is, of course, Kip.' She looked at the box again. 'What are you going to do with this?'

'Just get into it and stay there,' he said tightly, 'until this gang of ghouls gets out of me. Or until I die.'

'But you don't know it will work—'

'It'll work.' He bent over and squeezed himself crabwise into the crate. It was just big enough to contain him, head down, knees bent; he couldn't sit down in it, and he couldn't stand. 'There was something I forgot – didn't want to remember, maybe. Some things nobody likes, except masochists, and I haven't got any of them. The old formula. Flagellation. Rack, thumb-screw, water torture.' He tried to grin. 'This is the same thing, only more modern. Cheaper and just as efficient.'

He added, 'It takes a while, though, so if you want to go—'

She hesitated, looking down at him, sober and concerned. 'Kip, I *hate* to go— All right. I'll be back,' she said, turning, 'as soon as I can.'

She was dressed and gone in five minutes, and then the room was very quiet. Nancy sat on the couch, feet together, hands in her lap, watching and saying nothing. Kip crouched in his box.

After the first minute his knees and the back of his neck had begun to ache. His head was jammed into the angle between the top and side of the crate; he could lower it a fraction of an inch, but he couldn't raise it; his knees were as far down the narrow space as they would go.

Later the ache spread to his shoulders and chest. It was exactly like a heavy metal chest plate; he could feel the weight of it every time he breathed.

Still later, it was his ankles. He was able to move his feet a little, but each change of position relieved him only for a few seconds; then the knob of pain swelled again in each ankle, worse than before.

Then the cramps began: in calves, thighs, chest, groin.

He was breathing in short, sharp gasps. In his constricted chest his heart thudded irregularly like a trapped thing, and the pulse-beat slammed at his temples, as if it would burst the skin. The weight against his head and shoulders was Atlas' burden, the whole earth.

That's enough, the voice inside him kept saying; *you tried, you did all you could. Give it up – you just couldn't make it, that's all. Nobody could do a thing like this to himself.* His body sagged outward. It would be so easy – *Sure, easy,* the voices said; *just let go –*

Somewhere inside, deeper than the voices, he found a thing to hang onto. He moved his body the fraction of an inch that meant he was staying in instead of falling out. The torment went on.

After a long time Nancy came over and wiped his forehead with a cool, damp cloth. He squinted up at her.

'All right?' she asked.

'Sure,' he said thickly. 'Nancy.'

'What, Kip?'

'Light me a cigarette.'

She went away and came back with one. He could see her fingers shaking as she put the match to it. She held it out, and it was the one thing he wanted most in the world.

'Changed my mind,' he said. 'You smoke it.' After a moment she started to move away, and he said, 'No, stay here. Smoke it here.'

He watched the tip glow and saw the smoke curl out, blue from the burning end, fog-gray from her lips. He smelled it, and his racked body went hollow with hunger. She smoked it down to a half-inch of butt before he let her go.

Another idea stirred in him through the pain and the longing, and he said, 'Nancy. Go get me – bottle of rye. A fifth. And two quarts, beer. Go ahead.' Her skirts rustled away. He muttered to himself, 'Get swacked on boilermakers. Stand anything. Stay here forever, drunk.'

She was gone a long time.

She came back hurrying, door slamming behind her, and set the paper bag down clunk on the carpet, breathing hard. She looked at him wordlessly.

'Open it,' he said.

She took the bottles out and set them in a row. She reached into the bag again and pulled out a bottle opener. 'No,' said Kip, and paused for a breath. 'Break 'em.'

She stared at him a moment and then stood up with a bottleneck in each hand. Leaning over, holding them away from her skirt, she swung the two bottles together. The fifth shattered at the bottom; whisky splashed her ankles. She dropped what was left of the broken bottle, picked up the other quart of beer and bashed again, harder. Glass flew; Kip heard a piece of it rattle inside his crate, and saw a drop of blood well from the inside of Nancy's calf. She didn't notice it. She looked at the one bottle that was still stubbornly intact, and then she stooped for the opener, wrenched the cap off and held the bottle upside down while the beer glugged out.

Kip closed his eyes involuntarily. When he forced himself to look again, the frothy puddle was already soaking into the carpet. It smelled like all the distilleries and breweries in creation; there were jagged bits of glass and a soaked paper bag mixed up in it. It was a mess, and it was more than that: it was the pure instinctive essence of tragedy; the seized candy, the drowned kitten—

The waste, the waste …

Hot tears leaked out of his eyes. Then he felt a spasm of rage; then nothing but the slow waves of sensation that pulsed up and down his numb body.

Somebody was shaking his shoulder. 'Kip, Kip!'

He blinked and squinted. 'Wha—?'

'You were falling asleep.'

''S right.' He had been just about to dream something, too – something languorously pleasant, gone now like a burst soap bubble. Danger. That waiting stillness inside him – He scrubbed his face with his palms. 'Nancy, gimme pill. The li'l white ones.'

'Wait a minute.' She came back with the pills, two of them, a glass of water and a straw from God knows where – she must have brought it up with the beer.

The light from outdoors slowly brightened. He had been in the box – how long? Two hours? Three? Elsewhere men had suffered this same torment for days on end, and without breaking. If they could do it, he could.

I'll stay here forever, he told them. *If you get out and then come back, I'll climb into the box again. As long as you stay, as long as I live, it'll be just like this.*

There was a sense of pressures building up inside him … and something else, another almost-movement nearby. It was disquieting; he strained to feel what it was, but he couldn't.

The pressures grew.

'All right – sucker,' said one of the voices.

Something burst. There was a brief flurry of incorporeal motion.

The second group of tenants was out.

And the third was in.

V

When he had enough liquor in him, like now, he could still hear the voices, all right, but they were a long way away and he didn't have to listen. He saw the little blue faces gibbering wrathfully at him every now and then, when he forgot and looked in a bar mirror. They hated it when he didn't listen, but there wasn't much they could do about it. They *wanted* him to be drunk, most of them; they just didn't like how tough it was to make him do other things.

Funny how he'd never liked to get drunk before – only once or twice a year, maybe, and then more for the hell of it than anything else. This was the way to be, with the high thin singing in his ears, and his brain turning smooth and oily-bright to the pull of some cockeyed star.

And the liquor was free, because nobody knew he was there at all.

He choked and sprayed chewed peanut down the front of his jacket, over an old liquor stain. He rubbed at it automatically, noticing how thin his fingers had got. He'd been losing a lot of weight, the last few days, and his clothes hung on him funny. And he hadn't bothered much with shaving or washing either, but that was all right. That was fine, because when he did forget and look in the back-bar mirror, it wasn't a face he recognized at all, it was some other guy with those little blue monsters squatting on his shoulders.

The only trouble was –

The only *trouble* was –

The, only, trouble, was, there was nobody to fight. That was it. That was one of the things the voices wanted him to do the most, and he couldn't, because – Well, where was the fun in slugging somebody that didn't even know you were there, and couldn't slug back? Fish in a barrel. He could flatten any of them. That big guy in the leather jacket with his back against the bar, shot glass in his fingers like a thimble. He could stand in front of him and measure him and put him can over teacup over that bar, him and his leather jacket. But he wouldn't.

... hit him anyway HIT *the lousy ...*

Shut up.

There was another trouble, but he didn't remember what it was. He didn't *want* to remember that he didn't want to know what it was, that was the way it was. And that worked out perfect, because when he was as drunk as this he couldn't remember what it was that he didn't want to remember that he didn't know *what*. Only sometimes it bothered him, and it had something to do with—

Never mind her.

Her who?

Never mind.

Time he was getting out of this rotten joint, anyhow. *Break the mirror.* That's right. He picked up the bar bottle with its plastic spout, still heavy, he'd only had about four shots out of it, and swung it to a swift star of white glass tinkling icy echoes out of itself down among the bottles, clinketa clank. He saw the heads turning on one string all over the room, and that was that. He walked out of the place favoring his bunions in the same little island of clear space in the middle of the crowd that he walked in wherever he went. And the rainwet street was just as dark in between the cold bulbs and as shabby and lonesome as it had been before.

Let them figure that out.

He walked up the street looking in at bars, but they all had busted mirrors; that was how he marked them so he would know not to go in the same crummy joint twice. If they put in a new mirror, all right, he would have a few drinks and bust it again. But lately they were just boarding them up, and he was running out of bars.

The burleycue across the street was closed; that was the one where he threw the eggs that time, and then came back next night and squirted seltzer on the broads and started a riot, because they ought to know better than pass off a rotten sleazy show like that for burleycue. The one up the block was still running, but he'd seen the show and it wasn't much better. World was going to the dogs. Burleycue with three baggy strippers, each one old enough to be the other one's mother, good God, and a little spit of whisky for half a dollar, when it used to be all you could drink in one swallow out of a rubber hose for a nickel, and a man that knew how to hold his breath could fall down dead drunk when he let go. And nobody to fight an honest fight with.

He passed two cops walking tandem and looking fierce the other way, and then half a block later another two. There was the dirty-magazine store closed up and padlocked where he made the snowstorm with paper, and the record shop where he broke all the records. Boards on the pawnshop window; that was the time he saw a wristwatch he wanted, and where the *hell* was that wristwatch now? He felt his bony wrist. Gone. He must have thrown it down a sewer, or something.

Played out. Damn town never was any good, bunch of flatfooted hillbillies in flowered shirts, give a dime for the lot of them and get two cents change. Best thing to do be hop a coaster up to Frisco or Seattle. *Now about those movie studios, though? Go take a look at the starlets …*

No. Think I don't know when it's you talking, not me? Don't like how I do, get the hell out, you will anyway – can't even keep track of your names anymore. What am I, a lousy transient hotel?

Yes.

A flophouse? With dirt an inch deep on the old curved banisters, and damp peeling wallpaper, and the smell of cockroaches in the walls?

Yes. Yes. That's what I am. And you're all a bunch of no-good bums, worse than me.

Wasn't for this quarantine there's plenty he could do, he's broke in good …

There's no sense to it. If you guys aren't making the quarantine, WHO IS?

Silence.

They wouldn't answer. Scared of something. Stubborn. Unprint 'em. Squabbling with each other now like they usually did, fifteen or twenty of them all at once, drive a man crazy if he wasn't drunk enough not to listen. Scum of the earth. Scum of the earth.

He heard a cracked voice singing and caught a glimpse of somebody silver-spangled down the street, swaying and singing. 'A pret-ty girl – is like a –' That would be Nancy, and he didn't want to see Nancy right now; all things considered, he saw too much of Nancy. So he veered right at the corner and walked down into the darkness until the crowds thinned and his lone footsteps went flap against the housefronts, under a cold star.

And he started hearing the voices again.

The first light he saw, he blundered down into it and it was an empty poolroom with four guys playing cards under a naked bulb in the back. He kibitzed for a while but it was dull, they were playing for nickels and dimes and the cards were running slow, so he livened it up. The dealer dropped an ace bucking for a full house, and the fat-lipped little guy on his left had aces.

So he picked the ace out of the discards and put it back on top of the pack, and when the aces won there was a nice five-minute hassel that ended with the dealer on top of fat-lips choking him purple. But then the other two dragged them apart and took fat-lips away; and the dealer kicked a chair, and finally locked the door and went upstairs, leaving him alone with the mortuary slabs of the pool tables dismal under the one light.

He pitched billiard balls through the plate glass until he had a hole big enough to walk through zigzag, and went on up the street trying to sing a little, himself, but it was too lonely a noise. And the voices were bothering him again.

Then there was nothing for weary blocks until he hit a little art-jewelry store with a light in the window; it was closed, there was nobody there, but right next to it was a doorway with a dim bulb burning over a card that said 'Madam Rayma,' and he could see shadows moving against the windows overhead. So he went up the stairs in a hell of a hurry, and the door was unlocked, and he went in.

Somebody was moving around the room turning off lights until there was only the one left, forty watts in an old-fashioned lamp with a blue silk shade, right next to a woman leaning back in an overstuffed chair, chins up and eyes closed. There were other people in the place, men and women, about half a dozen, but they were all keeping quiet.

He was about to get up and go when the woman in the chair began groaning and spitting, and heaving herself around till the skinny guy who'd been turning out the lights had to come and hold her down. She quieted after a while. 'Who is there?' asked the skinny guy.

'Twixie,' she said in a peanut-whistle soprano, and giggled.

'Are there any others there, who wish to speak to us?'

'Yeff. *Wots* of 'em.'

The old malarkey. Soft soap and ectoplasm for the marks. And watch 'em eat it up!

The woman was speaking now in a deep masculine voice. 'Things are very different here, Dottie. There's no way to tell you – I couldn't make you understand. But your mother and I are happy, very happy. Some day we'll all be together, and then you'll see ...'

He squirmed restlessly. If he could just make them hear him, he'd give them spirit messages that would curl their toe-nails. But there wasn't any percentage in trying. You could back a man into a corner and holler at him, but he would just faint or go hysterically blind and deaf.

He could do it again. He could leave them laid out like St Valentine's Day. But there was no percentage in it. Fish in a barrel.

'Twixie' was back as he started to leave. 'Theas' fome-body heaw wanf to talk to K. M. Iff im*paw*tant.'

'Does anybody here have those initials?' the skinny guy asked.

'... Well, go ahead anyway, Trixie.'

'Thiff if the meffage. One dwink if haffa dwink, *two* dwinkf if a dwink too much, *fwee* dwinkf if *no* dwink ...'

Her voice faded to a ratsqueak behind him as he closed the door.

K. M. A coinfidenfe. But one drink was half a drink, all right – or eight, or ten. He went off down the hollow street, looking for a bedtime bottle.

When he got home with it he had to fight his way into the sitting room through a nightmare of twisted paper streamers thumbtacked to the walls, the door, the ceiling, everywhere. There was a kind of throne-like business over at the side of the room that he had to look at twice to recognize as a straight-backed chair on top of the coffee table; it was draped with satin from the windows and crumply sheets of aluminum foil, red giftwrap, pasted-on gold stars and festoons of what could only be pink toilet paper from the bathroom.

Nancy got down off it, switching her silver-spangled hips to make the ostrich plumes wag. She didn't look at him. She slow-marched across the room, arms out stiffly, little fingers curled, and put the playing arm down on a record that was already spinning in a portable phonograph. The volume was up all the way: it blasted at him, 'A PRETTY GIRL ...'

She rustled slowly back to her throne and climbed up again, graceful as an ape in her high heels, and sat there deadpan, her skin powdered white except for two fever spots on her cheekbones, silver-paper crown tipsy on her head, a battered scepter in her hands.

Kip sneezed, fumbled in an empty pocket, and wiped his nose on his sleeve. There were streamers criss-crossing the hall doorway, and it looked like too long a trip anyhow. He sat or fell, got his back to the wall, and scratched the worst and newest of his itches before he tilted the bottle up.

When it swung down again, sooner than he wanted, the door was opening. He got it in focus and tracked it, and it was Angelica coming in, leaning like a masthead over the slanty floor, lost in a mink jacket with the price tag still on it; embroidered slacks under that and the blank black umbilicus of a press camera gawping in between.

Angelica had about a million pictures of local officials in embarrassing poses, some politically compromising, some ludicrous, some lewd; her room was full of them. She had tried leaving them on her boss's desk, in newspaper morgues, on bus seats; nobody ever saw them, they were kicked around and thrown out with the garbage, but she kept on taking them just the same. The rest of her time she spent shopping; all the space in her room that wasn't full of pictures was overflowing with minks and ermines, Paris fashions, solitaires, necklaces, brooches and money, crisp in paper cummerbunds. She talked about moving a lot, but stayed, for the reason they all did: you had to have somebody to talk to, or you'd go crazier than you were.

'What's *this?*' she said, sweeping a strand of streamer aside, and took a long look at Kip and another at Nancy. 'The wino and the loony,' she said wearily, but with her throat pulsing hard against the banshee blather of the phonograph.

'... JUST LIKE A PRETTY TUNE,' the record screamed. It delivered itself of a final orchestral blurp, shut up, and began to skritch quietly to itself. Nancy climbed down off her throne.

'Turn it *off*,' said Angelica.

Nancy kept going, a traveling waxworks. She put the needle back on the lead-in groove and turned around, but before the thing could let out a squawk Angelica was there, lifting it off again. Nancy turned once more and came back.

'Look,' said Angelica, 'I've had a hard day—'

Nancy put the needle on.

Angelica yanked it off, lifted the record clear and whanged it into a dozen pieces against the phonograph lid. '– and I'm *tired*,' she said. 'Now do you understand?'

Nancy said nothing. She took the camera in both hands and hopped backwards, the strap pulling Angelica along with it till it slipped over her head. She dropped the camera and got in one kick before Angelica hit her low and they rolled over together, hands clawing for hair, shrieking like broken hinges.

Kip found the doorframe behind him and climbed it unsteadily. He sorted out his directions again, got to the middle of the floor and leaned for a grip on Angelica.

She was slippery as a fish inside that coat, but he got a double handful of fur and heaved her up kicking. Then somebody tripped him and he landed hard on the camera with warm flesh kneeing the daylights out of him. When he tried to sit up an elbow caught him under the chin, and on the way down again fingernails raked across his nose. The floor went crump against his skull, like a carpet-covered brickbat.

When he knew which way was up again, he crawled out from under, but the door he opened was the wrong one and he was sick in the hall.

Somebody kicked a garbage can and the echoes tolled down the dark street.

Kip sat on the cold stone steps with his head in his hands, the night air feathering through his fingers, listening to the emptiness inside him. He was sick lonely drunk, and his head was a bruise, but the voices were gone; he was a hollow house again, grimed and hollow, hollow and cold.

Too much for them. Wanted a fight but couldn't take the lumps; wanted the drunk but not the sick.

Or maybe they were just ready to go. None of them stayed long, any more; he'd had – how many gangs of them since Tuesday? Lost count.

But it never took long to replace them, either.

So he sat, in his five minutes of sanity, and faced the thing he didn't want to remember he didn't want to know.

Angelica.

He knew already what was happening to him; had known for a long time. Every new invasion was scummier than the last; he was getting warts and wrinkles and hickeys and heartburn and dandruff and scabby patches and ingrown toe-nails and probably worse to come. He was a run-down old mansion, subdivided into cold-water flats and then hall bedrooms full of transients with holes in their socks. He had been a valuable property once, and his owners had taken care of him. Now he was depreciating.

Down the rocky road to ruin. There was no use trying to kick them out any more; there wasn't time enough and they went when they were ready, anyhow. The way he was now, all he could do was hang onto the little scrap they had left him of himself, fight them off when they had something particularly scurvy for him to do. And soon enough, he wouldn't even be able to do that. Goodbye scrap; hello zombie.

And all that he had accepted. Because he was a coward, probably.

But Angelica.

Angelica had been following him down that road step by step, thoroughbred to cur, saint to slime. And now that he realized he had known it all the time, it was obvious enough: She was possessed too; so was Nancy, and he couldn't prove it, but he knew in his guts that so was nearly everybody. When you thought about how many people had died on this planet since Ug the Caveman, and how few of them would qualify for any heavenly establishment that there happened to be, it was a wonder they weren't swarming in every living human skull like maggots in offal.

How many damned souls could dance on the point of a pinhead?

And what was he going to *do*? Good God, no wonder they had quarantined him; he was a carrier of infection. No. He was a run-down house, and he was lowering the values of all the real estate around him, the whole neighborhood. And the neighborhood was Angelica, and Nancy.

Nancy didn't seem much changed – she was back to sub-normal, that was all, after that one day when she'd pulled herself together with both hands to help him. Maybe her tenants were the old maids, too stubborn to move, who live on in the old house when all around them has gone to tenements and weeds. But Angelica's weren't.

Slum clearance.

When a neighborhood starts downhill, can you stop it? Sometimes. Maybe.

If you tear down the right house.

Drunk … Thoughts spinning in his head, smooth and fuzzy-bright, every-thing clear now except around the edges, but he was top-heavy and tangled and when he went to stand up, his knees bent the wrong way. Couldn't find the drugstore without a searchlight … couldn't see to read the labels, find out what was poison. And his time was running out.

Up the steps, skinning his knee when he fell. Across the lobby by dead-reckoning, mothball and dust smell in his nostrils, and up the stairs because you couldn't get lost on a staircase as long as you could tell up from down; and because there would have to be something in the suite, razor blade, something; and if there wasn't, there would be the window.

And, all right, because he wanted to see them again before he died. Both of them, Angelica and Nancy, the woman he'd loved and the woman who'd loved him. All the world there was.

The sitting room was dark except when the reflected pink glow of a neon sign flickered into it. He lurched around the wreck of Nancy's throne and plunged into the cold hollow behind the couch, padding at the floor for his forgotten duffel bag. Hypo ought to be still in there; good as anything, if he could find the vein – barrelful of air, embolism, stop the heart quick and clean.

There was the bag, and the hypo wasn't in it, nothing but a bottle too big to have anything useful inside. He held it up to the window and squinted at it. Not drugs; what?

Prune juice and vitamin. That was right; he'd put the thing in the bag along with all the other junk for no reason except he didn't want to leave it behind. And here it was.

'One drink is half a drink …'

Who—? Oh, sure, the spirit message. Meaning the vitamins? K. M., Kip Morgan, one drink is half a drink –

'Two drinks is a drink too much …'

Sure. Why not? Little blue people sitting in the driver's seat in Madame Rayma's head, too. The wraiths of spiritualists – there was a laugh for you if you had room for it – making up that godawful childish gabble, contradict-ing each other sixty miles a minute. And once in a while, once in a long while passing on a message that meant something.

That would be what they wanted, too – 'they,' the things that made the quarantine to keep him from telling what he knew. A drink too much. The last one. Simple: An overdose of the vitamin would be poison.

With the cap off, he hesitated. Call them in? What for, to make a deathbed speech, ten immortal words with a hiccup in the middle?

The monkeys had died in convulsions. The hell with it, the hell with it he didn't have time to be nice.

He hesitated again. After he corked off, with his soul the dirty gray it no doubt was by now, would he find himself roosting in somebody's fusty cranium, scrabbling among the old habits and desires?

Ask me no questions and I'll tell you no lies. Never mind where the stuff comes from or what it's going to do to you; it's right off the bathtub; if you've got a weak stomach, hold your nose.

He put the bottle up, filled his mouth and swallowed. It went down like bile coming up, and some of it got caught in his windpipe.

Choking, he reeled to his knees and swept the lamp off the end table, the cord gripping him in the middle as he fell. He let it all go, legs, arms and the whole articulated bundle of guts: sorry now with a choked sorrow and glad with a bitter gladness that he was about to be rid of it.

He was beginning to feel a little dizzy and numb, and if this was dying it wasn't bad. But it seemed to him that this was a way he had felt once before; he was afraid of it without knowing why. Then he heard the murmuring begin, and even then he didn't understand, though he sensed that the voices weren't inside him—

The ceiling light blinked on. Nancy stood in the hall doorway looking down at him. And on her shoulders crouched four tiny smoke-blue figures.

Two on the left, witch-wives with trap-thin mouths, chanting, 'It's a sin! It's a sin!'

Two on the right, sluttish and slavering: 'Do it! *Do* it!'

The voices swelled, more of them and more, from every direction – through the walls, the floor, the ceiling.

Whatever Nancy was saying was drowned in the din. Now he saw Angelica coming up behind her, and *she* had ghostly shapes crowding her shoulders ...

A *drink too much.*

The street was no better. Hands futilely over his ears, mouth open in a silent shout, he ran loose-kneed and wobbling to his parked car, tumbled in headfirst, started the engine on the third try, clashed gears and drove like a madman down Figueroa.

Instinct had chosen the direction; twenty-odd blocks later he came to sanctuary – the U.S.C. campus. He drove into it as far as he could go and stopped, trembling over the wheel.

He was inhabited again. He could hear the nasty little voices yattering away inside him; but that was a thing he was used to, and by contrast it was almost pleasant.

He knew now that there were worse things than being infected by a corporal's guard of barflies, alley thugs and panders. It was a swift short slide down to where he was; there were depths below as black and hollow as a starless night, and people *lived* there, married and had children, paid their rent and taxes, walked in the free air, and nobody hauled them off to shock treatments or manacles.

What it must be like to have the curse of hearing in a hospital for the insane, he was unable to imagine.

It was no longer any cause for wonder that the books most normal people bought and the movies they paid to see were strictly and by definition psychoneurotic, nor that the laws made by the people for the people were an Iron Maiden, nor that a streetful of honest citizens could erupt into a roaring mob. The wonder was that there was any sanity in the universe.

Think. Think.

While one part of his mind scurried like a trapped rat, another part was coldly and curiously turning over the jumbled jigsaw pieces of his world, matching them to make a new pattern:

The curious blankness you saw behind the eyes of John Doe, the colorless, not-smart-not-stupid man who sold you groceries or filled your gas tank: the automatic ABC responses and the meaningless smile. X marks my window: a transient hotel. Too many tenants; too many faces superimposed make a blur.

Compulsive drinkers, rapists, desk-tidiers: they got no pleasure from it. But somebody did.

Déjà vu. You had never been there before; but somebody had.

Allergies, functional disorders, 'psychomatic' illnesses. Symptoms of struggle between the possessor and the possessed. Or: the tenant was a cotton farmer and hated wool, a housewife and hated dust, a bird-lover and hated cats.

The even dispositions, the inner assurances of people in caste trades and family seats. Memory is not inherited, but tenants can be, and over generations, inhabiting members of the same family, they might shake down into stable, well-adjusted groups that would cause no trouble.

The high incidence of neurosis, insecurity feelings, melancholia and all the skull-shoppers' bag of tricks in world-cities, where established groups of tenants break and mingle disastrously.

Homosexuality: the result of a sorority housed in a man or a fraternity in a woman?

The unearthly peace that you sometimes found in people who had suffered long and severely. Solution: to be unpossessed, be a house that nobody would want to live in.

Or jump out a window, or cut your throat with a razor blade.

Not yet. Follow the argument, add up the data.

If there isn't an answer, the quarantine was for nothing.

He had been thinking about the bottom half of the human pyramid, because that was where he was now and because the algebraic pressures squeezed out monsters there; it was natural enough. What about the top half?

There were people who had twisted circuits inside their heads, quirks that made them automatically the wrong shape to fit into any situation, square when they ought to be round and round when they ought to be square. And there were people who slipped through life as if all the doors had been cut and hung especially for them. The people who were born to prosperous parents in a prosperous country; who had sound bones and clear skins and white teeth; who never had to worry about the price of a meal; who never missed trains unless there was going to be a wreck; who lived a long time and enjoyed it all. The tall, straight, unwrinkled, lucky people.

The carefully built and tended mansions of the idle dead.

Item: The quarantine was not a thing imposed spontaneously by each new gang of tenants; it couldn't be, it worked too smoothly. It was organized, and that meant that somewhere there had to be an organizer.

Where?

Why, in the handsomest, the healthiest, the richest and happiest human being ...

The torrent of voices rustled down over him again as soon as he drove out of the campus. Each tiny crepitant note was distinct and clear; it was no good shutting his ears against them and they knifed through any distraction the mind made; he had to listen, writhing behind the wheel.

> *Rip her with your*
> *die in agony for they are*
> *dripping raw and eat it*
> *trying to breathe while*
> *where it's dark and the rats*
> *tell him to his face*
> *lights fire and KILL THEM ALL*

Thicker and thicker, more and more, as if the street were tilting downward into the more and more intolerable pressures of an ocean of voices. Straight back into the center, to the hotel, because that was where ...

But he mustn't think that.

Into the lobby, up the stairs against a turbulent river of voices. Lean against the door, heavy and slow, seaweed tendrils of sound weaving around him ...

In the underwater darkness he found the hard cold shape and put it in his pocket. Forget it.

When the light went on in Angelica's room she sat up in bed, her mouth opening with hard lines around it, but it closed again when she saw his face.

He dropped to his knees beside the stacks of photographs and spilled them onto the floor in a glossy kaleidoscope of faces and bosoms.

He pawed one out, then another. He tossed photographs aside in fluttering windrows, scrabbled again, stirred the mass with both hands. At last he had a thin sheaf of pictures in one fist; with the other hand he reached out to the dressing table, dragged Angelica's handbag off and shook it upside down.

He picked a fountain pen out of the resulting tangle, circled a face on each of his photographs, lurched to his feet and shoved the handful at Angelica.

'Addresses,' he said. 'On the backs.'

She hesitated. He leaned closer. 'Do it *now*.'

She glanced at the top picture, flipped it over, scribbled on the back, and went through the rest of the sheaf in the same way.

When he took them, she gave him a look of unwilling respect and said, 'What for?'

He didn't answer. The effort was too much; he was half-drowned again in the surge of voices, staggering out into the hall, down the murmurous stairs, into the night.

The world-famous director was not at home. Neither was the foreign-born, much-married writer, and Angelica's notation for the rising young beauty queen said only 'H'wood Hills, off Cahuenga.' But Taylor Spotswood III was asleep in his bed.

Spotswood, dark-haired and muscled like a swimmer, was built on a scale that dwarfed Kip, and the bed was big enough for six of him. Kip inched across the laundry-slick sheets and got the chloroform-soaked pad over his mouth and nose.

When his breathing slackened, the room was very quiet. Silver moonlight dappled the floor. It was a big sturdy house that stood on its own hundred acres, the servants were off in another wing, and the only voices Kip could hear came from the unconscious man's body. '... *verna effrenata mmmmmmm tant pis, on ne pent pas mmmm captus membris mmmmmm delenda est.*'

'Come out,' said Kip through dry lips. 'I want to talk to you.' He put the point of his open claspknife to the sleeping giant's chest and exerted a gentle pressure.

Three tiny heads popped into sight, glowing a swampfire blue in the darkness. They might have been brothers: all three had the same spiderweb tracery of microsharp wrinkles, the same lipless mouths, the same brilliant eyes. One turned to the others and remarked. '*Nequissimus.*' Another answered, '*Heu nefas!*' and added a short sentence in a totally unfamiliar language, at which all three briefly showed smiles like half-healed wounds; and the third asked coolly, 'What do you wish?'

'You know what I want,' said Kip, his hand white-knuckled on the knife handle. 'Don't waste time.'

'We have all the time in the world,' said the spokesman simply. 'You cannot cut any of it away with that tool. Therefore, be more respectful.' And his eyes glowed like spectral cigarette-ends.

'I can send you househunting, though,' said Kip. 'But the knife is just to make sure you hold still and listen. This is what I brought to bargain with.' He showed them a little bottle that had once contained sedative capsules; now it was full of a murky brown fluid.

The three glared at him, but the spokesman's voice was as cold and dry as ever. 'Even supposing that the power to grant your desire exists, which is absurd, we are only three retired gentlemen; we could not help you. What have you done with the rest of that, by the way?'

'Mailed it to myself,' said Kip. 'The power to make me and my friends invisible to every living soul in the City of Los Angeles exists, and if that's absurd, laugh now and get it over with. Somebody was afraid I'd tell what this stuff does. The same somebody only has to say frog and every spook in sight jumps twice. And if you're not that somebody, you're as near as I can get and you'll have to do. I think you are. I think the longer a tenant hangs around, the more he he learns about possession and dispossession, till the oldest ones can kick anybody out who doesn't toe the line. I think you're the oldest; if there were ever any older than you, they broke down into ash and stink a long time ago. But whether I'm right or wrong, either there'll be a new system of housing allotments – with everybody getting the tenants who'll do him the least harm and the most good – or I'll pour this stuff down the throat of your friend here. And when you move, as you'll have to, I'll follow you where ever-you go. I'll find you. I'll find you and I'll do it again. If I run out of the vitamin, I'll make more. And even if you do get out of my reach, I'll make such a stink and I'll give so many people the sight and the hearing that I'll pull your whole damned applecart down around your ears. Now. Yes or no.'

The three whispered together with a sound like dry twigs cracking and rattling in the wind. The spokesman said, 'We are disposed to deal gently with you, but a bargain that is all upon one side is no bargain. Next, the terms you propose are beyond reason and your need. We will restore yourself and the two women, no more, in exchange for certain services. Think how you answer; the offer will be made only once. And eternity is long.'

'Longer than common to a houseless haunt,' said Kip. 'Don't talk bar-room law to me; this is a *pactum donationis*, since you like Latin, or you can call it blackmail, I don't care. All or nothing. One.' He pried open the sleeping mans jaws. 'Two.' He lifted the bottle and twirled the cap loose with his thumb.

The three consulted with a glance.

'We agree,' said the spokesman.

It was too easy. 'Swear,' said Kip, 'by—' By what?

A whisper stirred in his mind, perhaps from the same – person – who had spoken through Madame Rayma; and he thought: *George?*

'Swear,' he said, 'by your hope of oblivion.'

The old ones had their ounce of revenge, after all; nature abhors a *pactum donationis*. The quarantine lifted when Kip left the house, newly equipped with a set of four chatty but good-natured ghosts; the caretaker spotted him, chased him to his car, and the State cops ran him down just outside the city limits. Nancy and Angelica were discovered by an astonished bellhop, and they were all three a one-day wonder in the newspapers: LAW STUDENT BURGLES ESTATE WHILE SWEETHEARTS SQUAT IN BRIDAL SUITE. Kip and Angelica lost their jobs; Nancy's mother threw seventeen successive catfits and placed herself under the care of a gentleman who combined Scientology with Yoga.

Kip got out of jail last; they hadn't been able to prove that he had entered the building or chloroformed the owner, but they had thrown the book at him for concealed weapons (the clasp-knife), leaving the scene of an accident (a broken gate) and resisting arrest.

He found Angelica packing. She had, she told him curtly, been offered a wonderful job with a trade mission in Chile. It was a great opportunity; it could lead almost anywhere. She was the same heartsqueezing Angelica, compact, graceful, honest, assured. But there was something wrong. She had hardened; she was a bisque doll with Swiss watch-works inside.

He listened to the voices that came from her – he had been waiting for just that; he wanted to be sure. And there was nothing wrong with the voices.

The bargain had been kept; there was no one inside Angelica whispering songs of ambition to her inner ear.

There never had been.

That was Angelica; that was what she was really like in the deepest deep of herself, and only the difference now was that she was free to be it without scruples or hesitations.

And the ounce of revenge was a pound.

… Until he met a redhead waiting in the pro shop at the country club when he went back to collect his things.

She had red hair: not carrot-color, and not henna-color, but the real, dark, glossy mahogany red that you see once in a lifetime. And she had the pale skin that goes with it, clear and fine, with that rose-in-snow flush glowing through it. And her eyes were big and bright and about to brim over.

He took a step toward her; there was a hurting in his throat. He said, '*Nancy?*'

She said, 'Kip,' the one word, and he knew; it was all there. It was the same voice that had said '*f* of *t*' when it meant more than 'the love of God'; those where the same hands, hardly changed though they were slender now where they had been thin, that had been about him all the time, praying, yearning to help. It was the same love, not bottled up now but flowing free.

A little later, he took the bottle out of his pocket; the police had given it back to him finally, not being able to find any poison, illegal drug or other contraband in it. It had just about a mouthful in it: one drink.

He had listened to Nancy's voices; he knew all he had to know.

He swallowed it.

Three drinks is no drink ...

The voices stopped.

GOD'S NOSE

'God's nose,' said my Zen Catholic friend, waving her expressive little hands, 'to begin with, must be the biggest nose you can imagine. In fact, theology and mathematics teach us that it must be infinite in size. Just think – bigger than the Sun, bigger than comets, galaxies – and still … a nose.'

The idea pleased her; she closed her eyes and smiled, squinting blindly up at the ceiling. Her neck was not quite clean. She was charming, black-haired, brown skinned, with a compact little body that was feminine without being unnecessarily soft. Her hands were like some small, friendly animal's – the palms wide, fingers and thumbs short, soft-padded, with sharp-pointed nails from which the red lacquer was peeling.

We were waiting in a friend's apartment for her lover to arrive, a man I had not met. We were sitting on cushions, tailor-fashion, since our absent friend owned no furniture. We had each had several glasses of Smirnoff's vodka mixed with orange soda. How the subject of God's nose had come up, I do not at this moment recall.

'Picture it in your mind,' she said. 'A good way to begin is to think of George Washington's nose.'

'Washington's nose?'

'On Mount Rushmore,' she answered impatiently. 'That big sunlit stone nose, tall as a building, with a little man swinging on a scaffolding beside it – looking like a fly. Now: think of that nose, only enormously bigger, out there in the light of the stars – a nose so huge that our whole solar system would be like a wart.' Eyes still closed, she shivered with pleasure.

'Does God's nose, then, have warts?' I asked her.

'No, evidently not, because a wart is an imperfection, and God's nose must be perfect. But pores? Hairs in the nostrils? Yes, obviously! And each pore, each hair, must be an absolutely perfect hair, or pore.'

'I'm not sure I like the idea of God having a nose,' I said.

'Then you're not getting the picture. Imagine being out there in a space-ship, near enough to see that nose looming over you – eternal, mysterious. You steer your spaceship parallel to the nose' – her hands showed me how – 'trying to get from the tip to the bridge. But you know you never can, because it would take too long – you'd die of old age first.'

She opened her eyes. 'Doesn't that make you feel pretty humble?'

'It certainly does,' I said. The tasteless vodka, or else the sickly sweet orange soda, had given everything in the room an unusual color and sharpness of outline. I felt that my Zen Catholic friend's words were nonsense, but a special, very valuable kind of nonsense which I must try to hang onto.

'People spend so much time worrying about the Creation,' she said abruptly.

'I don't.'

She made an impatient gesture. 'People who think, I mean. Where did all the stars and planets come from, they ask? All the clouds of gas in the Milky Way? All the comets and meteorites?'

'Well, where did they come from?'

'Do you know what I think?' she asked intensely, leaning forward. I half expected to see that her eyes had slitted yellow pupils, like a cat's, but they were brown, so nearly black that you could not tell where the iris left off and the pupil began. They seemed all pupil – two enormous round black holes staring at me.

'I think,' she said reverently, 'that God sneezed.'

There was a click and a sound of footsteps in the hall. My friend got to her feet in one eager motion. 'Hello!' she called.

'Hello!' a deeper voice echoed. A man came into the room, smiling, dressed in a torn white shirt, sandals, faded dungarees.

My friend put her arm around him, smiling. 'This is Godfrey,' she said.

We shook hands, and I am afraid I stared in fascination. Godfrey had the largest, most overbearing nose I have ever seen. It was nobly arched, thin, sensitive, with flaring nostrils. The rest of his face, with its pale brown mustache and beard, was hardly large enough to support it.

'We have to go now,' my friend said, smiling, holding Godfrey's bicep with one possessive hand. After a few minutes, discovering that I did not want any more vodka or orange soda, I followed them down the stairs into the warm sunlight, thinking very curious and pleasant thoughts.

CATCH THAT MARTIAN

The first person who got on the Martian's nerves, according to a survey I made just recently, was a Mrs Frances Economy, about 42, five foot three, heavy-set, with prominent mole on left cheek, formerly of 302 West 46th Street, Manhattan. Mrs Economy went to a neighborhood movie on the night of September 5th, and halfway through the first feature, just as she was scrabbling for the last of her popcorn, zip – she wasn't there any more.

That is, she was only half there. She could still see the screen, but it was like a television set with the sound off. The way she realized something had happened to her, she started stomping her feet, like you do when the sound goes off or the picture stops, and her feet didn't make any noise.

In fact, she couldn't feel the floor, just some kind of rubbery arms of her chair. They weren't there, as far as her feeling them went.

Everything was dead still. She could hear her own breathing, and the gulp when she swallowed that last mouthful, and her heart beating if she listened close. That was all. When she got up and went out, she didn't step on anybody's feet – and she *tried* to.

Of course I asked her who was sitting next to her when it happened, but she doesn't remember. She didn't notice. It was like that with everybody.

Not to keep you in suspense, the Martian did it. We figured that out later. There still isn't any proof, but it has to be that way. This Martian, the way it figures, looks just like anybody else. He could be the little guy with the derby hat and the sour expression, or the girl with the china-blue eyes, or the old gent with the chin spinach and glasses on a string. Anybody.

But he's a Martian. I don't see what else he *could* be. And being a Martian, he's got this power that people haven't got. If he feels like it, he just looks at you cockeyed, and zip – you're in some other dimension. I don't know what the scientists would call it, the Fourth or Fifth Dimension or what, but I call it the next-door dimension because it seems like it's right next door – you can see into it. In other words, it's a place where other people can see you, but they can't hear you or touch you, unless they're ghosts too, and there's nothing but some kind of cloudy stuff to walk around on. I don't know if that sounds good or what. It stinks. It's just plain dull.

One more thing, he annoys easy. You crunch popcorn in his ear, he doesn't like that. You step on his toe, same thing. Say, 'Hot enough for you?' or slap him on the back when he's got sunburn, serve him a plate of soup with your finger in it – zip.

The way we figured out it's a Martian was that it couldn't be one of us. No human can do a thing like that. Right? So what else could he be but a Martian? It figures. And nobody ever noticed him, so it must be he looks like anybody else. Some humans, they look like everybody else, but not because they want to. He *wants* to, I bet.

The way we know he annoys easy, there were eighteen 'ghosts' wandering around when the public first noticed, which was during the early morning of September 6th. That was about eleven hours after he got Mrs Economy.

Thirteen of them were up at Broadway and 49th, walking through traffic. They went right through the cars. By nine o'clock there were two wrecks on that corner and a busted hydrant gushing water all over. The ghost people walked through the water and didn't get wet.

Three more showed up in front of a big delicatessen near 72nd Street and Amsterdam Avenue, just looking in the window. Every once in a while one of them would reach in through the glass and grab for something, but his hand went through the pastrami and chopped liver, so none of them got anything. That was fine for store windows, but it wasn't so fine for the ghost people.

The other two were sailors. They were out in the harbor, walking on water and thumbing their noses at naval officers aboard the ships that were anchored out there. It was hell on discipline.

The first eight patrolmen who reported all this got told they would be fired if they ever came on duty drunk again. But by ten-thirty it was on the radio, and then WPIX sent a camera crew up, and by the time the afternoon papers came out there were so many people in Times Square that we had to put a cordon around the ghosts and divert traffic.

The delicatessen window up on Amsterdam got busted from the crowd leaning against it, or some guy trying to put his hand through the way the three ghosts did; we never figured out which. There were about sixty tugs, launches and rowboats in the harbor, and three helicopters, trying to get close enough to talk to the sailors.

One thing we know, the Martian must have been in that crowd on Times Square, because between one and one-thirty P.M. seven more ghosts wandered through the barrier and joined the other ones. You could tell they were mad, but of course you couldn't tell what they were saying unless you could read lips.

Then there were some more down by Macy's in the afternoon, and a few in Greenwich Village, and by evening we had lost count. The guesses in the papers that night ran from three hundred to a thousand. It was the *Times* that said three hundred. The cops didn't give out any estimate at all.

The next day, there was just nothing else at all in the papers, or on the radio or TV. Bars did an all-time record business. So did churches.

The Mayor appointed a committee to investigate. The Police Commissioner called out special reserves to handle the mobs. The Governor was understood to say he was thinking about declaring a statewide emergency, but all he got in most papers was half a column among the ads. Later on he denied the whole thing.

Everybody had to be asked what he thought, from Einstein to Martin and Lewis. Some people said mass hysteria, some said the end of the world, some said the Russians.

Winchell was the first one to say in print that it was a Martian. I had the same idea myself, but by the time I got it all worked out I was too late to get the credit.

I was handicapped, because all this time I still hadn't seen one of the ghosts yet. I was on Safe, Loft and Truck – just promoted last spring from a patrolman – and while I was on duty I never got near any of the places where they were congregating. In the evenings, I had to take care of my mother.

But my brain was working. I had this Martian idea, and I kept thinking, thinking, all the time.

I knew better than to mention this to Captain Rifkowicz. All I would have to do was mention to him that I was thinking, and he would say, 'With what, Dunlop, with what?' or something sarcastic like that. As for asking him to get me transferred to Homicide or Missing Persons, where I might get assigned to the ghost case, that was out. Rifkowicz says I should have been kept on a beat long enough for my arches to fall, in order to leave more room on top for brains.

So I was on my own. And that evening, when they started announcing the rewards, I knew I had to get that Martian. There was fifteen hundred dollars, voted by the City Council that afternoon, for whoever would find out what was making the ghosts and stop it. Because if it didn't stop, there would be eighteen thousand ghosts in a month, and over two hundred thousand in a year.

Then there was a bunch of private rewards, running from twenty-five bucks to five hundred, offered by people that had relatives among the departed. There was a catch to those, though – you had to get the relatives back.

All together, they added up to nearly five thousand. With that dough, I could afford to hire somebody to take care of Ma and maybe have some private life of my own. There was a cute waitress down on Varick Street, where I had lunch every day. For a long time I had been thinking if I asked her to go out, maybe she would say yes. But what was the use of me asking her, if all I could do was have her over to listen to Ma talk? All Ma talked about was how sick she was and how nobody cared.

First thing I did, I got together all the newspaper stuff about the ghosts. I spread it out on the living room table and sorted it and started pasting it into a scrapbook. Right away I saw I had to have more information. What was in the papers was mostly stories about the crowds and the accidents and traffic tie-ups, plus interviews with people that didn't know anything.

What I wanted to know was – what were all these people doing when the Martian got them? If I knew that, maybe I could figure out some kind of a pattern, like if the Martian's pet peeve was back-slappers, or people who make you jump a foot when they sneeze, or whatever.

Another thing, I wanted to know all the times and places. From that, I could figure out what the Martian's habits were, if he had any, and with all of it together I could maybe arrange to be on the spot whenever he got sore. Then anybody except me who was there every time would have to be him.

I explained all this to Ma, hoping she would make a sacrifice and let me get Mrs Proctor from across the hall to sit with her a few evenings. She didn't seem to get the idea. Ma never believes anything she reads in the papers, anyway, except the astrology column. The way it struck her, the whole thing was some kind of a scheme, like gangsters or publicity, and I would be better to stay away from it.

I made one more try, talking up the money I would get, but all she said was, 'Well, then why don't you just *tell* that Captain Rifkowicz he's got to *let* you earn that reward?'

Ma has funny ideas about a lot of things. She came over here from England when she was a girl, and it looks like she never did get to understand America. I knew that if I kept after her, she would start crying and telling me about all the things she did for me when I was a baby. You can't argue against that.

So what I did next, I took the bull by the horns. I waited till Ma went to sleep and then I just walked out and hopped an uptown bus on Seventh Avenue. If I couldn't get off during the daytime, I would cut down my sleep for a while, that was all.

I was heading for Times Square, but at Twenty-seventh I saw a crowd on the sidewalk. I got out and ran over there. Sure enough, in the middle of the crowd was two of the ghosts, a fat man with a soupstrainer mustache and a skinny woman with cherries on her hat. You could tell they were ghosts because the people were waving their hands through them. Aside from that, there was no difference.

I took the lady first, to be polite. I flashed the badge, and then I hauled out my notebook and wrote, 'Name and address please,' and shoved it at her.

She got the idea and looked through her bag for a pencil and an envelope. She scribbled, 'Mrs Walter F. Walters, Schenectady, N. Y.'

I asked her, 'When did this happen to you and where?'

She wrote it was about one P.M. the afternoon before, and she was in Schrafft's on Broadway near 37th, eating her lunch with her husband, and I asked her if the fat man was her husband, and she said he was.

I then asked her if she could remember exactly what the two of them were doing right at the moment it happened. She thought a while and then said she was talking and her husband was dunking his doughnut in his coffee. I asked her if it was the kind with powdered sugar and she said yes.

I knew then that I was on the right track. She was one of those little women with big jaws that generally seem to have loud voices and like to use them; and I always hated people who dunk those kind of doughnuts, myself. The powdered sugar gets wet and gluey and the dunkers have to lick their fingers right in public.

I thanked them and went on uptown. When I got back home that night, about four A.M. the next morning, I had fifteen interviews in my book. The incidents had taken place all over the mid-town area. Six got theirs for talking, four on crowded sidewalks – probably for jostling or stepping on corns – two for yelling on a quiet street at two in the morning, one for dunking, one for singing to himself on a subway, one, judging by the look of him, for not being washed, and one for coming in late to a Broadway play. The six talkers broke down to three in restaurants, two in a newsreel movie, and one in Carnegie Hall while a concert was going on.

Nobody remembered who they were next to at the time, but I was greatly encouraged. I had a hunch I was getting somewhere already.

I got through the next day, the eighth, in a kind of daze, and don't think Rifkowicz didn't call my attention to it. I suppose I wasn't worth more than a nickel to the City that day, but I promised myself I would make it up later. For the moment, I ignored Rifkowicz.

On the radio and TV, there were two new developments. In my head, there was one.

First, the radio and TV. I ate lunch in a saloon so as to catch the latest news, even though I had to give up my daily glimpse of the waitress in the beanery. Two things were new. One, people had started noticing that a few things had turned into ghosts – besides people, I mean. Things like a barrel organ, and an automobile that had its horn stuck, and like that.

That made things twice as bad, of course, because anybody was liable to try to touch one of these ghost things and jump to the conclusion they were a ghost, themselves.

Two, the TV reporters were interviewing the ghosts, the same way I did, with paper and pencil. I picked up four more sets of questions and answers just while I was eating lunch.

The ghosts came over fine on TV, by the way. Somehow it looked even creepier on the screen, when you saw somebody's hand disappear into them, than it did when you saw it with your own eyes.

The development in my head was like this. Out of the fifteen cases I already had, and the four I got from TV, there were eight that happened on the street or in subways or buses, five in restaurants, and six in places of entertainment. Four *different* places of entertainment. Now, at first glance, that may not look like it means much. But I said to myself, 'What does this Martian do? He travels around from one place to another – that's normal. He eats – that's normal. But he goes to four different shows that I know about in three days – and I know just nineteen cases out of maybe a thousand!'

It all fitted together. Here is this Martian. He's never been here before. We know that because he just now started making trouble. The way I see it, these Martians look us over for a while from a distance, and then they decide to send one Martian down to New York to study us close up. Well, what's the first thing he does, being that he wants to find out all about us? He goes to the movies. And concerts and stage plays too, of course, because he wants to try everything once. But probably he sees two or three double features a day. It stands to reason.

So there he is in the movie, watching and listening so he shouldn't miss anything important, and some customer around him starts making loud comments to somebody else, rattling cellophane, and snapping a pocketbook open and shut every five seconds to find a kleenex. So he flips them into the next dimension, where they can make all the noise they want without bothering him.

And that's the reason why there are so many ghosts that got theirs in the movies and places like that. On the streets of any city you can walk for miles without running into more than two or three really obnoxious characters, but in any kind of theater there's *always* somebody talking, or coughing, or rattling paper. You've noticed that.

I went even further than that. I checked with my notes and then looked in a copy of *Cue* magazine to find out what was playing at each of those theaters when the Martian was there.

I found out that the play was a long-run musical – the concert was musical, naturally – and one of the two movies was a Hollywood remake of a musical comedy. The other was a newsreel.

There it was. I as good as had him. Then I got another idea and went back through my notes to find out where the theater victims had been sitting. The guy in Carnegie Hall had been in the balcony; that's where you hear best, I guess. But the other five had all been sitting down front, in the first four rows.

The little guy was near-sighted.

That's the way I was thinking about him now – a little near-sighted guy who liked music better than Westerns, and was used to some place where everybody's careful not to bother anybody else. It was hard not to feel sorry for him; after all, some people that come from places closer than Mars have a hard time in New York.

But it was me against him. That night the total rewards were up to almost twenty thousand dollars.

I thought of one thing I could do right away. I could write to the Mayor to make an announcement that if people didn't want to be ghosts, they should keep from making unnecessary noise or being pests, especially in theaters. But one, he probably wouldn't pay any attention to me, and two, if he did, twenty thousand other guys would be following my lead before I could turn around, and one of them would probably catch the Martian before I did.

That night, I did the same as before. I waited till Ma was sleeping, then went out to a movie on Broadway. It was a first-run house, they had a musical playing, and I sat down front.

But nothing happened. The Martian wasn't there.

I felt pretty discouraged when I got home. My time was running out and there are over three hundred theaters in Manhattan. I had to start working faster.

I lay awake for a long while, worrying and thinking about it, and finally I came to one of the most important decisions in my life. The next morning I was going to do something I never did before – call in and pretend like I was sick. And I was going to stay sick until I found the Martian.

I felt bad about it and I felt even worse in the morning, when Rifkowicz told me to take it easy till I got well.

After breakfast, I got the papers and made a list of shows on my way uptown. I went to one on 42nd Street first – it was a musical picture about some composer named Handle, and the second feature was a comedy, but it had Hoagy Carmichael in it, so I figured I should stay for that too. I sat in the fifth row. There was plenty of coughing going on, only nobody got turned into a ghost.

Then I had lunch and went to another musical, on Broadway. I drew another blank.

My eyes were beginning to bother me a little from sitting so close to the screen, so I thought I would just go to a newsreel movie and then walk around a while before dinner. But when I got out of the newsreel I began to feel jittery, and I went straight to another double feature. The Martian wasn't there, either.

I had seen plenty of ghosts standing around on the streets, but they were all just standing there looking kind of lost and bewildered, the way they did after a while. You could tell a new victim because he would be rushing here and there, shoving his hands through things, trying to talk to people, and acting all upset.

One thing I forgot to mention. Everybody was wondering now how these ghosts got along without eating. In this dimension where they were, there wasn't *anything*, just the stuff like rubbery clouds that they were standing on. But they all claimed they weren't hungry or thirsty, and they all seemed to be in good shape. Even the ones that had been ghosts now for four days.

When I got out of that last movie, it was about eight in the evening. I was feeling low in my mind, but I still had a healthy appetite. I started wandering around the side streets of Broadway, looking for a restaurant that wasn't too crowded or too expensive. I passed a theater that was on my list, except I knew I was too late to get a ticket for it. It was the premiere of the newest Rodgers and Hammerstein show, and the lobby and half the sidewalk were full of customers.

I went on past, feeling gloomier because of all the bright lights and excitement, and then I heard something funny. Without paying any attention, I had been listening to one of these raspy-voiced barkers inside the lobby going, 'GETcha program here.' Now, all of a sudden, he said 'GETch—' and stopped.

I turned around, with a funny prickling up the back of my spine. The voice didn't start up again. Just as I started back toward the lobby, a ghost came out of the crowd. There was no doubt about him being a ghost – he ran through the people.

He had a bunch of big booklets with slick covers under his arm, and his mouth was wide open like he was shouting. Then he showed his teeth, and his face got all red, and he lifted the booklets in both hands and threw them away as hard as he could. *They* went through people, too.

The ghost walked away with his hands shoved into his pockets.

Running into that lobby, I shoved my badge at the ticket taker, and told him to find me the manager, quick.

When the manager came up I grabbed him by the lapels and said, 'I got reason to believe there's a dangerous criminal going to be in this audience tonight. With your cooperation, we'll get him.' He looked worried, so I said, 'There won't be any trouble. You just put me where I can see the front rows and leave the rest to me.'

He said, 'I can't give you a seat. The house is completely sold out.'

I told him, 'Okay, put me back in the wings, or whatever you call them.'

He argued, but he did what I asked. We went down the side aisle, through the orchestra pit and through a little door that went under the stage. Then we went up a little stairway to backstage, and he put me right at the edge of the stage, up front, where I could peek out at the audience.

There was a crowd of people running around back there behind the curtains, actors and chorus girls, guys in their shirt sleeves and guys in overalls.

I could hear the hum out front – people were beginning to fill the seats – and I wanted that curtain to go up. I just couldn't wait.

Finally the actors took their places, and the band suddenly started playing, and the curtain went up.

I understand that show is still playing to standing room only, even with all the trouble that's happened since then, but I didn't pay any attention to it and I couldn't even tell you what it was about. I was watching the front four rows, trying to memorize every face I saw.

Right in the middle there were three that I paid more attention to than the rest. One of them was a young blonde girl with blue eyes like the color of Ma's fancy china that she brought with her from the old country. Another was an old gent with a chin spinach and glasses on a string. The third was a little guy with a sour expression and a derby hat.

I don't know why I picked out those three, except maybe it was a hunch. Maybe I was looking at the blonde girl just because she was pretty, but then again, I never saw eyes that color before or since. It could be that Martians have china-blue eyes; how would I know? I might have had some wild idea that the old guy could be the Martian and was wearing the frizzy white whiskers because Martians don't have chins exactly like us. And I think I picked on the little guy because he fitted the picture I already had in my head. And the way he was clutching that derby in his lap, like it was made of gold – I was thinking to myself, maybe he's got some kind of ray gun built into that hat; maybe that's how he does it.

I admit that I wasn't thinking very logical – I was too excited – but I never took my eyes off that audience for a second.

I was waiting for somebody to start coughing or sneezing and get turned into a ghost. When that happened, I would be watching the people, and if I was lucky I might see who was looking at the victim when it happened.

That's what I was waiting for. What I got was a sniff of smoke and then somebody started screaming and yelling, 'Fire!'

Half the audience was on their feet in a second. I looked up, and sure enough there was smoke pouring out at the back of the room. Some more women screamed and the stampede was on.

The girls on stage stopped dancing and the band stopped playing. Somebody – some actor – ran out on the stage and started saying, 'Ladies and gentlemen, your attention please. *Walk*, do not run, to the nearest exit. There is no danger. *Walk*, do not run—'

I lost my head. Not on account of the fire. I knew the actor was right and the only bad thing that could happen would be people trampling each other to death to get out of there. But the seats were emptying fast and it struck me all of a sudden that I didn't know my way through that tangle of scenery backstage. By the time I got down the stairs and out into the auditorium, the Martian might be gone.

I felt cold all over. I didn't even stop to remember that I didn't have to go back the way I came, because there were little steps right at the side of the stage. I ran out from behind the wings and started to jump over the musicians. At that, I would have made it if I hadn't caught my toe in that little trough where the footlights are.

I had worse luck than that, even. I landed smack in the middle of the bass drum.

You never heard such a noise in your life. It sounded as if the ceiling caved in. Sitting there, with my legs and arms sticking out of that drum, I saw the people turn around and look at me like they had been shot. I saw them all, the girl with the china-blue eyes, the old gent with the whiskers, the little guy with the derby, and a lot more. And then, suddenly, all the sound stopped, same as when you turn off a radio.

The guy who owned the drum leaned over and tried to pull me out of it. He couldn't.

His hands went right through me.

Like I said, this Martian annoys easy. I don't know what he did about all those women screaming – maybe he figured there was a good reason for that and left them alone. But when I hit that bass drum, it must have burned him good. You know, when you're excited already, a loud noise will make you jump twice as far.

That's about the only satisfaction I got – that I probably annoyed him the worst of anybody in New York City.

That and being so close to catching him.

The company here is nothing to brag about – women that will talk your arm off and half your shoulder, and guys that say, 'Peaceful enough for you?' and back-slappers, and people that hum to themselves—

Besides that, the place is so damned dull. Clouds to stand on, nothing to eat even if you wanted to eat, and nothing to do except stand around and watch the new ones come through. We can't see much of New York any more, because it keeps getting mistier all the time – fading away, kind of, like maybe this dimension is getting a little farther away from the ordinary one every day.

I asked Mr Dauth yesterday how he thought the whole thing would wind up. Mr Dauth isn't bad. He's a big, cheerful guy, about fifty. The kind that likes good food and good beer and a lot of it. But he doesn't complain. He admits that his habit of sucking his teeth out real loud is aggravating and says maybe he deserved what he got, which you'll admit is big of him. So I talk to him a lot, and the other day, when we were watching a new batch that had just come through, I asked him where he thought it would all end, because we can hear each other, you see, being in the same dimension.

He pursed his lips and frowned like he was thinking it over, and then said that as far as he could see, there wasn't any human being that was perfect. Anybody is liable to do something aggravating sooner or later. That's the way people are.

'And this Martian of yours seems to be thorough,' he said. 'Very thorough. It might take him years to get through studying the Earth.'

'And then what?' I asked him.

'Well,' he said, 'eventually, if he keeps it up long enough, we'll *all* be over here.'

I hope he's right. Now that I come to think of it, that cute waitress I mentioned has a habit of setting down a coffee cup so half of it slops into the saucer. If Mr Dauth is right, all I've got to do is wait.

It stands to reason.

TURNING ON

CONTENTS

For Jim and Judy Blish
old and new friends

SEMPER FI

There was a brisk little wind up here, flipping the white silk of his trousers like flags against his body, ruffling his hair. Two thousand feet down past the dangling tips of his shoes, he could see the mountains spread out, wave after brilliant green wave. The palace was only a hollow square of ivory, tiny enough to squash between thumb and forefinger. He closed his eyes, drank the air with his body, feeling alive all the way to the tips of his fingers and toes.

He yawned, stretched with pleasure. It was good to get up here sometimes, away from all that marble and red velvet, the fountains, the girls in their gauzy pants … There was something about this floating, this complete solitude and peace.

An insect voice said apologetically, 'Pardon me, sir.'

He opened his eyes, looked around. There it was, the one he called the 'bug footman', three inches of slender body, a face half-human, half insect, wings a-blur, flying as hard as it could to stay in one place.

'You're early,' he said.

'No, sir. It's time for your therapy.'

'That's all I hear from you – time for therapy.'

'It's good for you, sir.'

'Well, no doubt you're right.'

'I'm sure I'm right, sir.'

'Okay. Get lost.'

The creature made a face at him, then veered away on the wind and diminished to a drifting speck of light. Gary Mitchell watched it until it was lost against the sunlit green background. Then he tilted lazily in the air, closed his eyes and waited for the change.

He knew to the second when it would happen. 'Big,' he said lazily, and felt the world contract suddenly around him. The wind was gone; mountains and sky were gone. He was breathing a more lifeless air. Even the darkness behind his eyelids was a different color.

He moved cautiously, feeling the padded couch under him. He opened his eyes. There was the same old room, looking so tiny and quaint that he snorted with amusement. It was always the same, no matter how often he came back to it. That struck him so funny that he rolled over, closing his eyes again, shaken with silent laughter.

After a minute he lay back, emptying his lungs with a grunt, then breathing deeply through his nostrils. He felt good, even though his body ached a little. He sat up and stared at the backs of his hands with amused affection. Same old hands!

He yawned hard enough to crack the cartilage in his jaw, then grinned and heaved himself up out of the hollow half-egg-shape of the couch. Wires and tubing trailed from him in all directions. He pulled the cap off his head, breaking it free of the tiny plastic sockets in his skull. He dropped it, let it swing at the end of its cable. He unfastened the monitoring instruments from his chest, pulled off the rest of his gear, and strode naked across the room.

There was a click from the master clock on the control board, and Mitchell heard the water begin to hiss in the bathroom. 'Suppose I don't want a shower?' he asked the clock. But he did; all according to routine.

He rubbed his palm over the stubble on his cheeks. Maybe he really should try to work out a gadget that would shave him while he was under the wire. A housing fitted to the lower part of his face, feedback to regulate the pressure ... But the damned thing might be more trouble than it was worth.

Staring at himself in the mirror, he saw a glint of delighted irony come into his eyes. Same old thoughts! He got out the razor and began to shave.

The clock ticked again as he came from the bathroom, and a tray slid out of the conveyor on to the breakfast table. Scrambled eggs, bacon, orange juice, coffee. Mitchell went to the closet, took out pale-blue slacks and shirt, dressed, then sat down and ate, taking his time. The food was food – nourishment; that was about all you could say.

When he was done, he lit a cigarette and sat with half-closed eyes, letting the smoke spurt in two streams from his nostrils. Vague images drifted through his mind; he did not try to capture them.

The cigarette was a stub. He sighed, put it out. As he walked to the door, it seemed to him that the couch and the control panel were staring at him reproachfully. There was something abandoned and pathetic in the empty egg-shape, the scattered wires. 'Tonight,' he promised it. He opened the door and stepped through.

Pale, yellow-tinged sunlight came from the big picture window overlooking the East River. The philodendron in the ceramic pot had unfurled another leaf. On the wall across from the window hung an enormous abstraction by Pollock, upside down. Mitchell gave it an ironic grin.

Reports in their orange plastic binders were piled on one side of the long mahogany desk, letters on the other. In the center, on the green blotter, lay a block of soft pine and an open jackknife.

The red light of the intercom was blinking steadily. Mitchell sat down and looked at it for a moment, then touched the button. 'Yes, Miss Curtis?'

'*Mr Price wants to know when you'll be available. Shall I tell him to come in?*'

'Okay.'

Mitchell picked up the top report, glanced at the sketches and diagrams inside, put it down again. He swiveled his chair around, leaned back and gazed sleepily out over the haze-yellowed landscape. A tug was moving slowly up the river, trailing puffs of yellow-white smoke. On the Jersey side, housing units stood like a child's building blocks; sunlight glinted from the tiny rows of windows.

Curious to see all that still here, still growing; on the other side, he had leveled it years ago, filled it in with jungle. There was something quaint about it now, like an old, yellowed snapshot. That was a little disturbing: coming back like this was always like re-entering the past. A faint sense of wrongness ...

He heard the door clock, and turned to see Jim Price with his hand on the knob. Mitchell grinned, waved a hand. 'Hello, boy – good to see you. Knock 'em dead in Washington?'

'Not exactly.' Price came forward with his heron's gait, folded himself into a chair, twitched, knotted his thin fingers together.

'Too bad. How's Marge?'

'Fine. I didn't see her last night, but she called this morning. She asked me to ask you—'

'Kids all right?'

'Sure.' Price's thin lips compressed; his brown eyes stared earnestly at Mitchell. He still seemed about twenty years old; to look at him, he had not changed since the days when Mitchell-Price, Inc., was an idea and a back room in Westbury. Only the clothes were different – the two-hundred-dollar suit, the perfectly knotted tie. And the fingernails; once they had been bitten to the quick, now they were manicured and shiny. 'Mitch, let's get down to it. How is that deep probe gadget coming?'

'Got Stevenson's report on my desk – haven't looked through it yet.'

Price blinked, shook his head. 'You realize that project has been dragging on thirty-six months?'

'There's time,' Mitchell said lazily. He reached for the knife and the block of wood.

'That's not the way you talked fifteen years ago.'

'I was an eager beaver then,' Mitchell said. He turned the block in his hands, feeling the little dusty burrs along the unfinished side. He set the blade against one edge, curled off the first long, sensuous shaving.

'Mitch, damn it, I'm worried about you – the way you've changed the last few years. You're letting the business slide.'

'Anything wrong with the earnings reports?' Mitchell felt the cut surface with his thumb, turning to gaze out of the window. It would be fun, he thought absently, to drift out into that hazy blue sky, over the tops of the toy buildings, still farther out, over the empty ocean ...

'We're making money, sure,' Price's thin voice said impatiently. 'On the mentigraph and the randomizer, one or two other little things. But we haven't put anything new on the market for five years, Mitch. What are we supposed to do, just coast? Is that all you want?'

Mitchell turned to look at his partner. 'Good old Jim,' he said affectionately. 'When are you ever going to loosen up?'

The door clicked open and a dark-haired girl stepped in – Lois Bainbridge, Price's secretary. 'Mr Price, sorry to interrupt, but Dolly couldn't get you on the intercom.'

Price glanced at Mitchell. 'Push the wrong button again?'

Mitchell looked at the intercom with mild surprise. 'Guess I did.'

'Anyway,' the girl said, 'Mr Diedrich is here, and you told me to tell you the minute—'

'Hell,' said Price, standing up. 'Where is he, in reception?'

'No. Mr Thorward has taken him down to Lab One. He has his lawyer and his doctor with him.'

'I know it,' Price muttered, prying nervously into his pockets. 'Where did I put those damn – Oh, here.' He pulled out some notes scrawled in pencil on file cards. 'Okay, look, Lois, you phone down and tell them I'll be right there.'

'Yes, Mr Price.' She smiled, turned and walked out. Mitchell's mild gaze followed her. Not a bad-looking girl, as they went. He remembered that he had brought her over to the other side, three or four years ago, but of course he had made a lot of changes – slimmer waist, firmer bust ... He yawned.

Price asked abruptly, 'Do you want to sit in?'

'Want me to?'

'I don't know, Mitch – do you give a damn?'

'Sure.' Mitchell got up, draped an arm around the other man's shoulders. 'Let's go.'

They walked together down the busy corridor. 'Listen,' Price said, 'how long since you've been out for dinner?'

'Don't know. Month or two.'

'Well, come out tonight. Marge told me to bring you for sure.'

Mitchell hesitated, then nodded. 'All right, Jim, thanks.'

Lab One was the showcase – all cedar veneer and potted plants, with the egg-shaped mentigraph couch prominently displayed, like a casket in a mortuary. There were half a dozen big illuminated color transparencies on a table behind the couch, to one side of the control board.

Heads turned as they walked in. Mitchell recognized Diedrich at once – a heavy-set pink-and-blond man in his early forties. The ice-blue eyes stared at him. Mitchell realized with a shock that the man was even more impressive, more hypnotic than he seemed on television.

Thorwald, the lab chief, made the introductions while white-coated technicians hovered in the background. 'The Reverend Diedrich – and Mr Edmonds, his attorney – and of course you know Dr Taubman, at least by reputation.'

They shook hands. Diedrich said, 'I hope you understand the terms on which I am here. I'm not looking for any compromise.' The pale eyes were intent and earnest. 'Your people put it to me that I could attack the mentigraph more effectively if I had actually experienced it. If nothing changes my mind, that's just what I intend to do.'

'Yes, we understand that, of *course*, Mr Diedrich,' said Price. 'We wouldn't have it any other way.'

Diedrich looked curiously at Mitchell. 'You're the inventor of this machine?'

Mitchell nodded. 'A long time ago.'

'Well, what do you think about the way it has turned out – its effect on the world?'

'I like it,' said Mitchell.

Diedrich's face went expressionless; he glanced away.

'I was just showing Mr Diedrich these mentigraph projections,' Thorwald said hurriedly, pointing to the transparencies. Two were landscapes, weird things, all orange trees and brown grass; one was a city scene, and the fourth showed a hill, with three wooden crosses silhouetted against the sky. 'Dan Shelton, the painter, did these. He's enthusiastic about it.'

'You can actually photograph what goes on in the subject's mind?' Edmonds asked, raising his black eyebrows. 'I was not aware of that.'

'It's a new wrinkle,' Price answered. 'We hope to have it on the market in September.'

'Well, gentlemen, if you're ready—' Thorwald said.

Diedrich appeared to brace himself. 'All right. What do I do? Shall I take my jacket off?'

'No, just lie down here, if you will,' Thorwald answered, pointing to the narrow operating table. 'Loosen your tie if it will make you more comfortable.'

Diedrich got up on the table, his face set. A technician came up behind him with a basket-shaped object made of curved, criss-crossing metal pieces. She adjusted it gently over Diedrich's skull, tightened the wing nuts until it fitted. She took careful measurements, adjusted the helmet again, then pushed eight plungers, one after the other.

Taubman was looking over her shoulder as she removed the helmet. At the roots of Diedrich's hair, eight tiny purple spots were visible.

'This is merely a harmless dye, Doctor,' Thorwald said. 'All we are doing here is to establish the sites for the electrodes.'

'Yes, all right,' said Taubman. 'And you assure me that none of them is in the pleasure center?'

'Definitely not. You know there is legislation against it, Doctor.'

The technician had moved up again. With a small pair of scissors she cut tiny patches of hair from the purple-marked spots. She applied lather, then, with an even smaller razor, shaved the patches clean. Diedrich lay quietly; he winced at the touch of the cool lather, but otherwise did not change expression.

'That's all of that,' Thorwald said. 'Now, Reverend Diedrich, if you'll sit over here—'

Diedrich got up and walked to the chair Thorwald pointed out. Over it hung a glittering basketwork of metal, like a more complicated and more menacing version of the helmet the technician had used.

'Just a moment,' Taubman said. He went over to examine the mechanism. He and Thorwald spoke in low voices for a moment, then Taubman nodded and stepped back. Diedrich sat down.

'This is the only sticky part,' Thorwald said. 'But it really doesn't hurt. Now let's just get your head in this clamp—'

Diedrich's face was pale. He stared straight ahead as a technician tightened the padded clamp, then lowered the basket-shaped instrument. Standing on a dais behind the chair, Thorwald himself carefully adjusted eight metal cylinders, centering each over one of the shaved purple patches on Diedrich's skull. 'This will be just like a pinprick,' he said. He pressed a button. Diedrich winced.

'Now tell me what sensations you feel,' said Thorwald, turning to a control panel.

Diedrich blinked. 'I saw a flash of light,' he said.

'All right, next.'

'That was a noise.'

'Yes, and this?'

Diedrich looked surprised; his mouth worked for a moment. 'Something sweet,' he said.

'Good. How about this?'

Diedrich started. 'I felt something touch my skin.'

'All right. Next.'

'Pew!' said Diedrich, turning his face aside. 'A terrible smell.'

'Sorry. How about this one?'

'I felt warm for a moment.'

'Okay, now this.'

Diedrich's right leg twitched. 'It felt as if it were doubled up under me,' he said.

'Right. One more.'

Diedrich stiffened suddenly. 'I felt – I don't know how to describe it. *Satisfied.*' His cold eyes went from Mitchell to Thorwald. His jaw was set hard.

'Perfect!' Thorwald said, getting down from the platform. He was grinning with pleasure. Mitchell glanced at Price, saw him wiping his hands with a handkerchief.

The cylinders retracted; the technician unfastened the head-clamp. 'That's all of that,' said Thorwald heartily. 'You can step down.'

Diedrich got out of the chair, his jaw still set. One hand went up to fumble at his skull.

'Pardon me,' said Taubman. He parted Diedrich's hair with his fingers and stared at the little gray plastic button, almost flush with the scalp, that had covered one of the purple spots.

Mitchell drifted over to stand beside Price. 'Our friend didn't like that jolt in number eight,' he murmured. 'Careful, boy.'

'I know,' Price answered in an undertone. Across the room, Thorwald and the technicians had seated Diedrich in another chair and put the cap on his head. One of the technicians began showing him big sheets of colored pasteboard, while another, a pale young man with big ears, read dials and punched keys at the control console.

'This is a pretty big gamble you're taking, son,' Mitchell said. 'You know if we just make him mad, he can really smear us. How'd you get so brave?'

Price scowled, shuffled his feet. 'Don't bury me yet,' he muttered.

A technician was passing vials of scent under Diedrich's nose, one after another.

'Something up your sleeve?' Mitchell asked; but he had lost interest, and did not hear Price's reply. The technicians were walking Diedrich up and down, getting him to bend, raise his arms, turn his head. When they finally let him sit down again, his face was slightly flushed. Mitchell was thinking dreamily that he could use Diedrich on the other side – make a Teutonic knight out of him, noble, humorless and fierce. But reduce him to about half-size … that would be funny.

'We won't try to calibrate the emotional responses this time, Mr Diedrich,' Thorwald was saying. 'That's more difficult and complicated – it takes quite a while. But you've got enough here to give you a very good idea of the device.'

Diedrich put up a hand to feel the cap on his head, the cluster of wires emerging from the middle of it. 'All right,' he said grimly. 'Go ahead.'

Thorwald looked a little worried. He motioned to the technician at the console. 'Input one, Jerry.' To Diedrich he said, 'Just close your eyes, if you will, and let your hands relax.'

The man at the console touched a button. An expression of surprise crossed Diedrich's face. His right hand moved spasmodically, then lay still. A moment later he turned his head aside. His jaws made slow chewing motions. Then he opened his eyes.

'Amazing,' he said. 'A banana – I peeled it and then ate a bite. But – they weren't my hands.'

'Yes, of course – that was a recording made by another subject. However, when you learn to use the other circuits, Mr Diedrich, you can run that through again and change it until they *are* your hands – or make any other changes you like.'

Diedrich's expression showed controlled distaste. He said, 'I see.' Watching him, Mitchell thought, *He's going to go home and write a speech that will blister our tails.*

'You'll see what I mean in just a moment,' Thorwald was saying. 'This time there won't be any primary recording – you'll do it all yourself. Just lean back, close your eyes, and imagine some picture, some scene—'

Diedrich fingered his watch impatiently. 'You mean you want me to try to make a picture like those?' He nodded towards the transparencies ranged along the wall.

'No, no, nothing like that. We won't project it, and only you will see what it is. Just visualize a scene, and wherever it seems vague or out of proportion, keep on changing it and adding to it … Go ahead, try it.'

Diedrich leaned back, closed his eyes. Thorwald nodded to the man at the console.

Price moved abruptly away from Mitchell, strode over to the chair. 'Here is something that may help you, Mr Diedrich,' he said, bending close. He looked at the notes in his hand and read aloud, 'It was now about the sixth hour, and there was darkness over the whole land until the ninth hour, while the sun's light failed; and the curtain of the temple was torn in two.'

Diedrich frowned; then his face relaxed. There was a long silence. Diedrich began to frown again. After a moment his hands moved spasmodically on the arms of the chair. His jaw muscles lost their tightness; his chin dropped slightly. After another moment he began breathing quickly and shallowly, lips parted.

Taubman stepped over, frowning, and attempted to take his pulse, but Diedrich knocked his hand away, Taubman glanced at Price, who shook his head and put a finger to his lips.

Diedrich's face had turned into a mask of grief. Moisture appeared under his closed eyelids, began to run down his cheeks. Watching him closely, Price nodded to Thorwald, who turned towards the console and made a chopping motion.

Diedrich's tear-filled eyes slowly opened.

'What was it, Mr Diedrich?' Edmonds asked, bending towards him. 'What happened?'

Diedrich's voice was low and hoarse, 'I saw – I saw –' His face contorted and he began to sob. He bent over as if in pain, hands clasped so tightly that the fingers turned red and yellow-white in patches.

Price turned away, took Mitchell by the arm. 'Let's get out of here,' he muttered. In the corridor, he began to whistle.

'Think you're pretty slick, don't you, boy?' Mitchell asked.

Price's grin made him look like a mischievous small boy. 'I know I am, old buddy,' he said.

There were four of them at dinner – Price and his good-looking red-haired wife; Mitchell, and a girl he had never met before. Her name was Eileen Novotny; she was slender, gray-eyed, quiet. She was divorced, Mitchell gathered, and had a small daughter.

After dinner they played a rubber of bridge. Eileen was a good player, better than Mitchell; but when he blundered, once or twice, she only gave him a glance of ironic commiseration. She did not talk much; her voice was low and well modulated, and Mitchell found himself waiting for her to speak again.

When the rubber was over, she stood up. 'I'm glad to have met you, Mitch,' she said, and gave him her warm hand for a moment. 'Thank you for a lovely dinner and a nice evening,' she said to Marge Price.

'You're not going already?'

'Afraid I have to – my sitter can only stay till nine, and it will take me a good hour to get up to Washington Heights.'

She paused at the door, glancing back at Mitchell. He could well imagine how it might be with this girl – the long walks, the intimate little restaurants, holding hands, the first kiss ... Price and his wife were looking at him expectantly.

'Good night, Eileen,' he said.

After she was gone, Marge brought in some beer and excused herself. Price settled himself in a relaxer and lit a pipe. Squinting at Mitchell over the bowl, he said mildly, 'You might have given the girl a taxi-ride home, old buddy.'

'And start all over again? No thanks, old buddy – I've had it.'

Price flipped out his match, dropped it into an ashtray. 'Well, it's your life.'

'So I've always imagined.'

Price shifted uncomfortably in the chair. 'So I'm a matchmaker,' he said, scowling. 'Dammit, I don't like to see what's happening to you. You spend more time under the wire than out of it. It isn't healthy, it isn't good for you.'

Mitchell grinned and held out a hand. 'Indian rassle?'

Price flushed. 'All right, all right, I know you work out at the gym every week – you're in good shape physically. That's not what I'm talking about, and you know it damn well.'

Mitchell took a long pull at his can of beer. It was lighter and maltier than he liked, but it was cold, at least, and felt good going down his throat. What about a green beer for St Paddy's day? Give it a suggestion of mint – just a touch …

'Say something,' Price said.

Mitchell's eyes focused on him slowly. 'Hmm. Think Diedrich will stop being a nuisance now?'

Price made a sour face. 'Okay, change the subject. Sure, I think Diedrich will stop being a nuisance. We're sending him a complete rig – couch, control board, library of crystals. And he'll take it. He's hooked.'

'Dirty trick?' Mitchell suggested.

'No, I don't think so.'

'You planted that picture of the three crosses, didn't you? Then, just to make sure, you stepped up and read him a paragraph from the crucifixion scene in Matthew. Pretty foxy.'

'Luke,' said Price. 'Yeah, pretty foxy.'

'Tell me something,' Mitchell said. 'Just for curiosity – how long since you've been under the wire yourself?'

Price looked at his hands, clasped around the pipe-bowl. 'Four years,' he said.

'How come?'

'Don't like what it does to me.' He folded his free hand around the one that held the pipe; his knuckles cracked, one after another.

'Made you twenty million,' Mitchell said gently.

'You know I don't mean that.' Price unclenched his hands, leaned forward. 'Listen, the Pentagon turned down that contract for forty thousand training crystals. They decided they don't like what it does to people, either.'

'Keeps them from being eager little beavers,' Mitchell said. 'My back aches for the Pentagon.'

'What about the contract – does your back ache for that?'

'You know, James, I don't understand you,' Mitchell said. 'One minute you're telling me the mentigraph is worse than hashish, heroin, booze and adultery, all put together. The next, you're complaining because we don't sell more of 'em. How do you explain that?'

Price did not smile. 'Let's say I'm a worry-wart. You know I keep talking about pulling out – maybe I'll do it some day – but till I do, I'm responsible to the corporation and I'll do my best for it. That's business. When I worry about you, it's friendship.'

'I know it, old buddy.'

'Maybe I worry about the whole world once in a while, too,' Price said. 'What's going to happen when everybody's got a private dream-world? Where's the old Colonial spirit then.'

Mitchell snorted. 'Have you ever done any reading about Colonial times? I did some research on it years ago. They used to drink a horrible thing called flip, made out of rum and hard cider, and they'd plunge a hot poker into it to make it froth up. You could tell the drunkards just by seeing who had an apple orchard.'

Price swung his legs off the relaxer, put his elbows on his knees. 'All right, what about this? You've got it made, haven't you – you can spend half your time in a world where everything is just the way you like it. You don't need that sweet kid who walked out of here half an hour ago – you've got twenty better-looking than her. And they're on call any time. So why get married, why raise a family? Just tell me this – what's going to happen to the world if the brightest guys in it drop out of the baby-making business? What happens to the next generation?'

'I can answer that one too.'

'Well?'

Mitchell lifted his beer can in salute, staring at Price over the shiny top. 'The hell with them,' he said.

THE BIG PAT BOOM

The long, shiny car pulled up with a whirr of turbines and a puff of dust. The sign over the roadside stand read: BASKETS. CURIOS. Farther down, another sign over a glass-fronted rustic building announced: SQUIRE CRAWFORD'S COFFEE MILL. TRY OUR DOUGHNUTS. Beyond that was a pasture, with a barn and silo set back from the road.

The two aliens sat quietly and looked at the signs. They both had hard purplish skins and little yellow eyes. They were wearing gray tweed suits. Their bodies looked approximately human, but you could not see their chins, which were covered by orange scarves.

Martha Crawford came hustling out of the house and into the basket stand, drying her hands on her apron. After her came Llewellyn Crawford, her husband, still chewing his cornflakes.

'Yes, sir – ma'am?' Martha asked nervously. She glanced at Llewellyn for support, and he patted her shoulder. Neither of them had ever seen an alien real close to.

One of the aliens, seeing the Crawfords behind their counter, leisurely got out of the car. He, or it, was puffing a cigar stuck through a hole in the orange scarf.

'Good morning,' Mrs Crawford said nervously. 'Baskets? Curios?'

The alien blinked its yellow eyes solemnly. The rest of its face did not change. The scarf hid its chin and mouth, if any. Some said that the aliens had no chins, others that they had something instead of chins that was so squirmy and awful that no human could bear to look at it. People called them 'Hurks' because they came from a place called Zeta Herculis.

The Hurk glanced at the baskets and gimcracks hung over the counter, and puffed its cigar. Then it said, in a blurred but comprehensible voice, 'What is that?' It pointed downward with one horny, three-fingered hand.

'The little Indian papoose?' Martha Crawford said, in a voice that rose to a squeak. 'Or the birchbark calendar?'

'No, that,' said the Hurk, pointing down again. This time, craning over the counter, the Crawfords were able to see that it was looking at a large, disk-shaped gray something that lay on the ground.

'That?' Llewellyn asked doubtfully.

'That.'

Llewellyn Crawford blushed. 'Why – that's just a cowpat. One of them cows from the dairy got loose from the herd yesterday, and she must have dropped that there without me noticing.'

'How much?'

The Crawfords stared at him, or it, without comprehension. 'How much what?' Llewellyn asked finally.

'How much,' the alien growled around its cigar, 'for the cowpat?'

The Crawfords exchanged glances. 'I never *heard*—' said Martha in an undertone, but her husband shushed her. He cleared his throat. 'How about ten ce— Well, I don't want to cheat you – how about a quarter?'

The alien produced a large change purse, laid a quarter on the counter and grunted something to its companion in the car.

The other alien got out, bringing a square porcelain box and a gold-handled shovel. With the shovel, she – or it – carefully picked up the cowpat and deposited it in the box.

Both aliens then got into the car and drove away, in a whine of turbines and a cloud of dust.

The Crawfords watched them go, then looked at the shiny quarter lying on the counter. Llewellyn picked it up and bounced it in his palm. 'Well, say!' He began to smile.

All that week the roads were full of aliens in their long shiny cars. They went everywhere, saw everything, paid their way with bright new-minted coins and crisp paper bills.

There was some talk against the government for letting them in, but they were good for business and made no trouble. Some claimed to be tourists, others said they were sociology students on a field trip.

Llewellyn Crawford went into the adjoining pasture and picked out four cowpats to deposit near his basket stand. When the next Hurk came by, Llewellyn asked, and got, a dollar apiece.

'But why do they *want* them?' Martha wailed.

'What difference does that make?' her husband asked. '*They* want 'em – *we* got 'em! If Ed Lacey calls again about that mortgage payment, tell him not to worry!' He cleared off the counter and arranged the new merchandise on it. He jacked his price up to two dollars, then to five.

Next day he ordered a new sign: COWPATS.

One fall afternoon two years later, Llewellyn Crawford strode into his living room, threw his hat in a corner, and sat down hard. He glared over his glasses at the large circular object, tastefully tinted in concentric rings of blue, orange and yellow, which was mounted over the mantelpiece. To the casual eye, this might have been a genuine 'Trophy' class pat, a museum piece, painted on

425

the Hurk planet; but in fact, like so many artistic ladies nowadays, Mrs Crawford had painted and mounted it herself.

'What's the matter, Lew?' she asked apprehensively. She had a new hairdo and was wearing a New York dress, but looked peaked and anxious.

'Matter!' Llewellyn grunted. 'Old man Thomas is a damn fool, that's all. Four hundred dollars a head! Can't buy a cow at a decent price anymore.'

'Well, Lew, we do have seven herds already, don't we, and—'

'Got to have more to meet the demand, Martha!' said Llewellyn, sitting up. 'My heaven, I'd think you could see that. With queen pats bringing up to fifteen dollars, and not enough to go 'round – And fifteen *hundred* for an emperor pat, if you're lucky enough—'

'Funny we never thought there was so many kinds of pats,' Martha said dreamily. 'The emperor – that's the one with the double whorl?'

Llewellyn grunted, picking up a magazine.

'Seems like a person could kind of—'

A kindly gleam came into Llewellyn's eyes. 'Change one around?' he said. 'Nope – been tried. I was reading about it in here just yesterday.' He held up the current issue of *The American Pat Dealer*, then began to turn the glossy pages. '*Pat-O-Grams*,' he read aloud. '*Preserving Your Pats. Dairying – a Profitable Sideline*. Nope. Oh, here it is. *Fake Pats a Flop*. See, it says here some fellow down in Amarillo got hold of an emperor and made a plaster mold. Then he used the mold on a couple of big cull pats – says here they was so perfect you couldn't tell the difference. But the Hurks wouldn't buy. *They* knew.'

He threw the magazine down, then turned to stare out of the back window towards the sheds. 'There's that fool boy just setting in the yard again. Why ain't he working?' Llewellyn rose, cranked down the louver, shouted through the opening, 'You, Delbert! Delbert!' He waited. 'Deaf, too,' he muttered.

'I'll go tell him you want –' Martha began, struggling out of her apron.

'No, never mind – go myself. Have to keep after 'em every damn minute,' Llewellyn marched out of the kitchen door and across the yard to where a gangling youth sat on a trolley, slowly eating an apple.

'Delbert!' said Llewellyn, exasperated.

'Oh – hello, Mr Crawford,' said the youth, with a gap-toothed grin. He took a last bite from the apple, then dropped the core. Llewellyn's gaze followed it. Owing to his missing front teeth, Delbert's apple cores were like nothing in this world.

'Why ain't you trucking pats out to the stand?' Llewellyn demanded. 'I don't pay you to set on no empty trolley, Delbert.'

'Took some out this morning,' the boy said. 'Frank, he told me to take 'em back.'

'He what?'

Delbert nodded. 'Said he hadn't sold but two. You ask him if I'm lying.'

'Do that,' Llewellyn grunted. He turned on his heel and strode back across the yard.

Out at the roadside, a long car was parked beside a battered pickup at the pat stand. It pulled out as Llewellyn started towards it, and another one drove up. As he approached the stand, the alien was just getting back in. The car drove off.

Only one customer was left at the stand, a whiskered farmer in a checked shirt. Frank, the attendant, was leaning comfortably on the counter. The display shelves behind him were well filled with pats.

'Morning, Roger,' Llewellyn said with well-feigned pleasure. 'How's the family? Sell you a nice pat this morning?'

'Well, I don't know,' said the whiskered man, rubbing his chin. 'My wife's had her eye on that one there,' he pointed to a large, symmetrical pat on the middle shelf – 'but at them prices—'

'You can't do better, believe me, Roger. It's an investment,' said Llewellyn earnestly. 'Frank, what did that last Hurk buy?'

'Nothing,' said Frank. A persistent buzz of music came from the radio in his breast pocket. 'Just took a picture of the stand and drove off.'

'Well, what did the one before—'

With a whirr of turbines, a long shiny car pulled up behind him. Llewellyn turned. The three aliens in the car were wearing red felt hats with comic buttons sewed all over them, and carried Yale pennants. Confetti was strewn on their gray tweed suits.

One of the Hurks got out and approached the stand, puffing a cigar through the hole in his – or its – orange scarf.

'Yes, sir?' said Llewellyn at once, hands clasped, bending forward slightly. 'A nice pat this morning?'

The alien looked at the gray objects behind the counter. He, or it, blinked its yellow eyes and made a curious gurgling noise. After a moment Llewellyn decided that it was laughing.

'What's funny?' he demanded, his smile fading.

'Not funny,' said the alien. 'I laugh because I am happy. I go home tomorrow – our field trip is over. Okay to take a picture?' He raised a small lensed machine in one purple claw.

'Well, I suppose—' Llewellyn said uncertainly. 'Well, you say you're going home? You mean all of you? When will you be coming back?'

'We are not coming back,' the alien said. He, or it, pressed the camera, extracted the photograph and looked at it, then grunted and put it away. 'We are grateful for an entertaining experience. Goodbye.' He turned and got into the car. The car drove off in a cloud of dust.

'Like that the whole morning,' Frank said. 'they don't buy nothing – just take pictures.'

Llewellyn felt himself beginning to shake. 'Think he means it – they're all going away?'

'Radio said so,' Frank replied. 'And Ed Coon was through here this morning from Hortonville. Said *he* ain't sold a pat since day 'fore yesterday.'

'Well, I don't understand it,' Llewellyn said. 'They can't just all quit—' His hands were trembling badly, and he put them in his pockets. 'Say, Roger,' he said to the whiskered man, 'now just how much would you want to pay for that pat?'

'Well—'

'It's a ten dollar pat, you know,' Llewellyn said, moving closer. His voice had turned solemn. 'Prime pat, Roger.'

'I know that, but—'

'What would you say to seven fifty?'

'Well, I don't know. Might give – say, five.'

'Sold,' said Llewellyn. 'Wrap that one up, Frank.'

He watched the whiskered man carry his trophy off to the pickup. 'Mark 'em all down, Frank,' he said firmly. 'Get whatever you can.'

The long day's débâcle was almost over. Arms around each other, Llewellyn and Martha Crawford watched the last of the crowd leaving the pat stand. Frank was cleaning up. Delbert, leaning against the side of the stand, was eating an apple.

'It's the end of the world, Martha,' Llewellyn said huskily. Tears stood in his eyes. 'Prime pats, going two for a nickel!'

Headlights blinding in the dusk, a long, low car came nosing up to the pat stand. In it were two green creatures in raincoats, with feathery antennae that stood up through holes in their blue pork-pie hats. One of them got out and approached the pat stand with a curious scuttling motion. Delbert gaped, dropping his apple core.

'Serps!' Frank hissed, leaning over the stand towards Llewellyn. 'Heard about 'em on the radio. From Gamma Serpentis, radio said.'

The green creature was inspecting the half-bare shelves. Horny lids flickered across its little bright eyes.

'Pat, sir – ma'am?' Llewellyn asked nervously. 'Not many left right now, but—'

'What is *that?*' the Serp asked in a rustling voice, pointing downward with one claw.

The Crawfords looked. The Serp was pointing to a misshapen, knobby something that lay beside Delbert's boot.

'That there?' Delbert asked, coming partially to life. 'That's a apple core.'

He glanced across to Llewellyn, and a gleam of intelligence seemed to come into his eyes. 'Mr Crawford, I quit,' he said clearly. Then he turned to the alien. 'That's a *Delbert Smith* apple core,' he said.

Frozen, Llewellyn watched the Serp pull out a billfold and scuttle forward. Money changed hands. Delbert produced another apple and began enthusiastically reducing it to a core.

'Say, Delbert,' said Llewellyn, stepping away from Martha. His voice squeaked, and he cleared his throat. 'Looks like we got a good little thing going here. Now, if you was smart, you'd rent this pat stand?'

'Nope, Mr Crawford,' said Delbert indistinctly, with his mouth full of apple. 'Figure I'll go over to my uncle's place – he's got a orchard.'

The Serp was hovering nearby, watching the apple core and uttering little squeals of appreciation.

'Got to be close to your source of *supply*, you know,' said Delbert, wagging his head wisely.

Speechless, Llewellyn felt a tug at his sleeve. He looked down: it was Ed Lacey, the banker.

'Say, Lew, I tried to get you all afternoon, but your phone didn't answer. About your collateral on those loans …'

MAN IN THE JAR

The hotel room on the planet Meng was small and crowded. Blue-tinged sunlight from the window fell on a soiled gray carpet, a massive sandbox dotted with cigarette butts, a clutter of bottles. One corner of the room was piled high with baggage and curios. The occupant, a Mr R. C. Vane of Earth, was sitting near the door: a man of about fifty, clean shaven, with bristling iron-gray hair. He was quietly, murderously drunk.

There was a tap on the door and the bellhop slipped in – a native, tall and brown, with greenish black hair cut too long in the back. He looked about nineteen. He had one green eye and one blue.

'Set it there,' said Vane.

The bellhop put his tray down. 'Yes, sir.' He took the unopened bottle of Ten Star off the tray, and the ice bucket, and the seltzer bottle, crowding them in carefully among the things already on the table. Then he put the empty bottles and ice bucket back on the tray. His hands were big and knob-jointed; he seemed too long and wide-shouldered for his tight green uniform.

'So this is Meng City,' said Vane, watching the bellhop. Vane was sitting erect and unrumpled in his chair, with his striped moth-wing jacket on and his string tie tied. He might have been sober, except for the deliberate way he spoke, and the redness of his eyes.

'Yes, sir,' said the bellhop, straightening up with the tray in his hands. 'This your first time here, sir?'

'I came through two weeks ago,' Vane told him. 'I did not like it then, and I do not like it now. Also, I do not like this room.'

'Management is sorry if you don't like the room, sir. Very good view from this room.'

'It's dirty and small,' said Vane, 'but it doesn't matter. I'm checking out this afternoon. Leaving on the afternoon rocket. I wasted two weeks upcountry, investigating Marack stories. Nothing to it – just native talk. Miserable little planet.' He sniffed, eyeing the bellhop. 'What's your name, boy?'

'Jimmy Rocksha, sir.'

'Well, Jimmy Rocks in the Head, look at that pile of stuff.' Tourist goods, scarves and tapestries, rugs, blankets and other things were mounded over the piled suitcases. It looked like an explosion in a curio shop. 'There's about forty pounds of it I have no room for, not counting that knocked-down jar. Any suggestions?'

The hellhop thought about it slowly. 'Sir, if I might suggest, you might put the scarves and things inside the jar.'

Vane said grudgingly, 'That might work. You know how to put those things together?'

'I don't know, sir.'

'Well, let us see you try. Go on, don't stand there.'

The bellhop set his tray down again and crossed the room. A big bundle of gray pottery pieces, tied together with twine, had been stowed on top of Vane's wardrobe trunk, a little above the bellhop's head. Rocksha carefully removed his shoes and climbed on a chair. His brown feet were bare and clean. He lifted the bundle without effort, got down, set the bundle on the floor, and put his shoes back on.

Vane took a long swallow of his lukewarm highball, finishing it. He closed his eyes while he drank, and nodded over the glass for a moment afterwards, as if listening to something inside him. 'All right,' he said, getting up, 'let us see.'

The bellhop loosened the twine. There were six long, thick, curving pieces, shaped a little like giant shoehorns. Then there were two round ones. One was bigger; that was the bottom. The other had a handle; that was the lid. The bellhop began to separate the pieces carefully, laying them out on the carpet.

'Watch out how you touch those together,' Vane grunted, coming up behind him. 'I wouldn't know how to get them apart again.'

'Yes, sir.'

'That's an antique which I got upcountry. They used to be used for storing grain and oil. The natives claim the Maracks had the secret of making them stick the way they do. Ever heard that?'

'Upcountry boys tell a lot of fine stories, sir,' said the bellhop. He had the six long pieces arranged, well separated, in a kind of petal pattern around the big flat piece. They took up most of the free space; the jar would be chest-high when it was assembled.

Standing up, the bellhop took two of the long curved pieces and carefully brought the sides closer together. They seemed to jump the last fraction of an inch, like magnets, and merged into one smooth piece. Peering, Vane could barely make out the join.

In the same way, the bellhop added another piece to the first two. Now he had half the jar assembled. Carefully he lowered this half jar towards the edge of the big flat piece. The pieces clicked together. The bellhop stooped for another side piece.

'Hold on a minute,' said Vane suddenly. 'Got an idea. Instead of putting that thing all together, then trying to stuff things into it, use your brain. Put the things, in, *then* put the rest of the side on.'

'Yes, sir,' said the bellhop. He laid the piece of crockery down again and picked up some light blankets, which he dropped on the bottom of the jar.

'Not that way, dummy,' said Vane impatiently. 'Get *in* there – pack them down tight.'

The bellhop hesitated. 'Yes, sir.' He stepped delicately over the remaining unassembled pieces and knelt on the bottom of the jar, rolling the blankets and pressing them snugly in.

Behind him, Vane moved on tiptoe like a dancer, putting two long pieces quietly together – *tic!* – then a third – *tic!* – and then as he lifted them, *tic, clack!* the sides merged into the bottom and the top. The jar was complete.

The bellhop was inside.

Vane breathed hard through flared nostrils. He took a cigar out of a green-lizard pocket case, cut it with a lapel knife, and lit it. Breathing smoke, he leaned over and looked down into the jar.

Except for a moan of surprise when the jar closed, the bellhop had not made a sound. Looking down, Vane saw his brown face looking up. 'Let me out of this jar, please, sir,' said the bellhop.

'Can't do that,' said Vane. 'They didn't tell me how, upcountry.'

The bellhop moistened his lips. 'Upcountry, they use a kind of tree grease,' he said. 'It creeps between the pieces, and they fall apart.'

'They didn't give me anything like that,' said Vane indifferently.

'Then please, sir, you break this jar and let me come out.'

Vane picked a bit of tobacco off his tongue. He looked at it curiously and then flicked it away. 'I spotted you,' he said, 'in the lobby the minute I came in this morning. Tall and thin. Too strong for a native. One green eye, one blue. Two weeks I spent, upcountry, looking; and there you were in the lobby.'

'Sir –?'

'You're a Marack,' said Vane flatly.

The bellhop did not answer for a moment. 'But sir,' he said incredulously, 'Maracks are *legends*, sir. Nobody believes that anymore. There are no Maracks.'

'You lifted that jar down like nothing,' said Vane. 'Two boys put it up there. You've got the hollow temples. You've got the long jaw and the hunched shoulders.' Frowning, he took a billfold out of his pocket and took out a yellowed card. He showed it to the bellhop. 'Look at that.'

It was a faded photograph of a skeleton in a class case. There was something disturbing about the skeleton. It was too long and thin; the shoulders seemed hunched, the skull was narrow and hollow-templed. Under it, the printing said, ABORIGINE OF NEW CLEVELAND, MENG (SIGMA

LYRAE II) and in smaller letters, *Newbold Anthropological Museum, Ten Eyck, Queensland, N. T.*

'Found it between the pages of a book two hundred years old,' said Vane, carefully putting it back. 'It was mailed as a postcard to an ancestor of mine. A year later, I happened to be on Nova Terra. Now get this. The museum is still there, but that skeleton is not. They deny it ever was there. Curator seemed to think it was a fake. None of the native races on Meng have skeletons like that,' he said.

'Must be a fake, sir,' the bellhop agreed.

'I will tell you what I did next,' Vane went on. 'I read all the contemporary accounts I could find of frontier days on this planet. A couple of centuries ago, nobody on Meng thought the Maracks were legends. They looked enough like the natives to pass, but they had certain special powers. They could turn one thing into another. They could influence your mind by telepathy, if you weren't on your guard against them. I found this interesting. I next read all the export records back to a couple of centuries ago. Also, the geological charts in *Planetary Survey*. I discovered something. It just happens, there is no known source of natural diamonds anywhere on Meng.'

'No, sir?' said the bellhop nervously.

'Not one. No diamonds, and no place where they ever could have been mined. But until two hundred years ago, Meng exported one billion stellors' worth of flawless diamonds every year. I ask, where did they come from? And why did they stop?'

'I don't know, sir.'

'The Maracks made them,' said Vane. 'For a trader named Soong and his family. They died. After that, no more diamonds from Meng.' He opened a suitcase, rummaged inside it a moment, and took out two objects. One was a narrow oval bundle of something wrapped in stiff yellow plant fibers; the other was a shiny gray-black lump half the size of his fist.

'Do you know what this is?' Vane asked, holding up the oval bundle.

'No, sir.'

'Air weed, they call it upcountry. One of the old men had this one buried under his hut, along with the jar. *And* this.' He held up the black lump. 'Nothing special about it, would you say? Just a piece of graphite, probably from the old mine at Badlong. But graphite is pure carbon. And so is a diamond.'

He put both objects carefully down on the nearby table, and wiped his hands. The graphite had left black smudges on them. 'Think about it,' he said. 'You've got exactly one hour, till three o'clock.' Delicately he tapped his cigar over the mouth of the jar. A few flakes of powdery ash floated down on the bellhop's upturned face.

Vane went back to his chair. He moved deliberately and a little stiffly, but did not stagger. He peeled the foil off the bottle of Ten Star. He poured himself a substantial drink, added ice, splashed a little seltzer in. He took a long, slow swallow.

'Sir,' said the bellhop finally, 'you know I can't make any diamonds out of black rock. What's going to happen, when it comes three o'clock, and that rock is still just a piece of rock?'

'I think,' said Vane, 'I will just take the wrappings off that air weed and drop it in the jar with you. Air weed, I am told, will expand to hundreds of times its volume in air. When it fills the jar to the brim, I will put the lid on. And when we're crossing that causeway to the spaceport, I think you may get tipped off the packrat into the bay. The bottom is deep silt, they tell me.' He took another long, unhurried swallow.

'Think about it,' he said, staring at the jar with red eyes.

Inside the jar, it was cool and dim. The bellhop had enough room to sit fairly comfortably with his legs crossed, or else he could kneel, but then his face came right up to the mouth of the jar. The opening was too small for his head. He could not straighten up any farther, or put his legs out. The bellhop was sweating in his tight uniform. He was afraid. He was only nineteen, and nothing like this had ever happened to him before.

The clink of ice came from across the room. The bellhop said, 'Sir?'

The chair springs whined, and after a moment the Earthman's face appeared over the mouth of the jar. His chin was dimpled. There were gray hairs in his nostrils, and a few gray and black bristles in the creases of loose skin around his jaw. His red eyes were hooded and small. He looked down into the bellhop's face without speaking.

'Sir,' the bellhop said earnestly, 'do you know how much they pay me here at this hotel?'

'No.'

'Twelve stellors a week, sir, and my meals. If I could make diamonds, sir, why would I be working here?'

Vane's expression did not change. 'I will tell you that,' he said. 'Soong must have been sweating you Maracks to get a billion stellors a year. There used to be thousands of you on this continent alone, but now there are so few that you can disappear among the natives. I would guess the diamonds took too much out of you. You're close to extinction now. And you're all scared. You've gone underground. You've still got your powers, but you don't dare use them – unless there's no other way to keep your secret. You were lords of this planet once, but you'd rather stay alive. Of course, all this is merely guess work.'

'Yes, sir,' said the bellhop despairingly.

The house phone rang. Vane crossed the room and thumbed the key down, watching the bellhop from the corner of his eye. 'Yes?'

'Mr Vane,' said the voice of the desk clerk, 'if I may ask, did the refreshments you ordered arrive?'

'The bottle came,' Vane answered. 'Why?'

The bellhop was listening, balling his fists on his knees. Sweat stood out on his brown forehead.

'Oh nothing really, Mr Vane,' said the clerk's voice, 'only the boy did not come back. He is usually very reliable, Mr Vane. But excuse me for troubling you.'

'All right,' said Vane stonily, and turned the phone off. He came back to the jar. He swayed a little, rocking back and forth from heels to toes. In one hand he had the highball glass; with the other he was playing with the little osmiridium knife that hung by an expanding chain from his lapel. After a while he said, 'Why didn't you call for help?'

The bellhop did not answer. Vane went on softly, 'Those hotel phones will pick up a voice across the room, I know. So why were you so quiet?'

The bellhop said unhappily, 'If I did yell, sir, they would find me in this jar.'

'And so?'

The bellhop grimaced. 'There's some other people who still believe in Maracks, sir. I have to be careful, with my eyes. They would know there could only be the one reason why you would treat me like this.'

Vane studied him for a moment. 'And you'd take a chance on the air weed, and the bay, just to keep anyone from finding out?'

'It's a long time since we had any Marack hunts on this planet, sir.'

Vane snorted softly. He glanced up at the wall clock. 'Forty minutes,' he said, and went back to his chair by the door.

The bellhop said nothing. The room was silent except for the faint whir of the clock. After a while Vane moved to the writing desk. He put a printed customs declaration form in the machine and began tapping keys slowly, muttering over the complicated interstellar symbols.

'Sir,' said the bellhop quietly, 'you know you can't kill a biped person and just get away. This is not like the bad old times.'

Vane grunted, tapping keys. 'Think not?' He took a sip from his highball and set it down again with a clink of ice.

'Even if they find out you have mistreated the headman upcountry, sir, they will be very severe.'

'They won't find out,' Vane said. 'Not from him.'

'Sir, even if I could make you your diamond, it would only be worth a few thousand stellors. That is nothing to a man like you.'

Vane paused and half turned. 'Flawless, that weight, it would be worth a hundred thousand. But I'm not going to sell it.' He turned back to the machine, finished a line, and started another.

'No, sir?'

'No. I'm going to keep it.' Vane's eyes half closed; his fingers poised motionless on the keys. He seemed to come to himself with a start, hit another key, and rolled the paper out of the machine. He picked up an envelope and rose, looking over the paper in his hand.

'Just to keep it, sir, and look at it now and then?' the bellhop asked softly. Sweat was running down into his eyes, but he kept his fists motionless on his knees.

'That's it,' said Vane with the same faraway look. He folded the paper slowly and put it into the envelope as he walked towards the message chute near the door. At the last moment he checked himself, snapped the paper open again and stared at it. A slow flush came to his cheeks. Crumpling the paper slowly in his hands, he said, 'That almost worked.' He tore the paper across deliberately, and then again, and again, before he threw the pieces away.

'Just one symbol in the wrong box,' he said, 'but it was the right wrong symbol. I'll tell you where you made your mistake though, boy.' He came closer.

'I don't understand,' said the bellhop.

'You thought if you could get me to thinking about that diamond, my mind would wander. It did – but I knew what was happening. Here's where you made your mistake. I don't give a damn about that diamond.'

'Sir?' said the bellhop in bewilderment.

'A stellor to you is a new pair of pants. A stellor to me, or a thousand stellors is just a poker chip. It's the game that counts. The excitement.'

'Sir, I don't know what you mean.'

Vane snorted. 'You know, all right. You're getting a little dangerous now, aren't you? You're concerned, and the time's running out. So you took a little risk.' He stooped, picked up one of the scraps of paper, unfolded it and smoothed it out. 'Right here, in the box where the loyalty oath to the Archon is supposed to go, I wrote the symbol for "pig". If I sent that down, the thought police would be up here in fifteen minutes.' He balled up the paper again, into an even smaller wad, and dropped it on the carpet. 'Think you can make me forget to pick that up again and burn it, before I leave?' he said amiably, 'Try.'

The bellhop swallowed hard. 'Sir, you did that *yourself*. You made a slip of the finger.'

Vane smiled at him for the first time, and walked away.

The bellhop put his back against the wall of the jar and pushed with all his strength against the opposite side. He pushed until the muscles of his back stood out in knotted ropes. The pottery walls were as solid as rock.

He was sweating more than ever. He relaxed, breathing hard; he rested his head on his knees and tried to think. The bellhop had heard of bad Earthmen before, but he had never seen one like this.

He straightened up. 'Sir, are you still there?'

The chair creaked and Vane came over, glass in hand.

'Sir,' said the bellhop earnestly, 'if I can prove to you that I'm really not a Marack, will you let me go? I mean, you'll have to let me then, won't you?'

'Why, certainly,' said Vane agreeably. 'Go ahead and prove it.'

'Well, sir, haven't you heard other things about the Marack – some other test?'

Vane looked thoughtful; he put his chin down on his chest and his eyes filmed over.

'About what they can or can't do?' the bellhop suggested. 'If I tell you, sir, you might think I made it up.'

'Wait a minute,' said Vane. He was swaying slightly, back and forth, his eyes half closed. His string tie was still perfectly tied, his striped moth-wing jacket immaculate. He said, 'I remember something. The Marack hunters used this a good deal, I understand. Maracks can't stand liquor. It makes them sick.'

'You're positive about that, sir?' the bellhop said eagerly.

'Of course I'm positive. It's like poison to a Marack.'

'All right then, sir!'

Vane nodded, and went to the table to get the bottle of Ten Star. It was still two-thirds full. He came back with it and said, 'Open your mouth.'

The bellhop opened his mouth wide and shut his eyes. He did not like Earth liquor, especially brandy, but he thought he could drink it if it would get him out of this jar.

The liquor hit his teeth and the back of his mouth in one solid splash; it poured down both cheeks and some of it ran up his nose. The bellhop choked and strangled. The liquor burned all the way down his throat and windpipe; tears blinded him; he couldn't breathe. When the paroxysm was over, he gasped, 'Sir – sir – that wasn't a fair test. You shouldn't have poured it on me like that. Give me a little bit, in a glass.'

'Now, I want to be fair,' said Vane. 'We'll try it again.' He found an empty glass, poured two fingers of brandy into it, and came back. 'Easy does it,' he said, and trickled a little into the bellhop's mouth.

The bellhop swallowed, his head swimming in brandy fumes. 'Once more,' said Vane, and poured again. The bellhop swallowed. The liquor was gathering in a ball of heat inside him. 'Again.' He swallowed.

Vane stood back. The bellhop opened his eyes and looked blissfully up at him. 'You see, sir? No sickness. I drank it, and I'm not sick!'

'Hmm,' said Vane with an interested expression. 'Well, imagine that. Maracks *can* drink liquor.'

The bellhop's victorious smile slowly faded. He looked incredulous. 'Sir, don't joke with me,' he said.

Vane sniffed. 'If you think it's a joke—' he said with heavy humour.

'Sir, you *promised*.'

'Oh, no. By no means,' said Vane. 'I said if you could prove to me that you are not a Marack. Go ahead, prove it. Here's another little test for you, incidentally. An anatomist I know looked at that skeleton and told me it was constricted at the shoulders. A Marack can't lift his hand higher than his head. So begin by telling me why you stood on a chair to get my bundle down – or better yet, just put your arm out of the neck of that jar.'

There was a silence. Vane took another cigar out of the green-lizard case, cut it with the little osmiridium knife, and lit it without taking his eyes off the bellhop. 'Now you're getting dangerous again,' he said. 'You're thinking it over, down there. This begins to get interesting. You're wondering how you can kill me from inside that jar, without using your Marack powers. Go ahead. Think about it.'

He breathed smoke, leaning towards the jar. 'You've got fifteen minutes.'

Working without haste, Vane rolled up all the blankets and other souvenirs and strapped them into bundles. He removed some toilet articles from the dresser and packed them away in his grip. He took a last look around the room, saw the paper scraps on the floor and picked up the tiny pellet he had made of one of them. He showed it to the bellhop with a grin, then dropped it into the ash-receiver and burned it. He sat down comfortably in the chair near the door. 'Five minutes,' he said.

'Four minutes,' he said.

'Three minutes.'

'Two minutes.'

'All right,' said the bellhop.

'Yes?' Vane got up and stood over the jar.

'I'll do it – I'll make the diamond.'

'Ahh?' said Vane, half questioningly. He picked up the lump of graphite and held it out.

'I don't need to touch it,' the bellhop said listlessly. 'Just put it down on the table. This will take about a minute.'

'Umm,' said Vane, watching him keenly. The bellhop was crouched in the jar, eyes closed; all Vane could see of him was the glossy-black top of his head.

His voice was muffled. 'If you just hadn't had that air weed,' he said sullenly.

Vane snorted. 'I didn't need the air weed. I could have taken care of you in a dozen ways. This knife' – he held it up – 'has a molar steel blade. Cut through anything, like cheese. I could have minced you up and floated you down the drain.'

The bellhop's face turned up, pale and wide-eyed.

'No time for that now, though,' Vane said. 'It would have to be the air weed.'

'Is that how you're going to get me loose, afterwards?' the bellhop asked. 'Cut the jar, with that knife?'

'Mm? Oh, certainly,' said Vane, watching the graphite lump. Was there a change in its appearance, or not?

'I'm disappointed, in a way,' he said. 'I thought you'd give me a fight. You Maracks are overrated, I suppose.'

'It's all done,' said the bellhop. 'Take it, please, and let me out.'

Vane's eyes narrowed. 'It doesn't look done to me,' he said.

'It just looks black on the outside, sir. Just rub it off.'

Vane did not move.

'Go ahead, sir,' said the bellhop urgently. 'Pick it up and see.'

'You're a little too eager,' Vane said. He took a fountain pen out of his pocket and used it to prod the graphite gingerly. Nothing happened; the lump moved freely across the tabletop. Vane touched it briefly with one finger, then picked it up in his hand. 'No tricks?' he said quizzically. He felt the lump, weighed it, put it down again. There were black graphite smears in his palm.

Vane opened his lapel knife and cut the graphite lump down the middle. It fell into two shiny black pieces. 'Graphite,' said Vane, and with an angry gesture he stuck the knife blade into the table.

He turned to the bellhop, dusting off his hands. 'I don't get you,' he said, prodding the oval bundle of the air weed experimentally. He picked it up. 'All you did was stall. You won't fight like a Marack, you won't give in like a Marack. All you'll do is die like a Meng-boy, right?' He shook his head. 'Disappointing.' The dry wrappings came apart in his hands. Between the fibers a dirty-white bulge began to show.

Vane lifted the package to drop it into the jar, and saw that the bellhop's scared face filled the opening. While he hesitated briefly, the gray-white floss of the air weed foamed slowly out over the back of his hand. Vane felt a constriction, and instinctively tried to drop the bundle. He couldn't. The growing, billowing, floss was sticky – it stuck to his hand. Then his sleeve. It grew, slowly but with a horrifying steadiness.

Gray-faced, Vane whipped his arm around, trying to shake off the weed. Like thick lather, the floss spattered downward but did not separate. A glob of it hit his trouser leg and clung. Another, swelling, dripped down to the carpet. His whole right arms and side were covered deep under a mound of white. The floss had now stopped growing and seemed to be stiffening.

The bellhop began to rock himself back and forth inside the jar. The jar tipped, then fell back. The bellhop rocked harder. The jar was inching its way across the carpet.

After a few moments the bellhop paused to put his face up and see which way he was going. Vane, held fast by the weed, was leaning towards the knife he had put there. The carpet bulged after him in a low mound, but too much furniture was holding it.

The bellhop lowered his head and rocked the jar again, harder. When he looked up, Vane's eyes were closed tight, his face red with effort. He was extended as far as he could reach across the table, but his fingers were still clawing air an inch short of the knife. The bellhop rocked hard. The jar inched forward, came to rest solidly against the table, pinning Vane's arm against it by the flaring sleeve.

The bellhop relaxed and looked up. Feeling himself caught, the Earthman had stopped struggling and was looking down. He tugged, but could not pull the sleeve free.

Neither spoke for a moment.

'Stalemate,' said Vane heavily. He showed his teeth to the bellhop. 'Close, but no prize. I can't get at you, and you can't hurt me.'

The bellhop's head bowed as if in assent. After a moment his long arm came snaking up out of the jar. His fingers closed around the deadly little knife.

'A Marack *can* lift his arm higher than his head, sir,' he said.

THE HANDLER

When the big man came in, there was a movement in the room like bird dogs pointing. The piano player quit pounding, the two singing drunks shut up, all the beautiful people with cocktails in their hands stopped talking and laughing.

'Pete!' the nearest woman shrilled, and he walked straight into the room, arms around two girls, hugging them tight. 'How's my sweetheart? Susy, you look good enough to eat, but I had it for lunch. George, you pirate' – he let go both girls, grabbed a bald blushing little man and thumped him on the arm – 'you were great, sweetheart, I mean it, really great. NOW HEAR THIS!' he shouted, over all the voices that were clamoring Pete this, Pete that.

Somebody put a martini in his hand and he stood holding it bronzed and tall in his dinner jacket, teeth gleaming white as his shirt cuffs. 'We had a show!' he told them.

A shriek of agreement went up, a babble of did we have a *show* my God Pete listen a *show*—

He held up his hand. 'It was a good show!'

Another shriek and babble.

'The sponsor kinda liked it – he just signed for another one in the fall!'

A shriek, a roar, people clapping, jumping up and down. The big man tried to say something else, but gave up, grinning, while men and women crowded up to him. They were all trying to shake his hand, talk in his ear, put their arms around him.

'I love ya *all*!' he shouted. 'Now what do you say, let's live a little!'

The murmuring started again as people sorted themselves out. There was a clinking from the bar. 'Jesus, Pete,' a skinny pop-eyed little guy was saying, crouching in adoration, 'when you dropped that fishbowl I thought I'd pee myself, honest to God—'

The big man let out a bark of happy laughter. 'Yeah, I can still see the look on your face. And the fish, flopping all over the stage. So what can I do, I get down there on my knees –' the big man did so, bending over and staring at imaginary fish on the floor. 'And I say, "Well, fellows back to the drawing board!"'

Screams of laughter as the big man stood up. The party was arranging itself around him in arcs of concentric circles, with people in the back standing on sofas and the piano bench so they could see. Somebody yelled, 'Sing the goldfish song, Pete!'

Shouts of approval, please-do-Pete, the goldfish song.

'Okay, okay.' Grinning, the big man sat on the arm of a chair and raised his glass. 'And a vun, and a doo – vere's de moosic?' A scuffle at the piano bench. Somebody banged out a few chords. The big man made a comic face and sang, 'Ohhh – how I wish … I was a little fish … and when I want some quail … I'd flap my little tail.'

Laughter, the girls laughing louder than anybody and their red mouths farther open. One flushed blonde had her hand on the big man's knee, and another was sitting close behind him.

'But seriously—' the big man shouted. More laughter.

'No seriously,' he said in a vibrant voice as the room quieted, 'I want to tell you in all seriousness I couldn't have done it alone. And incidentally I see we have some foreigners, litvaks and other members of the press here tonight, so I want to introduce all the important people. First of all, George here, the three-fingered band leader – and there isn't a guy in the world could have done what he did this afternoon – George, I love ya.' He hugged the blushing little bald man.

'Next my real sweetheart, Ruthie, where are ya? Honey, you were the greatest, really perfect – I mean it, baby—' He kissed a dark girl in a red dress who cried a little and hid her face on his broad shoulder. 'And Frank—' he reached down and grabbed the skinny pop-eyed guy by the sleeve. 'What can I tell you? A sweetheart?' The skinny guy was blinking, all choked up; the big man thumped him on the back. 'Sol and Ernie and Mack, my writers, Shakespeare should have been so lucky—' One by one, they came up to shake the big man's hand as he called their names; the women kissed him and cried. 'My stand-in,' the big man was calling out, and 'my caddy,' and 'Now,' he said, as the room quieted a little people flushed and sore-throated with enthusiasm, 'I want you to meet my handler.'

The room fell silent. The big man looked thoughtful and startled, as if he had had a sudden pain. Then he stopped moving. He sat without breathing or blinking his eyes. After a moment there was a jerky motion behind him. The girl who was sitting on the arm of the chair got up and moved away. The big man's dinner jacket split open in the back, and a little man climbed out. He had a perspiring brown face under a shock of black hair. He was a very small man, almost a dwarf, stoop-shouldered and round-backed in a sweaty brown singlet and shorts. He climbed out of the cavity in the big man's body, and closed the dinner jacket carefully. The big man sat motionless and his face was doughy.

The little man got down, wetting his lips nervously. Hello, Harry, a few people said. 'Hello,' Harry called, waving his hand. He was about forty, with a big nose and big soft brown eyes. His voice was cracked and uncertain. 'Well, we sure put on a show, didn't we?'

Sure did, Harry, they said politely. He wiped his brow with the back of his hand. 'Hot in there,' he explained, with an apologetic grin. Yes I guess it must be, Harry, they said. People around the outskirts of the crowd were beginning to turn away, form conversational groups; the hum of talk rose higher. 'Say, Tim, I wonder if I could have something to drink,' the little man said. 'I don't like to leave him – you know—' He gestured towards the silent big man.

'Sure, Harry, what'll it be?'

'Oh – you know – a glass of beer?'

Tim brought him a beer in a pilsener glass and he drank it thirstily, his brown eyes darting nervously from side to side. A lot of people were sitting down now; one or two were at the door leaving.

'Well,' the little man said to a passing girl, 'Ruthie, that was quite a moment there, when the fishbowl busted, wasn't it?'

'Huh? Excuse me, honey, I didn't hear you.' She bent nearer.

'Oh – well, it don't matter. Nothing.'

She patted him on the shoulder once, and took her hand away. 'Well, excuse me, sweetie, I have to catch Robbins before he leaves.' She went on towards the door.

The little man put his beer glass down and sat, twisting his knobby hands together. The bald man and the pop-eyed man were the only ones still sitting near him. An anxious smile flickered on his lips; he glanced at one face, then another. 'Well,' he began, 'that's one show under our belts, huh, fellows, but I guess we got to start, you know, thinking about—'

'Listen, Harry,' said the bald man seriously, leaning forward to touch him on the wrist, 'why don't you get back inside?'

The little man looked at him for a moment with sad hound-dog eyes, then ducked his head, embarrassed. He stood up uncertainly, swallowed and said, 'Well—' He climbed up on the chair behind the big man, opened the back of the dinner jacket and put his legs in one at a time. A few people were watching him, unsmiling. 'Thought I'd take it easy a while,' he said weakly, 'but I guess—' He reached in and gripped something with both hands, then swung himself inside. His brown, uncertain face disappeared.

The big man blinked suddenly and stood up. 'Well *hey* there,' he called, 'what's the matter with this party anyway? Let's see some life, some action—' Faces were lighting up around him. People began to move in closer. 'What I mean, let me hear that beat!'

The big man began clapping his hands rhythmically. The piano took it up. Other people began to clap. 'What I mean, are we alive here or just waiting for the wagon to pick us up? How's that again, can't hear you!' A roar of pleasure as he cupped his hand to his ear. 'Well come on, let me hear it!' A louder roar. Pete, Pete; a gabble of voices. 'I got nothing against Harry,' said the bald man earnestly in the middle of the noise, 'I mean for a square he's a nice guy.' 'Know what you mean,' said the pop-eyed man, 'I mean like he doesn't *mean* it.' 'Sure,' said the bald man, 'but Jesus that sweaty undershirt and all ...' The pop-eyed man shrugged. 'What are you gonna do?' Then they both burst out laughing as the big man made a comic face, tongue lolling, eyes crossed, Pete, Pete, Pete; the room was really jumping; it was a great party, and everything was all right, far into the night.

MARY

Thirty sisters, alike as peas, were sitting at their looms in the court above the Gallery of Weavers. In the cool shadow, their white dresses rustled like the stirrings of doves, and their voices now murmured, now shrilled. Over the courtyard was a canopy of green glass, through which the sun appeared to swim like a golden-green fish: but over the roofs could be seen the strong blue of the sky, and even, at one or two places, the piercing white sparkle of the sea.

The sisters were ivory-skinned, strong armed and straight of back, with eyebrows arched black over bright eyes. Some had grown fat, some were lean, but the same smiles dimpled their cheeks, the same gestures threw back their sleek heads when they laughed, and each saw herself mirrored in the others.

Only the youngest, Mary, was different. Hers was the clan face, but so slender and grave that it seemed a stranger's. She had been brought to birth to replace old Anna-one, who had fallen from the lookout and broken her neck sixteen springs ago: and some said it had been done too quick; that Mary was from a bad egg and should never have been let grow. Now the truth was that Mary had in her genes a long-recessive trait of melancholy and unworldliness, turned up by accident in the last cross; but the Elders, who after all knew best, had decided to give her the same chance as anyone. For in the floating island of Iliria, everyone knew that the purpose of life was happiness: and therefore to deprive anyone of life was a great shame.

At the far side of the court, Vivana called from her loom, 'They say a new Fisher came from the mainland yesterday!' She was the eldest of the thirty, a coarse, good-natured woman with a booming laugh. 'If he's handsome, I may take him, and give you others a chance at my Tino. Rose, how would you like that? Tino would be a good man for you.' Her loom whirled, and rich, dark folds of liase rippled out. It was an artificial fiber, formed, spun, woven and dyed in the loom, hardening as it reached the air. A canister of the stuff, like tinted gelatin, stood at the top of every loom. It came from the Chemist clan, who concocted it by mysterious workings out of the sea water that tumbled through their vats.

'What, is he tiring of you already?' Rose called back. She was short and moon-faced, with strong, clever fingers that danced on the keyboard of her loom. 'Probably you belched in his face once too often.' She raised her shrill voice over the laughter. 'Now let me tell you, Vivana, if the new Fisher is as handsome as that, I may take him myself, and let you have Mitri.' Mounds of apple-green stuff tumbled into the basket at her feet.

Between them, Mary worked on, eyes cast down, without smiling.

'Gogo and Vivana!' someone shouted.

'Yes, that's right – never mind about the Fisher! Gogo and Vivana!' All the sisters were shouting and laughing. But Mary still sat quietly busy at her loom.

'All right, all right,' shouted Vivana, wheezing with laughter. 'I will try him, but then who's to have Gunner?'

'Me!'

'No, me!'

Gunner was the darling of the Weavers, a pink man with thick blond lashes and a roguish grin.

'No, let the youngsters have a chance,' Vivana called reprovingly. 'Joking aside, Gunner is too good for you old scows.' Ignoring the shrieks of outrage, she went on, 'I say let Viola have him. Better yet, wait, I have an idea – how about Mary?'

The chatter stilled; all eyes turned towards the silent girl where she sat, weaving slow cascades of creamy white liase. She flushed quickly, and bowed her head, unable to speak. She was sixteen, and had never taken a lover.

The women looked at her, and the pleasure faded out of their faces. Then they turned away, and the shouting began again:

'Rudi!'

'Ernestine!'

'Hugo!'

'Areta!'

Mary's slim hands faltered, and the intricate diapered pattern of her weaving was spoiled. Now the bolt would have to be cut off, unfinished. She stopped the loom, and drooped over it, pressing her forehead against the smooth metal. Tears burned her eyelids. But she held herself still, hoping Mia, at the next loom, would not see.

Below in the street, a sudden tumult went up. Heads turned to listen: there was the wailing of flutes, the thundering of drums, and the sound of men's rich voices, all singing and laughing.

A gate banged open, and a clatter of feet came tumbling up the stair. The white dresses rustled as the sisters turned expectantly towards the arch.

A knot of laughing, struggling men burst through, full into the midst of the women, toppling looms, while the sisters shrieked in protest and pleasure.

The men were Mechanics, dark-haired, gaunt, leavened by a few blond Chemists. They were wrestling, Mechanic against Chemist, arms locked about each other's necks, legs straining for leverage. One struggling pair top-pled suddenly, overturning two more. The men scrambled up, laughing, red with exertion.

Behind them was a solitary figure whose stillness drew Mary's eyes. He was tall, slender and grave, with russet hair and a quiet mouth. While the others shouted and pranced, he stood looking around the courtyard. For an instant his calm gray eyes met hers, and Mary felt a sudden pain at the heart.

'Dear, what is it?' asked Mia, leaning closer.

'I think I am ill,' said Mary faintly.

'Oh, not now!' Mia protested.

Two of the men were wrestling again. A heave, and the dark Mechanic went spinning over the other's hip.

A shout of applause went up. Through the uproar, Vivana's big voice came booming, 'You fishheads, get out! Look at this, half a morning's work ruined! Are you all drunk? Get out!'

'We're all free for the day!' one of the Mechanics shouted. 'You too – the whole district! It's in the Fisher's honor! So come on, what are you waiting for?'

The women were up, in a sudden flutter of voices and white skirts, the men beginning to spread out among them. The tall man still stood where he was. Now he was looking frankly at Mary, and she turned away in confusion, picking up the botched fabric with hands that did not feel it.

She was aware that two Mechanics had turned back, were leading the tall man across the courtyard, calling, 'Violet – Clara!' She did not move; her breath stopped.

Then they were pausing before her loom. There was an awful moment when she thought she could not move or breathe. She looked up fearfully. He was standing there, hands in his pockets, slumped a little as he looked down at her.

He said, 'What is your name?' His voice was low and gentle.

'Mary,' she said.

'Will you go with me today, Mary?'

Around her, the women's heads were turning. A silence spread; she could sense the waiting, the delight held in check.

She could not! Her whole soul yearned for it, but she was too afraid, there were too many eyes watching. Miserably, she said, 'No,' and stopped, aston-ished, listening to the echo of her voice saying gladly, 'Yes!'

Suddenly her heart grew light as air. She stood, letting the loom fall, and when he held out his hand, hers went into it as if it knew how.

'So you have a rendezvous with a Mainland Fisher?' the Doctor inquired jovially. He was pale-eyed and merry in his broad brown hat and yellow tunic; he popped open his little bag, took out a pill, handed it to Mary. 'Swallow this, dear.'

'What is it for, Doctor?' she asked, flushing.

'Only a precaution. You wouldn't want a baby to grow right in your belly, would you? Ha, ha, ha! That shocks you, does it? Well, you see, the Mainlanders don't sterilize the males, their clan customs forbid it, so they sterilize the females instead. We have to be watchful, ah, yes, we Doctors! Swallow it down, there's a good girl.'

She took the pill, drank a sip of water from the flask he handed her.

'Good, good – now you can go to your little meeting and be perfectly safe. Enjoy yourself!' Beaming, he closed his bag and went away.

On the high Plaza of Fountains, overlooking the quayside and the sea, feasts of shrimp and wine, seaweed salad, caviar, pasta, iced sweets had been laid out under canopies of green glass. Orchestrinos were playing. Couples were dancing on the old ceramic cobbles, white skirts swinging, hair afloat in the brilliant air. Farther up, Mary and her Fisher had found a place to be alone.

Under the bower in the cool shade, they lay clasped heart to heart, their bodies still joined so that in her ecstasy she could not tell where hers ended or his began.

'Oh, I love you, I love you!' she murmured.

His body moved, his head drew back a little to look at her. There was something troubled in his gray eyes. 'I didn't know this was going to be your first time,' he said. 'How is it that you waited so long?'

'I was waiting for you,' she said faintly, and it seemed to her that it was so, and that she had always known it. Her arms tightened around him, wishing to draw him closer to her body again.

But he held himself away, looking down at her with the same vague uneasiness in his eyes. 'I don't understand,' he said. 'How could you have known I was coming?'

'I knew,' she said. Timidly her hands began to stroke the long, smooth muscles of his back, the man's flesh, so different from her own. It seemed to her that her fingertips knew him without being told; they found the tiny spots that gave him pleasure, and lingered there, without her direction.

His body stiffened; his gray eyes half closed. 'Oh, Mary,' he said, and then he was close against her again, his mouth busy on hers: and the pleasure began, more piercing and sweet than she had ever dreamed it could be. Now she was out of herself again, half aware that her body was moving, writhing; that her voice was making sounds and speaking words that astonished her to hear …

Near the end she began to weep, and lay in his arms afterwards with the luxurious tears wetting her cheeks, while his voice asked anxiously, 'Are you all right? Darling, are you all right?' and she could not explain, but only held him tighter, and wept.

Later, hand in hand, they wandered down the bone-white stairs to the quay-side strewn with drying nets, the glass floats sparkling sharp in the sun, spars, tackle and canvas piled everywhere. Only two boats were moored at the floating jetty below; the rest were out fishing, black specks on the glittering sea, almost at the horizon.

Over to eastward they saw the desolate smudge of the mainland and the huddle of stones that was Porto. 'That's where you live,' she said wonderingly.

'Yes.'

'What do you do there?'

He paused, looked down at her with that startled unease in his glance. After a moment he shrugged. 'Work. Drink a little in the evenings, make love. What else would I do?'

A dull pain descended suddenly on her heart and would not lift its wings. 'You've made love to many women?' she asked with difficulty.

'Of course. Mary, what's the matter?'

'You're going back to Porto. You're going to leave me.'

Now the unnamed thing in his eyes had turned to open incredulity. He held her arms, staring down at her. 'What else?'

She put her head down obstinately, burying it against his chest. 'I want to stay with you,' she said in a muffled voice.

'But you *can't*. You're an Islander – I'm a Mainlander.'

'I know.'

'Then why this foolishness?'

'I don't know.'

He turned her without speaking, and they stepped down from the prom-enade, went into the shadow of some storehouses that abutted on the quayside. The doors were open, breathing scents of spices and tar, new cord-age, drying fish. Beyond them was a pleasant courtyard with boats piled upside down on one side, on the other a table, an umbrella, chairs, all cool in the afternoon shadow. From there they took a shallow staircase up into a maze of little streets full of the dim, mysterious blue light that fell from cano-pies of tinted glass between roofs. Passing a house with open shutters, they heard the drone of childish voices. They peered in: it was the nursery school – forty young Bakers, Chemists, Mechanics, fair skins and dark, each in a doll-like miniature of his clan costume, all earnestly reciting together while the shovel-hatted Teacher stood listening at the greenboard. Cool, neutral light came from the louvered skylights; the small faces were clear and inno-cent, here a tiny Cook in his apron, there two Carters sitting together, identical in their blue smocks, there a pale Doctor, and beside him, Mary saw with a pang, a little Weaver in white. The familiar features were childishly blunted and small, the ivory skin impossibly pure, the bright eyes wide. 'Look – that one,' she whispered, pointing.

He peered in. 'She looks like you. More like you than the others. You're different from all the rest, Mary – that's why I like you.' He looked down at her with a puzzled expression; his arm tightened around her. 'I've never felt quite this way about a girl before; what are you doing to me?' he said.

She turned to him, embracing him, letting her body go soft and compliant against his. 'Loving you, darling,' she said, smiling up, her eyes half-closed.

He kissed her fiercely, then pushed her away, looking almost frightened. 'See here, Mary,' he said abruptly, 'we've got to understand something.'

'Yes?' she said faintly, clinging to him.

'I'm going to be back in Porto tomorrow morning,' he said.

'Tomorrow!' she said. 'I thought—'

'My work was done this morning. It was a simple adjustment of the sonics. You'll catch plenty of fish from now on … There's nothing more for me to do here.'

She was stunned; she could not believe it. Surely there would be at least another night … that was little enough to ask.

'Can't you stay?' she said.

'You know I can't.' His voice was rough and strained. 'I go where they tell me, come when they say come.'

She tried to hold back the time, but it slipped away, ran through her fingers. The sky darkened slowly from cerulean to Prussian blue, the stars came out and the cool night wind stirred over the jetty.

Below her, in a cluster of lights, they were making the boat ready. Orchestrinos were playing up the hillside, and there was a little crowd of men and women gathering to say goodbye. There was laughter, joking, voices raised good-naturedly in the evening stillness.

Klef, pale in the lights, came up the stairs to where she stood, his head tilted as he came, his grave eyes holding hers. 'I'm not going to cry,' she said.

His hands took her arms, gripping her half in tenderness, half impatiently. 'Mary, you know this is wrong. Get over it. Find yourself other men – be happy.'

'Yes, I'll be happy,' she said.

He stared down at her in uncertainty, then bent his head and kissed her. She held herself passive in his arms, not responding or resisting. After a moment he let her go and stepped back. 'Goodbye, Mary.'

'Goodbye, Klef.'

He turned, went quickly down the steps. The laughing voices surrounded him as he went towards the boat; after a moment she heard his voice too, lifted in cheerful farewells.

In the morning she awoke knowing that he was gone. A frightening knowledge of loss seized her, and she sat up with her heart leaping.

Down the high dormitory, smelling faintly of cinnamon oil and fresh linen, the sisters were beginning to rustle sleepily out of their cubicles, murmuring and yawning. The familiar hiss of the showers began at the far end of the room. The white-curtained windows were open, and from her bed Mary could see the cream and terra-cotta roofs spread out in a lazy descent. The air was cool and still and mysteriously pure: it was the best moment of the day.

She rose, washed herself and dressed mechanically. 'What is it, dear?' asked Mia, bending towards her anxiously.

'Nothing. Klef is gone.'

'Well, there'll be others.' Mia smiled and patted her hand, and went away. There was a closeness between them, they were almost of an age, and yet even Mia could not be comfortable long in Mary's company.

Mary sat with the others at table, silent in the steaming fragrances of coffee and new bread, the waves of cheerful talk that flowed around her. Carrying her loom, she went down with the rest into the court and sat in her usual place. The work began.

Time stretched away wearily into the future. How many mornings in her life would she sit here, where she sat now, beginning to weave as she did now? How could she endure it? How had she ever endured it? She put her fingers on the controls of the loom, but the effort to move them appalled her. A tear dropped bright on the keyboard.

Mia leaned over towards her. 'Is there anything the matter? Don't you feel well?'

Her fists clenched uselessly. 'I can't – I can't' was all she could utter. Hot tears were running down her face; her jaw was shaking. She bowed her head over the loom.

Iliria was neither wearisomely flat, nor cone-shaped nor pyramidal in its construction, like some of the northern islands, but was charmingly hollowed, like a cradle. The old cobble-stoned streets rose and fell; there were stairways, balconies, arcades; never a vista, always a new prospect. The buildings were pleasingly various, some domed and spired, others sprawling. Cream was the dominant color, with accents of cool light blue, yellow, and rose. For more than three hundred years, the island had been afloat, just as it now was: the same plazas with their fountains, the same shuttered windows, the same rooftops.

During the last century, some colonies had been creeping back on to the land as the contamination diminished; but every Ilirian knew that only island life was perfect. Above, the unchanging streets and buildings served each generation as the last; down below, the storage chambers, engine rooms, seines, preserving rooms, conveniently out of sight and hearing, went on functioning as they always had. Unsinkable, sheathed in ceramic above and below, the island would go on floating just as it now was, forever.

It was strange to Mary to see the familiar streets so empty. The morning light lay softly along the walls; in corners, blue shadow gathered. Behind every door and window there was a subdued hum of activity; the clans were at their work. All the way to the church circle, she passed no one but a Messenger and two Carters with their loads: all three looked at her curiously until she was out of sight.

Climbing the Hill of Carpenters, she saw the gray dome of the church rising against the sky – a smooth, unrelieved ovoid, with a crescent of morning light upon it. Overhead, a flock of gulls hung in the air, wings spread, rising and dipping. They were gray against the light.

She paused on the porch step to look down. From this height she could see the quays and the breakwater, and the sun on the brightwork of the moored launches; and then the long rolling back of the sea, full of whitecaps in the freshening breeze; and beyond that, the dark smudge of the land, and the clutter of brown windowed stone that was Porto. She stood looking at it for a moment, dry-eyed, then went into the shadowed doorway.

Clabert the Priest rose up from his little desk and came towards her with ink-stained fingers, his skirt flapping around his ankles. 'Good morning, cousin, have you a trouble?'

'I'm in love with a man who has gone away.'

He stared at her in perplexity for a moment, then darted down the corridor to the left. 'This way, cousin.' She followed him past the great doors of the central harmonium. He opened a smaller door, curved like the end of an egg, and motioned her in.

She stepped inside; the room was gray, egg-shaped, and the light came uniformly from the smooth ceramic walls. 'Twenty minutes,' said Clabert, and withdrew his head. The door shut, joining indistinguishably with the wall around it.

Mary found herself standing on the faintly sloping floor, with the smooth single curve of the wall surrounding her. After a moment she could no longer tell how far away the big end of the ovicle was; the room seemed first quite small, only a few yards from one end to the other; then it was gigantic, bigger than the sky. The floor shifted uncertainly under her feet, and after another moment she sat down on the cool hollow slope.

The silence grew and deepened. She had no feeling of confinement; the air was fresh and in constant slight movement. She felt faintly and agreeably dizzy, and put her arms behind her to steady herself. Her vision began to

452

blur; the featureless gray curve gave her no focus for her eyes. Another moment passed, and she became aware that the muffled silence was really a continual slow hush of sound, coming from all points at once, like the distant murmuring of the sea. She held her breath to listen, and at once, like dozens of wings flicking away in turn, the sound stopped. Now, listening intently, she could hear a still fainter sound, a soft, rapid pattering that stopped and came again, stopped and came again … and listening, she realized that it was the multiple echo of her own heartbeat. She breathed again, and the slow hush flooded back.

The wall approached, receded … gradually it became neither close nor far way; it hung gigantically and mistily just out of reach. The movement of air imperceptibly slowed. Lying dazed and unthinking, she grew intensely aware of her own existence, the meaty solidness of her flesh, the incessant pumping of blood, the sigh of breath, the heaviness and pressure, the pleasant beading of perspiration on her skin. She was whole and complete, all the way from fingers to toes. She was uniquely herself; somehow she had forgotten how important that was …

'Feeling better?' asked Clabert, as he helped her out of the chamber.

'Yes …' She was dazed and languid; walking was an extraordinary effort.

'Come back if you have these confusions again,' Clabert called after her, standing in the porch doorway.

Without replying, she went down the slope in the brilliant sunshine. Her head was light, her feet were amusingly slow to obey her. In a moment she was running to catch up with herself, down the steep cobbled street in a stumbling rush, with faces popping out of shutters behind her, and fetched up laughing and gasping with her arms around a light column at the bottom.

A stout Carter in blue was grinning at her out of his tanned face. 'What's the joke, woman?'

'Nothing,' she stammered. 'I've just been to church …'

'Ah!' he said, with a finger beside his nose, and went on.

She found herself taking the way downward to the quays. The sunlit streets were empty; no one was in the pools. She stripped and plunged in, gasping at the pleasure of the cool fresh water on her body. And even when two Baker boys, an older one and a younger, came by and leaned over the wall shouting, 'Pretty! Pretty!' she felt no confusion, but smiled up at them and went on swimming.

Afterwards, she dressed and strolled, wet as she was, along the sea-wall promenade. Giddily she began to sing as she walked, 'Open your arms to me, sweetheart, for when the sun shines it's pleasant to be in love …' The orchestrinos had been playing that, that night when –

She felt suddenly ill, and stopped with her hand at her forehead.

What was wrong with her? Her mind seemed to topple, shake itself from one pattern into another. She swung her head up, looking with sharp anxiety for the brown tangle of buildings on the mainland.

At first it was not there, and then she saw it, tiny, almost lost on the horizon. The island was drifting, moving away, leaving the mainland behind.

She sat down abruptly; her legs lost their strength. She put her face in her arms and wept: 'Klef! Oh, Klef!'

This love that had come to her was not the easy, pleasant thing the orchestrinos sang of; it was a kind of madness. She accepted that, and knew herself to be mad, yet could not change. Waking and sleeping, she could think only of Klef.

Her grief had exhausted itself; her eyes were dry. She could see herself now as the others saw her – as something strange, unpleasant, ill-fitting. What right had she to spoil their pleasure?

She could go back to church, and spend another dazed time in the ovicle. 'If you have these confusions again,' the Priest had said. She could go every morning, if need be, and again every afternoon. She had seen one who needed to do as much, silly Marget Tailor who always nodded and smiled, drooling a little, no matter what was said to her, and who seemed to have a blankness behind the glow of happiness in her eyes. That was years ago; she remembered the sisters always complained of the wet spots Marget left on her work. Something must have happened to her; others cut and stitched for the Weavers now.

Or she could hug her pain to herself, scourge them with it, make them do something … She had a vision of herself running barefoot and ragged through the streets, with people in their doorways shouting, 'Crazy Mary! Crazy Mary!' If she made them notice her, made them bring Klef back …

She stopped eating except when the other sisters urged her, and grew thinner day by day. Her cheeks and eyes were hollow. All day she sat in the courtyard, not weaving, until at length the other women's voices grew melancholy and seldom. The weaving suffered; there was no joy in the clan house. Many times Vivana and the others reasoned with her, but she could only give the same answers over again, and at last she stopped replying at all.

'But what do you want?' the women asked her, with a note of exasperation in their voices.

What did she want? She wanted Klef to be beside her every night when she went to sleep, and when she wakened in the morning. She wanted his arms about her, his flesh joined to hers, his voice murmuring in her ear. Other men? It was not the same thing. But they could not understand.

'But why do you want me to make myself pretty?' Mary asked with dull curiosity.

Mia bent over her with a tube of cosmetic, touching the pale lips with crimson. 'Never mind, something nice. Here, let me smooth your eyebrows. Tut, how thin you've got! Never mind, you'll look very well. Put on your fresh robe, there's a dear.'

'I don't know what difference it makes.' But Mary stood up wearily, took off her dress, stood thin and pale in the light. She put the new robe over her head, shrugged her arms into it.

'Is that all right?' she asked.

'Dear Mary,' said Mia, with tears of sympathy in her eyes. 'Sweet, no, let me smooth your hair. Stand straighter, can't you, how will any man—'

'Man?' said Mary. A little color came and went in her cheeks. 'Klef?'

'*No*, dear, forget Klef, will you?' Mia's voice turned sharp with exasperation.

'Oh.' Mary turned her head away.

'Can't you think of anything else? Do try, dear, just try.'

'All right.'

'Now come along, they're waiting for us.'

Mary stood up submissively and followed her sister out of the dormitory.

In bright sunlight the women stood talking quietly and worriedly around the bower. With them was a husky Chemist with golden brows and hair; his pink face was good-natured and peaceful. He pinched the nearest sister's buttock, whispered something in her ear; she slapped his hand irritably.

'Quick, here they come,' said one suddenly. 'Go in now, Gunner.'

With an obedient grimace, the blond man ducked his head and disappeared into the bower. In a moment Mia and Mary came into view, the thin girl hanging back when she saw the crowd, and the bower.

'What is it?' she complained. 'I don't want – Mia, let me go.'

'No, dear, come along, it's for the best, you'll see,' said the other girl soothingly. 'Do give me a hand here, one of you, won't you?'

The two women urged the girl towards the bower. Her face was pale and frightened. 'But what do you want me to – You said Klef wasn't – Were you only teasing me? Is Klef—?'

The women gave each other looks of despair. 'Go in, dear, and see, why don't you?'

A wild expression came into Mary's eyes. She hesitated, then stepped nearer the bower; the two women let her go. 'Klef?' she called plaintively. There was no answer.

'Go in, dear.'

She looked at them appealingly, then stooped and put her head in. The women held their breaths. They heard her gasp, then saw her backing out again.

'Crabs and mullets!' swore Vivana. 'Get her in, you fools!'

The girl was crying out, weakly and helplessly, as four women swarmed around her, pushed her into the bower. One of them lingered, peered in.

'Has he got her?'

'Yes, now he's got her.' Stifled mewing sounds were coming from the bower. 'Hang on to her, you fool!'

'She bit!' came Gunner's indignant voice. Then silence.

'Sst, leave them alone,' whispered Vivana. The woman at the bower entrance turned, tiptoed away. Together the women withdrew a few yards, found themselves seats on the old steps under the portico, and sat down comfortably close to one another.

There was a scream.

The women leaped up, startled and white. Not one of them could remember hearing such a sound before.

Gunner's hoarse voice bawled something, then there was a stir. Mary appeared in the entrance to the bower. Her skirt was ripped, and she was clutching it to her lap with one hand. Her eyes were filmed, pink-rimmed. 'Oh!' she said, moving past them blindly.

'Mary—' said one, reaching out a hand.

'Oh!' she said hopelessly, and moved on, clutching her garment to her body.

'What's the matter?' they asked each other. 'What did Gunner do?'

'I did what I was supposed to,' said Gunner, sulkily appearing. There was a red bruise on his cheek. 'Gut me and clean me if I ever do it with that one again, though.'

'You fool, you must have been too rough. Go after her, someone.'

'Well, then serve her yourself the next time, if you know so much.' Prodding his cheek gently with a finger, the Chemist went away.

Up the slope, an orchestrino began playing. '*If you would not be cruel, torment me no more. Do not deny me ever; let it be now or never. Give me your love, then, as you promised me before ...*'

'Shut that thing off!' cried Vivana angrily.

Her ageship, Laura-one, the eldest Weaver, was pacing up and down the seawall promenade, knotting her fingers together in silent agitation. Once she paused to look over the parapet; below her the wall dropped sheer to blue water. She glanced over at the blur of Porto, half concealed in the morning haze, and at the stark hills above with their green fur of returning vegetation. Her eyes were still keen; halfway across the distance, she could make out a tiny dark dot, moving towards the island.

Footsteps sounded in the street below; in a moment Vivana appeared, holding Mary by the arm. The younger woman's eyes were downcast; the older looked worried and anxious.

'Here she is, your ageship,' said Vivana. 'They found her at the little jetty, throwing bottles into the sea.'

'Again?' asked the old woman. 'What was in the bottles?'

'Here's one of them,' said Vivana, handing over a crumpled paper.

'"Tell Klef the Fisher of the town of Porto that Mary Weaver still loves him,"' the old woman read. She folded the paper slowly and put it into her pocket. 'Always the same,' she said. 'Mary, my child, don't you know that these bottles never can reach your Klef?'

The young woman did not raise her head or speak.

'And twice this month the Fishers have had to catch you and bring you back when you stole a launch,' the woman continued. 'Child, don't you see that this must end?'

Mary did not answer.

'And these things that you weave, when you weave at all,' said Laura-one, taking a wadded length of cloth from her apron pocket. She spread it taut and held it to the light. In the pattern, visible only when the light fell glancingly upon it, was woven the figure of a seated woman with a child in her arms. Around them were birds with spread wings among the intertwined stems of flowers.

'Who taught you to weave like this, child?' she asked.

'No one,' said Mary, not looking up.

The old woman looked down at the cloth again. 'It's beautiful work, but—' She sighed and put the cloth away. 'We have no place for it. Child, you weave so well, why can't you weave the usual patterns?'

'They are dead. This one is alive.'

The old woman sighed again. 'And how long is it that you have been demanding your Klef back, dear?'

'Seven months.'

'But now think.' The old woman paused, glanced over her shoulder. The black dot on the sea was much nearer, curving in towards the jetty below. 'Suppose this Klef did receive one of your messages; what then?'

'He would know how much I love him,' said Mary, raising her head. Color came into her cheeks; her eyes brightened.

'And that would change his whole life, his loyalties, everything?'

'Yes!'

'And if it did not?'

Mary was silent.

'Child, if that failed, would you confess that you have been wrong – would you let us help you?'

'It wouldn't fail,' Mary said stubbornly.

'But if it did?' the older woman insisted gently. 'Just suppose – just let yourself imagine.'

Mary was silent a moment. 'I would want to die,' she said.

The two elder Weavers looked at each other, and for a moment neither spoke.

'May I go now?' Mary asked.

Vivana cast a glance down at the jetty, and said quickly, 'Maybe it's best, your ageship. Tell them—'

Laura-one stopped her with a raised hand. Her lips were compressed. 'And if you go, child, what will you do now?'

'Go and make more messages, to put into bottles.'

The old woman sighed. 'You see?' she said to Vivana.

Footsteps sounded faintly on the jetty stair. A man's head appeared; he was an island Fisher, stocky, hark-haired, with a heavy black mustache. 'Your ageship, the man is here,' he said, saluting Laura-one. 'Shall I—?'

'No,' said Vivana involuntarily. 'Don't – Send him back—'

'What would be the good of that?' the old woman asked reasonably. 'No, bring him up, Alec.'

The Fisher nodded, turned and was gone down the stair.

Mary's head had come up. She said, 'The man—?'

'There, it's all right,' said Vivana, going to her.

'Is it Klef?' she asked fearfully.

The older woman did not reply. In a moment the black mustached Fisher appeared again; he stared at them, climbed to the head of the stair, stood aside.

Behind him, after a moment, another head rose out of the stairwell. Under the russet hair, the face was grave and thin. The gray eyes went to Laura-one, then to Mary; they stared at her, as the man continued to climb the steps. He reached the top, and stood waiting, hands at his sides. The black-mustached Fisher turned and descended behind him.

Mary had begun to tremble all over.

'There, dear, it's all right,' said Vivana, pressing her arms. As if the words had released her, Mary walked to the Fisher. Tears were shining on her face. She clutched his tunic with both hands, staring up at him. 'Klef?' she said.

His hands came up to hold her. She threw herself against him, then, so violently that he staggered, and clutched him as if she wished to bury herself in his body. Strangled, hurt sounds came out of her.

The man looked over her head at the two older women. 'Can't you leave us alone for a moment?' he asked.

'Of course,' said Laura-one, a little surprised. 'Why not? Of course.' She gestured to Vivana, and the two turned, walked away a little distance down the promenade to a bench, where they sat looking over the sea wall.

Gulls mewed overhead. The two women sat side by side without speaking or looking at one another. They were not quite out of earshot.

'Is it really you?' Mary asked, holding his face between her hands. She tried to laugh. 'Darling, I can't see … you're all blurred.'

'I know,' said Klef quietly. 'Mary, I've thought about you many times.'

'Have you?' she cried. 'Oh, that makes me so happy. Oh, Klef, I could die now! Hold me, hold me.'

His face hardened. His hands absently stroked her back, up and down. 'I kept asking to be sent back,' he said. 'Finally I persuaded them – they thought you might listen to me. I'm supposed to cure you.'

'Of loving you?' Mary laughed. At the sound, his hands tightened involuntarily on her back. 'How foolish they were! How foolish, Klef!'

'Mary, we have only these few minutes,' he said.

She drew back a little to look at him. 'I don't understand.'

'I'm to talk to you, and then go back. That's all I'm here for.'

She shook her head in disbelief. 'But you told me—'

'Mary, listen to me. There is nothing else to do. Nothing.'

'Take me back with you, Klef.' her hands gripped him hard. 'That's what I want – just to be with you. Take me back.'

'And where will you live – in the Fishers' dormitory with forty men?'

'I'll live anywhere, in the streets, I don't care—'

'They would never allow it. You know that, Mary.'

She was crying, holding him, shuddering all over. 'Don't tell me that, don't say it. Even if it's true, can't you pretend a little? Hold me, Klef, tell me that you love me.'

'I love you,' he said.

'Tell me that you'll keep me, never let me go, no matter what they say.'

He was silent a moment. 'It's impossible.'

She raised her head.

'Try to realize,' he said, 'this is a sickness, Mary. You must cure yourself.'

'Then you're sick too!' she said.

'Maybe I am, but I'll get well, because I know I have to. And you must get well too. Forget me. Go back to your sisters and your weaving.'

She put her cheek against his chest, gazing out across the bright ocean. 'Let me just be quiet with you a moment,' she said. 'I won't cry anymore. Klef—'

'Yes?'

'Is that all you have to say to me?'

'It has to be all.' His eyes closed, opened again. 'Mary, I didn't want to feel this way. It's wrong, it's unhealthy, it hurts. Promise me, before I go. Say you'll let them cure you.'

She pushed herself away, wiped her eyes and her cheeks with the heel of one hand. Then she looked up. 'I'll let them cure me,' she said.

His face contorted. 'Thank you. I'll go now, Mary.'

'One more kiss!' she cried, moving towards him involuntarily. 'Only one more!'

He kissed her on the lips, then wrenched himself away, and looking down to where the two women sat, he made an angry motion with his head.

As they rose and came nearer, he held Mary at arm's length. 'Now I'm really going,' he said harshly. 'Goodbye, Mary.'

'Goodbye, Klef.' Her fingers were clasped tight at her waist.

The man waited, looking over her head, until Vivana came up and took her arms gently. Then he moved away. At the head of the stairs he looked at her once more; then he turned and began to descend.

'Dear, it will be better now, you'll see,' said Vivana uncertainly.

Mary said nothing. She stood still, listening to the faint sounds that echoed up from the stairwell: footsteps, voices, hollow sounds.

There was a sudden clatter, then footsteps mounting the stair. Klef appeared again, chest heaving, eyes bright. He seized both of Mary's hands in his. 'Listen!' he said. 'I'm mad. You're mad. We're both going to die.'

'I don't care!' she said. Her face was glowing as she looked up at him.

'They say some of the streams are running pure, in the hills. Grass is growing there – there are fish in the streams, even the wild fowl are coming back. We'll go there, Mary, together – just you and I. Alone. Do you understand?'

'Yes, Klef, yes, darling.'

'Then come on!'

'Wait!' cried Laura-one shrilly after them as they ran down the stair. 'How will you live? What will you eat? Think what you are doing!'

Faint hollow sounds answered her, then the purr of a motor.

Vivana moved to Laura-one's side, and the two women stood watching, silent, as the dark tiny shape of the launch moved out into the brightness. In the cockpit they could make out the two figures close together, dark head and light. The launch moved steadily towards the land; and the two women stood staring, unable to speak, long after it was out of sight.

AUTO-DA-FÉ

The king of the world sat on a balcony, listening to the wind blow around his tower. He was drunk. He would get drunker still, and then he would be sick, and the dogs would take care of him. By tomorrow afternoon, he would be drunk and sick again.

The dog Roland lay near his feet – not quite near enough for a kick. The man felt his patient gaze like an itch, like the scab of an ill-healed wound that he could not scratch. Here we sit, he thought with blurred irony, the last man and the last dog. In a world of bitches.

He glanced down at the dog, and saw the grizzled fur above the great bloodshot eyes, the hanging dewlaps, the yellow teeth. You're old too, my lad, he thought with bitter satisfaction. You won't last another century.

Dogs and men, they all died eventually. The dogs lived five hundred years at most; all the art of their masters had not been able to give them more. But the race of dogs was not finished yet; the race of man was.

There were fifty-nine dogs left, fifty-eight females, one male.

There was one man, who could call himself the king of the world, or the Dalai Lama, or anything he liked, because there was no one left to dispute the honor with him. No one to talk to; no one to remember.

He was nine thousand and some odd hundreds of years old. Long ago, in the first fraction of that life-span, he had been given the organic catalysts that slowed down the process of maturity and decay almost to zero … not quite. At the age of one thousand, he had been a man of thirty, at two thousand, not quite forty. The golden years of full maturity, full powers, were multiplied until it had seemed they would never end.

But the years of decay were multiplied too. He had been a very old man for over a millennium. For a thousand years he had been dying.

The dogs kept him alive. They tended the machines, served him, did the work he was too feeble to do. The clever dogs, the faithful dogs, who would still be alive when he was dead.

He thought with bitter regret of his mother. He barely remembered her; she had died four thousand years ago. She could have had a daughter! he told himself. She needn't have left me to finish it all alone.

Perhaps she had tried. He thought he remembered vaguely that she had, that there had been miscarriages. The human strain was grown thin and sickly with too much care. He himself might have been incapable of fathering a child, even in his years of strength; now it was too late to wonder.

Not like the dogs, he told himself somberly. Bred for use, not for their own pleasure. *I* never wanted a child, when I was young. *They* think of nothing else.

He glanced again at Roland, and the dog's tail thumped against the paved floor.

A knot of pain gathered abruptly in the man's chest. He could well imagine the big-skulled whelps gathered around a fire in the evening, listening and looking while the older dogs told them of Man. He imagined their howls of dismay, when they learned there were no more men in the world.

Century after century … perhaps in time they would forget there had ever been a race of masters. Perhaps their sorrow and their loss would turn to a vague sadness, a restless urge that would drive them as Man's restless seeking had driven him. In time they might be great.

And then all the works of Man would be forgotten, lost to eternity – merely the unimportant prelude to the reign of Dog.

The thought sharpened his pain intolerably. He picked up the cool tube of the tankard that lay on the table beside him, and drew a long draft. The liquor lay heavily in him now. He was going to be sick soon.

He drank again, and sucked air. 'The tankard's empty,' he said. 'Fetch me another.'

Roland was up instantly, wagging his foolish tail. 'Yes, master,' and he was away, the tankard clutched in his clumsy fingers.

Roland hurried, ignoring the tight band of pain at the base of his spine, the complaining twinges in his legs. However altered and bred, the canine body was not designed to walk erect. You took the gift, and you gloried in it, but you paid for it. That was where old age first struck: very old dogs could not stand at all, but crept miserably on all fours, and the shame of it, Roland thought, shortened their lives.

The real agony came when duty pointed two ways at once; all else was of little account. For it was one thing to know what was best for the master – even to understand, in a dim corner of the mind, that the master was foolish, bitter, jealous, cruel. It was another thing to do what was best, when the master ordered otherwise. To obey was joy and utter necessity; even if the master commanded, 'Kill me!' even though the heart burst with remorse, a dog would obey.

Thus it was joy to fill the tankard, to serve, and it was pain, for the liquor was a slow poison. And even this was nothing. There was the question of breeding, which must be settled soon now.

Roland was the last male of his line. He knew how the others had died, one for clumsiness, one for a tail too big, others for a habit of drooling or for the wrong pattern of spots, or simply because the master was in a rage. He knew, even, that these deaths were not a matter of accident.

But Roland was coming to the end of his potent term, and still the order to breed had not been given. The food machine was still dropping, into every morsel of food the dogs ate, the chemical agent that kept them sterile.

The youngest bitch now living could not survive more than another three hundred years. The master, if he were well served could live another thousand.

As it had many times before, his mind skirted around the unvoiced thought of the death that would be the master's – the lonely, miserable death of an outcast cur …

The dogs must breed. The master must give the order.

He filled the tankard and climbed the ramp, panting as the strain told on his tired legs. Near the doorway stood one of the females, waiting for him. She did not speak, but there was a question in her anxious eyes.

Roland shook his head sorrowfully, and passed on.

He put the tankard on the little table, laid the drinking tube near the master's hand. The master did not appear to see him. Slumped among the cushions that filled the ebon and argent throne, he was gazing out into the sky. His bitter face was relaxed, almost peaceful.

Perhaps he was thinking of the days of his youth, when he had roamed the whole world and made it his. Perhaps he was musing on the greatness his ancestors had known – the globe-girdling engines, the mighty cities, the depth and daring of intellect that had plumbed the last secrets of the universe.

It was a good time; Roland dared delay no longer. His heart was thudding painfully and his throat was dry as he said, 'Master, may I speak?'

The man turned his head slowly and his red-rimmed eyes focused with surprise on Roland's face. 'You back?' he asked heavily. 'Where's the tankard?'

'Here, master,' said Roland, moving it forward. He waited while the man picked up the tube and drank. Then he said again, 'Master, may I speak?'

The man belched, and wiped his crusted lips with his hand. 'All right, what is it?'

The words tumbled out in confusion. 'Master, I am the last dog. I am near the end of my breeding time. If we do not breed, you will be left unattended when this generation is gone.'

The man looked at him with open hostility in his narrow eyes. 'Well, breed, then,' he said. 'Don't come to me for permission to play your dirty little games.'

Roland's throat was hot with shame. 'Master, to breed, I must stop the chemical in the food.'

'Stop it.'

They were playing a game, Roland knew. The master's memory was bad, but not this bad. His spirits lifted a little, even though he had little hope. If it was a game, then it gave the master pleasure. He said, 'Master, that is done by an automatic machine. The control cylinder is under your seal.'

The man stared at him silently for a moment, and scrubbed the bristles on his chin with one splotched and bony hand. 'So that's it, is it?' he said. 'You want me to unlock the cylinder, so you can make another generation of whining, dirty pups.'

'Yes, master.'

'You want your whelps to outlive me.'

'No, master!'

Volumes of unutterable things contended in Roland's mind. He felt shame, and horror, and a bottomless despair; and at the same time he knew that these were the things he was intended to feel, and he was glad. For a dog, however fine, is a dog, a man, however base, is a man.

The master said slowly, 'What do you want then, Roland?'

'I want you to live,' said the dog, and his voice broke. The slow, seldom tears of his race coursed down his cheeks.

The man was silent for a moment, then he turned away. 'All right, bring it here to me,' he said.

The female was waiting halfway down the ramp; two more were behind her. They shrank timidly at his approach, but their eagerness held them. He had no heart to reprimand them as they deserved.

'Did he—?'

'Yes!' said Roland. He hurried down the ramp, and the females followed him. More of them appeared at each stage of the descent, some racing ahead of him, some clustering behind. The corridor was filled with their involuntary yelps and whimpers of delight.

In the food room, a dozen of them were waiting for him, grouped around a cabinet against the far wall; they made a lane for him as he approached. Carefully, with ceremony, he unlocked the case and drew out the long cylinder, bound around with the wire and wax of the master's seal.

The king of the world sat in his throne of ebony and silver, and stared at the blank, meaningless face of the sky. Behind him, down the ramp that always smelled of dog no matter how it was disinfected, he heard the faint far echo of canine glee.

Roland had told them all about it, he thought. He felt hurried, cheated of his chance of decision. It was necessary to give them renewed life, he knew; he would suffer, otherwise; he would die painfully and alone.

But he could not prolong his life without sparing them also; and that was bitter as gall. Better to end all at once, dog and man ...

Roland came in, breathless, joy in his eyes, holding the cylinder carefully in his hands. Wordless, he held it out.

The man took it – a slender tube of silvery metal, dotted with line-up slots and the sockets of other components, and laced about with wire and the red wax of his own seal.

How long ago had he done that? a hundred, two hundred years – he had known even then that this day must come.

He glanced at the waiting dog – and remembered to his astonishment that in the days of his youth, this dog's ancestor and image had been his dear friend. They had been closer than brothers. He had mourned for years after that dog's death.

How was it possible that things had so changed? He looked at Roland again, saw the broad, crinkled brow, the worshipful eyes. There had been no changes here. It was incredible, to think how faithful that race had been. Millennium upon millennium, from the dawn of history until this day – all the thrown sticks retrieved, the households guarded, the blows accepted without anger. The weight of that loyalty seemed to him abruptly a crushing thing. What had his kind done to deserve it? And how could they ever repay?

It was Man, it was he himself who had changed. Man was the hopeless debtor, the flawed, the half-made. The dogs were worthier ...

And would survive.

In an instant that vision of the dog world that had forgotten Man came back to him, and his guilt receded, twisted upon itself, became a slow, bitter wrath.

He clutched the control cylinder in his fingers, as if their feeble strength could break it.

'Master—' said Roland falteringly. 'Is anything wrong?'

'Wrong?' he said. 'Not for you. Your whelps will inherit the Earth. A bunch of – dirty, flea-bitten, mangy *dogs*.'

The words were not enough; they came out in the quavering, impotent whine of an old man. He raised the cylinder, perhaps to strike; he did not know what he meant to do.

'Master? You will unseal the cylinder?'

Tears of rage leaked from the man's eye-corners. He said thickly, 'Here's your damned cylinder. Catch it, and you can have it!' And then the thing was done: he had flung out his arm with all its waning strength, and the cylinder was turning in the air, beyond the parapet.

Roland acted without thought. His hands and feet scrabbled on the flagstones, his muscles bunched in a pattern as old as the race; then he felt the smooth ivory of the balustrade for an instant under his feet.

He snapped once, vainly, at the cylinder as its arc passed him. Then there was nothing but the rushing wind.

The king of the world sat on his throne, and listened to the bitches howl.

TO THE PURE

'Jeff, please don't, you're hurting me.'

'Ah, you frigid dames give me a pain.'

Her voice altered, and he knew she was crying. 'Why did you marry me, then?'

'Sometimes I wonder. Come on, baby ...'

Monday morning when he showed up for work, there was an Antarean in the place. Jeff stopped in the doorway and looked at it. The thing was taller than him, slender, all golden down and feathers. It looked like one good belch would blow it away.

The super beckoned to him. Five or six of the other guys were standing around, looking uncomfortable. 'Jeff, this is Mr Nellith from the Antarean Technical Exchange Commission. He's going to find out what's wrong with our hyper-radio. Mr Nellith, Jeff Gorman, our circuits man.'

'Harya,' Jeff said warily, and stuck out his hand, then pulled it back. Somebody snickered. What was the thing going to shake with, for Christ's sake? It had flimsy golden wings, held close to its body, like a chicken's. The head was more birdlike than anything else – big cranium, great big glowing eyes, and a little thing like a bill, only soft-lipped. All the clothing it had on was a thing like a vest with pockets, but as far as Jeff could tell, there was nothing male about it.

'I am pleathed to know you,' Nellith said in a chirping voice. 'You are a thpethalitht in communicathionth thircuitth? Then we have thomething in common.'

Damned if we do, Jeff told himself, bunching the muscles in his arms and chest. Everything about him was short and thick – neck, fingers, his legs, his torso.

The super said hurriedly, 'Well, Mr Nellith, here's our problem.' He pointed to the big enamel-faced cabinet set up at one side of the room. It was an Antarean hyper-radio, one of the first items the Government had asked for when the technical exchange program started. They used it to monitor U.S. spaceships everywhere they went with the new Antarean drive. It had worked great for two years, then it had gone sour.

Jeff was a T5 and had studied the schematics. It should have been up to him to fix it, but there was no commonsense way to get into the damn thing. The cabinet was built in horizontal sections, with narrow spaces in between. Midway back in these spaces, running up into the machine, there were little access holes not even an inch in diameter, seven or eight inches deep. To get a component out, you would have to work with jointed tools and a periscope – and what if you dropped one into the machine?

The others followed the Antarean over to the cabinet, and after a minute Jeff went too.

Nellith's wings stirred; something like a stubby coil of rope appeared at the tip of each one, opened out – it was a tentacle, about seven inches long, with a bunch of weak-looking filaments at the end. Using them like fingers, the Antarean turned the power on, fiddled with the gain and tuning dials a minute. Then he bunched one set of filaments together and stuck them into an access hole. The tentacle flowed up into the hole, deeper, still deeper. It pulsed, as if the alien was feeling around there inside.

'You have been overloading the thircuith,' Nellith piped.

Everybody looked at Jeff. He felt his face getting red. 'Well, we had to try something, didn't we? What the hell, why don't you make these damn things so you can get into 'em?'

The super said hastily, 'The Antareans are building another rig to our specs. Meanwhile, we've got a service contract – it breaks down, they send a, hum, man, to fix it.' He coughed. 'What do you say, Mr Nellith, can do?'

The creature pulled out a component – one of the little Antarean hyper-resonators – clutched in the tendrils at the end of his tentacle. 'It may take thome time,' he said.

'Guess what Nelly did today?' Jeff asked sourly. He pulled off his tie, yanked his collar open.

'What?' Marge asked. She was clean and pretty as always – blond hair brushed, a touch of make-up – but her blue eyes were dull. She was two inches taller than he was, slender and fragile-looking. Maybe they were not especially well matched, physically or any other way, but he was proud of her. She was the kind of doll that made other guys eat their hearts out when they saw her on his arm. He had married her practically out of high school; he was the first man in her life, and he was proud of that too.

'One of the guys wrote down some parts numbers,' he said. 'Then he lost the paper like a damn fool. Nelly took the scratch pad and felt the next sheet, and read off the numbers. Then they asked him to read the date off a coin without looking, and he did that. So Andy Wolchak took him down to the Silver Grill for lunch and won twenty bucks betting on him. A bunch of us was going to go back after work and clean up, but Nelly wouldn't. Said he "didn't realize it was dishonest." Can you tie that?'

The beginning of the Antarean's second week on the job, the Department found him a room in one of the housing units right across the court from

Jeff. They threw a party for him that night, and invited all the Project personnel.

Marge spent practically the whole evening talking to Nellith, while Jeff gave her sour looks across the room. They had their heads together, eager and interested. Standing side by side that way, they even looked something alike – both tall and delicate, and Marge's blond hair was not so far off the color of Nellith's feathers.

'What the hell were you talking about all night?' he asked her when they got home.

'He's interesting – very spiritual,' she said. 'He's been all over the galaxy, studying religions. He says our Vedanta is very interesting.'

'Ah, for Chrissakes.'

Jeff started calling the Antarean 'Nelly,' first behind his back, to get a laugh from the other guys, then where Nellith could hear him. Finally he took to saying, 'Hey, Nelly – oh, sorry, I mean Mr Nellith.' But the alien was always polite and Jeff could not tell if it bothered him or not.

One day when they were alone in the room, Jeff crossed over next to Nellith and stepped on his fragile-looking foot, but the super came in at the wrong time, and he had to say it was an accident and would not happen again.

Next day he began making up to Nellith in a falsetto voice – praising the way he walked, his slender body, patting him on the downy top of his head. Once he even put his hands around Nellith's waist to show how narrow it was. One or two of the guys snickered.

Night after night, when he came home from poker or bowling with the guys, the same thing – Marge sitting up on the roof garden under the cool violet sky, side by side with Nellith.

'What in hell do you *talk* about all the time?'

'I told you – religion, mysticism, spiritual things like that.'

'Ah, hell.'

One thing he had found out. When Nellith was working on the circuits, with his tentacle stuck up deep into the insides of the cabinet, he was like an absent-minded professor – you could do damn near anything and he would not notice.

One lunch hour Jeff went down to the shopping area and picked out a wraparound beach skirt, white cotton with big yellow and blue flowers on it. He got it from the children's department.

He smuggled the thing in under his jacket and hid it. After about an hour, when everybody was busy and Nellith was probing away at the insides of the machine, he got up and tiptoed over. He got the skirt around Nellith's skinny hips and buttoned it. Nellith did not notice a thing.

He went back to his desk, and when one of the guys happened to look up and saw Nellith wearing the skirt, there was a roar of laughter.

The super was sore, and he knew Jeff was the one, but let him prove it.

'It ith not important,' Nellith said, looking at Jeff.

That was on the Monday of Nellith's last week. Tuesday, Jeff came home and found Marge gone – just gone, no note, all her stuff cleared out and the apartment tidied up.

On Wednesday he got a letter from a lawyer. She was suing him for divorce.

Friday afternoon, one of the guys said something he could not believe. He waited for the man out in the parking lot after work and pasted him good, but he still could not get it out of his head. That night there was a farewell party for Nellith. Jeff did not go, but stayed home by himself drinking beer and brooding.

Come eight o'clock, he put on a clean shirt and hopped on a cab out to the spaceport.

He found them there in the waiting room – Nellith the same as ever, all golden down and feathers; Marge looking young and pretty in a new blue suit, with an orchid on her lapel.

Two spaceport cops got in his way when he tried to walk closer, and some guy in civilian clothes moved up and flashed a badge in a leather folder. 'Let's not have any disturbance, please, Mr Gorman.'

'But damn it, that's my wife!'

The man looked embarrassed but determined. 'As I understand it, she's going to marry Mr Nellith as soon as your divorce comes through.'

'What are you talking about, marry – how can she marry that thing?'

There were reporters crowding around, and more cops, and more guys in civilian clothes. One of them said, 'Nellith has reciprocal citizenship rights under the treaty. According to Antarean law, there's nothing wrong with interspecies marriage. In fact, it's not uncommon.'

Jeff loosened his fists and said, 'Just let me talk to her. Okay? Just two minutes.'

They did not like it, but they let him get closer, sticking tight around him. He ignored the alien and looked at Marge. She looked back as if he was a stranger.

'Tell me why,' he said between his teeth. 'If it was some other guy maybe I could figure it, but how can you run off with a goddamn bird?'

Then the Antarean tender came down outside with a whoosh of jets, and the porters began picking up Marge's luggage. She gave him a look of contempt that took in his low brow, his thick hairy torso, his stubby hands and fingers. 'You wouldn't understand,' she said.

Then they all went away and left him standing there.

ERIPMAV

On the planet Veegl, in the Fomalhaut system, we found a curious race of cellulose vampires. The Veeglians, like all higher life on their world, are plants; the Veeglian vampire, needless to say, is a sapsucker.

One of the native clerks in our trade mission, a plant-girl named Xixl, had been complaining of lassitude and showing an unhealthy pink color for some weeks. The girl's parent stock suspected vampirism; we were skeptical, but had to admit that the two green-tinged punctures at the base of her axis were evidence of something wrong.

Accordingly we kept watch over her sleep-box for three nights running. (The Veeglians sleep in boxes of soil, built of heavy slabs of the hardmeat tree, or *woogl*; they look rather like coffins.) On the third night, sure enough, a translator named Ffengl, a hefty, blue-haired fellow, crept into her room and bent over the sleep-box.

We rushed out at the blackguard, but he turned quick as a wink and fairly flew up the whitemeat stairs. (The flesh of Veegl's only animal life, the 'meat-trees,' or *woogl*, petrifies rapidly in air and is much used for construction.) We found him in an unsuspected vault at the very top of the old building, trying to hide under the covers of an antique bed. It was an eerie business. We sizzled him with blasts from our proton guns, and yet to the end, with un-Veeglian vitality, he was struggling to reach us with his tendrils.

Afterwards he seemed dead enough, but the local wise-heads advised us to take certain precautions.

So we buried him with a steak through his heart.

BACKWARD, O TIME

He remembered the rain, and the white glare of auto headlights all around him. He could see nothing more, but he knew Emily was lying nearby, covered by someone's overcoat, not moving. It was painful, being born like this – a white knife, piercing him with each breath. All that drifted out of reach. When he woke again, they were both in the car, whirling violently back from the grinding clash of a collision. The other car receded; its head-lamps finally turned to a dim glow on the far side of the hill, and vanished. The road reeled back, silently, smoothly.

Sullivan watched the stars wheel through the night as he drove. He was tired and at peace, wanting nothing, accepting everything with a quiet wonder.

How strange and wonderful it all was, entering his home for the first time – five beautifully furnished rooms, just right for Emily and himself. The books with their leather and cloth bindings. The pictures, the boxes of cigars, the wardrobes and dressers full of rich, dark clothing cut to his measure. Life, thought Laurence Wallace Sullivan, was good.

That morning before the fire, his hand took a comfortably worn leather volume from the shelves, and opened it to a thumb-marked page.

> *Time's graven footsteps in the sands*
> *Behind us, if we but approach,*
> *Sublime our own lives we can make.*
> *Remind us, lives of all great men!*

Wonderful words … He glanced at his watch. The sky outside his study window was lightening, from deep azure to robin's egg, faintly green over the skeletal forest of antennas. He felt stuffed; it was time for dinner. He replaced the book on its shelf, and strolled into the dining room, sighing and stretching.

The firm of Sullivan and Gaynor, he found, operated an unprinting plant that filled a three-story building on Vesey Street. The enormous machines devoured every kind of printed matter and turned it into neat rolls of paper, cans of ink, metal ingots. Their operation was far too complex for Sullivan to understand fully, and he did not try, contenting himself with the correspondence and the financial reports that flowed across his desk. Gaynor, his partner, spent more time in the plant: a red-faced, dyspeptic man with a raucous voice.

Nevertheless, Sullivan flattered himself that he understood the romance of his business: words, words from all over the world streamed into this building in nature's senseless profusion – words endlessly repeated, words plucked from dead fires and from traschcans, to be carefully unprinted and reduced to one copy only of each sermon, pamphlet, book, advertising leaflet ... Like arrow-shapes, fan-shapes, of floating paper, each found its way unerringly to the one man for whom it was intended. Sullivan (in his humble way, of course) was a public servant, a guardian of regress.

The swift years went by. Summers, on Cape Cod, Sullivan began to feel a strange discontent, listening to the curlews piping on the sands, or watching a sudden evening squall carry water streaking up from the sea. In his lips the pale Havana cigars prolonged themselves behind their smooth inch-long ash, until at last they rounded themselves off, and he drew the flame, capped them with his silver-knife, and put them carefully away in the humidor. Emily's hair was darkening; they talked more now, and quarreled more. Sometimes she looked strangely at him. Where was it all heading? What was life for?

He was ten years old when he discovered sex, with Emily – a brief and unsatisfactory experience, not soon repeated. Two years later, he met Peggy.

It was in an apartment house in the fifties, where he had never been before. The door opened as he turned to it one afternoon, and she slapped his face, hard. Then they were inside, glaring at each other, breathing heavily. Sullivan felt a fury for her that was all mingled with disgust and desire. After a few minutes, sullenly, they began to take off their clothes ...

After Peggy came Alice, and after Alice, Connie. That was in 1942; Sullivan was fifteen, in the prime of his vigor. In that year the stranger who was his son came home from Italy. Robert had just been discharged from the army; he called himself R. Gaynor Sullivan at first, was gawky and insolent, but after he enrolled in college things went better. Then in a surprisingly short time he was home again, and the apartment was not big enough. They moved to a house in Long Island City: more confusion, and Sullivan's relations with his wife were strained. He was working too hard; the firm's business was booming, due partly to a heavy lump-sum repayment to Emily's father.

Each month, the check stubs. Money poured into the account, from grocer, dentist, doctors ... he was always hard pressed to withdraw enough to keep it balanced.

In the evenings his familiar face stared back at him from the mirror haggard and gray. His fingers rubbed the smooth cheek; the razor came riding diagonally up with a crisp sound, trailing lather and making the bristles sprout behind it. Then the warm brush to remove the lather, and the same face, with its beard restored. What if he should leave it smooth some day? But shaving was customary.

The firm had moved several times, finally settling in a loft on Bleecker Street. Their operations had simplified; more and more employees had been let go, until Sullivan, Gaynor and three printers could run the place themselves. Sullivan often took a hand at the job press; once you had learned the trick of it, there was a soothing, almost hypnotic quality in the rhythm that flicked a blank page from the platen and slapped a printed one in to be erased, all in the acrobatic movement of safety when the metal jaws gaped. Gaynor was a much more likable fellow these days; Sullivan's days at work were filled with pleasure, as his nights at home. The boy had grown incredibly dear to him, and he was in love with Emily: he had never, Sullivan thought, been so happy.

The last vouchers had been filled; the final entries had been erased from the ledgers. The workmen were unbolting the presses and dismantling them to be carried away. There was nothing more to do but to shake hands on it, and go their separate ways. He and Gaynor ceremonially locked the door together and adjourned to the bar downstairs, feeling a premonitory glow.

'Here's to success!'

'Maybe now this fella Roosevelt is going out, we'll see some changes.'

They clinked their glasses solemnly, set them down on the waitress' tray. Sobered, they left. Gaynor was going back to Minneapolis where he had job as foreman of an unprinting plant; Sullivan himself was going to have to hunt for a while before he found a job as assistant to a paper broker. But not for long; the Boom was coming up in a few years.

Sullivan uncrumpled the *Sun*, relishing the heavy feel of the gray pages. 'That woman is out of office in Texas,' he announced, adding, 'Good riddance!' Yes, that was what the headline said. Women governors – what was the world coming to?

Emily, folding diapers, did not seem to hear. She was losing her figure again; she seemed pale, tired and listless. Little Robert was grunting in his cradle; he had shrunk to a fat handful, more animal than baby. He slept nearly all the time, when he was not howling, or further distending Emily's swollen breasts. Life was a queer business. In another month it would be time to take them both to the hospital, and only Emily would be coming back. That was funny; he had loved the child, and took an affectionate interest in it even now, but it would be almost a relief to get rid of it. Afterwards, it would be a good six months before Emily got her figure back …

She glanced at him sidelong. She was still a lovely woman. Emily: but what did she secretly think of him? What was it really all about?

The minister's voice droned in his ears. Emily, looking more beautiful than he had ever seen her, gently moved out of his embrace. He took the ring from her finger, and handed it to Bob. 'I divorce thee with this ring,' he said.

Afterwards they went out together, many times, but never to bed except once, hastily, in the back room one night when her parents were away. At a party one morning they chatted inconsequentially; then a polite stranger said, 'Emily, I want you to say goodbye to Larry Sullivan,' and led him away. He knew he would never see her again.

From that day on, there was an emptiness in his life. He tried to fill it with amusements – too much liquor, too much music. He met girls, and kissed them, took them on dates, but he missed his wife. It was hard to get used to, living alone after all these years.

Still, life had its compensations. There was an endless interest in watching the changes the years brought – seeing it all work out.

Automobiles lost all trace of their former streamlines, became elegantly spare or even boxy, hinting at victorias and broughams to come. There were fewer machines on the streets, and fewer people; the air was purer. Garbo replaced Grable on the silver screen. Abruptly, then, the movies ceased to talk. The incomparable Chaplin came into his own; the Keystone cops were born. Sullivan watched it all with fascinated eyes. Technological regress was certainly a wonderful thing! And yet sometimes Sullivan found himself thinking nostalgically of the old blaring, bustling days.

Luckily there was still the War to come, Europe was rousing from her long sleep; and to the East, Holy Russia was being born.

Sullivan nervously fingered the scar on his shin. He was due to go to field hospital with it, he judged – it was tight and raw-feeling, and itched. It was the worst scar he had, puckered and stretching halfway up his shinbone; he would be glad to get rid of it, and go on to the front. War was not much like the movies, so far.

He walked out of the barracks tent into the sunlight, helping himself along with his slender cane. There were a lot of other casualties; he supposed this must be the prelude of the big battle of the Argonne that he had read about in the prophecies. That would be where his number came up. What would it be, a mortar shell, or hand-to-hand – or even something anticlimactic, like falling over a tent-rope in the dark? He wished the time would come, and get it over.

He met his father, briefly, when he came home from France. The old man was very gray and shaky, and they did not seem to have much in common; it was a relief on both sides, Sullivan thought, when he went off to Cornell.

He was enrolled as a senior, which meant he had to go the full four years.

Sullivan did not mind that; after all, the years you spent in college were the most important ones of your life. Here everything you had thought and read, all you knew, all you had been, poured out of you and funneled down to the instructee of that particular class. Then the instructee would sum it all up in one of his lectures, dry or brilliant according to who it was; and eventually the essence of it would get into the ultimate copy of a textbook, to be absorbed by the author and so returned to nature, used up, got rid of.

In the spring he went out for football. He was registered in the athletic prediction books as playing two full seasons on the varsity. The books did not say so, but probably that was where he was going to get rid of the crook in his nose.

Professor Toohey was an old duck who took a fancy to Sullivan before he had been in college a year. They used to spout beer, down in Toohey's dark cellar where he kept a keg for it, and talk philosophy. 'There's something to think about,' Toohey might begin, circling up to a subject they had discussed before. 'How can we tell? The reverse sequence of causation may be just as valid as the one we are experiencing. Cause-and-effect are arbitrary, after all.'

'But it sounds pretty fantastic,' Sullivan would say cautiously.

'It's hard for us to imagine, just because we're not used to it. It's only a matter of viewpoint. Water would run downhill, and so on. Energy would flow the other way – from total concentration to total dispersion. Why not?'

Sullivan tried hard to visualize that peculiar world: it gave him a half-pleasant shudder. Imagine never knowing the date of your death ... 'Everything would be backwards. If you meant "catch," you'd have to say "throw." All the words would have to mean different things – all the verbs that express duration, anyway. There are difficulties to it.'

'It all makes perfectly good sense in its own terms. Friction would be a factor to be subtracted from energy calculations, not added. And so on. The universe would be expanding; we'd heat our houses with furnaces instead of cooling them. Grass would grow out of seeds. And you would take food into your body and expel waste matter, instead of increting and exgesting as we do. That's right!'

Sullivan grinned. 'You mean, we'd come out of the bodies of women and be buried in the ground when we died?'

'Think about it for a minute. It would seem perfectly natural. We might live backward, death to birth, and never know the difference. Which came first, the chicken or the egg? Do wars cause armies, or armies wars? What do we mean by causation, anyway? Think about it.'

'Hmmm.'

And the formal end-question: 'Sullivan, what do you think about the principle of causation?'

He wished he knew.

The world was growing larger and brighter, now that he was fifty-two. Sullivan had a furious energy that drove him out of doors all day in good weather; even in winter he stood about, watching the freezing ground water rush up the drainspout, or letting the snow form on his head and shoulders, drifting up into the white sky as it did from the ground on which he stood. Whatever came he took without question; if his fingers and nose were bright pink with cold when he went out, the snow would warm them; if he awoke with a black eye, a friend would heal it with his fist. Sullivan climbed his friends' backs and leaped off, and they his, with peals of cracked idiot laughter. They fidgeted in class, made comical faces at one another from behind books, swarmed yelling up hill and down again. For repletion there was mealtime, and time was the cure for hunger. The hardest thing was that Mrs Hastings would not let him out of bed when he awoke early in the morning, though any fool could see he was not going to sleep anymore; after that his day was one long gallop.

There came a day when Sullivan and his father were seized with a nervous anticipation; it took the form of tears on Sullivan's part, scowls and throat-clearings on his father's. All day they were good for nothing, and could not look at each other. At last, in the late afternoon, they dressed to go out.

His father drove, following the roads automatically. When they got out, Sullivan saw that they were in a cemetery.

Something clutched tight at his heart. His father's arm came unwelcome around him, the strong fingers hard on his arm as he stumbled. Others were moving nearby: at last they all grouped, and turned, and were standing beside a half-open grave. Two men were uncovering the box already, expertly catching each shovel-load of dirt as it leaped, thrusting it sharply into the pile and waiting for the next.

Afterwards they raised the box with broad straps until it rested on boards laid across the hole in the ground. The minister, standing on the far side of the grave, unfolded his hands and spoke.

'... From dust thou comest, and dust thou art ...'

When he was finished, he coughed apologetically and was silent. The crowd began to flow away. The workmen stood beside the grave and the box, bareheaded in the sunlight, hands at their sides.

Sullivan was trying to get used to an unaccustomed pain that had come to live in his chest. It was like being sick, but he was not sick. It was not even an honest pain, caused by medicine; it was just a kind of persistent crying ache that would not go away.

He saw now, with the eye of disillusionment, that all his past gaiety had been foolish. Here he was in the last decade of his life, fifty-two years behind him, and what could he show for it? Nothing but this ache of loss. His hand worked reflexively at the contents of his pocket, and brought up a spiny handful: jackknife, pencil stub, assorted nails, a wad of grimy string, two marbles and an aggie, three pennies, a gray chip of rock with shiny specks in it, cracker crumbs, and over everything, pocket lint. Dust and ashes.

A hot tear crawled up his cheek.

The old man came into the room wearily, setting a broom down in the corner. He had been taking care of the house himself, these last few days; Mrs Hastings had disappeared and Sullivan did not think she was coming back.

'Put your coat on, Larry,' said his father with a sigh.

Sullivan did as he was told. In silence they went out to the corner and waited for the street car. Gradually Sullivan began to recognize the route they took. It was the same way they had gone that time when he had his tonsils put in. A touch of fear came to him, but he endured it and said nothing.

It was the hospital they were going to, all right. In the dark lobby, they did not look at each other. Sullivan's father stood with his bowler in both hands, talking to a doctor, while Sullivan walked mechanically past him down the hall.

Where was he going in this unpleasant dark place with its sharp smells of ether and formaldehyde, and its clicking sharp-heeled nurses with sour faces over their trays? The closed doors moved past on either side.

Sullivan stopped, and turned, with an unaccountable tightness in his throat, and found himself facing a door like the others. But this one was going to open.

The knob turned; Sullivan could not bear it. He wanted to run, but felt rooted to the spot. What, oh what was it? The door was opening, and inside, on the bed—

A gray woman. Her tired eyes opened, and she tried to smile at him.

A painful rapture swelled inside his chest. Now at last he understood; he understood everything.

'*Mother*,' he said.

THE NIGHT OF LIES

The desert hills hung dark over the town. It was early evening, and the wind was blowing gently across the long spaces. A cricket struck up its song, out in the darkness somewhere; then another. Down the long twisting streets the purple lights began to glow, like soft witchfires in the evening. They bathed the weathered false fronts with magical radiance, filled the empty windows and the dusty silent room. A store-sign swayed back and forth, creaking cheerfully. A breath of music floated up the street. A man's laugh rocketed up, full-throated and joyous.

A woman stepped out on to the boardwalk with a swirl of spangled skirts. She was slender in cream-and-gold; her face was as pale and her hair was as golden as her garments. 'Ken!' she called. 'Here!'

A man appeared under the distant arcade. He was lithe and slim, poised like a fighter. 'Lorna! We're alive – and they're gone!'

Her laughter rippled down to him. 'Of course! Isn't it wonderful?'

He came towards her with long strides. 'Where's Murray? And Louise?'

'Here!'

'Here!'

A stocky man came out into view, red-cheeked and grinning; then a woman in a glimmering ice-blue gown. They came together in the middle of the long street, the men clasping hands and slapping shoulders, the women embracing.

'Alive – and the invaders gone!'

'Clean away – back to Arcturus!'

'Forgot us!'

'We're alive!'

In the violet glow their faces were exultant, eyes bright, teeth flashing. The woman called Louise swung her dark hair, and her feet began to move to the music. 'It's too wonderful – I can't stand still – I have to dance!'

She seized Murray's hands and drew him protesting into a breathless polka, around and around to the music, while the other two laughed until they cried. 'Oh, Murray – if you could see yourself!'

'Never,' panted the stocky man, mopping his face with a bandana, 'never in my life did I dance like that.'

The others were silent a moment; the music had fallen into silence and the slow wind came lonely down the street. 'But come on!' said Murray. 'This is a night to celebrate – we've got places to go, and things to do, my friends!'

Fire fountained from the church spire, red sparks floating on the wind. Every cornice was a worm of blue light. Roman candles soared with a whispering rush overhead. Rockets went up, to burst into silent stars dripping and fading down the sky. 'To the watchtower!' cried Lorna.

'By the way of the wineshop!' shouted Murray. And their laughter echoed across the quiet town.

They mounted the clanging risers under the stairs.

'I was the greatest scientist in the world,' said Murray, looking out over the roofs.

'And I was the greatest singer,' said Lorna.

'And I was the best boxer.'

'And I was the most expensive whore.'

'Now, we four …' said Murray, and a silence fell upon them. The desert was empty and dark, all around the town.

'To us!' cried Louise, raising her wineglass.

'To us!' and they drank, standing high above the rooftops, while the dark wind ruffled their hair.

'Why should it be we four?' whispered Lorna to Ken. 'It seems so—'

'We're old friends,' he said. 'Who else would it be? Can you imagine the world without old Murray – or Lou?'

She touched his hair. 'I always loved you – really.'

'I know you did. I know that now, Lorna. And it's all right. I mean really all right, now, because we're alive, you hear – You stars, there, do you hear? We're alive!'

The echoes fluttered away across the silent roofs and died at the edge of the desert.

'Four out of billions,' said Murray, coming nearer, 'because I know we are the last.'

'It's better not to talk about it,' said Louise, following him.

'But we all saw the invaders' ships floating across the sky, burning and burning … rank after rank of them, as if they had nothing to do but float there, and burn. There couldn't be anyone else alive.'

'Well, then,' said Louise with a bright glint in her eye, 'four is enough, isn't it?'

'My dear –' said Murray, turning to her.

'Let's dance, then – let's sing!' cried Lorna. The music was skirling, and the lights pulsed up over the tower like phantom combers breaking.

Loudly their laughter rang out across the wasteland, and their untiring bodies whirled about the floor. They drank the red wine in great draughts, and were not drunken; they sang, and never paused for breath. The night flowed away across the mountains; the first edge of dawn appeared in the east.

The music had stopped, and only the distant crickets were singing in the darkness. 'I'm cold,' said Lorna, 'it's too cold here. Let's go down.'

'Four out of billions,' muttered Murray as they descended the tower. 'How could they have come to miss us? I can't remember – why were we here, the four of us?'

'We drove,' said Ken.

'Yes, at night,' said Louise. 'With the invaders up over the horizon – I remember. We came out across the desert, and then—' her voice trailed away.

'I can't remember any more,' said Lorna.

'No. Only a dream, a darkness, until we woke up.'

'But we're alive – what does it matter? We're alive ...'

'Suppose they had all died,' Murray muttered. 'All, the whole planet recently dead.'

'Don't talk about it.'

'No, but think of the dead people lying in their thousands and millions, all night long – would they dream?'

'Don't talk about it.'

'No, but would they dream? With no live people to interfere, to blot them out – such a refreshing thing, only the dead. Dreaming, in thousands, their one last night.'

Lorna shuddered. 'A nightmare.'

'Yes.' Murray nodded vehemently. 'A terrible thing – it's good that we're not there, that the desert protects us. All those dead people, dreaming freely at last, but so many at once! One dream overlapping the next, fragments tearing fragments apart! A terrible last night, for the dead people in their billions.'

They were silent, imagining the fretful voices, out beyond the mountains. *I was the greatest ... I could have conquered the ... men worshipped my beauty ... I, I was the king ... no, listen to me, to me!*

They shuddered. Lorna said, 'Why are we going this way?'

Ahead, in the town square, a car was overturned beside the old iron war monument. The hood was crumpled, the windshield smashed and scattered; there was a body lying, half in and half out.

'I saw it from the tower,' Murray said dismally.

'Let's not go any nearer.'

'But we have to, don't you understand? The night's almost over.'

The purple witchfires were dying, all down the street. The light in the east was rising.

'One of us?' whispered Ken.

They drew closer together, huddling in the cold dawn.

'But which one?'

They looked at each other. Lorna saw that Ken was turning misty, half-transparent; a morning star burned through his breast. Seeing her stare, he crouched and said fiercely, 'I'm real – me, I'm real!' And he struck his chest with his fist, but it made no sound.

'I'm dreaming you all,' said Lorna disbelievingly. 'I'm pretending. That must be me – my car, I was trying to get away, I crossed the desert and smashed up.' But her voice was thin, and the morning light blazed through her as if she were made of paper.

'All dead? All dead?' said Murray's plaintive voice. He was gray as smoke, like all the rest. They drifted, they floated towards the monument.

They came together around the body that sprawled out of the wreck. 'I was the greatest scientist in the world,' said Murray's voice, fading.

'I was the greatest boxer,' echoed Ken's, and he was gone.

'I was the most expensive whore—' A faint voice, dying on the wind.

'I was the greatest singer—' A murmur, rustling away into silence.

The four were gone. Only the one sprawled figure remained – a slight young man, dead, with blood on his jacket, and his weak face twisted up at the stars. A last thought, fading: *And I – I was nothing at all.*

MAID TO MEASURE

Côte d'Azur sunlight, filtered by the jalousies, made a golden dimness in the room. On the green brocade chaise lay a slender blonde in tennis costume, swinging a racquet in her hand. Each time she swung it, it went *thump* on the floor.

'I wish you wouldn't do that,' said the bearded young man irritably. 'I've spoiled this damn postcard twice.' He threw a colorful bit of cardboard at the wastebasket, and drew another towards him across the writing desk.

'*I* wish you wouldn't make cow's eyes at aging brunettes in bars,' said the girl. There was a gleam of spite in her big blue eyes.

'Aging!' said the young man automatically, pausing in his work.

'She must have been thirty if she was a day,' said the girl. *Thump* went the tennis racquet.

'Umm,' said the young man, looking up.

'*Umm,* hell!' said the girl. Her expression had grown definitely unpleasant. 'I've got half a mind—'

'What?' asked the young man apprehensively.

'Oh, nothing.' After a pause, she said, 'Mother would have known what to do with you. She was a witch.'

The young man clucked his tongue disapprovingly, without looking up. 'Shouldn't talk about your old mother that way,' he said.

'She was a *witch*,' the girl said. 'She could turn herself into a wolf, or a tiger, or anything she liked.'

'Sure, she could,' said the young man, signing his postcard. 'There we are.' He put the card aside, lit a cigarette, and glanced rather nervously at his watch. 'All kidding aside, Yana – we've had a pretty good time—'

'But all things come to an end?' the girl asked in a dangerous voice. 'We're both grown-ups? We ought to be realistic? Is that it?' She stood up and went to the closet.

'Well—' said the young man uncomfortably. His expression brightened. 'What are you doing?'

The girl pulled out a pigskin suitcase and opened it with unnecessary vehemence. She rummaged in one of the pockets, drew out a worn chamois bag. 'Looking for something,' she said over her shoulder.

'Oh,' said the young man, disappointed. He watched while the girl opened the drawstrings, took out a small object wrapped in a dirty red cloth and tied with string. He glanced at his watch again; when he looked up, the girl had a small, oddly shaped bottle in her hand.

'What's that?'

'Something my mother left me,' the girl said. Her fingernails gritted unpleasantly on the glass as she scraped the wax off and removed the stopper. She gave him a narrow look. 'So you won't change your mind?'

'Now, Yana—'

'Then here's luck.' She put the bottle to her lips, tilted her head back and swallowed.

'Now then,' she said, lowering the empty bottle, 'let's see ...' She flexed one hand experimentally, looking at her long nails.

The young man was inspecting his watch. 'Almost three o'clock,' he muttered. 'Yana, didn't you say you were going to the hairdresser's this afternoon?'

'I changed my mind.' She looked at him thoughtfully. 'Why – are you expecting anyone?'

'Oh, no,' the young man said hastily. He stood up energetically. 'Tell you what, Yana – no hard feelings – let's go for a swim.'

'I see,' said the girl. 'Tell me, what about tonight – no plans? No one coming over?'

'No, not a thing.'

'So, we'll be all alone – just the two of us.' She smiled, showing her pointed eyeteeth. 'That will give me plenty of time to decide. What shall I be, darling – your great big stripey pussycat ... or your faithful, hungry dog?'

The young man, who was peeling his shirt off over his head, did not hear. His voice came indistinctly. 'Well, if we're going for that swim, let's get moving.'

'All right,' the girl said. 'Wait a minute, and I'll change into a bikini.'

Emerging from the shirt, the young man said, 'Glad you decided not to be—' He looked around, but the girl was not in the room. 'Yana? Yana? That's funny.' He crossed the room, glanced into the bedroom, then the bath. They were empty.

A light tapping came at the French doors as the young man turned. They opened, and a pretty dark-haired young woman put her head in. 'Robert? I am not intruding?'

'Giselle!' cried the young man, smiling with pleasure. 'No, come on in – you're right on time. I was just thinking about going for a swim.'

The young woman advanced with a charming smile; her figure, in a low-cut blue sun dress, was also charming.

'Oh, it's too bad,' she said; 'I have no suit.'

'Here's one,' said the young man cheerfully, picking up two candy-striped bits of material from the chaise. 'Try that one for size.'

'But doesn't it belong to your – little friend? Won't she mind?'

'No, no – don't give her another thought.'

As they were leaving, the young man glanced with an odd expression at the striped bikini, which fitted the dark girl admirably.

'What is it, anything wrong?'

'Just thought of something Yana said before she left … No, it couldn't be. Well, come on!'

Arm in arm, laughing, they went out into the sunlight.

COLLECTOR'S ITEM

Dreams and memories mingled inextricably in Firefoal's mind now, so that the object of his search was not always the same ... Sometimes, with penetray scanner and keen listening devices, he stalked the last specimen of *hidden twitterer,* that saucer-eyed mouselike creature spawned from a mutated ovum twenty million years after the last acre of raw earth had been covered over and sealed away, while life went on in the steel honeycomb above it ... Sometimes, with atavistic hair sprouting like fungus from his weather-marked face, he hunted the dodo, or the okapi, or searched for the secret nesting grounds of the passenger pigeon. But always he knew these fantasies for what they were, so that he hunted not for specimens so much as for Meaning. He sought the reality behind the symbol.

Sometimes the search would be interrupted by long, brilliantly lighted scenes of seeming irrelevance, and Firefoal bore them patiently, waiting for the slow tilt of blue into gray that heralded a change in the dream.

Once he stood, a child, before the silent effigy of a great, proud creature that posed with head lifted and nostrils widening to a vanished breeze. Satiny brown it was of coat, and jet of mane and tail, and in its huge eyes were distances and open space such as he had never seen. His father, a vague figure in a long robe, moved his hand across a spot of light that glowed on the wall, and instantly the great animal vanished and a parched white skeleton stood there instead. He screamed then and would not be comforted, though his father made the animal come back again. He knew that he would never pass his fingers over those delicate nostrils or mount that wide back, for the animal was dead. And it was the last.

But that was when he was a child, and before he understood that he had been born into the world for one thing, and one thing only. He studied the sciences, and one day he knew, as his father had known, that they were all imperfections, all blunted instruments, leading finally to the one science that capped all.

Geology changed the faces of continents, before man rendered them forever changeless.

Medicine wiped out many species inimical to man.

Metallurgy forged weapons. Chemistry and physics armed them.

Comparative biology explained the beginning and the end.

Natural history, the oldest of all, replaced them all when they had done their work and faded. At the very apex of human endeavor, it explained everything, justified everything, fulfilled everything.

He was fifteen, sitting before a screen from which stared the deep-sunken eyes of a man long dead. He took no notes and needed none, for already his eager brain had mastered the principles of total recall. 'Consider,' said the dead man's voice. 'From the sterile beginning life struggled outward, forms proliferating upon forms until the earth swarmed and crawled with living organisms of every shape and size and color. The air was filled with their hum and the earth rustled to their coming and going, and the sea silently rippled with their multitudes.

'In every cubic centimeter of dirt and in every breath of air, in every drop of water, swam uncountable lives. Then, slowly, the pendulum swung.

'The ant and the termite survived, but the trilobite and the dinosaur did not. Fewer and fewer new forms took the place of those which died in natural catastrophes or exterminated each other. And then man was born, the great destroyer.

'For millions of years, man killed only those life forms which offered him competition on a gross scale, or which supplied him with things he needed. See, on this chart. Now van Leeuwenhoek; Pasteur; and the competitors in the microcosm are recognized and the battle is joined. Now preventive medicine. Now the electron microscope. Now the world city beings.

'And now, for the first time, it is realized that *all* other living organisms are man's enemies. Where is there place for horses and cattle, fields and forests, in a world of instantaneous transport and synthetic food? Here, note the emergence of durable flower replicas. Cereal plants are long since gone; now flowers go too, and there are no more bees.

'And so it goes. Here is Wildwing the Elder and pangermicide; here biosynthesis. Now the natural atmosphere of the planet is utterly sealed off and the wastes poured into it destroy all the remaining beasts of the air.

'Now we approach the present day. Sea water was the most efficient source of elements for conversion … It is gone. The number of species coexistent with man is three thousand, five hundred and eight, and of these all but approximately nine hundred are nearing extinction. The day is not far off when we shall see Earth swept clean of all life inimical to ourselves … that is to say, all life but our own …'

But this was a biologist who spoke; one of the last biologists. To Firefoal, the natural historian, all this frantic life was not dead but triumphantly alive. 'The proper study of mankind is Man' … yet no other history of man was adequate to describe him but the tale of the organisms he had vanquished. Here they were, in this great robot-tended museum which was the work of Firefoal's line. Not all of them, for many upon many had vanished unnoticed and unknown. But what man could do, man had done. Here was the last surviving member of nearly every species, elephant and emu, walrus and wapiti, dragonfly and dog, the great and the small, preserved, analyzed and documented, each in its place. The last work of man; his monument and his justification.

Now the half-dream shifted again, and the tension returned. The quarry still floated before him, elusive and dim, shape melting into protean shape, and he still pursued.

Time. Time was growing short. How old was he now? Five hundred years? A thousand? That question trailed off unanswered like the others, but he was old, he knew, and his lifework almost done ... *almost* done.

The world would not let him rest; he pressed on, though his heart thudded painfully and his breath was a knife in his breast. Again and again he glimpsed the creature he followed, and each time it melted, a phantasm or a memory. He was no closer to his goal; and time was short.

The pain caught him in a maze of color then and he fought it, struggling upwards like a drowning man, till the dream shapes faded and the dream colors dimmed ... Gently a pale light floated down upon him, and in it he saw an army of his victims, rank upon rank, each exquisitely clear and perfect in its cubicle. The picture strengthened as the pain receded and dropped somewhere below him; and now he saw—

Saw the empty cubicle he had prepared this morning before the sickness took him, and the mechanisms waiting beside it, and the tall robot which bent over him.

The robot took him up in careful arms, as the last of the pain dropped away into coldness. Only a spark now, Firefoal watched as he was carried into the cubicle – watched, fading, as the mechanisms began their work. He stood there, proudly erect, his old eyes looking into long-ago distances, his nostrils dilated to catch a vanished breeze. The last specimen. The greatest. The end and the cornerstone. Coldness now, fading. Darkness.

Satisfaction.

A LIKELY STORY

That was the damnedest December I ever saw in New York. Whatever the weather is, Manhattan *always* gets the worst of it – frying hot in summer, snow or slush up to your ankles in winter – and all along the seaboard, it was a mean season. Coming in from Pennsylvania the day before, we'd been held up twice while the tracks were cleared. But when I stepped out of the hotel that night, the Saturday after Christmas, it was like a mild October; the air was just cool, with a fresh hint of snow in it. There was a little slush in the gutters, not much; the pavements were dry.

I was late, or I would have gone back and ditched the rubbers; I hate the foolish things to begin with, one reason I moved to the country – out there, I wear house slippers half the year, galoshes the rest; there's no in-between. I took off my gloves, opened my scarf, and breathed deep lungfuls while I walked to the corner for a cab. I began to wonder if it had been smart to move ninety miles out of town just because I didn't like rubbers.

The streets didn't seem overcrowded. I got a cab without any trouble. Nobody was hurrying; it was as if the whole population was sitting peacefully at home or in some bar, in no rush to be anywhere else.

'Listen,' I said to the cabbie, 'this is still New York, isn't it?'

He jerked his chin at me. 'Hah?'

'Where's the crowds?' I said. 'Where's the rotten weather? What happened?'

He nodded. 'I know watcha mean. Sure is funny. Crazy weather.'

'Well, when did this happen?'

'Hah?'

'I said, how long has this been going on?'

'Cleared up about three o'clock. I looked out the winda, and the sun was shinin'. Jeez! You know what I think?'

'You think it's them atom bombs,' I told him.

'That's right. You know what I think, I think it's them *atom* bombs.' He pulled up opposite a canopy and folded down his flag.

In the lobby, I found an arrow-shaped sign that said MEDUSA CLUB.

The Medusa Club is, loosely speaking, an association of professional science fiction writers. No two of them will agree on what science fiction is – or anything else – but they all write it, or have written it, or pretend they can write it, or something. They have three kinds of meetings, or two and a half. One is for club politics, one is for drinking, and the third is also for drinking, only more so. As a rule, they meet in people's apartments, usually Preacher Flatt's or Ray Alvarez', but every year at this time they rent a hotel ballroom and throw a whingding. I'm a member in bad standing; the last time I paid my dues was in 1950.

Rod Pfehl (the P is silent, as in Psmith) was standing in the doorway, drunk, with a wad of dollar bills in his hand. 'I'm the treasurer,' he said happily. 'Gimme.' Either he was the treasurer, or he had conned a lot of people into thinking so. I paid him and started zigzagging slowly across the floor, trading hellos, looking for liquor.

Tom Q. Jones went by in a hurry, carrying a big camera. That was unusual; Tom Q. is head components designer for a leading radio-TV manufacturer, and has sold, I guess, about two million words of science fiction, but this was the first time I had ever seen him in motion, or with anything but a highball in his hand. I spotted Punchy Carrol, nut-brown in a red dress; and Duchamp biting his pipe; and Leigh MacKean with her pale proto-Nordic face, as wistful and fey as the White Knight's; and there was a fan named Harry Somebody, nervously adjusting his hornrims as he peered across the room; and, this being the Christmas Party, there were a lot of the strangest faces on earth.

Most of them were probably friends of friends, but you never knew; one time there had been a quiet banker-type man at a Medusa meeting, sitting in a corner and not saying much, who turned out to be Dorrance Canning, an old idol of mine; he wrote the 'Woman Who Slept' series and other gorgeous stuff before I was out of knee pants.

There were two blue-jacketed bartenders, and the drinks were eighty-five cents. Another reason I moved to the country is that the amusements are cheaper. Nursing my collins, I steered around two broad rumps in flounced satin and ran into Tom Q. He snapped a flashbulb in my face, chortled something, and went away while I was still dazzled. Somebody else with a lemon-colored spot for a head shook my left hand and muttered at me, but I wasn't listening; I had just figured out that what Tom had said was, 'There's no *film* in it!'

Somebody fell down on the waxed floor, there was a little flurry of screams and laughter. I found myself being joggled, and managed to put away an inch of the collins to save it. Then I thought I saw Art Greymbergen, my favorite publisher, but before I could get anywhere near him Carrol's clear Sunday-school voice began calling, 'The program is about to begin – please take your seats!' and a moment later people were moving sluggishly through the bar archway.

I looked at my watch, then hauled out my copy of the little mimeographed sheet, full of earnest jocularity, that the club sent out every year to announce the Party. It said that the program would begin somewhere around ten, and it was that now.

This was impossible. The program always pivoted on Bill Plass, and Bill never got there, or anywhere, until the party was due to break up.

But I looked when I got down near the bandstand, and by God there he was, half as large as life, gesturing, flashing his Charlie Chaplin grin, teetering like a nervous firewalker. He saw me and waved hello, and then went on talking to Asa Akimisov, Ph.D. (A-K-I-M-I-S-O-V, please, and never mind the Akimesian, or Akimisiov.)

Maybe it *was* them atom bombs. I found a vacant folding chair with a good view of the platform, and a better one of a striking brunette in blue. Akimisov got up on to the platform, with his neck sticking out of his collar like a potted palm (he had lost forty pounds, again) and began telling jokes. Ace is the second funniest man in Medusa, the first being Plass; the peculiar thing is that Plass writes humor professionally, and delivers his annual set-pieces the same way – the rest of the time he is merely a perfectly fascinating morbid wit – but Akimisov, who writes nothing but the most heavily thoughtful fiction in the business, bubbles with humor all the time, a poor man's Sam Levenson. I was going to write an article once proving that a writer's personality on paper was his real one turned inside out, but I fell afoul of some exceptions. Like Tom Q., who was still flashing his bulbs over at the side of the platform, and being noisily suppressed – you could paper him all over with his published stories, and never know the difference.

The program was good, even for Medusa. Ned Burgeon, wearing a sky-blue dinner jacket and a pepper-and-salt goatee, played his famous twenty-one-string guitar; a dark-haired girl, a new one to me, sang in a sweet, strong contralto; there was a skit involving Punchy Carrol as a dream-beast, L. Vague Duchamp as a bewildered spaceman, and B. U. Jadrys, the All-Lithuanian Boy, as a ticket agent for the Long Island Railroad. Then came Plass's annual monologue, and there is just nothing like those. I'm not exaggerating out of parochial pride (once a year is enough Medusa for me): the simple truth is that Plass is a comic genius.

He had his audience laid out flat, gasping and clutching its sides. Why should a man like that waste his time writing fiction?

Towards the end he paused, looked up from his notes, and ad-libbed a biting but not very funny wisecrack about – well, I'd better not say about what. A certain member in the audience stiffened and half got up, and there was a little embarrassed murmur under the laughter, but it was over in a minute. Bill looked flustered. He went back to his prepared speech, finished, and got a roar of applause.

I did my share, but I was worried. Bill can charm the rattles off a snake; if he wanted to go in for quack-doctoring, nut cultism or Canadian mining stock, let alone night-club comedy, he could be a millionaire. That *gaffe* simply hadn't been like him, at all. Still, it was Bill's Dostoevskian soul that made him the funny man he was, and God only knew what had been happening to him in the year since I'd been in town ...

Akimisov, as m.c., delivered the final words. He bowed, straightened, and his pants fell down.

In the dressing room, when I got back there, Bill was busy apologizing to the member on whose toes he had trodden – that apology would have soothed a tiger with a toothache – and Akimisov, with a bewildered expression, was holding up his pants. That was what I was curious about; it was another false note – I didn't think Ace would stoop that low for a laugh. The pants were too big for him, of course, but Ace had always struck me as the kind of guy who wears a belt *and* suspenders.

He did; but the tongue had come out of the belt-buckle, and all the suspenders buttons had popped, all at once. Scouts were being sent out to look for a belt that would fit.

I wandered out into the hall again. I was beginning to get a peculiar feeling on one drink. Too many fresh vegetables; I can't take it like I used to. So I went to the bar and got another.

When I came out, the brunette in the blue evening gown was standing near the doorway listening to Larry Bagsby. Next thing I knew, she let out a whoop, grabbed her bosom, and fetched Larry a good one on the ear. This was unfair. I was a witness, and Larry hadn't done a thing except look; her overworked shoulder straps had simply given way, like Akimisov's suspenders.

Curiouser and curiouser ... The noises around me were picking up in volume and tempo, for all the world like a dancehall scene in a Western movie, just before somebody throws the first table. There was a thud and a screech off to my right; I gathered that somebody else had fallen down. Then a tinkle of bursting glass, and another little chorus of shouts, and then another thud. It went on like that. The crowd was on the move, in no particular direction; everybody was asking everybody else what was going on.

I felt the same way, so I went looking for Ray Alvarez; you can always count on him to tell you the answer, or make one up.

Tom Q. went by, flashing that camera, and it wasn't till the mob had swallowed him that I realized he wasn't replacing the bulb between shots – the same one was blazing over and over.

Well, a few years ago it was silly putty; the year before that, Diarrhetics. This year, everlasting flash bulbs – and no film in the camera.

Ned Burgeon passed me, his grin tilting his whiskers dangerously near the lighted stub in his cigarette holder; he was carrying the guitar case as if he were wading ashore with it. I saw Duchamp off to one side, talking to some-body, gesturing emphatically with his pipe.

It isn't so, but occasionally you get the impression that science fiction writers are either very tall or very short. I watched H. Drene Pfeiffer stilt by, Ray Bolgerish in an astonishing skin-tight suit of horse-blanket plaid, followed by Will Kubatius and the *heldentenor* bulk of Don W. Gamble, Jr. I lowered my sights. Sandwiched between the giants there ought to have been half a dozen people I'd have been glad to see – if not Alvarez, then Bill Plass or his brother Horty; or Jerry Thaw; Bagsby; Preacher Flatt, who looks too much like a marmoset to be true … But no: down on those lower levels there was nobody but an eleven-year-old boy who had got in by mistake, and the ubiquitous fan, Harry *You*-Know, the one with the glasses and all that hair. I tacked, veering slightly, and beat across the room the other way.

There was another crash of glass, a *big* one, and a louder chorus of yells. It wasn't all automatic female shrieks, this time; I caught a couple of male voices, raised in unmistakable anger.

The crowd was thinning out a little; droves of friends of friends appeared to be heading for the coat room. Across one of the clear spaces came a pretty blonde, looking apprehensive. In a minute I saw why. Her skirt billowed out around her suddenly and she yelled, crouched, holding the cloth down with both hands, then sunfished away into the crowd. A moment later the same thing happened to a tall brown-haired girl over to my left.

That was too much. Glancing up, I happened to see the big cut-glass chandelier begin swaying gently from side to side, jingling faintly, working up momentum. I moved faster, buttonholing everyone I knew: 'Have you seen Ray? Have you seen Ray?'

I heard my name, and there he was, standing like stout Cortez atop the piano, where he could see the whole room like an anthill. I climbed up beside him. Alvarez, to quote Duchamp's description, is a small rumpled man with an air of sleepy good-nature. This is apt until you get close to him, when you discover he is about as sleepy as a hungry catamount. 'Hi,' he said, with a sidewise glance.

'Hi. What do you think's doing it?'

'It could be,' said Ray, speaking firmly and rapidly, 'a local discontinuity in the four-dimensional plenum that we're passing through. Or it could be poltergeists – that's perfectly possible, you know.' He gave me a look, daring me to deny it.

'You think so?'

'It *could* be.'

'By golly, I believe you're right,' I said. This is the only way to handle Alvarez when he talks nonsense. If you give him the slightest degree of resistance, he will argue along the same line till doomsday, just to prove he can.

'Mmm,' he said thoughtfully, screwing up his face. 'No, I don't – think – so.'
'No?'

'No,' he said positively. 'You notice how the thing seems to travel around the room?' He nodded to a fist fight that was breaking out a few yards from us, and then to a goosed girl leaping over by the bar entrance. 'There's a kind of irregular rhythm to it.' He moved his hand, illustrating. 'One thing happens – then another thing – now here it comes around this way again—'

A fat friend of a friend and her husband backed up against the platform just below us, quivering. There was something wrong with my fingers; they felt warm. The collins glass was turning warm. Warm, *hell* – yelled and dropped it, sucking my fingers. The glass looped and fell neatly on the flow-ered hat of the friend of a friend, and liquid splattered. The woman hooted like a peanut whistle. She whirled, slipped in the puddle and lurched off into the arms of a hairy authors' agent. Her husband dithered after her a couple of steps, then came back with blood in his eye. He got up as far as the piano stool when, as far as I could make out, his pants split up the back and he climbed down again, glaring and clutching himself.

'Now it's over in the middle,' said Ray imperturbably. 'It *might* be polter-geists, I won't say it isn't. But I've got a hunch there's another answer, actually.'

I said something dubious. A hotel-manager-looking kind of man had just come in and was looking wildly around. Punchy Carrol went up to him, star-ing him respectfully right in the eye, talking a quiet six to his dozen. After a moment he gave up and listened. I've known Punchy ever since she was a puppy-eyed greenhorn from Philadelphia, and I don't underestimate her anymore. I knew the manager-type would go away and not call any cops – at least for a while.

I glanced down at the floor, and then looked again. There were little flat chips of ice scattered in the wetness. That could have been from the ice cubes; but there was *frost* on some of the pieces of glass.

Hot on the bottom, cold on top!

'Ray,' I said, 'something's buzzing around in my mind. Maxwell's demon.' I pointed to the frosted bits of glass. 'That might – No, I'm wrong, that couldn't account for all these—'

He took it all in in one look. 'Yes, it could!' he snapped. His cat-eyes gleamed at me. 'Maxwell had the theory of the perfect hat pump – it would work if you could only find a so-called demon, about the size of a molecule, that would bat all the hot molecules one way, and all the cold ones the other.'

'I know,' I said. 'But—'

'Okay, I'm just explaining it to you.'

What he told me was what I was thinking: Our unidentified friend had some way of changing probability levels. I mean, all the molecules of air

under a woman's skirt *could* suddenly decide to move in the same direction –
or all the molecules in a patch of flooring *could* lose their surface friction – it
just wasn't likely. If you could *make* it likely – there wasn't any limit. You
could make honest dice turn up a thousand sevens in a row. You could run a
car without an engine; make rain or fair weather; reduce the crime index to
zero; keep a demagogue from getting re-elected …

Well, if all that was true, I wanted in. And I didn't have the ghost of a
chance – I was out of touch; I didn't know anybody. Ray knew everybody.

'Spread out, folks!' said a bullhorn voice. It was Samwitz, of course, standing on a bench at the far wall. Kosmo Samwitz, the Flushing Nightingale; not
one of the Medusa crowd, usually – a nice enough guy, and a hard-working
committeeman, but the ordinary Manhattan meeting hall isn't big enough to
hold his voice. 'Spread out – make an equal distance between you. That way
we can't get into any fights.' People started following his orders, partly because
they made sense, partly because, otherwise, he'd go on bellowing.

'That's good – that's good,' said Samwitz. 'All right, this meeting is hereby
called to order. The chair will entertain suggestions about what the nature of
these here phenomena are …'

Ray showed signs of wanting to get down and join the caucus; he loves
parliamentary procedure better than life itself; so I said hastily, 'Let's get
down with the crowd, Ray. We can't see much better up here, anyway.'

He stiffened. 'You go if you want to,' he said quietly. 'I'm staying here,
where I can keep an eye on things.'

The chandelier was now describing stately circles, causing a good deal of
ducking and confusion, but the meeting was getting on with its business,
namely, arguing about whether to confirm Kosmo by acclamation or nomin-
ate and elect a chairman in the usual way. That subject, I figured, was good
for at least twenty minutes. I said, 'Ray, will you tell me the truth if I ask you
something?'

'Maybe.' He grinned.

'Are you doing this?'

He threw his head back and chuckled. 'No-o, I'm not doing it.' He looked
at me shrewdly, still grinning. 'Is that why you were looking for me?'

I admitted it humbly. 'It was just a foolish idea,' I said. 'Nobody we know
could possibly—'

'*I* don't know about that,' he said, squinting thoughtfully.

'Ah, come on, Ray.'

He was affronted. 'Why not? We've got some pretty good scientific brains
in Medusa, you know. There's Gamble – he's an atomic physicist. There's Don
Bierce; there's Duchamp; there's—'

'I know,' I said, 'I know, but where would any of them have got hold of a
thing like *this*?'

495

'They could have invented it,' he said stoutly.

'You mean like Balmer and Phog Relapse running the Michelson experiment in their cellar, and making it come out that there *is* an ether drift, only it's *down*?'

He bristled. 'No, I certainly don't—'

'Or like Lobbard discovering Sectiology?'

'Ptah! No! Like Watt, like Edison, Galileo' – he thumbed down three fingers emphatically – 'Goodyear, Morse, Whitney—'

Down below, the meeting had taken less than five minutes to confirm Samwitz as chairman. I think the chandelier helped; they ought to install one of those in every parliamentary chamber.

The chair recognized Punchy, who said sweetly that the first order of business ought to be to get opinions from the people who knew something, beginning with Werner Kley.

Werner accordingly made a very charming speech, full of Teutonic rumbles, the essence of which was that he didn't know any more about this than a rabbit. He suggested, however, that pictures should be taken. There was a chorus of 'Tom!' and Jones staggered forward with his war-cry: 'There isn't any *film* in it!'

Somebody was dispatched to get film; somebody else trotted out to telephone for reporters and cameramen, and three or four other people headed in a businesslike way for the men's room.

Ray was simultaneously trying to get the chair's attention and explaining to me, in staccato asides, how many epochal inventions had been made by amateurs in attic workshops. I said – and this was really bothering me – 'But look: do you see anybody with any kind of a gadget? How's he going to hide it? How's he going to focus it, or whatever?'

Ray snorted. 'It might be hidden in almost anything. Burgeon's guitar – Gamble's briefcase – Mr Chairman!'

Duchamp was talking, but I could feel it in my bones that Samwitz was going to get around to Ray next. I leaned closer. 'Ray, listen – a thing like this – they wouldn't keep it to themselves, would they?'

'Why not? Wouldn't you – for a while, anyway?' He gave me his bobcat grin. 'I can think of quite – a – few things I could do, if I had it.'

So could I; that was the whole point. I said, 'Yeah. I was hoping we could spot him, before the crowd does.' I sighed. 'Fat chance, I suppose.'

He gave me another sidelong look. 'That shouldn't be so hard,' he drawled.

'You *know* who it is?'

He put on his most infuriating grin, peering to see how I took it. 'I've, got, a few, ideas.'

'Who?'

Wrong question. He shook his head with a that-would-be-telling look.

Somebody across the room went down with a crash; then somebody else. 'Sit on the floor!' Ray shouted, and they all did it, squatting cautiously like old ladies at a picnic. The meeting gathered speed again.

I looked apprehensively at the narrow piano top we were standing on, and sat down with my legs hanging over. Ray stayed where he was, defying the elements.

'You know, all right,' I said, looking up at him, 'but you're keeping it to yourself.' I shrugged. 'Well, why shouldn't you?'

'O-kay,' he said good-naturedly. 'Let's figure it out. Where were you when it started?'

'In the bar.'

'Who else was there? Try to remember exact-ly.'

I thought. 'Art Greymbergen. Fred Balester. Gamble was there—'

'Okay, that eliminates him – and you, incidentally – because it started in here. Right, so far?'

'Right!'

'Hmmm. Something happened *to* Akimisov.'

'And Plass – that booboo he made?'

Ray dismissed Plass with a gesture. He was looking a little restive; another debate was under way down below, with Punchy and Leigh MacKean vociferously presenting the case for Psychokinesis, and being expertly heckled by owlish little M. C. (Hotfoot) Burncloth's echo-chamber voice. 'It's too much,' I said quickly. 'There's too many of them left. We'll never—'

'It's perfectly simple!' Ray said incisively. He counted on his fingers again. 'Burgeon – Kley – Duchamp – Bierce – Burncloth – MacKean – Jibless. Eight people.'

'One of the visitors?' I objected.

He shook his head. 'I know who all these people are, generally,' he said. 'It's got to be one of those eight. I'll take Kley, Bierce, Jibless and MacKean – you watch the other four. Sooner or later they'll give themselves away.'

I had *been* watching. I did it some more.

A wave of neck-clutching passed over the crowd. Cold breezes, I expect. Or hot ones, in some cases. Tom Jones leaped up with a cry and sat down again abruptly.

'Did you see anything?' Ray asked.

I shook my head. Where, I wondered, was the good old science-fiction camaraderie? If I'd been the lucky one, I would have let the crowd in – well, a few of them, anyway – given them jobs and palaces and things. Not that they would have been grateful, probably, the treacherous, undependable, neurotic bums ...

They were looking nervous now. There had been that little burst of activity after a long pause (even the chandelier seemed to be swinging slowly to rest), and now the – call it the stillness – was more than they could stand. I felt it too: that building up of tension. Whoever it was, was getting tired of little things.

A horrible jangling welled out of Burgeon's guitar case; it sounded like a bull banjo with the heaves. Ned jumped, dropped his cigarette holder, got the case open and I guess put his hand on the strings; the noise stopped. That eliminated him ... or did it?

Take it another way. What would the guy have to be like who would waste a marvel like this on schoolboy pranks at a Medusa Christmas party? Not Jibless, I thought – he abominates practical jokers. Bierce didn't seem to be the type either, although you could never tell; the damnedest wry stories get hatched occasionally in that lean ecclesiastic skull. Duchamp was too staid (but was I sure?); MacKean was an enigma. Gamble? Just maybe. Burgeon? Jones? It could be either, I thought, but I wasn't satisfied.

I glanced at Ray again, and mentally crossed him off for the second or third time. Ray's an honorable man, within his own complicated set of rules; he might mislead me, with pleasure, but he wouldn't lie outright.

But I had the feeling that the answer was square in front of me, and I was blind to it.

The meeting was just now getting around to the idea that somebody present was responsible for all the nonsense. This shows you the trouble with committees.

A shocking idea hit me abruptly; I grabbed Ray by the coatsleeve. 'Ray, this cockeyed weather – I just remembered. *Suppose it's local.*'

His eyes widened; he nodded reluctantly. Then he stiffened and snapped his fingers at somebody squatting just below us – the invisible fan, Harry Somebody. I hadn't even noticed him there, but it's Ray's business to know everything and keep track of everybody – that's why he's up on his hill.

The fan came over. Ray handed him something. 'Here's some change, Harry – run out and call up the weather bureau. Find out whether this freak weather is local or not, and if it is, just where the boundaries are. Got that?'

Harry nodded and went out. He was back only a couple of minutes later. 'I got the weather bureau all right. They say it's local – just Manhattan and Queens!'

Something snapped. I did a fast jig on the piano top, slipped and came crashing down over the keys, but I hardly noticed it. I got a death-grip on Ray's trouser leg. 'Listen! If he can do that – he doesn't have to be in the same room. Doesn't Gamble live out in—'

There were cries of alarm over by the open courtyard window. The room was suddenly full of cats – brindle ones, black ones, tabbies, white ones with pink ribbons around their necks, lunatic Siamese.

After them came dogs: one indistinguishable wave of liquid leaping torsos, flying ears, gullets. In half a second the room was an incident written by Dante for the Mutascope.

I caught a glimpse of a terrier bounding after two cats who were climbing Samwitz' back; I saw Duchamp asprawl, pipe still in his mouth, partially submerged under a tidal eddy of black and white. I saw Tom Q. rise up like a lighthouse, only to be bowled over by a frantically scrambling Leigh MacKean.

Ray touched my arm and pointed. Over by the far wall, his back against it, Gamble stood like a slightly potbound Viking. He was swinging that massive briefcase of his, knocking a flying cat or dog aside at every swipe. Two women had crawled into his lee for shelter; he seemed to be enjoying himself.

Then the briefcase burst. It didn't just come open; it flew apart like a comedy suitcase, scattering a whirlwind of manuscript paper, shirts, socks – and nothing else.

The tide rushed towards the window again: the last screech and the last howl funneled out. In the ringing silence, somebody giggled. I couldn't place it, and neither could Ray, I think – then. Stunned, I counted scratched noses.

Samwitz was nowhere in sight; the crowd had thinned a good deal, but all of the eight, thank heaven, were still there – MacKean sitting groggily on a stranger's lap, Werner Kley nursing a bloody nose, Tom Q., camera still dangling from his neck, crawling carefully on hands and knees towards the door …

He reached it and disappeared. An instant later, we heard a full chorus of feminine screams from the lobby, and then the sound of an enormous J. Arthur Rank-type gong.

Ray and I looked at each other with a wild surmise. '*Tom* lives in Queens!' he said.

I scrambled down off the piano and the platform, but Ray was quicker. He darted into the crowd, using his elbows in short, efficient jabs. By the time I got to the door he was nowhere in sight.

The lobby was full of large powdery women in flowered dresses, one of them still shrieking. They slowed me down, and so did tripping over one of those big cylindrical jardinieres full of sand and snipes. I reached the street just in time to see Ray closing the door of a cab.

I hadn't the wind to shout. I saw his cheerful face and Tom's in the small yellow glow of the cab light; I saw Tom Q. raise the camera, and Ray put out his hand to it. Then the cab pulled away into traffic, and I watched its beady red tail lights down the avenue until they winked out of sight.

Some time later, walking down the cold morning street, I discovered there was somebody with me, keeping step, not saying anything. It was Harry Er-Ah.

He saw I had noticed him. 'Some party,' he remarked.

I said yeah.

'That was pretty funny, what happened in the lobby.'

'I didn't see it.'

'He came tearing through there on all fours. Right into the middle of all those women. They probably thought he was a mad dog or something.'

I took two more steps, and stopped, and looked at him.

'That was *all* he did?' I said.

'Sure.'

'Well, then,' I said with mounting exasperation, 'in the name of – Oh. Wait a minute. You're wrong,' I told him, calming down again. 'There was the gong. He made that gong noise.'

'Did he?' said Harry. One nervous hand went up and adjusted the hornrims.

I felt a little tugging at my shirt front, and looked down to see my necktie slithering out. I swatted at it instinctively, but it ducked away and hovered, swaying like a cobra.

Then it dropped. He showed me his open hand, and there was a wire running up out of his sleeve, with a clip on the end of it. For the first time, I noticed two rings of metal wired behind the lens frames of his eyeglasses.

He pulled his other hand out of his pocket, and there was a little haywire rig in it – batteries and a couple of tubes and three tuning knobs.

Fans, I was thinking frozenly – sixteen or eighteen, maybe, with pimples and dandruff and black fingernails, and that wonderful, terrible eagerness boiling up inside them … slaving away at backyard rocketry experiments, wiring up crazy gadgets that never worked, printing bad fiction and worse poetry in mimeographed magazines … How could I have forgotten?

'I wasn't going to tell anybody,' he said. 'No matter what happened. If they'd *looked* at me, just once, they would have seen. But as long as you're worrying so much about it—' He blinked, and said humbly, 'It scares me. What do you think I ought to do?'

My fingers twitched. I said, 'Well, this will take some thinking about, Harry. Uh, can I—'

He backed off absent-mindedly as I stepped towards him. 'I've been thinking about it,' he said. 'As a matter of fact, I haven't been to bed since yesterday morning. I worked on it straight through from four o'clock yesterday. Twenty hours. I took caffeine tablets. But go ahead, tell me. What would you do if you' – he said it apologetically – 'were me?'

I swallowed. 'I'd go at it slowly,' I said. 'You can make a lot of mistakes by—'

He interrupted me, with a sudden fiendish glint in his eye. 'The man that has this is pretty important, don't you think?' And he grinned. 'How would you like to see my face on all the stamps?'

I shuddered in spite of myself. 'Well—'

'I wouldn't *bother*,' he said. 'I've got something better to do first.'

'Harry,' I said, leaning, 'if I've said anything …'

'You didn't say anything.' He gave me such a look as I hope I never get from a human again. 'Big shot!'

I grabbed for him, but he was too quick. He leaped back, jamming the gadget into his pocket, fumbling at the spectacles with his other hand. I saw his feet lift clear of the pavement. He was hanging there like a mirage, drifting backward and upward just a little faster than I could run.

His voice came down, thin and clear: 'I'll send you a postcard from …'

I lost the last part; anyhow, it couldn't have been what it sounded like.

Just over a month later came Palomar's reports of unaccountable lights observed on the dark limb of Mars. Every science fiction reader in the world, I suppose, had the same thought – of a wanderer's footprints fresh in the ancient dust, his handprints on controls not shaped for hands, the old wild light wakened. But only a few of us pictured hornrims gleaming there in the Martian night …

I drove over to Milford and had a look through Ham Jibless' homemade telescope. I couldn't see the lights, of course, but I could see that damned infuriating planet, shining away ruddy, there across thirty-six million miles of space, with its eternal *Yah, yah, you can't catch me!*

Medusa meetings have been badly attended since then, I'm told; for some reason, it gives the members the green heaves to look at each other.

DON'T LIVE IN THE PAST

I

Bernard François Piet Fu-Tze Vargas had a clear and sustained feeling that there ought not to be days like this. Four of his wife's cousins from Callisto had descended upon him that morning at the ungodly hour of ten o'clock (they required special diets and were obscenely fat); he had been seated below a sub-assistant minister of finance at the High Commissioner's dinner last night, a manifest insult; the power beam had failed twice on his way into the office, once over Sancisco and once over the California Garbage Conversion Area; and he had a splitting headache.

Vargas was a youngish man with large, ruddy features now contorted into a heavy scowl. He sat half-leaning across his desk, chin on his fist, moodily thrusting folded sheets of metal fiber into the automatic letter-opener.

Abruptly the ceiling light dimmed and something swatted him on the rump three times in machine-gun tempo, jarring him all the way up his spine. Vargas found himself canted across his desk with his head in an overturned flower vase. The lights flickered again, went out altogether; and in the brief interval before they went on again a fourth shock, more violent than the others, lifted Vargas all the way across his desk and on to the thick body-temperature carpet.

He sat up slowly, inarticulate with rage. It was at this moment that his assistant, Knut Everett Roku LaSalle Choong, chose to burst into the room. He tripped over the doorsill, lurched wildly and brought up against Vargas' totem post, saving himself by clutching a white silk banner which carried the names and honors of two hundred and fifty-nine of Vargas' most distinguished ancestors.

Hanging dramatically from the banner, Choong bleated, 'Chief! The pipelines have busted!'

Vargas' face, which had been flushed a moment before, took on a blotchy appearance. 'What, all of them?' he whispered.

'All,' said Choong. 'We're right over a fault, you know. The quake must have snapped the pipelines like – like pipestems.'

Vargas scrambled up and clutched the other man by the slack of his sunflower-colored robe. 'Did they cut transmission?' he demanded.

'Yes, but—'

'How long before the flow stopped?'

'About two seconds, Chief. Possibly a little more. I didn't stop to get the meter readings—'

'Don't interrupt me!' said Vargas in a restrained shout. He took a firmer grip and brought his pop-eyed face close to Choong. 'What was being transmitted?'

'Flangs,' said the assistant in a barely audible voice. He gulped. 'Tweedle-dums. Collapsed flooring. Argo paste. Rozzers. And – and—'

Vargas had been puffing heavily. Now he held his breath for an instant. 'Well?'

'And mangels,' said Choong in terror. 'Three pipes of mangels.'

Vargas collapsed on the floor and looked at Choong through his fingers. 'Oh, Great Blodgett, no!'

'Yes.'

'Mangels!'

Bedlam was growing in the outer offices. There were running footsteps, shouts, shrieks of dismay.

'We'll be excommunicated,' said Vargas. 'They'll hang our totems upside down.'

A red-faced man appeared in the doorway. His expression was not pleas-ant. Vargas scrambled to his feet; both he and Choong stood at attention.

'Two and five-sevenths seconds,' the red-faced man remarked. 'Not a very good response for trained monitors, is it? Too much Rhine beer the night before, perhaps? Or reading a tape – composing poetry? Catching a little nap? Or was it –?' He stopped, wincing, and looked at a white-metal dough-nut strapped to his right wrist, above his ruffled sleeve. A tiny voice spoke at some length; Vargas could only catch the words 'jackass' and 'cretin.'

'Yes, sir,' said the red-faced man, whose name, for the record, was Wallace Hyacinth Manuel Chiang Llewellyn. He barked at Vargas. 'Turn on the tri-D!'

Vargas stumbled over to his desk and obeyed. A five-foot disc set into a low platform on his right glowed faintly, sparkled and then spat a vertical stream of color. The image steadied and became the all too convincing three-dimensional replica of a portly man with a bulbous nose and long gray hair.

'Enlarge your image!' it said sharply.

Vargas jumped a foot and tremblingly adjusted the controls on his desk. The portly man frowned at them and said, 'I happen to be Representative John Hsi Bright-Feather Wilson Woodcock, Chairman of the Committe to Investigate the San Joaquin Disaster, which was formed in emergency session five minutes ago. Now, are you all of the scoundrels who were immediately responsible for this outrageous dereliction of duty? If not, get the rest of 'em in here. We'll get to the bottom of this if it's the last—'

*

The Chief Executive, His Honor Ibrahim L. Btandu Eriksson Dickey, frowned an executive frown. 'Now let me get this straight,' he said. 'The goods are put into one end of the tube and they are turned into some kind of temporal flow?'

'That's it approximately, your honor.' Representative Rowland Mokai DeJonge Baruch Schemkov, Chairman of the Plenary Committee which had replaced Representative Woodcock's Emergency Committee (Woodcock having been impeached) glanced at a few notes in his palm. He had briefed himself thoroughly.

'In transit, your honor, the goods are in a special state of matter, in which they are partially out of our frame of spaciotemporal reference, and are carried along by the universal drift, thus apparently by-passing the laws of inertia and conservation of energy. We apply no force once they enter the tube; that's why tube transport is so cheap.

'Moreover, the size and shape of the goods to be transported make no difference, since the spacial coordinates are not fixed with reference to normal space. You might say that the net result is the same as if you had melted everything down to a kind of thin mush.

'There is just enough contact between the two matter states so that the material being transported will not go through a solid of any thickness. In other words, we can lead the shipments anywhere in the world through a tube, even a very small one – the tubes we use are three-eighths inch in diameter. At the end of the tube, the expansion of the material releases it from the special state and it comes out in its original form, ready to be processed, stored, consumed or whatever.'

'I see,' commented the Chief. 'That's all very well, Representative, but what I want to know is this. Just why were we caught with our robes up in this situation?'

Schemkov cleared his throat. 'There appears,' he admitted, 'to have been some theoretical possibility of this happening all along. I have several abstracts, which I will turn over to your office, of articles and scientific papers in which reference is made to the possibility. It—'

The Chief looked down his long nose in a manner which suggested that the Representative was not quite human. He said slowly and earnestly, 'And this possibility was given no consideration when the transport tubes were built? Is that it?'

Representative Schemkov had been a member of the Sub-committee to Pass on Recommendations for the Erection of Soong-Wiley Transport Tubes, and he quaked in his sandals. 'No safeguard was possible, your honor. What occurred was that the rupture in the lines took place at exactly the instant when that section of the planet was revolving directly opposite the line of universal drift – an event which astronomers assure me is very rare – and, in addition, I understand that the temporal displacement at that moment was exceptionally great. Under these conditions, the material released from the end of the tube did not reform normally but was carried some distance back along the temporal line—'

'How far back? I mean *exactly*, not a guess.'

'The mathematicians are still working on that, your honor, and the best they can say now is that it was probably somewhere between the mid-twentieth century and the late twenty-first. However, there is a strong possibility that none of the material reached any enclosed space which would attract it, and that it may all have been dissipated harmlessly in the form of incongruent molecules.'

'But those materials,' said the Chief grimly, 'included what?'

'Flangs,' said Representative Schemkov, 'and tweedledums, and collapsed flooring, and argo paste—'

'And *mangels*,' added the Chief. 'Isn't that correct?'

'Yes, your honor.'

'And you tell me that there is a possibility that these things did *not* suddenly appear in the homes and business places of persons of *Blodgett's own time*' – he touched his forelock, and Schemkov automatically did the same – 'causing Blodgett knows how many neuroses, how many psychoses, how many lost contracts, how many broken homes—'

'But, your honor—'

'Representative, the men responsible for this catastrophe are going to be sorry they were ever born into the public service. We're going to get to the bottom of this, and when we do—'

'Here's what it boils down to,' said the square man in the gray diamond-dusted robe. He made a triangle with his hands on the desktop. 'The kick went all the way upstairs and now it's come all the way down again. Everybody in fifteen echelons has a sore tail, the blame has been passed around, and now you're it. That's all.'

Ronald Mao Jean-Jacques von Hochbein Mazurin wore a slightly stunned expression on his normally cheerful, pug-nosed face. The face, up to now, had been his fortune; it bore a slight but perceptible resemblance to that of Blodgett, the Father of the World, as he appeared in early prints and paintings. Mazurin had learned to emphasize the resemblance by assuming a soulful look, once he discovered that it usually earned him the juicier and less messy jobs in the Bureau.

He said, 'Now wait a minute. How do they know they can get me to the right time line with this new gimmick of theirs? Isn't that a contradiction in terms? If I'm in it, that's a new line, isn't it? I mean—'

'I know what you mean,' said the square man. 'Every displacement moves the observer to a new time line. But remember you're not required to *do* anything once you get there; all you have to do is see what happened. As I understand it, you won't be attached to that time line at all; you'll just be partially in it, the same way stuff in a transport tube is partially in this line. You can't possibly affect anything that happens there. Therefore, from a mathematical point of view, you're not in it at all. You'll be able to see, because light quanta have binding extensions on either side of the plenum-line proper, but you can't influence anything that happens there.'

Mazurin was feeling uncomfortable. 'How do I get back?'

'Don't worry,' said the square man. 'You'll be at the end of a pencil of temporal energy all the time. That's what will be holding you in the partly-there state. After a few days, they'll send an impulse along it to bring you back.'

'Sounds like deep-sea diving at the end of a piece of string,' said Mazurin. 'What happens if the power fails, or the contact is broken some other way?'

'Then I suppose you'd be stuck in that line – which would, of course, immediately become another line. Not that it matters. But you wouldn't be too badly off if that did happen, I'd say. That was a pretty interesting period, not too uncivilized, and you'd see a lot of action.'

'Umm,' said Mazurin. He rapidly calculated his chances of getting another job if he were discharged and blacklisted by the ISC Intelligence Bureau – zero. 'All right, I'm your boy.'

The square man came around the desk and patted his shoulder with a hand like a jeweled bunch of sausages. 'Good man,' he said emotionally. 'I knew you'd come through, the Bureau knows how to pick 'em. Get your affairs wound up and report to the Physics Bureau at twelve o'clock tomorrow.'

Mazurin turned up in the white-tiled laboratory ten minutes late, with traces of lipstick still adhering to his right ear and exuding an enviable odor of good rice wine. In the interests of truth, it must be stated that he did not entirely absorb all the briefing he received before he was thrust unceremoniously into the temporal projection machine.

He retained a definite impression of the machine itself, which was of an unpleasant hollow-cube shape and emitted a disquieting hum, together with a sharp smell of ozone. He remembered that, once arrived at his destination, he would be able to walk about on any available surface, but unable to move any solid object or enter into any sort of communication with the inhabitants.

The breathing apparatus strapped over his mouth and nose was reminder enough that he was dependent upon his own air supply. He recalled being asked if he had been checked out in lip reading and Twentieth Century English, and of replying, with hurt dignity, that he most certainly had. There was some more talk, during which he had been distracted by a tendency of his knees to swivel sharply, and then he had been grasped by the nape of the neck and his heels and slung into the machine.

It was a Lysenko-begotten silly business, altogether. He seemed to be sitting now on nothing in particular, in the middle of a bright blue sky with clouds in it, while an obviously spurious landscape (flat, with antique square houses and a lot of palm trees, the whole being tilted at a forty-five-degree angle) gently rose towards him. He watched this process with growing disapproval until the scene grew to full size and he bumped gently against a sidewalk which felt like sponge rubber.

He stood up and soared some twenty feet into the air, coming down in an approximately upright position. He looked around him, breathing heavily. His head was clearing, and he didn't like it. What had seemed idle nonsense a few moments ago was now assuming the aspect of an incredible reality. The buildings around him were angular and massive, with an appalling quantity of extremely ugly embellishments in the way of glass bricks, chromium statues, walls of enormous windows. The people were all either walking or driving antique fourwheeled vehicles, and most of them were dressed in garments constructed on a curious cylinder principle, also with a great deal of angular detail work.

This period, he recalled, had been addicted to what its denizens termed 'the functional' in design. Not a curved line anywhere.

Culturally, this was a dismal era, yet being in it gave Mazurin a holy thrill. There was practically no doubt about it – Blodgett himself was alive at this actual moment!

Directly in front of Mazurin, the street widened into a sort of village square, in the center of which a wooden platform was erected. A man in black stood on this platform, evidently making a speech to a small crowd assembled around him. Mazurin saw several instruments which were evidently crude vision cameras. He watched the speaker's lips, and made out a few phrases: '... the principles of loyalty and obedience to which we are all dedicated ... one world, one people, one leader, one glorious ideal ...'

Interested, he walked closer. A gentleman approaching the crowd on a tangential course strode into him before he had time to get out of the way, and Mazurin found himself violently propelled several yards away, to bounce from still another moving spectator and come to rest finally sprawled on the pavement.

He got up determinedly, soaring as before, and this time leaped squarely into the thick of the crowd before any other outriders could get at him. The crowd was close-packed, and he stood with very little difficulty on their heads. Now he was near enough to read the speaker's lips easily, and he followed the speech with attention.

'On this, our youngest but not least hallowed day, we must dedicate ourselves in our hearts to the eternal principles for which so many brave men and women died. For if we do, those men and women are not ten years dead, but gloriously living in the eternal atmosphere of our truth. If we do this, the world did not end for them on that terrible day, August the seventeenth, nineteen eighty-one. The world will never end – for them and for ourselves!'

A man to the right of the speaker's platform, dressed in an ugly green uniform, raised a brass instrument to his lips and blew on it. Mazurin leaped nimbly as the citizens on whom he stood took off their hats and bowed their heads. The musician got through with whatever sounds he had been producing, and a row of similarly dressed men behind him raised antique rapid-fire rifles to their shoulders, aiming diagonally upward.

Mazurin, directly in the line of fire, automatically threw himself flat, but he was still unused to his new condition and the motion sent him in a lazy parabola five feet over the crowd's heads.

The guns fired in unison. From three-quarters of them leaped streaks of fire; from the other quarter issued something else entirely. At the end of each barrel, a dark blue bubble appeared. The bubbles swelled rapidly, more and more of them extruding, until they became ovoids three feet long and two feet wide, dotted with stumpy tentacles. Then they dropped out of Mazurin's vision, but he could judge their activity by the way the crowd scattered.

Mazurin leaped and watched the square empty itself beneath him. The uniformed men broke ranks and fled, some dropping their guns. The crowd was spreading out as quickly as those in the center could force the others back. In the cleared space, the blue ovoids were leaping like frogs, pausing and leaping again. At each pause, a toothless mouth gaped, and Mazurin could almost hear the bass 'Urk!' they emitted.

Nobody was left on the speaker's platform except the speaker himself, who had misjudged his vault over the railing and got himself tangled in the large black-and-red flag which draped it. While Mazurin watched, one of the blue ovoids bounded on to the speaker's back, settled down and began contentedly munching his jacket.

As he floated down, Mazurin took a notebook from his pocket and wrote: *Tweedledums: probably pineapple-flavored; very unripe and active; emerged without damper controls and broke up large religious gathering, frightening approx. 500 persons.*

II

Mazurin sat alone in the sun-washed and empty square, letting the full enormity of the scene he had just witnessed seep into him. After a while he took out his notebook again and tried to calculate the probable number of surviving descendants, in his own world, of the five hundred people who had just been introduced to tweedledums. He had got up to five generations, and reached the utterly discouraging figure of 20,420, when he gave up.

He shuddered. He was not a devout man by nature, but he had had the usual training as a child, and the idea of so much as being disrespectful to ancestors – much less confronting them unexpectedly with a troop of tweedledums – made him cringe as if he had touched something unclean.

And the other things had still to be accounted for: the rozzers, the collapsed flooring, the argo paste, the—

No. It was better not to think of that.

He got morosely to his feet and watched as the first of a long line of archaic ground-vehicles zoomed into the square and skidded to a stop. Green-uniformed men got out and ran off in all directions, till the square and the surrounding streets were covered with them. Presently a group of them came running back to the cars, carrying a tweedledum which was struggling furiously to escape. After a while they captured another one.

I hope they get them all, Mazurin thought; but he doubted that they would. Free of the projected energy that ordinarily kept them quiescent, a live tweedledum was the most active and elusive artificial food product ever invented. They had been one of Mazurin's favorite dishes; but he suspected now, with a sliding lurch in his stomach, that he would never, never eat one again.

Something else seemed to be going on at the far side of the square. Resignedly he propelled himself that way. A large knot of the green-uniformed men had collected near a doorway to one of the square buildings and was slowly moving back towards the cars. Mazurin leaped on to the heads of the crowd for a better view, and, approaching the center of the group, found that the quarry was not tweedledums this time, but people. A young man and a girl, to be exact. They were staggering along with their heads down, pushed and dragged by many hands. As Mazurin watched, someone reached over someone else's arm and struck the girl in the face.

Mazurin's first reaction was horror; his second was bewilderment. He saw now that what his superior had described as an 'interesting' era could only be painful to any person of normal sensibilities; for all of these people, without exception, might be ancestors!

And why were these officials, who were possibly ancestors, maltreating two young possible ancestors in this manner, instead of running down tweedledums as they had evidently been sent to do? Could it be that the boy and the girl were suspected of being responsible for the catastrophe?

It was absurd, but the only explanation he could think of. He followed, soaring over the rooftops, as the car containing the two zoomed off again.

He managed to keep in sight of the car, though it moved much too fast for him, and saw the two captives half-dragged, half-carried up the steps of a large, cubical black building.

Once inside the building, however, he was lost in a maze of corridors full of hurrying, worried-looking people. The place was three stories tall above the ground, and ten stories below, and there were hundreds of separate offices and suites. It was not till a full hour later that he found them, in a brilliantly lit cell facing a white-enameled corridor, in the lowest level of all.

If it weren't for the bruises and cuts on their faces, Mazurin thought, they would have been a handsome couple. The boy was tall and lean, with a dark, thoughtful face; the girl was neatly rounded and had a charming head of almost-platinum hair.

They were sitting side by side on a hard, narrow bench that ran from wall to wall of their five-by-five cubicle. The harsh glare that illuminated them was hard on Mazurin's eyes; he put his polarized goggles on. They themselves had shut their eyes tight against the fierce light, and their heads were close together, their hands clasped.

Mazurin watched their lips. The girl was saying, 'We must be guilty, of course. I mean guilty of *something*.'

'Or they never would have arrested us,' the young man finished after a pause.

'Yes,' said the girl. 'They are always right. *Always*. So we must be guilty, and yet it's hard to see—'

'Hush, dear. It isn't for us to question what they do. Perhaps we have committed some crime without even being aware of it. Or maybe—'

'Yes?'

'Well, maybe they are just testing us, or – or something.'

The girl's eyes opened for a second. 'Oh, Rob, do you suppose that's it?'

'It might be. Certainly we didn't cause any disturbance at the patriotic meeting that we *know* of.'

'But it's not for us to judge.'

'No.'

For some time, while he watched this conversation, Mazurin had been increasingly aware that the two young people were doing something rather odd. It had to do with their hands. He stopped watching their lips altogether and concentrated on the hands.

They were clasped loosely together on the bench between the two, half-covered by the drape of the girl's flowered skirt. Between the boy's palm and the girl's, Mazurin could see a constant flicker of motion, fingers flashing back and forth, first hers, then his.

Now this, thought Mazurin, was extremely interesting. Beyond a doubt, the two prisoners were communicating by means of some ancient form of the finger-code he had learned as a raw cadet in the Internal Security Commission. If he could only get closer, he was almost sure, he could read it …

Cadenced footsteps came down the corridor. It was a white-robed attendant, flanked by two of the green-clad officials, each with a drawn missile gun. The attendant was carrying something on a white enamel tray, probably food, and in his other hand he had something that looked like the key to an old-fashioned mechanical lock.

Clearly they were going to open the young people's cell, to feed them, most probably. If he could slip in while they did it ... Caution urged him back, curiosity drew him forward. There was no danger, he told himself. If the cell was opened once, it would be opened again, and he could get out. He made up his mind.

The two guards stepped back, guns ready, as the attendant opened the door and stepped inside, depositing the tray – which did, indeed, contain food of some sort – on a shelf. As he stepped out again, Mazurin, lithe as a rozzer, squeezed in past him. Simultaneously, three things happened.

The door shut with a clang.

Mazurin toppled to the metal floor under a totally unexpected access of weight.

The two prisoners, the attendant, and the guard turned to stare at him with saucer eyes.

While he sat there, feeling as if someone had slugged him from behind, the three men outside exploded into activity. The attendant fled with hoarse cries down the corridor, and the two guards threw themselves flat, aiming their curious weapons at Mazurin. The two people in the cell with him, he was vaguely aware, had moved as far away as they could get and were sitting in stricken silence.

Mazurin said weakly, 'Kamerad, Tovarich. Ami.' Then it occurred to him that these men spoke English and, anyway, they apparently didn't intend to shoot. Not as long as he didn't move, at any rate. He shut up and tried to think. What the Blodgett had happened to him?

The metal floor of the cell was hard and cold under his palms. He was here, all right, and not on the end of any pencil of temporal energy. It had happened when the cell door shut behind him.

He looked at the door. It was a grid of stout chrome-plated bars, with an interval between the bars of about three centimeters. A nonsense phrase came into his mind, 'Eve and Agrid,' which meant nothing. It wasn't Eve and Agrid; it was Eve and Adam. Eve and Agrid. Eve and Agrid. Eveandagrid –

Even a grid.

Mazurin shut his eyes and groaned. He opened them again when one of the guards made a warning sort of noise, and stared miserably at the limited vista before him. 'Above all,' one of the technicians had said, 'don't get yourself completely surrounded by metal, *even a grid*. It will break the temporal beam and you'll be marooned there ...'

Running footsteps approached down the corridor and a squad of the green-uniformed men hove into view. Two of them had a thing on a wheeled tripod that looked as if it were capable of blowing out the side of a building. The rest spread out with drawn hand-guns. The two on the floor got up, saluted and joined the semicircle.

'Stand up!' said one who seemed to be in command.

Mazurin obeyed with alacrity.

'Remove that mask! Put your hands behind your head! Face the wall!'

When he had done all that, the cell door opened, someone took two swift strides inside, and then colored lights detonated inside Mazurin's head.

He couldn't have been entirely out, because when he came to he was already thinking. *Very efficient police methods. They didn't take any chances. Just the way an ISC man would have handled it. …*

His head ached abominably, and his hands and feet seemed swollen. Green-trousered legs were scissoring back and forth in front of his eyes, and the gray concrete floor was moving rapidly backward under him. He was, he realized, trussed up like a rozzer, being dragged down the corridor.

His head cleared a little and he glanced to either side. The boy and the girl were in the party, in approximately the same condition as himself.

They reached an elevator, and Mazurin got a view of its scuffed metal floor before they carried him out of it again. More corridor, black-tiled this time. Several turns. Then a doorway with an ebony sill, followed by flooring of some brown composition, probably a primitive pressed fiber.

Finally he was set upright against a slender metal post and manacled there. The boy and girl were similarly disposed of to his right.

A round man in the green uniform stalked quickly in and stared at Mazurin. His little blue eyes darted quickly from Mazurin's cloth-of-platinum robe to his face, then to the equipment hung at his belt.

'All right,' the round man said, 'who are you?'

Mazurin opened his mouth, then shut it again. Tell the truth? Oh, no.

His training as a law officer told him exactly what would happen to him if he did. But what lie could he invent that would save him the pain of being questioned? For he had no doubt that being questioned in this era would be painful, despite the rudimentary methods.

The best thing, he decided, was to say nothing. He tried it.

The round man nodded decisively. 'We'll see,' he said. He turned as a second and a third officer strode in. All three stared at Mazurin, then turned and went to the far end of the room. Mazurin could read their lips easily.

'We knew they were cooking up something, but we had no reports that even hinted at anything like this.'

'I don't like the smell of it. Why would they materialize him in that cell and then let us capture him? Better get him out of the city as fast as possible.'

The round man got in the way at that point and Mazurin missed some of it. Then all of them turned to come back, and he caught one more sentence: 'Put them all in one cell, and we may learn something.'

The three of them were detached from the pillars, efficiently trussed up again, and hurried outside to the waiting maw of a long black paddy-wagon.

It was a long ride and an uncomfortable one. Not being able to talk under the eyes of the guards, Mazurin had plenty of time to think, and, by the time half an hour had gone by, he was shoulder-deep in gloom.

He was roused out of himself when the car suddenly leaped six inches off the road, came down and leaped again. Looking back through the barred window, Mazurin could see that they had left the smooth concrete highway and were rushing down a cowpath of some kind. He and the two young people, all with their wrists manacled around a horizontal bar, bounced like popcorn. The two guards crooked their free arms around stanchions.

Glancing down, Mazurin noted that the two kids were at it again with the fingers. He looked away miserably, then peeked back. It was his damned curiosity that had put him there; he might as well satisfy it while he could – if he could.

The code was the same, all right: five standard positions for each of the five fingers gave you twenty-five letters, and a clenched fist was 'X' if you needed it. After a moment, he could read what the boy was saying without difficulty.

'... in my shoe. If they give me a chance ...'

'Charlie, I'm scared!'

'Only way. They'll get it all out of us otherwise. They know how to. Would have done it before now if he hadn't turned up.'

'Think he's one of ours?'

'Can't be; we haven't anything like that. Don't understand it, but can't take any chances. He might be a spy.'

The girl again: 'Okay. I guess it's worth it.'

It occurred to Mazurin, with an ineffable shock, that it must be poison Charlie had in his shoe ... They were going to kill themselves, to keep the authorities from putting them to the question. Evidently either a large and fanatical fraternal society or else a revolutionary group; all kinds of secrets. But he couldn't let them commit suicide! Such a thing would be an ineradicable blot on the totems of their thousands of descendants. Even worse, he didn't know their surnames; they might be his own great-great-great-great grandparents.

He could alert the guards, of course, but the more he thought about that, the less he liked it. Questioning, this far back in history, would be sure not to be subtle. From one point of view it was perfectly sensible of them to prefer poison. *Bump!* If only the car would stop bouncing for a minute so he could think ...

The car abruptly outdid itself. Mazurin found himself whirling around the horizontal bar like a demented acrobat, while two green blurs that were guards soared airily to the forward end of the compartment. Something struck Mazurin a dizzying blow on the head, the car bounced twice more and came to rest, while the echoes of a thunderous explosion died away in his ears.

III

The car was canted, half in a ditch. The guards, piled up against the forward wall, were not moving. Charlie and the girl were half-stunned but conscious. Mazurin pulled futilely at his wristcuffs; they were too tight even for his trained hands to slip.

Acrid fumes drifted into the car through a burst seam in the rear. Mazurin sniffed, and felt a cold dew break out on his forehead.

'Oh, what is it?' asked the girl faintly.

'Argo paste,' said Mazurin. 'It must have started coming out of the exhaust or the jet tube – whatever these vehicles use. Oh, sacred name …'

'What's argo paste?' demanded the youth groggily. 'I never heard of the stuff.'

'I know you haven't,' Mazurin said. 'They use it to burn through metal. It's supposed to come out into glazed vats. If only it's stopped—'

The fumes grew thicker. Mazurin looked out the barred rear window.

'We're in a pool of it,' he said. He turned. 'Can you reach those two?' he asked, nodding towards the two unconscious guards.

The boy shook his head. 'They haven't got our keys, anyhow. The guard up front with the driver has them. And he's knocked out, or he'd have been back here by now.'

The car lurched and settled. A section of the floor began smoking and dripped away, leaving a puckered gap through which they could see a slowly heaving pool of gray paste.

'Can you get your shoe off?' Mazurin asked suddenly.

Charlie gave him a look full of suspicion.

'Your shoe,' Mazurin repeated with agonized patience. 'Either one, it doesn't matter.' He slipped his left foot out of his own elastic-topped sandal, grasped it between his toes and held it up. 'Mine's no good, you see? Too thin. Yours is made of thick leather. Can you take it off?'

'I don't get it,' said Charlie, baffled. A heavier drift of choking fog came up through the vanishing flood. 'But—' He grunted, raising and twisting his leg until his manacled hands could reach the laces. 'Here.' He dropped the shoe and kicked it along to Mazurin.

The car settled again. The pool of gray slime was now only a foot below them. Mazurin grasped the shoe with his toes, shifting his grip till it was as firm as he could manage. Then he held on like grim death and lowered the shoe through the gap in the floor, into the gray pool underneath. He brought it up quickly.

There was a good gob of the stuff in the heel end of the shoe, about two inches from his own bare foot, but it was smoking furiously. In another second, the leather would be eaten through.

He brought the shoe up, under the horizontal bar, over it again – and dumped the paste on the bar just as the leather gave way. The metal smoked acridly and melted.

Mazurin jettisoned the shoe, jammed his foot back into his own sandal, and peered at the bar through watering eyes. There was a hearty bite out of it, but a slender tongue of metal still united the two sections.

'Now!' said Mazurin. 'Pull!'

He braced his back and shoved at the bar till his muscles cracked, while Charlie, his face white with strain, pulled from his side. The car lurched once more, and the gray surface beneath leaped up to the level of the floorboards. Mazurin got his feet up on the bar and gave one last desperate shove. The metal gave a *ping* and moved a fraction of an inch. Through the smoke, Mazurin saw that the narrow part had snapped. He pushed some more, until the bar reluctantly bent a full three inches out of its original line.

Kneeling on the bench, Mazurin held his wrists carefully away from the smoldering ends of the bar and slipped his arms free.

'Nice work so far,' said Charlie, 'but what about the door?' He slid down to the end of the bench and moved his own arms free of the bar. The car tilted again as the girl moved to follow him.

'Get back!' said Mazurin urgently. He motioned Charlie to the forward end of the car. 'Balance the weight while she gets loose.' He looked at the door that still barred their way to freedom. The lock, naturally, was about halfway up, better than two feet from the level of the argo paste. 'Other shoe,' he told Charlie. 'Can't be helped.'

Charlie took it off and handed it down to him. The girl had got her arms free now and was leaning forward with the wristcuffs spread, evidently intending to touch the connecting piece to the smoking end of the bar.

'No!' yelled Mazurin, and she started back. 'Horrible stuff – get a drop of it on your flesh, no way to stop it. Get back with Charlie, please.'

Squatting on the bench, he leaned forward precariously and dipped the second shoe into the seething gray mass. He got a bigger quantity this time, and he could control it better. He brought it up swiftly and carefully poured it over the lock, peering through the haze to make sure he had the right place.

Smoke gushed out, and he couldn't see what was happening; but he pushed the door outward, and it gave. He stood up, put one foot on the opposite bench, and got the other wedged into the barred opening of the door. A push and a twist, and he was precariously balanced outside, directly over the center of the viscous, smoking pool.

The car settled again under his weight. He scrambled to get both feet on top of the door, lunged and sprawled across the smooth top of the car. Panting, he got his feet under him again and flung himself forward, feeling the car tilt slightly under him as he moved.

'All right,' he called, 'come out quickly!'

He saw a motion beneath him, and turned as the door of the cab opened and a head thrust itself out. The head shook itself, dazedly. Mazurin, flat on his stomach, leaned out and slammed his manacled wrists under the man's ear.

'Sorry, Sacred Ancestor,' he said regretfully.

The guard dived slowly and gracefully out of the open door and sprawled on the grass outside. Mazurin, overbalanced by the blow, felt himself slipping, grabbed for a hand-hold, then let himself go. He landed on his shoulders, rolled quickly and stood up, poised to leap into the cab. But the second uniformed man was still hunched over with his flattened face pressed against the windshield. A trickle of blood trailed from his ear.

Mazurin looked up as Charlie appeared on top of the car, followed by the girl. 'All secure here,' he said. 'You two all right?'

'We're just fine,' said Charlie grimly, 'and we're certainly grateful to you for saving our lives. But would you mind giving us a hint of what this is all about?' He and the girl jumped down beside Mazurin, and Charlie gestured towards the dwindling rear end of the car. 'Argo paste,' he said. 'And those things back in Welfare Square.'

'Tweedledums,' Mazurin supplied helpfully. 'Pineapple-flavored, I think.'

'Tweedledums,' repeated the boy. 'And you. What are you, the Mad Hatter? If so, what are you going to pull out of your hat next?'

'There's lots more,' Mazurin said gloomily. 'We haven't seen the flangs yet, or the collapsed flooring, or the rozzers, or—'

'Wait a minute,' Charlie interrupted. 'Just one minute. One thing at a time. What are flangs?'

Mazurin searched his mind for the archaic word. Castards? Something like that. Ces, cis, cos – 'Custards,' he said. 'From the French *flan*, although I believe there was some influence dating from the Early Hollywood Era. They're mobile, but not as much as the tweedledums. They only creep around, and they like to crawl into any dark enclosed space they find. So you just leave them with a bunch of open pastry shells, and—'

Charlie interrupted again. 'All right, I knew it was going to be something like that. I won't ask you what rozzers are.'

'Like a very slender pig,' said Mazurin promptly. 'Fast as lightning. Some people like to race them.'

Charlie looked at him, breathing heavily. 'All I want to know,' he said, 'is where all these things that nobody ever heard of came from.'

'Well, I'll tell you,' said Mazurin reluctantly, 'but I have a feeling you won't believe me.'

He squatted and began going through the pockets of the guard who lay on the greensward at their feet.

'No,' said Charlie, and gave him a push that sent him sprawling. Charlie knelt quickly and removed the guard's handgun from its holster. Backing up, he handed the gun to the girl and then went back to the guard. 'Sorry, but I don't see how we can trust you.'

He found the guard's keys, stood up and held the gun trained on Mazurin while the girl unlocked his wristcuffs; then they traded while he unlocked hers. It seemed, Mazurin thought ruefully, that they had no present intention of unlocking his.

'Can I get up now?' he asked mildly.

'Yes,' said Charlie. He gestured with the gun to their left, across an open field that ended at a wooded ridge. 'We've got to get under cover.' He glanced at the gun in his hand, then back at the smoking rear of the paddy-wagon. 'What do you think, Eve?'

'It would be nice to have it,' the girl said regretfully, 'but it's a sure tipoff.'

'Right,' said Charlie, and he returned the gun to the guard's holster. Then he pulled the keys out of his pocket and replaced them as well.

'Hey,' objected Mazurin, 'when do I get out of these things?'

'Later – maybe,' said Charlie. 'By the time anybody finds the car, there's a good chance that the whole rear end will be gone, and they'll figure we went with it. But not if we take anything from this guy.'

Eve started walking. 'Let's go. Someone may come along and ask why we're not helping our gallant lads out of danger.'

They headed across the field, Mazurin in the lead. He felt a little sick. In his own time, he tried to tell himself, he's seen men killed often enough for exactly similar reasons. But this wasn't his own time; this time belonged to his Sacred Ancestors, some of whom were being left to die in argo paste. He felt a wave of resentment against the two youngsters behind him, and then recoiled from that too. *They* could be his ancestors. Now just what in the name of Blodgett could a man do in a situation like this?

They pushed through a tangle of saplings and undergrowth for what seemed like several hours, until they reached a little stream. Eve sat down, gasping, and the other two followed suit.

'It's getting too late to go much farther, anyway,' said Charlie. He inspected his shoeless feet glumly, then turned to Mazurin. 'All right,' he said, 'let's have your story, improbable or not.'

Mazurin told them, from the beginning. They listened in discouraging silence. Finally, 'Is that all?' Charlie asked.

'That's all,' said Mazurin. 'What happens next *I* don't know, except that we'll probably run into the rozzers committing a nuisance in City Hall or somebody triggering a section of collapsed flooring and getting knocked into the next canton, or—'

'What makes you think you're going to see any city hall?' asked Charlie ominously.

'No reason, except that defiling a public building is one of the few supreme crimes I haven't been responsible for yet.'

'How's that again?' said Charlie, confused.

'Don't you remember what he said about ancestor worship?' asked Eve. 'It makes sense. He feels directly responsible for all these things that have been happening to people who, for all he knows, may be his own ancestors.' She frowned at Mazurin, opened her mouth to speak again. 'How—'

'Now wait a minute,' Charlie burst out. 'You're not assuming that he's telling the truth, are you?'

'You wait,' she told him. Then, to Mazurin, 'See if I've got this right. You come from about four centuries from now, and in your time the World State is an established fact. There never was any successful attempt to overthrow it. Is that right?'

Mazurin nodded.

Charlie snorted. 'Well, if we fell for *that,* we'd simply knuckle under and let Blodgett's hoodlums have it all their own way.' He peered at Mazurin puzzledly. 'Is that what you're for, to convince us we can't win? It seems a little too simple-minded to deserve all this buildup.'

Mazurin shook his head. 'You don't quite understand,' he said. 'This is a different time-line from the one I came from. It's different because I'm in it, here. Anything can happen now.'

Charlie looked more baffled than ever.

'Listen,' said Eve, 'just suppose he is telling the plain truth. And as you said a minute ago, if the Worstas had all that new stuff – materializing in our cell, and those green things in the Square – why would they waste it on a silly trick like this?'

'All right,' said Charlie. 'What then?'

'Then he might be able to help us win,' said Eve.

'Just for the theoretical interest of it – suppose you could help us overthrow the Worstas, Mazurin, would you do it?'

'The who?'

'The Worstas – the World Staters. Blodgett and his gang. You've seen the kind of tyrannical crew they are. All right, would you help us if you could?'

'Well, no,' said Mazurin honestly.

'Why not?'

'Because, for one thing, if I help you I hurt them, and vice versa. I couldn't help either side. It would be irreligious.'

Charlie stared at him contemptuously, and Mazurin felt his ears getting red. It did sound stuffy, at that. Why couldn't they have let him stay in his own environment, where a man could take his religion on sacred days and forget about it the rest of the time?

'There's another good reason,' he said defensively. 'You seem to forget that I come from the world that grew out of this one. Well, it's a pretty good world. It's peaceful; there hasn't been a war in more than three centuries. Nobody has to work hard, as a general rule. No more race or nationality problems – everybody's interbred so much, as a result of the lowering of national barriers, that there's only one kind of people. Why should I want to change all that?'

'No reason, maybe,' said the girl, 'but you can see why we want to change our world, can't you?'

Mazurin thought about it. 'No.'

'Well, look,' said the girl. 'Ten years ago there was a world war, the ninth in sixty years. There was a world-wide organization that was fighting the war, had been fighting against war since about nineteen sixty. They had a lot of followers, on paper, but they weren't strong enough to do anything until the people finally got fed up. After all, it had got to the point where you'd have two or three months of peace after the armistice was signed, and then the whole bloody mess would start all over again.

'Civilization was going straight downhill. That had been happening for a long time, but now it was happening so fast that you could *see* it happening. There was a spontaneous wave of revolt all through South America, where the fighting was going on at that time. It started with a French Regiment that turned around and shot its officers. Then the Canadian regiment they were fighting did the same thing, and after that it spread too fast to figure out how the idea got around.

'All the armies in South America sent delegates to a conference – the Conference of Acapulco – and the Worstas put over their program. Then all the armies went home, kicked out their governments, held general elections, and ten months later we had the World State.'

'Well,' said Mazurin, 'what's wrong with—'

'Wait. For five months everything went fine. All the important nations were in, and it was a sure thing that the others – the ones that hadn't been in this particular fighting – would come in later. We had a swell Constitution and we were disarming like fury. Then there was a *coup d'état*. Blodgett and his gang moved in, kidnapped Provisional President Carres, drugged him and made him sign orders appointing Blodgett's gang to key positions.

'It was logical enough; Blodgett himself was the number two man in the

Worstas movement to begin with. By the time anybody found out what was going on, they were so firmly entrenched that they've been able to stamp out every rising against them ever since. They've got the best propaganda line since Stalin, and the people as a whole won't move because there's peace, and they're sick of war. So all we've wound up with is just another damned dictatorship. *Now* do you see?'

'Wait a minute,' said Mazurin. He had been listening with growing horror to Eve's use of the Sacred Name. 'This Blodgett you're talking about – that can't possibly be Ernest Elwood Vernon Crawford Blodgett, can it?'

'His name is Ernest, and his mother's name was Crawford,' said Eve. 'Where you got those other handles from, I don't know.'

'It's the way we name ourselves,' Mazurin explained. 'Your own given name, given names of two prominent ancestors, one from each line, then mother's and father's line names. Anyway, if that's the Blodgett you're talking about, you must have your facts all wrong. Blodgett' – he touched his forelock – 'was the founder and first President of the World State. Kids learn about him in the first course. The Father of the World and so forth. He wasn't any dictator and there wasn't any president before him.'

'Blodgett is busy revising the histories right now,' said Eve grimly. 'I'll bet the big ham hasn't got buck teeth in the pictures you've seen, either.'

'Of course not,' said Mazurin. 'Have you ever seen him in person?'

Eve reddened. 'No. But I've seen smuggled pictures of him before he got his dentures—'

'Then,' said Mazurin triumphantly, 'how do you know the pictures *you* saw weren't faked?'

They kept it up for another hour, ruffling tempers all around, until Charlie told them both to pipe down and get some sleep.

IV

Mazurin awoke feeling as if he had spent the night hanging by his thumbs. His hands were completely numb, and the rest of his body was so stiff and painful that it took him ten minutes to stand up.

The other two had made out a little better, but they were all cold, hungry and short-tempered. They drank water from the stream, ate some wild berries they found after an hour's search, stuffed leaves into Charlie's socks, and then started off again through the woods. Charlie, when Mazurin asked him where they were going, politely requested him to keep his graphically described questions to himself.

An hour or so later, when the sun was higher and exercise had loosened their muscles, they were feeling a little better. They had struck a path of sorts under some kind of fragrant trees that were unfamiliar to Mazurin. The branches made a comfortable pattern against the sky, and there were birds calling pleasantries back and forth. Mazurin moved up beside Eve and walked with her for a while in silence.

'I suppose I was kidding myself last night when I thought you might be able to help us,' she said finally. 'We've got a fair chance as it is, but it's awfully risky. It would be nice to know that the Marines were going to ride up at the last moment.'

Mazurin made sympathetic noises, feeling a little embarrassed.

'How do you feel about being cut off from your own time?' she asked suddenly. 'You're in a pretty tough spot too.'

Mazurin realized that he hadn't had time to wonder how he did feel about it. He imagined the technicians back at the Physics Bureau searching through the time-lines, finding him by some improbable chance, and yanking him back. He had a clear vision of the expression on the face of his square-jawed superior when that worthy read his report.

He shuddered.

'What's the matter?'

'If I got back now,' said Mazurin, 'they'd give me one year in the Black House and then turn my totem upside down and demote me to the Cleanliness Inspection Squad.'

'Why? Because your mission wasn't successful?'

'Well, that isn't exactly the way my chief would put it. He'd say I was a disgusting ghoul with the moral fiber of a cuckoo, who would pick his teeth with a splinter from his uncle's coffin.'

'But you did all you could, didn't you?'

Mazurin conscientiously reviewed his activities of the day before. 'I guess I did, but that doesn't matter. They go by results.'

'H'm,' said Eve. 'So does Buck-tooth Blodgett. How did you happen to go to work for the – what is it?'

'Internal Security Commission,' said Mazurin.

'It would be. Fancy name for secret police, isn't it? Well, how did you happen to join up?'

'Why,' said Mazurin in astonishment. 'I was selected. When I was fifteen. Those decisions can't be left to individuals.'

She stopped and stared at him, wide-eyed. 'And you think *that's* the best of all possible worlds? Even Blodgett hasn't pulled anything quite as rank as that yet. But he will, I can see.'

She moved on, and Mazurin followed her, puzzled. 'How else would you do it?' he inquired.

'Free choice,' she said curtly. 'Government does its best to provide equal opportunities for everybody, and you choose what you want to be.'

'Ah,' said Mazurin shrewdly, having swiftly found the illogicality, 'but who would want to go into the ISC?'

'Yes,' she agreed, 'who?'

Half an hour later, Mazurin was still thinking about the implications of that remark.

They stopped when they got to another small stream that Charlie and Eve seemed to recognize. Charlie washed his face and hands, swore because he had no razor, and looked suspiciously at Mazurin's pinkly beardless chin.

'Depilatory cream,' Mazurin told him. 'Stuns the follicles for a month. Invented about 2050, I think.'

Charlie grunted, but looked half-convinced.

'Let me have those sandals,' he said. He put them on and climbed along to the top of the next ridge. He looked cautiously over, then waved to Eve and disappeared over the top.

'What now?' asked Mazurin.

'We wait here,' said Eve shortly. 'There's a town up ahead where one of our contacts lives. Charlie's going in to see if it's safe.'

He was back in an hour, wearing shoes and carrying Mazurin's sandals wrapped in a bundle. He looked worried. 'There's hell to pay,' he told Eve, then turned to Mazurin. 'I guess you're on the level, all right. Those cockeyed things of yours – the tweedledums and so forth – have been popping up all over this area for the last twenty-four hours. The Worstas are going crazy. They can't figure it out, and it scares them. The place is swarming with troops and no-goods.'

'National Guardsmen,' Eve explained to Mazurin, seeing his puzzled look. 'N. G. – no good. They're a bunch of picked stinkers, probably about like your ISC.'

Charlie made an impatient gesture, cutting off Mazurin's reply. 'Here's what we're up against,' he said. 'Bauernfeind got through to H.Q. all right, and they'll send a copter in time to get us to rendezvous. But the woods are full of patrols – we're lucky we haven't been picked up before now. The only place we'll be safe is in Bauernfeind's subcellar.'

He stared at Mazurin's outlandish costume. 'You and I probably can get through all right, one at a time,' he said to Eve, 'but he's a problem. I was ready to ditch him if we had to, but Bauernfeind says we've got to take him along; the Central Council wants him. We couldn't figure out any way to take those cuffs off, without bringing a machine shop out here. Best we could think of was this.'

He unfolded his bundle and produced a long-sleeved robe, a pair of scissors, needles and thread. 'There are two or three different sects in the hills around here,' he explained. 'This isn't quite the color any of 'em wear – Bauernfeind got it from a theatrical costumer's – but he thinks it will pass. We'll have to cut it open, so he can get his arms into the sleeves, and then sew him into it.' He picked up the scissors and spread the robe out over his knees.

'No, not that way,' said Eve, and took the scissors from him. 'Underneath, where it won't show.' She rapidly snipped the robe apart, starting in the middle of the chest, upward to the end of each sleeve.

The result looked like nothing that would ever serve as a garment again, but she slipped it over Mazurin's head, brought the dangling top part over his shoulders and, working swiftly, sewed it into shape again.

'That'll hold,' she said, '*if* you don't wave your arms around. Remember, you've got your hands clasped in meditation, and you keep your eyes down. What about those sandals, Charlie?'

'Half the crackpots in California wear them,' he said. 'And that long hair of his looks natural in this getup. Let's move along.'

Mazurin did as he was told. His head ached miserably, and it seemed to him that his situation was getting worse by the minute. From the time he had been captured by the Worstas, he'd had no power of decision whatever; and, even worse, he still had no idea what he could do if he were free to do it.

Just suppose he were to settle down in this century – providing he could get out of this present mess alive. Suppose he married and had progeny. That would obviously make *him* an ancestor, from the viewpoint of his own time. Then it would be just as important to save his own neck as anybody else's! ...

Wait a minute, there was something funny about that line of reasoning. Everybody, theoretically, could continue his own line. So when was an ancestor an object of veneration and when was he just a person? It couldn't be merely a matter of elapsed time, could it? Because elapsed time was subjective, an abstraction, a point of view. From where he was now, the world he came from didn't even exist; it was just a remote future possibility. But—

It was too much. Mazurin thought he saw the glimmer of a final answer, but he couldn't pursue it. It made him feel dizzy when he tried.

They clambered cautiously up to the top of the ridge, reconnoitered, and went down the other side to where a dusty road showed through the trees. Directly ahead of them, when they reached the road, were the outskirts of a small, weatherbeaten town. They waited for twenty minutes before a squad of soldiers hanging around in front of a warehouse decided to go elsewhere. Twice they heard distant shots, and once a confused sound of yelling.

Mazurin sighed with relief when they finally reached a fairly well-populated street. Mingling with the crowd, Charlie in front, then Mazurin, and Eve bringing up the rear, they weren't conspicuous, but as a group they had been decidedly peculiar. And if they looked nervous, he decided, it was in character; so did most of the people he saw around him. Every block or so they passed a patrol of green-uniformed men, hands on the straps of their slung missile weapons, looking alertly to each side as they walked.

The three bunched momentarily as they waited for a traffic light to change, and Charlie murmured, 'Two blocks more, then half a block to the right. It's the place called "Hi-Tone Tailors." Go straight to the back and down the stairs.'

He stopped talking as a green-uniformed officer paused nearby and glanced at them. The light changed and they started across the street. Mazurin kept his eyes down, as directed, even when a loud whirring noise approached him from behind and hovered over him. Immediately thereafter, something mushy hit him on the head and slithered down his face, blinding him momentarily.

He heard startled cries around him. The next instant, the mushy something had reached his nose and was trying to crawl up it. Strangling, Mazurin unwarily opened his mouth, and the stuff crawled into that too. He swallowed as much as he could – it was lemon-flavored – and spat out the rest.

He looked up just in time to see another glob hurtling towards him. He flung up his hands instinctively, and heard the popping threads as Eve's hasty stitching gave way.

Above him the flangs were raining down. The whirring noise, he found, proceeded from the blades of a helicopter that was hovering over the intersection. Two green-uniformed men in its cab were leaning out to peer in amazement and horror at the four loudspeaker horns fixed to its underside. From these, in an apparently endless flow, issued the flangs. They were piling up underfoot now, climbing up people's trouser legs, squirming in a custardy wave towards the comparative darkness of doorways.

Desperately Mazurin warded off another yellow blob, leaped the writhing form of a fat citizen who had flangs in his pants, and then lost his own footing, skidding half the width of the street and fetching up against a green-uniformed soldier. He saw the soldier's eyes widen as he caught sight of the wrist-cuffs. Then there was a shout and a whirl of motion, and something hard struck him solidly on the back of the head.

Light brought him to: blinding, hot yellow light that shone through his closed lids and made his eyes water fiercely. He tried instinctively to turn his head aside, and found he couldn't. For a moment he couldn't orient himself; he was being put to the question, that was obvious, but what for? He hadn't done anything – or had he? How had he made out on that time mission? He had a dim recollection of something unpleasant …

The rest of the memories came back then, and Mazurin groaned. He was in the hands of the Worstas again, those peculiarly unpleasant ancestors who were incredibly the founders of his own state; and some of the police methods in this century were crude, he remembered.

They'd get the other two, undoubtedly. They'd all been close together when the flangs started falling, and the soldiers would have rounded up everybody in sight after they caught him. Now it was going to be bad. Now it was going to be *very* bad.

He heard a sudden 'Ouch!' and then a stifled shriek. A moment later he understood the reason; something needle-sharp was jabbed an inch into his left buttock. He added his outcry to the others, whereupon a voice said, 'They're ready, Mr President.'

'Proceed,' said a slightly lisping voice. 'Begin with the girl.'

'Your name is Gertrude Meyer?' said the other.

Mazurin heard the girl gasp. She said, 'Yes.'

'You are a member of the underground society of wreckers and assassins known as the Freedom Party, and you are known to your co-conspirators as Eve?'

Again the gasp, and again, 'Yes.'

'You are aware of a plot to assassinate the President?'

The gasp, a pause, then another gasp. 'Yes!'

'What is the nature of this plot?'

This time Eve sobbed. 'Oh, *don't* do that – *oh!*'

'What is the nature of this plot?'

'Oh! I don't know—' She shrieked and then Mazurin heard her weeping. 'I'll never tell you – *oh!* – anything. *Oh!*'

Mazurin found himself struggling like a wild man against his shackles. He had an idea he knew what they were doing to Eve; it was a traditional method of interrogating females, so they'd probably had it even this early. It was very nearly infallible, and very unpleasant to think about.

Eve's cries grew louder and more frequent. Finally she screamed and there was silence for a while. Then the interrogation began again. After twenty minutes, Eve began telling all she knew.

It was a primitive plot, and it seemed to Mazurin that it could have had only a slender chance of success even in so barbaric an era as this one. In his own time, nothing whatever would be gained by assassinating the Chief Executive; the next eligible member of the Executive Families would simply take over. What you had to watch out for was thought subversion and heresy.

Here, apparently, the critical area was at the top. Blodgett was so obsessed by the idea that someone in his hierarchy might kick him out, as he'd done to Carres, that he'd made sure that the whole structure would collapse without him.

The Freedom Party knew this, or guessed it, according to Eve. They didn't know exactly what would happen if they killed Blodgett, but they were pretty sure it would be fatal to the present dictatorial group. In any case, they'd be rid of Blodgett and would, at worst, take their chances on his successor being less brutal.

The time they'd picked was an annual celebration at which Blodgett traditionally showed himself. It was always held in a big outdoor arena, and there would be thousands of spectators. Blodgett would be well guarded, of course, but they couldn't possibly screen everybody who got into the arena. All the revolutionists needed was an inconspicuous weapon, and it seemed that the underground's scientists had perfected one about eight months ago and had been turning them out in quantity in a hidden factory. Eve didn't know where the factory was. She and Charlie were the liaison agents, who were to pick up the completed weapons from other agents and take them to distribution points.

The weapon was a miniature bazooka. Only two inches long, it could be concealed so well that only the most rigorous search would find it, and its range was more than adequate for the job they wanted to do. Accuracy would have been too much to ask for, but they had intended to concentrate the fire of several hundred weapons on the rostrum, and hope that Blodgett would be killed.

The questioners took Eve through the whole story again, then started on Charlie. He held out for a few minutes, but he talked. He knew no more than Eve.

Then it was Mazurin's turn.

The first question was: 'What is your name?' and it was followed instantly by the touch of warm metal on the back of his hand.

Only a reminder, Mazurin guessed. They thought he was valuable and wanted to be very careful not to injure him seriously; but if he didn't answer satisfactorily, the iron would get hotter.

He answered the question with his full name. The next was, 'Where do you come from?' He told the truth, not expecting to be believed, but unable to think of any lie that would be more credible.

There was a muttered consultation, then, 'Do you maintain that you can tell us about events which are to us in the future, because of your knowledge of what is to you history?'

Mazurin said, 'Yes, only—'

Blodgett's lisping voice interrupted him. 'That's enough. General, this information is restricted. Take him into my private office. I will continue the interrogation personally.'

The light clicked off, and Mazurin felt the shackles being loosened.

'Prisoner, have you given any of this information to these other two?'

Mazurin hesitated, trying to figure out which was the dangerous answer, yes or no. The President's voice said, 'Never mind, General. I will assume that he has. Bring all three of them into my private office. Here, give me those manacle keys.'

Someone hauled Mazurin off the table on which he had been lying and locked his wrists together. He was able to open his smarting eyes after a moment, but he could see nothing except the after-image of the brilliant interrogation light. Hands turned him, pushed him, caught him when he staggered and kept him moving. He heard the shuffle of other feet. Eve was crying quietly.

A door was opened ahead of them. Mazurin was led forward a few steps and then shoved into a deep cushioned chair. Footsteps receded and the door shut again. Deep silence fell instantly, punctuated by their breathing and the President's soft footsteps, then the slight creak of a swivel chair.

'Now,' said Blodgett's voice, apparently from some little distance. 'We are entirely private here; this room is sound-proof and spyproof. Tell me all about the future of my regime, Mr Mazurin – and, I warn you, tell me the truth.'

Mazurin's vision was clearing rapidly. Directly ahead of him, twenty feet away across a deep carpet and a huge polished desk, sat Blodgett. He didn't look anything like the pictures in the histories. He was short and plump, and he looked crafty and nervous and worried. Mazurin glanced to his right. There was a row of chairs like his own, and in two of them, manacled like himself, were Eve and Charlie. Eve was bent over with her head in her hands; Charlie was rigid and stony-faced.

Perhaps the history books had idealized Blodgett's appearance. It didn't matter. Mazurin was in the Presence and he was awed.

'In case any of you are thinking of attempting violence against me,' remarked Blodgett, 'don't.' He showed them a heavy little machine-gun, mounted on a wheeled frame, that stood on his desk. 'You are too far away, and those extremely comfortable chairs are ingeniously hard to get out of. Also, this room contains a minor arsenal. I could fight off a regiment here, if I had to. Now, Mr Mazurin, talk. You needn't be afraid of telling the truth, whether you think I'll like it or not. You're a mine of information, and I expect to be able to use you for a long time to come. So tell me the unvarnished truth.'

Mazurin told him.

Blodgett smiled at the end of it. 'One thing more, Mr Mazurin. At what age will I die?'

'I don't remember exactly, your honor. About eighty, as I recall.'

'Good, good,' said Blodgett. 'Surprisingly good.' He took a seedless grape from the bowl in front of him and popped it into his mouth. 'You are sure, Mr Mazurin, that you have not colored this tale to please my fancy? No, I can see that you are sincere; you have no reason to lie.'

He ate another grape, smiling, pushed the bowl aside and leaned confidentially over the desk.

'If you had prophesied disaster, Mr Mazurin,' he said, 'I should never in the world have believed you. Do you know why?' The pause was rhetorical.

'Because I belong to the ages. I know it. I have felt it since I was a young man. I was born to rule the world. Would you believe that I have known that since I was twenty? And my rule is destined to endure; I knew that.

'Why? Because I started with what every other conqueror tried in vain to achieve – a world dominion. It is all the world or none, Mr Mazurin. Napoleon knew that. Hitler knew that. Stalin knew that. And that was the inexorable law that humbled each in his turn. They tried to achieve peace through war – fatal, fatal. They had to try, of course. They were born to rule too, but at the wrong time.'

He talked on interminably, his face growing flushed and his eyes glistening. He gestured, he smiled, he frowned. Didactic, he stood up and leaned earnestly over the table. Self-satisfied, he sat back and popped grapes into his mouth. Mystical, he stared at the ceiling.

It was during the latter phase that Mazurin – like the other two, half-stunned by oratory – suddenly came awake. From the muzzle of the squat weapon on Blodgett's desk, a tiny green bubble bulged. As Mazurin watched, the bubble grew to half an inch, dropped to the desk and rolled until the edge of the fruitbowl stopped it.

Mazurin felt suddenly cold all over. He darted a glance to his right. Eve was looking at the floor and had seen nothing; but Charlie was looking at him with one eyebrow raised, an expression that said plainly, *What is it?*

Mazurin looked back at the President. Blodgett brought a rolling period to a close, smiled soulfully, sighed, and became stern.

'As for you, sir,' he said, 'your destiny is allied with mine. To this favor you must submit. I do not ask, I give. I give you a living god, as you have yourself justly described me, to worship and follow faithfully all your life. And I give you what is immeasurably more precious than the schoolboys' history you give me – I give you a place beside me in all the history that's yet to be written!'

For an instant, that idea captured Mazurin's imagination. What a fantastic end to his assignment that would be – the Chief Executive, and the ISC Intelligence chief, and everybody, worshipping every holy day at his shrine!

Even while that thought raced through his mind, Mazurin watched the tiny green globule in utter fascination. If Bodgett reached for that globule, thinking it a grape, then for the first time in this whole misbegotten affair Mazurin would have reached a point of decision. And to save himself he couldn't tell whether he wanted that or not. He knew what he wanted to do, well enough, but he felt the first premonitory stirrings of a guilt that he knew would plague him for years. What right had he to interfere with the lives of millions still unborn?

Mazurin, he told himself, *you're an ancestor!* He glanced at Eve's pale, drawn face. *I'll see to it,* he added.

Blodgett's open palm came down on the desk, sideswiping the fruit bowl. The bowl wobbled elliptically around the desktop, spilling grapes. But the nearest to Blodgett's hand was still the globe that was not a grape.

'How say you, sir?' demanded Blodgett. 'Destiny or death?'

His hand hovered, as ready for one gesture as another. He glared at Mazurin.

Mazurin took a deep breath. 'I choose destiny, your honor.'

Blodgett's features relaxed. His hand dropped gently on the table, the pudgy fingers curling. Gently they closed on the green sphere. Smiling benignly, Blodgett popped it into his mouth.

He stayed that way, without changing posture or expression, for three long seconds. Then his eyes bulged. A shout formed itself on his lips, but no sound came out. He – *withered* somehow, shrank indescribably in his uniform. There was a look of horror and of passionate appeal in his eyes. And then, suddenly, *Blodgett was not there any longer.*

To the others, it looked as if he had simply vanished out of the world of men. But Mazurin, shuddering, knew that his fate had not been that simple – or that pleasant.

Eve gasped, 'What was it? That grape he ate—'

Mazurin felt sick. 'A mangel.'

Charlie demanded, 'What's a mangel? What did it do to him?'

Mazurin said shakily, 'You could torture me in the subtlest and cruelest ways and I would not tell you. This civilization is not ready to know.'

He put his head in his hands. One part of him knew that Blodgett was a stinker; the other part was simply saying, *You let him eat a mangel. You killed him. The most sacred ancestor of all, the Father of the World.*

He heard the other two talking in low, tense voices. Eve said, 'Are you thinking what I'm thinking?'

'Blodgett had already started making himself up to look like his propaganda pictures.'

'Yes. We could put it over, Charlie. They'd have no choice. It's either agreement or total collapse.'

'Gone,' Mazurin moaned. 'Blodgett. The beautiful society he built with his giant intellect—'

'No,' said Charlie. 'None of it's lost. Except the worst part of your civilization.'

'And certainly not the most sacred ancestor,' Eve added. 'Not the Father of the World.'

Mazurin, lost in misery, looked up. 'But the mangel got him. Blodgett is gone.' He touched his forelock absently.

'You're here,' said Eve. 'You know what the future is supposed to be like. You'll build Blodgett's world – with a few important changes.'

'You'll put one of your men in Blodgett's place?'

Charlie leaned over his chair. 'One of our men – one of everybody's.'

'Isn't it obvious?' asked Eve, squeezing Mazurin's arm. 'The Father of the World, the most sacred ancestor, will be a descendant.'

'He doesn't get it,' Charlie said.

'You,' Eve stated, 'will be Blodgett.'

Mazurin started to touch his forelock. 'Me?' he asked dazedly, then finished the reverent gesture.

He *was* an ancestor, after all.

Damon Knight (1922–2002)

Damon Francis Knight was born in Oregon in 1922. He is regarded as one of the most important figures in modern science fiction, having made significant contributions to the field as an author, editor and critic. Knight co-founded the Milford Writers' Conference, the influential Clarion Workshop and the Science Fiction Writers of America, serving as its first president from 1965–67. Around this time he also made his reputation as one of the field's foremost anthologists. Beginning with reprint collections, in 1966 he launched the influential Orbit series of original anthologies. Starting with Orbit 1, the series would continue for over a decade, concluding in 1980 with Orbit 21. Orbit was the longest running and most influential anthology series in SF up to that point, showcasing such important authors as Gene Wolfe, R.A. Lafferty and Knight's third wife, Kate Wilhelm. A master of short fiction, Damon Knight is best known in wider circles as the author of 'To Serve Mankind', which was adapted for *The Twilight Zone* and later spoofed in a Hallowe'en episode of *The Simpsons*. He was granted the SFWA's Grand Master Award in 1995, and in 2002, SFWA renamed it the Damon Knight Grand Master Award in his honour. He died in 2002.

If you've enjoyed these books and would
like to read more, you'll find literally thousands
of classic Science Fiction & Fantasy titles
through the **SF Gateway**

∗

*For the new home of
Science Fiction & Fantasy . . .*

∗

*For the most comprehensive collection
of classic SF on the internet . . .*

∗

Visit the SF Gateway

www.sfgateway.com